S0-AAO-145

WYVERN

A. A. ATTANASIO

WYVERN

TICKNOR & FIELDS

NEW YORK 1988

Library of Congress Cataloging-in-Publication Data

Attanasio, A. A.
Wyvern / A.A. Attanasio.
p. cm.
ISBN 0-89919-409-5
I. Title.
PS3551.T74W9 1988 88-4936
813'.54—dc19 CIP

Printed in the United States of America

P 10 9 8 7 6 5 4 3 2 1

For
your father
and mine — and their journeys
exiled in us

When people die there awaits them
what they neither expect nor even imagine.
— HERACLITUS, frg. 27

Walking with the Beast That Walks in Us

The Lord has said that He would dwell in thick darkness.

— Solomon

DAWN BUILT A TEMPLE of clouds above the jungle. The north wind, tangled with stars, blew west, and the clouds followed into the mountains. A sudden, brief torrent crashed over the peaks, clattering across ledges of black slate and rushing down the rocky slopes toward the forest.

On a mountain ledge where the deluge tattered to silver veils, a narrow figure stood, peering down at an immense maze of crooked chasms. The enormous vista swarmed with vapors, valleys exhaling like graves.

The mighty cumuli lifted and vanished in the purple sky among the last wind-shaken stars, and the slim shadow stepped from the cliff darkness into the dawnlight. He was black and angular, wearing only a snakeskin loincloth, the flesh of his chest and shoulders beaded like tar where ritual scars linked their proud stories. Serpent tattoos coiled up his legs, and on his flat head the bristly hair was braided in viper loops. His breath smoked violet in the cold light.

The mansnake scanned the terrain below until he spotted the high valley where the giant trees of the forest came to their knees before the stone peaks. There, a day's hike away, a demon dwelled. For seven years, the mansnake had watched this valley to see that the demon did not escape, and he had entered the glen to bring offerings only when he was certain that he would not be seen. But now the drum songs of the neighboring tribes spoke of sighting the dread creature, and the time had come at last for the mansnake to go down from the cold paths into the hot frenzy of the jungle and confront the demon.

The sun climbed the sky as he descended the planet's wall. Ahead, bald outcroppings of rock loomed and twisted pygmy trees squatted among cobbles and boulders. Farther down began the flower fields, knolls and braes drumming with color as the upsailing mists dispersed in the sunlight. Ferns walled the forest where the big trees ended, at the top of the demon's valley.

The valley was dark. Here and there where trees had fallen, sunlight lanced the dense canopy and ignited flights of tiny emerald birds and swarms of blue butterflies. Even as the sun mounted to noon, the gloom persisted here, and the tocking of frogs teemed in the famished light.

On the far side of this dusky valley, naked children, boys of the migrant Rain Wanderer tribe, splashed in the amber water of a stream. Their camp lay beyond a grove of thornbark trees. Several days ago a foraging party had glimpsed the demon that lived in the mountain-shadowed valley. The women who saw it declared that the demon was itself a child, but with poisonous moonflesh, sunfire hair, and blue eyes bright as stars. The men would not talk about it, so the bravest of the boys had set out to see for themselves. In a clearing at a bend in the stream, they had found a run-off pool free of crocodiles, where they could frolic without fear of being swept away or eaten. Yet no one forgot that this was the demon's pool. The fretful cry of every bird and monkey stalled their games and brought them apprehensively to their feet, ready to dash back to their mothers, foraging for the evening meal along the forest paths. Each time, the eldest child laughed at the fear of the younger ones and pointed to the animal that had cried.

Among the rubbery leaves above the stream, the demon watched. He was a young boy, and he seemed to glow in the shadows. His blond hair, bowl-cut and greased with nut paste, shimmered like sun-beaten metal, and his smudged skin leaked light. Only the cast of his bones was visibly tribal. His face had the feline contours of the children he watched, but from under his native brow span, blue eyes stared.

The boys in the stream were about his age, and he gazed with fascination at their waterplay. Their laughs and shouts were a new music. Never before had he seen children playing. For the seven years of his life, he had lived in the valley alone with Mala, his mother. Only lately had he heard the drum songs of the Rain Wanderers and been inspired to defy Mala's warnings and hike the length of the valley to find the music. He had seen the Rain Wanderers' camp from a distance and had followed the women as they gathered berries and kindling. Today was the closest he had ever come to the tribesfolk. Now he was certain: they were no different from him.

Suddenly he heard a frightened cry of "Demon-child!" and one of the children pointed to the underbrush. The oldest child rushed forward while the others cringed. A termite-riven log rolled into the mud shoals to the frenzied chant of "Demon-demon-demon-child!"

The boy crouching in the brush frowned. He knew they were calling to him. The previous day, when the women had spotted him peering through the draperies of pea vines, they had shrieked, "Matubrembrem — demon-child!" and run away.

But Mala called him Jaki. She had told him that his father was a man from a far-distant land, as her father had been, and that they lived apart from the tribes because their fathers' spirits belonged to other lands. But he could not see now why he should be called a demon.

Jaki wanted to explain this to the taunting children, but he had promised Mala that he would not show himself, and reluctantly he stepped back, determined to find out why the spirits of their fathers could find no home in the tribes. As he turned to go, his foot snagged on a root, and he pitched forward. Arms outstretched, he crashed through the screen of leaves and tumbled down the streambank.

Screams jumped from the children in the pool at the sight of the monster flying at them. They fled in panic, clutching at dangling vines to pull themselves up the bank. Only the oldest of the children, the one who had laughed before at the others, stood fast. He was not laughing now. While the others clambered up the embankment, he returned the demon's stare. He saw that the creature was but a boy, wearing a bark loincloth like other boys, but that his flesh, hair, and eyes were born of fog and sunfire. He picked up a river cobble and edged into the stream.

"Ferang! Come back," the children called after him, but he advanced heedless of their cries. Jaw set, white-knuckled fingers clasping the stone, he moved sideways toward the demon and kicked his foot through the water to startle the repugnant child.

Jaki did not move. He was confused by their terror. What frightened them? Could they not see that he was no different from them? And who was this one called Ferang who raised a stone to him as if he were a viper?

"Put that rock down," Jaki called out. "I will not harm you. I am a boy just like you."

Ferang halted his advance and shook his head. "You cannot fool me. I know who you are, Matubrembrem. Be gone!" he shouted, and let fly the cobble. It hurtled straight for Jaki, and the golden-haired boy ducked. The stone glanced the side of his head, and his vision flared blindly. The impact knocked him into the mud. Ferang hooted and ran back to the gravel bar for another rock.

Jaki's sight jarred back, and he touched the pain. His fingers came away hot with blood. He staggered to his feet, starpoints swimming around him, and collapsed. Dizzily, he crawled up the mud slope as the emboldened children pelted his back and legs with rocks. On his hands and knees, he scampered into the brush, lunged to his feet, and dashed with all his might into the dark valley.

Stunned and frightened, Jaki darted like an animal through the pillared gloom. He had never been struck before, and the stoning left him mindless with shock. He ran until exhaustion tripped him, and he flopped into the leaf-moldering shade, heaving for breath. His jumping heart shouted, "Matubrembrem — demon-child — demon — " Pain raged in his head. Above him, a starved-faced monkey laughed derisively. Its cackle twisted in his booming ears to "Matubrembrem!"

Jaki rolled to his feet and ran again, exploiting all the strength left in his child legs. A covey of pink birds flapped up from the sepia darkness screeching "Matubrembrem!" An opossum leaped away from his reckless flight with a mocking squeal.

Fatigue dropped the boy again, this time under the prop roots of a cobwebbed tree. He was alone at last. After catching his breath, he gently explored the wound at his temple and found it to be slight. He rose and walked on, befuddled and angered by the hostility of the children. Was he truly a demon-child? Had his mother lied to him then? He hurried through the dank shadows, swiping angrily at vines and saplings in his way, his anguish mounting, until the land began to climb and the heat of the jungle began to relent. Mala's whistle chimed from the clearing where they lived. Until he heard her voice, he had thought his pain was taking him to her. Now he realized that he could not face her yet.

Jaki continued through the forest, the leaf mulch underfoot becoming rockier, the air cooler and braced with resin scents. By midafternoon, he had climbed to the back of the valley where the jungle thinned out and the ferns unfurled their plumes. He stepped out of the forest under the open sky and winced against the bewilderment of clouds and the sudden sun.

Rhododendron fields soared up the steep slopes, groggy with pollen. Beyond the ranges of flowers, he was forbidden to go. The broken rock pitch was the domain of spirits. Jaki breathed in. The blossoms mixed their ethereal fragrance with the lonesome, pungent camphor of wind-rubbed rock. The granite slabs above indeed looked haunted: feldspar veins and amber patches of lichen outlined hideous faces. Always before, those evil stares imprinted in the rocks had kept him away. Now he climbed toward them, heedless of his mother's calls as she shouted after him from their grass house in the glade below.

He did not look back until he reached the jumbled slabs. Mala's cries had dimmed away by then, and when he looked down from this height she was but a grain of color. All around her, the world floated in vast green swells as far as he could see. Blue smoke rose from the Rain Wanderers' camp. Egrets winged north over the dense hills, and at the far side of the sky, the sun burned like a white star above a line of lakes.

Jaki climbed toward an island of tundra, and that exertion spent the last of his hot emotion. When he sat down on a rock shelf among pink tufts of grass, he was soaked with the peacefulness of fatigue. Who was he that others loathed him as he loathed the krait? He looked around for the evil faces that had stared back at him as he gazed up from the jungle. Nothing here but loose black rocks splattered with silver mold. He was the only demon to be found.

Jaki put his fingers to his face and outlined the world inside him. The mirroring touch on the dull bones witnessed the love of his parents — the hollows in his cheeks where his father lay down with his mother, and the jut of nose between the eyes where they stood up again. Mala said that he looked like his father. The old sorrow for that golden-haired man lit up as he traced the tall forehead so unlike his mother's narrow brow.

His fingers fell away, and he spoke aloud the name of his father, "Pieter Gefjon." The name was beautiful in the cold, a name made for the wind. He hugged himself against the icy breeze breaking over the rocks and remembered his mother's story of how his father had caught the wind with sails and voyaged in a big ship across the sea. Because he had never seen the sea, a ship, or the wind stretched out to a voyage, Mala had built a toy boat from a coconut husk and a shred of nipa palm and they had sailed it on the green pond near their home.

Happy thoughts of his mother, the cold rivering from the peaks, and hunger bristling in his stomach stood him up. He surveyed the confused tangle of ranges and valleys beyond the familiar dale where he lived. He would journey those distances someday, he promised himself, just as his father had. The tribes that believed him a demon he would leave behind, and he would travel with the weather over the horizon until he found his father's people. This determination softened the humiliation of his head wound and bruises, and he began the steep trek home.

From above, sheltered by a brash of jagged black granite, the man-snake watched Matubrembrem descend toward the jungle. With a hand flexed to a claw, the sinewy man carved a sigil in the air to protect him from the demon-child's invisible radiance. And then, like black smoke spilling down the broken slopes, he followed.

"Pirates!" a voice cried from the crow's-nest.

The cry from the top spun the captain on the heels of his cordovan boots. Pieter Gefjon, a gaunt, bearded man in blue knee breeches, ruffed blouse, and wide-brimmed captain's hat, stood on the quarterdeck staring hard into the glare of morning fire. Behind him, the Makassar coast of Celebes filled the eastern horizon. Along the shoreline slurred with mist, jumbled green masses of mangroves hunched below immense cliffs laced with waterfalls. Squinting against the barbed sunlight on the water, Gefjon could discern the distant mountains of Celebes. Pinpricks of light jiggled in the air. When he held his hand before his eyes and stared through the slit of his fingers, he spotted the pirates.

Three *djong* — Javanese junks — were tacking toward him. With their dragonhead bulwarks the ships had the swayback look of breaching sea serpents. Their lugsails were green, which meant they were Muslim and no friend of a Dutch trader like Gefjon's *Zeerover.* "Lanun," the captain muttered.

The Lanun were the fiercest pirates in Indonesia. Their Muslim faith was merely a convenience, left over from the jihad that had conquered Asia centuries before, and there remained nothing holy about them. Gefjon knew from other captains who had hunted the Lanun that they topped their masts and bowsprits with the skulls of their victims. He looked for and spotted white flashes of bone among the spars.

Gefjon reached in the pocket of his long coat for his Bible and began to pray. God knew his need. By 1607 the Dutch had been in Asia twelve years, Pieter Gefjon a captain in these alien waters from the first. In that time, his life had become a prayer — first to bring home glory to match the honor of his father and brothers who had fought in Europe to win their country's independence from Spain. But that prayer had died cruelly at Java in his first year as a young captain in the infamous Bloody Armada. Gefjon's admiral razed Jakarta for refusing the Dutch suzerainty, and Gefjon's man-of-war had sunk scores of paper-sailed *djong* attempting to flee the burning city. The screams of the drowning curdled his prayer for glory. Since then, he had lived only to bring useful goods to the primitives in trade for the raw treasures of creation they ignored or hoarded for their forlorn gods.

The captain continued to gauge the speed of the predators. The lighter *djong* were closing fast. He searched the jungle-strangled cliffs for a cove where he could stand off his attackers. Few European eyes had seen this garish coast. The maps described Borneo as a green desert, surrounded by dangerous shoals and infested with pirates. Gefjon emptied the dread in his lungs with a loud sigh. The maps were right.

Zeerover was an eighty-foot, three-hundred-ton *fluit,* a flat-sterned, round-bellied cargo ship. It was the first Dutch vessel to sail the eastern coast of Borneo, lured into these treacherous straits by the promise of diamonds big as walnuts in the silt of the Mahakam River, the Eater of Men.

The promise had been tendered by a fierce, square-faced man with ear lobes like pulled taffy and sharp red tattoos on his throat and the palms of his hands. Without a lash of hair on his face, Batuh's mien was harsh. But sea travel sickened him, and now he lay on the quarterdeck, beige with nausea, staring at the captain.

"Why am I here?" Batuh muttered under his breath as his gorge jostled with the roll of the ship. "I am a Tree Haunter. Tree Haunters have no boats. We are hunters. I do not belong here."

"Larboard reef!" a sailor cried from the foremast, and *Zeerover* lurched as the pilot leaned into the whipstaff.

Batuh moaned. "This must be the curse of the wise crones of my village, staring through me with one eye because I pleased myself among the women without marrying! They are laughing now! Batuh, Taker of Heads! Ha! Courage, Batuh! Here comes Death flashing on the reef. Courage, now! I am already dead — dead two years now, since the chief took my weapons and exiled me to the jungle for killing his holy pig. Exile has led me to this. So now I will die again — and I am not afraid. Just sick."

He could no longer watch the sailors dangling among the clouds or scuttling over the tilting decks, readying *Zeerover* for battle. He closed his eyes, trying to soothe his queasiness with memories of the many heads he had taken from rival tribes to nourish the fields of his people. Once, during a long drought, he had dared to journey far from the Tree Haunters' realm of the green butterfly, north, beyond the fog creeks and the turtle pools, beyond the shining brow of the eagle cliffs, seeking a stronger life force to revive the exhausted paddies. From among the strangely tall and fair-skinned people of the north shore, he took three heads and captured a girl. On his return, the rice grew thick and the hunting was easy.

The girl was named Malawangkuchingang — Bright Air Between the Palms — and though she appeared ugly to the Tree Haunters for not shaving her eyebrows or stretching her ear lobes or cutting her long hair to the bowl shape beautiful to the forest people, she had power over Batuh. He tolerated her ugliness because she had seen the big ships and the red-faced, large-nosed men who sailed them, and she enthralled him with tales of gleaming swords stronger than the finest-honed ironwood weapons and thundersticks that killed at a distance far greater than arrows. Indeed, she claimed that she herself had been fathered by one of those godly men, who had entrusted her to the care of a priest before returning to the sea. From the holy man, she had learned the gods' language, their faith, and many of their secrets, which she shared with Batuh for sparing her life.

Inspired by Malawangkuchingang's tales of the wider world, Batuh believed himself more worthy of leadership among the Tree Haunters than the traditional elders. He declared his peerage by daring to hunt the royal pigs — and was exiled for his arrogance. Intrepidly, he headed south toward where the drum songs of other Shadow Tribes spoke of sighting the big ships and their brightly garbed men with red, big-nosed faces.

At the end of his first night of exile, Batuh met a sorcerer called Jabalwan, a mansnake in knotted skins and bear teeth. "Go back," Jabalwan warned, pointing a needlebone at Batuh. "The way ahead belongs to the dead." For the first time in his life, Batuh was truly afraid. The mansnake was smoke thin, emaciated from a lifetime of fasts and trances. His body, naked except for a snakehide loincloth, pantherskin crown, and fang necklace, was scarred from ritual incisions and tattooed with twin serpents, caught in a dance across his flesh. Others would have scurried back. Batuh slipped sideways into the jungledark and rushed past the sorcerer. He was the hawk's shadow, the wind's gossip, a spark. "It is forbidden" was the last he had heard from his tribe.

In the third moon of his exile, Batuh found the gods he sought. He had defied the mansnake, trespassed the dead, endured the greed of the swamp, and evaded the fierce Muslim tribes of the coast to reach the Dutch trading factory of Bandjermasin. Mazed with streams and silver canals was a garden village of fern-roofed longhouses raised on stilts. At the south end where the rivers flowing through the village spilled into the sea, giant bamboo walls enclosed the trading post. Enormous trees had been lashed together among the mangrove islets to create a wharf, a giant spiderwork of scaffolding and winches among log platforms loaded with bales, barrels, and crates. Elephants carried cargo from the walled factory to the wharf and small boats conveyed the lading out to the deepwater bay where the big ships waited. For one day, these bearded, red-faced men were truly the gods in Batuh's eyes and their village the commerce of heaven. The finery of their clothing, the size of their ships, and the eeriness of their sky-colored eyes bespoke kinship with spirits.

The people of the village told him the truth about the monkeyfaced men. And soon enough he saw them drunk and witnessed a brawl between two of them that left one dead, his skull clubbed open and his brain glittering like a shucked sea creature. They were men, just as Malawangkuchingang had told him, but their hunger was more fierce and made them stronger than most men. He was ashamed that he had ever thought them gods, these loud, ugly men. Yet they were a powerful tribe. Thunder smoked from their ships, Dutch glass cut sunlight into stars that raised flames from leaf tinder, and the metal of their blades was keener than the best knives that the Muslims traded the Tree Haunters for skins.

Batuh decided to work among the bearded foreigners in the trading factory, in the secret hope of luring them back with him to the kingdom of the green butterfly, where their power would win him supremacy and their golden heads adorn his longhouse. He made no money cleaning boots and fetching water for the commonest of the sailors, but he was given food and he learned some Dutch from them. Within a year he was telling tall stories of his village to the sailors, baiting them with tales of what they most wanted to find — diamonds big as betel nuts in the river silt. Pieter Gefjon was the only captain to take him seriously.

The war cries of the pirates jarred Batuh loose from his memories. The Dutch soldiers stood at the rails on all sides of the ship, their matchlocks propped on aiming forks, fuse coils smoking. The cannon boomed, knocking *Zeerover* to one side. Batuh pulled himself to his feet to watch.

The cannon shot had splashed harmlessly among the spry *djong*, and the pirates swooped closer, waving their swords and taking aim with their bows. The severe, sun-blackened faces gleaming with sweat looked like dark beetles ready to burst into flight. The Dutchmen fired their matchlocks as the Lanun archers released their shafts. Batuh swung to the deck, and an arrow whistled through his shadow.

Grapnel hooks crashed over the rail, and crewmen converged to cut them away. An arrow struck one of them through the eye and threw him to the deck at Batuh's feet, where he lay writhing and wailing. The aborigine crouched over the screaming man, who with one hand gripped the lethal arrow piercing his eye and with the other tried desperately to free an amulet about his neck. Batuh tugged the iron talisman free of the sailor's shirt and saw it was a cross with a tiny man nailed to it. The wounded crewman kissed it and stiffened.

Batuh pocketed the dead man's amulet, taking the man's life strength for his own, and tried to stand to join the fight. But nausea stymied him, and he fell back and retched bile over his Dutch clothes. When he looked up, the grapnel lines had been cut away and the crew were cheering, routing the pirates.

Captain Gefjon had taken out his Bible and beat it against his chest while he shouted orders. "Ready cannon to catch them as they flee," he hollered. An arrow stabbed his side, throwing him against the quarterdeck skylight.

Batuh reached Gefjon first. He lay the Bible near the captain's hands so he would have something to grip. Then he took the shaft in his blunt fingers and felt through the blood-soaked cloth to where the arrow had cut between the captain's ribs. Relief rose in him as he felt the barbed head snagged on the bones. It had not pierced any organs. If the poison was not too strong, the captain might live.

Gruff hands seized the aborigine and heaved him aside. Batuh huddled against the gunwale and watched the sailors crowd about their captain and finally carry him off to his cabin. From the pocket of his oversized doublet, he removed the black silver cross with the image of a man in great agony nailed to it. Apparently, this was the monkeyfaces' strongest god, since they all swore by him, calling his name in times of fear as well as disgust. This was the god of the captain's black book, the very god that Gefjon had spoken of so often. Batuh turned the silver cross in the fingers of one hand, feeling the shape of the tortured body, the shape of pain that these devils worshiped. With this amulet, he too could talk with the pain god. He prayed that the captain would live and that *Zeerover* would not turn back to Bandjermasin but proceed, unhampered by pirates, to the Eater of Men.

The amulet felt powerful in Batuh's hands, and he believed his prayer had been received. He believed, too, that when the time came for him to take the Dutchmen's golden heads, in order to assure more abundant life in the land of the Tree Haunters, this god, who the captain fervently assured him was a god of forgiveness, would forgive him.

Under the scarlet evening, Jaki entered the clearing where he lived. Mala's silhouette waited for him in the doorway of their stilt-raised hut. Whispers of twigsmoke and simmering broth wafted on the cool wind, and the boy ignored his fatigue and quickly climbed the notched log to the verandah.

"You have disobeyed me, little man." His mother's unhappy voice stopped him in her shadow. She smelled of firewood, and her slender shape bowed over him, weary with concern.

"Is there meat tonight?" he asked cheerfully, but to no avail.

"Thrice I have forbidden you to leave our valley," Mala remonstrated, her fingers searching through his hair for burrs, insects, and spiders. "Thrice you have disobeyed me. What am I — " She stopped abruptly as she felt the blood-caked knot at the side of her boy's head. He flinched, and she stood aside so that the wan light from the hut illuminated the welt. "How did this happen, Jaki?"

Before he could answer, she hurried him inside and sat him by the cooking fire where a savory broth boiled in an iron pot and a coil of snakemeat crisped on a spit. While his mother cleansed his wound with a wad of moss soaked in nut oil, Jaki told of his encounter with the Rain Wanderer children. "Why do they call me a demon-child?" he asked, looking into her wide face. Her calm eyes, set deep as the black shine in a jungle pool, answered the hurt in him without her speaking a word.

"Your father is different from the fathers of the forest. The children of the tribes do not understand. To them, whatever does not look as they do is a demon. They are ignorant. They were ignorant with me when I was a child. My father, too, was from a distant land . . ."

Into bowls carved from root burls, she ladled the soup, diced the snakemeat into it, and they ate together. She told him the old stories of his father and the pirates who had killed him, of her father and the big ship that brought him and the fever that had carried him away. Afterward, she took out Pieter Gefjon's Bible and by moonlight read to him about the apocalypse from the Book of Daniel. When he lay down on his grass mat to sleep, his mind was awhirl with images of kings stern-faced as cliffs and nations warring like red and black ants jamming a carcass. The frown that had shadowed his childface since Ferang had raised a stone to him relaxed, and he was no longer troubled.

Mala watched him until his eyelids fluttered at a dream's verge. This was the third time recently that she had been left alone all day by her son, and she knew that signaled a lonely change — an ending that she had feared from the day Jaki was born. At seven, boys in the forest tribes were taken from their mothers by their fathers' brothers and were circumcised. Now that Jaki was seven, she knew that his destiny would take him elsewhere.

She lit a string of waxfern to ward off mosquitoes and stepped out onto the verandah. Clusters of stars flitted like mist among the moonstruck clouds, and swarms of fireflies flashed in the black doors of the jungle. The night breathed light. Distantly, Rain Wanderer drum songs rippled in the wind, but she did not understand them. She was a woman from the north coast, a fisherwoman's daughter who had been kidnaped by the forest people nine years before when she was a child. She did not understand most of what had happened to her since, but her faith in her father's God had helped her to endure her solitude and ignorance while she mothered Jaki.

Moonshadows crossed the clearing wearily as the shades of her past. Though she had never seen him in life, she recognized her father, because he was the one pale stranger among the dark wraiths of her tribe. The fisherfolk and her father vanished in the moonsmoke, gone as soon as she stared hard enough to see if they were really there.

She was alone with her son as she had been for seven years. Nothing had changed. The wind turned and carried out of the forest the perfume of the night-blooming jasmine and a chill from the mountains.

Pieter Gefjon did not die. Though a ferocious pain invaded his body and fever wracked him, his greed for diamonds would not be thwarted. He ordered *Zeerover* to continue up the unknown coast.

Strapped to his cot and clutching his Bible to ward off the demon visions of his fever, Gefjon could no longer oversee the expedition. Command devolved to Jan van Noot, an agent of the ship's owner, the Dutch East India Company. Van Noot was a tall, handsome man with white-gold hair. Unlike the others, he was clean-shaven and always meticulously dressed in the latest finery of The Hague: silk breeches, pearl-studded jerkin, white high-heeled boots with red soles, lace cuffs, lace collar, lace at the knees, lace on the brim of his black velvet hat, and lace-fringed gloves scented with frangipani.

Command of *Zeerover* had no appeal for van Noot, and he was content to leave all nautical decisions to the pilot while he contemplated the fortune in raw materials that awaited them on the Mahakam. An aristocratic debaucher, van Noot's greatest strength was his indomitable lust. Now he was fleeing the wrath of a powerful merchant in Amsterdam whose wife and daughter he had seduced. The merchant had arranged, through his considerable influence in the company, to have van Noot assigned to the most parlous venture available.

Danger did not daunt van Noot so long as he had a cabin in which to hide and other men to do the fighting. Denied an outlet for his rapacious sexuality, he invested all of himself in his ambition to return to Europe a rich man.

With loud chants into the jungle at each stop along the coast for fresh water, Batuh declared his victory among the deities in the south. When *Zeerover* reached the Eater of Men, drum songs had already announced Batuh's return to the Shadow Tribes of the interior. Numerous tribes, including the Tree Haunters, converged at the mouth of the Mahakam to witness the glorious homecoming.

Natives with red-streaked faces hopped and jumped to brattling drum music in welcome of the returning exile and the gods who accompanied him. In a fervent display of greeting, men and women, their bodies glossed with nut oil, coupled in the sand; others pierced their cheeks with long palm needles and danced quill-faced in tranced circles. The Dutchmen, splashing out of the longboat that had carried them to shore, acknowledged the performance with tense, nervous smiles and nods, uncoiled the fuses of their matchlocks, and looked to Batuh for reassurance that the aborigines were indeed happy.

The first of the tribesfolk to confront the Dutchmen and the European-dressed Batuh was the mansnake Jabalwan. Jabalwan had traveled among all the tribes of Borneo, and he knew that the monkeyfaced gods were truly men.

He led Batuh and the monkeyfaces up the beach among the frantic tribespeople to an ironwood throne. There sat the chief who had exiled Batuh two years earlier. The chief was a lean-faced man, sleepy-looking now that his time in the world was done, for the return of the ambitious

Batuh among the gods signaled the end of his reign. As a last defiant act, he had prepared a gift that he knew would gall his usurper.

Before the throngs of gathered tribes, the monkeyfaced deities were presented with three bamboo crates of varying sizes. The smallest contained hammer-dented gold plates. These delighted the Dutchmen. The largest crate was jammed with elephant tusks. The middle crate opened to reveal a naked woman.

The Dutchmen could immediately see that she was not like the other tribal women, who wore their short hair shiny with nut paste above their pendulous ears and whose dark faces had thick contours. This woman's skin was the tone of ground cloves and her features fine. Her brown hair fell in waves past her long shoulders to the flat curve of her belly and the dark feathery tuft below.

Instantly enamored of her, van Noot felt his heart dent when he learned from the chief that she was meant as a bride gift to the captain of *Zeerover*. But his disappointment was tiny beside Batuh's dark emotion, for the chief was giving away his own Malawangkuchingang, the girl who had first taught him of the monkeyfaces, the ugly child now grown to a gruesome woman whom the Dutchmen obviously found stunning.

By right, Malawangkuchingang was Batuh's property. But one look at her bruised and calloused hands showed that the Tree Haunters had put her to work in the fields after his exile. The chief's disposal of her was all the excuse that Batuh needed to snatch van Noot's sword and bound to the throne. The chief rose and met the luminous blade as it cut through the tufts of his monkey-fur vest and pierced his heart. Batuh grabbed him by the hair beneath his leopardskin crown and yanked him forward, bending him over the ground. The sword was a lightning stroke in his hand. In silence, he raised the chief's severed head, and a din of blood swirled over the sand.

A roar boomed from the massed tribes and collapsed at once into confused yammerings. Tree Haunter warriors, who had been guarding the flanks against the other tribes, pushed toward Batuh, knives drawn.

Batuh swung the head about, shouting, "See me! See me! The gods see me! I have come back and taken what is mine! The gods are my witnesses!"

The Dutchmen were appalled but helpless to do more than stand before Batuh, swords drawn, matchlocks primed to defend themselves if the tribes rioted. Their presence was all the authority Batuh needed. From that moment, he was chief of the Tree Haunters.

The agitated crowd made way for Jabalwan, who strode up to Batuh and stood in the shadow of the sword. "Will you kill the soul-catcher, too?"

Batuh lowered the sword and presented the head to the mansnake. "This is the only blood the gods want, Jabalwan."

"Leave the head here," Jabalwan ordered, "and come with me into the forest." He walked back through the crowd toward the emerald archways of the jungle.

Batuh squinted after him, pondering his choices. If he went with the soul-catcher alone into the forest, he would have to face down the sorcerer's poisons and tricks, which in an eyeblink could cost his life. Yet if he did not go, all the tribes would witness his cowardice.

With authority, Batuh ordered the tribes to gather their finest offerings for the gods. To van Noot, he lifted the ornate hilt of the sword. "I will keep this."

"And my blessing with it," van Noot said, grateful to see the tribes calming down and putting aside their weapons, the drum music resuming.

The sorcerer had disappeared into the dense brush, and Batuh moved quickly toward the tattered shadows of nipa palm and mangrove. The green light enveloped him in its damp heat, and the excited music and voices of the people on the beach were immediately muted.

Batuh was exultant despite his fear. This was his home, and he peered with nostalgia at the great trees, their buttresses draped with pallid tentacles of liverwort, their heights meshing in a sunshot canopy of dangling lianas and moss veils. The cries of the birds told him in which direction Jabalwan was moving.

Batuh followed, clambering noiselessly over the soggy hulk of a felled tree. He wished then that he was not wearing the monkeyfaces' clothes he had donned to impress his people, for they hampered his speed and held his body heat close to him so that after only a few minutes his garments were slick with sweat.

The mosquitoes swarmed, and he longed for the root and mud paste that the tribal peoples used to ward off the biting insects. He passed tilted, man-high ant towers, blood-mottled flowers wide as a full stride and stinking of dead meat, and a field of pearl-sized mushrooms.

Deep in the jungle where night lingered in chambers of chilled air, Batuh found Jabalwan sitting on the ground in the dark shadow of a massive tree gilled with fungi. "Z-z-zhut!" the sorcerer called as Batuh passed by without seeing him. The sound so perfectly mimed the twang of a bowstring that Batuh flung himself to the ground and rolled in the black, fusty duff.

"*You* want to be chief of the Tree Haunters?" The sorcerer laughed.

Batuh scrambled to his feet, brushed the leaf rot from his clothes, and swung his sword. "I have returned with the gods." His voice sounded froggish to him, and he waited a moment before using it again. In the interval, he stared boldly down the length of his sword at the sorcerer and noticed that the mansnake's eyes were closed. Red serpent eyes tattooed onto the lids were watching him. Batuh lowered the saber. "The gods are my witnesses."

"They are men, Batuh," Jabalwan said in his smoky voice. "I know about them and their big ships. They are men like us."

"They are different."

The sorcerer snorted. "They stink. You have their stink. You smell of something that doesn't like the sun. I think your shadow is already among the shades, Batuh."

Anger flinched in Batuh's chest. "I *am* the rightful chief of my tribe. I have taken more than any other in the hunt. I have offered more heads. I have wandered as far as the rains, to the sea, to the village of these monkeyfaced men. *I* have returned — and I bring their gifts."

Jabalwan smiled, his red-stenciled eyes flinching. "You and I have known each other from the beginning of time."

"Then you will help me? You will make peace with the elders?"

"Peace?" The sorcerer's eyes opened, and the suddenness of their intent stare jolted Batuh. "You are not talking to a chief or an elder. What do I care for peace or strife?" He snorted, and his face lifted, proud as a cobra's. "I am a soul-taker. I live in the spirit world outside the tribes. I watch the clouds in the hands of heaven, their backs to the earth. I talk with the forest and learn from its madman's grip on the earth how to reach for the clouds."

Batuh pointed his sword at Jabalwan. "If you do not help me, I will kill you."

Jabalwan sneered, held up his left hand in a fist. When he opened the hand, a leopard coughed from behind Batuh, and the warrior spun about, sword ready to block a pounce.

"No leopard wants your sour flesh, Batuh." Jabalwan folded his hands in his lap. "If I help you, what will you give me?"

Batuh faced the soul-taker again, his jaw clamped, the sword trembling in his hand. His anger felt radiant in the wake of his fear. Then his anger quelled as an idea struck him. He reached into his pocket and took out the crucifix he had taken from the dead Dutchman who had fallen at his feet during the pirate attack. "This is the god of the monkeyfaces," he announced. "Would you have it?"

Jabalwan stared somberly at Batuh, then closed his eyes again. When Batuh was at the point of admitting his failure, the sorcerer's hand lifted, slow as a watchful viper, and waited, palm up.

A smile expanded in Batuh, but he kept it from his face. He placed the crucifix in the soul-taker's hand, but he did not let it go. "I will need one thing more than your guarantee of peace with the elders."

Jabalwan opened his eyes but did not remove his hand.

"The chief of the monkeyfaces was wounded in the chest by a Lanun arrow," Batuh said.

"He was blessed it was Lanun," Jabalwan answered. "They make their poison from the blue squid of the reef. The poison goes weak quickly, and they're too lazy to make it often."

"Will you give me medicine for the wound?" Batuh asked.

Jabalwan's fist closed around the crucifix. He nodded to Batuh. "What you seek is under your feet."

"The leaf rot?" Batuh asked with a skeptical frown.

Jabalwan smiled. "Is that all you see?" The sorcerer brushed his fingers through the compost and came up with the writhing body of an ant. "Gather me a handful of these red ants. I will get everything else we need."

Batuh picked up a broad, newly fallen leaf and rolled it into a cone, one end of which he pinched off. With the gummy sap from a branch of a nearby shrub, he glued the seam and began collecting the stinging ants in the cup.

While he worked, Jabalwan foraged around the giant tree where he had been sitting for blue, filament-sized fungi. When Batuh came to him with his leaf cup milling with ants, the soul-catcher put a hairy tuft of fungi in the cup, squeezed off the open end, and rolled the cup against his thigh, thoroughly mashing the ants and filaments to a paste.

"Pack the wound with this," Jabalwan ordered. "It will burn, and he will fever overnight. By dawn, he will grow stronger. The wound will heal cleanly."

Batuh slid the sword between his belt and hip and took the leaf-wrapped mash with both hands. "I will never forget that you have helped me, Jabalwan."

The sorcerer held up the crucifix. "I accept this amulet for my medicine. But for peace with the elders and their families, you have not yet paid me."

"What do you want?"

"A life."

Batuh scowled.

"Not yours," the sorcerer said. "And not now. One life, when I call for it."

Batuh nodded once, and Jabalwan turned and walked into the green darkness of the jungle. A monkey screamed, and a flying snake lashed across a rent in the forest canopy. The sorcerer was gone.

Jaki woke in the night, jerked upright by the ache of his wound. Ferang's churlish grin and the Rain Wanderer boys with their fist-held rocks fell away before the familiar shadows of the hut, and the dream's derisive laughter slurred to the gabbling of toads. He jumped up and hurried to the hammock where his mother slept. He needed her solace against the ugly feeling the stone had nailed in his head. He wanted her assurances, though already he knew, in a wordless way, that he was beyond her help — and that frightened him more and made him yearn for her embrace.

Yet when he reached for his mother, his hands would not touch her. Seeing her asleep, breathing peacefully, the ache of his bruises lifted into his heart. She was as beautiful as the highland vista he had seen yesterday, where the world stretched out under him.

He backed away so that he could see all of her lying before him, her knees drawn up, hands folded together under her chin. She looked like a child, as small as he. A gasp of love held him still while shadows inched through the hut. And in that tranceful watching he felt something of the forefearing that had troubled her when she had sat over his sleeping body.

He, too, was aware that a change had come upon them. He had felt it for the first time earlier when he had climbed above the flower fields and had looked back to see her tiny shape against the immensity of the jungle. Someday he would leave the valley and wander that immensity to fulfill his time in the world, just as his father and her father before them. And what then would become of her, this child who was his mother?

A moth tapped his cheek and broke his stare. His lungs filled with the dewy chill of night and lifted him backward into the darkness.

By the time Batuh emerged from the forest, the Dutchmen had discovered, to their amazement, that Malawangkuchingang spoke a language they could understand. Though Spanish was the tongue of the Netherlands' enemy, her ethereal beauty won their sympathy. Van Noot could barely keep his hands off her and had ceremoniously helped her to cover her nakedness with a wrap of broad cloth.

Malawangkuchingang was happy for Batuh's triumphal return, for the Tree Haunters had mistreated her during his two-year absence. He was her abductor, yet he had always treated her well out of respect for the knowledge she offered him. Now, when he ordered her to go with the Dutchmen aboard their big ship and administer the medicine Jabalwan had given him, she objected but could not refuse.

Batuh had seen the adulation in the eyes of the Dutchmen and realized at once how useful this ugly woman from the north could be in the completion of his ambition to own Dutch heads — heads that would assure his authority among all the tribes. He promised van Noot that she would heal the wounded captain and that he would in the meantime organize the goods of the tribes for trading.

The Dutchmen were leery of the native medicine. But to van Noot, the tall, clove-skinned woman was even more enticing than the gold plates and the ivory, and he ordered her brought aboard, though he had no hope that she could help the ailing captain.

*

In Pieter Gefjon's smithering vision, the native girl was ablaze, the air around her head shaggy with golden brilliance. In the two days since he had been wounded, the pain had grown stronger and the fever more devastating.

"He's very ill," Malawangkuchingang told van Noot in Spanish. She was breathing through her mouth, not to smell the stink of putrid flesh that clogged the cabin.

Gefjon stared at her with fevered eyes. "I have medicine for your wound," she said in the language of the enemy, and he knew then that she was the seductive shape of death come to deliver him from his suffering. He squeezed his Bible tighter. She was death, the lioness the Lord had sent to sniff out his soul. Her claws had been in him since the arrow pierced his ribs. Brightening with this revelation, he lifted his face toward her, and the charred pain in his lungs ignited. He flopped back with a strangled cry.

Van Noot bent over the captain. "This medicine, it could be poison."

"The best medicine." A smile sparked in Gefjon's sweat-runneled beard. "Let the lioness have me."

Malawangkuchingang opened Gefjon's shirt, her wonder at the cloudy touch of silk and the oiled colors in the abalone buttons spinning away at the sight of the wound. Its black cauterized lips grimaced around a puckered hole, blood-raw with clots and seeping yellow syrup. The young woman looked up at van Noot. "We may be too late. You must hold him down."

She opened the leafroll, and a slithery stink swirled through the cabin. Quickly, she pressed the purple-brown mash into the wound. Harrowing pain clouted Gefjon and with one blow beat him black.

The next afternoon, after the first successful day of trading Dutch cargo for the riches of the jungle, the captain's fever broke. He awoke briefly and found the native woman beside him. Despite van Noot's impassioned entreaties to join him in his cabin away from the wound's stench, she had stayed beside the captain, aware that he was a man probably not unlike her own father, a foreigner whom she had never known.

Gefjon studied the brown sweep of her hair, the haughty bridge of her nose and the Palestinian depths of her dark eyes. He wanted to thank her for easing the pain, but her touch disembodied him, and his voice did not fit. She smelled of the afterlife, sweet and blue as snow, thundery, like a remote typhoon. He shut his eyes, and her Moorish face went with him into the darkness. *Why are you afraid?* her puzzled expression seemed to be asking. *The grave is a cradle. The earth is the nest of heaven.*

He peered at her through the slits of his lashes and saw her eyes gleaming with the grace of a devil determined to keep him in this world, to dull his fear of the crossroads, and to parcel his soul back into his cold flesh. She was going to heal him. He would not resist.

During the night, the Bible had fallen from his hand, and she had picked it up and cradled it, remembering the Book as the comfort of her orphaned years. It was as heavy as the priest's Bible she had known as a girl, and like the priest's it was bound in leather and printed in Latin, the only language she could read. She opened the book and, to calm the restless captain, read aloud the first line that caught her eye: "Rejoice, because your names are writ in heaven."

The captain was fading, and Malawangkuchingang's voice went with him into his swoon. Echoes clustered and droned: *writ in heaven.* The darkness he was falling into was cracked with light. Each tiny tendril of fire, Gefjon saw, was a name, a whir of letters scrawled in light the color of water or stars.

By dawn, the pain had abated and he was strong enough to get out of bed and relieve himself at the head. In gratitude for his restored health, he knelt beside the cot that had almost been his deathbed and prayed with the native girl who had saved him. To repay her for her help, he granted her wish to be returned to Batuh, and she was taken ashore with the first longboat.

Gefjon was delighted with the progress of the trading. The tribes were eager for Dutch goods and had bartered large quantities of ginger root, nutmeg, rhino horn, and silver. But the diamonds that Gefjon had suffered to possess were not to be found. Batuh promised him that they existed but had been gathered for ritual use in the interior and would be delivered within two days. As proof, he handed the captain a fish-bladder pouch, saying, "The girl Malawangkuchingang was given to you by the old chief. With these, I will buy her back from you."

Gefjon opened the pouch. His fingers twitched when he saw two chunks of smoke-colored stone within. "Diamonds," he breathed.

"Yes, Tuan. These were a tribute presented to me at last night's feast by the Rain Wanderers, a tribe from far in the interior. They call these stones the mountain god's tears."

"Will there be more?" Gefjon asked, trying to gauge the stones' weights and realizing, with mounting astonishment, that they were of excellent quality.

"Oh, yes — many more," Batuh promised. In truth, no other diamonds were expected. Instead, he had secretly arranged by drum song with the Lanun to take *Zeerover,* planning to relinquish the ship to the pirates and claim the golden heads for himself.

Even with the promise of more diamonds, the captain was uneasy about staying in the wilderness estuary too long. He did not wholly trust Batuh, and he feared that pirates could appear at any time. He gave orders to have the ship ready to leave that night when the tide came in.

Sitting alone at his desk in his cabin with the diamonds and the Bible in his hands, wealth and the afterworld in his grasp, the vestiges of fever honing his clarity, Gefjon contemplated a vision he had endured in his sickness. His fever had dropped him into a black pit veined with fire. The tiny flames of the fire were actually letters, and the letters spelled minute names, each name a branch of the fiery tree. *No — not a tree but a network of veins in the black rock of the fever pit, wormings.* What did those images mean?

Opening the Bible to the inside cover, he read the names of his parents, Kee and Jaki, written beside their birth dates. The space where his name belonged remained blank. Since he had been given the Bible twenty years before, when he left home for the naval academy, he had carried the common superstition that if he wrote down his name in the Book before his parents' natural deaths he would doom himself to an early grave. Now, as he uncapped the desk's inkwell and drew his quill, he realized that the space had been waiting not just for his name but for his vision. He signed his name and birth date and below it wrote in Latin: *I have seen the lion of the final moment — it guards the mine of signature.*

When Batuh learned that *Zeerover* was to depart that evening with the tide, he despaired. The tribes were too awed by the monkeyfaces to rise up against them and take their heads, and the Lanun would not arrive to assist him until the following dawn. Only one way remained to keep his prey in position until his trap was ready.

Batuh in his big clothes, his headdress a fountain of bouncing feathers, came striding toward Malawangkuchingang where she sat on the beach apart from the other women.

"Bright Air Between the Palms," he said, and she was frightened to hear him use her full name. The last time he had called her that he had explained to her his need to defy the chief and risk exile. "I need your help."

"Whatever I can do for you, my chief, I will." Her fingers touched his chest, and he lay his hands over hers.

"What I must ask of you now is difficult for me, Bright Air." His half-moon eyes searched her face. "But if I am to be chief, if the land of the Tree Haunters is to be fruitful, I must keep the monkeyfaces here in the bay another night."

"Why, my chief? We have their tools, their cloth, their salt. Now they are trading furniture and trinkets. If they leave now, we lose nothing but ornaments."

"I am a hunter. They are my prey. I have brought them here for more than their goods. The people have their goods. But what does the land have?"

Malawangkuchingang's hands tightened in the lace of Batuh's shirt as she comprehended. "Can you do this?"

"I can do it. But only if they stay one more night."

"Batuh, their guns, their cannon . . ."

"We are all orphaned to the dead, my Bright Air. This is not a thing for a woman to understand."

Malawangkuchingang's nostrils flared. "I am not a Tree Haunter woman. I know of the dead. I do not wish to see you among them." She pressed her body closer to him, hoping to fill him with her heat and reason. "The tribes will not defy the monkeyfaces, Batuh. They will flee at the first loud noise. You stand alone."

"There are others — fierce warriors. They are coming and will be here with the morning. I must keep the monkeyfaces here until then. The ship will leave tonight — unless you help me."

"But how can I keep the monkeyfaces here? The captain does not obey me."

"There is a way." Batuh breathed deeply to clear the dread in his lungs. "The one called van Noot desires you . . ."

Malawangkuchingang stepped back from Batuh with a horrified gasp. "He is so ugly!"

"This is so. That is why I can barely find the breath to ask you to favor him tonight — "

Malawangkuchingang gasped again and hid her face in her hands.

Batuh stepped closer and with one arm around her and another easing her hands from her face explained: "Do not give yourself to him until he convinces the captain to stay till morning. You will know this is so if the big ship does not sail before twilight. By then the tide will have withdrawn and the reefs will keep the ship in the bay until morning."

"I cannot give myself to him."

Batuh put his hand under her chin and gazed with yearning at the bold bones of her face. "You have taught me that we can do anything."

"Not this, Batuh. Do not give me to that ugly man."

"I am not giving you to him. You are mine. Always. But I can think of no other way to keep them here. I can think of no other way to be sure I will have the power I need to hold the land — for us, for our children."

The thought of children by Batuh lightened her fear, yet her heart still prickled with cold. "No man but you has ever wanted me."

Batuh reached into the pocket of his doublet and withdrew a necklace of dragonfly wings, iridescent and more delicate than any Tree Haunter jewelry. "From the Rain Wanderers," he told her. "You will have the most beautiful clothes and finery in the tribe. Never again will you have to work the fields." He pulled aside her long brown hair and tied the necklace about her throat. "Tomorrow, we will return to Long Apari together. You will be my wife."

"You will not hate me for this thing you ask of me?"

"I will hate you if you deny me this thing," he said coldly, and then tightened his embrace. "It is important. You will win prestige among the people for this. You alone will have been favored by a god. No one will ever call you ugly again. And you will be the first wife of the chief. Your story will enter the circle songs to be sung long after we have found our way to the afterworld. Will you obey me?"

Malawangkuchingang looked down at the slender body God had made from the earth's mud. Even among her own people in the north, she was despised for being a half-breed. Batuh had spared her a humiliating life by taking her away. God had made her from the mud, made her ugly, and yet given her to Batuh, a man of greatness. God had returned Batuh with the monkeyfaces. God was the glory and the power. She was but mud. She was not clever like the boar. She was not strong like the water buffalo. She was not brave like the hawk of Batuh's totem. She had no totem — yet she would die as the beasts die. That insight comforted her with the knowledge of how she must live, and she looked up at Batuh with the eyes of a free woman. "I will obey."

Night's jewelry sprawled above the jungle canopy. The moon was low in the east, and stars like bead glass gleamed from the embroidered seams of the sky. The dark itself was shiny as black feathers. Soon dawn would unfold its wings and night would fly.

Jaki sat on a branch in the canopy of the jungle. In the dim light he turned his face toward the atap hut in the clearing below him, where his mother slept. Wisps of burnt waxfern rose to meet him. The frosty smell kept insects away, and Mala burned coils of it throughout the night. The fragrance was comforting to Jaki, associated with night and his mother. But tonight, another scent hovered on the jungle's breath. Mala had not noticed it yet — the mountain whisper, the rain echo, the fog smell of the soul-catcher.

The scent meant there would be delicacies. Meat, rare nuts, and berries wrapped in offering leaves were right now being placed among the low tree elbows to be found in the morning. Mala said the soul-catcher brought these foods for them because he loved them. He was their guardian, sent by God to protect them from the jungle. Jaki did not believe that God had sent Jabalwan. God sent fruit and nuts to trees and meat to the bones of animals. The sorcerer was a man, though Jaki had never seen him. He had caught only glimpses, hurried motion-blurs gliding through the shrub at night, soft breathing in the trees' high places, and once a beetle-wing glint of eyes watching him through the wall of Mala's garden.

Tonight the boy had been roused by his bruises, but instead of waking Mala to comfort him, he had lain in the dark thinking about what had happened to him and why. Despite the Rain Wanderers, he had felt a primal pride in his small life. Mala loved him, and the animals who knew him frolicked and lulled with him every day. He had no need for the Rain Wanderers, who called him a demon, and he determined never to seek them again.

The rockmist scent of the sorcerer had risen while Jaki was making that resolve, and he had crept out of the hut into the forest's milky darkness, hoping to find this fabulous being whom he could barely imagine. Would the soul-catcher, with all his magical power, have fed him and Mala all these years if he had thought Jaki a demon?

He shimmied into a tree whose branches sprawled far enough for him to follow the scent across the grain of the wind. He scurried silently, pursuing the musty odor into the night. This was the closest he had ever been to the soul-catcher, and his heart pounded with excitement. A burst of wind whooshed past his face as he surprised a bird. The lamp of its cry flew ahead of him, and the rain-weary smell vanished.

He swayed with laughter. The soul-catcher was shyer than a mouse deer. A breeze veered off the forest floor, and a blur of the spoor mingled with leaf rot and pea flowers carried from the opposite direction. Jaki turned to pursue, and a brilliant whistle, like a bird's laugh, glittered across the glade. That was Mala. She had caught the soul-catcher's scent, too. Always she called the boy close when the soul-catcher was nearby.

Jaki paused, and the sorcerer's storm scent was gone. Briefly, he was tempted to ignore his mother and fly after the sorcerer, just to glimpse this mysterious man who had given them so much. But then he remembered how childlike Mala had looked asleep in the moonlight, and he could not bear to disobey her again. Assailed by a wave of love for her, he skittered out of the tree and dashed for the stilt-raised hut.

"She wants you," Batuh told van Noot in Dutch. They were standing at the edge of the forest in sight of the trading beach. Batuh had stepped directly up to him and spoken, gesturing to the shy native girl who held back in the shadow of the jungle.

"What are you talking about?" van Noot asked sharply.

"Bright Air Between the Palms wants you," Batuh said, thinking dire thoughts of the Lanun to keep himself from bursting into laughter at the joy and disbelief in the Dutchman's face. "She's too shy to speak herself. Afraid you will not want her. She asked me to ask you. Will you have her?"

"I — the — she's a gift to the captain," he finally blurted out.

"Tuan has given her freedom," Batuh replied. "You did not know?"

"No. I — I hadn't realized. She's free now?"

"Not in her heart. Not till you have her."

"I must hear this from her," van Noot insisted, and walked to the girl, bowed demure as a fern. "Mala — is what Batuh says true?" he asked her in Spanish.

Malawangkuchingang faced him placidly. "You must not tell the captain," she replied. "He is a Christian and will not understand my pagan desire." Breathing deeply to withhold her loathing, she put her hand on van Noot's sweat-gummed blouse. "Give me a secret night with you here in the forest and I can return satisfied to Long Apari."

Van Noot removed his big hat and wiped the sweat from his brow. "I had no idea."

"You do not want me?" A hopeful surge spurted in her, and she withdrew her hand.

"Of course I want you," he sputtered, and seized her hand. "But I had thought from the night you refused to come away from the captain — well, frankly, that you considered me repulsive."

"I was the captain's wife then, Jan." The sound of his familiar name nipped her tongue like vinegar. "I had no choice. Now I am free again. I have spoken to Batuh, my chief, about my desire. He approves." Close up, Jan's skin glowed like a freckled pear, and she turned her face.

"My lady, you do not seem very eager for this union." The company man glanced nervously about but saw no one else in the chapel darkness of the forest.

"Such unions are arranged differently in my tribe." Malawangkuchingang spoke to the green galleries. A garland of sunlight fluttered, and for a moment she saw a wet gleam among the tendrils of sunny pea vines, the heat of animal eyes. In the glare of a sunshaft, the sorcerer's ape-slanted brow flashed. Malawangkuchingang continued speaking as though she had seen nothing. "It is our custom when a woman desires a certain man for her to put some manioc in his hand. If he desires her as well, he will then come to her mat. If not, he will pretend to sleep." A sea breeze flurried the vines, and the sunshadow she thought was the soul-catcher lifted away with the wind. "A direct meeting like this is uncomfortable for me. Is it not for you?"

"Yes, but I am delighted to hear your true feelings. Won't you look at me?" She looked at him with an intensity he thought was passion, and in the amber of her eyes he saw his own face reflected. "I have wanted you from the first — when I saw you as the Lord made you."

"Do not speak of the Lord."

Jan frowned around a smile. "Certainly what we're feeling has the blessing of the Lord who blessed lepers, harlots, and his own betrayer?"

Malawangkuchingang searched van Noot's face for his meaning and was relieved to see his blue eyes shining with desire. "Then you will meet me here tonight?" she asked.

"If I can."

"You must." She lay her head against the ruff of his chest, tasted the milky aroma of his sweat, and heard the sprint of his heart. From behind the company man, Batuh appeared, smiling with satisfaction. Malawangkuchingang let the Dutchman go and turned away quickly to hide her shame.

"After the longboats are aboard, we weigh anchor," Captain Gefjon declared when the company man and the pilot presented themselves in his cabin. "We'll put into the strait and spend the night under sail. Van Noot, you'll set aside the company portion of our goods as described in our charter. I'll want the final manifest for the log by sunfall. Pilot . . ."

"Captain," van Noot interrupted, his tongue flicking over his lips anxiously. "We can't leave now. I assured Batuh we would continue trade tomorrow."

"Good." The captain stared at the company man, seeing the eagerness in his posture, in the lizard flicks of his tongue, in the whites around his eyes. "It's better for him to believe we are returning. That will forestall any desperate maneuver on his part. Batuh is ambitious."

"Batuh is desperate only for our goods, captain," van Noot pressed. "We have yet to barter our brandy. The natives have heard of our spirit water from Batuh. He's made it so famous they'll gladly trade gold for it."

"The crew needs the brandy more than the potatofaces," the first pilot protested.

Van Noot narrowed an irritated look at the pilot and continued speaking to the captain: "Batuh has assured us that baskets full of diamonds are on their way. Certainly that's worth our brandy."

"Batuh promised us gold today," the pilot retorted.

Van Noot pointed to the pouch tied to the captain's belt at his hip. "You have diamonds there, haven't you? Batuh has kept his word about them."

Gefjon removed the pouch from his belt and placed the two cloudy lumps of rock on his desk. Pale light squirmed through them in smeared rainbows. "Batuh gave me these when I returned the girl to him. He was buying her back, he said."

"Bait, says I," the pilot grumbled. "He wants us here till he can gather enough of the tribes to take back their gifts and our heads with them."

"Who knows what he's withholding," the captain added.

"Whatever he's withholding now, he'll give up for the brandy," van Noot said. "Let me bring them a few kegs tonight, as a gift. Once they've tasted it, they'll sell their gold idols. We'll leave the natives happy and return home rich."

"We're already rich," the pilot boasted. "We have over six hundred taels of silver in the hold. We have the gold plates and the ivory from the old chief. And we have crates of camphor, gutta-percha, rhino horn, enough total value to outfit a grand expedition. We can come back again. Let's take what we got."

"I agree with the mate," the captain said. "We leave as soon as the longboats are secure, while the tide is in."

"No." Van Noot swallowed and spoke stiffly. "The ship, the crew, and the cargo are company-owned, and I am the company agent. I will say when the trading is over. Your responsibility is to navigate and defend the ship. We stay until the trading is done. I insist on it." Van Noot had half risen from his seat, and he sank back with the weight of his conviction.

The captain was staring down at the diamonds. The rocks held sunlight in their oily interiors the way his sloppy life held him. Like them, he was incomplete, burdened by too much of himself, waiting to be perfected, gem-cut around his flaws, made more by less. His greatest flaw, in his own estimation, was his appetite for fortune. He had forgone a wife and family to make his fortune, and here it was, in these rocks exchanged for a sad mereling, a girl who knew the Book and yet still wanted her heathen lover. He chuckled humorlessly, and the pilot and the company man exchanged a baffled glance, which he caught. *Let them wonder.* The Bible was but a dream of men beside the actuality of these rocks. *God's tears. For the world is given to Satan, and here is the world's eternity.* He was but a dewdrop, his will the glint of the sun, shrinking across his moment of life. He wanted his share of eternity now, before he gave the lion's share of time back to God.

He faced the officers with a smile so weary it was hidden in his beard. "We leave tomorrow before noon, with the tide. Van Noot, when the manifest is done, bring Batuh one keg of brandy."

The evening rains had finished, the clouds were apricot-tinted, and the sea was a peacock's fiery blue when Jan van Noot rowed a skiff with a keg of brandy to shore. As he approached the fire-dotted beach, his heart was tripping loudly in his chest, more from fear than from the exertion of rowing. He was the first to go ashore alone, and the possibility that this might be a deception, a ploy to take his head, haunted him. Yet he did not stop.

A torch boat carrying Batuh in full feather and beastskin regalia met him near shore and escorted him with song and laughter to the first sandbar. There he was surrounded by natives. They attached torches to the stern and bow and splashed the skiff through the shallows to the beach. The natives looked bigger in the dusk, their greased bodies shimmering with energy, and he wished then that he had accepted the pilot's offer of a kris. Though little good any knife would do him among these hundreds of savages, he realized. The keg of brandy was lifted out of the skiff and disappeared at once into the throng of carousing, painted bodies.

Batuh said nothing to van Noot. He pointed up the muddy, weed-strewn beach toward the black tiers of the jungle, above which the first stars appeared. Van Noot began mouthing a question, but Batuh turned away and was carried off by his jubilant tribesmen, his white feather headdress swaying vigorously to the drum dance.

Van Noot headed up the beach, waving away mosquitoes and squinting into the falling light to keep from tripping over driftwood and seasnake holes. At the edge of the beach, he stopped. Dread hummed in him. The dark of the jungle was the black of the earth's interior. Fireflies twinkled, drastic odors luffed on the breeze that seeped from the dark, and demon cries tolled. Van Noot looked to the bay, and the sight of *Zeerover* strung with lights and perched on its slippery reflection urged him to rush back down the beach to the skiff. Before he could move, a voice called to him from the darkness: "Tuan."

He faced about and saw Malawangkuchingang standing before him. She took his arm and guided him into the jungle.

"Mala," he said in a hush, "all afternoon I've been in a dream, waiting for tonight."

"Say nothing more, Tuan," she begged him. She could not bear to speak with this devil. If he would only keep silent, her desire to please Batuh would not be thwarted by her repulsion. "Nothing we can say now will match what we feel. Please. Be silent."

Van Noot squeezed her hand more tightly and kept his seething sentiments silent. But his fear would not be contained. "Where are you taking me?"

The sound of his anxiety amused her, and she said around a giggle, "You will be pleased. Do not be afraid."

They walked a winding path through sheer blackness under the cackling of monkeys and the startled cries of birds. In the wake of Mala's sweet fragrance, the mosquitoes were biting less, and soon van Noot had adopted the native girl's low-slung gait. He felt as though he were flying with her through the night's plunging expanse. The whirs, clicks, and whistles of insects spun about them. High overhead, stars came and went like the tide of the wind, like exhalations of radiant smoke puffing through the black of the forest.

A luminous clearing opened before them. The trees were strung with lanterns — paper-thin, perforated gourds shining with trapped fireflies. At the center of the clearing was a hut raised on log stilts and covered with broad atap leaves. Mala led him up the lashed-bough steps into a dark interior thick with the scent of blossoms. She sat him down on a floor matted with fleecy ferns and tugged off his boots.

Mala's hair fell over van Noot as she undressed him, and his hands pulled at her sarong until her flesh was cooling his. Fearfully, she closed her eyes. His heat was the joy God's jealousy had denied her with the man she loved. She wanted to offer this monkeyface no more than a tuber would, but she had to act passionately or he would become suspicious and she would lose Batuh as well as her pride. The music of his touch surprised her. His lips sought hers, nip and tuck, and she trembled, her hands flying in the air, weightless.

Thicketed in the tangle of her hair, his fingers crawling a design between her legs, his face locked to hers, he slow-tugged her toward pleasure. Though she resisted and thought only to pretend, she could not repel the desire his clever touch stirred in her, and soon all pretense collapsed.

She surrendered to his smell of dead fire, his stink of underrocks, and the widening joy of her body, and her hands fell like sparks to his back. A mindless ecstasy was stirring in her limbs, blind and insistent. Not love. Not love but love. She felt her bones unlocking, her heart two-timing, her muscles etched with a deep good feeling. She trembled violently, a cry stung through her, and a stunning blow of passion kicked her legs straight out.

Jan lay her back on the ferns' wool and entered her. He was a tantrum rising and falling in the black, riding her the way the moon rides the wind, his sweat bright as phosphorus. She was whimpering beneath him. He rode his splinter of eternity hard, lit with her wetness, in full strut until his hunger burst free of him in a heave of bliss that sprawled him over her.

They made love twice more between spent interludes, lying on their backs listening to the sounds of the forest. Then van Noot slept, exhausted, replete. Malawangkuchingang wiped herself with a fern bough, wrapped her sarong over her body, and stepped swiftly into the night.

Batuh was waiting for her in the starlight. He took her face in his hands and kissed her eyes. That unlocked all her trepidations, and she clutched at him and sobbed.

"You have done well, Bright Air," he said to her with the gentleness of a father. "You have done well indeed. And if you will do for me one more thing, one more brave thing, you will have proven yourself a chief's wife."

Malawangkuchingang did as Batuh told her and woke van Noot and returned with him to *Zeerover.* She made love to him in the rolling darkness of his cabin, and when he had fallen asleep once again, she put on her sarong and crept up the narrow companionway to the quarterdeck.

The watch in the crosstrees and the drowsy man in his hammock at the bowsprit did not see her as she opened the scuttlebutt and filled a bucket with water. Limping with its weight, she found the stairs that led into the hold and lowered the bucket one step at a time while she followed after, down into the thick stink of the ship. On the gunnery deck, she had to pause until the dense darkness relented and she could discern the slung hammocks of the crewmen. All were asleep, and she slipped past the hulks of cannon to the center of the deck where Batuh had said she would find a large bin.

She reached in and felt the metal hoop and wooden circle of a barrel top. The lid of each keg had a cork stopper like a big petrified mushroom. Her hands were barely strong enough to uncork them, and when she had pulled the last one, the muscles in her arms were twitching from the exertion. A scent like cold ash rose from the bin. Grunting, she lifted the bucket and slowly poured the water over the kegs, gritting back the hurt of her tired muscles.

Done, she left the bucket inside the bin and closed the lid. Relief opened vividly in her, and she pranced up the companionway to the main deck and the guttering stars.

"Mala." A heavy voice descended, and she stopped in midstep, her heart squeezing like a caught animal's. "Why are you on board?" the voice asked in Spanish.

She looked up and saw the silhouette of the captain. "Tuan!"

Dreams of diamonds buzzing with the yellow light of hornets had fidgeted him awake, and he had come topside to calm himself. Diamonds were why he had come to Borneo. But now he realized that the diamond-bright lymph of the Milky Way was what he truly desired — God's grace, not God's tears, no matter how valuable. In the pit of night, sick with loneliness, he had decided he would give the diamonds to his pilot, who had a wife and the hope of a family, and he would return to the Low Countries with his share of the bartered wealth and begin a new life. *Diamonds,* he had thought, *only mime the soul's light. How much more valuable is the soul herself.* He had been walking the quarterdeck, breathing the pure light of the spheres, thinking about the gems Batuh had paid him for the girl, when he was startled to see her rising from the hold.

Malawangkuchingang scurried up the stairs to the quarterdeck and stood before the captain. He was hatless, his long hair floating in the steady breeze like seaweed. "I came aboard with the company man," she said, bowing her head, opening her hands innocently before her.

"He asked you aboard?"

"Yes."

"The pilot told me van Noot was enamored of you. But I did not think you cared for him." Mala said nothing. "Where is he now?"

"Asleep. I could not stay there anymore. It was too hot."

"Then he will not mind if you come with me."

She reached out and placed both of her hands on his chest and dared to raise her eyes. The captain looked solemn and white as a sleepy god.

He took her hands in his and removed them from his chest. "I do not want you in that way." Her gaze fell. "You saved my life. The medicine was the sorcerer's, yes. But you — you were the dread and the rapture that led me from the dead. Come to my cabin. Let *me* read to you from the Book and tell you what I saw in you when I was with fever."

Malawangkuchingang let herself be led through the captain's dim companionway to his stately cabin. He sat her in a lyre-back chair and opened the windows so that the ocean's breath swept into the corners of the room. On the bedstand, a glass bell the color of wind cupped an elegant flame, and by that light the captain opened his Bible and read to her in Latin the short passage about the names of the living being written in heaven. When he was done, he looked up. "What do you think that means?"

"I do not know."

He chuckled. "Neither did I. Until I was fevered and I saw you." The smile dimmed in his beard, and he was somber with recollection. "I saw you as death. I saw you as a magnificent lion of death. I had good reason then to believe that vision, naturally, for I *was* dying. That certainty wrenched me free of my most cherished illusion — that God abides our dreams, our ambitions — that through prayer, God helps us. I can tell you now, He does not. Through prayer, we help God by learning who we are, by learning our real names, which are written in the darkness from which all things have come." He shut the Bible. "Do you understand? I will be surprised if you do."

"I understand that you have seen truth," she answered, her eyes lustrous, her head framed by dawn's fire in the windows. "Father told us often, the truth sets people free."

"And so I am free. Until tonight, I was a slave of the company, seeking my fortune in these foreign lands — as if gold could free me from this world of suffering. But the world goes on until God frees us from it. Gold is luxury but not freedom. A simple thought, it would seem, yet only now, tonight, as I contemplate my own death, is that simplicity so clearly true. And that truth has set me free at last. Free of my hunger for wealth. For the first time, I can go home. I can leave Asia poor of pocket and return to Europe rich in acceptance of all that may await me. You understand that, you who have been a slave. You know freedom."

"There is a truth I must tell you." Malawangkuchingang spoke, her voice sounding far away. "At this moment, your life is forfeit. I have deceived the company man with his lust, and he has deceived you with your need."

Gefjon's benevolent face contracted. "What are you saying?"

Terror whirled in her to see the sudden alertness in his face, and she forced herself to speak. "At this moment, your ship is surrounded by pirates, Tuan. God has favored Batuh."

Gefjon leaped from his seat, seized the sword dangling from his chair, and rushed from the cabin. Malawangkuchingang took the Bible from the bedstand and hurried after him. They were in the cramped companionway when the alarm gonged wildly. Startled voices cried out. Gefjon kicked through the slatted doors and met the pilot scrambling across the quarterdeck toward him, kris blade in hand, face dark with fury.

"Lanun!" the pilot cursed. He pointed his knife seaward to where a flotilla of wind-slanted *djong* were converging on *Zeerover.* Back-lit by dawn, the fleet was a black swarm.

"Cannon!" Gefjon cried.

The pilot took his arm and stopped him. "The powder's been doused. The cannon are useless."

The first volley of arrows slashed over the decks, the alarm gong went silent, and the crewmen spurting up from the gunnery deck with krises and cutlasses dove for cover behind the longboats. An arrow stabbed into the plank between the captain and the pilot.

"Hoist anchor!" Gefjon shouted. "Men to the sails!"

The second volley from the closing *djong* felled the two men who scurried to the anchor winch.

"Cut the anchor line!" Gefjon bawled, and an arrow sickled past his head.

The pilot's stubbly face was shining as he seized Gefjon by his elbow and turned him about. "Good-by, cap'n. I will see you in heaven." With his free arm he hugged Gefjon mightily, pushed away, and bolted down the stairs to the main deck, bellowing: "Cut the slimy line, you drunkards!"

A plague of arrows swooped over the main deck. The pilot went down under them and lay pinned through his throat and chest to the mizzenmast. The first *djong* thudded against the hull. Grapnel hooks crashed onto the main deck, and war shouts leaped to the yardarms.

Gefjon unsheathed his sword and twirled about, slashing his blade in an arc to where Malawangkuchingang cowered against the companionway hatch. The point of the blade rested in the crook of her collarbones, and she stiffened. "You watered the gunpowder."

"Yes."

"Why? Why did you save me only to kill me?"

"If you died, the others would have left. Batuh wants your treasure."

"Treasure!" Gefjon cried out, and Mala's head banged backward against the hatch as the sword pricked her throat. "Is that my undoing? Greed!" His face was livid, but when he saw her clutching the Book to her breasts, he relented and stepped back. With a swipe of his arm, he drove the sword into the deck between them.

Behind him she saw the pirates, smudge-faced, viperish men, bounding onto the quarterdeck. Below, many of the crew had jumped overboard and were being speared like fish. Two of the men were praying and were hacked where they knelt. Jan van Noot's piteous wails echoed up the companionway from his cabin, where the Lanun had found him. Malawangkuchingang trembled with despair.

"My vision was right after all," Gefjon said, meeting her terror with a grim bemusement. "You are death — and all I've mined from my grave is greed. Christians and savages, all mining that dark lode! As if we could take enough out of the earth for all we must put in."

The pirates grabbed the captain, one snatching his hair in a clawed grip and jerking his head back. A blade flashed blue with dawnlight and in one stroke cut through Gefjon's neck. His body collapsed under a jet of blood, and his head was raised against the lustrous sky.

Mala fell to her knees, squeezing the Book to her body. The head had been sheared off so quickly that the eyes were still alert and certain, staring down at her with borrowed light.

Jabalwan waited among the scaly-leafed casuarina trees that grew in the low, swampy plains behind the shore. From there he could watch the pirates plundering the ship without himself being seen. Dawnsmoke flamed above the delta islands, and the figures scurrying on the decks of the ship were spectral and shadowy. The headless bodies of the Dutch were thrown overboard with jubilant shouts that crossed the bay and reached the soul-catcher like the squeaky sparks of bats. He lifted his stern face to the sky and intoned: "I watch the clouds in the hands of heaven, their backs to the earth. It is the clouds that carry away our spirits. It is the clouds that return prophecy with the rains. Their love is all I care for."

Only when Batuh and his warriors returned in their dugouts from the ship, bearing the heads of the captain and crew, did Jabalwan lower his stare from heaven and cross the bridge of fallen trees to the beach. At the sight of him, the warriors shouted their reverence and raised their trophies. The slavewoman, Bright Air Between the Palms, was with them. She cowered beside Batuh in their dugout, and she did not budge when her chief leaped to shore and strode triumphantly toward the soul-taker.

Batuh stopped before Jabalwan and presented the heads of the captain and the company man, holding one in each hand by their hair. The company man's face was locked in a rictus of horror, while the captain's features were quiet, his bloodless flesh gleaming like the underlight in a river.

Jabalwan took the captain's head and dismissed the Tree Haunters with his blessing. Batuh was disappointed to lose such a powerful head, bright with glory and bearded like a golden orangutan — but with the other nine heads and all the forest tribes waiting to see how he would dispense the bounty among them, he did not protest. The tribes were proud of him and eager for his leadership. His legend was already among the drum songs as the bravest of jungle wanderers, trapper of devil gods, slayer of Dajang, the old chief, and ally of the pirates. In fact, he was no ally of the Lanun. They would have fought him for *Zeerover*'s treasure, but he wanted only the heads. He had also demanded the return of Malawangkuchingang.

Mala's fingers gripping the side of the dugout felt like feathers. Her body was a slip of smoke. She stared hard at Jabalwan and Batuh standing among the dunes, not wanting to close her eyes, because behind her lids she still saw the captain's burst look, his whole life in his face. Inflamed as an orchid, the captain's shorn head stared from inside her and would watch her till her last day.

Batuh could see that Mala was troubled. He believed the land would heal her, and he took her back with him to Long Apari. His ambition to unite the tribes was more than a dream now that he had produced golden heads with the power to lure rice out of the mud and draw wild pigs into the forest clearings. He distributed the heads among the powerful families of the tribes that would agree to accept him as titular chief of the forest peoples. The Snake Walkers of the south and the Stilt Hunters, the Tree Haunters' archaic neighbors, were swift to agree, and their families immediately set to arranging marriages among the confederated tribes. The other jungle tribes were reluctant to accept a ruler who did not live in their own longhouses. They became Batuh's obsession, and he spent the first months of his return wooing them to relinquish their autonomy. Eventually, Batuh won the fealty of all the surrounding peoples except the most primitive and remote clan, the Rain Wanderers.

As Batuh was preparing a war party from among the allied tribes, hoping to intimidate the aboriginal Rain Wanderers into submission, Malawangkuchingang swelled with child. Since their return together to Long Apari, she had been his only wife, not so much out of affection, for she was colder than he remembered, but because his preparations for war had left him no time for his usual lasciviousness. Her impending motherhood infused him with pride. Though Mala was quieter and more withdrawn than when they had first been lovers, he cared for her. She had been his true friend and his teacher, daring him with her counsel of love to be loved. In his language the word for love meant trickle of water. Not the gush of the flood or the loneliness of clouds, those longhouses of nothingness, carrying their rains far away, but a trickle, enough to refresh. He had never thought of love as more than that nurturing trickle. She had made him see that what was small was great. Alone in the jungle during his exile, alone with the monkeyfaced men in their sour-aired wharf city, he had remembered her transcendent, inescapable faith in a life's trickle, and he had found strength. Now she would be the mother of his child; she would give him a son to inherit the kingdom he had carved with his trickle of life.

Mala's pregnancy was aswarm with premonitions. Shortly after her belly began to distend, a prodigious horde of dragonflies hatched in the surrounding creeks, and Long Apari flashed and clicked with so many of these iridescent insect eaters that for the first time in tribal memory meat could be hung from the trees to dry and not a fly would touch it. The pigs penned nearest Mala's end of the longhouse had litters of eight to ten instead of the usual four to six. The paddies facing her verandah grew plush green with rice even though the land was shaded and unfertilized. The elders wanted to carry Mala through their fields and into their pigpens, but Batuh would not allow it. He knew the omens presaged the birth of a mighty spirit, and he would not risk losing his heir to a slip in the mud or a bellicose pig. He forbade anyone to approach his wife closer than at arm's length, and he arranged for musicians and storytellers to amuse her during her lonely days while he trained his army.

Dreams of a clear light blowing like rain soaked Mala's nights, and by day the watertrace of the dreams stained her sight so that colors seemed stronger, shadows gluey, and the crosswinds over the rice paddies furry with half-seen shapes. The angels that Father Isidro, the priest of her childhood, had told her tended his earthly gardens had come to watch over her unborn. In secret, she studied the Bible that she had taken from Pieter Gefjon. When she could get away from the musicians and storytellers, she spent her days alone in the forest with the Book, reading, watching the bees lug their amber cargo, praying for the dead captain whose life she had saved only to betray. In the pollen-drenched air under the blossoming trees, she sat so long and so still entranced by her prayers that the bees tangled themselves in her hair and slumbered there. Later, when she made love to Batuh, the bees stung his hands, and they swelled like gourds so that he could not even draw a bowstring or hold an ax. For the rest of her pregnancy, he refused to touch her. The old women of the tribe, who had kept account of all Batuh's amorous conquests from his first adolescent blunderings, recognized the spirit work that denied him his own wife.

In deep daylight, under the blue flame of noon, Mala gave birth to a boy-child. Her labor was protracted and difficult, and the midwives chanted and sang to keep her alert. But at the crest of her birthing, with her lungs scorched from withheld screams, a baby's cry jumped, and the songs stopped. No joyous cry from the midwives joined the infant's wailing, and Mala defied her exhaustion to sit up and see what was wrong. Grimed with afterbirth, wrung from her effort, she reached for the hands that had comforted her in labor, wanting them to support her effort to rise, to see her baby. But they were gone. The infant was laid at her breast with its cord still uncut, and the midwives who had attended Mala stepped hurriedly from the longhouse, stumbling over each other, their hands over their eyes.

Batuh, who had been waiting with his brothers on the verandah, was baffled by the midwives' hasty retreat and commanded them to return and help his wife. No one would obey. When the eldest midwife was safely at the bottom of the notched log that served as a stairway, she looked up at Batuh and put her hands under her withered breasts to ward off evil. She grinned a toothless smile with scarlet, betel-stained gums, leering at the great man's misfortune. "The child is a demon," she said, then turned and scurried off.

Batuh found Mala bleeding and the child suckling. The infant was pale as a grub, its round head matted with pale lichen, its eyes like chipped glass. The cord was wound about the placental sac, and he lifted it and saw that the child was a boy. Mala was pallid with blood loss. Batuh shouted for his brothers, but when they saw the mushroom-skinned, white-haired baby, they would not cross the threshold. Batuh found the wads of sphagnum moss the midwives had gathered, and he used them to staunch the bleeding. "Bright Air, you have given me a son," he told her, and she smiled wanly.

"The child is *orang puteh,* a white man," she said in a whisper.

"Even so," Batuh answered, stroking the sweat-torqued hair from her throat, "he is of your blood — and he will be chief of the forest tribes. Let the people fear him, and his rule will never be questioned."

While Batuh was swabbing the umbilical cord with rice water, a shadow fell over them from the doorway, and they turned to see Jabalwan standing within the room, his black and red feather headdress brushing the lintel.

"I have come to take what is mine," he said in a voice like splintering wood. "You are chief of the Tree Haunters, as I promised. Now you owe me a life. I will take the mother-child."

Batuh stood defiantly between the soul-catcher and Mala. "The mother is my wife. The child is my son."

"They are mine now," Jabalwan replied with a soft hiss like a flame coming on. "They are one life, and they are mine. Will you defy me?"

Batuh thought of drawing the sword he had taken from the monkeyfaces and piercing the sorcerer through his heart as he had once done to the old chief Dajang. Jabalwan had only his small knife dangling from his hip. Batuh's hand twitched but would not move. The sorcerer's face was dark as a piece of night, his eyes notches of alertness. He stepped forward and put a spidery hand on Batuh's thick shoulder. His touch was bright and humming, like a blue link of the wind. "If you deny me, you will lose everything."

Batuh stood aside, and Jabalwan bent over Mala where she lay naked and blood-smudged on a reed mat. From a bamboo tube that dangled at his side he sprinkled a gray powder speckled with pink flecks into the burl cup filled with rice water. He lifted her head and made her drink. Immediately her eyes fluttered, and she glided into a plumbless sleep. With expert care he lifted the infant from the slumbering woman and inserted a black toe of a root in its mouth. The child, which had begun to cry, calmed. The sorcerer cradled it in one arm and with his free hand drew his knife and cut the birth cord. "You shall be called Matubrembrem, demon-child," he announced.

Batuh felt short of breath. "Where will you take them?"

Jabalwan looked over his shoulder and stared at the chief through his watery hair. "To where the next world meets this one."

Mala awoke in the longhouse to find herself cleansed and dressed in a blue silk sarong stenciled with chrysanthemum flowers and her baby asleep at her breast. A flagon of water and a bowl of fruit was at her side. The crone midwife was squatting beside her, her eyes brilliant with betel light. "You are the soul-taker's wife now," she gummed, and swallowed her cackle. "Nothing will be too good for you. Ghosts will watch after you and your demon-child. Beasts will bring you food. And the clouds themselves will dance for you."

Batuh came to Mala directly from his training field when he found out she was awake. He was dressed in his battle finery: brown breeches studded along the seams with hexagons of turtle shell, his billowy white blouse quilled at the shoulders with green feathers, his sword clacking behind him like a tail. Mala had slept two days and nights, and he expected to find her bleary and disoriented. Instead, she was alert and sitting up and already aware through the crone of all that had transpired.

"I will kill the sorcerer," Batuh promised her.

"No." Sunlight splashed in her lap where Matubrembrem slept, swaddled in white silk, his skin like porcelain, his hair silvery gold. "No one will murder for us. The old woman says you promised the sorcerer a life for his help. Is this so?"

Batuh's dark eyes nodded.

Mala reached out and touched Batuh's broad face. She was resigned to her destiny. The implacable melancholy that had penetrated her with the death of Pieter Gefjon stirred in her. "You will have many wives. All of them prettier than I. Among your people you are losing an ugly wife and a demon-child. Be happy."

Batuh was not happy to lose the one woman who had stirred his blood. That day Jabalwan appeared again in Long Apari, with a troop of huge apes and two Rain Wanderers. The presence of the Rain Wanderers, ghostly, bone-powdered men with adder-red eyes, alarmed the Tree Haunters and brought the warriors out with metal axes and knives. The sorcerer removed a needle-long dogbone from his headdress and held it up to the sky. Whoever he pointed it at would die, and the warriors scattered. The chalk-white Rain Wanderers carried on their shoulders a riding platform of bamboo with a nipa palm canopy, and they lowered it to the ground before the longhouse where Mala lived. Jabalwan motioned, and the troop of hulking apes bounded up the nicked log and into Mala's room. The chief's brothers and their wives rushed from the longhouse with shrill screams. Batuh, who had been at the latrine creek, came running toward the longhouse with his sword drawn. When he saw Jabalwan, he lowered his blade.

Mala was asleep, but the marl smell of the apes alerted her just as the largest of the beasts was lifting her baby from her arms. She screamed, and the ape dropped the baby back into her lap and retreated. When he reached again for her baby, Mala backed away with a horrified hiss.

Jabalwan strode into the room, barked at the ape, and sent it rushing outside. "They will not harm you," he assured her. "They are my children. You will come to love them." He held out his long-fingered hand. "Come away."

Mala and her infant went with the soul-catcher and his apes, riding on the shoulders of the dust-painted Rain Wanderers in their shaded litter. The last she saw of Long Apari was Batuh standing in the buzzing sunlight, his drawn sword a tusk of yellow fire, his free hand raised in parting, his eyes starry with tears.

Following serpentine riverbeds of slimy mud and then brambly ridges, Jabalwan led his troop through the jungle and into the mazy and jagged mountains, where sheet mist soon obscured the lowlands they had left behind. Three weeks they journeyed, stopping along the way at tiny villages to eat and rest. At every stop, the people stared in awe at Matubrembrem and presented his mother with their finest treasures: wide-mouthed ceramic jugs and silk sarongs from traders of the ancient north, a snakeskin comforter and squirrel-fur quilt for the child, a yakskin cloak, a hornbill feather blouse, resin candles to keep away insects, and leaf-wrapped bundles of rice cakes studded with honey-red beetles. The apes carried these treasures as the trek continued deeper into the mountains where only ghosts meandered.

In a high valley at the edge of the jungle, where the massive trees and the verdant blaze of lianas tattered to evergreens, meadows of rhododendron, and lunar heaths swooping up to stark black crags, the journey ended. In the heart of the valley was a glade where a hut of atap leaves and hewn wood was raised on stilts above ferny ground. Coconut palms crisscrossed each other among flowery fruit trees, and a sunspangled creek flashed at the far end of the clearing.

"Here you will live with your child," Jabalwan told Mala as the Rain Wanderers lowered her litter before the hut. "I will see that you have meat and foods you cannot forage for yourself. And I will protect you and your child from the biting ghosts of dead cobras." Those ghosts had killed Mala's mother and father and most of her childhood tribe, devouring them with blood-bruising fevers. "The powers of the world want the boy to live. As a man, he will be a soul-catcher. I will teach him myself."

Mala kissed the waxed knuckles of the sorcerer's hand. "Will you be living here with us?"

"You will not see me again until the time comes for Matubrembrem to leave you and learn from me."

Those words chilled her, and her voice shivered when she asked, "When will you come for him, then?"

"At the end of his seventh year his childhood ends. He is not as other children — and he will not be as other men. That is why you will live here at the top of the jungle far from all other tribes, alone with the spirits that are your child's teachers."

Jabalwan escorted Mala up the notched log and into the hut. A scent of cinnamon lingered in the air from the freshly cut wood. The apes had left her possessions and gifts on the reed mats. Among them she was relieved to see her Bible. The sorcerer read her gaze and said, "You will teach your child from this. He will know the language and stories of his fathers."

In one corner of the airy room, protected from mosquitoes by a gauzy veil of lake-colored cloth, was a cradle carved from the wood of a tree stump and glazed with hardened pine sap. In the opposite corner was the rattan crate in which she had been presented as a gift for the monkeyfaces. The soul-catcher opened its lid and removed a small object wrapped in red silk. "When the boy asks about his father, you will show him this and tell him of the man's bravery."

Jabalwan lifted aside the red cloth and revealed a tiny head in a nest of blond hair, its eyes sloped shut like an unborn child's. At the sight of it, emotions burst like weeds in Mala's heart, and she clutched her child tighter. "It is the head of the white chief!"

"Yes." The sorcerer stroked the roisterous beard of the shrunken head. "I prepared him myself. He will be your husband in the other world. Talk to him. He will recognize you."

The seven years that Malawangkuchingang spent with her son in the jungle valley at the top of the world were the happiest years of her life. Though she was a prisoner, she knew for the first time pure freedom, because she was undisturbed by the judgments of other people. Loneliness never touched her, because all that was dear in her life was with her in her child. She named her son Jaki after the captain's father, whose name she found in the cover leaf of the Bible. The boy was healthy, strong, and bright, and watching life splurge with animal fervor in him was her greatest delight. In the early years, she taught him of the earth, its green and many-colored jewelry and its creatures. She spoke to him in the two languages she knew, her native tongue and the Spanish she had learned from Father Isidro, which for her was the voice of angels and which she used only when she told him of God.

At first Jaki had no interest in God. God was invisible, and the boy, like all boys, was enthralled only by what he could see and touch. His friends were the jungle animals, the creatures he befriended with food offerings, gentle persuasion, and his own innate animality. Mala taught him nothing of hunting, and the animals of this remote valley knew no fear of him.

Jabalwan's apes were frequent visitors. The sorcerer had trained them to thrash the surrounding undergrowth with big sticks and drive away the cobra and the krait. They were docile beasts and liked to be preened and serenaded with the tribal songs Mala taught her son. Jaki rode on their broad backs, and occasionally they carried him up out of the valley into the expansive rhododendron meadows that sprawled like quilts in the lap of the rocky peaks. Lying among the sunclustered corollas, watching the clouds sculling over the mountain claws, listening to the apes humming their dolorous songs, Jaki's first memories congealed. He was three years old.

At night, by the pearly light of resin candles, Mala read him stories from the Book. And his dreamland became a desert of wandering prophets, exile, war, jeweled psalms logy with love for the unseen. By day he thought little, if at all, about these mysterious images — until the day in his fourth year when he found one of the apes dead. The beast was cradled in the buttress of a big tree, its club still in its hand. Its eyes had already been eaten out by rats, and the ants were busy in the sockets despite a driving rain. A krait had bitten the ape during the night. The red-and-yellow-banded serpent lay battered dead by the ape's side, its unhinged mouth grinning its empty victory. Mala and Jaki buried the ape beside a massive oak and then sat on a nearby log and read from the Book among the glass stems of the rain. For the first time, Jaki listened with his heart: "'The hand of the Lord has done this. In his hand is the life of every living thing.' Job, twelve: nine, ten."

Mala's heart caulked with grief to see in her boy's eyes the hungry need to understand. From that day, she strove diligently to teach him the magic of letters and words. He listened with an absorption that was painful to see in so young a child, and she questioned her capacity to teach him and prayed fervently that he would know what she herself could not explain.

Reading of lineage in the Book, Jaki wanted to know who his father was. His notion of fatherhood was uncertain. He had yet to see a man, and he imagined a theandric woman big-boned as an ape, hairy with beard and chest fur. Mala could not bear to tell him that his father was the salacious fool who had conceived him by her desperation to please the one man she had loved. Instead she told him of Pieter Gefjon, the noble sea captain who had given her the Book. Jaki was mystified by her descriptions of the sea and the big ships that had brought his mother's father as well as his to the jungle. He could not conceive of a body of water greater than the line of lakes he saw flashing from the high rhododendron meadows. She told him the sea was so big no man could see the end of it, and he went dizzy with the thought. After that he badgered her to tell him everything she knew of his father, the sea captain. She read him Gefjon's family tree from the Book and showed him his own name, the name of his grandfather, written before his father was born, and he himself puzzled through the captain's fevered scrawl and read the two abstruse lines he had entered below his own name. Mala could tell him nothing of the lion of the final moment or the mine of signature, and when he became frantic to understand, she revealed to him the captain's head. "He is your father," she told him. "Ask him." She explained that pirates had killed him and that Jabalwan the soul-taker had preserved his head so that she would still have a link with her husband and that her son would know the face of his father.

Jaki had thought little about Jabalwan until then: he was merely another of the jungle's mysteries, a scent of cliff dew that came and went during the nights before leaf-wrapped food appeared among the branch tines of the nearby trees. But the sight of the diminutive head with its placid features that still retained their wind-burnished authority filled him with respect for the recondite sorcerer. His mother showed him how she spoke with the captain by placing the head before the Book and opening the covers into the mountain wind that sluiced through the trees at twilight. As the pages flurried beneath invisible fingers, Mala dropped a tiny pebble among them. Where the pebble came to rest, she read the captain's message.

The first night that Jaki queried his father, the pebble landed in Numbers 31, where God commands Moses to slay the Midianites, and Moses admonishes the officers of the army for not killing all the women and children. *Now therefore, kill every male among the little ones, and kill every woman who has known man by lying with him.* Jaki was confused. "Did not Moses bring Israel the commandment from God not to kill?" he asked. Mala had no answer for him but to return to the Book and read further. After that, he never queried the Book again, though he continued to listen to his mother read the stories of the vengeful God. The stories thrilled him with their enormous weight of grief. The world was the history of grief — the dead ape he had buried beneath the oak, the dead father whose small face would never truly speak, the dead little ones and the dead women killed by command of a God with a heart as empty as the blue desert of the sky. This was a God of terror and mystery, of all that the boy feared. He would ask no questions of this God his mother loved. Even then, in the midst of his seventh year, he knew he was God's enemy.

Mala stood in the doorway of the hut. "Jaki," she called to him, and he sparked out of the black wall of the jungle. He spurted across the glade and pranced into the embrace of her long hair, breathing its grass flavor. "Why did you leave me alone in the night?" she asked, running her fingers through his hair, feeling for bugs.

"Is it night, mother?" Jaki asked impishly, pointing across the tattered roof of the forest at the first green wisps of dawn. "I thought it was morning."

"You thought you could see the soul-catcher." Mala ushered him inside with a scolding click.

"I have never smelled the soul-catcher so strongly," Jaki said. "I think he is very close. I want to see him."

"He is very close," Mala agreed, and went to the corner of the hut where she kept the rattan chest with all her valuables: her sarongs, the dragonfly-wing necklace Batuh had given her, the Bible, and Gefjon's head. She took out the Bible and the head and laid them on the rush-woven floor. The head was no larger than a pomegranate, and in the brightening darkness the great shocks of goldthread hair streaming from the scalp and beard looked like fog.

"Mother, why are you taking Father and the Book out?"

Mala hushed him with a stern glance. Jaki could feel a coldness spilling around her heavy as a mountain breeze. He was baffled. The sodden fragrance of the soul-catcher wafted stronger on the night air.

With the certainty earned from her seven years as Jabalwan's creature, she knew that he would appear to them for the first time soon, when the knives of dawn glinted over the horizon — moments from now. She had planned for this from the beginning, from the day she had arrived here, when she had last seen the sorcerer. After he had left, she had lain with her child, imagining how she would appeal to him when he returned. The tiny, warm body had inspired her imagination, and she had believed that when the time came, prayerful words would triumph in her. But now that seven years had lapsed and the soul-catcher was approaching, the words she had envisioned herself speaking did not come. Only anxiety volunteered itself in her. She knew what she had to do, and she put the Bible in Jaki's hands and laid the head atop it. "These are yours now, my son."

"Mother, why?"

"You will need Father more than I now, because the time has come for you to leave here."

Jaki almost dropped the Bible and the head. "Are you leaving, too?"

"No." She forced all her attentiveness into her face, trying to hold a smile. "I must stay."

Jaki put the Book and the head on the ground before his mother. "I don't understand. Why must I leave?"

"Only God knows," she answered, placing her hand against his cheek to still the tremor of panic there. "We must trust God. Always."

"I don't like God." Confusion surged in Jaki, and he reached for his mother. At that moment, a dark smell unraveled on the wind.

"Wait here," Mala ordered, and went to the door to peer outside.

"No," Jaki insisted, and he grabbed his bamboo spear from beside his sleeping mat. "The soul-catcher is coming for me."

Before either of them could move, they heard a heavy scuttling on the log stairway, and the door was suddenly filled with a black, hulking shape. The beast lurched forward into the hut, filling the small space with a pummeling roar.

Jaki and Mala collapsed in fear before the frenzied animal. Then it was gone, leaving behind a stink like wood evil with worms.

A bear, Mala thought, remembering Batuh's tales of the big beasts that lived in the mountains. She looked about for a way to block the door, and as she was sizing up her rattan chest, a human figure silently appeared in the doorway.

"Bright Air Between the Palms, I have come for the boy. Bring him out here."

The figure stepped away, swiftly as a swerve of water so that it seemed to the mother and child as if they might have imagined him. Jaki looked to Mala with alarm. He had never thought of the soul-catcher as dangerous, only as a guardian and provider.

"Our time has come, little warrior," his mother said quietly. "We cannot fight it."

"I will kill him," Jaki vowed. "And I will kill his beast," he added with less assurance.

Mala shook her head, her face dark with concern yet smiling. "Does not the Book say killing is wrong?"

"Unless one kills for God — like Jacob or David or Moses with the Midianites."

"God does not want you to kill the soul-catcher. He is your guardian — and now your teacher. You will go with him. You will do whatever he tells you to do. Understand?"

"You told me he would come for me when I was to be a man. Am I a man now?"

Mala stroked his hair. "If you are brave enough to leave me and go with him to learn all you must learn, then you are a man."

The muscles in Jaki's small face twitched with thoughts. "Mala, I don't think I am that brave yet."

"Yes, you are." She hugged him and turned him to look at Gefjon's head on the Bible. "Your father will be with you. He will watch you as he always has from the spirit world. Whenever you wonder if you are brave enough, remember him. He has gone ahead of you. He has already suffered everything you will ever endure. Take him and the Book and go now to the soul-catcher."

Limned in dawnlight, the head was a golden apple. Its life was with the spirits — but Mala was here, warm, familiar as sleep. He reached for her, and she seized his hands. Sternly, she said, "You are a man now. Take your father and the Book and go."

Her abruptness squashed the boy's will, and he shriveled into sobs. She released his hands, stood up, and turned away. If she stayed with him a moment longer, she would succumb herself to the anguish of their parting.

Mala stood at the head of the notched log and stared down at the soul-catcher waiting in the clearing, leaning on his tall blowgun. He was exactly as she remembered him: naked but for his black waistcloth, snake-sinew armbands, and headdress of sacred red and black plumes. He did not acknowledge her. Instead his gaze was fixed beyond her in the doorway where the boy emerged holding the Bible like a tray with the head perched atop it.

Jaki stopped beside his mother and looked up at her, seeking her dark eyes. But she would not look at him. She kept her attention deep in the dawn where the pain softened on its way into her heart. The boy faced the soul-catcher below him.

The man looked nothing like what he had imagined. He was dark, darker than Mala, almost black skinned as though charred. His hair, too, looked singed and ashen. The boy saw the twining serpent tattoos coiled about his legs and the puckered, glossy ridges of ritual scars on his chest and shoulders.

"Come closer, boy," the soul-catcher said in his strong voice.

Jaki stopped before him and looked back at his mother on the platform of the hut. The first ray of sunlight had lit the peak of the house like an offering flame.

As he looked away, the soul-catcher stepped closer and snatched the Bible and the head from the boy's grasp. "These are mine now," the gaunt man said. "As you are mine." His fierce, ugly face seemed soaked with a shadow that would eat noonlight. "Go to the kapok tree where you searched for me before your mother called you. Wait there."

The tone of command in the sorcerer's voice was impossible to ignore, and Jaki scurried across the clearing to the giant tree. From there he watched the soul-catcher climb the steps to the hut. Malawangkuchingang did not step back when Jabalwan approached her. Instead she bowed her head and waited until he called her name.

"Bright Air Between the Palms," he said in a voice that surprised her with its gentleness. "You have done well. The boy is healthy and alert. He will be a soul-catcher."

Mala raised her head and met the benevolent smile of the sorcerer. In one hand he held the Bible and Gefjon's head; in the other he offered a deer-antler vial. "Drink this," he said, tenderly as a father, "and you will know peace."

Mala accepted the vial. "Will I see my son again?"

Jabalwan shook his head so narrowly it barely moved. "You return now to your people. You are going to where we all go. But you are blessed for being the mother of a soul-catcher, and you will know no pain. Someday we will all gather again where there is no pain — but not all of us shall arrive without suffering."

"Then I am to die," Mala said with resignation. "For all the love I have given, you are killing me."

"The heart does not die when we think it does," Jabalwan replied, and nodded to the vial in her hand.

The sorcerer waited, and Mala took the vial and smelled the smoke of absolute loneliness, a sweet pungency like crushed petals. Curiously, she felt no fear. She recognized the intractable will in the sorcerer's stare, and the figure of her small son standing beneath the massive trees was all that was left of her life. "You will return the Book and his father's head to the boy?" she asked.

"When he has attained, they will be returned."

Malawangkuchingang nodded her acceptance and looked once more to her son. She raised the antler vial to him and quaffed the icy liqueur. The blossom-heady taste of it filled her sinuses and chilled a track to her stomach like a long road of moonlight. The vial fell from her hand as her strength flew from her muscles, and she dropped backward, falling to the verandah.

Jaki saw her collapse, and he dashed across the clearing for her.

Jabalwan met him at the bottom of the nicked log and caught him by his arm. A swipe of sunlight illuminated Mala where she was sprawled with her back to the woven wall of the hut, and she raised her hand and waved to him. He let the soul-catcher take his hand.

Mala smiled as her son was led across the glade, backward like a child caught in an undertow. Her son was to be a soul-catcher. She had done well by him during their time alone in the glade. On the blue sward before the atap hut her baby had learned to walk, romp, chase butterflies. She had taught him to read the Book as Father Isidro had taught her.

The thought of the black-robed priest shifted the patterns of her hallucination, and she was suddenly staring into the priest's rumpled face with its wizened beard and benign eyes. He was pleased that her child had been given over to the life of a soul-catcher. Jesu had come into the world to teach men to be catchers of souls. Her son knew this, because she had taught him. Father Isidro's smile brightened with kindly regard, and she blazed like a gnat in the sunshaft at the end of its life.

The poison was swift. Her hallucination vanished, and she felt her life rushing into the gaze of the sun, all her strength soaring with the jungle mist, vanishing at the sky's edge into blinding light.

The wing beats of her heart slowed, and with each pulse, the glare of sunlight concentrated to shadows, blurring as her vision lost focus. She was back on the quarterdeck of *Zeerover* in the silver dawn eight years ago when she had knelt before the severed head of the captain. That scene wrinkled into Batuh's face, the one man she had loved. He was staring at her with the same grief that he had displayed on the morning she had left Long Apari with the sorcerer and his troop of apes.

Batuh's face whisked away. Had his dreams of uniting the tribes come true? She would never know. Where Batuh's face had loomed, bars of twilit clouds were dissolving into sunsmoke. Morning mist swirled above the treetops, and she rose with it, silent as the sun.

At the edge of the glade, Jaki stopped to look back at his home and his mother. Jabalwan saw Jaki's leg muscles coiling before the boy knew he wanted to run back. The soul-catcher spat like a viper, and Jaki sprinted to the hut.

Jabalwan waited for the boy to realize that his mother was dead. When the shriek came, the soul-catcher faced downwind to where the bear waited. With tongue-clicks he commanded the beast to attack the hut and kill anyone in it.

Jaki was pressing his face into Mala's neck when he glimpsed a large movement from the corner of his eye. The bear had burst into the clearing, shimmering with raven-blue fur as it charged the hut, its black muzzle a snarling froth.

Jaki clung to his dead mother. Though death was flying directly at him he could not let go of his past, of the woman who had been his whole life. The sorcerer had forced other demon-children to this terrible decision. All had died.

Jaki's blood crawled in him. He nudged his mother, but she stared on, unblinking, at the sun in the trees. The sight of the bear's fanged muzzle slashed him with fear, and he tried to tug Mala to her feet. But she was dead — dead as the ape the krait had killed, dead as any of the God-murdered children and women of the Book. The bear's claws dug into the log stairway, and in one bound it rose like a wall of night. Before he knew what he was doing, Jaki was leaping over the railing. He bounced off the soft turf and turned to see the bear pawing his mother, swiping her limp body flat. He could not watch; he dashed across the glade away from the soul-catcher and into the trees, running with his full might.

Jabalwan let him go. He whistled the bear away from the hut and slowly crossed the clearing, his face the stern mask life demanded, but his insides bright. After decapitating Mala and starting a fire under the hut, he returned to the forest.

From his refuge in the jungle, Jaki watched the ladder of smoke climb from the blazing hut to heaven, sparks like beings of light, rising, going back to the sun. He did not know it yet, but he was as close now to the meaning of power as anyone gets in this life.

The Rain Wanderers lived deep in the mountainous interior. They were ill regarded by the other forest tribes because they kept entirely to themselves and traded with no one. What little metal they had was stolen or won in battle. They were masters of poison and roamed the high stony creeks, lacing the water with pulped tuba vine, which killed the fish they collected for their meals. Occasionally the poison drifted into the tributaries where other tribes bathed, sickening and sometimes killing them. The lowland tribes blamed all their unexplained illnesses on the Rain Wanderers, and Rain Wanderer heads were the most coveted of prizes, more so because of the tribe's elusiveness. To seek them out meant to dare the journey into the mountains of the big bears. Few returned — not only because of the churlish bears but also because the Rain Wanderers were eager themselves for heads to assure the fertility of their numerous clans.

Jabalwan was himself a Rain Wanderer. His father had been a master poison chemist and reader of bird omens, and he had recognized in his son the trance-strength of a soul-catcher. At Jaki's age, after he had learned all his father could teach him, he had been given to a sorcerer, a clench-faced man who stabbed the boy with poison thorns whenever he made a mistake. The brutal poisons had tormented him, wracking his brain and opening his head to the wind. By the time he attained manhood, Jabalwan was a twisted cypress, grown strong on pain, tied by his roots' mad vibrations to the earth, and shaped by the invisible.

Instructed by Jabalwan, the Rain Wanderers had sent a party of hunters into the forest. Within minutes they found the golden-haired demon-child hiding under a pepper shrub and carried him back to their village trussed like a tapir. His head would have been an important contribution to the land's wealth, but the soul-catcher had forbidden that. Instead, the boy was thrown in a pigsty, a low logwood structure with tight vine-mesh to protect the pigs from panthers.

Jaki curled into a corner, fended off the pigs with kicks until they left him alone, and sank back into his grief. The villagers had gathered to study him, and for several hours faces came and went, gazing with disbelief. The strange faces only thickened the sorrow in him. That night, sleeping fitfully in the pig dung, the beasts rooting aggressively about him, he dreamt he was with his mother again. Her fingers were licks of flame, her dark hair lavish as night, and she was saying, "It's all right, it's all right, little warrior."

The next day, Jaki was removed from the pigsty. His blue silk waistcloth was taken away, and he was bathed in a stream of chilly mountain water. Jabalwan had informed the tribe that Matubrembrem was to live as a slave among them, and after they had replaced his waistcloth with a crude loincloth of rough gray fabric he was taken out to the paddy field and taught the menial work of weeding and spacing rice plants in the mud. Twice that first day, he tried to flee. The first time that he was captured, he was punished with a blow to the back of his head that set his vision fluttering like a branch of yellow leaves. The second time, he was beaten, then leashed and tied to a rock. At nightfall he was fed rice gruel and locked in a squat pen with a captured gibbon. The animal was destined for the village stewpot, but it had not been killed yet because it was pregnant. That night it birthed two young. One it ate immediately. Jaki swooped up the second and kept the mad mother at bay with angry shouts and kicks. In the morning he shared his rice milk with the infant. The animal was pink and small as his hand, and he named it Wawa after his mother's dialect for gibbon. That day in the field, the tiny creature clung to the back of his neck under his long blond hair while he crawled through the mud doing his work. The villagers were amused, and when he was returned to the pen that night he found a small bowl of rice milk beside his gruel. The mother had gone to her fate.

The Rain Wanderers quickly became accustomed to their new slave and soon took no special notice of him, although the children were intrigued by the devil child and tried to outdo each other in their brave attempts to harass him. The worst of them was Ferang, the boy who had stoned him at the stream on his last day with his mother. He was a son of the village's fiercest warrior, a sinewy youth, older than Jaki, with stringy black hair and eyes like drops of mischief. While the other boys pelted Jaki with pebbles and insults, Ferang dared to touch him, tripping him into the mud while he worked, holding his head underwater when he bent to drink at the river, smearing his leash-rock with pig dung so the flies gathered and pestered him. Jaki had no sense of how to defend himself, and the warrior's son laughed at his futile efforts to strike back. Bruised and wearied by day's end, Jaki lay on his back in the pen with his baby gibbon under his arm, staring up into the sky and praying as his mother had taught him. The cadence of his prayers would lull him to sleep and invariably to dreams of the atap hut, the bee-knitted glade, and the air full of the flowery wind from the mountains.

Of the faces that came to stare at him, one smiled without malice or mockery. It was that of a young girl, with hair unstrung by the wind and eyes just rubbed free of sleep. When no one was looking, she brought him pieces of cooked meat wrapped in rice. She never spoke to him, and he saw her rarely, yet his days were lighter for her memory. Among the women he worked with in the paddy fields, a few were friendly toward him because his hard work made theirs easier, and he casually asked them who the girl was. "Riri," he was told, "the chief's daughter." *Of course,* the void in his heart rang — who else would have the self-possession to feel pity?

At harvest time, while their parents celebrated, the children hung Jaki in a wicker between the branches of a giant koompassia tree and pelted him with monkey pips and mudballs. Wawa whined and protested under the tree to the enormous amusement of everyone except Riri, who watched quietly from her father's shadow. At the ritual's end, Ferang lowered the wicker and a troop of howling boys dragged it to the river. They threw it in and let the current pull the line taut, until the basket snagged among the fisted rocks of the fish traps. When Jaki emerged spluttering and confused, they carried him back to his pen and threw his terrified pet in with him.

That night, Riri came to his cage. "Little demon, you have suffered enough," she said, and she cut the vine binding on the cage. Jaki stood up for the first time at night since his capture, and the incandescence of the sky seem to swim in his head. Riri did not back away when he reached to touch her. Her cheek was slippery with tears. "Go quickly, demon-child, before the others see what I have done."

"My name is Jaki," he said. "I will not forget you, Riri."

She looked surprised to hear her name, and he smiled. "Go now, Jaki."

He scooped up Wawa and jumped from the pen in one bound. At the edge of the village clearing he stopped and looked back; she was watching him. A dog yapped an alarm, and she vanished into the dark. He turned and ran. As weariness rose in him, he held to his nostrils the fingers that had touched her tears. The honeysuckle scent of her spurred him on, and he ran hard under the small stars.

At night's ebb, Jaki was thoroughly lost. He stopped by a stream and listened to its flat voice, trying to calm himself. He would not be afraid. Wawa sensed his uncertainty from his perch behind Jaki's head and stroked his cheek. "Where to go, Wawa? Where in the world are we to go?"

"Come here, Matubrembrem."

The voice seemed to come from everywhere. "You belong with me," the deep, soothing voice said. "Don't you understand that yet?"

"Sorcerer!" the boy cried in despair.

A manshadow drifted like smoke into the morning light, a jump away. "Where do you think you are running, Matu?"

The boy backed off. "How did you find me?"

"The whole jungle knows where you are, child. You've been running like an elephant. If you do not come with me, the Rain Wanderers will have you again and you'll be back in the paddy. Is that what you want?"

"You killed my mother."

The man stepped closer, and Jaki retreated several paces.

"Are you going to kill me, too?" he asked. "You want to take my head like you took my father's head, don't you?"

"I will make you a catcher of souls. That is what your mother wanted."

"Then why did you kill her?"

"Her time was used up. I blessed her."

"You killed her."

"You look with the eyes of a boy. When you become a soul-catcher, you will thank me for my gift to your mother."

"Never!"

The sorcerer shrugged. "Then run. Make your own way in the jungle. Have your head become a trophy in some tribe's longhouse." He turned and walked off downriver.

"Wait!" Jaki shouted, running after the soul-catcher. He knew he could not live alone in the forest. He had never hunted, but he had been hunted, caught, penned, and enslaved. He would not go back to that. And if he stayed with the sorcerer, he would at least have the opportunity to avenge his mother's death someday.

Jabalwan did not look back. He continued his stately pace along the riverbank, his blowgun resting on his shoulder. By the time the sun had risen, they had reached the fern grove where Jabalwan knew the Spider lived. The boy was still behind him, several reluctant paces back.

The sorcerer whistled him closer, and when he approached, the man pointed a bony finger at a dew-pearled web among the ferns. A spider, like a splash of pitch, hung at the web's center. "If you are going to be more than my shadow — if you are going to be a soul-catcher — you must give your hand to the Spider."

Jaki was aghast. "It will bite me."

"Yes. And when you are bitten you will suffer a vision. That is a soul-catcher's first sincerity. Maybe you will die because the powers of the world are not ready for you. But if you live, you are one of the Life's own, and you will be your own guide. Now touch it."

"No."

"You must. Only sincerity brings power. How will the world know you are sincere if you do not offer yourself?"

"You want to hurt me."

The soul-catcher turned from the spider and faced the boy. The lines in his face looked knife-carved. "A soul-catcher is the living pain of the world. The pain lives in him. It is not ignored. It is not frightened away. Because the pain lives in him, he knows how to draw it out of other people. That is why the soul-catcher is welcome in any village of any tribe. That is why you must give yourself to the pain before anything else can happen. Touch the Spider."

The Spider was as big as Jaki's outstretched hand, and when he stared closely at it, he saw the fine tufts of black hair on its jointed legs and the oil glow of its bulbed body. He could not bring himself to touch it; he could not even raise his arm. The soul-catcher saw the fear in him, and he spat with disgust. "Did you learn nothing among the Rain Wanderers?"

"I am afraid."

"Fear is its own danger. It never goes away. Act! Touch the Spider."

Damp heat flushed through the boy, and his stomach twisted.

"Bah!" The soul-catcher spun away and returned to the mudbank. He stopped there and looked back at the boy, still rigid with fright. "Matubrembrem," he called, and the boy jumped. "Walk away from it. This is not the time for that. Come. I will show you the Life. Then you will see how small a thing fear is. Come."

The gentle tone of the soul-taker's voice lured Jaki away, and he followed Jabalwan into the river's blue mist.

"Everything we see around us knows just what to do," Jabalwan taught Jaki. "But we can't remember enough. So we must watch. Always we must watch. Always." Journeying under the sun-basted canopy of the jungle, the sorcerer showed Jaki how to observe with all his senses. Some days the soul-catcher stoppered the boy's ears with wasp wax, and they wandered in silence until colors sharpened and shadows grew in depth. Other days Jaki was blindfolded and led through the tunnels of the forest by a baffled Wawa and Jabalwan's rare sounds. The forest spoke, and Jaki learned its laws — the animals' hungers, the spoor of their meals, the hooks of their sex. He was bedazzled by the jungle's straightforwardness. Simply by watching, he was learning the world's secrets. The Book his mother had taught him to read was a dim dream compared to the vivid clarity of just watching.

One day a new scent appeared in the air, a moist meaty smell. "A Stilt Hunter village is a day's walk away," Jabalwan informed him. "They call me to heal their sick."

"How do you hear them, teacher?"

Jabalwan touched his flat, flared nose, a gesture that meant *watch.* "At dawn, when the wind turns and comes up the mountain with the day's first heat, I sit in the highest tree I can find, and I listen. The drum music comes then, in scraps, but enough for me to understand what the villages are saying down below. You will learn this. But it takes time and comes later." He cuffed the boy affectionately behind the ear. In the weeks since leaving the Rain Wanderers, Jaki's ire had dulled and he had come to a truce with the soul-catcher. The man had shown him how to find food and how to avoid becoming food for the ravenous beasts that lurked everywhere. That trust mitigated his fear of the sorcerer, but the boy still cherished the hope of one day avenging his mother's death. How he would attain his hope he had no idea, yet he knew that with each new day of knowledge he came closer to his day of vengeance.

On the way to the Stilt Hunter's village, Jaki caught a scent of bear. A tongue of wind licked him from a brake of feather cane carrying the greasy scent of a big beast. He clutched at Jabalwan's arm as he was about to stroll on the mudbar beside the cane. "Teacher, wait! Beast ahead!"

Jabalwan nodded and smiled with satisfaction. "Very good, Matu. Your watchfulness will lengthen your life." The sorcerer clicked, and the brake burst apart around a giant, black-furred bear. Wawa screamed, and Jaki flew backward and splashed into the stream, sprawling to his back with shock. Jabalwan laughed aloud, and the big bear lumbered to his side and nuzzled the nape of his neck. "This is Papan, my guardian. Like your Wawa, she has been my companion since her birth. She knows all my tricks. She stays downwind of those I don't want to see her. But I have called her here today so that you may meet her."

Jaki rose from the river, and Wawa followed him timidly to the mudbank. "She is the bear that attacked me at the hut."

"Yes. And she would have killed you then if you had not fled."

"Why?"

"You need to ask?" Jabalwan shook his head with bemusement. "Unless your life meant more to you than your bond with your mother, you could never become a soul-catcher. For you it would be better to be dead than to live motherless and alone in the jungle. It was the only merciful thing to do."

Jabalwan showed Jaki how Papan could imitate sounds. When the sorcerer held his fist up and opened his hand, the bear coughed like a leopard so realistically that Wawa whimpered. With a nod of his head, the soul-taker elicited bird chirrups from the closed muzzle of the beast. Jabalwan waved, and the massive creature slumped off into the underbrush. Eventually, Jabalwan promised, he would teach Jaki how to use Wawa for making sounds so that his enemies would be confused.

"Animals are far greater than people," Jabalwan explained. "The tribes think they are more powerful because they have fire and weapons. But those are the very implements of their weakness. The animals are strong in themselves. A sorcerer knows this and learns from the animals. Wawa is your circumference."

Matu squinted with incomprehension.

"Wawa is your soul," Jabalwan said. "He encompasses you. You are inside his circle of wandering, and he will touch the world around you deeper than you can."

"Is not my soul inside me?" Matu asked.

Jabalwan scowled. "*Inside* you? Like blood and bones? No. The soul belongs to the world, not to you. Wawa is not your pet. You must let him go into the forest, to wander his own life. He will return when you need him. That is the strength of our animal souls. They hear our needs and they walk with us among all that does not need us."

Built directly over the river on vine-lashed piles, the Stilt Hunter village was accessible only by raft. As they approached it, the tribespeople gawked at Jaki, reminding him of his slavery among the Rain Wanderers. Walking the planks up to the wide verandah of the circular longhouse, he tried to stay in Jabalwan's shadow, but they were quickly surrounded. The Stilt Hunters bedecked the sorcerer with flower necklaces and sprinkled him with blossom water. The murmur *Matubrembrem* rippled through the crowd, and people hanging from the wide windows pointed at him. Those closer reached out to touch his sun-colored hair.

The clotted smells of so many people and penned animals disturbed Jaki, and he was ready to leave the village even before Jabalwan had begun his healing rounds. Even so, Jaki watched carefully as the sorcerer treated those afflicted with fevers, snakebites, and animal wounds. His touch alone brought relief to many of the sick, and his root powders, plant resins, bark teas, and mudpacks sufficed to alleviate most of the ills they encountered. Yet some were beyond help, and these he spoke to softly and with caring. The boy stuck close to his side and heard Jabalwan's words: "Rest. The wind knows your name now. You are part of the song it sings to the stars. Rest."

For several days, the pair traveled downriver, from village to village. At each settlement the soul-catcher healed the sick, comforted the dying, and shared a meal with the clans. After they had visited several longhouses, news of Jabalwan's eerie companion traveled ahead of them. In the hill and lowland villages of the Snake Walkers, the people brought their infants and young children to the demon-child, that he might touch them and bestow on them the favor of the solar spirits of which he was believed to be an avatar. At the feast that followed the healing rounds, Jaki would be favored with the choicest cuts of meat after the sorcerer. Wawa, because he hid in Matubrembrem's sun-yellow hair and so was obviously a familiar, was given food usually reserved for human guests.

One day in the rain forest lowlands, Jabalwan signed for Papan to cry a high, whining song. The wind wafted a scent the boy did not recognize. Jaki's apprehensions mounted, and he stepped behind the sorcerer and gripped his black waistcloth. A giant horned beast, gray as a boulder, broke out of the jungle and shambled toward them. "Don't be afraid, Matu," Jabalwan reassured him. "Like Wawa, like Papan, this is another of our friends. She is a rhinoceros I call Emang. She will carry us to our next destination." Emang bowed her massively horned head before the sorcerer, and he grabbed one of her ears and mounted, then held out a hand to Jaki. The soul-taker turned the beast back into the jungle, and they set off down a boar run with a speed that rushed the surrounding undergrowth to a glassy green.

The rhino slowed at the edge of the jungle, where the enormous trees fell away to blue shrubs, man-high grass, and swampy plains. Over the next several days, the flatlands unraveled their beautiful surprises — herds of elephants trumpeting their affections, hordes of wild pigs following trails of fallen fruit among oases of mango thickets. At night, fireflies sifted the darkness and the sky was a ghostly riverbed cobbled with starclusters.

One night, in a coppice of moss-shawled trees, they encountered a specter, a tall, lightning-shaped giant sheathed in blue-white flame and seeming to breathe with the wind. It was a fire tree, Jabalwan explained, a place where the spirits communed with earth. All night the sorcerer sat before it, chewing roots and speaking with the spirits. Jaki fell into a trance as the soul-catcher's strange words snicked like raindrops in dust. The luminous vigil ended at first light, when the specter dulled into the graying dawn and became a termite-hollowed tree trunk. Jaki rubbed the sleep from his eyes and timidly followed the sorcerer up to the possessed tree. The dead wood was sodden with hair-thin fungi, which in the cupped shadow of Jabalwan's hands emitted a frosty, billowy glow. He collected several handfuls and put the spongy stuff in a bamboo tube, which he slipped into the leather medicine bag he always carried slung over his shoulder.

Emang crossed the coppice in a day and took them to a grass plain as wide as a desert. Far-off mountains slept in their purple haze under the great clouds. Crossing the plain, Jabalwan explained to Jaki about the three degrees of sorcery. "My father read bird omens. That is the beginning of sorcery, and already I have taught you as much as he knew." That was true. Jaki had learned to find water by the circular flight of honeysuckers, and by listening to the varying cries of the forest birds he could track the movements of creatures in the brush and predict oncoming storms. "Knowing the bird omens well is all one needs for a long life in the forest. But out here one needs something more. One must look to the higher powers." Jabalwan gestured with his blowgun at the clouds. "I am a cloud sorcerer. I understand their cold blossoms. Up there is the spirit world outside the tribes. Together we will watch the clouds in the hands of heaven with their backs to the earth, and we will learn about the Life — for it is the clouds that carry away our spirits. It is the clouds that return prophecy with the rains. I will teach you to know what is yet to be."

For several moons they roamed the grasslands, eating grains, insects, and the small animals they trapped at waterholes. Jabalwan made good his promise and taught the boy how to read the clouds for weather and insight. Weather was easy, even the subtle seasonal changes were easy, compared with the visions that the sorcerer claimed the clouds carried. For a long time, Jaki saw nothing but weather — the fever days presaged by low-running tufty clouds, the dry blow of high serifs, the approaching great rains in the whorl-patterned puffballs. Standing in the rain-born light, prickled with the first gust of rushing showers and watching lightning dancing on the horizon, the sorcerer said, "See what I see. Look for the flash of joy in the coming storm front, the color of pain in the hot coils of wind-ripped clouds. Here comes the wind again. Smell. What do you sense?"

"Tapir, about thirty of them, to the southeast, three hours' walk."

"Food — is that all you can think of? Smell deeper. Breathe the light — smell past the blood. What is there?"

Jaki was confused. He knew he was right about the tapir. What more was there? The wind was wetter than the rain. It faintly carried the tallow stink of a delta. "A day's walk away is a river."

"Yes, that's good. But there's more. Don't you smell the burdens? The wind is choked with sorrows."

"I don't understand."

Jabalwan's smile was neither happy nor sad — a mysterious, slim smile, as if he wanted to share a secret. "Someday you will know. Death for you is still just a corpse." The sorcerer took the boy's shoulders under his arm, and they ran ahead of the downpour to a thornberry covert where Emang and Papan were already sheltered from the rain.

Jabalwan set Emang free on the morning that they first glimpsed the wood-tiled roof of a Windbone longhouse. The Windbone people, with their strange ankle-thong sandals, broad-bladed parangs, and knee-length waistcloths, greeted the soul-catcher with the same reverence that the northern tribes had displayed. Jabalwan completed his medical rounds, treating boar wounds, fever, and the ailments of the elders. Jaki was less warmly received. The Windbone tribe had seen Matubrembrems before, children of the devil gods who had built a city of walls to the south. They had no respect for these demon-children because when they appeared the devil gods themselves were near — and with them came the Star-and-Moon tribes, fire-spears, and war. No one tried to touch Jaki's solar hair, yet none of the people were malicious.

Following streambeds southward, Jabalwan and Jaki met another sorcerer. He was waiting for them under the gold-mist flowers of a snakebark tree, and he greeted Jabalwan with raised hands and closed, red-tattooed eyelids. The stranger wore the knee-length waistcloth of the local people, and he had the squat stature, long eyes, and broad lips of the Windbone people — yet his legs, like Jabalwan's, were tattooed with twining red serpents, and his naked torso, too, was raised in glossy bumps in an intricate pattern that Jabalwan had said depicted the wanderings of the moon and the sun in their endless romance across the sky. The sorcerer's name was Dano. He had heard that they were in his forest, and he wanted Jabalwan's assistance.

Dano led them to a fig grove laden with purple leaves and an atmosphere of pollen languor. Soaking in a scooped-out tree stump filled with a foamy green liquid was a recently severed head. Jabalwan studied it admiringly. "This will bring much power to your fields."

"Alas, we need more than that," Dano lamented. "The Star-and-Moon tribes encroach on our fishing pools, shoot our men on the river, and steal our women and children for slaves. For the chief and his warriors, war is inevitable. When I learned that you were here, I knew that the clouds had brought you to help us. You are a Rain Wanderer, Jabalwan. You know the way of making a head an amulet. So I have preserved this head here, waiting for your help. Will you make a war amulet for us?"

"These are the times of iron, Dano — you know that."

"I know — these are the times of iron. Matubrembrem is here, is he not?" Dano looked to Jaki with a sorrowful gaze. "The prophecies bloom. We are the last. Yet we must strive as if we were the first. Is that not the teaching?"

"It is, Dano," Jabalwan said sadly. "And I will help you."

From his leather pouch he removed bamboo tubes and gnarled tubers, which he pressed between rocks to extract a few silver drops of juice. The drops were mixed with powders from the tubes to form a green paste. "Without your bone-softening gum, the head would never be more than a longhouse head," Dano said as they mixed the paste with the volatile liquid in the tree stump, producing an oil-sheened broth. The head was reimmersed in it and covered with a swatch of cotton grass.

Over the next ten days, Dano led Jabalwan and Jaki through the tribal villages of his territory. Among the southern longhouses, which traded with the devil gods, a wasting plague was shriveling the population. Neither of the sorcerers had seen the likes of it before: high fever, noises in the chest like crackling fire, bluing of the fingertips and toes, and death. Jabalwan's cures were no more effective than Dano's, and the soul-catchers were reduced to witnesses, drifting among the villages, helping the people die, and blessing the deathrafts as they carried corpses downriver to the afterworld.

At their return to Dano's fig grove, Jaki fell ill. At first he thought that the sight of so many dying and dead had sickened his soul, but soon chills were blowing through him and his flesh became hot to touch. Wawa scurried through the grove, bringing him figs, but when he saw that the offerings were not being eaten, he paced nervously over and around the boy's prostrate body, plucking at his fingers and ears, trying to rouse him. Finally Jabalwan tied the gibbon to a tree, where it sulked disconsolately. Jabalwan himself began a healing fast, hoping for a vision that would enable him to cure the boy. The helplessness of the soul-taker allied with the hopelessness he felt for the Shadow Tribes. *The shapes of the world change,* he had learned early as a cloudreader, yet he had never accepted with his heart that all the Shadow Tribes would die in the times of iron, though the prophecies told him that was true. Why did the Life have suicidal yearnings? Why was death a hunger of the living? Even the monkeyfaces, who were the instruments of death for his people, believed in a god who became a man so that he would die. *Reborn — yes. But not in this world. This world is death's. I have looked. I know. The agony of will, our striving, is all we have while we have it. And so nothing is enough — for that is all we get. The rest is terror and emptiness. The sages did not lie.* Jabalwan decided then that if Matubrembrem died, he would fast until he was dead, too.

Lying on his back in a bed of fig leaves, shivering as the fever's dew collected on his flesh and staring up at the fume track of clouds, Jaki understood at last what Jabalwan had meant by seeing the Life in the sky. The seaward clouds were the fever dreams of the earth. Everything around him was also above him, mirrored in the wind. The blue of the sky was the emptiness of life — in his life, Mala's absence. His loneliness for her was the upward surge of the clouds, sweeping the blazing emptiness — for what? The cloudshapes surged around their own heat, and each moment was the beginning. There was sadness where the high wind sheared the tops of the clouds and the vapors shredded and thinned away. There was hope in the magisterial billowing, faces and animals in the streamers, visions in the sliding brightness. All of it was blowing away through an emptiness taller and wider than anything on earth. *Mother!* he cried aloud, frozen in his loneliness, and tears mixed with his sweat.

In the fourth day of his illness, Jaki's fever broke, and Jabalwan ended his fast. The boy was well enough by the afternoon to sit up and watch Dano and Jabalwan remove the head from the tree-stump keg. The flesh looked glazed, the hacked neck bloodless, dangling white strings. The solution Jabalwan had prepared had softened the bones, and under Jabalwan's direction Dano scooped out the brains and the skull like handfuls of soggy rice. Meanwhile Jabalwan heated white river sand in a cauldron. He laid out the deboned head flat as a pelt until the sand was hot; then he hung it from a small bamboo scaffold by its tattered neck strings, stitched its eyeholes shut, and filled the upside-down head-husk with hot sand. The sand sizzled as it filled the wet sack. Done, the head had the contours of a living man. Even the deflated nose was erect again, the thorn-stitched eyelids bulging as if with dream-held sight. Jabalwan turned the head upright in the scaffolding, and adjusted the twine and vine strings to hold it in place while sand trickled from the neck. Within a few hours, the flesh of the head had shrunk with the cooling sand, and they repeated the process. Over the next few days, while Jaki recouped his strength, the head was shrunk until it was no larger than a man's fist.

A great festival was conducted by the Windbone tribe to celebrate the new war amulet. Steel rang on steel as the people clanged their weapons together to arouse the spirits of their ancestors as witnesses to their power. Arrack, their rice wine, was passed around in gurgly boar bladders, and by nightfall, when the sorcerers returned to the forest, the tribe was wild with drunkenness. Jabalwan and Jaki left Dano at the fig grove, and they went deeper into the jungle, away from the war songs and laughter of the Windbone revelers. Once they had settled down for the night, Jaki said into the darkness, "Before we came to the Windbone villages, when we were still in the grass plains with Emang, you told me that the clouds were filled with visions. You are right, teacher."

In a voice just louder than the insects, the sorcerer whispered back, "So I haven't been fooling myself all these years."

Jaki laughed. Since his illness, the soul-catcher had been gentler with him, more watchful that he ate well and did not exhaust himself walking. "You told me then that there are three ways of sorcery. Bird omens and cloud-watching you have taught me. What is the third?"

"The most advanced and true of all sorceries," Jabalwan answered. "I know little about it, other than that it exists. It is an art higher than the clouds. It is star reading. Those who can discern the movements of the stars can read the world's destiny. While we see only our own fates, the star reader sees the fates of tribes. But in these days even a meager sorcerer like myself can see the world closing in. And I am grateful for what I do not see."

Jabalwan led Jaki south. They avoided the plague villages and saw few people during their long trek.

One day a bitter odor trailed on the morning breeze. Jaki thought the stink was burned flesh from a plague village. "Worse," Jabalwan corrected him. "It is the plague itself." He pointed toward the crushed shape of chalk hills on the horizon. "Beyond that white wall is the village of the monkeyfaces themselves. Tomorrow we will see them."

The thought filled Jaki with unexpected foreboding. "Teacher — am I not the child of a monkeyface?"

The flesh between the sorcerer's eyes twitched. "You are. But you belong to the forest. You know the bird omens and you understand the clouds. You are not a monkeyface."

"Then why have you brought me here?"

"You are Matubrembrem — the devil's child. Boy, the people have waited for you in dread from the beginning of time. You are the last witness of the remembered earth. You must see what we are coming to. Surrender yourself and be glad. You will know both worlds."

The bitter stench grew stronger as they traveled, and that night Jaki could not sleep. The wind was smoky with the acrid scents of the monkeyface village that they would see at dawn. He remembered the tent villages and stone-walled cities of the Book, yet he knew that what he imagined and what he would see could not be the same. He thought of asking Jabalwan for the Book, but though he had come to respect and even cherish the man, he was still wary of discussing his earliest childhood and Mala's teachings with him. While healing the sick, the sorcerer often reached into his medicine bag and left it open while administering his cures, and Jaki had peeked in from time to time and seen the icon of Jesu nailed to his cross. He was impressed that the god of his mother and of the monkeyfaces had a place in the medicine bag of the sorcerer, but they had not talked about it.

At first light, from the crest of a chalk ridge, Jabalwan and Jaki stared down at Bandjermasin. Dawn glowed over the paddies and shone in the serpent-coils of river streams that untangled across the delta to the sea. The clusters of stilt-raised longhouses were as frail-looking as dead leaves. At the far end of the delta, nearest the sea, giant walls made of lashed-together trees surrounded a city of domes and spires, minarets and battlements. Just discernible in the shadow of the great walls were elephants ridden by men whose turbans were sparks in the brightening air. The elephants, laden with crates, were marching toward the sea. As it grew lighter Jaki could see the ocean, a barren expanse blue as the sky, ruffling near the shore into waves like clouds. Several big ships were anchored just offshore, and their spiderwebbed shapes emerged from the dark like immense baskets trimmed in gold. His father had captained such a ship, Mala had told him. He strained to see people on the decks but could barely follow the elephants as they trudged to the loading docks.

The stink was coming from there. Fires flapped beneath cauldrons along the shore, uncoiling wind trails of gray smoke. "Tar," the sorcerer said. "The monkeyfaces heat the trees until they bleed their black blood. They use the tar to seal their big ships. The air stinks with it, and the land is scarred." He pointed to the swatches of jungle that had been cleared on the far banks of the river. "Their own land must have no more trees, else why would they come so far to take ours?"

Jaki wanted to go closer, but Jabalwan refused. "The monkeyfaces are allied with the Star-and-Moon tribes. If we go to them, they will kill us or, worse, make us slaves. This is as close as we will go. So look carefully — and remember."

The sun had risen, and the river plain had found its colors. Jabalwan whistled softly and walked away, and the boy dipped his gaze toward the sea for one last look at the big ships. They were his father. They had defied the depths and crossed the distances to be here, to make him. He raised his hand to the monkeyfaces, to the stories his mother had told him, stories that had always seemed more real than life, and then he turned away and loped back toward the jungle.

The stink of melting trees came and went like a bad memory as Jabalwan and Jaki headed toward the villages of the Claw tribe, just north of Bandjermasin. Many of these people made the short journey to work in the paddy fields around the walled city. Some had returned with parangs, turbans, and sandals and lived like chiefs, making and enforcing their own laws in their old villages. They defied the elders and hunted only for themselves. Jabalwan avoided them and ministered to the people who kept the old ways. He ignored the insults that the men in turbans and sandals cast at him and his devil's son, and he never met their gaze.

Jaki was troubled. "We must leave here," he told Jabalwan. "You can smell the evil."

"Evil!" Jabalwan said with disdain. "When you give your hand to the Spider you will see there is no evil. Only fear."

"I *am* afraid." The boy had grown since leaving the Rain Wanderers, and his lanky white frame was as tall as the sorcerer's. Even so, his face was still that of a child.

"You are right to be afraid, little devil," Jabalwan said, squinting lazily as a turtle. "These people are rotting on the inside. They have forgotten themselves. We must be careful."

"But why do we stay?"

"You are Matubrembrem," Jabalwan answered with a pang of disquiet. "You must see what is coming."

"Why?"

"The Spider will tell you when you give it your hand."

The plague had killed many of the Claw people, and those who survived lived precariously by foraging and hunting or by working in the paddies of the new lords. Only a few of the families continued to plant their own rice, and most of it was stolen by the lawless gangs from the south. Jabalwan sought out these families and urged them to move deeper into the forest. But the Claw people would not leave their fishing pools and their salt spring. Still, they honored the sorcerer, for though he was strange to them, he healed their sick, spoke their language with a dreamy cadence, and knew the old stories. They fed him and his devil, though they barely had food for themselves.

One late afternoon, the sorcerer held the tribe spellbound with a tale of the world's creation. He described how the hawk, the predatory Night itself, jealous of the sun, had tried to swallow heaven's light. But the sun was faster than the nighthawk and ran around it and shattered its skull with one blow from behind, spilling the world. "That is why the sun runs across the sky each day," the sorcerer said. "The sun is spinning a victory dance over the fallen body of its enemy, the night." He gestured at the silver rib of moon shining above the trees. "The moon and the stars are the broken pieces of the hawk's skull. The ocean is its blood. And its feathery corpse is the land and its forests. Our breath is the hawk's death cry, echoing down the generations, dimmer and dimmer."

At that moment the dark hollows of the forest shimmered with movement, and a war party of twenty men stepped into the clearing. They wore turbans and headcloths and some even had tar-stained breeches. Their soot-streaked faces seemed sunken from years of anger and despair.

The Claw headman, who had been entertaining the soul-catcher, stood up and demanded the intruders leave. Instead they strode to the longhouse, their gazes not wavering from the sorcerer. "Come down here, snakeman," one of them called. His rat eyes met the soul-taker's, and he showed chipped and rotten teeth. "You tell the people to leave here," he said in a broodful voice. "You tell them to go deeper into the forest. But if they go, who will work our fields?"

"Each tribe works its own fields," Jabalwan responded tautly.

"You speak of tribes, snakeman," the leader cried out. "This is not your tribe. You are not a Claw."

"I have invited him," the headman called down from the verandah. "He has healed the sick among us. He has told the old stories. He is more a Claw than you."

The gang hooted derisively, and their leader scuttled up the notched log and stood toe to toe with the headman. "My father was a hunter," he said vehemently. "My mother worked the fields. I am Claw. But I do not believe anymore in sorcerers. I do not believe in headmen. I have been south. I have melted trees for the big ships. My eyes are open now."

The headman did not flinch when the leader's parang came up under his jaw.

"The old ways are dead," the new lord said. "The Star-and-Moon tribes drive us from the fish pools and the salt spring. They have weapons from the monkeyfaces. We must get our own weapons from the devils in the south. No more talk of sorcery. No more running from the Star-and-Moon tribes. We are a new people now. We make our own laws."

"The law is inside," Jabalwan said from behind the headman.

The new lord shoved the headman aside and closed to within a pace of the sorcerer. "What nonsense are you spitting up?"

"The law is inside," the sorcerer repeated, calmly, gazing into the back of the man's eyes. "Your fathers before you knew this. They obeyed the law — and so you are here now. But if you ignore the law, you will die. Evil consumes itself."

"*This* is the law." The new lord raised his parang. "And it is you who will die."

"Fool!" the headman shouted. "You raise your sword to a soul-catcher? You are doomed."

The crowd jeered, and a war cry slithered among them. "I am not your enemy," Jabalwan said loudly. "We are all here now because our fathers observed the paths. They chose wisely. Why do you throw away their wisdom?"

The new lord spat. "You want to confuse us. You want us to stay ignorant like our fathers — beaten back into the jungle by the Star-and-Moon tribes. We will not! If our fathers were so wise, why are we hunted like animals by our enemies? Let us take the weapons we can get from the monkeyfaces and kill our enemies!"

"The monkeyfaces are your enemies," the soul-catcher said. "They are simply buying you to serve them — like the Star-and-Moon tribes serve them. What will become of your children? You must leave this place."

"Who are you to tell us anything, snakeman? Look at the devil you think is your son!" He jabbed his parang in the air at Jaki. "He is a monkeyfaced whorechild. We will not listen to your lies."

Jabalwan pushed the man's swordarm aside. "Then leave here and go back south."

"Not without your head." The new lord's parang blurred an iridescent arc in the falling light, and Jabalwan ducked aside, dodging the blade by a hair's breadth. The headman's family had retreated inside, and the sorcerer grabbed Jaki's arm and pulled him the length of the verandah, Wawa racing ahead of them. The rest of the gang leaped and surged up the notched log, and their leader charged Jabalwan with his parang spinning.

"Jump," the sorcerer whispered to Jaki, dropping his hand into his medicine bag. He whirled about as a blade sliced past him and his hand came out of the medicine bag gripping an open-fanged snake's head. The viper struck the leader between his eyes, biting reflexively into the flesh of his brow just beneath his headband. The new lord screamed and fell back, the snake still stabbing his face.

The crowd flinched to a stop and watched the man roll on the floor in agony, ripping the fangs from his flesh. But the poison was already shooting into his brain. He bucked and kicked, and then lay dead. The war party howled with rage and leaped over the side of the verandah, pointing their parangs at Jaki and Jabalwan's fleeing shadows.

Up ahead, Jabalwan pulled Jaki to a stop.

"Wait," the sorcerer panted. "We cannot elude all of them. We need help."

"Papan!"

"No. It is too dangerous for him this far south. I sent him back." Jabalwan opened the stopper on a bamboo tube and shook out the shaggy barkdust of the fire tree. The fungi had thrived and multiplied in the tube, and the blue light in Jabalwan's hand rang like a crystal. "Rub this in your hair. Be swift."

As Jaki did so, Jabalwan removed his headdress and shook the tube over his own head. From the headdress he removed long black splinters and buried several in the ground, their points slanted to pierce. He stuck a scarlet feather in the ground as a warning.

The war party came flying toward them as Jabalwan stood up. When they saw the sorcerer and the devil child lit with blue fire they slammed into each other in their eagerness to stop. The sorcerer pointed at the scarlet feather on the trail, shook his hand in a warding sign, turned with his arm around the boy, and strolled silently away.

Jaki could hear the men arguing whether to pursue or retreat, and then feet scuffling through the damp duff in pursuit. His legs tightened to run, but the sorcerer restrained him with a heavy arm across his shoulders. The next instant, a scream was heard, and the chase ended in a confusion of alarmed voices. Jabalwan swiftly led Jaki off the path and into a tangled darkness of waxy leaves and pliant branches. Arrows flew blindly through the forest avenue where they had been walking, and again Jaki flinched to run. "Relax, little devil," the soul-taker advised. "The chase is over. One of those who pursued us is wounded and in great pain. The others will not leave him. Remember this night. Remember not to kill your pursuers. The dead can be left behind. The wounded demand care and slow the chase."

That night the sorcerer and the devil child traveled through the dark, slowly, meticulously, until the swipe of branches and vines had shaken free all the firebark from their hair. Only then did they crawl into a root cove and curl up. "Remember this night, little devil," Jabalwan whispered. "You have seen real demons. You have seen men who have lost their tribe — men who have lost their souls. Remember."

"I have no tribe," Jaki said to his teacher the day after their escape. "Where is *my* soul?"

They had followed a ridgeback up from the lowland forest toward the mazy hills to the north. Though a hill trek would slow their progress, the tortuous highland trails, slashed by torrential streams and mudslides, would make pursuit impossible. Sitting on a rain-pitted limestone rock overlooking the jungle plain where they had been, they shared mushrooms and tender radish shoots. "Your tribe is the Rain Wanderers," Jabalwan answered.

"But I am not a Rain Wanderer," Jaki protested. "I lived alone with my mother. I grew up in the valley."

"Until you were taken as a slave by the Rain Wanderers. They hold your soul now. You belong to them."

"I escaped from them."

"You were set free, by the Princess Riri. And for that offense, she was made to sit with the pigs a day and a night."

At the sound of the princess's name, Jaki saw again her drowsy angel eyes, her rainwashed hair, and her dawn-touched flesh.

"You would be her slave, wouldn't you?" Jabalwan read Jaki's expression. "Oh, child, you have so much to learn."

"I am a child," Jaki snapped, "but I am no slave."

Laughter fell away from the soul-catcher's face. "You are a slave until you free yourself and become a sorcerer."

"Teacher, I have followed you everywhere. I have learned the birds' omens, and I have seen the floating truth of the clouds. I am learning."

"You can learn all your life and you will still not be a sorcerer. Learning is the way of all people. The sorcerer does more than learn. The sorcerer seeks sincerity. Only through sincerity does one acquire power."

"How do I find sincerity?"

"Have you forgotten already?"

The food Jaki was chewing felt suddenly rubbery. "The Spider."

"Yes." Jabalwan's slanted eyes flared with heat. "Will you give your hand to the Spider?"

In the many moons since he had last faced the Spider, Jaki had changed. The journey with the soul-catcher had changed him. All that his mother had taught him through the Book had come to pass with this strong man. *He hath torn that he may heal us,* Hosea had promised. What the boy had seen of death and suffering on this tour of the tribes had revealed the gentleness of his mother's death. That she had to die at all was still confusing to him, yet he had no doubt now that the soul-catcher had eased her passage to the afterworld. And the Psalms had said, *The Lord is our guide even unto death.* The more Jaki knew of the sorcerer, the more he respected the man, enough at last to forgive what he could not yet understand. Had not Isaiah and Micah written, *He will teach us of his ways?* "Teacher, I have no real understanding of the birds or the clouds. I know only what you have told me. I am just a child, as you say. But I will not be a slave. I love the freedom you have shown me." Jaki forced himself to go on: "I will give my hand to the Spider."

Jabalwan smiled without mirth. Between them was all the terror of the world. Could he bring Jaki deeper into that terror, to the collective memory of suffering that made pain magical? Jabalwan wondered if he had that power with this child. Sometimes he could not even bear to meet the boy's gaze; his blue eyes seemed a declension of the sky, the blue breath of heaven peering through the mask of a human head. Jabalwan had to continually remind himself that this was still just a boy, though his eyes were frightening and his words often unnerving. He was secretly glad when Matu misstepped in the hunt or wept at night remembering his mother. He was human; he needed care. Like all beings of this temporary earth who strove to be more, he needed care.

The journey north to seek the Spider was less playful than the southern trek. Emang carried them quickly across the flat plains, eager to return to the jungle before the big rains came. When they did, Jabalwan let the beast go, and he and the devil child continued their journey on foot. Sometimes the downpour was a blinding silver wind, and they crouched under whatever shelter they could find. Hunched under a stunt-tree or a tabard of clustered shrubs, they told each other stories. At last Jaki began to speak of the religion he had learned as a child, and when he told the story of the Flood, the sorcerer was fascinated. In turn, the soul-catcher explained how the rains that came each year were the old songs of the tribes from the year before, echoing back from heaven and shaking loose the sweet water of the celestial sea.

During a lull in the torrent, when they had climbed from the grassland to a dry haven in a cranny beneath a waterfall, Jabalwan reached into his medicine bag and came out with the Book. He handed it to Jaki. "Teach me what your mother taught you," the sorcerer said.

Jaki took the Book and almost dropped it. It had the heft of an animal and a fragrance like leafsmoke — a feel and a smell that swayed through him with memories, a dizzy nostalgia that turned the breath in his lungs to a withheld cry. Tears shot to his eyes before he knew he was going to weep, and Jabalwan restrained a shudder of misgiving. Jaki regained his composure quickly, reminding himself that he was already promised to the Spider and would probably soon be joining his mother. Opening the Book to its first page, he began to read aloud, touching each word as he translated it to the native tongue he shared with the soul-catcher. Jabalwan watched closely, astounded to realize that each word had a shape, and that each shape was crafted from elements, the immutable powers of the alphabet. Each letter, he grasped immediately, had meaning within its sound. "Each word is a shrunken spell," he said with awe, and his fingers touched the page reverently. "How skinny speech is."

Jaki was surprised by the sorcerer's fluency, by how quickly he learned the alphabet and by the intensity with which he listened to the boy's favorite stories. He became intrigued by Elijah, sensing in him a fellow soul-catcher who had been fed by ravens, had heard the still, small voice of the hidden world while wandering in the wilderness, and had finally been hoisted free of earth in a whirlwind.

Hoping to inspire the youth with the written language of his own tradition, Jabalwan taught Jaki how to read the jungle scrim that other sorcerers left as messages. What before had seemed merely a black creek became a page where a casually bent weedstalk was a passer-by's name and the scattered weave of a fallen nest a sentence describing the route to the nearest fish pool. This language was harder to learn, because it faded so quickly. "The vanishing is part of the script," Jabalwan explained. "How long ago it was written often tells more than the message. The Book's words are timeless. Ours never leave genesis."

The monsoons had transformed the already plush landscape to a magically dangerous terrain. A hum would become a roar, and a cascade of mudbroth and shattered trees would stampede through the slopes of the jungle, driving the wanderers up into the forest galleries. Wawa was keenest at detecting these abrupt floods and became their leader as they wended north among rainbow arcs and floats of tiny red-winged butterflies. The biting insects swarmed in brown, gray, and black auroras, and Jabalwan and Jaki painted their bodies with root paste and leaf dyes that made them impervious to the insects and appealing to the animal spirits. Hunting was easier as Jaki became expert with the blowgun, and they had more time to sit among the spreading tree limbs, high up where the light was radiant, and read the Book. The air was abundant, strange with birdsongs and monkey-chatter, mists and sunstruck squalls. Plants opened, outlandish flowers ignited, and the boy's apprehensions about the Spider were eased. The hours spent teaching his teacher to read the Book quieted his dread even more; for the first time he felt a calm trust in the unknown.

At dawn one morning, they heard Papan call. The big bear was wounded, its right haunch matted in dried blood stuck with flies. When they had cleansed the spot with gourd juice, they realized that it was a gunshot wound. Jabalwan concocted a sleeping potion, and while the bear slept, they dug the metal pellets from its flesh and swabbed the injury with leafsap to inhibit infection. Jabalwan held up one of the pellets and stared into its silver roundness, then dropped it into his medicine bag.

"The Star-and-Moon tribes are close," the sorcerer said. "They are reaching deeper into the forest."

For five days, they waited for Papan's wound to heal, always listening for enemies. When he was able to walk without pain, they continued their journey. Soon they came to a riverbend jammed with deathrafts. The stink of the corpses was lost almost wholly in the jungle steam, and the bodies were mostly bone, the flesh given up days before. Blue and yellow birds scattered as the soul-catcher began his chant for the dead, shoving the deathrafts free. When they had all drifted downstream out of sight, he waded back to shore. "Those are Rain Wanderer dead," he told Jaki. "They were killed with fire-spears."

"I cannot believe the Star-and-Moon tribes have come this deeply into the forest — especially now that the rains are here," Jaki said in a voice muted with respect. "I have listened for drum songs warning of the enemy, and I have heard nothing."

"That means something terrible," Jabalwan agreed. "The Rain Wanderers are not using their drums because their enemy understands their songs." The sorcerer's face was grim with realization. "They have been attacked by another forest tribe."

Jaki was stunned. Except in the south, where the tribes were crazed by plague, war with the Star-and-Moon intruders, and the domination of the monkeyfaces, all the forest people were benign. Headhunting flourished among them, but a war seemed unthinkable. The fierceness of the Rain Wanderers had always dissuaded other tribes from attempting more than rare forays for heads. Jaki preferred to believe that somehow a Star-and-Moon war party had endured the rain-veiled trails, because the idea of all tribes stalking each other with fire-spears was nightmarish.

Yet the nightmare was true, as he and the sorcerer learned when they finally found the Rain Wanderers in a mountain valley far from their customary fish pools. The longhouse was quickly constructed and the rice fields bare, since anyone old enough to carry a weapon had been dispatched to guard the trails against the approach of the enemy. "Who?" Jabalwan asked the chief.

"The Tree Haunters," the chief answered. He and his men were decked in war regalia — white body mud, clawstrokes under their eyes, black feathers splashing at their ankles. "They surprised us at our salt spring. We fended them off as best we could, but they had new weapons, sorcerer. Weapons no one has ever seen. Short blowguns that shoot lightning clouds and stab our warriors with metal rain. Look." He opened an amulet sack dangling from his neck and poured out a handful of gunshot.

"Call all your warriors in," the soul-catcher ordered. "Begin the rice planting, continue the hunt."

"But, sorcerer, the Tree Haunters destroyed our old fields." The chief's eyes glowed with angry tears. "That is why we are here. We have lost our fish pools. We have yet to find a new brine spring. Unless we accept the rule of the Tree Haunter chief and trade with him, he will hunt us and destroy whatever we build."

Jabalwan pointed to the rice fields. "Plant the rice. Continue the hunt. I will show you another brine spring not far from here. We will build new fish pools."

"But, sorcerer, the Tree Haunters — "

The soul-catcher silenced the chief with a frown. "I will visit them. I will face their great warrior Batuh and make him understand that the Rain Wanderers are not to be molested."

The chief embraced Jabalwan with relief, and the two walked together to the longhouse to plan the new settlement. Jaki followed, quivering with excitement to be back among the first people he had known as a tribe. Familiar faces hovered in the crowd — faces that he had last seen scrawled with mockery, derisive and harsh. Now those faces were dull, numb with grief and uncertainty. He observed the rude clearing that was their new home, noting the overgrown tangles of flower vines among the vegetable patches, the few scrawny pigs tied to a stake, the fire pit clogged with half-charred logs and palm-leaf litter from flames quickly doused. The signs of a people living in fear.

Among the women and children who had gathered on the verandah a pretty face floated that tripped his heart and sent his blood surging.

Riri was no longer a girl but a young woman. She studied him with dark, quiet eyes, the wind blowing strands of her long hair across her face.

A man blocked Jaki's way so abruptly that the boy slammed into him and almost toppled backward. The warrior was resolute as a tree and did not budge. "Ferang!"

"You remember your master, slave boy." Ferang scowled at Jaki's appearance. "How pretty you look, painted like a slink lizard. Get down in the mud and show us how you crawl."

Jaki tried to step around Ferang, but the young warrior blocked his way.

"Just because the chief's daughter freed you, you are no less a slave."

"I am the sorcerer's student."

"Fah." Ferang spit. "Everyone knows you did not give your hand to the Spider. You are the sorcerer's slave as you are our slave. Crawl in the mud, slink lizard."

Jaki skittered left and dodged right, but the warrior swept the ground with his leg and tripped him into the pig dung.

The chief shouted Ferang's name, and the boy reached under his waistcloth, wagged his penis at Jaki, and strode away.

Jaki stood mired in pig ordure. Jabalwan, who had watched from the log stair, pointed to the river. "Cleanse yourself." Jaki ran from the clearing, his insides burnished with anger, the nerves in his neck and face burning with shame.

At the river, he did not even bother to check for crocodiles or kraits but threw himself into the water as if off the end of the world. The water cooled his hot emotions, and he floated to the surface and drifted on his back in an eddy circle, watching the clouds towering above him. He *would* give his hand to the Spider. He would die before he would let Ferang humiliate him again. A yellow dartbird flashed overhead with its tickled call, as if confirming Jaki's determination, before he realized that it had been startled. He splashed upright and saw Riri standing on the mossbank smiling at him.

"Riri!" he blurted.

"You must call me princess, like all the tribespeople."

"Princess," he said, standing. His heart buffeted and steadied. "Thank you for setting me free."

She dismissed that with a toss of her head that spilled her hair into the breeze off the river. "That was two years ago. You were just a child. So was I. I wouldn't do that today. Why did you come back?"

"The soul-catcher brought me here." The breeze tilted, and he smelled her odor of crushed raspberries.

"Then you will be our slave again." Her eyes brightened.

"No." His certainty pushed into words. "I will never be a slave again. I have seen the spirit tree burning at night. I've worn its fire in my hair to escape our enemies. I've learned to understand the birds and read the clouds. I'll not be a slave again."

"I want to see you without your paint." She nodded toward a brake of amole cane.

Jaki snapped a cane, thumbed out the gelatinous interior, and frothed it in the water. He dipped his face into the suds, scrubbed free the paint, and looked up. She was gone. A laugh came from above him, and he shot a glance upward and saw her hanging overhead on a shaggy branch. Her breasts swung with her laughter, and for the first time in his life he felt a splurge of desire. He flopped backward into the water and floated, staring up at her with wonder, a soft hammer knocking inside his body. Her face was like music: it kept changing yet stayed the same.

"You are ugly," she said, and giggled into her hand.

The soft hammer clunked against his ribs.

"Oh, don't look so hurt." She dropped a nut, and it splashed beside his ear. "It is not your fault. You're a devil child. That's how the spirits formed you. That's why I like you. You're like the people and yet not. And that's why Ferang hates you. He thinks your ugliness is a bad omen. He's a warrior. Everything's an omen to him. He doesn't see you're just a person, too."

Jaki sloshed out of the river and whistled for Wawa, who flew out of a blossom-tufted tree and tumbled to his side.

"Come back!" Riri shouted, scrambling down from her perch as he moved off into the woods.

Jaki kept walking until the girl ran up to him and seized his arm. Her touch stopped him, and silence rose in him like joy, quieting his hurt feelings. Her pretty face muted all sounds except her voice: "You can't walk away from me. You're a slave."

"I am Matubrembrem," he said, his words coming from the stillness her touch had opened in him. "That is why I am ugly. And that is why I am free." He stroked her cheek as he had the night she had helped him to escape, and the quiet in him alloyed with a warmth that pooled in his belly. Her hair was hoarding light, her lips shimmered on the brim of a smile, and her hand reached up and fingered his wet blond hair where it touched the pale curve of his shoulder.

"My father made me sit for a night with the pigs after I let you go," she told him. "But I'm glad I let you go. You look more like a sorcerer than a slave."

"Riri!" a woman's voice shrilled from the camp, and the girl dropped her hand and skipped backward with a laugh.

"My mother," she said and dashed off.

Jaki stood staring at the spot where she vanished into the brush, until Papan's cough startled him. Jabalwan emerged from the cane brake where he had been watching. "She likes you," he said.

"She says I'm ugly."

"She's right. But she still likes you." Jabalwan put his arm across Jaki's shoulders. "You're lucky we're leaving immediately. She'd have you slaving in the fields again before sunfall."

They walked to a grove a short distance downriver. Jaki knew the place. This was not the same fern holt where he had first faced the Spider — and yet it was timelessly the same. "Teacher," he croaked, and swallowed hard to clear his throat. "Ferang says I am a slave until I give my hand to the Spider. How does he know that I haven't?"

"He should know," the soul-catcher said. "Before you, he had selected himself to be a soul-catcher. He faced the Spider once and backed away."

"Why? He is a warrior."

"It is easier to face men than to face the Spider." The sorcerer's gaze fell on Jaki. "Ferang's older brother was to be a catcher of souls — and the Spider killed him. If you had given your hand to the Spider, the watchful Rain Wanderers would have seen and the drum songs would have announced a new sorcerer." Jabalwan signaled the boy to wait, and he stepped softly over the clumped grass and through the fronds. Jaki listened to the flashings of bird and monkey calls, followed the swirl of wispy clouds like flimsy thoughts in the sky's mind, tried and tried to steady his piling anxiety — and still jumped when Jabalwan whistled for him. The sorcerer had found a large, bright web studded with dew and hung with a red-splotched black spider. The air around it gleamed softly.

"You know what to do." Jabalwan stepped back. Wawa hung from a branch above, his round black face in its corolla of silver fur watching with bafflement.

Jaki approached the Spider, extended his left hand — and fear paralyzed it. Clamping his jaw and pushing his arm forward with the strength from his legs, he touched the dew-silvered web. Wawa shouted a warning cry. The Spider jigged swiftly at him, and he snapped back his hand, leaving the web shivering. Jabalwan was stunned. He had never seen a movement that swift, and he stepped a pace closer. Jaki looked at him with woeful eyes and thrust his hand back into the web. Again the Spider attacked, and again he whipped his hand away with amazing speed as the black legs closed on his shadow. Terror howled in him, but he remembered Ferang's mockery and shoved his hand toward the Spider, which was vibrating with rage.

Jabalwan had already begun to rush forward to stop the boy; the furious Spider would certainly inject more of its lethal poison than even a grown man could survive. As he reached Jaki's side, he saw the Spider flailing its mad legs over the hand, and the boy holding it there even though his muscles were clearly strumming with pain. Jabalwan's bamboo knife blurred and struck the Spider away. The fang marks were a red welt in the meat between the thumb and forefinger, and already the flesh had begun to swell. The sorcerer hid his alarm and gently pushed the boy down. "Lie here quietly," he instructed. "Do not move. I will be back at once."

"Did I do well, teacher?" Jaki asked, afraid that his reluctance had botched the initiation.

"You did very well, young sorcerer." The sound of his new title dispelled all the boy's apprehensions, and a glow of satisfaction suffused his chest. "Now wait quietly. I must gather plants to help with your vision."

The soul-catcher was gone, and Jaki waited, the pain in his hand throbbing darkly. Wawa swung down from the branches and sat beside him, one long-fingered black hand on his forehead. He blinked curiously, and Jaki smiled. "Don't worry. You heard the teacher. I am a sorcerer now. Nothing bad will happen to me."

Jabalwan himself was not convinced of that. Always before when a hand was offered, the Spider pounced, bit, and quickly retreated — and even then sometimes the venom killed. Jaki's unexpected swiftness had frenzied the creature, and now death seemed certain. The sorcerer quickly gathered the plants he needed to help counter the poison. As he hurried along, dropping leaves and lichen shreds into his medicine bag, Jabalwan realized how much he had given his heart to this strange-looking child. Perhaps because the boy was truly strange, with eyes like metal and hair like the wind, he had become dear to Jabalwan, who had also lived his life apart, strange among his own people. Always before, the soul-catcher had watched dispassionately as the Spider selected candidates for the Life and killed its rejects. But to think of this boy dead hollowed his heart.

Jaki saw the hot tracks of wasps like amber ribbons against the tilting sky. A noise was coming from inside the trees, a sound like rain. The pain in his hand was gone. His hand was gone. He could feel nothing in his arm, very little anywhere in his body. His vision began to fog, and he realized that he had stopped breathing. He had to drag at the air willfully, laboriously. His sight cleared, splintered with light and slivered rainbows. *Be brave,* a woman's voice said. That was curious, for he had felt no fear since the Spider's hooks had seized his hand. Silence pawed at him between flares of noise. The thought occurred to him that the Spider's venom had killed his fear with the rest of his sensations, and he watched the wind feathering the fern fronds and wondered if he was going to die. *Be brave, little warrior.* The voice was his mother's, and when he recognized it, he remembered her dying day, the light clicking in her eyes and the cold stealing over her flesh. She stepped out of the tree at his feet, and although she looked exactly as he remembered her, she was breaking up, scattering and regathering like a reflection in water. She smiled wearily, her long hair caught in the river breeze, her calm voice floating ahead of her: "Be brave, and I will show you something wonderful." Vision began to fog again, yet now his mother appeared more lucidly than ever. He could not remember if he was breathing out or in, and that stymied his effort to cross from one breath to the next. "Come," Mala said, offering her hand. He reached for her, drawn by the star-flakes of her eyes. Her touch was the thrill of rushing water, and he stood up in the white blare. "Where are we?" he asked. "This is the medicine cloud," his mother explained. "This is where the dead go." Just visible as a tracery of vitreous colors was a landscape like the rhododendron slopes above the valley where he had lived with Mala. The harder he stared, the clearer the scene became. Stars shone in a sky rippling with light like river waves — a twilight more beautiful than any he had ever seen. He pulled away from his mother and tried to walk out of the fog and into the luminous dusk. "You can't go there, little warrior," Mala said. "Not yet. Only the dead belong there. You must stay here in the medicine cloud." A figure had stepped down the mountain slope from the stitchwork of stars, a tall, big-shouldered man. "That is your father," she told him. "He has come to greet you, to give you power for your time in the world." The man came closer, fireflies tweaking around him and trailing a vapor shadow the color of water. Jaki stepped up to him, straining to see through the moony haze. He was blown backward in a gale of horror. The man was a one-eyed monkeyface, his right eye patched with red feathers, his good eye gorged with light, staring madly. His long gray hair, knotted in numerous skinny braids, rippled like quills as he charged forward, a mouth of yellow teeth gaping open, thick black clothing crackling like lightning as his arms wheeled and legs pumped. Most horrible of all, emerging from a hole in the monkeyface's forehead, was a snakehead, spitting venom. Its fangs snapped, and its venom laced the air. A cry shook, a booming war cry leaping from the gulf of hell, and Jaki's heart quopped as if stabbed. He turned and ran. "Mother!" he cried, but could find her nowhere. Behind him the hell-thing was hurrying, hot to seize him, its wild scream smothering his call for help. He squandered all his strength running through the endless erasure of the fog, its weight slowing him to within a pace of the pursuing monster. Globules of venom flicked past him, grazing his cheek like hot, stinging sand. Ahead the fog shredded about a shadow. "Mother!" he called, his breath slamming through his body. "Matu," he heard distantly in Mala's frightened voice. She had never called him that before, and the sound of it almost stopped him except that the snake acid was burning the backs of his legs. The shadow ahead was an immense tree, bigger than any he had ever seen. Closer, he saw a root tunnel big as a cave. Twig shoots like mighty boughs swayed in an unfelt wind, their leaves charred black and glinting. With the monkeyface bellowing like a boar and sharp clawfingers plucking at his back, Jaki rushed toward the tree, only to realize that the leaves were mouths with needleteeth chewing at the air. That instant a roar louder than thunder hit the boy and stopped his desperate run. A giant lizard, white as a grub, crawled from the tree on pincered legs. Its head was transparent, and Jaki could see a tiny blue flame, no bigger than his hand, floating in the core of the lizard's skull. The white lizard hurled itself at the one-eyed man and seized him in its jaws. "Matu!" Mala's voice echoed from the root tunnel. The leaves like mouths gnawed frantically as Jaki dashed beneath them and into the cave. "Mother!" he yelled, and the echoes came back in Mala's singsong: "Matu — ma-tu — ma-tu — tu . . ." The darkness was too thick for him to run farther, and he crept forward, arms outstretched, his feet like hands, feeling for direction, calling again and again for his mother. Each time, his echoes came back as Mala's call for the devil child. Jaki sensed that the darkness around him was not empty; there were presences here. He could feel their body heat, smell their foreign scents. A wink of light flashed ahead of him and the lumbering shadows withdrew. Moments later, another flicker lured him deeper. "Who are you?" he whispered, and the echo rolled back, "We — are — you — " He stared with aching intensity into the black and saw gray shapes, hulking forms scattering into particles. The particles were people, he realized then, the great hulks crowds. He was seeing tribes wandering in great throngs across the blowing ash of time. The horde of people were dropping their possessions behind them — cookpots, hunting bows, headdresses, salt bags, pelts. Children were left straggling, their bellies swollen, eyes sunken. They were leaving everything behind and wandering into a desert horizon, blowing forward into the wasteland like so much dust. Behind them, gathering their droppings, picking over their fallen weapons and furs, were the monkeyfaces in their bulky clothes. Swarms of them billowed after the tribes, and then the whole roiling rush of shapes blurred into darkness. Relieved to be free of that sickening vision, Jaki listened closely for the dark presences and was glad not to feel them. "Matu!" his mother cried, and he hurried forward into the blindness. The licks of white fire came more frequently as he continued, sighing like heat lightning until the cave was flickering with its silent music. The sparks whittled away the blackness, and he saw that he was in a bowel of the earth. The walls glistened, reflecting the sparks' heat. At first he thought the sudden flametips were glowworms because they writhed briefly while they burned their cold light. But when he bent down and stared hard at the pinscrawl phosphorescence under his feet, what he saw stood him upright. Each squeak of light was not a worm but a word! He bent again and this time saw that the words were names, written in the same language as the Book. The elegant swirls and serifs spelled out endless names: *Old Crow, Watermelon Pit Eyes, Baboon Head, Walk On Thin Ice, Crazy Horse, Blood Beard, Iron Thighs, White Maiden* . . . A sizzling howl poured through the cave, and Jaki looked over his shoulder to see the white lizard, burning like ghostfire, slithering toward him, its scales hissing blue sparks as they rubbed the cave walls. Jaki bolted, running by the light of the fiery names. "Matu, hurry!" his mother called from ahead. He ran with all his might. Ahead, the cave walls vanished in a wash of pure white light. The radiance lustered like fire, white hot fire eating all shadow, all shape. He was blinded by the brilliance of the names. The lizard crackled louder, and the boy bounded with all his terrified strength into the glare. Suddenly then, the blaze curdled to shadows, and Mala was leaning over him, pressing air into his lungs. Blue sky swooped overhead, and his mother's hair lifted in the wind, her smile dazzling.

"Matu!" her voice croaked, and her image teetered and became Jabalwan's panther crouch.

Jaki sat up in pursuit of his vision and fell back in a sweel of dizziness. The spell of love that had guided him out of the terror of the medicine cloud was gone. In its place was the man who had killed his mother — the man who had been his only real father. The clash of love and hate almost overwhelmed him, and he lay back, shaking with tears.

Jabalwan rolled off Jaki and lay on the leaf mulch, staring up through the trees. All yesterday and all night he had squatted over the boy, breathing for him by pressing on his chest. During the night the sorcerer's body had gone beyond fatigue into trance, and he had become the sky itself pressing breath into the earth. The boy would live now because the sky had come down to save him. Gratitude and pride mixed in the soul-catcher, and he listened to the youth's sobs with satisfaction.

Wawa, who had scurried from the trees to Jaki all day and night, frantic with helplessness, squealed and flipped backward somersaults over and over. The gibbon's racket penetrated Jaki's confusion, and in midsob the last gray smoke of the medicine cloud cleared from his soul. His tears bleared away, and a stupendous clarity rang through him; it was as though the world were a bell that had been struck by his return. He blinked. The core of hate he had felt for the sorcerer who had poisoned his mother was gone. *No — not gone.* The core of hate had become so heavy it had dropped out of his body and into the earth. He belonged to the world now — not to his grief or his anger or his fear or even his life. His life was the life of the world, the slipstream of being that belonged to no one. That was why his mother had told him to be brave. She had introduced him to the world. *Yes, mother, I will be brave,* he said to the faraway medicine cloud that had dropped him like dewfall into this world. And he thought the truth but could not find words for it: love, the love he had learned about from the Book, was so much bigger than he; it was everything that did not need him. He was streaming now, he was gushing with the Life.

Matu, his mother had called him. He understood. Jaki was his closed self; Matu was the Life that wore Jaki like a mask. Jaki was a corpse feeding on memories and dreams, eating even the worm-dirt glow of the words in the Book. Matu was adamant with being, not memories. He read the clouds in the wild sky. Even now he could hear the trees drinking rain, could see wasps crisscrossing on their roadless wandering under the cloudpath. Wawa blinked at him almost audibly, the Life lifting the bristles of the gibbon's silver fur in the wind's shift, lustrous strings of remembering twining in his perfectly round, black eyes.

"You cannot hold it all, young sorcerer." The soul-catcher's low, steady voice grazed his ear. "You hear, you feel, you see, and you smell the Life all around you. But as you get stronger, the Life will fit more snugly. Already your senses are returning to their holes. You must choose one direction and ignore the others or you will lose them all. Choose now while the power is strong with you."

Matu looked up through the trees. He saw. As never before, he saw the balm of clouds soothing the sky's open wound. That was his wound, the vast emptiness of being, the lack of handhold, the lack in him of everything but what was there in the gust of the moment. He knew that what he saw in the clouds was what was seeing through him. That's what Jabalwan had meant all along. There was more than weather in the wind. Heavenward the dreams of the Life were stepping from the dust that shaped him. The dreams were rocking with the wind, shriven of his small hungers and memories. Up there, the clouds were the shapes of the looker's reach. He reached out from the Life ascending in him, and he saw gullies of heath grass and the tribes roaming deeper into their exile, dropping their weapons, their sacred garments, their children. And behind them — there, in the firefall of the rising sun — the big-nosed people were coming, throngs of them, the golden stitch of their hair and the red of their faces wild with greed.

"You have chosen well, young sorcerer," Jabalwan said, and placed a hand over the boy's eyes. "Now you see the truth, the spirit world outside the tribes. Now you see how the clouds with their backs to the earth carry our spirits and return prophecy with the rains. From this day forth you will hunger more for them than for food. You will fast and you will wound yourself to be near them. All your suffering will be their long calling, all your needs their necessity. The clouds are the weight of your life and the shapes of your destiny. Whenever you rise to them, in prayer and in pain, they will carry you. For now, you are a sorcerer."

Jabalwan let his words drift into the boy before speaking again. "I will always be your teacher. I carry the weight of more days. Other than that, and that is very little now, we are equals. We are both sorcerers. We are both given to the Life."

Matu looked at Jabalwan floating above him, his sinewy face dusted with morninglight, and tried to grasp what the man was saying. His words were sweet, and tense, and gone even as he spoke them, like threads of wind whistling through a hollow bone.

"I have listened to you read the Book," the soul-catcher went on. "I have come to understand something of the vision in the Book, which is so different from the Life here in the forest. I understand the rage you must feel toward me for blessing your mother with an easy death."

Matu sat up, wanting to share with Jabalwan his insight about the world's hate, but his tongue was still asleep.

The soul-taker reached among the feathers of his headdress and removed a needlethorn long as finger. "I have soaked this thorn in a red toad's sweat. One stab will kill a man. I am giving it to you because we are both sorcerers now. If the Life instructs you to kill me, use this." He handed the thorn to Matu, who took it only because Jabalwan's dark face insisted.

Matu shook his head no.

For several days Matu lived in the fern dell, drinking riverwater and eating moss, watching as the cloud-drifts revealed their secrets. "The time of the tribes is ending," he announced to Jabalwan the first day that he ate meat again. "The children are being left behind. The monkeyfaces are making them their own."

Jabalwan nodded wearily. "I have seen it."

"Then the whole world *will* become a monkeyface village like we saw in Bandjermasin?"

"Yes. The whole world one day will be a wall. We will not live to see it, but it is certain as the sky is blue."

"Is that good?"

"Good?" Jabalwan smiled joylessly. "You are thinking like the Book again. For sorcerers there is no good and evil. Remember?" He looked up at the clouds floating above them. "The sky is deep. It carries everything. No matter where."

As soon as Matu's strength had returned, Jabalwan led him downriver past the funerary rafts of the Rain Wanderers. Matu's senses had closed in on him again as the soul-taker had foretold, yet with his mounting strength came a burst in physical growth and the first pummeling waves of puberty. Hunkering on a mossbank spearing fish in the tide pools, he saw himself in the silvered water and was astounded by the changes. He had his mother's high, solemn cheekbones and small, docile ears close to his head. With horror he observed that his nose was long and straight — the big nose of a swamp monkey and not the flat, broad, and beautiful nose of the forest people.

"You will never eat if you are waiting to spear your nose," Jabalwan chided, coming out of the forest behind him.

"I am becoming truly ugly, teacher," Matu groaned.

"The uglier the sorcerer, the greater his power. You will be less tempted by women — for they will certainly not seek you out with a nose like yours. And good riddance," the soul-catcher quickly added, seeing the consternation on the youth's face. "You belong to no tribe now. The Rain Wanderers have no claim to you anymore. You are a sorcerer, and so you are married to yourself. Your wife is the stately sky. She is naked only to your gaze."

Matu heard this with alarm. In the weeks since his initiation by the Spider he had endured his first emergencies of lust. Dreams of Riri, her naked, dusk-colored body, polluted his sleep. He would wake fevered, laminated in cold sweat, and could return to sleep only after touching himself where the heat of her body still gripped him though he was awake. Orgasm only deepened the dreams. Alone in the forest, while Jabalwan sewed feather-fins to his cane arrows or sat chewing roots, entranced by the sky's tapestry, Matu thought of Riri and stroked himself until his seed flew from him and a peace soft as the inside of a cloud filled his limbs. "Only the sky will be my wife?" he asked Jabalwan. "I will never have a woman?"

"You are a sorcerer," the soul-catcher said in a gust of laughter. "What woman would want a sorcerer? We have no tribe. Our life is endless wandering without roof or garden. Who would protect our wives and children while we hunt? We would have to build longhouses and pigpens and paddies. There would be no time for cloudreading or healing those who need us."

"But what about desire?" Matu asked, churning with uneasiness. "Don't you have desire?"

"Everyone has desire. But when a man thinks too much about desire, a stink of death becomes apparent in his movements. He becomes hesitant. He whines for pleasure, and his mind is not in the wind but in his memory. Even the future becomes a memory. He is already dead but thinks he aches with life. He aches with the madness of the insatiable dead. Desire is not the Life — but the Life *is* desire."

"Is there a root or leaf I can chew that will blunt the desire?"

Jabalwan smiled. "No, young sorcerer. Your desire is your endless prayer. It is the plaint of your life, the wish of your soul for what is unfinished — for what the stars are finishing."

"Is that why my desire is so strong at night?"

"Yes. All our hungers are the echoes of the Hawk's cry before the Sun killed the Hawk and scattered its skull into stars and moon. When the Sun's back is turned in the circle dance, the cry is loudest. Listen to it — without memory, without hope. Just listen to it twanging your muscles. It has its use, like the hawks that circle over the forest again and again, keeping the wind clean."

Matu nodded as though he understood perfectly, though he was troubled. Did not the Psalms sing: *All my desire is before thee . . . the desire of every living thing*?

"No sorcerer has a wife," Jabalwan said with a shadowy smile, "but the unmarried women are always eager to make love with a sorcerer because our fortune rubs off with our embrace. Except at night. At night we become panthers."

Jabalwan understood Matu's urgency, and days later when they arrived in a Stilt Hunter village he indicated to the chief that the devil child was ready to bless the paddies. While the soul-taker visited the afflicted, the young man was led into the forest skirting the paddies by a gang of giggling young women crowned with flowers. They stripped off his waistcloth, threw it into the paddy, and knelt staring with amazement at the gold wires of his pubic hair before pulling him into their midst. In their laughing, love-wise play, Matu learned the delirious wonder of coupling, and when they carried him into the paddy exhausted, eyes uprolled, and grinning like the blessed dead, the tribe, who had gathered at the hem of the field, cheered. They dropped him in the mud and covered him with ooze. Plastered with earth, he staggered among the fields scattering blessings, his legs still tremulous from his ardent initiation.

At the feast later in the day, Jabalwan smiled to see Matubrembrem gorge himself on food, the grace returned to the boy's features and gangly limbs after weeks of restlessness. The soul-taker was glad for their detour. *Life is the journey of beasts, not the hopes of men,* he thought, remembering his promise to the Rain Wanderers that he would confront the Tree Haunters' great warrior, Batuh.

Night lapped in red sunlight on the windy shoulders of the trees and a black moon edged in silver hung over the smoky jungle when the sorcerers left. The shouts and laughter of the young women trailed after the men as they went to meet the night.

Matu's Spider vision haunted him. Some nights he woke torn by howling fear. The nightmare was always the same. He was being chased by the one-eyed monkeyface with the snakehead writhing from his forehead. The one-eyed man chased him deeper into the cave, but this time there were no wriggling lights, no reassuring call from his mother, only the monkeyface's breathing and the spit of his snake as Matu bolted headlong into the darkness. Lying awake then he would hear the monkeyface's whisper in the wind, calling him: *Jaki — Jaki Gefjon —*

"He is Death," Jabalwan explained. "Death is always more plausible than life, in song, in story, even in act. What more can your dream offer? He is one-eyed because Death is not ambivalent. There, before the single vision of Death, is what goes deeper. That cave he is guarding is important. Your father wrote about it in the Book, but you could never understand it until now. If you stop playing with yourself when you think I'm not looking — *if* you listen well to everything I tell you, you may get past Him and be amazed. You will see, He guards the mine of signature."

Jabalwan had been profoundly moved by what Pieter Gefjon had written in the cover leaf of his Bible. Though the sorcerer had never seen a lion, he understood when the boy had first translated the Latin script and had read as his mother had taught him: *I have seen the lion of the final moment.* The lion was the shadow-beast of all people, the panther soul that stalked everything living — though only people knew they were stalked. That knowing was a living death. And only by going past it could one reach the depths of one's identity.

The soul-taker talked to Matu about this on new moon nights, when the forest was too dark for scavenging and the darkness emerald with waking dreams. They would chew a black knuckle of root that Jabalwan kept in his medicine bag in a pocket stitched with a staring eye, and the spirits would swarm like gnatfire. As the soul-taker spoke of the Longhouse of Souls, the ghostworld began to drizzle all about them, and Jaki saw that they were inside the Longhouse of the Ancestors, where fogged shapes wafted with great weariness among black hives and indigo faces with char mouths swerved close. Jabalwan's droning narrative quickly carried them deeper into the rainhaze of the Dead. The soul-taker's goal was the cooking pot at the center of the longhouse. There he sat with his spirit ancestors and listened to their stories in the light of the first cooking fire. But Matu could never go that far with him. Standing at the cooking pot was the one-eyed monkeyface, his serpentheaded brow blowing venom.

"Death has sat with you twice," Jabalwan told him one morning. "The Plague and the Spider let Death into your body, and yet It remains a stranger and an enemy, keeping you from the cooking pot where all our visions boil. The insights that come from that stew are cooked for us by the old sorcerers. They are the food by which our souls grow strong enough to catch other souls from the claws of sickness and sometimes Death. Without that food, you will not live long as a sorcerer. We must go meet this Death who keeps you from us."

That day Jabalwan led Matu to within sight of Long Apari. In all their travels, Matu had never seen such a village. Six longhouses zigzagged the curves of the mighty Great Dawn Running River. The verandah of each house was hung with heads, and colorful banners flew from the roofs. On the riverside, the houses extended into wharves where baskets and crates were passed between shore and a flotilla of dugouts. No paddy fields or vegetable gardens were visible. Instead, the cleared land was stamped flat and warriors splashed in the dust practicing fighting drills. The women congregated in the shade of the verandahs, supervising the dockwork and chewing betel. Children played in the fish pools, spearing animals for sport and letting their bodies spin downriver.

For days Jabalwan had Matu sit in the high trees in the bluffs above the river, watching Long Apari the way they had sat in the deep forest watching animals. "Watch carefully," the soul-taker demanded. "You must know this beast well before we go down there to tame it."

Matu knew about tribes from his year as a slave among the Rain Wanderers and from the Book, but he had never truly watched them the way he had watched elephant herds and tapir packs. The routines of the village intrigued him with their regularity: into the sun-sheeted river at dawn the dugouts that had been loaded the day before were launched. The nightwatch straggled in from their forest posts, and day patrols of a dozen warriors each left the longhouses for the boar runs and creek trails. By noon another fleet of dugouts labored upriver to Long Apari loaded with crates, barrels, sacks, mounds of vegetables, and scaffolds hung with dead animals. In the afternoon, while the wharf-work went on, the warriors drilled.

With Wawa scouting ahead for the sorcerers, Jabalwan and Matu were able to elude the redoubled guard force around the village and come to the edge of the clearing before the longhouses without being seen. "The central house with the banners is the one where the chief lives," Matu said. "I have seen him come out to review the cargo rafts and to exhort his warriors. He is a powerful-looking man."

Jabalwan agreed with a nod, his wary eyes continually scanning the undergrowth and the longhouses. "His name is Batuh. He is the man who brought your mother and father together. We will go speak with him now."

Matu laid a hand on the soul-taker's forearm. "Perhaps we should wait awhile. Each morning I see the chief go to the women's end of his longhouse to pleasure himself before the boats arrive. He must be in there now."

Jabalwan smiled a joyless grin and strode into the clearing. The moment he rose, Papan bellowed from the far side of the village where the forest swept closest to the clearing, and all heads turned in that direction. Swiftly, Jabalwan, Matu, and the large ape that had followed them down from the bluffs ran across the clearing. Musketfire boomed from the forest, and the roaring ceased.

Jabalwan put a finger to the frown creasing the space between Matu's eyes. "Don't worry, young sorcerer. Papan was wounded once by the fire-spears. She knows better now than to get close enough to be hit." They were under the longhouses where the air stank of offal and pigs. "Give me the poison needle."

Matu drew the black-tipped red needle from the back band of his waistcloth and handed it to the soul-catcher. Jabalwan held it before the ape, gestured, and the ape took it and ran into the shadows among the pigs. Jabalwan reached into his medicine bag, removed his head-dress, and put it on. "Say nothing," he warned Matu. "Simply watch. Watch. Watch."

Jabalwan signed for Matu to follow and walked around the pilings so they arrived at the notched log stairway with its parang-bearing guard as if out of thin air. The guard grunted in alarm, and the sorcerer signed for him to be silent and stand aside. The guard readily complied, and they mounted the stairs to the verandah, where smoked leathern heads hung by their hair from the crossbeams. The women on the verandah jabbered with dread at the sight of the sorcerer and his gold-headed escort and were silenced when Jabalwan drew a dogbone needle from his hair and pointed it at them.

Silently, the sorcerers paced the length of the verandah and stopped outside the doorway to the wives' chamber. Batuh was within. They could hear him admonishing: "Bend over and forget the commotion outside. I will deal with that when I am through."

Jabalwan growled. Women shrieked, bodies scuffled, and Batuh barged out of the doorway. He was a stout man and had grown more stolid and muscular in the twelve years since Jabalwan had last seen him. The measure of his leadership was that he did not cry out at the sight of the sorcerer and the devil child, but instead opened his hands in greeting. "Jabalwan," he said. "Your ugly face has haunted my nightmares since you took my Mala from me." He looked at Matu, the black borès of his clever eyes widening. "And this is her bastard son, fathered by a monkeyface in a flash of lust." He saw eyes he hated and feared in the boneshape of the one woman he had loved. "Even a child is known by his doings," he said in a tone of memory to what he saw of Mala.

Matu was uneasy, yet a response sparked in him, and he looked to Jabalwan for permission to speak. The soul-taker nodded. *"Instead of fathers, children will rule."*

The claw of a grin lifted one corner of Batuh's mouth. "Yes, your mother told me that once, too. She read it to me from the Book. I believed her and defied my fathers. I even defied you, Jabalwan." He swung a harsh look at the soul-catcher and held his lazy stare. "Do you remember meeting an exiled hunter moving downriver to the land of the dead? Do you remember warning me that it was forbidden?" His laugh showed yellowed teeth filed to points. "Come with me where we are not a spectacle for the whole village," he said, stepping back inside.

Matu trailed after Jabalwan and Batuh into the longhouse, through the muscadine shadows of the wives' quarters to the central chamber. Heads with time-charred flesh and black curled lips hung in a cluster from the main pillar. One of the heads had hanks of blond hair dangling past its mouth hole and the yellow butterfly of a vertebra.

"Your father," Batuh announced, gesturing with mock deference to the skull-staring head.

"You lie!" Matu blurted, and Jabalwan touched his arm and clicked like a cricket.

Batuh came at Matu. "You call me a liar? I who *gave* your mother to this man?"

From the doorways, women were peeking in. Jabalwan clicked again and risked a glimpse at the boy. His face was pale as soft gold, and his eyes said that his brain was moving like a swollen river, lost in itself.

"The boy's father is the squall," Jabalwan said loudly. "The clouds with their backs to the earth. This boy is a sorcerer. The Spider has bitten him, and he lives."

Batuh's face shriveled as if smelling a stink. "The clouds piss on you no differently than on any of us."

A murmur passed through the women at the doors, and Jabalwan spoke sternly. "You will curse the whole village if you speak ill of the spirits, Batuh. What kind of chief are you who cares so little for your own people?"

A vein beat on Batuh's brow, and he stepped close and spoke in a whisper. "Have you come to destroy me, sorcerer?" A twisted smile showed the points of his teeth. "You already did that when you took Mala from me. She was my weapon, she was the one woman I loved. Now *I* am the dead you taught us to fear. Fear me, Jabalwan. Only my care for the Tree Haunters keeps me from killing you and this monkeychild now."

"Batuh, we have not come to destroy you or your head would already be free of its body." Jabalwan stared past the chief to the women and the few warriors who had dared mingle with them. "Matubrembrem and I have come to bless the Tree Haunters. The healers I meet in the forest speak well of the people. They say you are so strong you need not grow your own rice or hunt your own meat. The other tribes pay you tribute for mediating with the monkeyfaces. You have grown wealthy. The other tribes are in awe of you. I have come to acknowledge that awe. To bless you with the wisdom of the ancestors that you will remain strong."

Batuh stomped an angry circle through the wide room, chasing off the onlookers. Alone with the sorcerers, he peered at them with his adder eyes. "You are cunning, Jabalwan. You will use my own people against me. Though I've given them freedom from famine, heads from every tribe, and the wealth of the monkeyfaces, they would still defy me to honor you."

"I am the mansnake. They are my children."

Batuh shook his head. "What do you want from me, mansnake?"

"You will never again kill Rain Wanderers," Jabalwan said with the timbre of thunder. "You will immediately withdraw all your warriors and hunters from the lands west of here. You will never encroach there again."

Batuh's jaw muscles throbbed. "You say this loud enough for everyone to hear. You are not talking to one of your foolish children. I am Batuh, the chief of tribes. I am Batuh, beloved of the devil gods. I am not afraid of your deceptions, mansnake. Why should I obey you?"

"If you do not heed me, the Tree Haunters will lose everything you have given them. Their children and their children's grandchildren will be slaves to the tribes you now dominate."

Batuh shouted something in a foreign tongue, and four men in turbans with beard-hackled faces lunged into the longhouse, scimitars drawn. "The forest people are too afraid to free themselves from your ancient slavery, but the Lanun will happily take your heads."

"Lanun!" Jabalwan said in surprise. "So you trade not only with the monkeyfaces but with their enemy. Do you sell them to each other?"

"The monkeyfaces will not trade their fire-spears with the forest tribes," Batuh answered. "To get guns to rule the other tribes, I tell the Lanun what they need to know to find the monkeyfaces' fat trade ships." Batuh grinned proudly. "Now, for knowing this — and for enslaving the people with your sorcery — I kill you." He signaled the Lanun, and the furious men pounced.

Jabalwan had drawn his dogbone needle from his hair, and he pointed it at the closest Lanun and stamped toward him. The pirate screeched with pain, his sword wrenching free of his hand. He hopped blindly and collapsed before the sorcerer. Jabalwan moved his dogbone in an arc, and another Lanun bounced from the longhouse.

Batuh's face was stupid with what he had seen.

"By betraying me," Jabalwan said, "you betray your people and their ancestors. Your father and the fathers before him will not recognize you in the Longhouse of Souls. Unless . . ." He put the bone back in his headdress and signed for Matu to step for the door. "You will do no further harm to the Rain Wanderers. Each new moon you will go personally to the fork in the river west of here and leave a raft with a full sack of salt, twenty sacks of rice, and a rack of fresh meat. This you will do for two years. After that the ancestors will be content if you leave the Rain Wanderers alone."

Jabalwan walked to the cooking pot and threw it over in a clatter of metal knives and spoons. "In this house the spirits themselves were assaulted and forced to kill a man." He snatched a stalk of bamboo and thrust it into the smoldering embers of the nightfire. "This house cannot stand." He passed his hand over the embers, dropping a cube of coal tar, and flames hopped like rats. "Get out. Have your warriors cut the pilings. Quickly, before the other houses catch the cleansing fire."

Batuh shambled toward Jabalwan, but the sorcerer lifted the flaming bamboo lance and shook it at him. The chief faltered, sweat sparking from his face. "I will kill you, snakeman!"

Jabalwan thrust the burning staff into the thatch ceiling, and the dry grass ruffled with fire. "If you kill me, I will come back from the dead and kill you!" The flames flew across the roof, and the sorcerer screamed the snake's greasy cry, a coiling eeriness that shook the flesh on his skull and split Batuh's rage to gaping fear.

The chief grabbed his ceremonial sword from the pillar where fire was already licking the hung trophies, glimpsed a tongue of fire laughing in van Noot's head, and bolted.

Matu hopped aside to let Batuh pass. The chief leaped from the verandah and tumbled into the dust, his sword spinning from him. All the women had already fled; the pigs under the house were unpenned, and the pilings were being hatcheted. Jabalwan seized Matu's hand and ran with him the length of the verandah, ducking through coils of smoke. Together they leaped off the end of the platform as a wall collapsed to a flaming nest behind them.

The Tree Haunters cut through the pilings, and the burning longhouse sagged to a mound of churning smoke and fiery gushes. Matu squeezed his hand urgently. "Is that my father's head that hung as a war trophy?"

"Your father is a thunderhead. You are his flash." Jabalwan guided Matu away from the flames. "How can you think otherwise after feeding your blood to the Spider?"

The people stood back from the sorcerers as they walked away from the destroyed building. Matu stopped and caught Jabalwan's gaze. "Is that the head of my seed father?"

"The edge of death is not a gamble," the sorcerer replied. "Fate is ancestral energy. You know that."

"My mother lied to me," Matu said, coldly.

Jabalwan shook his head with morose disappointment. "Jan van Noot is your seed father."

"Why did Mala lie to me?" Matu asked in a pang of hurt.

"Did she lie?" Jabalwan's flesh knotted between his eyes.

"Who is Pieter Gefjon, then?"

"Your spirit father," Jabalwan answered sharply. "He is the one who watches you from the medicine cloud. Mala is with him now while van Noot crawls with the animals. Wake up to your mother's sincerity, Matubrembrem. Did you suffer the Spider blindly?" He walked away, and Matu faced the pyre alone. The possibility that Mala had lied to him unfurled like nausea. Who was that blond man? How had Batuh taken his head? He looked for the soul-catcher and saw him striding toward a knot of warriors.

Jabalwan beckoned to a warrior with a fire-spear, and the man ran to him and bowed his head. "Give me your gun," the mansnake ordered. "You will show me how to use it." The warrior obeyed.

Batuh glowered from among his nervous guard, the Lanun keeping safely behind him. The acre of smoke between him and the soul-catcher were the bounds of the earth they had trespassed together. Time was shredded among the flying vapors, and Batuh understood, mired in his anger and humiliation, that he was fighting not only the backward Rain Wanderers and Jabalwan but the dead hordes, the ghost tribes of the ancestors. The future, like the past, was shaped by power — and he knew with unbearable certainty that the power was with the monkeyfaces' fire-spears. In the widening clarity of his defeat, Batuh saw that eventually he *would* kill Jabalwan, he would slay the past, and he would be the future's first ancestor.

Jabalwan and Matu journeyed deep into the mountainous forest, far from the tribes, to practice with the fire-spear. While they practiced, Jabalwan told Matu the story of *Zeerover* and what he knew of Jan van Noot. Van Noot had spoken incessantly about himself the night Mala received him, and later she had relayed everything to the mansnake. "Your seed father was more mask than man," the soul-catcher said. "His mind knew nothing of spirit, so nothing could keep his body from the knives."

The story of his mother making love to a man she did not love so Batuh could take heads and begin an empire destined to destroy the tribes sickened Matu with grief and rage. Over the following days, he shuffled among his chores, absorbed in the reality that he existed only because of his father's carnal passion and his mother's duplicity. He was himself one of the first casualties in the destruction of the tribes.

Jabalwan sensed Matu's torment, but he was helpless to do more than keep the youth busy and prevent him from sinking into complete torpor. The sorcerer wanted to explore the secrets of his new weapon, and they spent weeks in the yellow hills, mixing the powders of his flash-dust until it was as potent as the gunpowder that had come with the musket. Matu assisted patiently, although morosely, building twig-fires for charcoal, scooping sulfur from the stinking hell-vents, scraping saltpeter from cave walls, and foraging for each day's meals while the soul-catcher flashed his powder concoctions in coconut shells.

When the rainy season began and the blowing mists made the powder experiments more difficult, Jabalwan decided to go northwest, deep into the mountains, to meet other sorcerers and show them what he had learned. Matu was still shaken by the revelation that he had no lineage but a sexual spasm and a deceit. In demonic accord with this legacy, his own dreams had become poignantly lubricious, the lapping sounds of the rain thickening into images of women gamboling naked with him. Even awake, the world began to look feminine. Skirts of rain, vulval blossoms, and the perfumes of wet earth made every day a soulful meditation on women. Yet the knowledge of his loveless fathering soured the idea of gratifying himself with the eager maidens of the river villages. He wanted more than an afternoon of rutting, indiscriminate hands groping for him, giggling girls vying to straddle him. He desired the heat of one face, a laugh he would recognize, a touch with a name, a look of caring. "I want a wife," he told Jabalwan.

Jabalwan shrieked with laughter, then blinked away his astonishment. "You can't take a wife. You are a sorcerer."

Matu had brought up the subject on a silver evening in the highlands, when gleaming gusts of rain were sweeping the valleys below and the sky overhead was a blue haze shot with the mica of stars. The world was a woman. The woman was a chasm, the very fallen land before him furred with trees, perspiring mists, glistening streams and cascades. The mountainous contours, the winding descent through the forests, the fleshy grass ranges, and the pubic heat of the swamp leading to her belly in the sea seemed to hold the very shape of all the travels he would ever make. She was his fate. And he wanted to meet her in a real woman. "My dreams insist I am a man first, not a sorcerer," he told Jabalwan.

The sorcerer raised his shoulders and closed his eyes with weary resignation. The tattoo circles on his lids saw the infallible images, and his body sagged. "Well, you are Matubrembrem. The tradition cannot hold you. Go. Take a wife. I must trek higher into the mountains to find this year's convocation of sorcerers. Those of us whom the simplicities of destiny allow are already gathering. We are to meet in a cave at Kinibalu the first new moon after the rains. I will go there with the fire-spear and news of your initiation."

Matu's heart bobbed. "And I?"

Jabalwan's eyes clicked open. "You will find the Rain Wanderers and give the headman this." He took from his medicine bag a pink snail shell with a brown-banded lip and handed it to the youth. "What does it look like?"

"A flower bud, a fresh-laid swiftlet egg . . . a sunburned turtlehead."

"It's your cock after the bamboo knife whacks off your foreskin!" Jabalwan choked with amusement. "This snail shell entitles you to be circumcised."

Matu's face knotted.

"That's the only way you can take a wife," Jabalwan assured him with a slack grin. "You must join the tribe."

The anticipation of that blow coiled Matu's insides tighter, yet he took the snail shell. "The Spider taught me the wealth in risk."

"And your wife will teach you the risk in wealth." Jabalwan sighed and extended his hand in blessing. "Never forget the Spider. Its will threads the moments. You've seen its webwork in the clouds, cobwebs of rain catching life out of the air and hanging it on earth in green trees and hungry animals. You *know* you are in the web. To forget that now is the worst crime. All evil comes from such forgetfulness."

Jabalwan left during the night, following the high, windy ridge trails that were secret to all but the sorcerers who had been initiated in the convocation. The raveling trails carried him above the misty valleys, and in two weeks he completed the journey it would take Matu four months of sultry, humid roaming to unriddle among the boar runs and rivers. Jabalwan found the Rain Wanderers and informed them of their monthly tribute from Batuh and also of Matubrembrem's desire for a wife. He imposed no strictures on the tribe in their behavior toward the devil's child and left again for the mountains that same day, believing that only the powers of the world could liberate Matu from a tedious tribal life and return him to the verge of mystery.

Back on the steppe the morning after, Matu woke to discover that Jabalwan was gone. One scarlet feather hung from a weed-claw above the niche where he had slept. In the leaf-stuffed fissure of the soul-catcher's bed, his blowgun and its darts lay beside the Book. Matu peered through the hanging gardens of mist above the valleys and saw shooting stars over the distant sea, green splinters in the sun's silver corona. No sign of Jabalwan's direction was apparent, so he bowed to the world's four corners — *in every direction, holy of holies* — and called to Wawa. The silver-colored gibbon swung from the bamboo grove in the rocks overhead, and the young sorcerer selected a vine-matted trail that led westward and down the green cliff face toward the dark, rain-smoky forests of the heartland.

Matu wandered the valleys for several moons, visiting sites of power recommended by local villagers. He went because he was lonely for

Jabalwan. He went because he was angry at himself for following his penis instead of his teacher. That was his seed father's way. It was leading him west to his tribe and his wife. Among the power sites — man-size anthills carved by the rains to resemble witches, or stone tigers among ancient ruins — he was with Jabalwan. He spent days perfecting the practical skills of watching and stalking that his teacher respected. He began his own medicine bag. He killed a crocodile with the soulcatcher's blowgun and took the white scales of the belly for his sack. Once the skin was cured he cut pockets and stitched flaps of varying skins and furs to them so he could tell each pouch by touch alone. Then he began collecting the plant parts, minerals, and animal pieces his teacher used for healing. Each village was a lesson in suffering. The injured and ill showed him the inconsolable limits of flesh, and in their damage he faced the greedy mouthparts of the Spider, so keen to devour what its web had snared. Sometimes he remembered enough to find the plant or crushed stone that repelled the avid spiderjaws and left bodies alive around their scars. Sometimes the jaws tore life apart, and he was left chanting the dirge poems Jabalwan had taught him. The work took days at each village, and early in his quest for the Rain Wanderers he saw the truth in Jabalwan's maxim that "there are no obstructions, only instructions."

The healers of the villages responded to his sincerity and helped him, adding to all that Jabalwan had taught him. And though his physical appearance was appalling to the natives, who usually shrank from him at first, he saved lives and won the trust of the people. He accepted the swift, illusory pleasures of the maidens whenever they would have him. He lived in the villages as he imagined Jabalwan would, working by day, cavorting in late afternoon, and returning to the forest at night. The drum songs called him the Sunstare Warrior. He told each village he was not a warrior, that he had no blade, took no heads, fought in no battles, and used his blowgun for game only. Yet the song went ahead of him anyway. To the people he looked minatory. His thin snake lips, raptor nose, deathly pale flesh, and clear eyes imparted a lethal mien to his tall stature. To ease villagers when he first arrived he would pluck gold whiskers from his chin and hand them to the most timid. In the late afternoons, he would entertain the tribe by reading stories from the Book. The people were enthralled by the strange and violent tales, and his reputation as a prophet of war and of supernatural intervention was added to his drum song.

As villages became more rare, the profuse valleys opened into solitary weeks of foraging and walking. Spirits walked with him. The dreams of the one-eyed monkeyface had stopped, and the world both seen and invisible seemed his friend. Wawa brought Matu berries and accounts of animals at neighboring sites each day, and once they met up with

Papan at the juncture of a river and a waterfall, where the fish under the echo-loud cliffs were bends of rainbow and big as forearms. Sometimes at twilight, Mala watched him from among the trees, smiling in a shaft of rose sunlight or gazing through the pummeling fog. Jabalwan visited frequently while he slept, suggesting routes through the jungle, commenting on the secret faces of the animals the boy had seen that day, and laughing at his daytime fantasies of Riri. She was the one he imagined as his wife among the Rain Wanderers. She was the only living woman he dreamed about. And the fear that she might already be given away spurred him on his journey. She had been marriageable six months earlier when she had come down to the river to meet him. The cumin of her complexion, the mischief in her imp-slanted eyes, her hot laugh, her gums pink as dusk haunted his waking. He fouled shots with his blowgun that could have been meals and lingered asleep to remain in her bewitchment. He could not stop fondling her in his mind. Pondering was not enough. He had to go to her, to be mocked or loved. And always there was the possibility that when he found her she would belong to someone else.

One muggy afternoon, Matu glimpsed in the shade of a vine-woven bough the frayed tail feather of an arrow. He picked it out of the branch, then began to search the area, soon discovering footprints that led toward the back of the valley. Under a root-arch, he found the bent grass sign of a healer from the Rain Wanderers.

Matu followed the mudpath and its prints to a buffalo path of another season. The jungle had already covered the ditchlike run with its pea vines and spangle-leafed creepers, yet Matu could discern the direction the healer had taken. Wawa chirruped from ahead, giving the signal for a waterfall. Mist breezed through the hanging vines and clung to the curtains of yellow bell-blossomed tendrils, shrouding the giant limbs of the primeval trees in haze. Colorful flowers glowed spectrally in the gloom, and the air was a suede of chilled moss scents. Under colossal cliffs fuming with falling water, Matu wound his way carefully among steaming boulders and churning pits of foam. Wawa shouted through the din, announcing people, and Matu pranced out of the wet smoke into the brilliant heat of broad riverflats.

Dazzling waterbirds strutted with stately aplomb in the sun-glinting shallows. Crocodiles sank to their eyeholes in the algal mud and copper grass of the banks. Just visible downriver, at the first wide bend where the current splashed among smooth stones, women were fishing in the rock pools. A high-peaked longhouse among bursts of fruit trees stood on the high bank almost invisible in the face of the forest. At the sight of Matu the women scattered up the embankment, and he sat down on one of the rocks and waited.

Among the first warriors to hop down the bank and confront him was Ferang, animosity vibrant in his strapping body. "So you have found us." Ferang smirked at his companions, who stood back in deference to the devil's child. "Jabalwan tells us you would be a man." His laugh was empty.

From above on the scarp, a voice called out, "Young sorcerer, welcome to your home."

Matu looked up past Ferang's quivering face to see the chief and his family gathered on the slope. The chief was beckoning him. Sunlight winced among his white feathers, and his broad features were lifted in a smile. His wives and children gawked down at the tall painted figure with sunspun hair. Riri was among them, and the sight of her made Matu's heart jump. She had sauntered closest to the edge and smiled widely at him. He shouldered past Ferang, handed the blowgun upward, and picked his way among the toeholds and rootsteps so that he passed closest to Riri.

The chief and the elders were impressed with Matu's new maturity, and he was ushered into the village with much hooting and yodeling. Matubrembrem's arrival from the headwaters of the Eater of Men seemed to the people a glad omen. Arrack was passed around, pigs were slaughtered, and a spume of music fell from the longhouse.

Matu was pleased to see the village looking healthier than it had at the last site. The paddy fields glistened like fur in the blue shade of the ancient trees, the vegetable garden flourished, and the clearing before the longhouse swirled with children. He plucked his gold whiskers for the young ones who shied from him and passed out colored stones and shells from his medicine bag. For Riri he produced a coil of rare white python skin.

Ferang watched with menacing attentiveness. When Matu offered him the skull of the python, a potent amulet for earthing power during the dance, he was irked. He would not accept this farce of a human. The Spider had killed Ferang's brother — and it had let this abomination live. Curse the spirits and the Spider. Curse the mansnake. To avenge his brother, to spite the hidden world that denied him, he would find an accident for this boy.

Matu was yet a sorcerer and before night he had to be circumcised. To the boisterous honking of bamboo flutes, the men of the tribe carried the boy through the forest to a glade of stones. He was offered a deer horn of liquid, but he refused because it had the soporific smell of night and he did not want to be stupefied his first day with his tribe. Grunts of amazement and concern among the men were silenced as the headman drew a short, black obsidian blade from an eelskin scabbard. Matu's foreskin was drawn, and the headman sliced it off in one hard stroke. Blood spat on the rocks, and Matu gnashed the pain. The men cheered, the flutes bleated, and an astringent leaf was wrapped about his wound. All night the Rain Wanderers celebrated, with music, acrobatic dances, heroic stories, and much arrack. At dawn, the tribe crawled into the shade and slept.

In his first weeks, Matu proved to be the tribe's supreme hunter, and he was favored with a room in the longhouse among the elders. The honor was burdensome for Matu. He had slept in the forest since Jabalwan took him from his mother, and he was stifled by the pall of cooking odors, body scents, and the noisome pigs. Soon he began sleeping outdoors again, explaining to the chief that his hunting skill was honed by the night air. Every night since his wound had healed, he had approached Riri's mat among the chief's other daughters in the longhouse and placed a piece of manioc in her hand. Other hunters, including Ferang, had done likewise, and he had seen her later going off with them into the bushes at the hem of the forest. She did not favor him in this way, though she continued to watch him with smiling directness, and she did not cringe from him when he sidled up to her at the fish pools or in the garden. Many of the maidens solicited his interest with lingering glances and affectionate gestures, but he never visited their mats. The precarious feeling Riri's garnet-brown eyes inspired did not open in him with any other. He wanted her.

For her part, Riri did not understand her feelings for this grotesque man. Her attraction was as strong now as the last time she had seen him, when he was washing the dung from himself in another river. But her gusty feelings for this pale, stone-faced youth were not love. They were the turmoil of fear and wonder in the magnetic field of her revulsion. She wanted to be near him the way she sometimes wanted to watch dogs root out a squirrel and its litter and devour the runt after the hunters took the rest. Her horror was cold but sexual, and she felt froth between her thighs when she breathed the forest stink of the wind-eyed boy.

Ferang took note of Riri's fascination and Matu's hopeless passion and devised a plan to destroy him with his own desire. He convinced Riri to spend a day working at the far end of the garden where a rill from the river had cut a deep, stony gorge. The narrow fissure was cluttered with lianas and fallen saplings. The day before Riri was to work there, Ferang cleared the gorge of all the saplings but one, which he slanted across the steep ditch to where Riri would be standing as she pruned the gooseneck gourds. He used a bone splinter to dig out the pith of the sapling at its middle, and then he turned the trunk so his work was not visible from above.

The Rain Wanderers were anxious to reassure Matu and his spirit allies that they now accepted as an equal the boy who had been their slave three years before. Every family invited him to their cooking fire, and in his first weeks he visited each of the clans, including Ferang's.

His was a hunter's clan, flying fox totem, with a great-grandfather who had been a sorcerer and had roamed among the tribes like Jabalwan. Ferang had pierced his ears with fox fangs and narrowed his face with red ocher streaks, beginning between his eyes and streaking his flat brow and the eminent bones of his sockets. A black line down his nose and the surly set of his long jaw gave him the brazen semblance of a fox. At Matu's visit to his clan's cooking pot, after the new tribesman had enthralled everyone with strange tales of the south, Ferang invited him to go hunting.

They were to meet on the north side of the village in sight of the garden, early, while the morning mist was still tattering. Matu arrived first and spotted Riri in the humid light among the gourd vines. She was on her tiptoes, reaching for the dangling fruit in the skeletal trees supporting the vines, her breasts with their tight dark nipples swaying, her long ear lobes bobbing beneath her cropped hair. Her stretch had pulled her soft bark loincloth to the downy shadow at the base of her spine, and the sleek length of her nut-oiled body shone like an eel. She saw him and adjusted her waistcloth. They waved at each other, the morning between them shivering with sunlight. He plucked a green orchid from the knee of a bumpy tree and ran to present it to her. On the sapling bridge, he stopped and toed the wood to be sure the termites had not found it. Seeing that the wood was green, he hurried over.

Ferang watched as the sapling snapped under Matu's weight and he plunged into the stone-fisted rill. The hunters heard Riri's alarmed cries, and they rushed to the gorge to find Matu unconscious, his right leg bent at an impossible angle where it had caught between two rocks and snapped above the knee. They carried him to the longhouse, laid him in a grass hammock, and fit the broken ends of his legbone together.

Matu woke basted with fever, his leg barbed in pain, throbbing knife-thrusts. He chewed the black toes of sleeproot, and the pounding agony softened. Riri wept at his swollen leg until her tears had soaked his silk grass bindings. She swabbed his fever-dew, fed him rice broth, and collected and prepared the leaves and roots he requested. The leaf mash she helped him concoct cleansed the infection from his gashed thigh and the blue milky drops squeezed from the roots dulled the pain and plunged him into a moribund trance for several days while the bone set.

In his trance, Matu returned to the medicine cloud. Mala was there, unearthly with moon-disc eyes and sunset-brindled hair. "Mother, help me," he bawled to her, and she knelt over his black-bruised leg and laid her icy hands on the lips of his wound.

The sound of her voice was exhausted as though it had traveled through miles of silence. "Now you are crippled. You will never hunt again." He groped for the pain of his snapped limb and instead felt dead meat. The medicine cloud darkened and brooded on rain. Jabalwan spoke from inside an alley of wind. "There is no true freedom in life, Matu. The more you struggle for what you want, the tighter the trap becomes. Where did you think you were going?"

Matu woke with the comprehension that he would never be young again. His body had been broken. He would never run or stalk again with effortless will. For weeks he lay in the longhouse, stewing in its cauldron of odors, the remorse for what he had lost a heavy sludge in his lungs. He was glad for the pain, and he listened to it knitting the splinters of his bone, ticking with hurt and mercy. Days of fever relented to days of absorbed watching, contemplating the clouds and the rain, remembering with silent anguish the jubilant love that had lured him here.

Riri's beauty was invincible, squeezing his heart all the more ferociously as she tended him with utter patience and extravagant common sense. He knew by the sad melody of her touch and her gracious smiles that she could never desire him. And over the flow of many days, he recognized her true desire, not for any of the young hunters who brought her delicacies from the jungle and serenaded her with sentimental flute passions, but for sullen Ferang who had kept aloof since Matu's injury. Matu had seen the heat in her tapered eyes when Ferang's fox-slanted face peered in at her during the sorcerer's afternoon trances. She thought Ferang was staying away because of the spell of bad luck she had inflicted on the sorcerer, and her meticulous care for Matu was actually a demonstration of contrition for Ferang.

Matu knew this. When Matu had fallen, Ferang had presented the elders with a termite-hollowed sapling, saying it had caused the accident. Matu clearly remembered the green sapling, but he confirmed Ferang's story. "Even a sorcerer can be a fool in love," he told them, and that satisfied their grave doubts and amused the gossips. Ferang was baffled. He began to visit Riri more often, hoping to learn more about this enemy who did not challenge him.

The sorcerer remained reticent. He had fashioned a crutch for himself, and he hobbled silently up and down the verandah, strengthening his withered leg. Riri accompanied him everywhere. Genuine respect competed with revulsion as she witnessed his quiet perseverance during his recovery. His lack of pride made him look ridiculous to her at first, especially when he insisted on bathing and swabbing his ripped thigh in herbal waters and root oils like some precious pet instead of defeating it with the indifference of a true man. But over time she saw the usefulness of his prideless devotion to his predicament. Two moons after splitting his leg, he walked without a crutch, hobbling stiffly, yet whole. He outlined his scar in a red serpent-swerve and put himself to work on his knees in the paddy fields and the kitchen to stretch and fortify his new muscle.

When the third moon had risen, Matu requested that the elders send him to the east river fork where the Tree Haunters left their monthly tribute. The headman was reluctant to send the sorcerer on such a venture because the last two tributes had been smaller, the salt dirty, and the rice mixed with pig dung. The Tree Haunters' belligerence was rekindling and a gimp-legged man just strong enough for women's work was not worthy of the danger.

"It is because I am a gimped man that I am worthy of the danger," Matu pleaded before the chief's cooking pot. "I will never be all that I was before. Why risk strong men? If anyone is to die, let it be me."

The elders were persuaded by his argument, and they agreed that he should guide the tribute raft to the tributary, whose currents would carry it to the village. They offered him one escort, and he selected Ferang.

Convinced that Matu meant to kill him in the forest in revenge for his injury, Ferang painted his body for battle. He stenciled amulets on the big bone behind his neck and over his heart to ward off evil energy and covered himself with white plaster. He strapped a bamboo blade to each thigh, freshened the poison on his darts, sharpened the wooden spearhead of his blowgun, and selected his most powerful sling gun and a pouch of knifetip rocks.

Matu shook his head when he saw him. "We are not fighting a war, Ferang. If we are attacked, we will hide." He insisted that Ferang paint over his battle-white with snakeleaf green and yellow and brown nut paste. Ferang complied reluctantly and followed Matu several wary paces behind when they entered the dark, narrow passages of the jungle. He considered spearing the sorcerer through his back and feeding his body parts to the crocodiles, but within moments in the cool gloom of the forest he sensed Matu's mastery. Favoring his right leg and striding slower than Ferang liked and with an occasional spasm of limp that made him hop like a deer, Matu was still quieter and left no trace. His feet infallibly found the callus of a root, the moss pad, or even the liana rope on a tree trunk where he could place his weight without pressing a print or molesting the random beauty of the leaf litter. He was the forest's precise center, ubiquitous with alertness. His signing of animals long before they came into sight and his knowing stare when they faced each other over the evening's leaf fire convinced Ferang he was in the presence of a spiritman. He purged himself of all thoughts of betrayal and concentrated on defending himself.

Matu was gratified by Ferang's wariness. The spirits of the waking world were punishing him, just as the Book assured. His weeks of pain had reminded him of the Spider's cunning and his own impuissance.

He was no different from everything else that was alive. The web of dying had fixed him when he dropped from Mala. The medicine cloud's reminder that there was no freedom except in limitation explained his wound. Loving Riri, loving any woman — Mala, the paddy girls, even the phantoms of his lewd dreams — was loving death. That was the fatefulness of women. *They are drowning us with blood.* He recalled the menstrual chants of the women when the Ceremony of the Wound greeted the sickle moon. Everyone knew this. It was common knowledge. The surrender of life to death, of men to women, and women to the bearing of the tribe was human destiny from the beginning of time. Except for those few men God made mad or too grotesque to love women. God had selected him from this, and he had yearned instead for a woman's love because it was denied. He had loved death. He had sucked from her bright tits. He had spurned God's will when he sought a wife, and his wound was God's brand, the sign of the covenant broken between them. He had loved death even after he had been shown the Life. He was eating his own death each day that he stayed with the Rain Wanderers. But with a broken leg, he could not leave. He knew then that he had to endure like a frail tree and reach deeper into the dirt of necessity, into the dark earth where he found himself, and he submitted to Riri's care and the uxorial chores his wound allowed. Only now that he was free to leave did he demand of himself one more withholdance. He had decided that the first challenge to his wound would benefit the Rain Wanderers or kill him.

Deep in the afternoon two days later, they arrived at the river fork where the tribute raft waited. Squirrels and red-winged manakins flicked over the rent sacks of rice, and the hung meat had already been carried off by beasts, testifying that the raft had sat undisturbed a long time. Matu stopped Ferang as he moved to approach the offering. "Wait. We must find the trail the Tree Haunters left by."

Ferang wagged his head with annoyance. "Any child can see that we are the only people here."

"Wait." Matu circled along the far bank of the fork where the raft was tied to trees by the river. He was listening with all his might for Wawa's call, but the gibbon had been distracted by a female in heat. "We will wait," Matu announced when his end of the circle met up with Ferang's.

The Rain Wanderer scowled. "The afternoon is already tired. How long can we wait?"

"Till morning if necessary."

"For what are we waiting?" Ferang threw a fist at the raft. "There is the tribute. Let us take it. We can float it to the riverbend and the homeward stream before nightfall — if we act now."

Matu stared into Ferang's face and said nothing. The warrior's eyes were too bright. His defiance was impenetrable. Matu called for Wawa, and his shrill whistle mimed a barbet so exactly it stiffened the hairs behind Ferang's ears. No answering call came.

Ferang shed his look of disgust for a mask of compressed determination. He stalked away, sliding through the underbrush along the bank that led directly to the spit in the fork where the raft was tied.

"Wait!" Matu ordered, and the warrior's amulet-painted back stared at him sternly before vanishing in the shrubs. Matu blew the dread out of his chest and went after him.

They descended through a brake of stunted bamboo where a mudslide had smothered an old grove, and had just entered the clearing before the bank, when Wawa's singsong rang from directly behind, warning of men. Before Matu could pull Ferang to cover, three Tree Haunter warriors in battle regalia crashed into the clearing from the surrounding brush.

Ferang's spear flew, impaling the nearest. Matu spun, and a long dart blinked over his shoulder. He put the momentum of his whirling dodge into his spear-arm and flung his dagger-tipped blowgun at the sniper, catching him through his chest.

Wawa screamed again, and Matu swung his attention across the wall of the jungle. Two Tree Haunters were charging across the clearing with metal-tipped spears and parangs. His blood jumped to flee, but Ferang was standing fast, a bamboo blade in each hand. Whimpering with urgency, Matu fumbled through his medicine bag searching for the flash-powder Jabalwan had taught him to make. A spear wobbled in the sunlight toward him; he threw himself aside, and it gouged past.

Ferang stabbed his knives into the ground, seized the thrown spear, and turned it on the assailants. He threw and missed, and the two Tree Haunters closed on them. Matu found the gritty soil, but there was no time to light it. A warrior with raised parang hacked at him, and he cast the black powder in his face and hopped away. Ferang had locked spears with his opponent, and Matu had to face the other Tree Haunter alone. He drew his bamboo knife and retreated as the man came at him with his swaying parang. His bad leg cramped with the effort, and he collapsed backward under the warrior's assault.

Wawa shrieked and flared out of the leafy grove, arms overhead gripping a stick, fangs bared. The gibbon clubbed the warrior over Matu, giving him time to slash with his bamboo sliver. The knife daggered the man's left shoulder, and Wawa's stick snapped against his hip. Berserk with pain, the Tree Haunter grabbed Matu's knife-arm and would have severed the sorcerer's throat if Wawa had not snagged his wrist.

Ferang was still pitting his strength against his enemy. He saw the chance for a feint, sagged suddenly, and exploded forward, breaking the spear-lock and knocking the Tree Haunter aside. Ferang's spear snaked after him, goring him between his ribs.

Matu had rolled to his feet and was trying to avoid the warrior's parang and break his grip. Ferang's spear snapped the warrior's back, dropping him with a gargled scream. Matu reeled away, splattered with blood.

Ferang laughed in relief at the sight of him, and Matu grabbed Wawa's tough hand in gratitude. But their smiles froze as a blowgun poked from the bamboo behind Ferang. Matu shouted in warning. The hunter wheeled about. A dart flashed and dug deep in the globe of Ferang's shoulder.

Matu yanked the spear from the spine of the man who had almost killed him and threw it vehemently into the grove, finding a scream. He rushed into the bamboo and saw the warrior pinned through his bowels to the earth. The man bared his throat and cried to be killed. Matu slashed with a hunter's precision, then jumped away and ran from the grove.

The Rain Wanderer had curled up in the mud, the dart in his hand, the puncture wound in his shoulder threading blood. Matu drew a finger-razor of volcanic glass from his medicine bag and sliced open the tiny hole with two deep cuts. He put a rubbery fish bladder to his lips, sucked it to a wrinkled vacuum, and attached its opening to the puncture. It drew spurts of blood.

"Leave me, sorcerer," Ferang mumbled. "I feel the poison on my heart. It is cold. I am dead."

Matu pinched the corners of Ferang's eyes until he squinted alert. "Listen, Ferang — you will not die. I have drawn the poison out."

"It is in my heart. I feel it." His eyes fluttered. "Cold."

"You will not die!" Matu asserted.

"My soul is leaving." His voice slurred. "Tell my family I sent three ahead of me."

"You will not die, Ferang." Matu pulled a gray tuft of heart-tripping leaves from his bag. "I will catch your soul. Stay awake!"

Matu squeezed open the hunter's mouth and pressed the broken bits into his saliva. The warrior shuddered mightily, his legs jerked straight out, and he stopped breathing. Fecal stench clouded up from him with his soul.

Matu beat Ferang's chest like a great drum, summoning the soul back in as he had seen Jabalwan do. Then he straddled the warrior's thighs and pressed against his chest, forcing air out of his body. The air sagged back in as he released, and he pressed again. Matu continued the rite as the day wilted, and the stink of the bodies lured bear cats and foxes. In the dark, Matu could no longer see the glister of life in the young man's eyes, and he had to judge the tenacity of Ferang's soul by the limberness of his ribcage as it surrendered to his push and returned with his release. Matu's arms were erased by fatigue, and he lifted his face to the bonechips of stars and rode the ritual of the stolen breath with mindless concentration. Somewhere in the middle of the night, long after rain clouds had masked the stars and a hot drizzle had driven off the mosquitoes and fireflies, Ferang coughed to life.

"Why did you do this, soul-catcher?" Ferang wanted to know when his alertness had fit his voice back in place. The humid night air stank of death, and his chest ached with bruised ribs, yet he was a wallow of joy. "Do you not know that it is I who tricked you into breaking your leg?"

"I may be a clumsy warrior, but I am not stupid."

"Then why?"

"Because, Ferang, you are right to hate me." Matu served him an invigorating infusion of barkchips that steadied his shivering heart.

"I don't understand. The Rain Wanderers love you. Even Riri was coming to love you. You could have her for your wife."

"Perhaps, for I love the Rain Wanderers in return. If not for you I would have remained trapped among them. You set me free. You broke my illusions with my leg, Ferang. I owed you a life."

"Then we are equal again." Ferang's brutal face relaxed.

Matu helped Ferang to the raft and guided it to the stream that flowed home. Ferang lay spraddled among the rice, the salt a pillow under his head. His heart was still outlined in cold, and the air shimmied with invisible mothwings around Matu's sun-furred head. "Where will you go?"

"To the roof of the world," Matu replied. "I will dance your triumph over the Tree Haunters in the sight of heaven." He waved as the current accepted the raft.

Ferang waved back and held the sight of the lanky sorcerer — his arms raised over his head, his long white hair burning in the early sun — until the river swerved and the jungle closed on him.

The memory of Matu's first kill lingered, and for years no day passed without images of the two Tree Haunters he had skewered to the earth with spears. The thought that he might have been killed himself that afternoon did not dim his memory of the despair in the warrior's face whose throat he had cut. The lucidity in the man's plea to be killed had chilled Matu. *Death is not a secret.* He would finally comprehend this several years later, when the killing was about to begin again. *Life is secret.*

Even before killing the warriors, Matu had realized that leaving Jabalwan and searching for a wife was the act that had awakened the dark future. Life's urge had led to death, and with the deaths of the

Tree Haunters he returned to the Life, forsaking his hope for a wife and a family tribe. He had known uncounted paddy girls and was not satisfied. He had loved one woman openly and maimed himself. He had killed to defend himself and been troubled. He was through with the unrelieved loneliness of his needs, and he set his heart on the mountains. Clouds calved from the black peaks, and waterfalls glinted among forests dark as sleep. Jabalwan was there, and the Life that he hoped would help him forget the taste of death. He was ready now for the borderland between rock and dream. He was thirteen years old.

The rains swept in silent waves over the valleys, beating against the doors of the forest. Rivers swelled over their banks and emptied among the trees, carrying snakes up from the sliding water. Matu collected enough snakeskin to make himself a rainhat with a brim that sloped over his back. He also trimmed his medicine bag with fangs and made a broad strap of white hide from drowned cave vipers.

Now he understood why the convocation of sorcerers took place on the highest mountain at the end of the rainy season. The paths up the slopes were gushing rivulets and flash floods boomed unexpectedly, sweeping away boulders and trees. Above the valleys, fog soaked earth and sky and erased vision like the medicine cloud. Only a sorcerer could find his way through this terrain. Secret signs scratched by other sorcerers into the moss on trees and cliffrocks indicated the path up the fog ledges and into the cold, brilliant world above the clouds.

That night Matu curled up with Wawa under a wind-polished escarpment and chewed on braids of dried meat as rain smashed among the great cliffs.

Toward dawn, fire spilled into their hollow with a roar, and Matu jerked upright, smacking his skull against the stone roof. He crawled out onto the pitched ledge. Above him, on the curve of a granite fin, Jabalwan stood, naked, his black hair streaming in the icy updraft, the fire-spear raised in salute.

"Come with me," he exhorted, stepping to a higher ledge. "Quickly now, before I freeze my manhood off."

Matu's fear startled to joy, and he scrambled after his teacher. Jabalwan led them up a gravel spill and along switchbacking trails no more than a palm's breadth away from the void and the dewdrop stars. Where the trail ended, dawn glowed like metal, and the only way to go was up a rock chimney hung with thick vines. Matu stood on the toehold at the world's edge and looked out over the violet thunderheads to where the sun squatted like an amber scorpion. He climbed into the chimney, and the air softened to ferny breezes lush with the ripe fragrances of pond grass and willows.

"Come in, sorcerer and beast," Jabalwan said from above, his voice gaseous in the draft. "This is Njurat — Heaven's Flight."

Matu crawled up the jagged chute and entered a misty grotto of percolating mud pools. The banks were luxuriant with giant, shiny ferns, ancient cypress and willow trees, and a busy confusion of air plants, orchids, and dusty pink birds.

"Leave your clothes here," Jabalwan ordered. Matu stripped and followed Jabalwan to a trail among the boiling mud pools. Men sat in the mud or squatted naked on the bank. They were sullen shapes cauled in wet black earth, slick serpent faces and tranced limbs in the foggy twilight, staring at the trees bending beneath their green yokes.

"These are sorcerers from many lands," Jabalwan said. "They will not see you until you have first seen the dragon."

Jabalwan strode through the smoky light, and Matu ran after him. Seeing again the soul-taker's lean, strong frame, the young man felt his life deepening. He wanted to express his joy at walking once more in the shadow of his teacher, to tell him he was sorry that he had ever left his side, but every phrase that came to mind weighed falsely on his tongue. At last, he asked, "What is this dragon we must meet?"

"The dragon is the earth," Jabalwan answered, stepping down into a fissure of moss and vines. The rock was sweating clear water and dripping roots and white flowers tiny as frost. "The steam pools are its breath seeping up through the rocks. As it dreams, its soul travels through the world as the power in the clouds. That is why cloudreading shows the dreams of the world."

At the bottom of the fissure, a black slab was wedged into the earth, and the mountain was pried open just enough for a man to crawl through. In the lintel was carved the sorcerers' sign for maw, barely visible among the gnarled roots of the black oak above the cave.

"You've changed in the year we've been apart," Jabalwan said, motioning for Matu to sit on a rock facing him. The youth was longer of shoulder, thicker jawed, and wore his hair plaited in tribal fashion. But Jabalwan was most curious about the ugly scar that strapped his thigh.

Matu read his stare and told him the story of his love for Riri and Ferang's jealousy.

"Then you have changed, young sorcerer. When last we met, the whole world was a woman to you. Now you have looked deep enough to know that for a man, woman is death. It is terrible you had to be injured to know this."

"Only pain could have freed me, teacher. Pain is the only answer to love."

"Now you must meet the dragon and join the sorcerers. Are you ready? Eat this." Jabalwan reached into a leafpouch that lay at his side and held up a flat circle of bread no bigger than his palm.

Matu recognized in the mushroom shavings and blue-tinged dough the curls of a fungus called strong eye. Jabalwan often gave it to people as they were dying. But Matu did not want to eat it. The terrible vision from the Spider was still harsh in his memory, and he dropped the bread so it fell behind him, where Jabalwan could not see. He bent swiftly, as though alarmed at his clumsiness, tucked the bread into a fracture in the wall, and plucked a tuft of moss which he stuffed in his mouth instead. He faced the sorcerer as he chewed it.

Jabalwan nodded toward the rock slab named maw. "We will crawl into the belly of the mother now. Come, before the strong eye begins."

Jabalwan lay on his back and inched into the cleft face up. Matu crept on his stomach after him, relieved that he had avoided the mushroom bread. The tight mouth of the cave hugged and scraped him, and several times he had to empty all of his breath before he could squeeze on. The hard rock scraped his skull and spine, and with his head turned sidewise, his cheek bleeding, he pushed with all his might. Suddenly the passage opened, and he could stand and feel the black breezes. A spark snapped, and a wriggling flame rose from a resin candle in Jabalwan's hand.

He looked into the damp of the youth's eyes to see that the mushroom bread was brightening in him. Matu asked where they were, but the older man motioned for him to keep silent. Each small sound, each footscrape and sigh, was barnacled in echoes. Jabalwan held the candle high and the wan light revealed a cavernous space flimmery with bats.

They walked down an incline of giant mushroom-shaped outcroppings, striated and glossy as meat, leading into dense heat that smelled of prophecy, incense, and torchsmoke. A black tunnel loomed ahead, and there the descent swooped into blackness. Jabalwan lifted a torch from where it had been turned head down in a stone wall. At the touch of the resin flame, the torchlight kicked the darkness back, and the tunnel's arch sparkled with mica-chipped glyphs.

"What does it say?" Matu asked, echoes washing up into the depths.

"No one remembers. The first sorcerers carved this tunnel in the times before. Now be silent. This is the dragon's chamber."

Jabalwan lowered the torch into the tunnel. "Go forward and meet the dragon of the earth," he commanded.

Grateful for his clear head, Matu stepped through the archway with Jabalwan a pace behind, the torchlight scattering in starbursts across the mica-vaulted ceiling. The tunnel led to a shallow rock pit with a thrust of boulder lifting into the dark among sharp, confused shapes. Jabalwan ignited the bowl of oil in the pit.

The sudden blue light illuminated the giant face of Death. Matu skittered backward, into Jabalwan's waiting arm, and was shoved toward a ferociously huge, fanged face. Matu held back a yell and gaped at the abomination. It was a malignant skull — bigger than three men. The caves of its sockets stared emptily; the jaw was a hollow wave of bone. Rippling vertebrae connected the colossal skull to a marl of stone in the pit, a stew of petrified mud, and the round, shattered-pottery shapes of eggs. Three gray eggs, each the size of a honey hive, lay smashed open. Inside these eggshell cradles were the stone bones of lizards, grappling shapes melted in rock. Matu unclenched and approached the dragon's nest.

At first Matu thought the monster crèche was a remarkable idol carved by the first sorcerers. But on closer scrutiny he perceived that the skeletons were too predatory to have been carved by human hands. "What is it?"

"The dragon of the earth. The mother of life. This is her true head, discovered here by the first sorcerers. These are her brood, hatched at the moment of death. You are at the center of the world."

Matu moaned, overwhelmed, and Jabalwan helped him to sit down in the pit, next to the eggs and the huddled skeletons. Above him the enormous mother reared, her monster grin suspended over her calves, ready to protect or devour them.

Jabalwan left him then, and soon a fathomless music began as the sorcerers piped hidden flutes and horns. If he had eaten the mushroom bread, Matu thought, this would have been the furious portal to the medicine cloud. Instead, the great bones before him seemed simply locked in their fate, their passion held in the flame-lit rock. Looking about, he spotted a path beyond the pit. He decided to explore. Matu lit a torch at the pit and then clambered into the shaft in the far wall.

The corridor was just large enough for him to walk bent over. Branching tunnels led to catacombs of racked heads, a devotional room mounded with the white stones called mountains' tears that the monkeyfaces desired, and a snake-painted crawlway that made him stop. The strong eye would never have let him see all this, and he was not sure he should cross these taboo serpent lines until the other sorcerers had accepted him. But that reluctance disappeared as he listened to the sounds of the sorcerers moaning the noises of the afterworld. They were laughable to him in his freedom, and his glee at having avoided their spell emboldened him. He crept over the stenciled floor and into the forbidden alcove.

Two heads were mounted side by side on a stone pedestal shagged with moss. One was the tiny, bearded head of Pieter Gefjon. The other was also tiny, a snail-small face wrapped in a smoke of black hair — his mother.

Matu flew howling from the alcove, beaten back by the sight of Mala's wee face with its eyes stitched shut. Back in the dragon chamber, he dropped to his knees, his head throbbing with hurt, fear, and dull rage.

He sat that way for what seemed hours. When he looked up, Jabalwan was standing before him in the slick blue light, Gefjon's small head dangling in his hand by its hair.

"You have mocked the earth dragon." The older man's face looked damaged. "You have mocked me."

Matu glared at him with sulky remoteness.

"Why have you done this?" Jabalwan asked.

"I am Matubrembrem."

"Don't feed me that dung. You have spurned a vision in the dragon chamber. If you had eaten the bread, you would have talked with the earth dragon. She would have told you what to do with your Spider vision."

The shock of meeting Mala was still rushing in Matu. "Forgive me, teacher." He listened to the silvery needlepoints of cave-dripping sounds, searching for what to say. "I did not mean to mock," he stammered, faltering before the sorcerer's disappointment.

"Take this." Jabalwan thrust the head into Matu's grasp. "I promised your mother it would be returned to you when you had attained. Now it is yours. You are not a true tribesman. You are not a true sorcerer. You have attained your destiny." Jabalwan shook his head and turned away.

Matu clutched the sacred head and shuffled after him, out of the dragon chamber, up the sloping path to the dark cavern. Matu breathed deeply, bolstering himself for the tight squeeze through the stone maw. But Jabalwan did not go to the cleft. Instead he wandered down a side corridor and shoved open a crawlhole in the cavern wall. Sunlight poured in. Outside in the numbing brightness, a rock trail snaked among the boulders and led down the slate ridges into the green mist of the forest.

"Call your beast," Jabalwan ordered. "We cannot stay in Njurat now that you have mocked the dragon."

Matu whistled for Wawa, and the gibbon appeared on the rock ledge above them, wreathed in fern fronds, a piece of pink melon in its hand, and jabbering annoyance at being pulled away from paradise.

Jabalwan and Matu camped that night on a mountain ledge under a sky huge with stars and the flaws of the moon. The older man had said nothing since Njurat. Matu thought he was angry, but the mansnake was sad. He had felt no grief when the boy had abandoned his work as a sorcerer to become a Rain Wanderer, but now that Matu had forsaken his place among the other sorcerers, Jabalwan feared for him. His voice surprised Matu with its sorrow. "You are a sorcerer in spirit. Why do you act as if you had never given your hand to the Spider?"

"I cannot believe as you do, teacher. I am the son of a monkeyface."

Jabalwan seized the youth's arm in his cold grasp. "You are Matubrembrem. You are the last of the sorcerers. You did not have to mock us."

"Yet I did."

"And because of that you have forsaken a life among others. You will have no place in the world but what you make for yourself. No one will walk with you now that you have left the Rain Wanderers and the brotherhood of sorcerers."

"And you, teacher? Will you not walk with me?"

Jabalwan's stare glittered in the dark like starlight. "You gave your foreskin to the Rain Wanderers, yet found no place among them. You risked your life to reach Njurat, yet scorned the sorcerers who received you. Matu, do you not see? You lose distinction with each insincerity."

"I am sincere for what I am."

"And you are alone."

"I have always been alone, except for Mala — and you. Will you not walk with me, teacher?"

Jabalwan gazed out over the moonlit forest. "I will not walk with you. I go alone into the jungle." He looked at Matu, and his face appeared swollen in the dark. "But if I meet you there in sincerity, then together we will walk with the beast that walks in us."

The next day, Matu followed Jabalwan as though nothing had happened to separate them, and the mansnake was glad that the boy had the heart to go on with him after his disgrace at Njurat. He loved Matu, for the devil's child was as near as he would ever come to a son, and he was determined to teach the youth to survive without the fellowship of sorcerers or the protection of the tribe.

He led Matu westward through mountain valleys teeming with jungles, dwarf forests of smoke-shaped trees, cactus-mazes, petrified woods where the sunlight plucked colors from the stones. Once they saw a green deer peer at them and then scurry dizzily into the vine-lash. But Jabalwan had not brought Matu on the high trails to see wonders. The sorcerer knew the magic design of these cliff paths, and he showed Matu how to find his way through the labyrinth of mountain corridors. From the peaks, the land looked confused. The terrain was a tangle of ranges, gullies, hillocks, derelict glens, and immense valleys. Swift travel was possible only on the high trails the sorcerers traversed.

On the highest verges, Jabalwan demonstrated spirit fist. "There is nothing supernatural about it," he stated, balancing on the selvage of a cliff that leaned over a chasm of clouds and rock spires. "There is a wind in the body — and not just farts, so drop that grin. The wind is an energy that moves in our bones. The first sorcerers called it spirit wind. It heals our wounds and grows our hair. If the body is clenched in a fight, the spirit wind becomes spirit fist. Every fight is a struggle with gravity, whether it is the struggle to climb a mountain or to kill a man. Balance judges the outcome. You must learn to clench your spirit fist."

When Matu tried to walk the paths Jabalwan crossed with ease, he slid and fell and would have plummeted to his death if not for the vine-rope secured to his waist and anchored by his teacher. Sometimes Jabalwan left Matu hanging for a day, twisting in the wind, contemplating the mysteries of spirit fist. Jabalwan had great hopes for his student, for Matu's reflexes were astonishingly swift; he had witnessed that with the Spider and in the hunt. He was glad that the youth had surrendered his fascination with God and the stories of God's heroes, because now they could concentrate on skill, which was a sorcerer's only true power. "Knowledge is worthless as a ghost," he instructed Matu, "unless it finds its way into the muscles and becomes skill."

The journey of memory and learning took three years and would have continued if the drum songs had not become sinister with news of the Tree Haunters' bloodiest war raids ever. The tribes neighboring the deep valleys of the Rain Wanderers had withheld their tribute, and Batuh had destroyed their longhouses. Jabalwan was convinced the Tree Haunters would assault the Rain Wanderers next. He and Matu hurried along the high trails to the cliffs above the valley where the Rain Wanderers were camped. To one side they could see a stream along the bluffs and a fleet of war boats swarming to shore; on the other was the Rain Wanderers' vale.

They had built their longhouse in the glade where Mala's hut had once stood. Matu floated downhill on ghostlegs, sliding like windsmoke through colorful meadows of flowers, among the tattered evergreens, and into the dark vale of great trees. The scent of jasmine splotched the air. The sounds of dog yaps, rice pounding, giggling children wove through paths that were exactly as he remembered them from childhood. He stopped beside the oak where he and Mala had buried an ape friend and stared past crossed palms and a sunspangled creek to the longhouse perched on its stilts.

"Batuh has sent his warriors all this way to destroy this longhouse because you and I are Rain Wanderers." Jabalwan lifted his headdress from his bag and put it on. It was vibrant, the plumage fresh from the birds they had hunted in the mountains. "The tribe has come here to this valley because it is your birthplace. When you became a Rain Wanderer, this valley became theirs. Do you see the marrow in this root? Batuh is attacking not just our tribe or us but the Life. Do you see that?"

Matu understood. "By destroying a sorcerer's tribe he destroys the spirit of all tribes. No one will resist him again."

"He will claim the authority of the ancestors. A warrior, a man of death, will claim the Life. As if he could live forever. Even in his seed." Jabalwan rocked his head moodily. "The people will become slaves of Batuh's masters."

"I have seen it."

"Yes. We will not stop it. This is the demon age when the Life shrinks to an infinitesimal seed — maybe even something inhuman." He squeezed his eyes shut to stay the tears of their certain defeat. The stencils on his lids throbbed. Then his eyes clicked open and glared with resolve. He stamped his blowgun and clicked its bamboo bayonet against Matu's. "Death is not a secret. We know what we must do now. We fight for the Life. We can *not* lose."

Jabalwan's words shot into him, sharp as darts. When the sorcerer knocked his weapon against Matu's an electric thrill brushed the length of his body. Today men would die. The terror of that certainty linked into images of shouting men, flying weapons, bloodspray, the eternities of war. Death was not a secret. They would fight as men had fought from the beginning of time.

As they walked together into the clearing, the headman came forth to meet them. His scouts had already seen the war party that had stalked upriver, and his warriors were assembling on the banks of the creek, readying a first strike.

Among the women on the verandah Matu spotted Riri. A toddler clung to her waistcloth and an infant suckled her breast. Memories of this place where his own mother had fed him ascended in his skeleton, and he felt lighter. Riri saw his look and smiled, and he tilted his spear toward her.

"My daughter is Ferang's wife," the headman said.

Matu grinned with the thought that if he had stayed, she might have been his. With her or without her, he had come to the same place. She would see him either kill or die today.

Ferang was at the creek. He was painted for war, like the other warriors, and his hands were moving keenly over his weapons, as though he could feel the wounds humming in them. At the sight of Matu, he leaped and charged. Jabalwan jumped to block the attack, but Matu stood aside and took the force of the collision with open arms. The two men staggered in a jubilant embrace. Ferang pulled back with a war yell. "Now the Tree Haunters must fight not only Rain Wanderers but the spirit powers!" he shouted to the others. "We cannot lose!"

The sound of the same phrase that Jabalwan had used but with different emphasis was ominous in Matu's ears. *We must not lose,* he thought and shared a knowing glance with Jabalwan.

"You have grown stronger," Ferang said, squeezing Matu's shoulders, thickened from three years of mountain climbing.

"And you have grown more respectable," Matu said. "I have seen Riri and your children."

"Yes, I no longer set bonebreaking traps for my own people. We cannot afford it. The Rain Wanderers need all our warriors now. There is no place left for us to run."

"In three days," the headman said, "the enemy will have marched through all the spring-traps and spike-pits we have laid in their way, and they will cross the mountain's skirt. We must go and meet them. They must never see our valley."

Jabalwan offered his strategy. Using the high trails, they would cross the cordillera in hours and descend on the enemy that very afternoon when they least expected it. The plan was unanimously approved, and the war party marched up the valley, following Jabalwan and Matu. The ground soon became sheer rock, the wind bragged of death with its cold, and the warriors huddled and clicked their weapons with hollow bravura. At the summit, they gazed down on the enemy.

The Tree Haunters were colorful ants in their war paint as they filed along the stone bed of a creek toward the cliffs that walled the high valley. Jabalwan pointed out the clearing of a withered pond. "In a short while, the enemy will reach that field. We will be waiting in the trees, in two groups. One will hold the cliffside of the clearing, and the other will cut off any retreat."

The war party descended on the twisted trails that dropped almost straight down through talons of rock. Once down among the trees again, the warriors moved swiftly, relieved to be under the familiar tangles of vine and bird noise. A roar crashed through the bramble, and the warriors quailed and fell into a defensive circle, spears jabbing at the shadows.

Jabalwan laughed and called for Papan to show herself. The shrubs shoved apart, and the man-size bear barged past the warriors and lay her black muzzle between the soul-catcher's feet for Jabalwan to scratch her ears. "I have been calling you for days," he chided the bear. "Where have you been?"

"Papan is the beast of your destiny," Matu said. "She knew where to meet you."

The stones in the drying pond glowed pale as bones in the green shadows. Jabalwan sent Papan into the dense foliage downwind and signaled Matu and Ferang to position their men in the trees at the back of the open ground. The headman and the soul-catcher took their men into the forest at the head of the creek.

The band of Tree Haunters hiked over the creek cobbles and into the glade with their spears and muskets on their shoulders. As the leaders were stepping toward a root path that led back into the forest, Papan bawled with rage, and the poison darts swarmed. The howls of the pierced men battered the air as the Tree Haunters scattered into the brush, to be speared and hacked by the waiting Rain Wanderers. Those who fled back down the creek met their deaths in a whirlwind of darts from Jabalwan's hidden warriors. The Rain Wanderers leaped from their hiding places and began killing the wounded and taking heads.

In the confusion of victory cries, no one heard Wawa's frantic call that other men were running up the creek. Matu had pulled himself into the bough of a tree to look for Jabalwan, seeking new orders. Standing apart from the kill-frenzied warriors, Jabalwan ignored the headman's urgings to join in the taking of heads. He was looking for a way back up the mountain when he saw the other Tree Haunters charging up the creek. The men they had killed, he realized at once, were an advance party sent ahead to flush out ambushes. The war party attacking now was many times larger, their bodies green with the jungle paint that had made them invisible from the high vantage of the cordillera.

Jabalwan shouted with alarm. Too late. The enemies' fire-spears were loaded, their fuses lit, and the first rounds of deadly thunder dropped the headman and the warriors around him. A shot cracked a rock between Jabalwan's legs and sent him skittering backward. He threw his spear and brought down the point man, exposing the enraged figure of Batuh. The chief of the Tree Haunters yowled with delight at the sight of the soul-catcher standing among corpses, a bamboo knife dangling in his hand. Jabalwan stepped back and then stopped, recognizing the moment's finality. He held Batuh's gaze and with his free hand drew his dogbone needle from his hair and jabbed its curse at him. Batuh laughed, leveled his fire-spear at Jabalwan's heart, and fingered the trigger.

Matu saw Jabalwan kicked backward by the impact, and he sprang from the tree. Ferang caught him with an arm around his chest. "No, Matu, he is dead. Quickly, we must escape. We need you to lead us back to the longhouse to save the women and our children."

The undergrowth beside Jabalwan's body heaved apart, and Papan lunged into the attacking swarm, saliva threading from his fangs, claws swatting, strewing gouts of flesh and bowels into the air. Batuh squealed and fell back as musketfire smoked around him. The big bear thrashed forward, blooming blood, mad with grief, and collapsed across the creek quilled with spears. Metal blades jolted, and the bear's head was lifted like a keg.

His brain rattling, his heart twisting, Matu spun away. Ferang kept a hand on him until they were far up the mountain slope. The only Rain Wanderers who escaped were the ones who had been waiting at the cliffside of the pond with Ferang and the sorcerer. They hunkered among the skinny mountain trees, shivering with fear and grief.

"We have barely a dozen men left," Ferang said, searching the forest for signs of movement. "The best warriors were killed with the headman. We must return at once to the longhouse and take our women and children away. You will show us the high trails to the west, and we will build a new longhouse far from the Tree Haunters."

"No." The tears streamed over Matu's cheeks, beading like dew on his red and white war paint. Woe pierced him. He closed his eyes, hugged his knees, and rocked his whole body. Finally he said, "You will go back and take the women and children into the forest behind the longhouse. From there you can climb quickly into the mountains. You will find your way to another valley without me."

"And you?"

Matu met Ferang's insistent stare. "I am going after my teacher. I have always followed him. When I did not I knew grief. I will follow him now. And many Tree Haunters will come with me. Give me your sling guns." He selected three of the dozen that were offered. "Do not leave the valley unless you see the longhouse burned. If it burns, you will know I am dead."

Ferang did not try to stop him when he rose and walked downhill and back into the dark forest.

The Tree Haunters camped for the night at the site of the day's battle. A fire hopped at the heart of the dry pond. Around it, the warriors had impaled Rain Wanderer heads on their spears and planted them in a circle just inside the grasp of the light. Now they sat beneath the heads, chewing betel nut, singing songs, honing their metal blades. Two crossed spears supported Papan's large head. Beneath it Batuh squatted, staring into the flames and seeing there the future rending itself from the darkness. His destiny was fulfilled. The one man he had feared was dead. No tribe would defy him now. He had become more than a chief. He was a spirit-chief, a slayer of sorcerers.

Jabalwan's corpse was laid before the fire, his chest caved in where the lead slug had smashed it. The blood had been drained from his body before it could clot, and all the warriors had drunk of it and become spirit-warriors. In the morning the corpse would be carried to the river and ferried to Long Apari, where it would be encased in salt and displayed on the battlefield at each village that raised arms against Batuh.

A weird yodel swooped from the trees, and Batuh lifted his head to listen. The men around him rose to their heels apprehensively, and when the strange wail cut again they looked about with twitching faces. The sound could not have been made by a human throat and no animal cried with such explicit bane. Lightning drilled far off among the trees, and in the lag the warriors waited for thunder that never came. The nearness of the next whistling howl swept everyone to his feet. Batuh grabbed his Spanish sword and swung it ferociously over his head, swiping the bear head that was spiked behind him. Tilting crazily, the wrathful black face seemed to be staring at him, in collusion with the wailing spirit of the dead sorcerer.

Seizing a loaded musket, Batuh shouted to the darkness, "It is a Rain Wanderer trick!" No one believed him, since no one, not even Rain Wanderers, moved through the jungle at night. Batuh recognized the challenge in the deflected glances of his men. He shoved warriors aside with his swordarm, and with a musket poised from his hip he strutted to the creek. A scream from the afterworld lashed from the bank and Batuh fired into it, the flare from the gun exposing the dark arteries tunneling among the trees.

Greased black from his hair to his toetips, Matu watched from a bough on the cliffside of the camp. Two of the three sling guns on the branch before him were packed with naphtha-soaked moss around stones of compacted flash-powder. The third had a pebble-weighted poison dart meant for Batuh if he missed with the first two. In the aftermath of Batuh's musketblast, he fired the first flash-powder stone at the fire and missed. The second stone disappeared in the darkness and then popped back into sight as it fell directly into the flames, hissing in the blue licks of fire. The Tree Haunters whirled around at the sound of it and saw their campfire explode. A gust of silver-hot fire billowed, kicking tinder across the clearing, whipping sparks and clots of flame into the black canopy. When darkness swooped in, Matu came with it.

The Tree Haunters had run from the blast and were huddled in the creek, poking their spears at the night as Wawa hopped among the sedges, shrieking the death music Jabalwan had taught him. Matu slung Jabalwan's body over his shoulders and disappeared into the forest.

Matu was certain that none of the Tree Haunters would pursue when they saw the sorcerer's body gone. He slept that night with the dead man in his arms, wrung with sadness, entranced by the grisly satisfaction of having him even as he was lost.

The next morning reinforcements arrived at the Tree Haunters' camp with much fanfare. These enlistees from other tribes had come to follow Batuh, hoping to win prestige and authority in their own villages. The story of the sorcerer's escape sounded wondrous in the light of day. Surrounded by so many heads — and a chief's among them — the new troops were even more eager to participate in the epic assault against the primitive and witchy Rain Wanderers.

Matu severed the head from Jabalwan's corpse and wrapped it in broad leaves with moss. He dragged the body to the river and floated it downstream, where he could burn it without alerting the enemy army.

No deathraft would carry his teacher to the afterworld, for Jabalwan had not died. The mansnake had only been changed, and the doorway of fire would be his exit from this world and his entrance into legend. No death chant rose from Matu's lungs, for he wanted to keep the soul-taker's soul with him. Silently he stacked logs and laid the headless body atop them. As the pyre accepted the flames from the dead wood, he turned to leave.

On his way up the valleys, Matu collected the plants he needed to make the bone-softening broth he had learned about from his teacher. Then he fashioned a watertight container of bark and gutta percha, brewed the broth, and immersed Jabalwan's head in it.

With the slogging sack strapped to the blowgun across his back, Matu climbed to the clifftops overlooking the valley of his childhood. For three days he paced those rocks, whistling down into the glens for the big beast Emang and balancing on the boulders soaked in the purple glow of the sky, wanting to feel the deep drive of the power Jabalwan had called spirit fist. He felt the balmy wind honeycombed with fragrances: the mint of the jungle and the char of Rain Wanderer cooking fires in the valley below. Far away as he was, he could sense the mourning of the tribe. He felt their grief, and he felt the stony earth, laced in nettles. But the crux of all feeling, the current of strength his teacher had talked about, was not there.

One night he dreamed of the medicine cloud, the whiteness invading his sleep, obscuring all images. Toward dawn, the medicine cloud folded back and Jabalwan was before him, light playing over his body with watery sounds. "Life is secret, Matu. Enormous space touches everything, and every move hurtles us through great distances. We can never stay where we are. Only death is known. Good-by, sorcerer." He smiled then. "Oh, yes — when you're through with my face, leave it in the forest for the small animals to chew."

Wawa woke him, scampering onto the ledge with the news that Emang was in the valley below. As the gibbon jabbered on, Matu looked past him to the longhouse far below, where the warning gong had begun to sound. People fled the building, flitting across the clearing into the forest and the traces of night. Far off, just visible in the morning mist, the army glittered in the trees at the mouth of the valley.

Matu slashed open the gutta percha and lifted the sunken head. With deft knife strokes, he severed jaw muscles and skull fascia and peeled the flesh from the softened bone. Matu whistled for Wawa to lead him to Emang. He slung his medicine bag over his shoulder, attached the rubbery flesh to his blowgun to dry, and followed the gibbon to a boar run through the forest that led to a black tarn. Sipping at the still, dark water was Emang. Matu scratched the fly-mizzled folds around the rhino's wet eyes and then climbed onto Emang's hulled back. Wawa hopped on behind him, and the big beast lumbered away from the tarn, taking its lead from the sorcerer's knees on its thick neck.

Matu pulled Jabalwan's face flesh over his head. The skin fit snugly, smelling of rotted wood and the menthol of the bone-softening broth. He tied its cut neck flaps with twine, covered that and his shoulders with Jabalwan's long black hair, and urged the rhino faster. Emang barged through a tangle of hanging creepers and bean shrubs, and astonished the Rain Wanderers cowering there, who shouted to see Jabalwan astride the rhino's back. Ferang recognized Wawa and guessed what was happening. With a war cry, he raised his spear and mustered the warriors hiding in the brush.

The longhouse showed among the trees in the distance, and Matu could see Batuh before the notched log stairway exhorting the troops, his sword stabbing at heaven. Matu goaded the rhino into a full charge with a lung-emptying cry. Emang ran at a full sprint, and the trees to either side blurred as they cannoned into the clearing.

The nearest men were trampled, swept under the hurtling hulk. Others leaped aside with amazed shouts, and the crowd of warriors scattered. Jabalwan's name jumped through the throng, growing louder and wilder with horror. Muskets barked, and powder clouds smoked on all sides. The pellets stung Emang's hide and spurred it faster through the raging noise and confusion.

Batuh stood fast before the longhouse. He drove his sword into the earth and lifted his fire-spear. The slug sucked past Matu's ear, and he raised his spear as the rhino approached the longhouse. Men leaped from the verandah, leaving Batuh standing alone.

Emang slowed to a trot and Matu leaped off, his spear leveled before him.

Batuh shouted his disbelief. "You are a trick!" He dropped the musket and grabbed his sword. With a slash he cut through the thrusting speartip.

Matu threw the blowgun aside and stood facing Batuh's naked sword.

"I see you in your mask, boy," Batuh taunted. "Come" — he waved Matu closer — "and you will join your teacher."

A rush of wind carried Matu forward, surprising him with the danger of his move. Batuh's sword swung, and Matu moved aside just as the blade gashed through the space where he had been standing. Exhilaration grabbed his heart with the awareness that the spirit wind was moving him.

Time seemed to stop. Matu saw every twitch of emotion in his opponent's face as Batuh turned the blade toward him again. "Go ahead, jump. I'm going to stick you with this even if you jump like a toad." He showed his pointy teeth, his nostrils widened, and his cunning face pushed forward. "This is your father's sword, Matubrembrem. He gave it to me when I became chief. And now it will kill his bastard." As Batuh began his stabbing lunge, Matu again nudged aside just enough for the blade to cut past his shoulder, glazing his flesh with its wind. The moment was a pivot of imbalanced forces, a stressed instant already exploding into the next movement as Batuh turned the blade to slash. Matu saw the weakness in Batuh's extended swordarm. He reached out, grabbed the stout man by his neck and shoulder, and heaved him into the ground.

Batuh sprawled in the dirt, his sword twisting from his hand and spinning loose. Matu grabbed it and flicked the blade at Batuh, who rolled away and rose to his knees, his face clawed with frustration. The sorcerer feinted with a jab that jerked the man's head back; then he brought the sword around in a whistling arc that hacked into the side of Batuh's neck. The chief collapsed face down. Matu put a foot on his back and with a double-handed blow, lopped off Batuh's head.

Anguished yells rose from the awed crowd as Matu lifted the still scowling face for all to see. Then the treeline rang with a war cry, and the Rain Wanderers came running into the clearing waving their wood swords and spears. The Tree Haunters ran for the mouth of the valley, and Matu, holding Batuh's head up with the sword, rode the rhino out of the glade with the fleeing army.

Sunlight was emerald in the canopy and gold bronze in the shafts that lanced to earth. Matu steered Emang through a wall of flowering lianas where a tree had fallen and light touched the earth. In the shadows on the far side, he removed Jabalwan's face, kissed its leathery mouth, and threw it into the leaf duff where small animals would devour it before dark.

Batuh's head he carried to Long Apari and posted on the wharf, where it remained until the birds had torn all the flesh from it.

Emang carried Matu from Long Apari east along the Great Dawn Running River, his father's sword at his hip, Gefjon's shrunken head angling from a twine looped about his neck.

Rage and sorrow beat in the boy's blood. Why had he lived and a true sorcerer died? Why must he endure each inch of pain on the pitiful road to death? For occasional scraps of orgasm? For the glutted satisfaction of an occasional full meal? For the weariness of old age? Why live at all? The Life was secret; only death was certain and easy to know.

Matu studied his own face in a languid river. He was grotesque. His features were harsh as lightning-chewed rock: his nose jutted instead of spreading wide and flat; his chin thrust out and was dented in the middle, so unlike the smooth curve of the beautiful people. And his eyes — so pale, so void, lacking all earth color as if hatched from the sky. Why should this face live? The hollows of his cheeks recalled his mother's image. Jabalwan had been right to bless her with an easy death. Now he wanted the same blessing for himself. But he knew he could not have it. He had given himself to the Life, and death would have to find him as it had found Jabalwan. He would live as his teacher had taught him — but he determined never again to haunt himself or others with this need to understand. Life was appetite and observation, and there was no more to the dream.

He soaked the Book in a river pool until the pages came apart. He carried them to a flat boulder and used a razorflake of volcanic rock to cut out each word. The task took days, and when it was done he had a grass sack full of words. Matu continued his journey into the rising sun. At each village he visited, he dispensed the words as charms against evil. He placed words on the tongues of the dying, pasted them with fever sweat to their foreheads, glued them with blood to their wounds. In plague villages he enlisted the help of all the able and pasted hundreds of words to all the tools, utensils, weapons, even the garden plants. By the time he reached the sea, he had used up every word. All that remained of the Book was its black leather cover, scrawled inside with the names of Gefjon and his family.

Matu said good-by to Emang on the beach where van Noot and Gefjon had first traded with the tribes. He knew he would never return to the Rain Wanderers. Remote and primitive, they were safe now from the monkeyfaces who had spawned him and empowered Batuh. Matu decided he would give his life to the southern tribes who were suffering the most from the scourge of the monkeyfaced invaders.

One moon later, on a white-rock beach known as the Snakehunter's Grave, Matu saw a Lanun *djong* ride into the bay light as a petal. He stood in the shadow at the fringe of the jungle and watched the pirates slosh ashore. They were too far away to hit him with their muskets, and he was fascinated by them. They wore red rags around their heads, their faces splotched with whiskers, their breeches filthy. They seemed to embody the very sickness that was killing the tribes. Their devil faces seemed to him mockeries of the human visage.

One of them spotted him and immediately unslung his weapon and aimed it. Matu waited for someone to hand the gunman a fuse. He had never seen a flintlock before. The gun smoked, blackness struck him between the eyes, and his body was flung into the lap of the jungle.

Silenos and The Fateful Sisters

Humanity must perforce prey on itself.

— Shakespeare

CAT'S-PAW CLOUDS filled the sky, smeared by a high wind and blue with watershine. Matu rocked awake. A sunburst daggered his sight, and he glimpsed a green lug sail bellied with wind. He raised his head, and the effort almost blacked him out. His skull felt broken — and a sharp needling in his ankles and wrists told him he was bound.

Through squinted eyelids he saw a grime-stained tiller and a gruesome helmsman missing fingers. He looked the other way along the deck and saw a crowd of scrawny men with hair hanging in tendrils from sweatdark headbands. Their eyes were bruised red, and their faces were sharp as rats'.

Lanun.

Rancid aromas twined in the wind, sour whisks of fish waste, sweat, and urine. He counted eighteen men. A harelipped face swung closer, the split mouth spitting words Matu did not understand. Other demented faces approached, and he saw the lice-scabs in their patchy beards and the gray stains of dried salt on their sun-black skin. The charred faces pulled back then pressed closer, amazed at his pale eyes. The pirates jabbered in a hacking singsong, asking him questions and laughing at his befuddlement. A shout in his right ear turned his head, and he confronted a face with a slimy hole where its nose had been. The crusty upper lip peeled back from a rotted smile, and the pirate held up the gold-tufted head of Pieter Gefjon.

Matu closed his eyes. His mind raced, and he had to speak strongly with himself to keep his terror from devouring him. *You are a sorcerer. No evil can defeat you. No matter the fear. No matter the pain. You are already dead to this world. Let the pirates have your body. You belong with Jabalwan now. No evil can defeat you.*

When he opened his eyes again, a knife was twisting before his face in rhythm to the choppy noise of the noseless man's voice. Matu looked past the man and the amused crew, to the sunclusters on the sea as the boat rose and fell with the chop. Nausea whirled in him, and he squeezed his eyes shut. Ripples of motion waved in the shadows under his lids and seemed to blend with the waves of stink from the men around him. His head throbbed where the lead ball had glanced his skull. His gorge shot into the back of his mouth, and he vomited saliva and bile.

The captain, a massive, bald man with a thistly beard, sliteyes under a tigerskin headband, and a scimitar strapped to his muscle-cobbled back, ordered the boy cut loose. Seasickness would be the blond aborigine's bonds now. Matu tried to stand, but his legs folded and dropped him to the rolling deck. The captain ordered that the boy be kept alive, for he wanted him for the slavers in Sangihe across the Celebes Sea, where a white youth as able-bodied as this would fetch twelve taels of silver.

Matu curled up at the stern and lay shuddering with queasiness, watching the noseless man comb the hair on Gefjon's head with his stained fingers. Beyond him, the sailors turned his medicine bag inside out, strewing its contents over the filthy deck: fingers of roots, hairy tubers, leafrolls, serpent vertebrae glowing like butterflies. The cover of the Book was nailed upside-down through its spine to the mast, and the gold cross that was embossed on it was smeared with fish blood.

Over the fifty years since the big ships had first appeared in the southern seas, Europeans had been scattered among the islands by shipwrecks and pirates. Some of this crew had white sailors among their aboriginal, Muslim, Hindu, and Oriental ancestors. A blond native, however, was rare. Most of the crew had seen blond hair only on scalps, and they plucked at the youth's long locks and tugged at his loincloth to examine his genitals.

His head pounding, Matu felt helpless against the pirates darting their hands at him, pointing at his nakedness. When the noseless one touched Matu's thigh, he shoved him away, but nausea stymied his movements and the crew hooted with glee. Two of them seized him by his arms and dragged him forward, bending him over a stinking barrel of gurry water. He struggled, and the pirates laughed louder, their hands grabbing and stroking him.

The captain ignored the crew, even when a man mounted the tribesman and jigged over him in a lusty frenzy. Several days under sail lay ahead of them, and he was glad for the amusement that the blond native provided. He would let three sailors have the boy today and maybe three more tomorrow.

Matu fixed his mind on his father's sword, which the captain had taken for himself when he recognized the Spanish swordmaker's mark at the base of the blade. The boy tried to draw strength from the weapon that had killed the enemy of his tribe, but the spirit wind did not rise in him. And the harder he bucked to throw off the bestial men grasping and debauching him, the louder the pain blared from his joints. He shouted the Rain Wanderers' war cry, and the pirates exulted.

After the third sailor had broken his lust against Matu's fierce struggles, the captain ordered him bound again. During the night, other men fondled the prisoner, and the captain, just to keep an eye on him and be certain he was left whole, finally had the youth tied to the mast, arms stretched out on the lower spar like the crucified god his pale ancestors worshiped.

At dawn, as the aborigine was being cut down to be passed to the men who had won him by lot for that day, the watch at the prow cried a sudden alarm. A large ship was swooping down on them from the south. With its black sails, it had not been spotted until it was almost upon them and now escape was impossible. The captain and crew squinted to make out the big ship's flag, but Matu saw it first — a black square stretched taut at the top of the masts and emblazoned with the image of a man-shaped winged dragon.

"Wyvern!" the watch screamed, and the whole crew moaned and seemed to shrink on their skeletons.

The sound of their dismay inspired Matu, and when they tried to bind him again, he shook off the torpor of his night on the mast and swung out with all his vigor, knocking aside two men. The crew were scrambling for their battle stations, and he leaped from the mast's scaffolding to the deck, his nerves sparking with the knowledge that this could well be his death. He snatched a parang from one of the crew and turned to confront six men with knives and swords converging on him. He faced them with a viper's concentration, parang tip trembling.

A rib-clacking roar rent the dawn, and the junk's mast was sheared away in a cloud of fléchettes. Two of the pirates were thrown to the deck. Matu shoved himself against the sudden tilt of the ship and attacked the pirates closest to him, hacking with furious blind speed. All at once he was before the noseless pirate, who wore Gefjon's head strung on its vine. The pirate had a machete in one hand and a kris in the other, and he grinned with the demented abandon of a man who knew he was already dead. Matu could see the huge, black-sailed ship behind the madman, rearing above the tiny junk. Men were swinging on lines and dropping to the decks with cutlasses flailing. Musketfire crackled from above, and pirates spun off their feet under spouts of blood. The sight flared the killing fire in Matu, and he threw his parang like a spear, stabbing the pirate before him through his nosehole. He drew the blade, and quickly removed the twine loop with Gefjon's head, put the amulet around his neck, and shouted like a warrior.

The huge ship slammed into the junk. Timber flew, and the deck lifted steeply, sending Matu toppling. He flipped over corpses and sprawled to the prow. As he staggered upright, he met the baleful lour of the Lanun captain. The hulking man had van Noot's sword raised over his head, and he brought it down so hard that it split the prow's rail as Matu leaped aside.

The captain twisted the blade free just as Matu swung at him, and their two weapons clashed in a ringing tremor. The pirate pushed Matu off his feet, slapping the breath out of him. Matu swung his legs, trying to kick the pirate's feet out from under him, but the massive man was sturdy as a tree, and he snagged Matu's legs between his ankles and held him tightly for the death blow. The sword hung up, barbing dawnlight at the peak of its arc, then stiffened as if hitting an invisible barrier. Blood spilled from the giant's ears, and he keeled to his side, the back of his head sundered, glittering with ropy brains. The junk lurched, and he dropped overboard, still clutching the Spanish sword.

Matu stared up at the big ship looming alongside and saw a scowling black figure with silver hair in flying rattails, a red patch over his left eye, and a long mustache dangling with bonebeads. The large man waved his musket, signaling Matu to come aboard. He pointed to one of the lines that had swung from the side of the warship where men were already hauling away the junk's meager provisions in a great net.

The one-eyed pirate could not believe what he was seeing: a naked, fair-haired youth with a shrunken head about his neck and a parang in his hand dripping Lanun blood. The day was too young for grog hallucinations, and he leaned over the rail to grasp every detail of the queer sight before him. Wind streamed Matu's long blond hair behind him, and the pirate frowned into the clear eyes and arrogant bones of the youth's face as if into a mirage.

All of the Lanun crew were dead now, and the junk was listing as the sea rushed in below deck. Matu bounded over the corpses of his tormentors to the jagged stump of the mast and found the Book's cover still nailed to the shattered wood. He pried off the black leather with his parang and tied it to him with a strip of cloth so his hands would be free. His medicine bag was nowhere to be seen among the heaped bodies and shattered planks, but he found his blowgun lying tangled in the nets under the gunwales. The deck tilted sharply, and Matu grabbed the blowgun and clambered for the dangling rope. Swirling like a monkey with the blowgun clasped between his legs, he squirmed up the rope, and the eyepatched man who had saved his life offered a sturdy, callus-barked hand and pulled him aboard.

Close up, Matu could see that the man's forehead was branded with the cicatrix of a snake coiled in a figure eight. His red eyepatch was studded with diamond chips in the shape of an asp's eye. An unearthly music chimed deep in the wells of Matu's ears as he realized that this was the one-eyed, snake-browed man he had seen in countless nightmare visions from the time he had given his hand to the Spider. He was even dressed in the shadow and blood colors he had worn in Matu's nightmares: a black doublet with silver buttons and slit seams exposing a red silk blouse beneath. His knee breeches were also black, above gray stockings and low, flaring brown boots lined in scarlet. A cutlass hung from his side, and a pearl dagger handle stuck from the cuff of a boot. Matu swayed before him, stunned by this collusion of vision and reality.

The pirate stared back with his one gray eye, scrutinizing the shrunken head dangling from Matu's neck. The rest of the crew had seen it, too, and they studied the sorcerer grimly. Matu leaned his blowgun on his shoulder and slowly raised his hands in tribal greeting. The one-eyed man grinned a thin, yellow-toothed smile and clapped the youth on the shoulder. "The lad doesn't look to be a villain, mates," he shouted in Malay to the crew. "I say we have him aboard."

Cheers leaped from the men. These were the first true monkeyfaces Matu had seen close up, and he was moved by their hideous faces and oversized bodies. The snakebranded pirate pointed to the Book's cover, and Matu untied it and handed it to him. The man's good eye widened at the sight of the clear Latin script within: *I have seen the lion of the final moment — it guards the mine of signature.* He leveled a hard stare at Matu and asked something in his thick voice.

Matu gestured his incomprehension and searched back for the phrases his mother had taught him lifetimes ago. "I speak some Spanish," he said hesitantly, the rust of the words catching in his throat.

The pirate's jaw jogged loose and the crew edged closer. "A naked jungle boy mangling Castilian!" he exclaimed in gruff Spanish, a laugh of surprise breaking across his face. He was by nature a suspicious being — Matu could see that from the squint lines around his narrow eye. Matu also saw the night gathered in that eye, a soul used to staring at hardship. Suffering eked from his gaze. Yet deep in the graven lines of his harsh face was a wondering expression, and Matu thought he heard a tinge of awe in his voice as he said, "Welcome aboard *Silenos*, young warrior. What will you be called?"

Matu understood the question, but he could not bring his tribal name into Spanish, so he reverted to the name Mala had given him from her ill-fated encounter with the Dutch. "I am called Jaki."

"Ah, as it says here in your family tree," the pirate said, running a thick finger over the faded writing in the Book's cover. "Your grandfather's name, aye? But your own birth is not recorded here."

Jaki's expression went sullen. "I am the son of nobody," he replied. "I had many fathers but belong to none."

The sly gray eye crinkled compassionately for a moment before it hardened again. "You will be Jaki Gefjon then," he said. "A Dutch lad — and with native blood in your face, I can see. How old are you?"

"I am in my sixteenth year."

"And how came you to this?"

"I was taken from my land by the Lanun," he answered softly.

"What happened to your parents?" the hulking man asked.

Jaki could not bring forward the words of his story. The ugly man slapped him brusquely on the shoulder again. "There will be time enough later for singing our strange tales. Your wound needs a clean dressing from the look and stink of it. And if you want, we will find you some sailor's clothes." He returned the Bible cover.

"Forgive me," Jaki said, inhaling the soft energies of the sea. "If the ship is called *Silenos*," he asked, "then are you Wyvern?"

The man threw back his head with a laugh and punched his hand in a salute to the mainmast, where the black flag stretched as a topsail, bearing the image of a two-legged serpent with wings. "*That* is our Wyvern, boy. A creature of dreams come to feed in the real world. And how have you heard of our beast?"

"The pirates cried that name when they saw this ship."

He slapped both of his hands on his chest with satisfaction. "I'm gratified that even the Lanun have learned to fear Wyvern," he said proudly, wholly liking this white savage — "though they're not our usual prey. We don't stalk the *djong* pirates, but when we meet them, we help ourselves to their cargo and ease them from this tormented world." He waved to the shattered junk, which was sinking from sight. "They're empty men, naked souls, better off without this world oppressing them — or them oppressing earth's innocents like yourself." He fixed his eye on Jaki. "My name is Trevor Pym," he said slowly, "designer and builder of *Silenos*, erstwhile privateer with Sir Francis Drake, with whom I raided the Spanish cities of the New World and thus acquired some facility with this tongue."

"Are you also the captain?" Jaki asked.

Pym turned to the attentive crew and bawled in Malay, "Am I the captain?"

The men shouted their affirmation, throwing caps in the air and whistling. Though their storm-beaten faces were malefic with scars, tattoos, and beards spiked with boneneedles, they were dressed cleanly in long gray trousers and full, puffed linen shirts. Most of them were barefoot, but some wore leather shoes frilled with rosettes.

"Yes, it appears I am still captain of this ship," Pym said and put an arm around a fire-faced man with red curls and beard who stood at his side. "And this is Mister Blackheart, the ship's quartermaster and my missing eye. He runs the ship whilst I spend my time visiting with the spirits." He raised the crocodile-skin flagon from under his doublet and took a draft.

Mister Blackheart nodded his sunburned face and grinned through his dense, bristly beard. He and the captain seemed to be the only blue-eyed monkeyfaces among the crew, the rest looking much like the Lanun except healthier and better dressed.

"Mister Blackheart is the only other European aboard," Pym said. "I don't usually abide Europeans. Or any who truckle to kings and queens. We're equals aboard *Silenos*. But you'll hear all about that later. For now you should know that Mister Blackheart is not your usual European. He's a Scot and a defender of his Orkney home against James — the king who decided *all* Scots should serve him. The king's men slaughtered his family, and our Mister Blackheart lost his eloquence for stirring up rebellion against kings."

Pym signed, and Mister Blackheart opened his mouth and revealed a blackened stump of a tongue.

"Cut out for rousing his fellow Scots against foreign rule." Pym shook his head at such barbarity. "He hates kings worse than I. Ah, but I'm chewing wind. I can see all this means little to a heathen lad like you."

"Kings are no different from you or me," Jaki said quietly. "I know, for I have slain the king of my people's enemy."

Pym pulled down the corners of his mouth and nodded as if impressed. "Is that so? Well, then, we've new stories to hear and new ears for our stories, Mister Blackheart. Take him below deck, patch his head, and find him some suitable attire. We'll hear his story after he's dressed and eaten." Pym took a long swig, winked his eye at Jaki, and stalked off to survey the plunder.

The quartermaster led Jaki across a deck blond with cleanliness and down a tight stairway that smelled like the inside of a tree. Jaki ran his fingers over the satin of the varnished wood, amazed at how the light seemed to seep from the grain like sap. The roll of the big ship was gentler than the junk, and he adjusted his gait to it.

The sight of the twenty-two cannon along the gunnery deck, their sturdy carriages strapped with elephantine ropes, filled Jaki with an incomprehensible ardor. It was the inheld might of the guns' black metal that impressed him. Never had he seen so much iron. Mister Blackheart had to lead him away by the hand.

The ship's surgeon swabbed Jaki's head wound with brandy as the boy ogled the saws and scalpels, phials and clear glass jars of herbal tinctures.

The surgeon gestured to himself. "Saja, call me," he said. He was a tiny Malay in a green turban, white pongee shirt, loose black trousers, and rush sandals. Fingering the amulet Jaki wore, he said in a crude imitation of a forest dialect, "From jungle sorcerer, lah? This headstyle ancient. Long time not seen. Who give this?"

"My teacher," Jaki replied, exuberant at the sound of his own language even though it was garbled. "It's the head of my spirit father, and my teacher took great care to prepare it in the correct way."

Saja's thin eyebrows shot up to hear the tribal tongue spoken lucidly by a European. "Teacher, lah? Headtaker, lah?"

"No, not a headtaker. My teacher was a soul-catcher. He trained me as a sorcerer."

Saja released the small head as though it were a live coal. "*You* a soul-catcher?" Disbelief sharpened to startlement as confirmation shone in the boy's blue stare. Saja backed away quickly, bumping into the cutting table on his way out the door.

Mister Blackheart tilted his head with bewilderment and signed for Jaki to follow him. They walked through narrow gangways lit by skylights to the stern of the deck beneath the gunners, where there was a small laundry chamber. Jaki scrubbed himself with a cake of pumice and lavender and rinsed off with a pail of warm fresh water lowered through a hatch from the galley above.

At the sight of Jaki's circumcision scar, Mister Blackheart grimaced and chopped his hand across his groin like a knife.

Jaki laughed, for the first time in the three moons since Jabalwan had died. The laugh cut through the callous pain of his grief, and his senses brightened. "I did it for a woman," he said in Spanish. "And it was not worth it."

Mister Blackheart understood. Shrugging with laughter, he led naked Jaki down another stairway to the fourth and lowest deck, where they entered a dark chamber big as a longhouse. The quartermaster opened port hatches, and the azure sunlight showed crates heaped with bolts of silk in brilliant junglebird colors. Red, blue, and black leather chests trimmed in brass were stacked atop each other in packed ranks the length of the deck. Amidships, in the crystal shine from the great skylight at the top of the cargo well three decks up, was a shrouded bulk. The sea breeze from the open ports had flipped the corner of a tarpaulin and revealed a large pile of smudged metal bars. "Silver," Jaki breathed, softly, as if in a holy chamber. He lifted his face toward the high skylight and saw the scaffolding two stories up that served as catwalks across the cargo well for the men on the gunnery deck. The benthic glow and the broad roll of the ship brought the Book's Jonah to mind, and he quoted aloud: "For thou didst cast me into the deep, into the heart of the seas."

Mister Blackheart regarded him for an instant, nodded thoughtfully, and guided Jaki through the capacious storeroom past casks and crates to the draft-cooled stern, where a rope ladder descended two decks from the galley. Ambrosial fragrances rose from large open bins of fruit and vegetables. Behind a paper screen were racks of clothing. Mister Blackheart riffled through kimonos, gowns, vestments, and court finery and selected a blue zibeline shirt with cartridge pleating, a fawnskin vest, and brown trousers with black stitching on the outer seams.

Jaki took the clothes with vague arms, amazed to feel the lambent fabrics. He held the trousers to his waist and trembled like a deer. These were his father's garments, he thought, and by wearing them he was putting on his father's soul. The sepulchral shadows of the low-ceilinged deck swerved with sealight and breezes. Presences circled him. Mystery had turned its circle again, and he looked to the quartermaster with his heart's blood in his face.

Mister Blackheart helped Jaki dress, providing a green satin pouch for the shrunken head and the Book's cover, and then led him through the timber-scented corridors and upstairs to the galley, where the rafters were hung with slabs of spiced meat, chains of garlic, and hands of gingerroot. A tureen of boiling soup sat on an iron stove with lionpaw legs; beside it, a long-haired Chinese was chopping vegetables. He scooped cooked rice into a wooden bowl and ladled hot fish broth over it. Blackheart left to take the wheel while the day's course was plotted. Jaki ate voraciously, and left the galley satisfied with the soup's promise and eager to get back above deck and learn more about his generous hosts.

He stopped in the empty companionway. Shafts of serene blue light stood beneath the hatches like pale tree trunks. Alone for the first time since the Lanun had captured him, he put down his green pouch and knelt. He thanked God for his deliverance from the Lanun, and he listened to the faint voices of his blood. "Jaki," Mala called, and he looked behind him. He was alone. But the immediacy of her voice had set his heart hopping. He listened again and heard the sea hugging the ship, foreign voices scooting through the hatchways, and the wind walking like an old man. He was no longer Matu. She knew that, and she was telling him she knew. Jaki had put on his father's clothes.

On this boat, in this boat's world, Mala was no secret. The sound of Spanish had pulled him swiftly into her shadow, but he saw that she was not near at all. She was far, far away in the green forest where the rains rose at night, and he was now a ghost to that world. He had died to his mother's forest life and been reborn in his father's womb. The strangeness of it broke over him like a stream, tasting of the weariness of the mountains.

His fingertips brushed the soft fabric of his new clothes. He closed his eyes and spoke to the invisible. "I'm alive in the afterworld, Mother! And you are dead in the forest. Speak well of me to my spirit father and do not forget me to my seed father, though he did not earn your love in this life. I am in their world now, at the mercy of their powers. And they are strange. My fathers are men of the horizon. Their father is the wind. They are as ugly as I. I am afraid among them — and I miss the forest. The forest is your mother as you were mine. I hope that I will see her again and meet you in the trees and rivers, touch you in the still waters and the long grass and know that I am safe and have never been away from you."

He opened his eyes and saw men watching him from the corridor. Solitude was a ghost of the forest. He bowed to the crewmen, picked up his green pouch, and climbed the narrow stairs into the light.

Pym was on the quarterdeck sighting the sun with a backstaff, and Mister Blackheart was at the big wheel. Jaki stood on the top step, watching the large man with his back to the sun holding the brass contraption with its flashing shard of mirror at the far end. The quartermaster's hand scrawled busily to record the captain's words. Jaki was as intrigued to see a man writing as he was by the odd apparatus.

Pym lowered the backstaff. "Those clothes suit you," he said. "You look like a lad from the island country where I grew up." Pym nodded at the congruity of the clothes and the youth's devil-handsome face. Yet there was an odd center of gravity to the boy, a wolf-slouch that made him look ready at each instant to pounce or flee. "Come here, lad. You don't need permission to walk the quarterdeck on this ship." He fit the backstaff into a cabinet built for it in the gunnel. Above the cabinet was strapped a whetting stone carved in the shape of a giant rat's skull. Pym rubbed it affectionately as he rose. "You and anyone else in this crew can go wherever they like on *Silenos*, even my cabin."

Jaki stepped onto the quarterdeck and scanned the giant ship. The rake-masted vessel had refitted her sails while he was below deck, and the black canvas had been replaced by smokegray sheets that caught the wind and skimmed them swiftly over the sparkling sea. Men dangled from the shrouds tightening the rigging, and Jaki's soul rode with them up into the mango-yellow clouds.

"The surgeon tells me that you're a sorcerer," Pym said. "Is that so?"

Jaki looked to the captain with the glare of the masts still in his eyes. "Yes."

Pym weighed this disclosure. "You speak with the dead?"

"Yes."

The captain's eyes screwed up intently. "What do they say to you?"

"They don't talk back."

Pym and Mister Blackheart laughed in unison, and when they saw the puzzlement on Jaki's face, they laughed louder. Pym brushed a tear from his eye. "Excuse us, lad. We're laughing with relief. Saja says you commune with the dead — and the last thing we want on this ship is ghosts wandering the decks. We've enough trouble with the living."

The quartermaster signed to Pym, and the captain said, "Mister Blackheart wants to know what kind of sorcerer you are."

Jaki pondered a response and finally said, "I was learning to catch souls before my teacher was killed."

"Souls, eh? And what do you do with them after you catch them?"

"I put them back in their bodies."

"Ah, then you're telling us you're a surgeon."

Jaki recalled the blades and saws on the wall of Saja's cabin and looked skeptical. "I am trained to heal wounds and fevers."

Pym winked slyly at the quartermaster. "And what do you think you can do for this wound?" He flipped up the gem-studded patch over his dead eye and revealed a socket of mangled flesh, syrupy with pus. The grin under Pym's mustache stalled when the youth did not blanch and look away.

Jaki stepped closer. He had seen eyewounds before, and he could tell from the red membrane filming the bone and the blisters of festering sores that the captain was in continual pain. "You are suffering," he said with concern and touched the captain's stubbly cheek to turn his head so that light fell into the back of the bone cave. A yolk of abscess smeared the socket's lining. "This could easily fever and kill you if you are not careful to keep it clean."

"I wash it with brine every day," Pym said, angrily, "though it burns like a peephole to hell. Let it kill me, I say. It's taken long enough. Eleven damned years now."

"I cannot return your eye," Jaki told him, "but I can clean the infection and stop the pain."

"Can you now?" Pym asked, and lowered the patch to keep the stinging sea breeze out. He lifted his flagon and sucked deeply at the coconut ferment. "I'd be indebted to you, lad, if what you say is true. But any number of leeches and ship's surgeons have plied their tricks on that hole. Some have numbed it, but it always gets worse again."

"I can help you," Jaki said with certainty. His stare had something unspoken in it. "The pain and decay will go away and not return. But I must go into the jungle to get the plants I need."

Pym's face clouded suspiciously, and he stepped back. "We're twenty miles north of Celebes. We can stop there."

"I don't know Celebes," Jaki said. "I know I can help you but only if you return me to the beach where the Lanun abducted me."

"And where might that be, young sorcerer?"

"The Snakehunter's Grave."

Pym looked to Mister Blackheart, and the quartermaster's hands shaped signs in the air. The captain's face hardened. "That's Borneo. We're over two hundred miles from there. I'll not backtrack that far now." He leaned closer to Jaki, a shadow in his gray eye. "You've seen our treasure. Silk, silver, rich clothing, artwork — the cargo of a thousand-ton Dutch carrack we took in the Java Sea on its way to Batavia from the Japans. I want that booty on land before a storm or the Spanish take it from me. The journey you're asking us to make will add four days of sailing."

The quartermaster signed, and Pym nodded grumpily. "Yes, yes. We can put our treasures ashore and then find your Snakehunter's Grave — if we want to miss harrying Hsi Hang's gold flotilla north in the China Sea. He sails only once every four years. That's too much to give up even for an eye. And after that voyage, it'll be monsoon time, and we'll be landlocked months." He rubbed his chin and cocked a furry eyebrow at Jaki. "You wouldn't be lying to me now, would you? If it's just that you want to get back from where you came, I'll get you there eventually, boy. In the meantime you'll have adventures with us. You needn't promise me a cure you can't deliver just to dupe me into taking you home. *That* would enrage me, and I would be using your bones for fishhooks. You understand?"

"I am not lying, Captain Pym. I know the jungles of my land very well. I can find plants there that will immediately stop your suffering. But we must not wait — not for anything you value less than your life." Pym's eyebrows knitted, and Jaki went on. "Unless we dry up the yellow blood that is eating its way to your brain, you will die. I don't know when. But that wound could fever at any time."

The pain behind Pym's eye socket winced, and he looked to Blackheart. The quartermaster, not wanting the responsibility, kept his hands on the wheel and his gaze on the sea. Pym thought of the booty in the ship's hold. He was carrying the riches to his wife, Perdita Iduna. When she saw him and his treasure, her amber face would ignite with joy, and he would lose his pain in her spiceskin touch, her cumin breath, her lips' shine.

He looked up, resolved to take *Silenos* to Perdita — but when he met the sorcerer's ingenuous stare, he believed the boy could heal him, and the hope was suddenly more than he could bear. He lunged to his feet. "Hard aweather, Mister Blackheart," he ordered, slapping the pate of the ratskull whetting stone. "I'll put our case to the men."

Silenos turned into the wind, and Pym bellowed the orders to strike canvas. The ship glided idly, and the crew of thirty-two gathered on the main deck. The faces of the men staring up at the quarterdeck were fixed on Jaki as Pym explained his offer to heal the festering wound. To them he looked too childlike to be a healer, and at last one sailor shouted in Malay: "And what happens to the bugger if we risk squalls and men-of-war to get to Borneo and he can do no more for your headhole than a shadow puppet conjurer?"

"Then we'll string him up like a puppet," Pym promised, "and you'll have your bonus from the captain's share of the booty for making this trip."

There were grumbles about Pym's foolishness, but the crew were enticed by the generous bonus the captain had promised and they took off their hats and headscarfs to acknowledge their assent. When the entire ship's company was bareheaded, Pym sent the men back to their stations and nodded to Jaki. In Spanish he said, "My men have agreed to help me." And he felt an icy twinge, a premonition of the rage he would suffer if, in the end, he had forsaken half his captain's share of the Japanese treasure, and Hsi Hang's gold to boot, for a foolish hope.

Jaki saw Pym's fear in the cold, black ember at the center of his eye, and he smiled placidly, the light in his own eyes holding their flame.

On the journey south, Jaki learned about his father's world. Pym showed him the ship's compass and its faithfulness to the invisible strength of the north. Only iron could break its spirit hold, and Jaki understood then how the Rain Wanderers and all the first tribes who eschewed metal and sustained themselves solely on the spirit powers of the earth were doomed — and how those who picked up metal instantly lost their animal souls and became men possessed by the invisible spirit powers themselves. Even more inspiring for Jaki was to witness Pym navigating by night. The captain pointed out the north star low on the horizon and showed him the planets, the shards of the hawk's skull still whirling from the sun's blow at the beginning of time. Pym read the stars like ore in the mute depths of rock. Jaki remembered Jabalwan telling him that greater than bird omens and cloudreading was the sorcery of the night sky. He listened attentively to all Pym had to say about the packs of stars, the twelve houses where they received the sun and the moon, and the beast shapes that wore the stars like ornaments in the black heavens.

Pym assigned Jaki a small cabin in the aftercastle, a handsome chamber with a narrow bay window, a Persian couch with lionhead armrests for a bed, and a three-legged stool of red lacquer from China. A crewman had died of fever there the previous year, and no one else would have the cabin, though it was comfortable and commanded a wide view of the stern. Jaki was fearless of the dead. The powers of the world had saved him from the cruelty of the living, and he was convinced that his fathers were guiding him. By day, he spent hours in the masts, reading the clouds, hoping to learn more of his fathers. The clouds showed him a far country, a land not of longhouses but of tallhouses, lifting like trees against the sky. The people rode up and down in winched crates like the basket and pulley the cook used to haul vegetables from the draft-cooled aft hold. He could not believe what he saw, and soon he watched the clouds less and the men around him more.

The crew were impressed by Jaki's agility on the shrouds. The regular net pattern of the rigging was simplicity to him compared to the riotously guileful canopy of the forest. Once the ship's veering balance became familiar, Jaki would crawl out on the topmast spars and execute the rigging knots the crew taught him. His temerity won him the crew's respect. Even Saja relinquished his apprehensions about the sorcerer as he noticed the benevolent magic Jaki had worked on their ash-blooded captain. Pym raged at the men not at all since they had plucked the blond savage from the Lanun, and Saja had no gashed scalps or split lips to stitch from the captain's blows. An infectious joy spread through the crew, inspired by Pym's hopeful tolerance of his pain. For the first time in eleven years, the captain joined the men at their meals and shared in their bawdy stories with gusto. Those who did not know him from the years before he lost his eye and soured with the pain of its chronic abscess were wary at first. His baleful eye, severe as steel, was suddenly sparkling with ironic insight and withheld laughter, and his bulldog mouth had relaxed to an easy grin. But those who had been with him the longest, and who remembered his laughter in the face of Spanish cannon and gale-force winds, relished with glee the return of his high-spirited soul, and the belief spread among the crew that the blue-eyed boy was indeed a sorcerer who had spelled the captain's bitterness.

Blackheart, who had known Pym from his first years in Asia, was delighted to see his captain's suffering abate once again — yet he was afraid. He knew that when the yellow-haired heathen fled back into the jungle and did not return with his apocryphal cure, Pym's fury would be terrible and probably the destruction of them all. With concealed foreboding, Blackheart watched Jaki win the affection of the crew. His childlike interest in everything anyone was doing on the ship burnished mindless routines to the ardor of rituals. Pym chuckled to see the swabbing of decks and the plaiting of hemp glorified by the virtuous attention of the handsome youth that everyone wanted to impress. In just a few days, he had become their witness from the primeval world, their jungle child hungry for what they knew so well that they had almost forgotten. And they were all fathers to him.

Under the rolling stars, the pirate captain and the sorcerer spoke of life, mystery, and the silt of destinies. Jaki was mesmerized by the large man's compressed voice, booming even in a whisper. "Hope is vain and reason is a joke," he said. "The world is a lie — a great deception. Does not the earth look flat and the sun *seem* to rise and set?"

"This is not so?" Jaki's weighing stare wobbled with bafflement. "My teacher could see the world's soul in the clouds, but he had no understanding beyond that. You do. You read the stars."

"I see the wind in the clouds," Pym replied, glad for someone with whom to share his learning. "And I see the weather the wind carries. I know nothing of soul but its conspiracy with death. The soul flies and we die. If your teacher saw the world's soul in the clouds, he saw death riding high over our spinning rock." He lifted his flagon to his lips. "I will tell you a thing that will set your savage heart soaring. The world is not the stretched-out corpse of the hawk as your people believe. The stars are not the shattered orts of its skull. Each star is a sun." He swept his arm across the glittering sky like a club. "Countless suns. And all of them so far away they look like chips of glass." With an unsteady hand, he snapped open a panel in the gunnel where the backstaff was stored and removed his largest spyglass. He pointed to a large yellow star. "Look there, lad."

Jaki held the tube to his eye. The yellow star gazed back at him like an amber eye, tiny pinpoints of light poised around it.

"Jupiter," Pym said. "Another world. And with its own moons — a handful of them."

Wonder lapped in Jaki's chest, and he regaled Pym with questions about the sky, the stars, and the planets. The boy's mind reeled before Pym's answers, and Jabalwan's voice whispered from deep within: *The sky is deep.* Deeper than the old mansnake could have guessed — or had he? *The sky is deep. It carries everything. No matter where.* Pym sucked on his rice wine and told the boy everything he knew of how the sun held the planets in sway, swinging them around itself while they spun like marbles through the days and nights.

"Now do you see the deception of our eyes?" Pym asked. "We cannot trust our senses. We cannot trust life itself. Does not the spider spin a web the color of air? Does not our lust promise us life even as the humors sour in our veins?"

"Only God is good," Jaki said, gazing through the spyglass at the crushed light of stars.

"God!" Pym's jaw snapped like an iron trap. "*You* speak of God? Do you think God has a place for you in His heaven?"

Jaki put down the spyglass and regarded Pym with incredulity. "I am here, aren't I?"

Pym hurled a laugh into the night. "You're here because *Silenos* pulled you out of hell."

"I am like you, captain. I am dust thrown into the wind. We don't have to call that God. It carries us anyway."

Pym grumbled. "Carries us where? From the pain of birth, through sickness to death, with frequent portcalls at hunger. It's a journey I'd not have chosen to make."

Jaki shrugged. "There is no true freedom in life."

"Why not?" Pym swigged at the wine. "If God is good, why is life a torment?"

"The Life is secret."

"No, jungle boy." He closed his eye and let the wine lug him toward sleep. "We are just ignorant."

The smell of land reached *Silenos* before the islands hove into view. The sharkfin mountains of Celebes smoked with distance off the portside, and a honey wind spilled from the cliffs of Borneo from the starboard. Jaki stood on the crosstrees with one of the bat-faced sailors, scanning the coast with the spyglass for the white rock of the Snakehunter's Grave. He recognized a black river and knew that the beach where the Lanun had seized him was nearby.

Jaki hollered his sighting, and Mister Blackheart steered *Silenos* through the reef gulch toward the narrow beach. Bringing his own spyglass to bear on the shaggy swamp trees, Pym searched for signs of people. He shouted orders to men in the rigging, and the sails were struck. The ship glided through the channel toward the green shallows, and Blackheart spun the wheel so she fell off from the wind and slowed. The anchor dropped with a bright splash.

"Have the cannon primed," Pym ordered Blackheart. "By now the Dutch and the Spaniards both know we took the fat bird from the Japans, and they'll be coming up and down the strait looking for us."

Blackheart signed for Pym to stay aboard and offered to go ashore himself.

Pym shook his head and selected a musket from the quarterdeck's gun rack. "I'm a better shot than you, Blackheart. And if our blond heathen means to desert us, I want the satisfaction. Stay alert now."

A skiff was lowered, and Pym selected his two best gunmen to row, though Jaki assured him the marsh was empty; he could tell by the amble of the big-nosed monkeys and the birds' scrawling flights that no people were nearby. Jaki had put on his spirit father's shrunken head and insisted on bringing his long, speartipped blowgun, but Pym kept it beside him, out of the boy's reach.

As soon as the skiff bit into the mud shoal, Jaki leaped from the prow and splashed ashore. Pym cocked his flintlock as he rose to follow, but there was no need for it. The boy threw himself to the sand and hugged the beach. He had never expected to see this land again. The forest aromas laved him, and he chanted a silent prayer of thanks to his guardian the Spider and another to his dead fathers.

Pym uncocked his gun, shoved it back in his sash, and lifted Jaki by his shoulders. "Come on, happy colt. I'm a target for every flag in Asia. I can't be standing here while you blubber. Get me the medicine you promised."

Jaki pointed into the forest and called out with a piping whistle. Pym clapped a hand over the boy's mouth and in a wink had the cocked flintlock pressed against his ear.

"What treachery is this?" the pirate demanded.

"No treachery," Jaki insisted. "I am calling my animal — Wawa. When the Lanun took me, he fled into the forest."

"That was well over a week ago," Pym said. "No animal but a dog would linger here that long."

"Wawa is not a dog. I don't know the name in Spanish for what animal Wawa is. But he will come. He is my animal soul. He will not have gone far."

"If this is a trick for calling the tribes down on us, you will die, Jaki Gefjon."

Jaki twisted his shoulder loose from Pym's grip and strode into the jungle. Pym and his two apprehensive sailors followed.

The languorous smell of the jungle enveloped them in its cool shadow. Looped lianas, pallid, fungal-gilled tree trunks, and miasmic vapors opened like a grotto. Sultry odors blundered about them as they disturbed the leaf rot, and the muted music of the bird and monkey jabber fell deeper into the lowering wilderness.

Jaki cried again for Wawa, and Pym hissed at him to shut up. Jaki faced about and looked deep into the pirate's one eye. "You are in my world now, Captain Pym. You may kill me here if you wish, and I will die happily. But if you want to be healed, you must do as I say."

Pym nodded and uncocked his flintlock.

"Do you see these mushrooms?" Jaki picked a bluewhite hair from a tree trunk. "Collect a handful of these and have your men do the same."

Pym commanded his sailors and watched Jaki lope deeper into the jungle, flitting like a shade over the root burls. "Where are you going?" he shouted, but the boy did not answer and in a moment had vanished in the steam of the jungle. His shrill whistle fluttered like a flag in the green darkness.

While Pym was busy collecting the blue fungus, Jaki circled back to the beach and retrieved his blowgun. Back in the forest, he fashioned himself several darts from a thorn shrub and found the poison he needed in a Strychnos vine high in the canopy. Now Pym lived at his mercy.

A chittering bark startled him, and he turned to face the silver-haloed black mask of Wawa. The gibbon tackled him and they both toppled over in exuberance. "Find me the forest people," Jaki instructed Wawa. But the gibbon would not leave his side, so they went together deeper into the forest until they found, on a nearby riverbank, a longhouse of Snake Walkers.

The legend of Matubrembrem was well known to the people, and they received him warmly, bowing to the golden head that hung from his neck. Jaki stripped off his vest and shirt and gave them to the headman in exchange for all the hide pouches of arrack he could carry. Back in the jungle, he collected the medicinal plants he needed, then ran to within a shout of where he had left the pirates. He used a Strychnos dart to kill a tapir that Wawa spotted from the canopy.

Pym had returned to the skiff and was berating his men for their cowardly unwillingness to go with him into the jungle to hunt down Jaki when the boy appeared, laden with pouches and dragging the tapir by his vine-lashed spear. Wawa peeked timidly from behind him. On the walk to the beach, Jaki had tried to explain — as much to himself as to his beloved companion — why they were leaving the forest: "Our time here is done, Wawa. A new world — the world of my fathers — has its claim on me now. Will you come?" At the Snakehunter's Grave, the gibbon timorously followed Jaki down the beach to the marsh shoals.

"By Christ's lopped foreskin!" Pym bawled in English at the sight of the half-naked youth. He signed for his men to take the tapir, and he slogged scowling up the beach. "I was a hair's breadth from leaving this festering beach. Where were you so long?"

Jaki grinned, revived by his foray into the jungle. "Getting your medicine, captain. Some meat, too. And some real rice wine." He held out a pouch and unstoppered it.

Pym sniffed the wine, and his frown fell away. "Those mushrooms you wanted — have we scraped up enough for my cure?" He opened a pocket on his doublet and showed Jaki a gray wad.

"Enough to kill a herd of boar," Jaki answered. "Now you can throw it away."

"What?" Pym's eye squeezed angrily.

"I had to keep you busy," Jaki explained and showed him the darker blue fungus he had gathered himself. "This will clear up the yellow blood in your missing eye." He took out a handful of white berries and round, silver-lipped leaves. "And these will keep your pain asleep long enough for the fungus to work. Lie back, and I will heal you."

"In the skiff," Pym said. "I smell danger in the wind, and I want *Silenos* on the high seas where she can at least give a good fight." He bent to pet Wawa, and the gibbon snapped at him and hid behind Jaki. "You're not bringing this devil aboard."

"This is Wawa," Jaki said. "He is my animal soul. I cannot go without him."

Pym snarled at the gibbon and gestured gruffly for them to get aboard.

On the ride back to the ship, Pym lay back, and Jaki squeezed the milky juices of the berries and leaves into the gaping socket. Immediately the captain's harrowing pain fled, and a frosty brightness gilded the eyerim of his skull. Jaki packed a mash of the fungus into the numbed socket. "We will do this every day for five days," Jaki said. "By the sixth day, you will suffer no more from this wound."

Pym regarded Jaki and his skitterish gibbon with a happy smile. "I did not trust you, lad — and I'm glad I was wrong. Now Trevor Pym is indebted to you. For as long as this pain stays away, I will have you for my friend. Yea, for the son the God you love never gave me."

"That pain will never return," Jaki assured him.

Pym's smile widened and showed his square, yellow teeth. "Then, Jaki Gefjon, you are my son for life."

Two days later, off the cliffwalls of Mangkalihat where the Strait of Makassar opened into the Celebes Sea, *Silenos* confronted three Dutch warships, squatting like black demons on the sea's shining altar. They had been dispatched to hunt down the pirates who had disrupted the Dutch monopoly with the Japans. Jaki was horrified that he had brought this doom upon his saviors. He knew that he almost certainly could have found the medicinal plants to heal Pym's lost eye in any nearby jungle, but he had insisted on returning to the Snakehunter's Grave only because he had wanted to retrieve Wawa. And Wawa hardly seemed grateful. The animal had immediately become seasick and lay swooning in Jaki's arms, eating nothing but fruit pulp and frequently vomiting that up. For his troubles they were all going to be destroyed.

Pym laughed at Jaki's consternation. The pirate held up the pouch that contained the medicine Jaki had culled from the jungle. The sorcerer's fungal concoction had put an end to Pym's pain, and for the first time in eleven years he felt whole and clear-headed. "Woe to the Dutch to find me as I am now," he chortled in Spanish for Jaki's sake, seeing the anguish on his golden face. "Mister Blackheart, battle stations! And let's hear some fighting music!"

Crewmen bustled over the decks, breaking out flintlocks and powderhorns. Port hatches clapped open loudly as the cannon were wheeled into firing position, and a driving rhythm throbbed from the afterdeck where a handful of men had clustered around kettledrums and were beating them with human femur bones. Fife notes trilled, and the pirates' faces shone with wildness as they brandished their weapons. A steady chant swelled from the men, riding the crest of the martial music.

"What are they saying?" Jaki asked, carrying Wawa onto the quarterdeck to be near Pym.

"We are Death's children — we suck Her tits of pain — and we grow strong — yes, we grow strong on Her bitter tits of pain." A grisly laugh shook the pirate captain. "The Dutch fight us for their money." With a blunt finger he tapped the purple serpent branded on his forehead. "We fight for this. They're dead in the water — and they don't know it."

"But there are three of them," Jaki piped. "They're bigger than we are. And they're coming right at us!"

"That they are, lad. The fools. Look there." He pointed into the sea, and Jaki saw kegs bobbing in the swells, swimming rapidly away from *Silenos*. "The strait current is running fast here where it empties into the sea. The Dutch favor us by running against it. So I sent some emissaries ahead as soon as I spotted them. The first should be arriving about now."

"What are they?" Jaki asked, and in answer an explosion leaped across the water. The lead Dutch ship nosed up in a blossom of flying timber and smoke. Another blast followed, ripping the echo of the first in a sundering roar. The Dutch leader bucked in a tormented shudder, and Jaki saw flames hopping to the sails and fire-whipped men leaping into the sea. Several more explosions boomed as the second ship in the line met the deadly floating kegs, and its timbers burst apart, its armory igniting in a billowy cloud of fire.

"Marksmen!" Pym shouted, seeing the third ship shifting sail and turning about to flee. "And the chase!" He howled with merriment.

Wawa hugged Jaki in terror at the thunder and the noise of the battle orchestra on the deck below. And Jaki hugged back, alarmed by Pym's mad intensity as he leaned against the quarterdeck rail, bellowing orders. Blasts spouted water in silver columns, and the pirate ship slashed through the strait in swift pursuit of the third Dutch warship.

"They're in a panic," Pym told Jaki. "In a moment they'll make their fatal error and turn about to stave us with broadsides. And so the hunter feels the claw!" He snapped his fingers and bit his lower lip to see his prophecy enacted. The Dutch warship dampened its sails and began to swerve. "Now you'll see the advantage of a wheel over a whipstaff. Blackheart! Hard alee!" He bowed over the voice tube and shouted to the gunnery deck, "Declaw the cowards. We're taking this prize home."

Silenos turned to her side swiftly and cleanly while the Dutch were still straining to bring their prow about, and the pirates fired the first volley. Each of the shots found its mark, smashing into the tiered Dutch gundecks. The second volley devastated the last of the Dutch cannon facing them, kicking in the gundecks and collapsing the gunwales of the main deck. The next volley would have clipped the masts, but the Dutch struck their colors. *Silenos* turned on Pym's command and swung to the side of the damaged vessel, bumping her hard. Grapnel hooks were thrown aboard the tall Dutch ship, and the pirates scurried aboard, blades in their teeth, flintlocks tucked in their waistbands.

The Dutch captain appeared overhead on the tall ship's quarterdeck and gazed down at Pym, gesturing frantically that he surrendered. Pym drew his flintlock and shot the man in the throat, dropping him into the water between the ships.

Jaki grabbed Pym's arm. "You killed a man who was gesturing peace!"

Pym glanced at him with annoyance. "Were they stalking us to preach us gospel? I'm not a gentleman, whelp. I'm a pirate, damn it. Stand back if you won't fight." Pym grabbed a powderhorn from the gun rack and reloaded. A rope ladder was lowered to the quarterdeck from the big ship, and Pym clambered up it.

Jaki looked to Blackheart, who had tied off the wheel, and the quartermaster raised a fist in victory. The screams of slaughter and the war music brattled louder, and soon only shouts of triumph came from the taken ship.

Jaki sat on the deck, Wawa pressed to his side. A cloud threw a shadow over them, and he shivered to feel his life becoming smaller.

The tide was falling. *Silenos* skimmed through the shallows of delta islands off the east coast of Borneo, bumping gently against the sandbars of Maratua. Giant kapok trees above the high dunes shed their powders into the low wind, and the red air of the westering sun swirled in dusty eddies. Jaki stood at the forecastle rail, sensing the deepening silence as the crash of the anchor stilled the birdsong in the swamp grove and the gulls wheeling above the ship lifted higher. He smelled no camp scent on the breeze and saw no sign of people on the mud flats.

In the day since *Silenos* had sunk the two Dutch warships and taken the third in tow, Jaki had tried to overcome his revulsion at the pirates' ruthless violence. The jungle was no different from the sea in its crux of talons and fangs, he told himself. The tribes with their headhunters and war parties were different only in scale, and now that they were acquiring muskets and cannon, soon they too would do more killing, and most of it from afar. Life bred malice among her abundance. The pirates were life's creatures, and Jaki had resolved to learn from them, because the captain and his mate were as northern and avian as his fathers had been. Staring into the gritty light of the falling sun, he searched for signs of other people, ghosts, and the future.

Pym climbed to the foredeck and stood still, appraising the white aborigine and his gibbon. The youth did not stir. What did he see? What could he forecast from tree dust? The gibbon ignored him, too;

it sat on the rail peeling bright red spines from a rambutan fruit and nibbling at the pulp.

The captain strode across the deck with loud claps of his brown seaboots. "We leave when the tide turns again," he said gustily, expansive with well-being. "At the odd-even hour in the midst of the night, we'll leave Maratua quiet as we came." He swung his gaze over the sour swamp of the coast. "We're alone here. The wilderness and her children."

Jaki nodded, his attention sliding to the fog pure as milk slipping through the culverts among the mangrove tussocks. Absently, he took another rambutan from the pouch hung from his hip and handed it to Wawa without diverting his gaze from the mist folding over the sills of the trees. He was looking for Mala or Jabalwan. He knew he was leaving the jungle for the sea, his mother's world for his father's, perhaps forever.

"You can go back now if you want," Pym said, exhilarated by his own good intentions. After eleven years of barbed pain, his body was a cloud again and his mind its hushed exhalation. Now he was prepared to make even exchange, one release for another. "You can have our best tender. Steer her west and the current will carry you home. Leave now and you'll sight Borneo by tomorrow's nightfall."

Jaki tilted his face to look at Pym, and the red rays made his eyes flash like smashed tourmalines. "I have no home."

"The jungle," Pym said, pointing toward the shrugging trees. "The story you've told me of your teacher and the Rain Wanderers says your home is there."

Jaki shook his head and looked again to where day spun its last threads in the forest. "That is just a story." A tall darkness stood up slowly in the grass. "It's done with me."

Pym grunted, considering this, then abruptly slapped Jaki's back. Wawa hissed, and the pirate edged a half step back. "Let a new story begin here. Why do you think we've landed here, boy?"

Jaki turned full about. The raised scar on Pym's brow flared crimson in the long light, and his ravaged face shone like a lantern. "I thought you came ashore for water, food."

"At night? Washed in with the tide? Any armed ship that comes over the horizon now and finds us beached can batter *Silenos* to tinder while we weep in the jungle." He hooked his thumbs in his doublet and shook his head in amazement. "You know nothing of the sea, child. Indeed, you belong in the jungle."

Jaki cocked his head. "I healed you."

"Aye," Pym said, with a satisfied squint, "and that's why we're here now. The highest honor I can grant you is to jeopardize my ship and crew to return you to your home."

"I've told you. I have no home. You know my story —"

"Aye. Your blood's three-quarters European and a mere quarter aborigine. You speak passable Spanish. You read Bible Latin. But you know your way in there." He nodded to the forest, where the sun melted among the trees. "Out here, life is very different. You cannot wander alone on the sea. This crew and I are brethren deeper than blood. We are a clan of exiles, brothers in suffering. We thrive because we live and die together."

"You are a tribe of the sea. I understand that," Jaki said, vibrant with alertness. "I want to go with you."

Pym arched an eyebrow, impressed by the boy's zeal. "You've proved your usefulness by me, sorcerer. I know all of us would benefit to have you aboard. But are you certain you belong here?" Her jerked a thumb at the captured Dutch vessel anchored farther out. "You saw our business yesterday. We roam the seas and we plunder ships — Spanish, Portuguese, English. Your daddy's ships, too. It doesn't matter whose ships. If they fly the flags of empire, they're prey. We kill those who fight us and maroon those who yield. If we fail, we die, for crowns show no mercy to pirates."

"And no mercy to tribes," Jaki said. "I have seen entire tribes dying in the shadow of empire. The best I can do for them is to fight the hawk-faced men with you."

"Well and bravely put, sorcerer." Pym stepped closer. "But first — if you are certain you belong with us — you must become one of us and take the oath before Wyvern."

"Initiation."

"Aye, that's it." His eye blinked warily. "Will you do it?"

"I have been to the center of the world," Jaki answered with a candor that chilled Pym's blood. "I have met this creature you call Wyvern. She is a frightful mother, Captain Pym."

"Mother of nightmare," Pym agreed, waiting for the youth's meaning.

"The most terrible nightmare of all," the sorcerer said. "Life."

Pym barked, and Wawa jumped. "Life! Mother of rats, wolves, and pirates! You lived under her skirts in the jungle. Out here on her heaving bosom, she is no kinder. Be sure. Wyvern is our mother as no country, church, or monarch could ever be, for we are life's bastards, we are, orphaned by the God that made us. Will you swear by that?" The captain clasped Jaki's shoulder with a hand big as a bucket. "Will you swear before Wyvern to be one of us?"

Jaki lay his hand on Pym's bison shoulder. "I will swear — but not for plunder. I am a sorcerer. My avarice is not for gold, Captain Pym." The darkness clasped the soul-catcher's face in iron. "I want mana."

"Mana!" Pym hurled a joyful laugh. "The strength beyond sickness that the island natives speak of. How will you find mana among pirates, man-child?"

"You will teach me," Jaki said earnestly. "You will teach me what you know about the stars and their directions. Teach me about the sea and her paths. There is mana."

Pym clapped the boy's shoulder so hard that Jaki staggered. "You amaze me, lad. You are a mereling of sixteen and already you know true wealth. I will give you mana. If you've wit for it, as I think you do, I'll make you a master navigator whose map will be the sky." His good eye wrinkled smaller. "Now will you swear?"

Jaki allowed a slim smile that in the darkening air could have been the beginning of a snarl. "Take me to Wyvern."

In two tenders fitted with torches, the crew of *Silenos* rowed to Maratua. The tenders bogged to a stop on the black mud shoals, and the men waded ashore, sunk to their knees in silt. They carried drums, their furled flag, and kegs of wine to a dune trammeled with sea grape. The tightly rolled banner was stretched between two gnarled trees and then men began tossing uncorked kegs among themselves, streaming long ribbons of wine, while jigging scraps of tribal dances and battle mimes. Within the cupola of torchlight, each remembered his own suffering that had brought him remorselessly to Wyvern.

Pym placed Jaki under the dune's vine-woven scarp, and then he and Blackheart stood at either side of their rolled pirate flag. They raised their hands simultaneously, as if in a dream, and waved for Jaki to approach. Wawa cringed as Jaki advanced. He ordered the beast to wait for him in the jungle, and it swiftly bounded away. The wild dancers whirled about him, and the kegs shuttled before and behind him, looping wine in the air, but no one touched him.

"Behold the sign of our suffering!" Pym shouted, and Blackheart unfurled the banner and tied off its lower corners, stretching the fiercesome image into the swirling torchlight. The pirates stopped their dancing at once and glided into two files before Pym and Blackheart, caps and hats doffed.

Jaki glanced to either side, but none of the enthralled men looked at him; their attentions were fixed on the gloomy ensign. Jaki faced it and recognized the scowl of the nighthawk that defied the sun. The eagle's frown and its clawed wings vibrated in the torchglow, and the twin serpent legs twisted with the fire's writhings. The monster's vivid eyes hooked Jaki's soul from a black distance, and he stepped toward it with weightless, otherworldly precision.

Knives flashed in the hands of the pirates, and they pointed the blades at Jaki with trembling fervor. He winced, and crouched in sudden fear.

"These are the knives that will own you if you betray us!" Pym bellowed in Spanish, his one eye bulging red. "No wound or scar marks this initiation, Jaki Gefjon. The pain that has led you to us is the only brand of our brotherhood. We are the world's exiles. We belong to no one but ourselves. And we have given ourselves to Wyvern."

At the sound of that name, the knives were sheathed, and the men faced forward again.

"You will speak one word," Pym continued, softer, conspiratorially, huge hands clasped before him. "You will say it in Malay so the crew will understand. That one word you must lift out of your flesh, sorcerer, for it surrenders your body to Wyvern and our brotherhood. Look on the sign of our exile." He raised a fist to the creature. "Is this the very shape of your suffering? Is this the design of all your loss? Do you swear by the grief that you have endured, by all that has cast you off, never to betray your brothers in Wyvern to any of our enemies? Do you swear before this monster that you yourself have named Life to die before you yield to our enemies? Do you forswear all other allegiances to every tribe, crown, or kingdom? Do you swear to take all empires as your enemy? Do you swear you will love death to save Wyvern and your brothers?" Pym's eye surveyed the group, seeking the affirmative look of every man in the crew and finally locking on Jaki. "Speak loudly the one word that will make you a pirate."

Jaki raised his arms. This was the immense instant of beginning, the reckless surge into a new life. Where this life was going already faced him right here at its start. The screaming visage of Wyvern, with its flame-locked eyes, was the conclusion of all striving, the guardian of unbeing who had owned him from the womb.

Jaki shouted the word in Malay that threw the pirates back into their drunken frenzy and named him the pirate that life had made him: "Yes!"

Silenos was towing the Dutch warship north to Panay, where Pym had his haven. Jaki returned to his apprenticeship in the rigging and devoted himself with the vigilance of a sorcerer to the ship's routines — holystoning decks, mending canvas, braiding hemp. Pym was good to his word and continued teaching Jaki the rudiments of navigation. The pirates treated his silver gibbon like a favorite pet, and Wawa was soon comfortable with this new and smaller world in the vastness of wind and rolling emptiness.

One morning Pym, sucking on a lime, pointed through the glare. "There" — he gestured loftily — "is Iduna." The jungle island loomed ahead, a netherworld of enormous green veils of hanging vines and strangled green shrubs. *Silenos* sailed through the afternoon, up a broad, deep river to a cove hacked from the verdant chaos. Seven big ships were moored, and a swarm of small boats skittered out on the river to greet them. "Here is where we stop being pirates and become men. Here I stop being a nameless pirate and become Trevor Pym, legate of Iduna. Here we can talk of soul, my young soul-catcher. And here you can berate me for my evil ways."

"Captain," Jaki said, holding the pirate's gaze, "you are no more evil than the panther that takes its prey."

"Ah, spoken like a poet." Pym put his hands on Jaki's shoulders. "Perdita is going to like you."

Pym was ignorant of the magnitude of truth in that prophecy. Perdita Iduna had been remorselessly faithful to her husband; the idea of infidelity was as alien to her as algebra. But as she walked toward the wharves to greet him and saw the tall, hawk-faced youth, her knees trembled, and her maids rushed to support her. Thinking she had been weakened by the sight of him, Pym bounded from the longboat onto the wharf and swept her into his powerful arms. She locked her gaze onto his familiar face, afraid to look again at the virile youth who accompanied him.

"Oh, Perdita, my love," he murmured, hefting her against his chest. "You wet the salt in my bones. Don't faint away on me now. I've prizes to astound you. A Dutch warship to be refitted for your argosy — a hold jammed with treasures from the Japans — and here —" He motioned for Jaki to disembark. "A blue-eyed sorcerer from the jungles of Borneo. A real sorcerer, too, who knows more about healing than any leech in Europe. My wound is not a hole of pain anymore, Perdita. He cured me of my suffering. And I'm looking upon you now for the first time unstricken by the wound that won you."

Jaki was astonished by Perdita's beauty. She was a copper-haired woman, slender as a first-week moon. Her complexion was tan with light from the end of day, smoky with clove dust; and when she looked at him, her eyes, the amber bright of tree resin, emptied him of days, and he was a child again with Mala.

"His name is Jaki Gefjon," Pym said, lowering her. "And, my Perdita, he speaks Spanish. Can you believe that? Show her I'm not a liar, Jaki."

"My lady," Jaki mouthed with a numb tongue, "I am blessed to meet you."

"And I, you," she answered, offering her hand timorously, as if to a fire.

Jaki looked to Pym, and the pirate nodded gruffly. "Go ahead and act the gentleman, jungle boy."

Jaki took her hand, and her living cold thrilled him.

"Welcome to Iduna," she said, her hand glowing with his heat. She had never imagined that men could look as this youth did, sun-laved, strapped with long muscles, noble-boned, and with cavepool eyes the color of tears. "We must honor you for delivering my husband from the claws of pain."

"You may let her hand go now," Pym said.

Jaki released her, but the cool of her touch stayed in his fingers.

Iduna was a great estate carved out of the jungle. Egrets, peacocks, herons, and parakeets decorated the expansive blue swards within the jungle walls. Oleander and white frangipani trellised winding walkways of pastel flagstones that connected gazebos of caged parrots and monkeys. The main house was a mansion with the fluted pilasters of a Greek temple, the rose windows of a Gothic cathedral, and the mosaic tiles and daedal tapestries of a mosque. Here Pym worshiped life, and the goddess of the living was Perdita herself. She dressed in colorful silk sarongs and walked barefoot through the marbled chambers, her body glinting with firepoints of gems, the rarest perfumes luffing from her hair and skin. And always from her delicate ears dangled gold ball earrings impressed with Pym's initials and reminding everyone whom she served. Dwarfs, African eunuchs, and sloe-eyed servant women attended Perdita, Pym, and their guests in large rooms hung with gently smoking censers and elaborate paper and ivory lanterns. All the treasures of Pym's twenty-five years of plundering were gracefully arranged throughout the great house, and an imperial aura pervaded the estate.

Over elaborate meals at which all the pirates partook, Jaki learned that Iduna was a kingdom unto itself, with its own flag and fleet. Under its banner of two interlinked bezants on a blue field, one gold, the other silver — representing the sun and the moon, pirate captain and his bride — Pym maintained a fleet of warships free from the harassment of the rival European powers in Asia. Since no pirate hunters who met him under the banner of Wyvern had survived, he was free to visit all the major ports in Asia as a respected trader when he flew the Iduna flag.

In the days that followed, Jaki devoted his full attention to the marvelously strange foods that were served in Iduna, the better to keep his mind distracted from his fatal attraction to Pym's wife. The jungle meats and fish were familiar, but the honey malt ale was a frothy delight and the grape wine left him giddy and yearning for the embrace of the long-haired lady of the kingdom. With the voracity of a locust, he sampled the bizarre vegetables from distant lands: cucumbers from northwest India, asparagus and cauliflower from Persia, wild peas, woody beets, turnips, and carrots from Flanders, tomatoes from the New World, haricot beans from Africa, cabbages, Brussels sprouts, and cherries planted in Gothland by Romans a century before Christ. When he could eat no more, he wandered the vast lawns of the tiny kingdom and sometimes ran naked with Wawa through the jungle in an attempt to exhaust his crackling desire for the untouchable Perdita.

At the end of one of his furious runs, he burst through a wall of jasmine vines into a high field overlooking the mansion, its lotus ponds and mirrored trees ablaze with twilight. Perdita was there in the waist-high grass, having climbed the flagstone paths to sit in solitude with her desire for the azure-eyed boy. When she suddenly saw him naked to the waist, aglow with sweat and clearly awed by the sight of her, the pull between them drew them into each other's arms.

They collapsed into the grass, only to have Wawa leap atop Jaki's back and screech loudly. Jaki flung himself away from Perdita in time to see her eunuch escort climbing the flagstone path to the wild field. His eyes lingered on her for a moment, and then he turned and followed Wawa back into the jungle.

Jaki spent that night sitting in a tree, filled with darkness for betraying the man who had saved his life. Was passion always an accident? Had he not already seen that woman was death? *Where have I been? I am numb to the Life. I am not a sorcerer anymore. Maybe I was never a sorcerer. I refused the strong eye at Njurat. Now I am blind. My belly is my face, and hunger is my only sight.* "Jabalwan!" he called into the darkness, and a char of silence blackened the jungle. "Who am I?" *The devil's son — with a belly for my face.*

Buffeted by guilt, he thought of killing himself, but the same necessity that had made him offer his hand to the Spider years before commanded him to confront Pym and let the pirate captain do with him as he would. When the first ash of dawn smudged the east, he walked out of the jungle and down the flagstone paths to the great house, Wawa trailing behind.

Pym was waiting for him, sitting on the white pillared porch in a giant fanback cane chair. He was alone, his big cuffed boots propped on a dragon-carved taboret, his hands gripping a cutlass. Jaki stood on the marble steps before him. "Captain, I have betrayed you," he said, somberly.

Pym's boots banged to the porch, and he lurched forward, swinging the cutlass in a hissing arc. The blade snicked the breath under Jaki's nostrils, and his whole body flinched but did not move. Pym guffawed and thwacked the cutlass into the taboret so the haft stood straight up. The pirate's laughter was voluble, and a tear silvered his eye. "Ah, Jaki," he said, cuffing the boy behind the neck and leading him onto the porch, "you really are a soul-catcher, aren't you? And you've plucked my soul from hell. If you had not come back to face me, you would have betrayed me."

"I have put my hands on your wife," Jaki blurted. "I have felt desire for her and would have —"

"Aye, but the fact is, you didn't." Pym brushed the tear from his eye. "I understand lust, boy — and I abide it. That eunuch was not there by accident. I keep my one good eye on what is mine. My heartbreak is that *she* wanted you. But with a heart as dark as mine, heartbreak is daybreak."

"I . . . I don't understand."

"It's one of those things you've got to feel to be true," Pym answered wearily. "You have cured my eye and let me know my wife for the first time without physical pain. And you have stirred a passion in my wife that hurts me with a bodiless pain I will feel whenever I am with her — for the rest of my bloody life." A blur of anguish shadowed his face — and was gone, replaced by a hard grin. "But your courage in coming to confront me proves the pain is my own and not the treachery I maybe wish it was. That's why I laugh. The gods toy with us, boy, trading pain for pain."

"I will never touch her again," Jaki promised, his voice incandescent with sincerity. "I will become a eunuch."

Pym laughed. "Keep fondling other men's wives and indeed you will."

"I mean it. I will cut off my offending part."

"Then it's your head you'll have to cut off." Pym grabbed Jaki's testicles and squeezed them just hard enough to send a jolt of pain up his spine. "Desire can't be cut away, you fool. Life will kill all of us soon enough. Be patient."

Pym let Jaki go, and the boy dropped his gaze to the ground. "I am nothing but hunger."

"Of course. You are a man. We must find you a woman."

"I'm luckless with women."

"So it seems. Still, we dare not let your lack-luck thwart nature too long," Pym said. He sniffed the brightening air. "The rains will be here soon. There'll be no prey in the trade lanes, so we will go touring. First, we will cruise the islands, and you will learn English, by God. Then, with the storms at the height of their rage, we will test our cunning and heaven's favor on the high seas. I will introduce you to the great courts of Asia, and you can do to their women on land what we do to their ships at sea."

Remorse smothered Jaki's passion for Perdita Iduna, and when they met in the mansion's dining hall during each day's boisterous feast, he did not meet her amber gaze. Yet he felt her stare even when he was alone in the suite Pym had set aside for him and Wawa. From the servants he learned that Perdita had been luminous with happiness since marrying Pym eleven years before and had only become languid since his own arrival. Her whole life had been devoted to the careful observance of her ancestral traditions, tribal rites expanded to accommodate the Christian faith of her Portuguese grandparents, and she had used her great wealth to educate the people of her parents' tribe. The tribesfolk were the citizens of Iduna who manned her trading ships and warehouses and who rivaled the kingdoms of the Spice Islands in their contacts with the European capitals. Even the humblest family had forsaken their tribal ways and converted to Christianity. And now the whole kingdom was praying to the nailed god for Perdita's salvation, for they believed that her unholy desire for Jaki would provoke heaven's wrath and destroy their new-won affluence.

Pym was less irate than heaven, however. He forgave his wife and blamed only himself for introducing her to the tall youth. Perdita was Pym's soul, and he understood the earthly temptations of a soul bound to so hideous a body as his. He forgave her and watched her more greedily thereafter.

The day that *Silenos* departed with Pym and Jaki aboard, the citizens crowded the wharves, waving frond crucifixes in the hot rain. Jaki stayed out of sight in his cabin, but he peeked through the bay window and saw Perdita standing alone at the end of the longest pier, her coppery hair strung with rain, the gold ball earrings swinging as she waved good-by.

Jaki assuaged his remorse by diligently attending to whatever task Pym was demonstrating. In their first weeks at sea, roaming the watery maze among the jungle isles of the Philippines, Jaki learned the use of maps and the secret of Mercator sailing, which few navigators of the time had yet grasped. Though all sailors knew the world was round, few knew exactly where they were on the sea even with an accurate map in their hands, because few had the mathematical ability to convert distance on a flat map to the course of a ship over the curved surface of the globe. Pym was a master at this, and he taught Jaki how to use a cross-staff to measure the altitude of a star from the instantaneous stillpoint at the crest of a swell and determine latitude. By day, they used the backstaff to avoid staring directly into the sun. Distance was gauged by running a line knotted at regular intervals behind the ship from a spool while singing a well-timed chanty or marking time on an oval verge watch taken from a Dutch prize. Soon Jaki became proficient at multiplying the east-west distance they had run by the secant of the latitude to get their change of longitude.

Pym's most important possession was a marine chronometer. While still a student at Oriel College in England, he had learned of a Flemish astronomer's discovery, a century earlier, that timed observations of heavenly bodies could be used to determine longitude. The difficulty was that no timepiece was accurate and sturdy enough to work aboard a ship at sea. Pym did not solve the mechanics of the problem until he saw a gimbal ring on a Chinese toy in Macao. The toy was a yin-yang globe of carved ivory, attached to two bearings at right angles, connected by a ring so that the yin-yang remained horizontal no matter how it was turned. He replaced the yin-yang globe with a clock mechanism and, by doing so, invented the world's first chronometer, a hundred and thirty years before it became commonplace.

Pym kept the chronometer in his cabin, a perpetually accessible, doorless stateroom with mullioned windows on three sides and map easels, a globe, and a mounted telescope arranged on a Persian carpet. Here Jaki received most of his European education, not only in navigation and English but in history and courtly manners. Free of his oppressive pain, Pym delighted in reviewing the knowledge that he had ignored for over a decade, and he sumptuously recounted what he knew.

Jaki learned the history of the Greeks and the Romans and the empires that followed, cut from the cloth of tempest by Charlemagne, the Saracens, and the feudal kings. But history came slowly to the jungle youth, and Pym found it easier to teach him folk songs and popular dances. To the amusement of the captain and his mate, Jaki became adept at court dances — the gavotte, the quick-tempoed courante, the stately allemande — all of which Jaki practiced with Blackheart while the ship musicians played their jaunty tunes and the sailors cavorted with each other in high-spirited imitation.

Under her silver-gold banner, *Silenos* called at Manila to trade surplus goods from her Dutch prizes for Spanish bullion. The red-tile-roofed city was the first true port Jaki had seen since Jabalwan had led him to the outskirts of Bandjermasin. He was awed by the galleon-crowded harbor, the stone-walled settlement with its clustered, three-storied buildings, its massive cathedral like a mountain with many eyes, its horse-drawn carriages, and its plumed cuirassiers with their bright metal shirts.

At a court function to which Jaki and Pym were received as emissaries of Iduna, they mingled with dignitaries from many nations. Jaki's striking good looks immediately attracted the attention of the court ladies. During the dances, Pym gloated to see the Spaniards' eyes flashing as the eager youth made advances with women that these aristocrats had been endeavoring for weeks to meet. Once, out of his ignorance of court protocol, Jaki almost provoked a sword duel with a jealous officer, and only Pym's intervention and apologies spared the boy. Though Pym had covered his serpent brand with a black headcloth and had replaced his red, gem-studded eyepatch with a simple gray one, he was still an imposing figure, and a few mollifying words from him were sufficient to put off the challenge Jaki had inadvertently inspired.

During the seven hundred and fifty–mile voyage from Manila to Macao across the China Sea, Pym supplemented his navigation, language, and history lessons with an introduction to sword technique. "The most important thing to know about sword fighting," he told Jaki as he handed him a rapier, "is to avoid it. Fighting for honor is an alp of stupidity. In a close fight on a ship, there is no formality, and a flintlock or a cutlass will serve you best. But if by some miscalculation you find yourself in a formal duel, you must obey the rules, for if you don't, then even if you win you will lose. The second and the witnesses will seize you, and you will be summarily executed. Always avoid fighting for honor. Or learn to do it very well."

From the mizzenmast, Pym dangled a coconut on a rope, and Jaki practiced jabbing it while it swung and the deck rolled under him. When he had become expert at thrusting, Pym demonstrated what he knew of parrying and feinting within a narrow compass. Pym was astonished by Jaki's speed. The boy had the reflexes of a mongoose in a cobra's shadow. The rapier was a chrome blur in his hand, intuiting blocks and attacks before Pym could voice them. The crew shouted encouragement as his silver flash of steel weaseled through the captain's strenuous defenses and tapped his heart. But swift as he was, Jaki was duped time and again by feints that confused his toetip reflexes, and Pym concentrated on teaching the boy to slow down and think.

Jaki's lessons were interrupted late one afternoon by the sighting of a large junk. Pym fixed his telescope on it and his hulking body quivered with delight. "Hsi Hang!" he shouted, and the crew cheered in anticipation. "Hard a-port your helm, Mister Blackheart! Break out Wyvern! Ready cannon!"

Pym handed Jaki his rapier. "Get below deck, lad."

"What's happening?"

"Hsi Hang, that shifty seasnake, is running his gold junks to Singapore and Jakarta against the monsoons, thinking we're landlocked somewhere. Who knows how many boats he's sneaked past us already. If you hadn't grabbed my wife, we might have missed even this one." He stung Jaki's cheek with a friendly slap. "Now get below till this is over."

"Let me help."

"No," Pym said adamantly. "Hsi Hang outfits his gold junks with opium-crazed Mongols. They fight like rabid wolves. There'll be no quarter. Get below."

Jaki seized Pym's black doublet. "This is my life now. I've taken the oath before Wyvern. I must see the worst of it."

"You may die," Pym snarled, "or, worse, be maimed. I won't be watching for you."

Jaki contained his excitement with cunning. "We're dust in the wind, Captain Pym."

Pym's grin shot straight back like a shark's. "Then you're more a pirate than I. For the gore of it then, put those toys away and get yourself a flintlock and a cutlass. And stay close to Blackheart."

Jaki locked Wawa in his cabin and rushed up to the quarterdeck in time to see Wyvern unfurled on the topmast. Its nightmare shape filled with wind, and it gaped with damned eyes, mad with the world's anguish, tar-winged, viper coiling to barbed legs and talon-loaded claws. The sight of it turned his stomach, and he wanted to go below deck again and hide with Wawa. Only the Spider held him fast beneath that banner of life's enemy. The nightmare was outbound, and his fate was here on the quarterdeck, in the fumaroles of the dying sun.

The gun rack was empty, but a bone-handled cutlass leaned against the sternpost behind the wheel where the quartermaster was steering. Blackheart read his look and nodded. The mute's face was intent, and Jaki felt a cold rush as he passed him. *Death's shadow.* He picked up the cutlass and faced into the red skein of the western horizon.

Silenos was running parallel to the junk, and it tilted sharply as its cannon boomed and gunsmoke snapped into the wind. The junk's lugsails blew away, and its cannon spit flame and puffed. The dark water splashed white alongside the pirate ship, and the scud of the impacting shot misted over the decks. The second volley's roar cut through the echo of the first shots, and the junk's gundecks flew into the air like a swarming hive.

Silenos veered sharply and cut across the wind to intercept her prey. Spars grinding, sails crackling, she descended on the smaller ship like a cat. Jaki stood at the rail with Pym and saw the infuriated Mongols waving their parangs and muskets. At Pym's sign, *Silenos* turned and fired a third volley from very close. Powdersmoke rose with the pitch of the ship, violet in the gloaming, and when the ship rocked back they saw the junk's gunwales sheared away, the decks shattered and sagging, the Mongols skeltering in a panic. The tiller had been snapped, and the junk was trolling.

Blackheart swung *Silenos* into the junk before the damaged ship could whirl about and bring its intact cannon to bear. A loud thump shook the big ship's timbers, and Pym howled, "Board!"

Grapnel hooks flew from the main deck and hooked the junk's shattered rails. Pym retreated to the wheel, and Blackheart took his cutlass and signed for Jaki to follow him. He dashed down the stairs to the main deck, Jaki close behind, leaped over the rail where a rope had been tied off, and shimmied down to the battered deck of the junk. A musketball intended for Jaki splintered the rail as he leaped over it and snagged the grapnel rope, landing in a crouch behind Blackheart.

The quartermaster had drawn his flintlock and was peering through the melee for a target. Men were locked in sword-clashing conflicts on all sides. A pack of Mongols erupted from a gangway, and Blackheart fired into them. One fell, tripping two others. Jaki cracked a spear with a bone-jarring blow and found himself face to face with a snarling warrior. Backhanded he struck and felt the man's skull crack like wood under his blow. *When you must kill,* he heard Jabalwan's voice amidst the screams and battered echoes of clashing metal, *let the animal in you do the killing.*

"Jabalwan!" Jaki shouted, hacking at the men scrambling to strike at him. His blade swooped through a sponge of flesh, and hot blood slammed against his face. "Jabalwan!" his lungs squeezed painfully, hysterical with the memory of his teacher's corpse slumped on the blood-daubed earth. Gaumy with gore, he swung at clenched faces and upraised weapons, cutting a path through the angry men stabbing at him. Lopped limbs flew aside, terror sirened around him, and he ran forward with a murderer's strength, sobbing now for the breath cut from his teacher, from the one man who had loved him.

Blackheart fell back, shocked by the man-eating fury beside him. Spools of blood spun in living coils and headless men fell away from the crazed killer. He was shouting something Blackheart could not understand. But the Mongols doubtless knew the demon, and for the first time he saw those kill-crazed warriors turn and flee. Amazed, he pursued them across the splintered deck. Most of the slaying was already done, and the pirate crew squatted among the corpses and watched in cold fascination as the death-hungry boy cut a meatroad across the deck. At the far rail he turned, mired in blood, his body heaving in great sobs.

Blackheart took the cutlass from his bloody hand and held it high. The crew cheered and stepped over the sprawled bodies to gather around him, touching him for the electric mana of lost lives steaming invisibly off his shivering limbs. Pym had seen the whole slaughter from the quarterdeck, and he was glad for the falling light that had masked the horror. His heart was twanging like a harp, and he did not know if he should turn away or kneel in awe. He shouted for the gold to be brought aboard.

In the junk's hold, the crew found seven hundred pounds of gold, the largest prize *Silenos* had ever taken. The crew wanted to turn about and return to Iduna, but the east was black with stormclouds, and starcrofts still glimmered in the west. Pym ordered Wyvern struck and the Iduna flag raised, and *Silenos* returned to her course, running ahead of the gale winds.

Back on the big ship Jaki scrubbed the blood swarf from his body in the laundry cabin, donned sailor's trousers and a leather vest, and climbed up into the mainmast to stare at the axle of darkness turning the stars. The angry power that had blown him into a killing frenzy had passed entirely away, and he lay on the crosstrees feeling wispy and unreal under the starfoam.

The lavender fragrance of the goat tallow soap lilted off his scrubbed flesh, yet he still smelled the blood of the men he had killed. *No, not I,* he corrected himself. *The animal you found in me, Jabalwan. That did the killing. The same animal with its face in my belly, its tongue in my loins, lapping at death in the scent of women. Its claws are in my feet, teacher, scratching for a place in the dance of the tribe. The dance I have no place in. Not in the tribe. For I am the devil's son. And not on the dancefloors in the great cities of my dead fathers, either. For I am a pirate. The Life is nameless, and yet It names me. Why can I not be as other men?* He listened for Jabalwan, for some memory that would disdain his pity, but he heard nothing.

Pym was especially strict with his charge after the slaughter of the Mongols. The fury that had possessed the jungle boy had frightened Pym deeply enough to stir the pain of his oldest rage, the rage that had made him a pirate, and he resolved to share his story with this primeval witness. One night after a twilight carnival of rowdy feasting and drinking, Pym and Jaki sat together on the quarterdeck.

"A lie branded me a traitor," Pym told the boy. "And that lie is the world. That is why I wear no hat. I have no rank in the world. So I allow myself no disguise for the lie branded on my forehead. It is my distinction before God to prey on the world, to feast on the lie. All nations are pirates. I alone am truthful, because a lie made me so." He sucked a breath through flared nostrils and began to tell how, for eleven years, he had been bound in a Lucifer's harness of pain — an obedient dog of hell since the afternoon he lost his left eye in a knife duel with a Spaniard. "The Spaniard lost his life," Pym confessed with a growl, "and sometimes, boy, I envy him for it."

Pain had been Pym's saga all his adult life, and he often thought on his youth, forty years past, when living was ruly and poetry came to him without brandy. His family was old as fishes and loaves, he said, a naval family who could trace their lineage back four hundred years to William of Wrotham, keeper of King John's ships. His father, a commander, died at sea in an engagement with the Spanish off the Azores when Pym was two, and afterward Pym had traveled with his merchant uncles, from Sweden's necklace inlets to the starfish sands of Greece and North Africa. He was educated in the academies of diverse ports and then at Oriel College, lordly Oxford, where he studied mathematics and architecture, read Petrarch's Latin for the pleasure of the sound, and composed cunning sonnets about youth's waste and the jealous undereye of death.

"Hah!" He grinned like a gnome. "My poems stirred passion in several courtly ladies, and I very nearly married and became a stanchion of the society I've spent the rest of my life defying. Imagine that — Lord Trevor Pym, shipbuilder for the realm. But that was not to be."

In 1585, at the age of twenty, Pym was commissioned in the Royal Navy and committed to his humbling fate. He sailed that year for the

Caribbean as a junior officer on one of a fleet of twenty-nine warships commanded by Sir Francis Drake.

Pym shook his head as though he could barely believe his own story. "Our mission was to raze the Spanish Main, no less, and it was during the sackings of San Domingo and Cartagena that I learned to kill and saw death astride whole towns. The stink of corpses became common as the briny smell of the sea. Heaps of bodies — the harbors clogged with their gas-bloated bodies."

The havoc of war seemed to him a wanton disputation of the Great Chain of Being, and of all the noble ideals he had adopted at Oriel, and he became surly with disillusionment and doubt. Soon he was ostracized by the exultant crew and the glory-swollen officers, and thereafter fulfilled his nautical duties silently and mechanically. Years later he would realize that this silence of horror was his first act as a pirate.

A short time later, Pym was selected by Samuel Quarles, one of the captains of the fleet, to accompany him ashore at Antro Cay on an eccentric search for a blue rose reputed to grow on the sand shelves of the Caribe. Anchored outside Antro Cay, Quarles was careful to record in his logbook a single perfidious sentence, which was to seal Pym's fate as an outcast forever: *Mister Pym,* he wrote, *has insisted on manning the tender into Antro Cay.*

"Insisted! Never!" Rage clawed the pirate's ghastly face. "I avoided that man, because he was imperious. He *ordered* me to take him ashore."

In truth, the search for the blue rose was a hoax, and Quarles's lie about Pym a treacherous and greedy plan: Quarles, for all his vanity, was a prodigal heir who had whittled away his ancestral fortune and gone deep into debt to finance his captaincy in Drake's fleet. His magisterial airs and personal bravura had disguised his plight, even to his superiors. No one suspected the man to be desperate or venal enough to sell the fleet's schedule to the Spanish. A chest of Incan gold promised him by the governor of Cartagena in remuneration for his treason lay in a tide pool cave on Antro Cay. (This Pym learned later from the Spanish governor himself.) Quarles chose Pym to row him there because Pym was a morose lad and openly disaffected: an easy and credible scapegoat for the betrayal.

He planned to shoot Pym as he lugged the chest from the cave. When the Spanish had finished ravaging the English fleet, they would return for him, a galleon would carry him to Europe, and he would quietly make his way back to England. With his Incan gold secretly secured in his coffers, he would then spin an adventurous tale of Pym's duplicity and his own miraculous, God-given survival. But as it happened, the Spanish attacked prematurely, while Pym was still in the cave grotto struggling with the chest, and the cannon thunder drew him out in time to see Quarles sending mirrorflash signals to the galleons. Outraged at the obvious betrayal, he attacked Quarles and they locked in a grim struggle. Only Quarles was armed, and Pym lost the top of his right ear in wresting the cutlass from the traitor.

The pirate fingered the remnant of his ear. "The pain made me crazy, and I drove the blade into the captain's heart."

A skiff of armed English crewmen had sailed for the cay to retrieve Quarles when the first Spanish warships rose on the horizon, and their arrival fixed Pym's destiny in hell, for the crew saw him slay the captain. Pym was immediately hauled back to the besieged ship and, after the Spanish assault had been repelled, he was tried and condemned to death for treachery and murder. The chest in the tide pool, which he frantically claimed was Quarles's payoff, was never seen by his accusers because the tide rushed in at that hour, and the court-martial would not wait for fear of another Spanish attack. A special iron kept on the gundeck to intimidate cowards was heated in a lead-smelting oven until it pulsed red; then Pym was branded on the forehead with the snake sign of perfidy.

As he stood on the arm of the mainmast, a rope about his throat, his brow bubbling like tar, the feared second assault came, a fleet of warships swooping out from behind the surrounding reef islands. Pym's ship was overrun by Spaniards, and he was carried aboard the admiral's galleon a hero.

For the ten years that followed his branding, almost daft with the irony of his fate, Pym lived in the Caribbean, first as a sailor aboard the galleons, though the Spanish never fully trusted him — especially after he returned to Antro Cay and discovered that the tortoiseshell chest that financed Quarles's betrayal was filled with sea coral. After that, his snakebrand glowed a violet-purple on his brow, and he refused to cover it with a headcloth. The world thought him a traitor, so he wore his Cain mark boldly.

Abandoned eventually by the Spanish in Hispaniola, Pym wandered into the forest and became a mountain bandit, robbing wealthy estates until the day he stole a slave ship in Isabella Harbor, trained the slaves as sailors, and began pirating under a flag emblazoned with the coiled serpent of his shame.

With the booty he accrued raiding Dutch, French, and Spanish cargo vessels, Pym designed and built for himself his own ship, the fleetest and most maneuverable warship in the Caribbean. At first he called it *Sin* and carved on the bowsprit lines he bastardized from Spenser's *Hymns*.

Running a finger over the serpent-coil burned into his flesh, Pym recited:

"I down descended, like a most demiss
And abject thrall, in flesh's attire,

That I might pay sin's deadly hire
And myself restore unto that happy state,
In which I stood before my hapless fate:
In flesh at first the guilt was committed;
Therefore in flesh it must be satisfied!

"And so it has been." Pym's eyes widened, and a smile shot from under his braided mustache.

In 1596, Drake returned, and Pym, after a decade of exile, had his revenge off Porto Bello. There he attacked Drake's fleet in *Sin*, gadflying the English ships until they gave him chase. His trim ship held back enough to let the English believe they were gaining on her, and he lured them into a pincered cove of gun-mounted cliffs, a Spanish trap in which Drake was killed.

After that, Pym's skill as a buccaneer was touted in all the European capitals, and the English offered a prodigious reward for his head. The Caribbean became dangerously small for him, and he followed the southern routes through the storm-lashed Straits of Magellan and across the chartless South Pacific to the Spice Islands. On the long sea crossing, short of provisions and hallucinating from hunger, he saw his snake emblem sprout legs and wings. Thus in the womb of madness *Wyvern* was conceived.

For seventeen years, Pym met little resistance as he plundered the great merchant ships that Europe sent to Asia to enrich her kings, queens, and companies. He never abandoned his nostalgia for the practical sciences he had learned in his college days, and his ship and crew were the most able under sail. Pym culled all his mathematical and design skills and applied them to perfecting a peerless man-of-war.

While other ships had clinker-built hulls laden with ornate carvings, *Wyvern* was carvel-seamed in a smooth line, sleek as a shark and painted to blend with the horizon. She had black sails for night running, and blue and cloudgray for day camouflage. Outfitted with one of the first steering wheels in the hemisphere, *Wyvern* easily outmaneuvered whipstaff ships, which had to be steered by altering the trim of their sails. *Wyvern* also had a rounded stern and a flanged keel — revolutionary in the age of the flat-sterned galleons — which made it agile enough to zip in and out of rocky coves and reef barriers. No ship could catch her when she fled. And when she pounced, none could elude her. *Wyvern*'s twenty-two short-barreled cannon burned corned powder, which flared faster and more evenly than the serpentine powder used by almost all other long-cannon ships. And Pym had trained his gunners to shoot thirty-pound balls so accurately that enemy gundecks were blown apart without damaging the cargo holds.

Pride owled his eye. "*Wyvern* is devilish with tricks. But her greatest weapon is her maps. Her maps, sorcerer — accurate and as new as science can fashion them. You see, knowing precisely where we are at all times, we have supremacy over our hunters and our prey. *Wyvern*'s infamy wins her numerous prizes without a fight. And that leaves us more time for this." He lifted his crocodile-skin flagon and drank deeply, then continued his story.

Pym's success had been spoiled eleven years ago, in 1613, when, already famous and immensely wealthy, he had lost his left eye during a brief skirmish with a Spaniard. The hurt wore him like a skin, and he drank to elude his wound. That was when he renamed his ship *Silenos*, after the lewd and drunken satyr of Greek myth.

"Why did you fight the Spaniard?" Jaki asked.

Pym smiled. "We fought over a woman, over the incomparably beautiful Perdita Iduna, the fifteen-year-old virgin daughter of the warlord of Iloilo in the Philippines."

The warlord had been an aborigine with Portuguese blood who was eager to win the favor of the powerful Spaniards in his island kingdom of Panay. He would gladly have given his daughter to the Spanish officer who had asked for her hand in marriage if Pym had not offered him the fortune of a prince — a casque big as a boar's head filled with pearls and gold. The warlord took the treasure, and Pym wed the girl in a Panay ritual.

During the ceremony, the Spanish officer arrived with a squad of armed soldiers. Pym's pirate crew faced them down, but to avoid a blood bath, Pym agreed to duel the officer for the hand of the girl.

The officer was a wizard with a knife, but Pym was bold, willingly taking cuts as he pressed his massive size close enough to overpower the officer and thrust his blade through his Spanish ruff and into his throat. But one of the cuts Pym took spilled his left eye down his face. He had Saja fire the wound with gunpowder and pack the socket with a wad of brandy-soaked silk, and then he went ahead with the wedding.

Pym never regretted losing his eye for Perdita Iduna. She was the ideal wife for a pirate, attracting men with her narrow body and her heathery scent — yet passionately loyal, forgiving Pym his long absences. She even claimed to be proud of his violent defiance of empires. And he spent all his wealth on her, building her an opulent estate in Panay and surrounding her with servants and luxuries. She bore him two sons and a daughter, but all died in childbirth, almost taking her into the afterworld with them. Pym cursed each one of them. He had not married her for children, and to protect her life he had had Saja remove his testicles. The pirate captain cast them in gold, and after that, Perdita Iduna wore them as earrings.

The dismayed look on Jaki's face brought a laugh from the pirate.

"Now you know why she was never without her earrings. Marring my body means nothing to me. I've never been a handsome body; I'll not be a handsome corpse. As well as missing this eye and the top of my right ear, I've lost joints of fingers on both hands. And this —" He tapped a stubbed finger to the livid scar of the snake. "Long before the Spaniard marred me, I was a ghastly-looking lad, and I regret the loss of my eye only because of the maddening pain that harpied me since my wedding day. Wine and murder were all that afforded relief — until you healed me, sorcerer." He stood up and leaned over Jaki. "You healed me — and now all my pain is exiled to my soul."

Jaki watched the pirate captain stomp drunkenly down the forecastle steps and across the main deck to his cabin. The sorcerer was not yet ready for sleep.

The captain's cruel story circled back on Jaki like a nagging song, and he could not ease his mind. *All evil from forgetfulness*, Jabalwan had taught. Pym was the evil of the world's fear and forgetfulness, and yet he had saved Jaki's life and was thus the nearest he had to kin. Like Mala and Jabalwan before him, he was the new life of pain for Matubrembrem, the Spider in the world's web — who would either kill him with his teaching or, in an agony of change, empower him to live as a sorcerer in his fathers' realm.

His very life was at stake; even so, these thoughts left Jaki cold. He was indifferent to Pym's rage against the world, and he was indifferent to his own life as a sorcerer. All ambitions — all wants — were lies before the truth of death. He wanted only to live the life of the animal with its face in his belly, and that simply because he found himself alive. From here, life led everywhere — and so nowhere.

Jaki gazed up at stars and listened to the deep-chested ship striving through the water. The passion and deep nobility of life grew from suffering. No matter the hurt he felt for all he had lost to death, he would endure as Pym endured and as Jabalwan had. The edgeless mystery demanded that of all life.

Jabalwan's soft laugh echoed from the repose of memory: *Shut up and get some sleep, Matu. The truth will still be there when you wake up. A soul-catcher is the living pain of the world.*

The morning Macao's bay came into view, Pym presented Jaki with a sword belt of Moroccan leather and a serpent-hilted rapier. "Eighteen years ago I took this off a Spanish man-of-war in the Banda Sea," Pym told him, "and I've never had to use it in a duel since. I hope you are as wise with it."

Jaki received the weapon with cold fingers, feeling the death in it. The leather belt was stained a dark blue, like the sea far from land, and constellated with tiny silver studs. The weight of the sword at his hip dropped his gravity's center deeper into his pelvis, and he had to practice moving with it, promenading up and down the decks. The crew laughed, thinking him vain, but he ignored them. The days he had spent shod in Manila had been uncomfortable because he was still not accustomed to the profuse clothing these people wore. His movements had been hampered, and that was dangerous. Yet even after leaving Manila, he had insisted on wearing the shoes Pym had given him. Slowly, the leather had surrendered to his splay-toed gait, and he had learned to move gracefully with those odd encumberments. Adjusting to the sword was actually easier than feeling the deck through shoe leather, and when *Silenos* docked in the palmetto-frilled bay among numerous galleons, junks, warships, and yachts, Jaki carried his weapon with ease.

Rain-wrung Macao was a gallimaufry of traders from every land. Turbaned, baggy-trousered Arabs, skullcapped Chinese, long-mustached Hindus, and cuirass-breasted Portuguese mingled in the boisterous wharfside markets. Bins of spices from the Moluccas and jugs of aromatic oils from Sumatra charged the air with rich fragrances, and pier stalls flashed with gold from Siam, silver from Burma, silks from Cathay, gems from India. In the winding alleys, swarthy men in travelworn apparel hawked the services of sybils, harlots of every race, young boys. *Silenos*'s crew melted into the bazaar eager to exhaust the fortunes they had not spent during their eight days in Manila.

Jaki accompanied Pym and Blackheart to pay tribute to the governor, so that he would allow them to conduct trade with the crown-sanctioned merchants who shipped the largest and most lucrative lading and did business only with heads of state. Iduna could not flourish on booty alone, and over the years Pym had established legitimate trade relations in port with many of the European companies he plundered at sea.

The governor's palace was richer even than the opulent mansions and cathedral of Manila, though its construction was not yet complete. Sculptured trees circled a courtyard of black marble fountains, and soaring columns lifted a red onyx cornice on bronze triglyphs. Scaffolds latticed an unfinished wall, and granite blocks lay heaped in dwarf pyramids among milling workers.

The cuirassiers guarding the one entrance to the palace crossed their halberds at the pirates' approach, and Pym presented a letter of introduction from Perdita. One of the guards disappeared and reappeared momentarily with a young bareheaded officer in a cavalry uniform, who returned the letter wrist up as if holding something soiled. "The governor will not receive emissaries from jungle kingdoms unrecognized by Lisbon."

The smoke in Pym's eye ignited. "Unrecognized? Iduna has conducted recognized trade with Spain and the Netherlands for over a decade now."

"Perhaps," the officer said. "But you are not in the catalogue of kingdoms favored by Lisbon. Please, go conduct your business in the market."

"By God we will not!" Pym roared, and the officer stepped back and clamped his jaw. The guards pressed closer, and Pym said in a modulated voice, "I will speak with your superior officer."

"*I* am Diogo Almeida de Cão, the commanding officer of the palace guard. My superior is the governor himself."

"I will speak with the governor then, Diogo."

The commander's nostrils flared at the affront of being addressed by his Christian name. "Sir, I tell you, you will not." He put his hand on his sword.

Pym and Blackheart stepped back, hands wide at their sides, but Jaki advanced, gripping the hilt of his rapier, his heart pounding with excitement.

Almeida faced him, ready to fend off an attack. Blackheart seized Jaki by his shoulders and pulled him away, grunting with alarm.

"Take your mute and your blond clown away from this gate," Almeida ordered. "The governor is not looking to be amused by freaks today."

Pym raised a conciliatory hand and smiled his humorless shark grin. "Please, commander, we have misunderstood each other. No harsh words need pass between us. We are both here to do honor to Macao's governor, you as his protector and myself as an emissary of a small but wealthy kingdom. I come with a valuable gift that the governor would be disappointed to lose over a mere misunderstanding." He removed the leather satchel slung over his shoulder and opened it to reveal a jewelbox of white jade that seemed to glow in the dark bag. Pym lifted the lid of the box and removed a knuckle of ruby from the cluttered jewels. "Please accept this as our acknowledgment of your authority and allow us to present the rest of these precious gems to the governor."

Almeida removed his hand from his sword hilt and, feigning indifference, accepted the large ruby. The gel of red light in the stone's heart cooled his anger. He looked to the guards. "Let them pass."

Enormous mahogany doors opened to an inner court of gray sentry stones scribbled with vines. Most of the construction was complete inside the unfinished walls, and they passed through tall archways with gold-sheeted intrados into a cedar-paneled hallway. "You realize, of course, you *were* a clown to provoke Almeida," Pym whispered sidelong to Jaki. "The Portuguese are devils with rapiers. He'd have cut all three of us down before we could say his name."

Jaki nodded absently, dazzled by the frescoed ceiling of a marble chamber that led to the governor's office. Pym, hatless, his branded forehead covered in his formal black headband, signed for the two men to remove their hats before he lifted the lionmouth knocker on the giant carved doors. He announced himself to the satin-clad servant as the ambassador from Iduna and handed him the intricately carved jade jewelbox. The servant opened the delicate box, glimpsed the fiery chunks of gems within, bowed, and closed the door. Moments later, he returned with an engraved invitation to the governor's court ball two evenings hence.

"That's all?" Jaki asked indignantly. "A box of jewels for an invitation to a dance? Not even an audience with the governor that he might thank you in person?"

"I want trade rights in Macao, lad, not some noise from a man no better than God's most common clay but that he's a king's cousin's nephew's son-in-law. Come, we've better things to do than to stand here dignifying this temple to greed. There's drinking and whoring to be done!"

Pym and Blackheart led Jaki among Macao's wynds and alleys, buying provisions for *Silenos* and haunting the wine cellars, where they listened to sailors' tales of ocean crossings, the African slave trade, the wars in Europe, and the frightful reports of the pirates plundering Asia's seven seas. That night, they visited an elegant palm-groved bordello with tapestried floors, mirrored walls, and silk-cushioned beds. Jaki's desire annealed with fright in the presence of the sophisticated and richly garbed women who laughed at his wide-eyed amazement and obvious inexperience. Like the paddy girls of the jungle, these Oriental and Portuguese odalisques were intent on pleasuring him, for Pym had paid handsomely for the boy to be treated with special consideration. Jaki's apprehensions fell away with his clothes.

Afterward, relieved of desire's burden, empty as a dream, he sat under a palm in the palazzo and thought back on the many women who had granted him respite from lust. The simple satisfactions he had known with the jungle women were, even in distant reflection, more precious to him than the ribald games he had played this night on the malleable bodies of these pleasure-wise prostitutes. He had been just another man here, humbled by his own passion.

Nostalgia wheezed in him. He was so far from his life as a sorcerer, and drifting further. He realized that the course he had chosen would never return him again to the immortalities of the jungle. He was lonely, and the loneliness soon turned to melancholy. It seemed to him that blind wanderings before time's furies were all that was left of his life. Perdita Iduna had shown him that: the animal with its face in his belly had almost devoured her and him — and Pym with them. Desire by itself was demonic.

Stung by this new clarity, Jaki swore that the next time he was stuck to a woman with sweat, love would be the weld.

The day of the court ball, the crew of *Silenos* watched with awe from their vessel, anchored at the mouth of the bay, as the largest man-of-war they had ever seen glided past them and entered the harbor. Three gundecks bristled with cannon — a hundred guns, most of them fifty-pounders. The hull was painted white, its strake long and clean of barnacles. The bitts on the rail were brass and bright as sundrops, and the stern rounded gracefully to window galleries without a wisp of baroque molding or gilt.

"It's the devil's own," Pym muttered as he studied the sleek lines and trim rigging of the ship. On its topmast, a flag of conquest snapped in the wet wind, the red cross of England's St. George laid atop the white cross of Scotland's St. Andrew — the Union Jack. "A floating fortress with the speed of a barracuda and bearing the flag I loathe more than any other." Pym's eye squinted with rage as he read aloud the name on her bow: "*The Fateful Sisters.*"

The rest of that day, Pym sat in his seachair, drinking Lisbon wine and staring at the huge ship where she had moored at the sea wall, studying her for any sign of weakness and sulking darker as her strengths became more obvious. He railed to Jaki. "No other ship in Asia had a jib sail but *Silenos*. And we took that sail off our bowsprit before entering harbors so others wouldn't guess its advantage. Now look at *The Fateful Sisters* with her jib in full view. Soon every warship will have that edge. And look there!" He pointed to the rope attached from the bowsprit to the hull. "She's got a bobstay. She's done away with her gammoning just as we have. God rot her! I'd not want to cross her at sea."

The British warship posted guards on the sea wall beside their gangway and would answer no questions for the curious sailors whom Pym had sent to find out who captained the modern vessel. Through his spyglass, he studied the British crew as they hurried about the business of unloading the holds and lading provisions. The mate, long-skulled and with a beard like a slap of tar across his jaw, supervised the hoisting of horses and cattle from between decks. The captain, in full-rosetted breeches, pinked doublet, and ruff, stood at the poop's gunwale, peering back at him through a telescope. Pym did not recognize the square, barley-bearded captain watching him, but he knew the crewmen of his ship — the ruddy faces and fair hair of Devon sailors; the angular features of Yorkshire men; the squat, dark men from Wales. Each face was a splinter in Pym's heart, stabbing him with forty-year-old memories of his exile. He passed the spyglass to Blackheart and reached under his seachair for his flagon.

Aboard *The Fateful Sisters*, the captain held his telescope so fiercely its leather casing crackled in his grip and he had to lower the instrument and stare for a moment into the barbs of sunlight on the bay to steady himself. The sight of the one-eyed pirate in the bright grip of the telescope's lens — his viper brand hidden by a black headcloth, his rattail beard gleaming with the wine that spilled from his upturned flagon — filled him with rage, and he held to the ship's rail as if buffeted by a stormwind.

The mate saw him and strode to the quarterdeck. "Sir — is something amiss?"

The captain turned a harrowed look on his mate. "Attend to the lading, Mister Montague," he said with a twisted voice that sent the mate hurrying away.

From his earliest years, Captain William Quarles had hated Trevor Pym. He had been five years old in 1586 when Pym murdered his uncle Samuel Quarles at Antro Cay and deprived his family of the wealth that his noble uncle was winning for them in his New World adventure with the Spanish. Misfortune under Queen Elizabeth had withered the Quarleses' family fortune, and Uncle Samuel had been striving to re-establish their prosperity when Pym slew him. All his life, William Quarles had struggled to regain the stature that Pym had snatched from his family, and now that he was facing the devil himself, he could barely restrain his wrath. But he would not allow Pym or his own fury to befoul his hard-won career — and though he craved to storm *Silenos* immediately and seize the villain, he restrained himself. Pym was a traitor to England, but they were in a Portuguese port, and Quarles needed proof that Pym was a pirate before he could break the man — otherwise, he would be charged as a brigand himself and outlawed from these waters, where he had come to establish diplomatic ties and trade agreements.

He searched the length of the pirate's ship for any sign of the notorious standard that haunted Asia's sea lanes. But Wyvern was nowhere in sight, unless the ship herself was regarded with a wary eye; only then was the monster apparent: the raked masts were her wings, the slender hull empty of ornament and curved for speed was her serpent glide. Her talons were well hidden: the gunports were closed, and several were draped with gammon nets as though the hatches hid not cannon but davits for craning cargo. She rode nosedown in the water, bespeaking an unusual keel, and Quarles noted her wheel where the whipstaff should have been. This was no ordinary merchant ship, though she wore her colors on her foremast as a ship of trade. That she would pretend that she was not a fighting vessel convinced Quarles that he had indeed found the dread Wyvern, and he scrutinized her for weaknesses.

Below him, through a bay gallery, another spyglass watched *Silenos*. From *The Fateful Sisters*'s stern window, sixteen-year-old Maud Rufoote scanned the big ship sitting in the bay, giggling at the sight of the half-naked men holystoning the decks and repairing the rigging. She was pretty, a chestnut-haired maid with capable hands and a lively freckled face. "Look, Luci," she called to her mistress, "there's one without ears!"

Lucinda Quarles, the captain's daughter, lay curled in her canopied bed, dolorously turning the pages of a thin volume of verse. With a wince of her blue eyes, she dismissed her maid's appeal. The telescope was a toy that had ceased to amuse her years before. And though she was no older than her maid, she could read — and the scenes she found in her father's library were more vivid than anything she had seen through the lens.

Maud, a country girl nostalgic for the croft in Devon where she had grown up, was giddy at every port of call. She delighted in the telescope's reach that lifted her from the ship's confinement without incurring the prodigious anger of her mistress's father, a severe man who never indulged his servants. "This crew looks healthier than most we've seen in Asia," she said. "But there's one with a snake tattooed down his back. And that one has a ring in his nose and one in each nipple! Oh, Luci, come see."

"Maud, I'm reading," Lucinda protested, then said in a stronger voice: " 'Long since I see my joys come to their evening —' "

"Sidney," Maud recognized with a groan, not budging from the eyepiece. "That's too sad. Don't read Sidney to me now. We've just made port. Are you going to pine for your lost love the entire tour?"

A year earlier, in Rome, Lucinda had fallen in love with her Latin tutor, a young poet with a starved face and enormous eyes. Before her love could be reciprocated, her father had been awarded command of *The Fateful Sisters* and, fully aware of her nascent passion, he ordered her to accompany him on this mission to Asia. The tour was to last three years, and on their return to Europe, she would be eighteen and expected to marry a gentleman of her father's choosing. That prospect had galled her for the entire yearlong voyage, and she took an adolescent's perverse pleasure in heightening her misery by reading melancholy passages from the poets.

> "Long since I hate the night, more hate the morning:
> Long since my thoughts chase me like beasts in forests,
> And make me wish my self laid under mountains."

Maud removed a hand from the spyglass to wave that morbid thought away. "Laid, yes, but not under a mountain, Luci, please. You *promised* we wouldn't die virgins." She beckoned Lucinda and steadied the telescope with both hands. "Come look at the Asians — one of them's playing a fiddle. And there by the binnacle! A European — with one eye and a knotted beard. He's ugly as a troll, but he looks English. And there's another, this one with red hair and a face like a boot. Oh, you must see."

"What's the ship's name?" Lucinda asked without looking up.

Maud swept the spyglass to the prow and read, "*Silenos* — what an odd name."

"Latin, Mousie — *The Man in the Moon*," Lucinda translated.

Sweat stung Maud's sight, and she wiped the eyepiece on her sleeve. "This heat is hateful. Why weren't you more melancholy in Italy? He would have left us in the care of some great house and we wouldn't be shriveling now like hags under this vile sun."

"You know better, Maud. Father doesn't care how I feel. He keeps me near because I am his and he cannot bear to relinquish anything that is his."

"Luci!" Maud shrieked as her sight found Jaki knotting hemp in the shrouds. "*Another* European — and a handsome one, this one is. His hair is fair as yours or more. Beardless — he's a boy, yet he has the limbs of a man. And his face — fine and strong as any statue's we saw in Rome. You must look for yourself, Lucinda."

Maud placed the telescope on the sill and hurried to her mistress. "Forget your poems and your lost love and come look."

"I'm coming," groused Lucinda, climbing out of bed.

Lucinda lifted her white gown to sit on the sill and picked up the telescope, and Maud pointed her toward the foremast topgallant shrouds. The beat of her heart deepened. He was all that Maud had said, his lanky arms and legs naked and solar dusted, his hair, white as a star, falling long over his thick, seaburned shoulders. He was the most complete being she had ever seen. His features were becalmed as marble, magnificently empty of the malice and harshness that stared from the faces of other men. Even intent on his work, he seemed free as the tumultuous clouds behind him, unhaunted by human feelings. That could not be true, she realized, and she yearned at once to know what emotions stirred the heart of such a man.

"Sad to think he's a pirate." Maud disrupted her reverie. "I pray your father won't have us watch his hanging."

Lucinda lowered the telescope and frowned at her maid. "Better you had left me with my poems than steepen my melancholy with such an apparition." She retreated to her bed and picked up her book again, but what she had seen through the telescope itched at the soles of her feet and sizzled through her legs like the brightenings of music. She watched Maud resume her post in the window gallery, telescope to her eye, and she breathed deeply to fill herself with strength against the shiverings from her vision.

Silly girl, she berated herself. *Only a child falls in love with an image.* She was smart enough to know that she really did not love the stranger she had glimpsed through the lens, but love itself. For the last year, she had loved love — and that had put her at terrible odds with her father. He wanted her to marry a gentleman of means, and she wanted love. A dim smile lit her face at the idea of what her father would think of her falling in love with a pirate. But that smile quickly faded, and she resolved to put the handsome sailor out of her mind. He was a pirate — and he was her father's prey.

That night, rains lashed the bay city, and Pym, Blackheart, and Jaki were carried in palanquins to the governor's palace.

Dressed in their finery, the pirates stood in the colonnaded entrance to the main hall while a heron-faced servant announced them as legates of Iduna, then they waded through the majestic crowd of bejeweled silk and rose-powdered faces to the polished chair of the governor. He was a plump, balding man with an aquiline nose, meticulously coifed beard, and red, parrot-beaked lips in the cup of an elaborate ruff. Behind him stood Diogo Almeida de Cão, the commander who had challenged the pirates two days earlier. He nodded to Pym and fixed Jaki with a haughty stare.

The governor tersely thanked them for their gift and introduced them to his special guest, sitting in the thronelike chair to his right — the Chinese merchant prince Hsi Hang.

Hsi Hang was a wizened mandarin with excruciatingly long fingernails. "Captain Pym," he said in excellent Spanish, "I have admired your ship, *Silenos*, which I have seen in the harbor. Its lines and raked sails suggest that it is a vessel of great speed and adroitness."

Jaki noted the beastlike wariness between the two men and heard the reserve in Pym's voice. "I am pleased to hear you say that, Hsi Hang, for your reputation as a master seaman is famous throughout Asia. I designed *Silenos* myself, and she is indeed fashioned to carry her cargo swiftly."

"The better to avoid pirates, yes, captain?" He smiled with what may have been slyness or admiration.

"The Lanun are troublesome along the Malay coast," Pym replied, "but I've had no trouble so far with predators on the high seas."

"Then you have not yet run afoul of Wyvern?" Hsi Hang inquired, widening his sleepy eyes incredulously.

Pym turned a puzzled expression on the governor, seeking a clue.

"Hsi Hang refers to a notorious pirate who has harried our trade routes for a quarter century now," the governor said, scrutinizing Pym and his two companions from under a cocked eyebrow. "You have not heard of Wyvern? I'm surprised, captain. I've been here merely a year, and that scourge has not escaped my notice."

"Yes, but you are governor of Macao," Pym said, nodding deferentially. "I imagine that very little escapes your notice. I am merely a merchant."

"How long have you sailed these waters, Captain Pym?" Hsi Hang asked.

Before Pym could reply, the herald stamped his mace for silence and announced, "Master of *The Fateful Sisters*, Captain William Quarles of the British Royal Navy, and his daughter Mistress Lucinda Quarles."

Pym stiffened as if stabbed, and Blackheart edged closer and laid a hand on his shoulder. " 'Tis the bastard's flatulent ghost!" Pym hissed under his breath in English. Blackheart tightened his grip on his captain's shoulder and looked to Jaki, but the boy's attention was at the far end of the room where the guests were entering.

A stocky man with flattened brown hair, a full oat-gray beard, and skin the color of pickled cedar stood in the entrance surveying the gathering with imperial hauteur. He wore an ermine-trimmed velvet jacket, blue knee breeches, pleated garters, and oxblood boots of polished leather. The young woman beside him, a silvery blond, pale as starlight, was dressed in a soft black chemise, a white satin skirt, and gray pearl-studded slippers.

As they approached the governor's chair, Pym shivered and backed off, but Jaki was enthralled by the first blond woman he had ever seen.

Captain Quarles bowed to the governor and nodded to Hsi Hang. Observing the friendly intimacy of that nod, Pym tried again to back away and meld into the festive gathering, but the governor was faster. "Master of *Silenos* — Captain Trevor Pym — this is the man who will assure that the sea lanes are free of the dread Wyvern: master of *The Fateful Sisters*, Captain William Quarles."

Quarles's hazel eyes met Pym's single one. "Do you know me?" he asked in bitter Portuguese. "I certainly remember you, sir. Your name is black in our family. Though I was but a mate's apprentice when I sailed with Drake in ninety-six to harry the Spanish in the New World, I remember well how you betrayed us. My uncle was Samuel Quarles, the captain you murdered on Drake's first foray."

Hsi Hang and the governor watched Pym closely and caught the hint of fang in his tight grin. "Sir, you are sadly mistaken," he said in Spanish. "In fact, it was your uncle who was the traitor. I was but the scapegoat he would use for his treachery, for no other reason than that I was callow and at that time had no taste for blood."

Blackheart gently pulled Pym back, but Quarles waved the quartermaster away. "Do not fear for your master," he said serenely in English. "I am a man who abides law and will not seek my vengeance here in the governor's court."

Hsi Hang and the governor exchanged glances as Quarles stepped close to the pirate. "But Trevor Pym, the snakebrand you hide under that headcloth will hang you if ever we meet in British territory. For certainly you do not deny your responsibility in luring Sir Francis Drake to his doom at Porto Bello?"

"Is this an inquiry?" Pym asked the governor. "I had assumed you invited us here to be entertained."

The governor nodded to Diogo Almeida de Cão, who glided forward and bowed first to Captain Quarles and then to his daughter. "The dancing is about to begin," he said. "Will you honor me?"

The girl curtsied and accepted, and they moved away to the first strains of the orchestra. Blackheart took that opportunity to lead Pym away, too, scratching his palm to remind the captain of the money represented by the many merchants and traders gathered in the great hall.

"Aye, we've Perdita's surplus to unload," Pym muttered in English and let Blackheart guide him toward the glittering banquet tables where the businessmen were dining.

Jaki let them go and then immediately sought out Almeida and Lucinda on the dance floor. "May I have the next dance?" he asked in Spanish.

"Sir, we have not been introduced," said Lucinda Quarles, looking inquiringly into the sandy haze of Jaki's features. He was even more striking in person than he had looked to her in the lens that morning.

"My name is Jaki Gefjon."

"Then you are Dutch," she said, though she was certain she saw something else in his dusky complexion. "Are you with that man my father remembers as a traitor?"

"Yes, m'lady," Jaki answered, dolefully. "He is my captain."

Almeida snicked a cruel smile, but before he could speak, Lucinda said, "I need refreshment."

Almeida and Jaki offered their arms simultaneously, and she took both, but kept her eyes on the boy with the wind-sprung hair and the riddling blue stare. "May I boldly introduce myself? I am Lucinda Quarles."

"You are British," he said in English. "Macao is a long way from England."

"And you are far from the Low Countries," she answered in English, intrigued by his accent, which did not sound Dutch.

Almeida poured her a crystal of sherry and led her into a yellow pond of lanternlight away from the serving table. "The Dutch seem very comfortable in the presence of pirates," he remarked icily.

"I'm sure I don't know what you mean, sir," Jaki said.

A small laugh chimed from Lucinda. "I think Commander Almeida means to refer to the strenuous competition between the Dutch and the Portuguese in the Spice Islands."

"Lady, you surprise me with your political astuteness," Almeida said coolly.

"My mother died of plague when I was an infant," she explained, "and I was reared by my father. I speak most of the trade languages at his insistence. And lacking a son, he has schooled me in the politics of trade. I know something of the European powers' Asian interests. But I'm afraid I am wholly devoid of feminine virtues."

"Then my eyes do deceive me," Almeida said, smiling warmly, "for you seem the very shape of feminine excellence."

"Shape is the least of a woman's virtues," she smiled back and looked to Jaki. "Don't you think, Master Gefjon?"

"A woman shall compass a man," he said, and the sound of his words embraced her, so gentle did they seem.

"Ah me," Almeida groaned, "if you're going to quote the Bible, I am outdone. I would not have expected such rectitude from a pirate."

Jaki spoke in a dry voice: "You call me a pirate because my name is Dutch. Small reason."

Almeida studied the lanky man before him. "I call you a pirate because this lovely lady's father believes your captain to be so. That is why the Bantam of Siam invited Captain Quarles and his warship into these Asian waters, to help us cleanse our empire of its sickly parasites. Isn't that so, my lady?"

Lucinda saw a fiery haze ruddle Jaki's cheeks, and she laid a hand on his arm. "A pact has been made between the Bantam and the British Crown to combat piracy in Asia for the benefit of all empires. My father has been ordered by his Admiralty to stalk these pirates, especially the infamous Wyvern that has plundered trade vessels with impunity for decades now. But my father would not accuse anyone of piracy without direct knowledge."

The heron-faced servant appeared and whispered in Almeida's ear. "Please, my lady, excuse me," the officer said with a bow. "My governor requires my presence." He turned to Jaki. "Your ruse is pitiful, Dutchman."

"*Are* you a pirate?" Lucinda asked when they were alone.

"If I were, you would be my first prize."

She smiled coolly. "Now you sound like that Portuguese sycophant."

"Forgive me." He blushed and put a firm hand over hers where it still rested on his arm. "Though we've just met, Mistress Lucinda, I am drawn to you. I know that I like you very much."

"How can you know that, silly boy? You can't begin to know me."

"What is there to know?" He put a thumb on her chin. "When a man stands on a height, he can see for miles. Standing here with you, I see as far as my life can go."

"Bold, impetuous words for a pirate." A reckless feeling whirled up in her as she stared into his topaz face. "By which I mean, I believe you really *are* a pirate, Mister Gefjon. My father is convinced that your captain is the villain whose standard is a wyvern."

Jaki's heart jumped, and he looked quickly into the crowd for Pym and Blackheart.

"I'm afraid it's too late," she said playfully. "Your captain will soon be undone; there is no way out."

Jaki faced her. "We are all on journeys toward wounds," he said with an intensity that startled her. "You must think me a fool, but if my journey doesn't end tonight, will you grant me the favor of seeing you again?"

"Why?" She held him with a hard-eyed stare. "Because I have a pretty face?"

"You are pretty," Jaki said. "But behind your beauty I sense a strong soul — a soul worthy of love."

"Love?" Her pixie face opened to laugh, but she did not laugh. "What does a boy like you know of love?"

"I know nothing of love," Jaki acknowledged with a candor that stopped her laughter again. "But I feel that whatever I could know of love I will find in you."

"We have just introduced ourselves and already you speak of love." She compressed her lips and shook her head.

"Lady," Jaki said with an urgent squeeze of her hand, "please do not be swift in your judgment. I am a fool to speak like this with you, I admit that. I am a fool. But I know my heart — and though I do not know you yet, I feel so powerfully that I know you in my heart. Please, favor me with a chance to see you again."

She regarded him with her steady gaze. Always, she had played coquettishly, teasing viscounts, naval officers, and all manner of heroes in every major European port and across Asia. The game was all preciosity and insignificance; she had just turned sixteen and enjoyed the tender speeches, the merriment, the anonymous sensuality of men's eager attentions. She had lost her heart once — to the poet in Rome — and had not believed she could love again. But now, suddenly, this man — this boy — had enchanted her with his smile, his Asian eyes blue as an afternoon's emptiness. He was very different from the pale, skinny poet in Rome. She would not love him — she was determined. His melancholy accent would not move her. Her certitude gave her the strength to continue her game. "*The Fateful Sisters*' port in Asia is to be Singapore," she answered finally. "Perhaps we shall meet there one day."

"If I seek you out there," he whispered, "you will favor me?"

Her face shone with curiosity, ambivalence, and a hint of ardor. "Yes." She leaned closer and added, "As I favor all courtly gentlemen who seek my company."

"Expect me, then."

"I will be constant as the zodiac," she said flirtatiously.

Jaki spun away, sliding like a breeze through the crowd as he searched for Pym and Blackheart. He found them approaching the governor's chair and slid between them, whispering to Pym, "Quarles knows."

"So it seems, lad," Pym answered without looking at him.

"We must flee," Jaki said, crouching as if at the smell of a panther.

Blackheart put an arm about him and braced him taller. "Stand up, sorcerer," Pym commanded. "We are in the governor's house. He'll not butcher us here. Nor can we escape. Too many guards. We must brass this out — see how they play us."

The governor waved to them impatiently, and Pym stepped forward.

Quarles, seated to the left of the governor and Hsi Hang, did not rise when Pym approached. "Your happy gathering here has helped me to sell all of my surplus from Iduna," Pym said graciously to the governor. "Festivities like this inspire good trade. Now how can I be of service to you?"

"Quite directly, Captain Pym," the governor said. He nodded to the Chinese merchant beside him. "My estimable guest, Hsi Hang, has expected for three days now the arrival of a junk loaded with one hundred bars of bullion. The fact that it has not yet arrived indicates to us that it has been lost."

Pym responded with consternation. "A hundred bars of bullion is a great deal of wealth to entrust to one storm-fragile junk."

"We suspect that no storm has sunk the vessel," the governor replied. "In fact, we are quite certain that it has been plundered by pirates."

"How can you be so certain during monsoon season, governor?"

The governor turned his elegantly coifed head toward Quarles, and the British captain thrust out his bearded chin. "We had arranged with Hsi Hang to escort his gold vessel into Macao, but when we sailed out to meet her, all we found was wreckage. And not just storm flotsam. Hsi Hang's ship was destroyed by cannon. And that means pirates."

"How terribly unfortunate," Pym said, shaking his head sadly. "Perhaps now with you here, Captain Quarles, such villains will be expunged. Still, I do not see how I can help you with this particular loss, governor."

"Hmm, but you can, captain." The governor stroked his beard. "You see, your ship arrived from the direction and at the time that we expected Hsi Hang's gold."

"I'm afraid we saw no piracy on our journey here from Manila. The China Sea is no small body of water, sir."

"Captain Pym," Hsi Hang waved a long fingernail at him with barely restrained fury, "perhaps you have plundered my ship."

Pym reeled toward Hsi Hang. "Sir, you accuse me of piracy?" The lilting music stuttered to silence.

The governor waved for the orchestra to continue, and the air paislied with sweet sounds again. "Forgive us, captain," the governor said. "We are not accusing you, but we suspect you. How could we not? We are not fools. You bear the serpent brand of a traitor. Your ship is a sleek man-of-war. And you have arrived at the right time and from the right direction to have intercepted Hsi Hang's gold junk. All we are asking is that you disprove our allegation."

"And how can I possibly do that?"

"You will let us search *Silenos*," the governor demanded.

"Never!" Pym shouted. "I am the master of *Silenos* and a legate from Iduna. I will not allow a search party of vain, importunate accusers aboard my ship."

"Then you prove yourself a pirate!" Hsi Hang yapped.

Pym swung toward him, and Almeida leaped between them and shoved Pym backward. Jaki seized the officer and slapped him twice before Blackheart could pull him away.

"I will remind you that I can have you imprisoned and hanged for striking an imperial officer," the governor barked at Jaki.

Pym raised his hands softly as a priest. "Governor, Hsi Hang gravely insulted me. My officer was only protecting me from yours. I am, after all, a true legate of Iduna, which has freely shared its wealth with Portugal. We are not pirates, I assure you, and we will not be treated as such. After all, did you not invite us here by your own hand? Will you now show that hand to be deceitful and treat us, your guests, as criminals?"

The governor's placid face frowned deeply. "Very well. Your anger was provoked. But I insist your ship be searched. A hundred bars of bullion is at stake here. That is no small matter."

Pym dug deep within himself for the appropriate response and felt cold emptiness. His stomach turned, and Jaki read his distress.

"Our honor is no small matter, either," Jaki said sharply, stepping forward. "For us, it is more valuable than mere gold. I insist on satisfaction for your officer's insult." Blackheart grabbed Jaki's arm again, but the boy threw it off. "This is not the first time your officer has insulted me this evening. I have overlooked his verbal abuse more than once, but I cannot abide his physical abuse of my captain. I demand a duel. Now."

The governor grinned with disbelief. "Young Dutchman, clearly you are a fool. Your master has taken no grievance he did not himself inspire."

"So you say," Jaki answered, ignoring Blackheart's urgent protests. "But he dared assault the official legate of the kingdom I am sworn to serve. I will have satisfaction. And I will have it now."

Pym searched Jaki's expression for his true intent and saw the stony will in his set jaw and a narrow stare that was a plea of cunning. He understood. Here was their one chance to buy the time to escape. But Pym could not spend Jaki's life, and Jaki saw that now in the sudden squint of his one eye. And so he turned brusquely and slapped Almeida's cheek. A blood-hungry light flashed in the officer's face, and he looked urgently to his superior.

"So, Dutchman, your death will be our amusement tonight," the governor decreed. "To the courtyard with you both, where you will not offend the women and those disinclined to see a life thrown away."

Almeida swept his arm toward the exit, and Jaki stalked off without glancing at Pym or Blackheart.

"He's a dead man," Pym mumbled, and pulled Blackheart to him. "We must not waste his death. Back to *Silenos* with you. Prepare to weigh anchor. We sail at once."

Blackheart's face was taut with desperation.

"No," Pym insisted, "there is nothing we can do for him. He's given us his death freely. Don't waste it. Go!"

Quarles sidled up to Pym. "That foolish boy hasn't bought your escape, traitor. My ship has orders to watch *Silenos*. If she tries to sail, I will blow her out of the harbor." He barged through the crowd that was hurrying to see the duel.

Pym arrived in the torchlit courtyard in time to see Jaki kick away his shoes and peel off his socks. Laughter twitched through the encircling crowd, but Almeida was not amused. Like the professional soldier he was, he stood bolt upright at the center of the cobbled yard, rapier drawn and pointing down, a gold thread of death in the flame light. The governor and Hsi Hang stood side by side under a lantern's radiant circle, but Quarles was not to be seen; Pym knew he would be hurrying back to *The Fateful Sisters* to be certain *Silenos* did not escape. Quarles's daughter was there, though, with a worried maid at her side. The young lady was watching boldly, though her features seemed filled with emotion.

Jaki stood ready and raised his rapier in salute. Almeida returned the salute with a sardonic grin, and they crossed blades. The Portuguese looked relaxed and poised, and Pym's bowels crawled with cold to see Jaki's hunched and amateurish posture. Almeida stamped forward swiftly, thrusting to skewer Jaki even before he could move. But the boy was gone, dancing sidewise with a swiftness that elicited a collective sigh from the crowd. His rapier flashed and scored air. Almeida had pivoted and come up under Jaki's extended swordarm, and only Jaki's great speed saved him again. Their rapiers spanged, and Jaki jumped away.

The fear coursing through Jaki gleamed brighter. His enemy seemed made of liquid in the firelight, sliding sinuously through the shadows. Jaki wanted to succumb to the animal instinct burgeoning in his nerves, but he knew that if he did, he would lose the delicate control necessary to win a formal duel. He could not be an animal now. He had to fight as a man, a man of his father's ilk. But this man in him was naked with terror.

Almeida pursued, lashing in a feint and jabbing. The deceptive shadows lured Jaki into his enemy's slide. Pym saw the miscalculation and cried out as Almeida's blade pierced Jaki's left shoulder.

Jaki wobbled quickly away, blood squirting from his gouged flesh. Then in midstride backward, he hurled forward, fluid as the pure release of an arrow, but ill timed, giving Almeida the margin to dodge. The swordmaster closed in at once, and Jaki parried downward. Their swords clacked, and for an instant they stood facing each other in a scuffling lock. Almeida grinned disdainfully, shifted his weight, and sent Jaki flying past him. The Portuguese whipped his rapier and spanked Jaki as he flew by.

The crowd keened with laughter. Jaki spun about, stung and angry, and glimpsed Pym in the swarm of faces, shaking his head. The pirate held one hand up, and Jaki reined in his rage. Ignoring the sting across his buttocks, he stepped to the attack slowly, watching his opponent's ink-dark eyes.

Almeida was a blur in the torchlight, determined to kill Jaki quickly now while he was still smarting with humiliation. But Jaki had dropped that pain, and with blinding defensive speed he caught his opponent's cutover, lifted his rapier, and delved sharply, scoring Almeida's cheek and sending him skidding backward, hand to face.

The mocking grin was gone from the swordmaster's lips when he closed again, and he assaulted remorselessly. Jaki met each of his blows, sliding backward and to his left — and then he was gone. He pounced to his right, crouched, and thrust upward, scoring Almeida again, this time in the hip.

The officer backed off, awareness dawning that though this Dutchman was not a skilled swordsman, he was a deadly fighter.

The man swung his rapier in a tight circle, focusing all his lethal intent on each movement. The swords touched with a rattle, and Jaki sprang to the side and slashed.

"Foul!" Almeida called out, and the crowd murmured their agreement. "Stand and fight, Dutchman!"

"Engage!" the governor commanded.

Jaki crept closer, suppressing his shouting instincts, and touched metal. "You cannot flee your death, pirate," Almeida said, and jumped, both feet flying forward, sword snaking out and up.

Jaki stood fast, managing to bring his sword up just before the enemy's point reached his heart. Metal sang, and with a frantic clashing Jaki pressed the fight. "Death is no secret!" he shouted, shooting stars of sweat flicking from his face. In his desperation, he had shouted in his native tongue, and the sound barbed him with all the hopelessness of his lost life in the forest. Abandoning all mental intent, he surrendered to his emotion, the release of that power propelling him mightily through the shadows. Only Almeida's expertise with the rapier kept him upright before Jaki's stunningly swift blows.

Almeida scrambled backward, forgetting his footwork, desperately seeking a fatal chink — and when it appeared, he thrust for it. His blade split Jaki's rib and would have skewered his heart had Jaki not already disoriented his opponent with the fury of his attack. The sword-tip slipped off his nicked rib and gouged the air beside him. Enduring his wound and heaving himself into it, believing, as he had with the Spider, that he was already lost, Jaki surprised Almeida, caught him unready to parry, and thrust his rapier through the man's chest.

Almeida shrieked and collapsed face down, gasping blood. The crowd roared and surged forward.

Pym shoved through the throng to Jaki's side and swept him up in his thick arms. He was badly shaken, soaked through with sweat, leaking blood from his shoulder wound and split rib. Pym yelled for the crowd to make way, but the governor pressed to Pym's side. "You are a sloppy swordsman," he said bitterly. "You won by rage alone."

"Yet he won," Pym said with hot admiration. "Now stand aside. He's wounded and needs tending." Pym sheathed the bloody rapier, threw Jaki's arm over his neck, and walked him through the crowd to the tall open doors of the yard.

Lucinda Quarles stood under the red mane of a torch, her face aglow with excitement and relief. Her maid was gripping her shoulders from behind, trying to move her away, but she stood fast, and when Jaki passed, she held out her hand.

Jaki stopped before her, his wild gaze softening at the sight of her face. "Time is blood now, lad," Pym whispered in his ear.

"Your journey continues," Lucinda said, holding her hand higher so he could see the amber brooch she held. "Take this as an emblem of your victory tonight — and as a hope that we may meet again."

Jaki accepted the brooch, and before he could speak, Pym hauled him away.

Pym ran with Jaki in his arms through the rainwet boulevards to the harbor. Each jolt was the lonesome singing of Jaki's life against the vaulting silence of death. The sky of fire behind his eyelids was shadowed with the souls of the men he had killed. Almeida's surprised black stare was closest, but his face was already receding with each belt of pain that assured Jaki that *he* was alive. Other eyes watched from the shadowy flames behind Almeida's deathmask — the faceless souls of the Mongols he had slaughtered on Hsi Hang's junk. And behind them were the merest glints in the nightrock of eternity, the dim ghosts of the Lanun he had slain and the Tree Haunter warriors he had trampled and brained. Batuh was there, a shadow in the face of the night, and behind him the vague shades of the first men he killed, the Tree Haunters he had speared to save himself and Ferang. His life, his pain, was carried by these deaths. His life was the manifest spirit of these dead. And all this was so, he believed, because he had abandoned the Life to find his place in the tribe, to be a man as other men.

The harbor air was dewy with the redolence of the sea. "Blackheart's ready for us," Pym said, guiding Jaki out onto the pier and into a waiting skiff.

Pym rowed, and Jaki lay back. "We'd not be here now without your risk," Pym said as he bent to the oars. "That dago governor was determined to board *Silenos*. But in the hubbub you left behind, he'll not gather his guard till we hoist anchor. Well done, lad. You handled that rapier like a born swordsman. I'll not call you a son again. From now, Jaki Gefjon, you are my brother."

At *Silenos* Jaki was hoisted aboard in a sling and laid out on the deck, while Saja examined him and determined that the wounds had cut no organs.

"Release the floaters, Mister Blackheart," Pym ordered when Saja was through. "The tide's coming in, and it will do most of our fighting for us." He trained his spyglass on *The Fateful Sisters* and saw the cannon, fifty big guns aimed at them. But the night was starless, and *Silenos* was a black target; even the best gunner would have trouble marking the range. Then he saw Quarles in the blazing lanternlight, watching them through his telescope. Certainly he would see the floaters that even now were being lowered overboard. Would he guess their lethal intent?

"Blackheart, throw over the bales of spice we collected in Manila. Let him think we're lightening for a run. And let's pray he holds his fire till we show canvas."

Minutes later when the first of the floating powder kegs reached *The Fateful Sisters*, Quarles ordered one retrieved to see what Pym was dumping. A grapnel line was thrown to it, the matchlock triggers were sprung, and the keg of corned powder exploded, sweeping several of the other mines into the hull of the big ship. A string of blasts ripped the night in rapid succession.

"Anchor aweigh!" Pym shouted with the first explosion. "Canvas!"

Silenos rose against the tide, caught wind with her black sails, and cruised toward the night sea. Behind her, the tide had carried the rest of the mines into the harbor and among the other ships. Fiery bursts tore apart the wharves and sundered the smaller ships clustered alongside Quarles's pirate hunter. *The Fateful Sisters* fired twelve rounds, but the blasts that had ripped her broadsides and flooded her lower decks spoiled the cannons' ordinance, and the fifty-pound balls splashed wildly in the bay.

Pym spied Quarles through his glass, flailing across his quarterdeck, shouting commands with frustrated ardor. The pirate captain howled with pleasure and ordered his cannon to fire a salute. The cannon spat fire and thunder, and Pym saw Quarles lean on the rail in an anguish of rage, watching *Silenos* draw away into the darkness and stormsmoke.

Blind with fury, Quarles stalked the busy main deck, and frightened sailors flitted out of his way, disappearing down holds and into companionways. The captain steadied himself on the starboard gunnel and glanced down at the scorched and shattered timbers along the hull.

The damage to *The Fateful Sisters* was slight but sufficient to prevent pursuit of *Silenos*. The pirate had escaped him. *Escape!* The thought branded his soul, but the floating mines had substantiated Quarles's suspicion that Pym was the infamous Wyvern; and now trade ports everywhere would be closed to Iduna and Quarles could stalk Pym freely.

"I will hang him from my own ship's yardarm," he swore aloud. "Pym has *not* escaped. There is no escape in this round world. I will run him down. And I will have him dead."

Quarles's words burned through him with the heat of a lifelong anguish. All his life he had raged against fate. Determined to avenge his family's suffering by regaining all that had been lost, he had become a model seaman and had earned a navigator's rank by his twentieth birthday. In 1607, royal friends of his fallen uncle had arranged for him to sail as a master mariner with King James's flotilla to supervise a truce between Denmark and Sweden. In Copenhagen, he met and married a wealthy merchant's daughter, and with his new fortune and the esteem he had won from his service to the king, he had attained the captaincy of his first vessel and sailed profitable trade routes from the North Sea to the Mediterranean.

For several years, Quarles's spite seemed wholly used up, leaving him an affluent and content man. He purchased back the estate in Devon where he had been born, the ancestral lands that had been lost early in his childhood, and he gloated that he had reclaimed his past without benefit of college or inheritance.

Then in 1610, the year his daughter was born, plague killed his wife in La Spezia. He had been at fault — he believed that to this day — because he had let her stay by his side when trade had brought him to the stricken port long after all other ships had fled. What success he had gained for himself in La Spezia had cost him his wife, the quiet, patient Dane who had taught him true felicity.

The next sixteen years had been a furor of withheld wrath at the injustice of creation. Committed to wresting order — his personal order — out of the chaos of his loss, Quarles refused to relinquish his daughter to his wife's parents in Denmark and took her and her maid with him on all his voyages. She was all he had left of family, and he was determined to make her worthy of the fortune he had devoted his life to creating. He spent his mounting wealth freely on her. The finest clothing and jewels were hers from infancy. Yet as soon as she could walk, she wanted nothing more than to be everywhere that he was. He indulged her even in that, and the toddler witnessed his brilliantly stern command of his ship and learned early the exigencies of will.

In her seventh year, Lucinda's nanny had been replaced by a maid her own age. Maud Rufoote was a little peasant girl from his Devon estate, who had been reared by her Aunt Timotha, a woman wise in herbal medicines. Quarles personally assumed responsibility for his daughter's education. But his resolution to imprint her with his jaded wisdom clashed with the romance of illusion that is every child's gift, and he forbade her any dreams but the most pragmatic and tactical. Lucinda was a willful child, however, and though she mastered her father's lessons in languages, mathematics, and cynicism, she would not relinquish her faith in inspiration, the heart's revelation — love.

As Lucinda grew into womanhood, they were constantly at odds, for she shamelessly opposed all the advantageous marriages with merchants' sons and noble-blooded officers that Quarles tried to plot for her happiness and security. She insisted that she would choose her own husband.

Remembering the dreamy look on Lucinda's face as she conversed with the blond pirate at the governor's ball, Quarles headed for her cabin to have it out with her. At the companionway he lifted his face into the stiffening wind and thought he could taste the heat of a typhoon. Time enough to discipline Lucinda, he reasoned, sensing threat in the hot wind. A new irony occurred to him: perhaps Pym's flight into the jaws of the big storm was his doom, and heaven would seize revenge from Quarles. He did not want Pym killed that way, for there was something vital he had to learn from the pirate first.

Years before, shortly after Quarles had been awarded his first captaincy, he was confronted aboard his docked vessel one day by several well-dressed men who claimed to be secretaries for a secret society to which his uncle, Samuel Quarles, had belonged. The society was called the Church of the Two Thieves, an interkingdom organization of affluent and influential gentlemen with papal connections. The Quarles family had been Roman Catholic from Norman times, but William, early in adulthood, had converted to the Church of England to gain favor in the court. He wanted no contact with the papists. But before they left, the men prevailed on him to examine correspondence between the Spanish governor of Cartagena and his Uncle Samuel that disclosed the betrayal by his uncle of Drake's war fleet during its 1585 raid of the Spanish Main.

Quarles refused to believe the documents. The letters were never revealed to the government or the public, and no effort was made by the papists to blackmail him. Any such effort would have failed as his fortune had been secured entirely by his own hard work and he was helpless to account for the honor of an uncle he barely knew. But from that day, the passion for revenge that had driven him cooled to mere cunning, and nothing again was ever what it seemed.

Pym hotly declared his own innocence in the governor's palace, and his protest hinted at a dark truth. Pym remained a scoundrel in any case, for he was still responsible for the murder of Drake in 1596 and for decades of piracy. But Quarles wanted to know what had really happened.

Then, three years ago, the secret society had divulged Trevor Pym's presence in Asia. A juvenile excitement gripped Quarles when he heard this, and he used all his accumulated favor and prestige to arrange a diplomatic mission to Asia. He was no longer certain that Pym had been responsible for his uncle's misfortune and his own indigent youth, but he was determined to find out. The very idea of advancing his career at Pym's expense inspired him in his plea to the Admiralty for an Asian assignment, and he was appointed captain of a modern warship, *The Fateful Sisters,* and dispatched to Asia to establish contacts of trade amidst the aggressive claims of the other European powers.

Not a day of the yearlong trading voyage around Africa, Arabia, and India to Siam and Malaysia had passed without Quarles anticipating his confrontation with the snakebranded pirate, and now fate threatened to cheat him once again.

As he clomped down the narrow stairway, the bustling sailors hauling pails of sand to the fires fell away from him as from a lion. He did not see them. His mind was already in the map room, intent on learning the precise location of the kingdom of Iduna.

The monsoon rains battered *Silenos,* shredded sails, cracked timber, swept men overboard, and would have sunk her had not her captain's will been as dark as the storm's. Pym had weathered gales at sea before, and he knew when to let the windy angels command his ship and when to defy them. As soon as *Silenos* had arrived in Panay and Hsi Hang's gold was melted, coined, and distributed, he was itching to sail again, to plunder the spice vessels in the Moluccas. But the crew, harrowed by the stormy crossing and the terrible apparition of *The Fateful Sisters,* were afraid. Few of the ablest seamen reenlisted with Pym; most believed his pirating days were spent, and they disbanded and took their wealth with them, some to Europe and the others to the small kingdoms of Asia where they could take up new lives as merchants, estate owners, and shipping potentates. Unable to find enough skilled sailors to replace them, Pym moped in the grand mansion of Iduna, drinking himself into a stupor, usually before noon.

Though Pym loved Perdita, he was a troubled man, haunted by the memories of all the men he had killed and seen killed. His own shame and fury — though greatly diminished since Jaki had relieved his eye-pain — was too onerous to allow him a gentle life. Each breath was a rage against the arbitrary authority of those who had stripped him of his dignity. And now that most of his pirate crew had abandoned him, he was bereft. He would need massive sums of money to induce sea-worthy men to sail with him — and he did not have those sums, unless he took back what he had already given Perdita, the very thought of which sickened him more than entrusting his beloved *Silenos* to an inept crew. Briefly, he toyed with the idea of borrowing the money from his wife, but he could not do that. Perdita ran her island kingdom as a Christian empire, and though he knew she would give him the money, he also knew she would be troubled by the thought of supporting his unholy adventures. Receiving his ill-gotten booty was a way of redeeming it, for she poured it all into her Christian dynasty, but lending the sanctified money back would make her complicit in his hellbent war against humanity. Stymied, he sulked and stewed, made even more restless by the fact that Quarles now knew his homeport was Iduna. Months passed, however, and the sentries posted at the promontories of Panay never sighted the fierce British destroyer.

Jaki fished and hunted with Blackheart to avoid Perdita's flirtations and Pym's dark moods. He fashioned a thumb ring of the amber brooch Lucinda Quarles had given him, and he fantasized about shipping himself to Singapore to find her. But that was death. Riri had taught him that. If Lucinda was to be his woman, the Life would lead him to her. So he contented himself with fishing the ancient rivers and wandering the jungle valleys with Blackheart and Wawa. Then one morning, in a tunnel of jungle fog, he remembered Njurat and his legacy as Matubrembrem, the last of the sorcerers.

"You want plunder?" he asked Pym over lunch that day. "I can lead you to a chamber filled with diamonds."

Pym lowered his glass. "Where?"

"Borneo."

"What is this treasure — and how can we get it with only half a crew?"

"The treasure belongs to me," Jaki told him. "I am Matubrembrem, the son of the devil and heir to the misfortunes and wealth of my tribal people. These diamonds to them are mountains' tears, shed for the grief in the clouds' spelled stories. All we need do is go to the mountaintop cave where these diamonds are kept and take them. No one will dispute my claim to them. No fighting is necessary. We need only enough crew to sail *Silenos* to the north coast of Borneo. I can lead us from there."

"How many diamonds?"

"Enough to buy a fleet of ships. Enough to build an empire of our own."

"And Perdita —"

"You know yourself that she will be safer from Quarles if you are not here when he arrives," Jaki reasoned. "Iduna is a sovereign kingdom and amply armed."

Pym's shark grin came and went. "Hmm, even if we succeed in getting the diamonds, we face the challenge of transporting them back here without a full crew."

"That's a challenge for a man the likes of Trevor Pym."

Pym fixed Jaki with a cloudgray stare. "Is it the Life?"

"For a pirate."

Pym swept the tabletop clear with a glass-shattering sweep of his arm and lurched upright. "To Borneo!"

With a skeleton crew, *Silenos* avoided the busy sea lanes of the Sulu Sea and sailed through the Cuyo Archipelago. The sky was ribbed with clouds the afternoon they drifted into a cliffhung cove on Borneo's north shore. No signs of the Muslim tribes had been seen for miles, and Jaki stood in the forecastle and shouted the traditional sorcerer's greeting into the whickering wind: "People of the forest, hear me! I am the soul-taker from the spirit world outside the tribes! I watch the clouds in the hands of heaven with their backs to the earth. I read the prophecy that returns with the rains. I am Matubrembrem — and I have returned to take what is mine. Show yourselves!"

A *kavon* bleated from the cliffs, and an answering cry spooled down with the wind. Jaki recognized the call of a western tribe that he and Jabalwan had once visited, and the legend of his early life brightened in him. He called down the tribe, and by sunfall, the beach was lit with a huge fire, and the pirate crew, who had never seen true forest people before, were being feted and regally entertained.

The savages, in their fur pelts, colorful plumes, and gleaming zigzag painted bodies, looked dangerously fierce to the pirates. They moved to the rhythms of their drums and gongs like licks of fire. When Jaki danced with them, incorporeal as smoke, Pym and Blackheart recognized the unpredictable movements of his fighting style — but all else that was familiar about him vanished, and he became a sinuous shape of flame in the ancestral night.

Once the feast was over, the crew retreated to *Silenos*, but Jaki stayed with the people, chanting the incantations Jabalwan had taught him in the light of the dying fire. The tribe wanted him to return with them to their longhouse to visit with the ailing, but he would not. He had come to escort the one-eyed monkey god straight up into the mountains to retrieve the mountains' tears and take away as much of the land's suffering as they could carry. Jaki's life as a jungle sorcerer was over, ended at the Snakehunter's Grave when the Lanun killed him. Since then, he explained, he had been reborn in the sea world of his fathers where the Life was teaching him new mysteries.

He did not tell them of his nostalgia for the forest. Smelling the orchid smoke coiling with the night breezes, he thought of returning to the jungle and staying. The amber ring on his thumb itched at those wistful thoughts, and he knew then he could never go back. *Freedom is effort,* he heard an echo of Jabalwan's voice in his memory. If he stayed, he would never be free. Even returning for this adventure was dangerous. Here the future was still unbegun and the past demanding, stronger than hope, stronger than question, almost stronger than life. The asphodel ring and its promise of a life of love, a future with a woman who would complete him as a man, was his talisman against the allure of the past. He clutched it to his breast, and Jabalwan's ghost-voice sharpened: *Freedom is effort — and it feeds on our hearts.*

At dawn, Pym relinquished command of *Silenos* to Blackheart with instructions to sail for Iduna if he did not return after the span of a moon. He selected three hardy sailors and rowed to the beach to meet Jaki. The forest people had taken Jaki's European clothes and given him a pantherskin loincloth and an anklet of tortoiseshell and snake sinew so he could strap his metal knife to his calf. He rubbed his blowgun with nut oil so it gleamed, and sharpened the white edge of the bamboo speartip. He had painted his body green and yellow with black contour lines, so that his limbs and torso were serpent slick and the bones of his face were skullsharp.

Pym faced him now with a tremor of apprehension. He seemed alien; only his blue eyes distinguished him from the heathens who surrounded him with proprietary closeness. The men with hair coarse as coconut fur and broad, flat, ugly features had empty, animal eyes.

"You look fearsome, lad," Pym said, his hand on his cutlass.

"This is a fierce land," Jaki told him, and handed him a gourd packed with yellow paste. "You'd best paint your hands and face with this, captain. Otherwise the insects will eat you before we get to the mountains."

The forest people led them into the jungle, and Pym and his men clung closely to Jaki, who seemed to grow thinner and almost transparent in the pelagic light.

Wawa flew through the canopy, ecstatic to be home after more than a year away, and he pounced upon favorite fruits and insects. Pym watched the gibbon disappear into the heights, and though he was accustomed to staring into the very cope of heaven from the topmast crosstrees, he dizzied to look up at the towering trees. He was a mite among the buttressed roots of these giants. Ant nests chimneyed taller than men, bromelias dangled in the gloom like hairy hung heads, and huge blood-red flowers with the stench of rotting meat hazed the air with flies.

Subhuman masks glared at them from the chaos of vines and air plants — monkey troops aghast at their trespass, screeching and barking and scattering into the verdant shadows. Fretful birdcalls tolled and clicked like mad knitting needles. Jaki whistled, and the noise ceased. An eagle flapped through the sunshafts and alighted on a thin branch above them, watching. Jaki whistled again, and it cocked an eye and whistled back at him before lofting above the canopy. Pym was clearly impressed. Jaki smiled to see the formidable pirate captain big-eyed with reverence.

The men slept that night on the leaf beds Jaki prepared for them, and after they were asleep he climbed up into the canopy and watched the stars feeding on the darkness, looking for a sign that what he had come to do was acceptable to the spirits of the sorcerers who had preceded him. The bone of moon set, and bats whirred. "What is hidden everywhere," he murmured in the darkness, "cannot be lost. Jabalwan, my teacher — are you anywhere but everywhere?" No sign came. A star fell, and clouds freighted by in black windwaves. No good omen showed itself — but then no bad one, either.

Days led the party through the forest; nights submerged them in exhausted sleep. Nine days after leaving the ship, they reached the steep trails that led up into the mountains and the sorcerers' high roads. The pirates were glad to leave the steamy jungle behind and feel again the commotions of the wind.

From his nearly fatal first visit to Njurat, Jaki remembered to bring an ample supply of water, and the cold desert crossing was less arduous than he had feared. They arrived at the hot spring oasis after only two days and a night on the barren slopes. But instead of the precarious chute Jaki originally had had to climb to enter Njurat, a grassy path led them into the paradisial grotto of willow and cypress trees.

Pym danced a jig on a blue moss sward and his men yodeled their amazement at this garden on the roof of the world. The pirates followed Jaki charily through the scaly fern trees and among the boiling mud pools to the crater rim paths, where pink, long-legged birds faced them fearlessly. Wawa rushed ahead into the warmth, and Jaki waited for him to call out the presence of other men. But the gibbon saw no others. They were alone in Njurat.

While the men luxuriated in the grove, Jaki and Pym searched for a way into the mountain of black slabs that backed the grotto. Together they crawled down into the fissure before the narrow cave entrance where Jaki had once deceptively refused the strong eye. Pym shook his head at the tight passage. "I'd never fit through there." Toward sundown they finally found the rockslab door that Jaki had exited through on his last visit, and Pym hollered for his men. Together, bent-shouldered against the rock, they nudged the monolith open a crack, just wide enough for them to squeeze through singly. The air smelled baked, and the men hesitated. "It's almost night," one of them breathed, and gestured to the apocalypse of sunfire and rain clouds on the mountain-finned horizon.

"It is always night where we are going," Jaki said, and led the way in. Pym grabbed the back of his loincloth and followed. The others edged after him, clutching on to each other's clothes.

Jaki fastened candles to the speartip of his blowgun and held the bright flame ahead of them. In the flimmering light, the stone walls looked glassy with rocksweat. Jaki and the pirates stepped lightly, yet the startled echoes of their movements throbbed like old aches. The tongues of candleflame wagged with the air sighing through the open portal, then went perfectly still as they moved deeper into the dark. The ground sloped around curves of leprous boulders and drool-shaped stalactites and pillars.

The darkness went darker as the walls fell away, and they entered a giant cavern. Jaki recognized the dragon pit where he had confronted the immense stone-shaped lizard skull and her brood of hatched eggs. The resin candles threw too weak a light to illuminate the pit, and Jaki led the men around the depression toward the corridor where the torches were kept.

All at once, the channels grooved into the rock floor ran with blue fire. Icy flames circled the cavern, and the bowl of oil in the pit ignited brightly. The grimacing dragon skull lunged from the darkness, ablaze in the blue light. Pym and his men shouted — the giant skull was the horrifying actuality of Wyvern, their emblem made real. "Truly this is the ninth circle," Pym gasped. "Where in this hell of hells are the diamonds?"

Jaki shook his head and pointed down. Human figures stood in the pit, their faces stark white, tempestuous ghost shadows, their eyes jerking with sparks.

Two of the crewmen screamed at the sight of the numbfaced specters, and one bolted, arms flailing. A dart struck him in the back of the neck, and he dropped, choked on a scream, and lay still.

"Don't move!" Jaki said, laying down his spear. "Take off your sword belts — quickly!"

Pym and the two sailors, numb with fright, unbuckled their swords and dropped them. The impassive white faces of the dozen men in the pit were fixed on Jaki. One of them spoke, and though they could not understand him, the pirates heard the stern command in his voice.

"Matubrembrem, you have returned for one purpose," the skull-painted face said.

"You know my purpose, soul-catcher?" Jaki asked, desperately trying to keep his voice steady.

"We know." The dozen faces looked like submerged bones in the wavery light. "We have waited for you from the beginning of time. You are the last of the sorcerers, the orphaned son, fathered of strange seed. The prophecies minted you in the pitiful first days of creation. You are the one who has shamelessly chosen death before the Life. In you, the prophecies have become history. Now we are the ghosts, dutiless in the sunken world. And you are what is left. You are the desperate life of the end, getting and forgetting all that we have been. Thus we knew that you would return. For you did not fulfill the prophecy here at the center of the world. You did not meet the mother of life." The soul-catcher raised skeletal arms to the enormous monster head slavering over her broodlings. "And the proud blood of the earth will not be denied."

"What does the mother of life want of me?" Jaki asked, his voice flat now with resignation.

"What you denied her when you were last here, with Jabalwan." The dozen men each held up a wafer of bread speckled with dark color. "The strong eye."

Jaki had scanned the chamber while the soul-catcher was speaking, and he had spotted the warriors in the rock crevices who had killed the fleeing crewman. Escape was unthinkable. The choice was death or the strong eye.

"I am Matubrembrem," he said forcefully, feeling the alertness in the many watchful eyes. "I have come to fulfill the prophecy. Escort these three men out of here, and I will wear the strong eye."

"Matubrembrem and the devil gods who have accompanied him will wear the strong eye," the soul-catcher said, stepping up from the pit and holding out the wafer of mushroom bread. "The mother of life will decide who leaves the center of the world — and who stays."

Jaki turned to Pym and the two crewmen, who were being seized by the sorcerers and were looking to him with anguished incomprehension. "They will not harm you," he told them urgently, "if you do exactly as they command. They want you to eat their mushroom bread."

"That's all?" one of the crewmen blurted, his face warping with withheld tears.

"It stinks of poison," Pym protested as the wafer was held before his lips.

"It is not a poison," Jaki assured them. "But it is a dreaming mushroom that is mixed with the bread. We will be sick together. But I promise you, no harm will come to you if you stay calm and let the mushroom have its way."

The crewmen whimpered and opened their mouths as the skeletal sorcerers pinned their arms behind them. Pym struggled, and his arms were twisted sharply until he screamed and the bread stoppered his cry. Jaki, being a sorcerer himself, was allowed to touch the holy bread with his hands, and he remembered with regret the strong eye that Jabalwan had presented to him on his first visit to Njurat and that he had slyly discarded. He ate the wafer that was given him — and was handed another.

"You will kill us," he said, staring harshly into the witchery of the soul-catcher's painted face.

"The mother of life will decide that, Matubrembrem."

Jaki ate the wafer, and another was handed to him. He ate that one, and accepted a fourth, then was led down into the pit and made to sit among the hatched eggs under the dragon mother. The pirates, too, were forced to eat four wafers, then brought into the pit and seated beside the bowl of blue-burning oil.

"You will stay here until the mother frees you," the sorcerer told Jaki. "If any of you vomits, you will be killed." He gestured to the twisted corpse of the pirate. "Now, devil's child, you will finally hear the prophecy you are perfecting, spoken as it came to us from the first sorcerers."

The ghost-painted native closed his eyes and intoned with ritual zeal: "The end circles from the beginning through the smoke of the air. The living dead arrive from across the sea, from the long night of the north, and the end circles from the beginning. Their history is the death of kings. Their god is a dead king. They bring with them the north bound in bright stone. They melt the north like wax. They melt the north and shape it into spears harder than stone. Their spears kill without leaving their hands. They are death's promise. Their hearts are axes. Their faces are flame-shaped. They strengthen our enemies. They defeat us. The dead are their triumph. They spawn on our women witnesses to our end — devil children whose eyes are the shadow of the sky, whose eyes are the color of tears. One will choose the Life above his mother and leave her though he is her only child, fathered of the living dead. When he appears, the bright anniversaries written on the clouds will be at their end. He will be the last of the people of the waking dream. He will be the end of revelation and shamelessly choose death before the Life. But he will look twice and see the many-born in the black night of the blood. He will see the end that is fire and the love that imagines the world and the wish of love that closes the world in fire. He meets us in Heaven's Flight where the future gathers its pieces. He meets us on the sacred ways in the meeting place of end and beginning. And mystery will descend with him and reclaim the ancestors. And the people of the waking dream will be no more."

The soul-catcher walked into the shadows, and the grotto shook, sizzling with trickles of loosened dirt. Jaki stared into the cowl of darkness above them. Vaporous colors flitted through the shadows, and a wave of nausea mounted in him. He knew that too much of the dreaming mushroom provoked convulsions, paralyzed breathing, and killed. But what could they do now? They would have to trust in the mushroom.

"I feel sick," one of the crewmen moaned.

"You must stay calm," Jaki said to him, laying a hand on his arm. The man's flesh was chilled and ripply with turgid energy. "Do not give in to your sickness. If we foul this sacred place, surely we will be killed. Stay calm. Soon the dreaming will pass. Remember that. Nothing you see now is real."

His words sounded muffled by the mourning noise of his heart. Pym was watching him with a sharp, knowing eye. They were going to die, and he would not be deceived.

Vertigo seized Jaki, and he had to lie back into the fathomless funnel of gravity. The ground below them was trembling — or his bones were vibrating. He gazed about wildly. A smell of death troubled his nostrils, a broken stink. A hysterical struggle ensued between his pounding heart and his breathing. He could no longer tell if he was drawing breath or exhaling, and fear howled in him.

The pirates were chattering with cold, clutching at one another and rocking. Pym had locked his face in his hands and was shaking with sobs. Jaki's muscles clenched and shivered, stropped with hot iciness. *Ease!* he commanded himself, but his body doubled up with extravagant pain. All of them were curled up now, squeezed tightly into their suffering.

Time was spasmodic. Seconds gonged for hours, blackening them with pain. Hours were a whirlwind, billowy with colors. Jaki strained against the constricted straps of his muscles and straightened enough to see the others hunched over their suffering. Fumes of radiance wafted from their quaking bodies. He looked away and zoomed in a spindrift of foaming brilliance toward the blankness of the medicine cloud. *That way is death,* he realized, and pulled back. The nightmare face of the dragon loomed over him, and he turned away. The chamber was a stormy racket of colors, spider spume, night-thick roaring, and the lonely splendor of his canceled life. The crystal air was bleeding him, and he saw again the medicine cloud and within it the Longhouse of Souls. One-eyed Pym was there, as he had been in Jaki's earlier visions, but not frightening now that Jaki knew the viper-browed pirate. In his vision they were sitting beside the cooking pot. The two other pirates were lolling there, too. They were alone, but the souls of the dead sorcerers were just visible through the wide windows, wandering into the midnight mist outside the Longhouse of Souls.

Jaki recognized Jabalwan. The sorcerer had his arm around a woman, urging her into the dark of the past. Her eyes were crystal, her hair the ash of twilight, and her flesh so long dead that it was the silver-black of the space between the horns of the moon. She had to be Mala — but she was gone . . . The others, just glimpsed, had vanished. Jaki looked back to the cooking pot, age-old black with soot from a fire that had blazed unremittingly for centuries. The fire was out. Inside the pot was a glowing lump of melted flesh. The glutinous lump stirred, and a troll's eyes opened painfully in a syrupy face. *Eat me,* a tortured voice begged, its mouth a burst blister.

Jaki yanked himself against the nightmare's horror and toppled out of the medicine cloud back into the dragon pit. He looked himself over, relieved to be awake. His hands were white, slack as dead meat. The skull face in the hatched egg beside him bayed with despair and shape-shifted in dazzling pastels to a murderous worm gnawing at his dead hands. The foul fiend ravenously chewed his ruined life, and he cried with torment.

Ease, Matu. The voice was Jabalwan's, casual as moonlight. *The prophecy is fulfilled. You have seen the end that is fire. The Longhouse of Souls is empty at last. Look at the mother. Look at her without desire or denial. Look at the face of life!*

The worm eating his hands had withered to a vanquished skeleton in an aura of sunlight. He rolled to his back and looked up at the mother of the earth. Terror staggered him. She was alive, knotted with flesh, her long fangs beseeching blood, her sockets swiveling with gelled sight, and her head and limbs prosperous with movement. He slammed his head backward, trying to squirm away from her, but his fastest reflexes were tiny before her gargantuan presence. Her mad face dipped, fangs gnashing, and she grabbed one of the crewmen. Jaki saw the man writhe like a hawk-snagged mouse, flapping with pain.

Jaki screamed, trying to stir Pym and the other two, but his cry was ash. The cavern was so loud with raucous noise, his yell had the beat of silence.

Why don't you listen to me? Jabalwan pleaded. *Look at the mother. Her beauty is terrible. She is the Life's beauty — the left side of the blood — what gives when we take back — what remains when nothing is left — primitive magic — mother of us all — night crawler — the beloved life and the unsparing hunger that takes no for an answer. Look at her, little man, corpse-to-be, look at her and see the terrible beauty of all departure.*

He looked. With dreadful queasiness, he looked and saw her squamous flesh peel away and the moist meat of her angry mouth melt like tallow in a glare of lightning that left behind only the scaffolding of bones. The beast's viciousness hung moistly in the spaces between the bones of the skeleton like dew mist, like a heat mirage. *Don't you see?* Jabalwan asked, derisively. *Death wants to be alive!* Jabalwan laughed, slowly, like a lament. *The other side of life is not death but more life. And the enemy of life is not death but indifference. Go now, nameless one, back to the edge of pain and numbness and bring your life to the full.*

Jaki reeled away from the huge skeleton and its skins of light. He drifted to his feet in a languor of shimmery music. The ground swayed with a grating roar, and dust and pebbles clinked from the high ceiling. Pym and the two other pirates were curled on themselves like rocks, and he floated to them and shoved the captain over. Pym's eye was tangled with tears, his face slack with deep sorrow. He had escaped the world and seen the unknown powers, secret and wild, wailings of wind looking for bodies in the stony dregs of the earth and finding people asleep behind their own faces, senile with greed, asleep before earth's savage beauty. And he saw himself, asleep behind his one eye, asleep in the infinite instant, a ghoul stitched with bitterness and cunning. "I cannot bear it!" he shouted. A vale of sorrowful echoes vaulted over them. "I am worm-dirt — and yet I live! I am death, and everything I touch dies."

"No!" Jaki shouted at him. "We are alive! And we are free."

The jostling bedrock settled, and the air stilled to a cathedral-like calm. Pym's hands trembled over his body, and he was amazed to feel himself whole. "The diamonds —" he rasped. "The diamonds are the price of our suffering. Jaki, we must find them."

Clairvoyant awe passed between them, and Pym stared with dumb amazement at the dark cavern scribbled with musical sparks. The blue fire had shrunk to a slim shine in the gutter. The oil bowl was empty of heat. The darkness glowed with the faintest luster and their own psychic fire. Pym shook the man beside him. "Awake, dreamer!"

The crewman jumped, then gazed about him with electric clarity. "Captain! Oh, captain! I saw the fathoms of infinity! I flew to the angel spheres and witnessed with mine own eyes the switchback of heaven and hell!"

"Aye — we were there with you." Pym shoved the fallen sailor, and the man rolled to his side and stared blindly at them. "He's dead."

Jaki closed the pirate's eyes and stood up, gazing about for the warriors and soul-catchers. There were none, and the air was still. He stepped out of the pit, lit the resin candles, and motioned Pym and the two crewmen toward the tight corridor that led to the cache of mountains' tears, as well as to the niche where his mother's head had been preserved.

Pym and the sailors retrieved their weapons and crawled in, following Jaki. His body felt hollow, diffuse as smoke, and the strong eye brushed his vision with whisks of sharp color. When they arrived at the kettle chamber, he placed his candle in a socket, and the room broke into a puzzle of oily lights. Pym and the sailors shouldered up to him and gasped at the sight: a rock cauldron mounded with chunky diamonds. Giddy now, Pym grabbed a fistful and clinked them between his palms. Windy lights still swirled in his vision from the mushroom bread, and he had to hold one of the thumbsized diamonds to the flame to be certain he was not hallucinating.

The nightmare that he had just endured of humanity asleep in its great moment of life faded before this radiance of incalculable wealth. The pirates stripped off their shirts and tied them into pouches; then, dragging their booty behind them, they crawled back through the tight corridors to the dragon chamber.

They could not tell what was seen or visioned in the wanly lit cavern. The bone faces of the sorcerers flickered, and the mother of life gazed down from her mortal limit, illuminated by a seraphic glow that made her jaws seem icicled and beautiful. "The Life is secret," Jaki said to her loudly in the tribal tongue, "until each of us faces your fury and finds the courage to make truth out of fate."

The earth shook again, vehemently, knocking the men off their feet and splitting the stone walls with jolting screams. Pym heaved himself upright on the rolling slabs, snagged Jaki by the wrist, and pulled him away from the pit as the walls erupted. Looking back, they saw the dragon mother knocked over and buried in a cascade of dust-streaming boulders.

Blindly they ran through the shaking tunnel, rock pillars shattering behind them with resounding force, the turbulent swell of rocksmoke stinging their flesh and snuffing out their wicks. The haze finally relented in a bright crystal shaft, and they shoved out of the mountain into the blinding sun staggering like drunks. Pym knelt over his bundle of diamonds like a child, giggling with disbelief.

Jaki searched the sky. Thunderclouds skewed overhead. Wawa barked shrilly from a fern tree and tumbled toward them in a terrified rush. Suddenly geysers of mud arced into the sky, stands of palm collapsed, and the whole grotto heaved. The gibbon charged down the mountainside, the men sprinting behind in headlong flight from the convulsed plateau.

The sky seemed to shatter, whirlwinding spouts of black rain, as Njurat quivered and collapsed into a cloud of rocksoot and steam. Pelting hail flogged the pirates as they scrambled over the bucking earth, not stopping until the desert sands sprawled before them. When they looked back, Njurat was gone. The mountain flank where it had stood was reduced to an angry cloud of smoke beneath the lash of rain and lightning.

The cold of the desert crossing was debilitating, and once in the highlands they had to rest for three days. Numerous times their cumbersome loads almost toppled them into the misty chasms as they picked their way down the cliffsides, and when they reached the jungle they were clumsy with weariness, and easy prey for snakes and cats. Without alcohol, Pym had become trembly as a doddering old man, and the crewmen, maddened by their many days in the jungle, began seeing death omens. The cry of a snake from the verdurous shade convinced even Jaki that death was stalking them. The startling destruction of Njurat had confirmed his role as the last sorcerer, and he suspected that even if he did escape the jungle, he would die.

That very day, the jungle relented, and the pirates crept into sight of the green bay and the bat's wing silhouette of *Silenos*. Pym splashed into the shallows in a burst of joy, hollering across the water. A skiff came for them rowed by Blackheart, and Pym kissed the startled quartermaster and rode to his ship standing, with his arms outstretched as though he could embrace the whole world with his new love.

No small boats came out to greet *Silenos* when she arrived on the river passage to Iduna, and Pym ordered the cannon readied for a fight, suspecting his homeport had been raided. He was right. The wharves were deserted. The big ships sat idle and empty. A charred hulk sat among them, its black ribs stiff as the clench of a corpse. Wisps of smoke fumbled above the treeline, and the crew rowed to shore speechless, dreading the evil that had befallen their kingdom.

The great house was empty, though all its treasures were intact. Pym stalked among the grand rooms, calling for Perdita. On the giant silk-sheeted bed that he had shared with his wife, he found the gold ball earrings and under them a letter in her hand: "Beloved husband —

"I know now I will never see you again. The angels have come for me. Only by their grace have I the strength to write you, that you may understand what terrible fate has befallen our kingdom.

"A month ago, two ships came. One was the largest English man-of-war I have ever seen, the very destroyer of which you warned me months before, The Fateful Sisters."

Pym had to lay the parchment on Perdita's dressing table and prop himself over it with both arms to continue reading:

"We prepared for a fight, as you had exhorted me that this warship would attack us. But the English vessel wore her colors on her bowsprit, signaling peace. The ship she towed was nameless it seemed, her name burned off and the char painted over with the mysterious admonition from Daniel: Mene, Mene, Tekel, Upharsin. *Her sails were black.* The Fateful Sisters *led her into harbor, and the English captain announced from his quarterdeck that the nameless ship's crew were ill and needed care. He refused to come ashore and accept our hospitality — and by that I should have suspected the grave extremis of the*

ill. The English captain declared that he had brought the ill to Iduna because no other kingdom would have them and they were doomed to die at sea. Iduna is the only Christian kingdom before Manila and unless we accepted the sick, they would die in transit.

"You will be angry with me, my Trevor, I know, but the Lord has said that what we do for the least among us we do for Him. I accepted the ship of sickness. Before we could even begin removing the ill, The Fateful Sisters *departed. We were appalled by what we found aboard the exiled vessel: a hundred souls, their flesh bloated purple and rent with festering wounds. Most could not speak, their tongues were that pus-riven. Those who could speak told us they had been a Danish merchant ship who had lost crew in a storm and taken on sailors in Halmahera — and there they contracted plague. No port would have them until* The Fateful Sisters *took them in tow and promised them sanctuary.*

"We tended them with all our skill and Christian care, yet within a week all were dead. Soon thereafter, our people began to fall ill. The illness spread rapidly. We had a continuous Mass read until the priests themselves were too ill to go on. We burned the dead. This last week there have been more corpses than people to manage the fires. Many have fled back into the jungle. I would have gone with them, just that I might see you again — but the illness is upon me. With my last strength and authority, I have arranged for a great fire to be prepared so that all the corpses, including my own, may be consumed and spare you our fate upon your return.

"Though I have been unfaithful to you in my heart, that was entirely my sin, my weakness for a boy of supernatural beauty. Forgive me and do not punish yourself. You have always been love itself to me, my husband, my soul. Your disbelief in the afterlife assures me that my suffering will soon end. And if you are wrong, then I will prepare your way back to me with my love.

"The angels remind me . . ."

The letter ended there, in a fit of illegible handwriting. Pym flew down the stairs, his face constricted, his mouth wide around a silent scream. Jaki, who had been waiting on the porch, moved to follow, and Blackheart stopped him and shook his head.

Perdita had been burned with the other corpses in a large pyre above the swan linns. Pym sat in the ashes and wept. A full day and a night he sat there while Blackheart and Jaki watched from the great house and the crew waited in *Silenos*, afraid to stay ashore.

Pym was wracked with grief. His vision in the dragon pit returned with renewed clarity, and he understood now that he had always been asleep when he was with Perdita, that only pain was wakefulness, and now that she was ash, he would never sleep again. On the second day, he rose and went straight into the house. He built a bonfire around the bed, and without taking a single item from the house, he left with Blackheart and Jaki and did not look back.

*

Aboard *Silenos*, Jaki and Blackheart watched the burning pyre of Iduna rise in coiling black billows. Pym ordered the ships in the harbor sunk. He watched from the quarterdeck as the cannon punched in the empty vessels' hulls below the water line. After all the ships had disappeared in frothy gurges, he turned the cannon on the harbor and blasted the wharves. With Iduna utterly devastated, he ordered *Silenos* to sea and retired below deck.

Jaki carried his pouch of diamonds to the captain's stateroom and spilled half of them on his rosewood tabletop. Then he turned and handed Blackheart the rest of the precious stones. Blackheart hefted the bag with surprise, clicking the gems, and Pym's somber eye fixed Jaki. "What is this?"

"Diamonds," Jaki answered with flat sincerity.

"I know that," Pym gruffed. "Why are you giving them to us?"

"I have no need for them," he said, speaking truthfully, for he had no use for the dragon's pelf, these mountains' tears that had been wept for the dumb immensity of the past. "The greatest wealth for me is to have lived the strong eye, don't you see? — the mother of life's initiation. Now I am truly a sorcerer as my teacher was before me."

"That's all well and good, lad, but even sorcerers need money when they leave the jungle."

"Then consider this my pay for my cabin and my board."

"Bah!" Pym dismissed that with a wave. "We achieved brotherhood on Macao — I don't want your bloody diamonds. I have my own — and I also paid for them with that cursed strong eye. That nightmare under the living bones of Wyvern still pollutes my sleep, thank you."

"It is what pollutes your waking that concerns me, captain."

Pym ground his teeth audibly and waited for Jaki to go on.

"The soul of Perdita haunts you," Jaki said, "and demands the blood of revenge. But does not revenge require weapons and a crew? Why are you making me tell you these things that you already know? My diamonds will help you get the men you need. That is all. And what I've given to Blackheart is his because he is you — your missing eye as you called him."

"Aye, you are a true sorcerer, Jaki Gefjon — to know my own soul fled with Perdita's and both walk homeless, disembodied, until we catch the cursed soul of William Quarles and damn it to hell!"

Blackheart heaped the diamonds Jaki had given him atop those on the table. He bowed to Jaki, touched his heart with his fist, and opened his hand before Pym.

"I understand, sir," Jaki said, "that the heart you have given your captain will serve him better than diamonds." He looked to Pym. "It is true — your enemy's doom is more strongly sealed with Blackheart's devotion than these rocks we lost lives to take. We are all of us committed to the destruction of our common enemy — but . . ."

"But what!" Pym snarled.

"Does it not say in the Bible that there is a time for everything? And is not now the time to grieve, to bury the dead, to cleanse our souls with silent prayer and God's grace? No one understands the fury of loss better than I. It blinds worse than fear. You will spell your own doom, captain — become prey to every trap — if you do not release Perdita's soul. These diamonds buy a time to mourn."

Pym lifted his flagon and splashed brandy over the jewels. "Fah! This grog is all I need to ease the loss of my dear wife. How often has it stilled the grief of the treachery that branded me for the murder of that true traitor, Samuel Quarles! How often has it stilled my grief at the murder and plunder my hand has been forced to — evils for which I once had no heart and no stomach, until they were burned into my flesh!" He slapped the viper on his branded brow. "And how often has it helped me forget Perdita's passion for you — adulterer!" He dropped back into his seat, drank deeply, and waved Jaki away.

Pym withdrew entirely into a wrathful trance, and he became as mute as Blackheart except when barking navigational commands. He could not bear to be near the sorcerer for more than moments, for the blond youth's quiescence mixed poorly with the choler inflaming him.

At last, Jaki left him alone and busied himself with shipboard chores as *Silenos* sailed north among the myriad islands of the Philippines to Manila, stopping frequently at brambly islets, searching for the rag-flags of marooned sailors. A handful of men were enlisted this way, although most were too weak or wild to be of any immediate use. Saja fortified the enfeebled with his herbal tinctures and the cook plied them with his broths. The dark souls Pym took aside, and his own redoubtable pain circumscribed their fates. Their shared wounds bound them tighter than brothers — and in the black throat of the ritual night when Wyvern was unfurled and the new recruits stood trembling before the demon visage of the viper bird, they stared into its mad eyes and swore their oaths with the vehemence of saints.

Shahawar Shirazi was one such recruit. Blackheart and Jaki had found him among the drunks under an abandoned pier at the far, garbage-strewn end of Manila harbor. The only sober one in a company of the blind, the lame, and the limbless, he wore his turban unraveled and knotted about his throat like a scarf; his long black hair, braided in a coil over his right shoulder and straggly with seaweed, was tied with an intertwining green band, attesting to his Muslim faith. The loose trousers he wore were streaked gray with wear, and his sleeveless black cashmere waistcoat was tattered, its embroidery rubbed to etched lines. At his side was a scimitar sheathed in a mold-chewed scabbard. When Jaki queried him in Spanish, he told them that he once had been a boatswain on the *Nur-e Siyah*, an Arabic name he translated as *Black Light*. At the sound of that name, Blackheart, aghast, lifted the man out of the vomit-splashed sand and took him at once to *Silenos*.

From Pym, Jaki learned that *Black Light* was a formidable Muslim warship in the employ of the Bantam of Siam. Thrice before it had stalked *Silenos* among the mazy islands of the Indonesian archipelago, but Pym's lighter ship had eluded the six-hundred-ton *Black Light* with its seventy-two big guns. Even so, the fear remained that one day the deadly ship would catch *Silenos* between shoals or in a cove where escape was impossible. Whatever information they could squeeze out of the sailor about the Muslim warship or its fanatical warrior-captain Rajan Kobra would be invaluable.

Plied with rice broth, the Byzantine-faced youth told them his story. Rajan Kobra had been a stern captain, intolerant of counsel from those of lesser rank and a fanatical stalker of pirates, driving his crew relentlessly. One day Shirazi, an impolitic upstart with a sharp tongue, had demanded more pay and incited the crew to unrest with his accusation that the Bantam himself was cheating them of their rightful wages. Instantly, Kobra set the youth adrift on the open sea, and by Allah's grace alone, Shirazi had landed in Manila, where he had tried to find employ aboard a galleon. But the Spaniards had no use for a Muslim boatswain, and so he had languished among the wharf rats until the day that Blackheart and Jaki found him.

Pym pummeled him with questions about Kobra and his *Black Light*, and Shirazi detailed the Muslim warship's patrol pattern in the Moluccas, the Banda, Flores, and Java seas, as well as the watering coves where it took provisions and was occasionally careened. Shirazi possessed vital information, too, about Rajan Kobra's faith in the holy calendar. *Nur-e Siyah*, he told them, had been named for a Sufi belief which claimed that things could be known only through their opposites — being only through nonbeing and celestial light only through the black shadow cast by the sun. Rajan himself had taken his name from a Muslim saint of centuries past, and his faith demanded pilgrimages to certain mosques in the Surabaja and Djambi regions that kept *Black Light* away from the sea lanes on specific weeks of the year. So pleased was he with this intelligence, Pym offered Shirazi employ aboard *Silenos*. Shirazi, intent on avenging himself against his erstwhile master, readily took the pirate's oath before Wyvern.

Outfitted with a newly bolstered crew, *Silenos* sailed south through the Celebes Sea to the cloud-scutted Molucca Passage and the fabulously wealthy spice vessels. Although wealth had never been Pym's objective — and was less so now that he had lost his Perdita — he knew that the seizure of ships was the only way to temper his crew for the eventual confrontation with the archfiend Quarles. In Manila, he traded a handful of diamonds for corned powder, shot, and the finest Swiss-machined flintlocks. For the first time, *Silenos* had enough handguns for each member of its crew to fight like a gentleman, including the cook and the surgeon. Each day, Pym held drills, emphasizing alacrity in reloading and accuracy in targeting, and in a few weeks, every crewman became a crack shot.

For Jaki, Shirazi proved the most interesting of the new recruits, for he was the only other man aboard who regularly spoke to God. Though several of the crew were Muslim, their faith was superstitious, talismanic efforts to protect them in battle and illness. Shirazi prayed fervently each day in his cabana, his berth ringing with musical utterances.

Hanging in slings over the side together to caulk the timbers, Jaki and Shirazi shared their visions of life. Shirazi spoke of *alam al-mithal,* the middle realm between mind and experience, ideal and real, God and the world. "We are like sparks," Shirazi said through the fumes of bubbling tar, "sparks that leap between heaven and earth. Our lives are that brief, our illumination that little. That is why we must always do what we dream. How else can our lives matter?"

The sorcerer described his vision under the strong eye. "I saw then, Shirazi, that the enemy of life is not death but indifference. Just as you say, we must do what we dream — despite the pain. Prayers and songs are well enough, but action is the highest good. Only by doing what we know is right are we the sparks of light you speak of. Otherwise we are little more than mud."

Shirazi listened to Jaki with a melancholy comprehension in his Arab eyes. "You speak like an *imam,* a man who has the fidelity of faith. I did not expect to find one such as you among pirates."

"Are we simply pirates?" Jaki asked. "We are sparks of the divine, too."

"But *Silenos* plunders cargo ships. That hardly merits divine sanction."

"Life plunders life." Jaki shrugged. "That is timelessly so. If God sanctions hawks, panthers, and wolves, why not us?"

"But we prey on ourselves."

"Could that be because we are made in the likeness of God? We mime our creator, Who destroys Himself in all He creates."

Shirazi nodded contemplatively. "Perhaps that is so. The Koran speaks of God's majesty, which sets being on fire. That majesty is the black light. All other lights illuminate, but the light closest to God, the black light, attacks, invades, annihilates." The Muslim's dark stare became more pensive. "You have given me much to consider, Gefjon."

Jaki liked the clean-shaven, turbaned young man who spoke of angels and who looked like one, with eyes dark as pools of scribe's ink, graven cheeks, and flesh the color of desert sand, unstained by tattoos. At

Sangihe and Manado, where *Silenos* was welcomed for her gold coin despite her recent renown as a pirate ship, Jaki and Shirazi sported together. They rented horses by the wharves, and Shirazi delighted at Jaki's clumsy efforts at riding on the beaches. They hunted with flintlocks and the blowgun in the jungle fringes and frolicked in the tree canopy, bounding with Wawa among the branches and swinging on lianas over green pools. Shirazi was Jaki's first true human friend. Under the rustling stars, picking lice from each other's hair by firelight, they exchanged stories of their homelands and laughed at the follies of their childhoods. Jaki was impressed by the Muslim youth's devotion to his faith, and frequently they knelt together before the God of mystery.

The sorcerer's admiration grew when he saw how brave a warrior Shirazi was. Once, off Ternate, *Silenos* maimed a Portuguese carrack and sunk her escort yachts, yet the cuirassiers aboard defended her cargo of pepper and cloves with their lives. Shirazi threw himself among the brawny Portuguese, his scimitar stealing lives through the narrowest chinks of armor. Time and again, only Jaki's swift intervention saved him from saber thrusts and blows of hatchets. Yet Shirazi's idle regard for his own life and his grandiose and precise savagery broke the enemy's defenses, and the carrack was taken with only a few pirates lost. The Muslim warrior was carried back aboard *Silenos* on the shoulders of the triumphant raiders, and he was rewarded by Pym for his courage with a fang of diamond from the dragon's hoard.

Twice more, Shirazi proved himself confident of heaven's embrace and threw himself into certain death only to emerge heroic thanks to the intercession of his comrades. The fourth time was the last. *Silenos* had pursued a well-armed Spanish warship on the sea north of Seram. The man-of-war had many more guns than the pirates, but *Silenos*'s smaller cannon, faster-burning corned powder, and bore-angled trunnions far outshot the Spaniards. With her broadside caved in and all decks ablaze, the warship struck her colors — yet Pym smelled treachery.

Shirazi volunteered to lead a boarding party, and Pym agreed, loading the skiff with powder-keg floaters to be used if there was duplicity. Jaki joined the half-dozen men who followed Shirazi, and they tacked for the wounded warship, shouting for the Spaniards to lay down their weapons. The captain appeared with his hands open before him, and a rope ladder was lowered, but before clambering aboard, Jaki tied twine to the matchlock on one of the powder kegs and unraveled it behind him. Once aboard, they were surrounded by armed Spaniards who intended to hold them hostage in return for their ship's freedom. The captain's steel-hard grin froze when Shirazi's scimitar flew. "Kill them!" he shouted. Jaki tugged on the twine, and the powder kegs exploded, rocking the boat and shattering the tiller. The musketmen's shots were spoiled, and the fight fell to swords.

Shirazi, washed in gore, plunged into the thick of the enemy, drawing blows away from his companions. Jaki followed, a cutlass in each hand, leaping like a panther. He would not sacrifice another human for himself—and when the Muslim slipped on a pool of spilled bowels and lay face up waiting for the cold crash of his doom, Jaki beat off the frantic enemy.

Silenos slammed into the man-of-war, and her pirate crew swarmed aboard. At the sight of Blackheart swinging a knife-barbed chain and the pirates firing their flintlocks with withering accuracy, the Spaniards conceded, laying down their weapons, and Shirazi looked to Jaki with dismayed surprise at finding himself alive. "You look disappointed," Jaki said, helping him to his feet.

"No greater glory awaits a man than to die in battle slaying the enemies of Allah," he answered glumly.

"If you continue to fight so recklessly," Jaki warned, "you will not be disappointed much longer."

The enemy survivors were set ashore on Seram with provisions; their warship was emptied of its cargo of gold, camphor, and spice tonnage and then sunk. That night Pym convened a council under the torchlit Wyvern. There he laid out *Silenos*'s itinerary and his plan for exchanging their booty for gold. After raiding the southern Spice Isles of Timor, Flores, and Sumba, they would beat west and north to Johore. Pym knew the sultan of Selangor, who would trade them bullion for spices. By then the rainy season would again be upon them, and they would sit out the big storms in Malacca and Kuala Lumpur, living like shahs with their stupendous wealth. The crew accepted his plan by unanimous vote.

Two nights later, in the wind-trampled Timor Sea, Shirazi was swept overboard during the midnight watch, while a starless wall of storm was rising in the south. Jaki and two crewmen lowered a four-oar to retrieve him, for even though he was within range of thrown floaters, he seemed too confused to grab on to them and was soon carried into the darkness. The storm kicked the sea into phosphorescent peaks before the four-oar could release her ties, and the two crewmen scrambled back aboard and shouted for Jaki to follow. But the sorcerer would not abandon the man who spoke of angels, and he threw off the lines and rowed into the night.

Silenos vanished from view, though the cries of the men came and went with the whirling wind. This may be *my* death, Jaki realized, facing into the black depth. In one sense, he felt almost grateful. Pym had become demonic and silent since Perdita's death, and Jaki's cloudreading had offered nothing less than cruelty: the future was toppling into a chaos of vaster and more devastating wars. And what were these wars deciding? All war was futile. Pirating was futile. There was no end to the violence and the madness. To give his life for another in this night storm seemed fitting for a man who was a slayer of men, a pirate, a sorcerer whose legacy was the mountains' tears.

Shirazi's bobbing head appeared in the froth-gleaming sea, and Jaki broke off his death reverie and quickly extended an oar for him. The warrior grabbed it and climbed aboard, huffing brine. He clutched Jaki ferociously, his face an anguish in the wind. "You! Again you keep me in this world!"

"Not for long, brother!" Jaki shouted and pointed to the lightning above the whitecaps and the black sea.

Jaki and Shirazi crouched in the battered boat while the night raged and the earth spun. Gusts of rain flashed in the lightning-glare like steel, and white-crashing swells tossed them high against the maniac night. Their hearts strained to splitting, and they wept with visceral terror, clasping each other until they sank into pain-smothering comas.

They woke in the sibilant dark to see the storm shredding to star vapors and a burgundy moon. "You were wrong, brother," Shirazi moaned. "We live."

"Yes —" Jaki answered, sitting up into a great clot of pain, "but without the provisions for life. No water."

"Too much water, I think." Shirazi scanned the horizon but saw no shadow of a ship.

Through their nightlong drift, they sat silent, each lost in the certainty of the slow death to come. At dawn, Shirazi said his prayers and held up his scimitar. "At your word, my weapon will cut you free."

Jaki shook his head. "That is not the way of my people."

"Nor of mine. Only Allah may kill us. And for that, He has a plenitude of ways. Sad for us He has chosen one of His longer paths."

The sun came hard across the world, hot and relentless. The men sat with their faces down, turned away from the fired sky, their shoulders draped with their long hair. Occasionally they looked up and searched the circling horizon. Remnant stormclouds lay on the north all day like scraps of iron. The rest of the sky was cloudless, a clear eye, perfect in its emptiness. Shirazi said his prayers at each of the sun's stations. Toward evening, the friends lay face up on the thwarts and slept.

With dawn, the wind rose. The world was the horizon, lordly and full of light, the flawless edge between heaven and earth. Shirazi broke the silence with his prayers, then said, "On the big ship, we spoke casually of *alam al-mithal,* the middle realm." He picked at the gray splinters of the gunwale. "Now that is all. That is all there is."

Neither of them looked up anymore to search the mute horizon.

The four-oar lifted and fell on wide, gliding swells. Shirazi mumbled his prayers. They were chilled in the parching sun, their eyes bloody red, their cracked lips scaled with salt. Shadows thrived in the air, heat shimmers gleaming off the sunstruck water. "Angels," Shirazi muttered. "Angels come to carry us to heaven." A lone cloud wandered the hard line of the sky. "Angels, here to take us —"

"Be still, Shirazi."

"No, I must tell you, Gefjon. I must say it —"

But he said nothing more that day. The sun fell, the wind banks in the western sky blazed briefly, and the sky filled with wild stars. Jaki touched his brow with the cool amber of Lucinda's ring, remembering her.

Both men slept through the night and dawn. When they woke, the sky was already white with sunfire. Jaki pulled himself upright, turned his face into the breeze musing from the west, and saw a dark shadow on the leaden water. "Shirazi!" he croaked.

The Muslim stirred and raised his head. When he saw the ship on the horizon, he moaned.

"*Silenos!*" Jaki cried.

Shirazi lay a cold hand on his arm. "No, brother. You are seeing with your heart. Look closely."

Jaki squinted into the hard glare and saw that the ship indeed was not *Silenos* but a larger vessel with green sails and the figurehead of a black angel with spread wings.

"*Nur-e Siyah,*" Shirazi breathed. "*Black Light.*"

Jaki sagged back into the bilges.

"As Allah is my master, now you must hear me," Shirazi spoke, leaning close, his black hair dangling like eels. "I have betrayed my oath before the winged snake. I have betrayed Captain Pym. And I have betrayed you, whom I call brother."

Jaki shifted so he could stare into the man's dark eyes. "What are you saying?"

"I am saying that I am a spy. I am a Muslim warrior, a servant of *Black Light* and of her captain Rajan Kobra. When the Bantam of Siam learned from the British pirate hunter, Quarles, that Wyvern was Trevor Pym of Iduna, a plan was invented. It was known Wyvern would need new pirates. So, the Bantam ordered Rajan Kobra to place men in key ports, in the hope that one or more of us would be recruited. I alone succeeded."

Jaki sat up, incredulous.

Shirazi's lips stuck to his dry teeth, and he rasped with belabored breath: "I was to learn all I could, then at the right time and place jump ship and be picked up by *Black Light,* whose whereabouts I have always known. But the mission did not sit well in my heart." He gasped, and breath caught in his dry lungs. "I expected to spy on pirates, not men who spoke of *alam al-mithal*. To spare myself the indignity of betraying men I admire, I tried time and again to die for *Silenos* in battle. But you — you kept saving me."

Jaki sank on himself with comprehension. "Why did you not stay aboard — stay with us?"

"I could not betray my first fealty," Shirazi answered, his hand falling away from Jaki's arm. "But again I tried to defeat myself. I jumped ship before the tempest, believing that would kill me before *Black Light* would find me. And again you saved me."

"Now *Silenos* is lost."

"Rajan Kobra is a hard captain," Shirazi replied, darkly. "He will not care that you speak of angels. He will do all he can to make you talk of Wyvern."

"He will learn nothing from me."

"I know you will cleave to silence, my friend — but there is no silence Kobra cannot break. You must trust me. We will pretend you are my ally in treachery. Soon as I can, I will find a way to free you. I owe you that."

"You owe me nothing, Shirazi." Jaki watched the green-sailed ship bearing down on them. "I have made my own fate. You must be true to yours."

"Rest assured — I will be true. Allah be my witness."

Black Light plucked them from the sea, and Shirazi lay prostrate on the deck, praising Allah. Jaki had no strength to stand, and he too lay on the deck staring up at the turbaned, sun-tarnished men and the ship's rigging. The shadow of Pym's voice flitted in the wells of his ears as he studied the ship: *Tight, clean planks buoy men's spirits; they're the face of the ship, more than the bowsprit or the hull, for the men see the planks day in and day out.* The planks under him were grimy, splintered, and ill joisted, warped from strain. His gaze rested on the nearby sheaves, the grooved wheels that were used in the blocks of the rigging and which carried the great strains of the sails, and he saw that they were gray and cracked. *The sheaves on most ships are made of oak, a sturdy wood — but on my ship the sheaves are carved from lignum vitae, living rock, the hardest wood in the world.*

Shirazi was on his knees, speaking rapidly. Jaki looked up and saw a gnome of a man with a long black mustache waxed to points that stabbed to the sides like a charred bone stuck through his nose. The man's face was cast iron, his jaw blue with stubble, the cheeks carved like an icon's, the eyes tiny black holes under a brilliant white turban. He grinned at something Shirazi said and showed sharp wolf's teeth.

"I am Rajan Kobra," the iron-faced man said in Spanish dense with a foreign flavor. "You have cast your lot well with Shahawar Shirazi, young Dutchman. My men will take you below, refresh you. Tonight we feast and celebrate the doom of Wyvern."

Jaki was carried down a gangway that stank of bilge water, sweat, and unclean timber. He was given tea in a flask and washed in sour water on the lower gundeck, while crewmen stood around marveling at the gold curls of his hair and the curry brown of his flesh. The tea burned a dry path to his withered stomach, and he retched, washed his mouth out, and drank more gingerly.

Shirazi was not with him, and Jaki worried that if he was questioned their stories would not match. He accepted the baggy gray trousers and sorrel blouse a crewman handed him and dressed. Dizzy and enfeebled from his two days under the pitiless sun, he sagged beside the barrel of scummy water where he had bathed. The crewmen lifted him and placed him in one of the hammocks strung above a cannon. Lying there, his body humming with refound life, he surveyed the ship as best he could. It was an ugly vessel, ill maintained and noisome — but then any ship would so appear after the immaculate and proud *Silenos*. New respect for Pym welled in him, and he was more determined than ever not to betray the pirate captain. The resolution was his last thought as exhaustion claimed him and he fell into a deep sleep.

He woke to lantern light and a grisly, toothless crewman shaking him alert. His legs were unsteady beneath him, but they carried his weight, and he followed the sailor to the poop deck and through the captain's companion to a spacious cabin, well lit with ruby-glassed oil lamps and appointed with luxuriant cushions and carpets. The wood panels of the cabin were inlaid with silver outlines of turrets, mosques, and arabesque loveknots, and the bay windows were a mosaic of intricacies that caught light like burning blood.

Rajan Kobra sat on a cushion under the windows, a sapphire gleaming like an eye on his turban. The satins and silks he wore breathed light. He gestured for Jaki to enter and sit before him and dismissed the toothless sailor. Alongside the tasseled cushion where Jaki sat was a satinwood tray of silver plates heaped with dates, orange wedges, bananas, almonds, green nut paste. A gem-crusted chalice brimmed with wine. "Eat, drink!" Rajan Kobra commanded. "Shahawar has told me your story. I am honored to meet a man who has endured the travails of the jungle and the sea and not lost faith in the one God."

Jaki ate heartily so he would not have to speak and was grateful for the sweet fruits. His body buzzed with joy to break its fast, and he nodded his satisfaction.

Rajan Kobra sat with his hands folded in his lap, observing closely. "Why have you decided to abandon your pirate companions?"

"Shirazi must have told you," Jaki answered.

"Shahawar has told me much," Kobra agreed, his eyes like puncture wounds. "You will tell me as much."

"I am with him because of *alam al-mithal,*" he answered, emboldened by the burn of the wine. When he saw the Muslim captain's ominous eyes brighten, he added, "I am a man of spirit, a sorcerer among the jungle people who reared me. If I am to serve at sea, I would serve men who understand that we are all just sparks between heaven and earth."

Rajan Kobra made a morose face. "What of the pirates you left? Have you no loyalty to them?"

"We are all pirates before God," Jaki ventured and drank more wine. "My first loyalty is to God — and Shirazi convinced me that you were a God-minded captain."

"Then you will tell me what you know of Wyvern?"

"I will tell you everything," Jaki replied, feigning enthusiasm. "Her name is *Silenos*, and her captain is Trevor Pym, a traitor snakebranded by the British."

Rajan Kobra's tiny eyes beaded with oil flame. "You will tell me her course plan."

"The whim of her captain."

The iron face shook *no* and the eyes squinched smaller. "You have heard of strappado, Jaki Gefjon?"

Jaki said nothing but did not drop his gaze.

"If you lie to me, young half-breed, you will be tied by your limbs and dropped from the yardarm. The first drop will crack your joints. You will sing with pain. The second drop will rip your limbs from your body. But you will not die. Hot tar will stop your bleeding. And you will live aboard this ship in the bilges, a living stump in the pisswater of your enemies. We will keep you alive many years and you will pray to the one God to die — but without hands or legs, you can do nothing but wait for Allah's judgment." He leered with awful pleasure. "And now again — what is the course plan of Wyvern?"

Jaki drained the goblet, sighed to remember the Spider, and faced Kobra with his blue eyes more luminous. "Among my people I am a sorcerer," he said, calmly, though his insides were prickling with terror. "I am not afraid of pain, not even a lifetime of it, if that is God's will. When I am convinced you are the God-minded captain Shirazi promised, I will tell you all I know."

Rajan Kobra sat back, grinning mournfully. "The strappado will be prepared, Jaki Gefjon, and you will tell me what I need to know." He barked, and the cabin door flew open. Two muscle-packed sailors entered and hoisted Jaki away.

They locked him in a tight, empty hold amidships on the lowest deck, where the sewer stink of the ship's bilges choked the air. There he sat for three days and nights, judging time by the chinked light that seeped through the ill-fitted planks. Scrap food that looked and smelled like garbage was tossed in to him, and he tried to catch it before it plopped to the excrement-puddled floor. When he could not escape into sleep, Jaki scythed hours with memories, pretending he was in the jungle canopy again with Wawa and Jabalwan or in the mountains listening to streams racing among cliff boulders. He placed Lucinda's amber asphodel to his lips and crooned promises of fidelity. He remembered the black stagger of trees on the forest edge of the mountains and the wide world with its cowl of storms and starlight.

The door whined and swung open, and Shirazi stooped over him. "Jaki — we must move quickly," he whispered, hushing his questions with a finger to the sorcerer's lips.

Jaki could barely move and Shirazi had to help him up the gangway to the top deck. Shirazi had already lowered a skiff. He pointed starboard to a black shadow on the horizon. "Sumbawa," he said. "You can reach there before Kobra knows you are gone. But you must hurry. And when you get there, you must go into the forest and hide, for they will surely search for you. My scimitar is in the skiff."

"Come with me," Jaki urged.

Shirazi shook his head. "I cannot. This minute I am to be attending Kobra in his cabin, detailing *Silenos*'s course plan. For three days, while he ripened you for torture, I have told him everything I know. But I have let him think I know more. If I go with you now, we will not even make it to shore. Please, leave now, while you can. I have made my peace with you."

Jaki clamped his friend's hand between his own. "Thank you for the gift of life," he said, tears rising in him.

"It is a fragile gift, Gefjon," Shirazi responded, helping him over the side and onto the rope ladder. "Just a spark."

Jaki summoned all his strength to row the skiff away from *Black Light* toward the massed darkness of Sumbawa. The stars crashed above him like surf, and he fixed his attention on them not to feel the suffering of his muscles.

Arriving at the black beach, he breathed the island's blossom wind with his whole body. Using Shirazi's scimitar for support, he climbed out of the skiff and collapsed under a palm. At dawn he watched *Black Light* sweep past the coast. When the skiff was spotted, the crew threw anchor and a longboat arrowed for shore.

Jaki thrashed into the jungle, sucking the sweet air of the forest with desperate lungs. He waited in a tall tree, letting the pain of his abused muscles twist silently, while the Muslim sailors beat the brush of the shore until the biting insects became unbearable. When they left, they took the skiff with them.

Jaki stayed in the high tree, watching as *Black Light* swung about to depart. Hanging from the bowsprit was the limbless corpse of Shahawar Shirazi.

*

The world-wanderer who arrived in Jakarta with the first monsoons looked barbaric, his hair tied back with eelskin bands, his long body naked but for a rag loincloth, his sun-grained flesh roughened by many winds. A scimitar hung from his side, strapped to his lean hips with snake sinew.

"Mister Gefjon!" a woman's voice belled in the rainy air.

Jaki looked about at the cluttered harbor. Sampans, lorchas, and junks crowded the mist-blown quay, and smells of cooking fires mingled with the stench of low tide. Over the last moon he had journeyed seven hundred and fifty miles across the swamp isles of Raba and Lombok, over the cliff ledges of Bali, and through the jungles of Java. After swimming the narrow channels between the swamp isles, he had stolen a canoe on Lombok and sailed it west, following the cloudpath streaming from the mountains of the Sunda Islands. His journey was relentless; he had to reach Johore in time to warn *Silenos* that Rajan Kobra knew she was hiding there. Caught in the narrow Strait of Malacca, the pirates would be easy prey for *Black Light*. Jaki had ignored his exhaustion in order to reach Johore in time, and for days he had been hearing shadowy voices among the silver wands of rain, seeing angel choirs in the swirls of sun that broke through the storm banks. Not until the woman's voice called him a second time did he truly believe he had heard her.

Jaki stared hard in the direction of the voice and saw a wharf where several Dutch carracks were moored. Beyond them the giant masts and white hull of an immense warship reared. He had been looking for the harbormaster's building, hoping to find work aboard any ship bound for Johore or its main port of Singapore. Now, peering through the gusty tail of the wind, he shivered as he realized that the big ship towering at the dock was *The Fateful Sisters*.

"Mister Gefjon!" The voice flitted through the blinking rain.

And he saw her — in a brag of lantern light at the stern castle window, he saw her, Lucinda Quarles. She waved her spyglass, and he raised his left hand in a fist so that the thumb ring he had made from her brooch was visible.

Lucinda had her maid distract the quarterdeck watch while she lowered a rope that she had tied off to the window jamb. Jaki slipped into the harbor's black water, seized the rope, and pulled himself into her cabin.

Lucinda stepped back with her hands to her mouth, startled and amused by Jaki's naked, gleaming strength.

"You look like you crawled across Asia on your belly," she said, her nose wrinkled. "When I saw you through the spyglass, I thought I recognized you. But, Mister Gefjon, you look different without your clothes."

"I hope I am not offending you, Mistress Lucinda," he said, his heart bouncing. Seeing her up close, his eyes ached for some sign of love in her shell-bright face. Instead, she was watching him with a blend of curiosity and remoteness. Her pale hair was longer than he remembered and fell in heartbreakers, long lazy curls, over her shoulders. "You've been an inch behind my eyes since I saw you last in Macao — a year ago."

"A year? Yes. I suppose it has been that long," she said, stepping closer. He was muscular, even more so than she recalled, and she looked for the shoulder and chest wounds from his duel with the Portuguese officer. Her curiosity dilated to an unexpected wonder, and the veil of remoteness fell away. He watched her with a zealous intensity that spun her blood harder through her veins. "I will confess," she said in a fearful voice, "there have been times in that year when I've wondered if I would ever see you again."

"Our journeys have crossed," he said ardently, and her breath fluttered. "But only briefly. I must leave here at once. I have been separated from my captain, and I must find him."

"Where are you going?" she asked, paler.

"Johore."

Her face lit. "But we sail for there tonight. We will reach Singapore within four days and five nights."

Lucinda's heart pounded with the hope of an adventure. The two years that she had lived aboard *The Fateful Sisters* had been miserable. Since poisoning the pirate kingdom of Iduna, almost a year ago, her father had become obsessed with clearing the sea lanes of pirates, and he had methodically crisscrossed Asia's seven seas seizing unmarked vessels and destroying them when they would not yield. Recent sightings of Wyvern had inflamed her father's mania, and all his time was devoted to charting patrols and coordinating tactics with the merchants and trade officials of the numerous ports that received him.

At each port, Lucinda was presented at court functions and expected to perform her role as loving daughter and marriageable maiden. But she had met no one worthy of her love, and her memory of the bold Dutch pirate had burned brighter with every ball. Lucinda loathed the men who courted her, ambitious for the rich captain's only daughter. She saw through their syrupy flattery, fully aware that her life as the wife of an important man would be as confining and unsatisfying as her existence aboard her father's ship. Her memory of the few luminous minutes she had spent with Jaki Gefjon became monumental for their sincerity.

She had been sitting despondently at the window in her stateroom when she spied him on the docks of Jakarta, and was startled by the ethereal passion that swelled in her. Now, facing into his lovestrong stare, she recognized the prodigious moment that could begin a new fate for her. "Please," she urged, "travel with us."

"How can I?" he asked, incredulous. "Your father knows I'm a pirate. He would hang me."

"*If* he knew you were aboard," she said, a giddy impulse mounting swiftly to resolve. "But why does he have to know? This is my private cabin. You will stay here with me."

"Lady, I cannot!" He looked haplessly about at the handsomely furnished cabin. In one corner stood a bed with a canopy and a velvet curtain; beneath a lace-fringed porthole was a scarlet-lacquered writing table, a majolica vase with fresh maidenhair, and two cushion-seated wing chairs. A cane-slatted door left slightly ajar revealed a copper-fitted latrine and a high-backed enamel tub. "If your father found me here your honor would be wholly compromised."

"My father never enters my cabin," she answered, holding his gaze, her insides burnished with the boldness of her intent. "Even when *The Fateful Sisters* sails to fight and I'm left ashore, this cabin is locked. It is kept for me alone."

"Your maid —" he began.

She hushed him with a finger to his lips. "Don't fret over Maud. She is my dearest friend and would not betray me for her own life. You must get to Johore, and this is the fastest ship in Asia. Stay with me — and let us not be strangers anymore. I want to see who you are."

Jaki listened for premonitory voices, heard only the tide slapping and his heart yearning — and he accepted. Lucinda was seventeen now, not much younger than Jaki, and the novelty of his manhood, the smell of him like a breath of split wood, confounded all caution. She decided then that she would make love with him. He was her handsome plaything, obviously in love with her and far more innocent and interesting than any of the jaded suitors at the many courts she had visited. She bathed him in lilac water and had her maid alter breeches and a blouse from her father's wardrobe. She cut Jaki's long hair in the French vogue with lengthy, uneven curls and a bow of blue ribbon knotted to the longest lock.

By nightfall, when *The Fateful Sisters* slipped its moorings, he was bathed, coifed, dressed, and well fed on braised fish, dumplings, mustard cabbage, and ale.

Maud was sent above deck to get some air for an imaginary headache, and Lucinda blew out the flame on one of the two lanterns chained to the rafters. Determined to divest herself of her virginity that night, she left the writing table cluttered with the dishes and mugs from their meal and led Jaki by the hand to the wing chairs.

Lucinda twined her fingers in the long locks of his sun-bleached hair, unhurried and playful, and asked about his dangerous journey among the islands. Words evaded him in the magnetic field of her touch, but he tried to recount the voyage until he recognized the puckish glint in her merry eyes. "Lady, you mock me," he blurted.

She laughed at his surprise. "I am playing with you, Mister Gefjon. Do you object?"

He took her hand from his face. "I'd rather move your heart than amuse it," he said.

"So serious." She arranged his hair so that his lovelock fell over his shoulder. "Your life has been too hard, Mister Gefjon. You have never learned to play."

"If we are just going to play," he replied in a whisper that faltered as her hand trailed across his shoulder to the warm flesh at the open throat of his shirt, "won't you at least call me Jaki?"

She frowned with mock solemnity. "That's so very personal — Jaki." With one hand she opened his shirt and with the other traced the curves of his bare shoulder.

"Lucinda —" His hands opened helplessly in his lap. "What you are doing is dangerous."

She leaned close and giggled in his ear. "For whom?"

Jaki felt like he was breaking in two, and he lifted his hands and touched her dress lightly, his fingers buzzing. She did not pull away as he had feared. Instead, she leaned into him, and his hands took her weight and were surprised by her size. She was bigger than the paddy girls and the Macao odalisques but as soft and with an unexpected smell of cool, rainwet fur.

Her hair tented their faces, and she stared down at him with the loveglow he had longed to see — and something more, an impish smile. She was laughing at his astonishment, at the drunken tug of implication pulling his eyes wide. His naked innocence enamored her, and she wanted him to be the first to have what the sophisticated royals her father admired had failed to win. He was the spirit of her childhood, sincere as a puppy, vulnerable to her every whim. She did not love him, not then as her face dipped to taste the mist of his breath. And when his arms drew her closer and their bodies met, love was still far away, overshadowed by passion, and she was glad when his breath came in gasps under her nibbling lips.

Jaki lifted her in his arms and carried her to the bed. They tugged at each other's clothes in an erotic game, until they were jubilantly naked. For her, the ensuing strokes of touch and feel that sparked her wet inside and out culminated moments later in a tantrum of pleasure, leaving her gasping and exhilarated. For him, the slick complicity of their bodies was love itself, and he entered her slow and tense as a predator, stalking her heart, reading her eyes, her murmurs, and her cries for inspiration. Then the bewilderment of passion overcame him, and he succumbed. With lyrical rapacity, they grappled around the prism of their lovelock — slow-motion somersaulting, bellybouncing, backcrawling, spilling through each other, and bounding back in verging arcs, weightless as rainbows.

Jaki had not disappointed Lucinda in her passionate expectations, and that night they made love again while the maid slept restlessly on the trundle bed outside their veiled bower, dreaming of seastorms.

The next four days were a conflagration of amorous adventures, each burning hotter than the last as the two lovers expended their desires with bright animal intensity. Lucinda was afraid that with the pleasure gained between them something would be lost — *phlogiston,* she called it, the fiery essence of their souls. Jaki listened patiently to her fears and allayed them with his forest tales of the inexhaustible love of the sky for the landlocked horizon and how their mythic hunger for each other was satisfied twice each day in the beauty of twilight.

Lucinda was intrigued by Jaki's jungle stories and he by her tales of Europe and the many ports she had visited with her father. Each day was a sharing of their worlds' enigmas and each night beneath the monsoon rains, a reconciliation of all differences and all mystery. At dawn, their bodies glazed with the shellac of their erotic abandon, they lay together and gazed serenely into each other's eyes, blue into blue, sharing their new-found intelligence about everything — trade and poetry, money and monarchy, God and free will — everything except the future.

Occasionally, Quarles's voice would bend through the creaking walls, and Jaki would shiver to hear the iron in his commands, the cold timbre of the will that had maliciously infected Iduna and robbed Pym's tormented soul of its last light. "What is he like — your father?"

"He's a cursed man," she answered dully. She lay curled up with her back pressed against him, his hand under her cheek. The spoon of Jaki's warm nakedness absorbed the chill that descended when she thought of her father, and she found the vigilance to peer deeper at herself and to admit what she could not confide even to her maid: "I am his curse."

Jaki tightened about her, and she told him what she knew of Quarles's struggle from poverty on the sordid Chatham dockyards to his triumphant captaincy, the retrieval of his ancestral estate, and the crushing loss of his wife. "I was too young to remember her. But he did love her — and still does. She must have been a strong woman to command his devotion, to have even gotten his attention. My father has cared for no one and nothing else since but his ascendancy. I impede that. My mother left me in her place, and every day I have reminded him of her absence. That is why he has never remarried; he is still married, he thinks — to my fate. He reared me as he would a son, sparing me no learning but manual labor. And now that I know something of this sad world, he demands that I behave as if I were an empty-headed woman, eager for a husband and a household."

"What are you eager for?"

"Something grand. I didn't know what — until now. But the way I have been living cannot go on, because it is taking me helplessly to some man I cannot love and to an obedient, dreamless house where I cannot live." She sat up, her eyes affright. "True child, I want to go with you."

Hope welled up in Jaki, but he dared not touch her until he saw that she was reaching for him in love and not fear. "I will use my mountains' tears to build us a home far away from everything that wants us apart."

She fell into his arms, and he hugged dearly this woman who filled the emptiness his life had crossed.

From far back in the wilderness of dreams, on an unfound path out of the canyon of memory, Mala chanted lines from Psalm 19: *Day to day pours forth speech — and night to night declares knowledge.*

When dawn came and the roll of the ship steadied to the anchored rhythms of her new moorings, they confronted their future. Love had found Lucinda sometime during the stormsea crossing, and all her playfulness had sharpened to a rueful need for her caring, carnal, forest-scented man. She did not want him to go, though she knew her father would kill him if he stayed. Jaki swore to return to Singapore at the next new moon, after he had warned his comrades and they had made their way to safety.

"I will come back," he said with his face in the heady fragrance of her gold-shadowed hair, "and this time never leave again. I will bring my fortune with me and ask your father for your hand. We will leave Asia, and you will show me Europe. Perhaps the Alps will be our home — we will have a chateau by a lake and rear our children in happiness and teach them to cherish beauty and peace."

"You dream more than I can believe," she said sadly. "Yet I will wait for you to return." She kissed the amber ring to seal her promise, and they agreed to meet next under the dark of the moon behind the stone lion that gazed over the harbor of Singapore, the City of Lions.

He secured a rope to the window jamb and nimbly swung down to the stone slipway of the landing stage. He waved and in a moment vanished in the amulets of morning mist dangling over the harbor.

William Quarles left Mister Montague on the poop deck to oversee the last stage of the mooring, and unfolded his spyglass to survey the other ships in the port. Behind him, the gangways were affixed, and the dockcrew noisily began unloading cargo. As the captain leaned on the taffrail and cocked his broad hat the better to use his glass, he glimpsed a blond youth swing from his daughter's castle window to the end of the mist-folded landing stage. Quarles would not have thought it possible unless he had seen it, for the leap demanded the precision of a panther to clear the distance from the stern to the sea wall without slamming into the cables. Eager to catch the youth's face, he swung the lens over the bloated images of barnacled stone walls, timber framing, and rusty winches and recognized the handsome Dutch pirate Lucinda had beguiled a year before in Macao. He rapped his spyglass on the rail, shattering it in his burst of fury, and shouted for his daughter.

Lucinda heard her father bellowing her name, but before she could reach the door, it burst inward and he entered with a roar of indignation. He stopped at the edge of the bed, glaring at his daughter as he assessed her complicity. Then his chest collapsed in a moaning cry, and he slapped her hard, sending her reeling back into the pillows.

Quarles stood and waited for Lucinda to sit up again. The maid crept toward the door, eyes averted. "Sit down, Maud," he commanded in a huge voice, and she fell into the nearest chair. His eyes never flinched from his daughter as she sat up and wiped the blood from her mouth, her eyes burrs of angry light. He had never hit her before, and he had just begun now. She saw that. Her insides crawled as she stared at her father and read his thoughts. She was *his* daughter, *his* girl-child. What mind she had, what will she flaunted, he had made — and now he would take that apart — *as he should have long before.*

"Who was the man in your cabin?" he asked through his teeth.

"The man I love!" she shouted, and he slapped her again. In a fury, he snapped a curtain rod from the bed's canopy, spilling drapes, then seized her arm, heaved her over, and slashed at her back with it.

Maud lunged from her chair, crying, "Stop! Stop it!"

Quarles turned on the maid and was satisfied to see abject fear warping her face. His anger had worked on her. He had known too well that his daughter's will was as obdurate as his own; she would never divulge the truth about the pirate. But Maud, gentle Maud, would tell him all she knew. "Go to my cabin," he ordered the maid, and she went to the door and waited, afraid he would attack her mistress again. But he only stood over his daughter's sobbing body and silently cursed the day he had let cruel life seduce him with love.

For days, Jaki wandered the marshy coast of Johore in a skiff that he had purchased with a few gold coins Lucinda had given him. He was anxious to find *Silenos* as quickly as possible, yet he was also grateful for each hiatus in his search that allowed him to contemplate the enormous joy he had found with Lucinda, the woman who would be his wife, who would mother his children and anchor him in creation's sealash of light and darkness.

Under a green twilight off a cove beyond Malacca, a horde of sampans swept out of the shadows and surrounded Jaki's skiff. He stood with scimitar brandished, peering anxiously for firearms among his enemy, and shouting his war cry.

A familiar guttural laugh came in return.

"Blackheart!" Jaki yelled, lowering his scimitar.

"You will die bravely, Jaki Gefjon." Pym's voice hammered from behind him, and he jumped about to see the big pirate bound from a sampan into the skiff, almost knocking Jaki from his feet. "I could use a man like you."

They embraced like bears, the stink of brandy on Pym like perfume to Jaki. Blackheart grunted and steadied the skiff with his booted foot.

"My only prayer in thirty years," Pym grumbled, "was that the four-oar you threw into the storm saved you."

"It did, captain," Jaki answered in a rush. "And it carried me with Shirazi to *Black Light,* where I learned he was a spy." Pym's mirth brittled. "Rajan Kobra knows we are here and is planning to pincer us in the strait with *The Fateful Sisters.*"

Pym clasped Jaki's shoulder, absorbing this irony. "So the very trap you warned me about on *Silenos* you've returned to prize me from." He pursed his dark lips, and the bonechips dangling at the ends of his mustache clicked together. "I treated you poorly in our last days together, Jaki — and I've been in anguish over that since. If *Silenos* carries us to freedom, I will reward you for your intelligence — and to redeem my bad faith." He looked over Jaki's shoulder. "Mister Blackheart, to the ship. We sail tonight."

Blackheart swung his hands before him, indicating that the ship was still careened.

"I don't care!" Pym rumbled. "We'll right the ship by torchlight. Triple pay in gold for the men who work. We won't be gutted belly up by muck-blooded Quarles *or* the Bantam's Muslim stooge. We're away before dawn!"

The sampans turned back into the cove and towed the skiff to a covert where *Silenos* was beached and turned on her side. By torchglow, Jaki could see that most of the barnacles had been scraped from her bottom, and the hull was partially tarred and caulked. "Devil take it, we've another two days' work here," Pym said. "But we can't wait now. You must tell me the rest. Come to the watchtower."

Wawa was there, peeling limes for Pym, and at the sight of Jaki, he ran to him squawking. Once the animal was finally gentled, the sorcerer related his story while the captain oversaw the righting of the ship. "Love is the deadliest trap," Pym warned disapprovingly when he heard about Lucinda and their four days and nights of romance aboard *The Fateful Sisters.* "Look what became of my Perdita — because of love. If I had relinquished her to the Spanish officer who first asked for her hand, I'd have my left eye still wed to my right and she would be a duchess in Manila. What a cursed fool I was to think I could make a life for her." His ugly face shook with remorse. "And you're a fool, too, if you think that beast Quarles will give his beauty to the likes of you. You're a pirate and a half-breed. No English gentleman would consent to have you as a son."

"Then we'll steal away."

"Hah! He'll track you to the ends of the world," he said. His words brought a small smile to Jaki's lips. "You think I jest. I do not. Quarles is here in Asia because I am. He has come here to avenge the death of his uncle, that faithless dog Samuel Quarles, whom he and the rest of England still believe to be a hero. How much more passionate would he be to recover his daughter, eh?" He saw the smile slip from Jaki's face. "Listen to me, young lover, and trust not your heart to the seed of your enemy. Asia abounds in beautiful women. You'll sate your soul in Jakarta, Macao, Manila."

"I will see her again at the dark of the moon in the City of Lions."

"Aye." Pym sighed, seeing in the blond youth before him the look that was need absorbed in itself. "You will see her again — if we survive her daddy's cunning and might. And when you do, Jaki boy, hark to this — don't expose yourself. Not at first. Listen to an old snake who knows his way among the hawks. Test your love, and if she's true, then I say, damn creation that made men sinners, and go with her. But test her first. Mark me, now."

Pym concentrated on readying his warship for the sea, and Jaki was left to steep in his heart's madness. At dawn *Silenos* glided from the cove and beat north along the coast to where the strait widened at Klang. There they sighted *Black Light,* bearing down on them full speed.

Jaki stirred from his brooding and stood beside Pym at the binnacle. Blackheart was at the helm, and he grunted a nervous request for orders.

"Keep our sails full, Mister Blackheart," Pym commanded. "Point the ship right at *Black Light.* And don't veer a whisker."

"Captain," Jaki said in a voice shadowed with apprehension, "when I was aboard that ship, I saw her cannon."

"Aye, you've told me. Fifty-pounders, most of them."

"Yes!" Jaki swelled with fright. "Shouldn't we turn to lee and tack back down the coast?"

"And have a six-hundred-ton man-of-war chewing at our rudder?" Pym shook his head and grinned with a devil's bravura. "We've the wind to our backs and the best helmsman in Asia at the wheel — the only wheel in this match. We'll run straight for Rajan Kobra and pray he veers. Then, if we're lucky, we'll swing with her prow, empty our broadsides into her nose, and scamper past her and into the open sea."

"Kobra's as cruel as he is determined," Jaki said, hearing the sails crackle with wind as the ship heeled over and gathered speed. "His is the bigger ship. He'll ram us for sure. And if we swerve before he does, his giant guns will blow us to splinters."

Pym slapped Jaki on the back. "Your encouragement is my strength, boy!" He bent over the voice tube beside the sternpost. "Battle stations all! Prepare cannon!" He looked to Jaki with his hardset shark's grin. "You're a sorcerer. I've seen your devil's ilk with my own eyes and eaten your unholy mushroom bread. Beseech the spirit powers to help us, sorcerer. Place a curse on *Black Light* and you can have your mountains' tears back."

They were doomed, Jaki feared; close enough now to see the Muslim sailors in the shrouds adjusting canvas to sidle *Black Light* directly into line with *Silenos*. All his efforts to find Pym and warn him had been in vain. He would never see Lucinda again. Rage mingled with despair, and a deathly calm saturated him. This was the quiescence the Spider had imparted to him. He gazed up at feathery cirrus, expecting to see the sky's sorrow, the soot of the future. Instead, he saw scimitars full of silver speed, streaked with noon. The sky was an army of wind angels. The sight of it numbed him to his bones, and the calm of stymied rage and despair in him expanded to hold the whole sky. Jaki was suddenly a chord of sunlight above the stunned animal of his body. And he prayed: *Powers of the world — protect my long journey. Cast aside my enemies and carry me free of their malignant will. As I have served you with my very life, so carry my life now in your shadow, free of the might and shrewdness of my enemies. Let your will be done — powers of the world!*

The fervor of his prayer returned him to his body, and the numbness of the trance whisked away, leaving him prickly with alertness.

The wind stiffened behind *Silenos*, and the rush of their flight tasseled seaspray and bleared their eyes. At the same instant, the backwash off the mountains dampened, and *Black Light*'s canvas went slack.

"Steady so, Blackheart!" Pym clacked open his spyglass, scrutinized the Muslim bow for prow cannon, and found them above the winged angel figurehead. They were thirty-pounders, but their range would not match *Silenos*'s precision-bored guns. He saw the Muslim crew scrambling among the shrouds, unfurling the studding sails to tack and bring the big cannon to bear. But the sudden gust of wind behind *Silenos* carried the pirate ship into firing range first, and Pym shouted the commands gleefully. "Left handsomely, Blackheart!" The ship slashed to port, and he stepped to the voice tube. "Mark and fire!"

Silenos's broadside sheared *Black Light*'s foremast, bashed in her angel figurehead, and exploded the powder of her prow guns, kicking the forecastle into the sky in a gush of timber and flames.

The fight was over. Blackheart steered *Silenos* out of range of *Black Light*'s guns, and Pym fired a mock salute to the crippled ship as they flew by. He lifted Jaki off his feet in an enormous embrace, Wawa clinging to the sorcerer's legs.

A terrified cry dropped from the crosstrees. "Ship aft!"

Pym dropped Jaki and bounded to the sternpost. Full sails set, pearl bright in the sunlight, *The Fateful Sisters* gleamed from around the Klang promontory, riding the same strong wind that had carried them past *Black Light.*

"We're at hell's gate once more!" Pym cursed. "We'll need your sorcery again to outrun that devil hound."

Jaki squinted up at the scimitar clouds, saw them blunted and blurring to windy vapors. His magic was spent, and he passed a woeful stare to Pym. The pirate captain nodded, patted the sorcerer's back. "You proved your worth," he said, tugging contemplatively at the gray bones in his mustache. "Now we'll test mine." He stepped to Blackheart's side. "Wean her from the coast slowly. We'll get fewer crosswinds in the open water. We need every knot now."

Pym paced from the quarterdeck to the forecastle, studying the set of his canvas, quickly replacing rent sails and reading the wind precisely so he could order swift changes on the yards and catch the most speed. *Silenos* flew through the channel. Even so, by noon *The Fateful Sisters* was closing to within cannon range. Through his spyglass, Pym could see Quarles in the forecastle staring at him. Pym waved, but Quarles did not wave back.

The first round from *The Fateful Sisters*'s prow cannon splashed into *Silenos*'s wake. Pym tried trailing gunpowder floaters, but Quarles would not be fooled twice by that. Marksmen on the prow detonated the kegs before they could reach their target. *Silenos*'s stern cannon, firing into the wind, did not have the range of her pursuer's guns, and the shots fell short. Flight was the only option, but with each hour, the enemy drew closer.

Midafternoon carried *The Fateful Sisters* within cannon range, and the prow guns blazed, again and again. Thirty-pound iron balls smashed *Silenos*'s stern castles, disabling her aft guns, shattering the cabin rafters, and collapsing the back ends of the two inner decks. Two shots punched holes at the water line, and the sea flashed in.

The pirates staunched the flow with bolts of canvas, but the gaping holes still bled water, and the bilges flooded. Pym rushed below deck to supervise the bailing, relieved to see that the tiller and rudder were undamaged. The British ship's heavy firing had blunted the speed of her pursuit, and *Silenos*'s crew could expect an hour's reprieve before the next assault. Jaki joined the bailing crew. Water was bucketed and spilled out port hatches; tar was melted and gobbed over the weeping canvas. The work was nearly done when the thunder of cannon gloated. The hull above the bilges blasted inward, spraying whole timbers. The bulwarks shredded with a deafening roar, and brazen sunlight flooded in.

A wave of doom rose up in Jaki. He scrambled over the debris and crushed bodies, ignoring the wails of the wounded to reach the gangway. He was determined to meet his death in the open.

The quarterdeck was in shambles. The sternpost was cracked, most of the taffrail was missing, the rat god whetting stone lay in pebbles underfoot. Blackheart was gone. The planks before the helm had dropped away, and Pym was steering with his legs spread wide on the beams that supported them. His face gleamed with tears. Wawa cowered beside the binnacle and scurried to Jaki's side when he stepped to the quarterdeck.

"Blackheart," Pym wept. "Cannonball took his head off!" Jaki saw the trail of blood across the tattered planks. "I threw his head after his body! I threw his head into the sea after his body!" He brushed tears from his face with the cuff of his red shirt. "I thought you were dead below. The last rounds caved in the castles. There must be carnage below."

"There is." Jaki stared aft at their stalker, fallen back now after the fury of her last barrage, and wondered if Lucinda was aboard. "We're done, captain."

Pym grimaced. "We're done when we're dead! Never forget that, lad, and you'll live until you die. Look at the men."

Jaki saw the pirates hard at their stations, hanging in the shrouds, keeping the rigging tight.

"I'll not give up my life — nor theirs." Pym's one eye was wide and staring. "Quarles is death. And we might as well be a dying man in a sickbed fighting the croup. We'll hold on till it strangles us! By God, we'll hold!" He pointed west to the slouching body of Sumatra, where the sun barbed the distant mountains. "In an hour we'll be running with the twilight. An hour more and it'll be night. Take the helm, boy. I'm going to shoot the sun."

Jaki jumped astride the broken gap of the deck and seized the wheel while Pym got out his backstaff. Blotting tears from his eye, he sighted the sun in the backstaff's mirror and shouted the markings as though Blackheart were there to note them. Then he collapsed the staff and unfurled the charts.

"Here we are off Tandjungbalai," he said, jabbing the chart. "Ahead is a bluff and a pride of reef islands. We'll reach there after dark and lose Quarles. Mark me, if this doesn't happen, my soul will stand for yours in hell."

Pym was right. The sun sank, and night rains shrouded the stars. *The Fateful Sisters* fired her prow guns into the twilight. One shot crashed into the starboard rail and kicked out the poop deck's gunwale, carrying another seaman to his death, but the others flew wild. By dark, the British vessel was lagging behind the intrepid *Silenos*, and Pym ordered the day sails reefed and the black canvas set, all in running sequence so little headway was lost. With every light doused, *Silenos* sailed by soundings into the reef islands, and they watched *The Fateful Sisters*, with her sprigs of light blazing from her lantern-hung bowsprit and rails, float by within musket range. When her lights were sparks on the horizon, *Silenos* drifted out into the open water and then made sail northeast for Selangor, where Pym knew a sultan who, for diamonds and gold, would help him refit his vessel.

Planks were laid over the hole before the helm, but no one would stand as helmsman where Blackheart had lost his head until Pym offered triple pay. Jaki accompanied Pym below deck to survey the damage. Saja was busy with the wounded and would work the night through; the dead were buried hastily at sea. Pym's cabin had collapsed to the deck below, and he and Jaki rummaged through the debris searching for an ivory map case that Pym was adamant about finding. Shortly after midnight they found it among the stalks of Pym's crushed rosewood desk. It was a truncated tusk, big as a forearm and carved with human-faced Byzantine lions. Pym handed the carved tusk to Jaki. "This is yours now, sorcerer," he said in a voice slurred with fatigue and grief. "There are maps inside, drawn from my time in the New World, thirty years gone. They're yours, now that my time is done."

"Done? I thought you weren't done until you were dead. You look hale enough to me."

"Aye, but I've a foretaste of my doom," he answered. "Losing Blackheart took the wind out of me. Without my pneuma I won't be going much further, boy." Then briskly, "I'm resolved to it. Life has been abundant with me, and freer than anything except love could redeem." His face darkened. "I touched that love briefly in Perdita." He gazed round at the devastated cabin and met Jaki's rueful stare. "And that love touched me again with the naked world's beauty after you healed me of my headpain. When I thought I'd lost you in that storm, I grieved that I had ever raged at you. For you have shown me that love is its own truth." He paused. "The truth of love soaked me at Njurat when I met the very embodiment of Wyvern in your cursed mother of life. What a monster she is, eh? She woke me up to the truth. And yet I fell asleep on my bones after I lost Perdita. Only now do I see that to be truly awake is to be in pain — and pain makes us want to sleep. The mother of life loves us to death, doesn't she? You know that better than any man I've met. And that is why I'm giving you this —" He held out the ivory canister. "My charts of the Caribbean. They show in great detail its numerous islands, reefs, and seaways. When I'm gone, leave Asia. The likes of Quarles own this corner of the world now. Empire is voracious. You showed me that in the clouds. Don't let it devour you as it has me. Go to the New World, where there's room yet for unknown pirates to harry empire. And harry them fiercely, boy. Harry them in the name of the darkness that holds all light. Harry them for Wyvern, the mother of life."

Jaki did not have the heart to inform Pym that his pirating days, too, were at an end. There was no rage in him like that which had fueled Pym's career. He yearned for love, for his love, Lucinda, whose ring he touched to his heart to remind him of life's inestimable promise. With his other hand, he took the tusk carved with the shape of lionmen.

"Captain, you are alive," Jaki said with a force that echoed too loudly in the ruined cabin. "*Silenos* will be rebuilt."

Pym lifted a twisted piece of metal from his shattered chronometer and laughed mournfully. "Take my offering and leave me to grieve my quartermaster."

Jaki took the tusk of maps topside with him, and he and Wawa climbed into the crosstrees to relieve the watch there. He touched the amber ring to the tusk and tingled to feel two destinies exclusive of each other meeting in his lap. He was Asian, and he wanted Europe, and for Lucinda and his children to live under the silver peaks of the Alps. The tusk was a tooth of the unknown with its maps of mystery, and he almost threw it overboard. He did not want anything of the New World. He wanted life and love, a fate simple with self-indulgence. He wanted Lucinda. But he knew he could not have her now — his fate as a pirate had not quite finished.

"Love solves distance," Pym said to Jaki once *Silenos* was anchored in a cove in Selangor. A noon storm rolled fire and purple smoke over the seaward horizon, and green clouds hung over the jungle flats.

Jaki was dressed in buckskin breeches, brown stockings and flat ankle-slung shoes of tanned cordovan, a gray sleeveless suede jacket that fell below his hips, and a blue billow-sleeved shirt without a collar. At his hip he wore Shirazi's scimitar, and around his neck dangled Pieter Gefjon's shrunken head. He was hatless, and his hair was swept back and hung in lovelocks over his shoulders. With Wawa at his side and his blowgun leaning on his shoulder, he was ready to begin his journey south to meet Lucinda.

Pym and Jaki stood together a last time on the quarterdeck. The wounded ship was already under repair, and the air rang with the sounds of hammering and sawing.

"No matter we will never see each other again," Pym said, his one eye glossed with sorrow. "I'll never see Perdita or Blackheart again either, but my parting with them was not so sweet as this. Love solves distance, lad. Whatever separates us, we share the love that healed the pain of my lost eye and that taught you all you know of the sea."

"Won't you even consider coming with me?" Jaki asked, gesturing to the blue-hulled skiff with furled sail bobbing alongside *Silenos*.

"What, and spend the rest of my days landlocked while you sire your family?" He swept his arm at the shore. "This is as close to land as I want to be. If I'm lucky, I'll die at sea." He winked and took a swig to fortune. "One word of advice to the lovelorn, lad." He lifted the dangling shrunken head with his stubbed fingertips and shook his head. "I wouldn't be wearing this when I went calling on my ladylove if I were you."

Jaki chuckled politely. "I'm wearing it only to help me with our parting, captain — to remind me of where I came from, so I can see clearly where I'm going."

"And where is that, Jaki Gefjon?" Pym asked, raising a hand to his face to wipe away rain and tears.

"I was fathered by money," he answered, "and reared by a people who had no word for money. I grew up in the morning of the world. I grew up restrained by instincts, though my teacher tried to free me from them. But always I have wanted my place in the world. And my instincts were not enough to save me from the guns and the gunmen who wanted money. And so I met you — my last father. Everything is pain, is it not? We rage against empire and its greed for money. And our rage is the only real love in this wounded world. But the new age is loveless, captain. I thought you saw that in the clouds with me."

"Aye, lad, I saw that," Pym admitted, the rattails of his hair gleaming with rain. "But my fate is different from yours. I never knew the morning of the world. I was born to money and did not know its evil until it turned on me. At least I was privileged to feel the strength of mystery in my suffering and know that there's more to the Life than money. I fear that in times to come the wound will worsen, we will lose that mysterious strength, and all that will remain is money and its clever geometry of bought people."

A frown creased Pym's serpent-scarred brow, yet he smiled. "Let us say no more. The truth cannot be added to." He hugged Jaki. When they separated, he reached into his pocket and removed the black leather Bible cover pierced by the Lanun pirates' nailhole.

"Keep that for me," Jaki said. "I found my place in the tree called family — with you. From here, by your training, I can leave the dark mine of my past and enter the light of the world, where I will find my own home."

"*Make* your own home, lad," Pym said, and lifted a duffel bag from beside him. "You'll find nothing but trouble if you go looking in this world. Might makes right here as in the jungle — as always. Dare to make your own way. But use your head, not your heart. And let this remind you ever more of heaven's evil joy." He opened the bag. Inside was the ship's flag, folded to a triangle, and a silk pouch big as a coconut. "Wyvern," Pym said, and passed the duffel to Jaki. "A Chinese artist stitched her for me three decades gone. I want you to have her. And the pouch, too. It has what's left of the mountains' tears. I owe you that for your magic. If you're going to take a wife and live in the world's wound, you'll need a fortune." He embraced Jaki again and pushed away. "Go now. We'll be together in our wanderings."

Pym turned away and shouted commands to the men hoisting timber to the main deck. Jaki stared a last time at his broad back and wild silver hair and lowered himself into the waiting skiff. Wawa swung down after him, and they untied and set sail into the rain-glimmering afternoon. When he looked back, he saw Pym aboard an empty piragua with Saja and two crewmen, rowing to shore to secure more medical supplies and provisions. Jaki was tacking into the wind when he glimpsed the snout of a big ship rounding the jungle-strewn bluff of the cove. His heart lurched.

The Fateful Sisters glided into view.

Jaki turned and looked to shore in time to see Pym pulling up to the beach and a bevy of armed men lurch from the shrubs at the edge of the sand. The pirate captain was seized before even a knife could flash and Jaki could hear Pym's roar of protest. The captain threw a fist toward *Silenos* and was subdued, his arms pinned back by three men. He struggled mightily, and Jaki was certain they were going to shoot him. A flintlock rose and fell, glancing his head, and he went down.

A signal fire glinted on the bluff overlooking the beach — and Jaki understood then that Pym had been betrayed by Selangor's sultan. *The Fateful Sisters* was too far away for them to see Pym, but Jaki was certain Quarles had orchestrated this drama. Pym was a prisoner and *Silenos* the prize.

Jaki cried out in a wrack of fury and futility. His impulse was to turn about and fall on the men who had seized the pirate. Yet even in his rage, he knew that was certain death and would accomplish nothing. He saw the desperate men on the decks of *Silenos*, waiting for their ship to be taken. Four-oars were being lowered, and some of the crew were preparing to flee, while on the shore, piraguas were loading with British soldiers to give chase. *She won't be taken!* Jaki brought his skiff about and aimed her for the pirate ship.

Riding the wind, Jaki reached *Silenos* and tied off as the British piraguas shoved into the bay. He clambered up a rope the crewmen lowered, Wawa on his shoulders, and shouted orders for the men to gather the wounded and abandon ship. Then he had five of the gunners follow him below and help him stoke the cannon. "Wait until you're certain of blowing them to hell," he commanded, and grabbed a long coil of fuse. He hurried below deck to the powder room. Frantically, he crawled in headfirst and was halfway through when the ship's cannon boomed and the timbers shook.

In the dark of the powder room he unstoppered a keg, knotted the end of the fuse, and thumbed it into the keg's opening. When he reached the gundeck, the fuse stringing behind him, the gunners had already left. Through the ports he saw that several piraguas had been blown apart, but several more were closing in. He took one of the smoldering cannon tapers the gunners had left behind and lit the fuse.

Cannon thunder rolled across the cove from *The Fateful Sisters* as Quarles tried to disable *Silenos*'s guns and prevent her crew from escaping. The gunmen were in the skiff, arguing about leaving Jaki behind, when he appeared at the rail. He swung into the boat on the loose rope, and Wawa skirled down after him.

The Fateful Sisters fired her broadsides, and the two escaping four-oars that carried the wounded were blasted to shards. Jaki unfurled the skiff's sail, and as they luffed from *Silenos*, more shot struck the pirate ship, collapsing her masts, shearing her bowsprit, and crushing her quarterdeck. The British piraguas reached *Silenos*, and the men climbed aboard and raised the Union Jack on the poop deck.

Suddenly, a gargantuan explosion tore through *Silenos* and lifted the ship off the water in a fireblown cloud. The blast spun flaming timbers into the sky, and the gray waters of the cove were tattered with fiery groats. Smoke-streaming chunks of the blasted ship crashed into the bay, splashing water over the skiff. The crewmen ducked into the bilges, but Jaki stood tall, staring hard at the glut of fumes and rubbish spluttering in the chewed water where *Silenos* had just been.

He took the tiller and steered the skiff through the debris. A bright wind slashed from a radiant break in the storm banks, and the small boat sliced through the flogging rain toward the iron horizon of the sea.

The explosion of *Silenos* rattled the timbers of *The Fateful Sisters*, and Lucinda's seventeen winters rose up in her all at once. She had been sitting curled in her bed for days, thriving on the pain from her cut back while *The Fateful Sisters* pursued *Silenos*. Her father, who had never taken her on a military expedition before, insisted she attend the chase and destruction of her pirate-lover's ship. At the clangor of bells and whistles that called the crew to their battle stations, she had curled under the bedsheets, trembling with each cannonblast as if struck. But when the explosion that shattered *Silenos* shivered the planks of her cabin, she rushed to the box windows. Smoke rolled by like fog, and a damp gust speckled her with the acrid char of gunpowder. Leaning her head out the window, she could see nothing but two four-oars and a blue skiff sliding through the rain toward the sea.

The timbers shook again as the two trailing four-oars were caught in range and flew apart like smashed jugs. Lucinda turned away, aghast to see the scattered, torn bodies. Suddenly Maud cried, "I see him!"

She pointed through the open window. "There — standing in the sailboat."

Lucinda looked again, her hand cupped against the wet wind, and saw a blond figure who had to be Jaki. Quarles saw him, too, through his spyglass from the poop deck. The skiff was already beyond range and too spry to pursue along this lacy coast. *Small difference*, Quarles told himself, knowing that the new moon would deliver him the hopeful defiler of his daughter. From Maud he had extracted the time and place of the lovers' next meeting and, with a welting blow across her face to allay Lucinda's suspicions, had sworn the maid to silence. For now, Quarles would content himself with the capture of Asia's premiere plunderer. He ordered Lucinda on deck for the arrival of the prisoners. He wanted her to see her handsome pet's cohorts.

Quarles waited until night, until *The Fateful Sisters* was running south through the black strait and Pym's cries had withered to silence, before he collected a skin of brandy and climbed down to the orlop deck to see his prisoners. The three pirate crewmen were stowed below in the stinking heat of the bilges. Pym was locked in a bamboo cage above them, on the lowest deck, and though the cage was too small for him to stand or stretch out, and no hatches vented the fecal stink from the surrounding animal pens, he was less likely to contract the hemorrhaging sickness that sometimes killed people bitten by rats. Quarles did not want to lose the murderer of his uncle to simple happenstance, no matter how grim. The elusive pirate king had been captured by William Quarles and so would be dispatched by him. The public execution of the legendary Wyvern would be a political coup for the British presence in Asia.

Quarles thumped the bamboo bars with his boot, and Pym roused from his stupor. His one eye peered from under a heavy lid and closed as nausea ascended in him. He curled tighter on himself. Quarles unstoppered the brandy and swigged from the skin. The ruby fragrance opened Pym's eye and he watched Quarles in the lantern light, savoring the bouquet. "Pomace brandy," Quarles said, squatting and offering the skin. "Crushed *grapes*, captain. From Europe. Veneto."

Pym rose to a crouch, ugly with hate. "Your Uncle Samuel betrayed the fleet," he snarled. "Not I!"

"I know," Quarles said. "I have seen my uncle's letters to the Spanish governor. He sold the fleet's schedule, it seems. Yet, he was not betraying his country so much as defending his faith."

"Bah!" Pym recoiled from the proffered drink and squeezed his trembling hands between his knees.

"My uncle was not naturally a treacherous man. It would appear that he was led to his misfortune by a secret society that employs deceitful and immoral means toward noble achievements. The Church of the Two Thieves —"

"Papist shrews!" Pym cried. "They've been threading their intrigues in Europe for centuries."

"And you were one of their victims." Quarles sloshed the liquor. "Drink with me to the innocence of your youth, Captain Pym, which so utterly denied me the innocence of mine."

Pym fought back the thirsting chills tremoring his muscles, and scrutinized his captor. Under the curve of his flat-crowned hat, Quarles's stocky face glowed with maliciousness. His coifed beard could not hide the smirk on his lips, yet he said without disdain, "We share a suffering, you and I. We were both challenged by fate, captain. You were branded a traitor. I was condemned to a life of poverty at the dockyard. Neither of us was prepared for or deserved our fates. You became a pirate. I became equally hard, and perhaps as predatory. But I chose to serve and not defy. Now, sir, I have a captaincy, a beautiful daughter, and the respect of my peers. While you —" He swilled the brandy in a gulping gasp. "You will hang within the week from the yardarm of this ship — hang by your neck, your only legacy after forty years of piracy."

Pym loomed against the bars. "To that, I will drink." He reached from the cage.

Quarles placed the skin on the deck, two inches from Pym's groping hand. He stood up and smilelessly watched Pym strain for the brandy. "*We* are the two thieves, Captain Pym. Your pirates loved you and were faithful to death. Not one surrendered. Yet the world despises you. My crew fear me. My own daughter loathes me. But I am respected in every port and honored in England. We are thieves, the two of us, for we have stolen our lives from fate and made our own destinies. You, unfortunately, made your destiny too much your own."

Pym's reach shrank, and he withdrew his arm with a disgusted snort. "You killed my wife."

"*You* had a wife?" Quarles's face inflated with surprise, and he squatted again. "You startle me, Pym. I did not realize you were capable of fidelity to anyone but yourself. But then, indeed, a wife is one's self." He removed a wooden cannikin from his pocket, poured brandy into it, and placed it beside the cage where Pym could reach it. "I assure you, my action at Iduna was entirely tactical. Your wife's death was a casualty of my strategy to flush you out. I would have met you honorably at sea, but you avoided me. I, too, have lost a wife to plague. I understand your pain. Drink up, Pym — you will be with her again soon enough. Or do you not believe in the afterlife?"

Pym dashed the brandy down before his trembling hands could spill a drop. *Festina lente, Trevor!* he admonished himself for his thirst. He closed his eyes and pressed his head back against the cage, grateful for the stinging relief of the liquor sharpening his blood.

"I am amused by the cover of a Bible I took from the pocket of your coat," Quarles said, holding the leaves open to reveal the handwriting of the Gefjon patriarchs. "Who is this Jaki Gefjon whose family tree you carry?"

Pym squinted. "Is the boy alive?"

"And wooing my daughter." Quarles's tight smile glinted like metal behind his whiskers. "He thinks he has escaped. But I have trapped him with his heart."

"Homo homini lupus," the pirate said in a burning whisper.

"Yes, man is a wolf unto man," Quarles agreed. "That is what converts us to Evil."

Pym conceded with a fatigued nod.

Quarles, relishing his victory, read aloud Pieter Gefjon's Latin inscription. "What do you make of that, docent, now that you are facing the lion of the final moment yourself?"

"Are you too ill educated to know of the Doctrine of Signatures? The depths that death guards are the correspondences. We cannot see our relation to the all until we die. And so fools like you are doomed to live partial lives and believe heroes villains and true villains heroes."

A laugh huffed from Quarles's belly. "You think too much of yourself, pirate."

"I do. I am an alchemist. I read the manuscripts at Oriel, and I learned to live their truths so that life's pain would not reduce me to the benighted varlet it has made of you. I worked my ship like an alembic, converting the dross of empire's outcasts to the gold of self-strong men. That's Trevor Pym's work — dared because I could accept myself for what fate made me."

Quarles's smile brightened to have guessed this about his enemy. "You delude yourself."

"Perhaps. But the man whose tree you hold is a true alchemical spirit, Mercurius himself, the son of darkness."

"You weary me, Pym. The boy is a heathen. I will snare him as I have snared you."

Pym shook his head and steered a finger through the bars to touch the Bible cover at the blank space where Jaki's name was absent. "Fear him."

Quarles's smile blinked out, and he slapped the cover shut and pocketed it. "He will be joining you in hell. You do believe in hell? Look around you, Pym. This is heaven."

Pym leaned back and shut his eye. "You killed my wife," he said with eerie gentleness. "Your vengeance against me was perfected then, William Quarles. What you do to me here is a favor — and the death you promise a boon."

Quarles rose, empty in his bones, disappointed by Pym's sudden composure. He kicked the skin of brandy close enough for the pirate to reach and turned away.

"William," Pym called when Quarles reached the companion ladder. "When I'm clothed in seaweed, with fish for eyes, I will be like a king. But you will never be more than what you are now." He tipped the skin and poured the liquor straight down his throat. "Mark me," he gasped.

Jaki stood in a cage of rain on a pier in Serangoon Harbor. Singapore ranged before him like a constellation that had smashed into a swamp. Torchlights from the bamboo-walled settlements of Changi, Serangoon, Seletar, Siglap, and Bedok glimmered among the black shadows of mangrove belts and marsh copses. The lion stele in the Strait of Johore, where the harbor widened to deepwater wharves, glared in the lanternglow from *The Fateful Sisters*. The decks were well patroled, and the wharf around the warship had armed men stationed in groups of three.

Beyond the stele were ancient flowering trees, terraced hanging gardens, and the lion plaza where Jaki was to meet Lucinda at the new moon in two more days. But now his attention was turned to the stone garrison inside the bamboo wall of Changi. There, Pym was a prisoner. Jaki and the twenty surviving crewmen of *Silenos* had followed *The Fateful Sisters* south from Selangor in the skiff and whatever canoes, prau, that they could buy or steal from the swamp tribes. The big ship had quickly vanished ahead, and the five-day pursuit had wrung Jaki with the apprehension that Quarles intended to take his prisoner to the British settlement at Surabaja across the Java Sea, inaccessible to the fragile prau. He was relieved when they reached Singapore and found *The Fateful Sisters* at anchor. Here, at least, there was a chance of freeing Pym.

Jaki had moored the pirates' prau in the cane brush around Changi, and after leashing Wawa, he and the others had come to the unlit pier before the garrison to barter for Pym's life. Now he stood in the rain, his men hidden in the swamp behind him, and shouted his ransom offer to the guard. His promise of diamonds brought several turbaned soldiers to the garret, and they beckoned him closer. Instinct prickled in him, and he decided not to budge. Instead he threw one of the diamonds to the guards, and they disappeared with it. Minutes later, the gate of the settlement swung open, and a band of mounted warriors charged out, parangs whirling. The guards reappeared on the garret, and their arquebuses flared in the dark. A ball swiped past Jaki's ear, and he drew his scimitar and threw his body into his war cry. The pirates crouching in the cane brakes fired their flintlocks, and the charging horsemen were flung from their saddles.

The pirates broke from their cover, charging the open gate. Seizing the reins of a frenzied horse, Jaki pulled the animal around and sent it flying back into the settlement, the pirates rushing behind it. The arquebuses again spit fire from the garrets, killing the horse and tearing the ear off a pirate. Three of the pirates took aim and dropped the garret guards.

Inside the settlement, Jaki led his men to the garrison. Pym appeared in a barred window of a tower overlooking the front courtyard, his silver hair shining in the dark, and the men cheered for him. Hoof-thunder rumbled, and more horsemen galloped from the stables behind the garrison, a squad of turbaned guards charging behind them.

"Fall back to the prau!" Jaki yelled, and they scrambled for the gates. Musketfire dropped three of the men, and four more were cut down by horsemen. At the gates, the pirates turned and emptied their flintlocks. Their long practice with the weapons made each shot count, and the pursuit faltered, allowing Jaki and the others to escape into the rainy marsh.

Cowering in the muddy fields, they watched the gates close and the guards double on the garret. There would be no rescue for Pym, and when the pirates realized that, they decided to go their own way. "The captain is not dead until he's dead," Jaki told the men passionately, and they did not dispute him. They simply turned silently and disappeared into the many doors of the night. Only five wild faces remained, staring at him like rays from the center of darkness.

The six of them haunted the marsh around Changi, searching for a way in, scurrying low in the tule grass until they discovered holes in the bamboo fence big enough for them to crawl through. Once inside, they were stymied by the garrison's stone walls and the Muslim guards. But they overheard a guard saying that Pym was being held until the Bantam of Siam and a delegation of local sultans could arrive to witness the execution — and so behold the superiority of the British in protecting the Bantam's interests. Two days later, by the night of the new moon, the crewmen had not succeeded in getting any closer to their captain, and Jaki decided to meet Lucinda as he had promised.

That night the rains abated, and aisles of stars led the way to infinity. Making his way toward the lion plaza through the hanging gardens of Serangoon that walled the harbor, Jaki was flushed with heartglow. Memories of the days and nights he had spent with Lucinda aboard *The Fateful Sisters* lightened his grief over Pym's capture, and he continued to hope that he would find a way to free his captain.

Thinking now of Pym, he remembered the captain's warning from days before, not to trust the seed of his enemy. He wanted the satisfaction of meeting that warning fairly, and he approached the plaza cautiously, avoiding the cobbled walkways. He was wearing black breeches and doublet to hide him well in the shadows of the torchlit plaza and a black headcloth to cover his bright hair. Monkeys chittered noisily in the branches above him, and as he sidled through the wrangle of jasmine and mimosa shrubs, he spied figures in the adjacent trees. His heartbeat smudged when he saw that the crouching shapes were men, long-trousered monkeyfaces with drawn sabers. They had not yet seen him, and he was able to approach closer and recognize them as English sailors. He whirled silently into the deeper darkness, stung that Pym had been right.

Once hidden in the shadows, Jaki looked for Quarles, his mind racing with thoughts of capturing him and bartering him for Pym, but he did not find the British captain among the lurking men. Instead, on the winding path that climbed up from the harbor to the lion plaza, he spotted Lucinda and her maid on their way to meet him. That baffled him. Why would they endanger themselves — unless they were unaware of the ambush? But, then, who had betrayed him?

Dashing through the aqueous shadows of starlight, he followed the paths along tiers of sandalwood and kumquat trees toward the women. Their pastel gowns glowed like specters in the dark. From his vantage, he could see that they were unaccompanied by guards, and he waited until they reached a bend in the path where the sailors in the trees could not see them. He wanted to see the women's faces clearly. When he stepped onto the path before them, he removed his headband to be certain that they would recognize him.

"Jaki!" Lucinda called with jubilant surprise, and he knew at once that she had not betrayed him. She rushed to him, and his blood spun swiftly. "You came back. I knew you would."

He pulled her closer, then jolted suddenly and drew a loaded flintlock from under his doublet, aiming it at the maid who was slipping away, edging around a myrtle tree. "Stop or I will slay you, betrayer."

The maid's eyes went round and pleading. "Don't kill me! I beg you, sir! I only did what was best for my mistress."

Lucinda looked at the frightened maid without understanding and turned her perplexity on Jaki. He told her about the sailors hidden in the trees ahead.

"I had to tell him, my lady," Maud said, sobbing. "But I told him nothing of the passage from Jakarta. He thinks your swain came aboard as we docked."

"But why did you tell Father about my tryst?" Lucinda demanded.

"Had I any choice, my lady? If Mister Gefjon had met you only at dockside, it must have been to arrange a meeting. Why else would he stay so short a time? And I could not say you had refused, for you yourself declared to your father that this is the man you love. If I had lied, we would be found out and worse off."

"Nothing would be worse for me than to lose this man." She clutched at Jaki, who had lowered his flintlock but was staring into the jasmine shadows for movement.

"Please, my lady, forgive me." Maud's face crumpled, and tears flicked to her cheeks. "I could not bear to see him beating you."

Lucinda put her arms about her, and Maud pressed her face to her mistress's shoulder. "I should have known," Lucinda said. "We've sneaked off ship many a time, but this was the easiest. Father arranged for the watch to shift early, did he not?"

Maud nodded. "He wanted you to see your swain captured."

Jaki touched Lucinda's arm. "If your father knows you left ship, he will have sent a guard behind to meet with those ahead. We must leave the path quickly."

"You will stay here, Maud," Lucinda ordered. "If you love me as truly as you say, then watch the path faithfully and use our whistle should anyone approach."

Maud nodded and peered into the black flutters of shrubbery. "Come back for me, Luci," she called in an anxious whisper as Lucinda and Jaki stepped into darkness. Jaki took Lucinda's hand and guided her through hedges of mimosa to the top ledge of the garden, high above the big ships, lorchas, and sampans in their halos of lanternlight on the black water. "Until tonight, I did not know if you would be here," Jaki breathed, embracing her. She flinched, and he saw the welt on her shoulder where her gown had slipped in his eager hug. "You have been beaten."

"It is nothing," she said, fiercely.

"This is what Maud meant," Jaki said with anguish. "Your father truly beat you."

"He is my father, yet he loves me with an iron heart." In the dark, her golden hair was ablaze with starfire, her eyes bright pieces of the night in her pale face. She smelled like wind in a meadow, and her bones felt light and fragile as glass.

"Then you will come away with me?" he asked, caressing her cheek.

"I've already arranged for our passage on a Swedish frigate to Surabaja. From there we can ship to Europe. I will sell my gems, and we shall find a place to live."

"But look. You won't have to sell your gems," Jaki said, drawing a pouch out of his pocket and opening it to show a cluster of uncut diamonds, each big as a man's thumb. "This is only a few of what I have — my tribe's legacy. Money will never own us."

They kissed, and the taste of her mouth was the consolation he had yearned for since the green days of his jungle childhood. "Then quickly, get the rest of your treasure now, my love," she said. "The carrack sails at dawn."

Jaki slumped, his breath drooped drowsily in his lungs. "I cannot," he replied almost inaudibly. "I must stay and save my captain."

"Pym?" she asked in a blare of disbelief. "Father will hang that rogue tomorrow at noon. Dignitaries have arrived from all over Asia to see it. You can do nothing."

"I have no choice in this, I swear it," he replied thinly, afraid to break the spell of their pledge. "I must try. I've told you how he has cared for me."

Lucinda shook her head. "I know he has earned your love — but he is yet a pirate. Don't you see?" She gave him a wide-eyed, imploring look. "You will be captured and hanged beside him."

"Then that is my fate."

"No! No talk of fates!" Her jaw was set, her face rigid. "We are not children anymore. Our fates are in our own hands now. I beg you, before God, do not leave me, not for this brigand."

Jaki did not flinch. "Lucinda, I too am what he is. I cannot abandon him. Surely you understand that." Tears lit his eyes. "Faith is all I have of the Life. Without that, you would be marrying a living corpse. Forever after, you would regret leaving the life of promise with your father for me."

Her face buckled, and she bit her lip not to weep. "You belittle me, Jaki."

"Lucinda —" Jaki's expression was frantic with caring. "After I have saved Pym, I will come for you. Nothing will stop me."

She shook her head. "Maud has betrayed me. If I go back now —" Her voice quavered. "I will never see you again. There is a Dutch carrack departing for Batavia with the dawn tide. Father has booked my passage. If we do not flee now, he will send me back to England."

"I will find you," he said with haunted resolve. Her expression told him she thought he was throwing his life away, and he did not dare ask her to come with him. "I will find you wherever he sends you."

A whistle trilled from the path below.

Lucinda's hands fell away from Jaki, and the radiant persistence in her eyes dulled. "If you think so little of me that a pirate means more, then truly, I was mistaken to come here. What a fool you must think me." And she turned away abruptly and started down the path, toward Maud and the imperial blaze of *The Fateful Sisters*, hoping with every step that Jaki would rush after her and call her back.

Jaki stood in the threads of starlight and watched her silk-ruffled shape drift away from him, and could not move.

Turbaned and with his face smudged with bonechar, Jaki watched at dawn from a covert of indigo bales mounded along a pier as Lucinda and her maid, accompanied by an English guard, boarded a Dutch carrack. After their trunks were carried aboard, the gangways were hoisted, the moorings slipped, and the big Dutch ship eased away from the quay wall, riding the tide into the strait. Jaki's heart wheezed with helplessness.

Toward noon, he and the five faithful pirates mingled with the large crowd in the harbor plaza, watching as Pym, arms shackled behind him, was led through a phalanx of musket-wielding British sailors to *The Fateful Sisters*. He was drunk, gustily singing a sea chanty as he was half carried through the jeering assemblage, the serpent brand on his brow glowing scarlet. Plume-capped sailors stood him on the main deck, while the Bantam of Siam and the sultans of Johore, Trengganu, Kelantan, Selangor, and Kedah sat in judgment on the quarterdeck in carved mahogany thrones.

The Bantam was thin and ashen as a wooden post, but in his silk finery studded with rubies and emeralds, he was imposing as a pontiff, and he presided over the court with imperious aplomb, serenely ignoring Pym's noises. The sultans watched dispassionately, already thinking ahead to the feast to follow. Their oiled beards glinted in the sunlight, and their eyes batted drowsily, unaccustomed to noonfire. Hsi Hang was in the gallery behind them, alongside Rajan Kobra, who grinned beatifically throughout the ceremony and laughed aloud when Pym doubled over and vomited. Three sailors lifted him and propped him to the mainmast by hooking his shackles to a cable truss.

Quarles paraded before the dignitaries and the gallery, his stout girth emphasized by the large ruff of his collar and his wide-hipped breeches. The flamboyant feather in his cocked hat shook as he recounted Pym's crimes, and his sunburned face grew hotter with his passionate declamation. Pym swayed with anger, his one eye now soberly fixed on his accusers.

Jaki pressed through the crowd until he was standing before the gangway guard. All morning he had surveyed the ship, seeking some way to extricate Pym. They had cruised past the warship in a prau, under the nose of *Black Light* with her new forecastle and Hsi Hang's opulent junks, but Quarles had posted musketmen on the seaward rails of his ship. Saja and the two crewmen captured with Pym had been tried and hanged from the bowsprit the previous day, and their bodies were tarred and stobbed upright on the levee as an example to all pirates. The sight of the stiff, black-resined corpses assailed Jaki's hope. The ambition to sacrifice himself in a raging attack dulled at the sight of so many ready weapons. If there were some chance of killing Quarles and the Bantam he would have been able to muster the vitality for an assault. As it was, he could barely empower himself to watch.

Pym's time to speak came, and he was unhooked from the truss to stand between two sailors. With a defiant scowl he stood tall, fierce and dignified, and steadied himself. He spoke in English though he knew that most of the heckling faces in the crowd would not understand him. Even so, none dared breech the last words of a condemned man, and the silence of the harbor was violated only by the cries of sea birds.

"Bantam, sultans, self-appointed and majestically self-righteous judges, listen well to the one you drive ahead of you into oblivion. You accuse me of treason and piracy. I plead innocent to both. As to the count of treason, I did indeed kill Samuel Quarles. I admit it with the averred freedom of a man facing his death. But *I* was not the traitor. Samuel Quarles betrayed Drake's fleet to the Spanish, and it was God's curse upon me to witness it and slay him for his betrayal. This his vainglorious nephew knows to be true. And this I declare before God and all His fallen angels." Pym's thick features trembled with the passion of his veracity, and he looked in turn at each of the sultans and the Bantam, meeting their stares with his arrant eye.

"Now that you greedy minions of empire are to murder me, I will admit that it was I who harried you under the flag of the monster Wyvern, I who hampered your rape of Asia — but in vengeance, you bloodfat devils. Never in greed. In vengeance only did I war with you, because you are evil and no one stands against you. You are evil, for you and your kings walk on the backs of people. You trample them naked into the earth for your greater stature. Your allegiance is not to God but to gold. The curse of your plundering is on your heads and the heads of your children." He shook his shackles at the gathered throng, then saw the laughter in their faces and dropped his arms. "There is no true freedom in life," he said less forcefully. "All of us are chained to mystery and misery. And all of you are going where I am going."

"But not as quickly!" Quarles called out. "Or as vilely!"

Pym ignored his captor's taunts and turned to the mainmast. His hands were unbound, and he climbed the shrouds to the crosstrees, where his wrists were bound again. A rope was placed about his neck as he stared up into the soaring cloudflow. The moment it was secure, he threw himself into the air. His body fell a short distance and jerked to a frantic spasm at the end of the taut rope, as the soul of Trevor Pym wrenched to be free of his body.

A cheer went up from the crowd, and William Quarles faced the Bantam with an exultant expression. Most of the gallery guests were already stirring, eager for the banquet, but the Bantam and Hsi Hang remained seated and watched with glowing faces while the pirate captain danced his death jig.

Jaki did not blink until Pym's body stopped writhing in midair. Then he closed his eyes and watched the bloodlight behind his lids scrawl its immemorial and indecipherable promises.

Once the hanging was over and the festivities in the palace of Serangoon began, *Black Light* dropped her lines and slipped out of the harbor.

Jaki and his five men followed in their prau, unnoticed among the armada of junks, carracks, and sampans crowding the inlet.

Black Light traveled west, along the broad Johore Strait. Jaki surmised that she meant to follow the inland strait to take on fresh water and meat before launching into the ocean. A strategy unfolded in him, shaped by his hot grief as he watched *Black Light* drift slowly along the jungle shoreline.

Relinquishing the prow to one of the crewmen, he joined at the oars with lusty fervor, driven by rage. The prau skimmed close to the mud-banks opposite the Muslim man-of-war. At the riverbend it quickly overtook the big ship and flew ahead.

Jaki was furious that death had robbed him again, but he knew from grim experience that he could not relent to that fury. The men who had killed Pym would kill him too easily if he gave free rein to his feelings and attacked like a rabid animal. Only a sorcerer's trance could give him the necessary calm to stalk men, and he breathed from his pith to draw his violence deeper and steady his exertion. His face went deathly white, and his stare hardened. He relented reflexively to the centuries of murder that informed all vengeance, relented to his need to catch Pym's soul. The men, seeing his paleness, thought simply that his grief consumed him. But when they witnessed the inhuman strength in his muscles as they rowed over the shallows, they were confounded.

He stopped rowing, and the others bent to their strokes while the soul-taker sat lifeless, listening to the jungle shore with his whole body. A chill seeped out of his heart, stilling his anger. He felt the half-hinged breezes swinging from the forest wall, heard the coughs of the trees, smelled the incense from the algal pools — and knew just where to stop the skiff.

Jaki ordered the men to take the prau farther up the strait until they were out of sight around a bend. Before they left, he took the shrunken head from his duffel bag and looped its twine around his neck. "Wait for me under cover," he commanded the pirates. "I will meet you at nightfall."

"Where are you going?" one of the men asked suspiciously.

But the sorcerer was gone.

Wawa rushed ahead, and the gibbon's cries assured Jaki that no large animals or men were near. He moved among the trees, searching the leaf litter intently. Here and there he stopped and collected small plants, pink flames that licked the crevices of silvered deadwood. The solitude of the jungle and its familiar scents eased his grief. He felt Jabalwan nearby, in the minty sighs of the ripe earth. The invisible presence guided him, and he followed his hunches through the forest wrack, picking more of the poisonous pink plants — starwort, famous among sorcerers for its tasteless toxicity and delayed action. When he had a handful of the deadly blossoms, he paused to gather a tuft of twistbane, then hurried back to the creek glade.

Jaki knelt over a clear freshwater pool where the creek emptied before silting into the brackish shallows. After pounding the starwort and twistbane into a paste on the pool rocks, he stirred the mixture lightly into the water without disturbing the algal lace. He finished as the warship floated into view, and with one backward step he disappeared into the tall grass along the creek.

But *Black Light* did not stop at the firth as he had been sure it would. It drifted up the strait, and Jaki cursed himself. His intuition had been so certain that its failure ached in him like a bad heart. "Damned fool," he berated himself.

Wawa barked, signaling that the big ship was returning, and Jaki popped up. The jungle tangle ahead and the sight of stormclouds gathering with the dusk had prompted Rajan Kobra to reconsider the creek glade he had just passed, and he had ordered his ship hard about. Jaki watched with relief as the restored black angel figurehead hovered over the channel. Weightless with expectation, he slipped deeper into the grass and observed the lowering of the warship's gig. The men who came ashore unloaded muskets, longbows, spears, and buckets. While the officers stamped into the forest to hunt in the falling light, the oarsmen tasted the water of the pool and, finding it satisfactory, filled their buckets and began loading water into the large barrel in the gig's midship.

Musketfire splotched the jungle silence, and the hunting party returned with a tusked boar railed on their spears. They loaded the game, splashed a couple more bucketfuls of pool water in the transport barrel, and shoved off.

Jaki clutched the shrunken head hanging beside his heart and raised it to the humming mist where the dead were watching. "May God's justice be done," he whispered, and lifted his face toward the clear oil of night spreading across the sky. In the last light, he foraged for more poison plants, Strychnos berries and strangle vine. He packed the pockets of his doublet with pigment roots and dye leaves, then returned to the pirates huddled in their prau at the water's edge. He told them of *Black Light*'s deadly water and promised them a great slaughter at dawn. That night, they lay silent in their mourning and fingered their weapons, remembering Pym.

When the first blister of dawn appeared, Jaki took out the pigment roots and dye leaves and painted his and the pirates' faces in predatory warstreaks. Their cutlasses and sabers he edged with Strychnos resin and strangle vine sap. Then the pirates sculled into the strait and drifted to *Black Light*. By now almost everyone on board would have drunk the lethal water, yet the warship still looked formidable. The watch sat in the crosstrees and forecastle, and lanterns blazed on the rails. Jaki ordered his men to ready their flintlocks and he unraveled a loop-ended rope. He snagged the nub on the main deck's railpost, the rope snapped tautly, and Wawa and Jaki led the climb up the beveled hull to the deck.

The watch in the crosstrees stirred but did not notice them as they rolled onto the ship. Wawa scampered up into the shrouds to the mainmast and charily approached the watch. The man lifted an arm at the approaching beast, then withered. Wawa poked at him and leaped away, but the sailor did not budge. The forecastle watch was slumped backward against the bobstay pinion, unconscious. The quarterdeck watch was sprawled before the whipstaff, his tongue swollen in a blue bulge between his teeth. Jaki guided the pirates to the gundeck, where the crew were asleep. Many were dead. Some who had not drunk the water were slumbering, and their throats were easily cut — until a restless sleeper awoke and shouted an alarm.

A dozen men stirred from their hammocks, and the flintlocks cut half of them down. The sluggish ones were no threat for the savagely painted warriors, and while the pirates hacked at the impaired crew, Jaki ran for the officers' quarters.

Three officers staggered into the companionway and confronted him. "Shahawar Shirazi sends me for your lives!" Jaki shouted.

The officers did not understand him, but they recognized Shirazi's name as they attacked. The companionway was too narrow for all three to converge on Jaki, and he screamed his war cry and parried the blow of the first assailant so ferociously he fell back into the other two, throwing them off balance. Jaki chopped at them remorselessly, and their blood sprayed. With the scream of the last of them cut loose from his life, Jaki bounded over their corpses and climbed the gangway to the poop deck and the captain's cabin.

The door was swung wide and showed an empty chamber. A wash of ice wind spilled over his scalp, and Jaki looked up to the quarterdeck in time to see Rajan Kobra pointing two flintlocks at his head. He dove into the cabin as one gun discharged, smashing the plank of the threshold.

Jaki whirled back out the door, and Rajan Kobra fixed him in his gunsite, his black eyes bright nails of murderous intent. A shriek from above startled them both, and Wawa flew out of the shrouds and collided with the captain. The flintlock went off, and the ball shot into the green dawn. Jaki sprang up the stairs to the quarterdeck, blade high.

Kobra's squint went wide as Jaki came closer. "You! The aborigine!" He waved his scimitar.

The two paced each other, circling, their scimitars wavering, searching for an opening to strike. With a side-slashing blow, the Muslim warrior charged, and their swords clanged. Jaki was shoved back by the power of the strike, and fear burst through him. Kobra was maniacal, and the force of his horror matched Jaki's anger. Their weapons clashed in a brattling frenzy, Jaki falling back, Wawa screeching.

Jaki cat-footed sideways, breaking the captain's lunging advance. But the reprieve he had expected did not follow: Kobra, trained in the treacheries of the scimitar, pivoted agilely, feinted, double-feinted in a blur, and thrust for Jaki's heart. Outwitted, Jaki stepped falsely and lurched about as Kobra's blade snaked toward him. The tip grazed his left shoulder and snicked for his throat.

Frantic to retreat, Jaki staggered, and the edge nicked his ear and scored him across the back. He whipped around and blocked a slicing maneuver that would have cut his throat. The block locked their swords, and they pressed against each other. Kobra's fist banged into Jaki's temple and dropped him to the deck, stunned. The Muslim howled victoriously and drove down with his scimitar. The blade jolted as it pierced flesh.

Rajan Kobra viciously swirled the blade so it would cut vitally inside his enemy's chest — and only then did he see that his sword had struck not Jaki but the shrunken head.

Before his startled adversary could leap back, Jaki swiped his scimitar at the Muslim's gaping face, and the razored tip slashed his throat. Blood sheeted over Jaki, and Rajan Kobra heaved backward. Jaki rose and lopped off his enemy's head. He removed the turban, tied the long hair to the unwound headcloth, and used the cloth to secure the severed head to the sternpost.

The slaughter below decks was over, and the handful of pirates, flushed with killing, appeared on the main deck. At the sight of Rajan Kobra's grimacing head and Jaki splashed with his blood, they cheered and raised their swords to him.

Jaki silenced them with crimson hands uplifted. "We insult our captain by rejoicing while his body still hangs in Serangoon Harbor. Weigh anchor and set the mainsail. We will give Trevor Pym a burial that befits a pirate king!"

Jaki steered the huge ship into the seabound current. Once *Black Light* was under sail and flying downwind toward Singapore, he turned the whipstaff over to a crewman and took the quarterdeck.

The shrunken head of Pieter Gefjon had been gashed open by Rajan Kobra's sword, and the fine sand in it had bled away. The head was now just a scrap of skin and knotted hair, its features indistinguishable. Jaki removed it from around his neck and tied it to the sternpost above Kobra's head. His dead father had saved his life, and the spirit in the head had gone, taking the threat of his enemy with it. Jaki lowered a bucket overboard and drew up seawater to wash the blood and war paint from his hands and face. As he had once put on the clothes of his father, he now had to shed himself, he realized, and looked up at the hank of hair and the shred of skin that had once held his father's spirit. Shed himself and be renewed.

Wawa, who had climbed into the crosstrees, shouted at the sight of the first lorchas, and Jaki yelled to the men. "Keep to the deep water! Unfurl all the sail you can! And steer this ship straight for Captain Pym!"

Jaki ran down into the hold, following his cruel memories of captivity through the blood-puddled companionways to the gunnery deck. Dead men lay everywhere, and the sour stink of the ship was overlaid with the gummy smell of spilled lives.

Scattered among the big guns, Jaki found kegs of serpentine powder, and he rolled them into a stack above the narrow fire door that led down into the powder room. Through open gun hatches he could see sampans, swamp willow, and the thatched huts of Seletar, and he knew Serangoon Harbor was not far ahead. He implanted two coils of fuse into an unstoppered powder keg and ran the fuse after him. Once out of the hold, he stood on the skylight and searched ahead for the harbor.

The cannon crew that Quarles had stationed at the harbor entrance fired a salute to *Black Light*, and the British sailors waved at the pirates, mistaking them for Kobra's crew. By the time the commander saw the Muslim captain's severed head gaping on the sternpost, the warship had already flown past him.

Jaki wanted to unfurl Wyvern, but the crowded harbor had already swung into view. There was little time to spare. He ignited the two fuse lines and dropped them into the hold. The wind was blowing briskly behind them, and the ship was shooting along the strait so fast that foam peeled from the prow in luminous wings.

The Fateful Sisters's lofty masts and glamorous white hull appeared ahead, still moored before the lion stele, still displaying Pym's hanged body. The decks were busy with crewmen, who rushed to the rails to marvel at *Black Light* soaring into the harbor at a fatal velocity. Men scampered in alarm, and the stern gunports clacked open.

"Drop the prau and abandon ship!" Jaki shouted, and the pirates swung down from the masts. Jaki signed for the helmsman to join his companions in the prau, and he took the whipstaff and cried for Wawa. The gibbon tumbled out of the shrouds and scampered to his side. Jaki threw his medicine bag into the prau and commanded Wawa to get in, but when the animal realized Jaki was not following, he refused to go and finally Jaki signaled for the men to drop their line. He saw the skinny ship jettison away and put his full alertness into holding course straight for *The Fateful Sisters*.

The British warship opened fire. *Black Light* lurched as cannonballs bashed into the bow, her new forecastle splintering, shooting timber shards upward and ripping shrouds and canvas. The hurtling ship was slowed but not diverted. Jaki fought the whipstaff to keep the behemoth vessel from veering into the junks and sampans clustered along the banks. Spars screaming like a grieving beast, *Black Light* reeled forward.

Peering ahead, Jaki saw the tiny figure of Quarles on his quarterdeck. The captain held his spyglass to his eye and spotted Rajan Kobra's hacked-off head and below it the tall figure of Jaki Gefjon at the helm, his wild hair flying in the wind. "Abandon ship!" Quarles cried before the second round could be fired.

Jaki grinned as he watched the sailors spewing over the decks of his target. "Death to empire!" he shouted. He tore off his doublet and used the ripped fabric to tie the whipstaff to the binnacle, locking the rudder, and he grabbed Wawa and sprinted to the taffrail. With a last look at Pym's corpse dangling from the yardarm, he leaped with Wawa into the strait.

Jaki swam hard through the blue chop of the channel, Wawa clinging to his back. At the uproarious sound of the collision, he rolled over and saw *Black Light* smash into *The Fateful Sisters*'s stern and glance along her port broadside, plowing timbers, planks, and rails ahead of her. The monstrous impact hove the British ship to its side and snapped her masts. Shouts reached across the harbor and the sky shook as the landing platform was sundered by the force of the slammed vessels.

In the shock of silence that followed, the screams flurried louder. Jaki backstroked to the mud beach and sat in a nest of kelp and drift scrap with Wawa in his lap. The powder hold in *Black Light* ignited, and the two ships heaved into a fireball. Flames gushed through the roil of flying debris, and a moment later the powder hold of *The Fateful Sisters* detonated, blowing the levee and the lion stele into a gray cloud of rubble. The surge of blasted stone immolated the harbor, smashing lorchas, crushing junks with a colossal roar. When the haze cleared, *Black Light* was gone. *The Fateful Sisters* was a flame-gutted pyre, and Serangoon Harbor was a web of devastation, the main wharves collapsed, the levee broken, and numerous fires raging.

Jaki stood up wearily and turned from the fiery havoc. The marsh bowers opened before him like a cave, the vaulting depths rimed with trapped sunlight and the ore of homesickness. Wawa danced ahead, leading him past the watertrace into the arrow grass, the vinelap, the somber trees — leading him back to his first life, far away, at the river's edge of the heart.

Sleeping with Satan

Heaven and earth are not humane.
They treat people like things.
— TAO TE CHING, 5

JAKI LAY DOWN on the rootweave, his body and mind numb. Smudges of black smoke from the burning harbor unraveled in the sea wind. High above the char, clouds were forming animal faces, looking down at him as if they watched to see which way he would go now.

Lucinda was far away and getting smaller. If he got up now and ran with all his might through the swamp to where his comrades waited with the prau, and if he used root magic to give himself strength to row through the marsh isles and through the night — he might be able to catch her. The Dutch carrack that was carrying her to Bantam had left yesterday at dawn, but it was a sag-bellied vessel and could not sail directly south through the shoals to Java. But even if he did find some way to get aboard the carrack without getting killed, would Lucinda want to see him? Remembering the anger in her face from the night before, he was not at all sure she would.

Wawa appeared nearby, clicked querulously and slinked closer. But Jaki lay gazing upward, oblivious. His mind floated above his body, up through the treetops to the clouds. He wanted some sign from them of what to do next. The fury that had impelled him to destroy *Black Light* and *The Fateful Sisters* was spent, and he had broken into stillness. Pym, dead not even a day, was as far away as Mala or Jabalwan. A slow wheel turned in his chest as he thought of those well-known faces gone into rain. *The dead return with the prophecies of the rain.* But where was the prophecy in the clouds above him? The faces of the creatures surging in the clouds were impassive as real animals, indifferent as the powers of the world. Distantly the sea was shrugging, the wind muttering its prayers. Whatever he decided, the world was simply watching.

The gibbon's long fingers touched his face, and he blinked and turned to stare at the animal. Wawa wagged his head, motioning him to go deeper into the jungle, away from the tumult that had almost taken their lives in the strait. Jaki told him to sit and wait, but the gibbon, still skittish from the explosion, chattered nervously.

Jaki was aware that Wawa wanted to take him back to the jungle, to the past they knew. He regarded the animal sharply for the first time in a very long time, and his annoyance faded. The gibbon had endured a great deal. He longed to be back in the trees, drifting through the speckled air among the branches. Wawa sat trembling softly in the shadows like a tribal woman who had lost a child.

In his mind Jaki followed Wawa into the forest to where blue-nosed deer pronked mulchy paths with their hoofs and sunlight sparked from shadows. That thought returned him to his body, more numb than ever. He knew he could never return to the land of his childhood. He had heard the prophecy of the devil's child at Njurat. *When he appears, the bright anniversaries written on the clouds will be at their end.* He was a devil's child; he was the end of revelation. In the medicine cloud, the Longhouse of Souls was empty. He was the last of the sorcerers. If he returned to the jungle, he would be returning to death. He could live as Jabalwan had, treating the ill and injured, easing the dying. Yet for all he healed, his father's weapons would destroy more. Pym had revealed that inevitability. For all Matubrembrem could offer, he would be no more than a witness to the end of the tribes. The prophecy would be fulfilled, and he would see the people of the waking dream meet their end in fire. He had nothing else to offer the jungle and its people but this death. Is that what the powers of the world wanted?

Jaki sagged. He could no more imagine his own future now than he could two years before when Jabalwan had died and he had wandered embittered among the tribes, dispensing words from his mother's Holy Book. But now the emptiness was even thicker, for he was truly alone, without even the tribes to receive his pain.

He stared at the amber ring on his thumb. Lucinda was his only future — if she would have him. The anger he had seen in her gnawed at him, and his hand flopped to his side. *What I've hurt in her,* he thought, *I've hurt in myself.* Then a new thought opened: *Maybe that works the other way, too. Maybe I'm only hurting myself and my denial is also hers.*

That hope tingled through him, and he looked more closely at the amber ring. The gold light breathing there was all of life — even if that life was pain and the anger of the woman he loved. *Yes!* The enemy of life was not death but numbness. The vision he had suffered in

Njurat was alive in him. The emptiness that had stretched him out here was his enemy, and even Lucinda's wrath and rejection were preferable to this. He sat up.

Wawa muttered hopefully and stepped closer.

Jaki held out his arm, and the gibbon leaped into his embrace. He whispered soothing noises, then, sighing, he said, "I cannot go with you back into the forest, Wawa. I know that was our life once. But now I belong in my father's world. And I am going back to it. Will you come?"

Wawa stared at him with black sequin eyes, not comprehending. But when Jaki rose and took his first step toward the sea, Wawa squawked with disapproval. Then, reluctantly, the animal shuffled after him.

As he made his way through the swamp, Jaki thought of how his father's head had saved his life under Rajan Kobra's sword, and suddenly a vibrant clarity opened within him. His life to this moment seemed of a piece, whole. But from here, he was on his own. No ghosts were glimmering among the skeletal marsh trees to warn or counsel him now. And the clouds drifting above the treetops were not animal faces anymore, just smoke. He had come this far by following others — neither betraying friends nor yielding to enemies. But now, for the first time, he had a goal and no teacher. The choice to be bold, to be happy, or alone, was his own. Disappointment and fulfillment mated noisily just ahead in the glare of the future. But here, on the marly path among the mangrove and casuarina trees, where the air was splintery with sunlight and redolent with seasmoke, he felt almost drunkenly free. For the first time, he was free to choose his own way.

Free. He said the word to himself in the several languages that he knew. Each sounded strange. "Am I free, Wawa?" he asked the gibbon. "Freedom must belong only to God, I think, because people and animals are too small for it. We live in our hearts, not our freedom. Do you see? The powers of the world have set me free today. And what do I want?" He held up his thumb, and sunlight murmured in the amber of his ring. "I want to tie myself to another's fate. I don't want to be alone with my freedom."

His decision to find Lucinda, no matter the consequence, filled the vacuum of his shock and grief at losing Pym, and he moved with unerring swiftness over the root-woven tidal flats. Minutes later, a cry from Wawa alerted him to men ahead. With relief, he realized as he came upon them that they were not enemy, but the last of the pirates from *Silenos*. The prau they had used to take *Black Light* was tied off to a fallen tree, and two men were lying inside it under a gray cowl of mosquitoes. When Jaki stepped out of the arrow grass, the men jumped with alarm, then lowered their flintlocks as they recognized him.

"You have come back, lah!" said Kota, a bow-legged stump of a man who had served on *Silenos*'s gundeck as a powder-runner. Pym had saved him from a swamp-pit where he had been buried up to his chin and left for the mud-skippers to eat his eyes after his Celebes village had been sacked and destroyed by the Lanun. His square face was pocked with white crescent scars where the snakes had gnawed at him. Fanatically loyal to Pym, he had led the throat-cutting in the hold of *Black Light*. He regarded Jaki now with cautious relief.

"We knew you were alive," the other one said. Mang was a tall, humorless Javanese, hollow-cheeked as a monkey and sly-eyed as a gargoyle. Jaki knew he was cunning, equally able to read subtle wind-shifts and the thoughts in a man's face. His scalp was scabrous; most of his hair had fallen out, and he wore a black headcloth knotted about a human fingerbone.

"Where are the others?" Jaki asked in Malay and looked in the prau to see that his medicine bag and blowgun were still there.

"We were mindful of your treasure, sorcerer," Mang said. "The other three said you died at Serangoon. They want the diamonds you have in that bag. Smart of you to put Wyvern on top. None touch it once they see that." Three sets of wide-spaced footprints scuttled away downstream from the prau. "There was a small fight," Mang acknowledged.

"Why didn't you go with them?" Jaki inquired, lifting the medicine bag out of the prau. He knew from its heft that it had not been tampered with.

"I am a thief to my tribe," Mang answered. "Pym made me a sailor, taught me to read weather and catch the wind. He did that." The tall man knocked his knuckles against the hull of the prau, to ward off the influence of the dead man he was praising.

"You are the captain's sorcerer," Kota added. "Great power, lah." He made two fists and held them to his temples. "We will follow you."

Jaki assessed the men before him. They had clearly proven their loyalty, but their motives were very different. Kota's slavish attentiveness reminded Jaki of the tribesfolk who had respected him and Jabalwan for their magic. Kota was bound to him by awe.

Mang was more pragmatic. Pym had taught him the mysteries of the sea. Perhaps Jaki would teach him the mysteries of poisons and stalking that had so ably avenged Pym's death.

"Do you know what this is?" Jaki held up his thumb ring.

They both nodded. They had been aboard at Macao when he had dueled the Portuguese and won, and they knew the ring had come from Quarles's daughter. "Your prize from the English captain's daughter," Mang said.

"I would have that woman for my wife," Jaki told them.

Kota grinned with approval, and Mang frowned doubtfully. "We saw the woman leave yesterday," he said. "A Dutch carrack took her downriver past Changi. She has gone far to sea now."

"The carrack is bound for Bantam," Jaki replied. "She has to run east first to clear the delta isles. If we leave now and bear due south through the marsh, we can meet her as she pulls around."

"No prau can run that hard," Mang said with finality.

Jaki met his narrow stare. "This one will." He dropped his medicine bag in the bilges.

Maud rose from sleep to a smell like the threshold of a stable. Groping toward the lantern with drowsy fingers, she touched fur, and her eyes snapped open to see before her a bestial black face. She screamed. The animal flashed fangs, then bounded into the dark.

Lucinda sat up and peered groggily at her maid. "Maud, what is wrong?"

"My lady!" Maud gasped, leaping to her knees in her bed. "An incubus braced against me! I saw its devil face!"

Lucinda fumbled for the flintstriker on her bedstand to light a candle. The striker was gone, and she sat up straighter.

A spark jumped in the dark, and a yellow flame lifted into gummy radiance. Maud screamed again.

"Hush, Maud," Lucinda said, with awed breath. "It's Mister Gefjon."

Jaki placed the lit candle on the bedstand and knelt beside it. His face was an angel's shadow, weary with wanting, eyes bright with zeal, wet and star-webbed from looking too long into the wind. A fever glaze glistened on his brow. "I traveled hard to find you."

A knock thudded dully on the door.

"Maud's screams have alerted the guard," Lucinda whispered. She lifted the covers and Jaki got into the bed, whistling gently for Wawa. Lucinda crept out and drew the curtain tight before going to the door. "It's all right," she said to the burly English ship's mate. "My maid has suffered a nightmare. That is all."

The mate stuck his head in the cabin and stared at Maud. "Nothing to be afeared of, ladies," he said, and pushed the door open. "I'm here to see to it no harm befalls you." He eyed the open window. "But I can't help if you be leaving your windows open and letting the flux in." He strode into the cabin, went to the window, and pulled it closed.

Water splattered the sill and the floor. The mate touched and tasted it. "Seawater," he muttered, and looked inquisitively at Lucinda. "What's this?"

Lucinda stared at him, dumbstruck.

"Seawater, you oaf," Maud blurted. "My lady lowered a rag with her sash and soaked it to soothe the heat from my nightmare. I would not have her waste our drinking water on that. We thought you'd be asleep and we'd have to fetch more ourselves and face the Dutch in the night."

The mate guffawed. "We've a treaty with the Dutch now — and you, a captain's daughter, unaware? We are allies."

"Even so," Lucinda piped up. "Only four years ago they massacred our factors in Amboina. We have not forgotten that savagery and never shall. We want little to do with them, thank you. Now, if you will leave us alone, please, we will return to our sleep."

"Do," he said with an amused smile. "And should your pretty maid chance to have any more night fevers, have her knock on my door and I'll soothe her myself."

When he was gone, Lucinda pushed her nightstand against the door and opened the bed curtains. Jaki smiled at Maud. "Thank you," he whispered.

"Do not flatter yourself that I lied for you," Maud said, indignant. "I am my lady's servant."

"I well remember," Jaki said, dropping his smile. "Two nights ago you would have had me strung up alongside my captain to serve your lady."

"To spare me my father's wrath," Lucinda said. "I've come to think she was right. Now get out of my bed."

Jaki let Wawa go, and the gibbon scurried up the bed curtain to the top of the canopy. Jaki took Lucinda's hands.

"How did you find us?" she asked, deliberately removing her hands from his grip, though her eyes were large with amazement.

"A prau carried me through the shoals with two shipmates. They're alongside now in the dark. They're cutting ahead through the shoals and will meet us in less than an hour. We must leave here quickly."

"Leave?" Lucinda stepped back a pace.

Jaki stepped closer. "I came back for you, Lucinda. I want you to be my wife. To come to Switzerland with me, just as we planned."

"And Pym, your captain — what of him?"

The glow on Jaki's brow glinted sharply as he lowered his face against the wan candlelight. "Dead. As you said."

"So now you've room to fit me into your life." She laughed and swung her eyes to her maid. "Am I a toy, Maud, to be put down and then picked up at his leisure?"

"No, my lady," Maud answered without looking at her.

Lucinda looked more closely at Jaki. "Are you going to steal me away forcibly?"

She half hoped he would and was disappointed when he slumped and sat at the edge of the bed.

"I traveled hard to find you," Jaki said, quietly and urgently. He searched Lucinda's face, seeking his fate, and saw a cloud of hope there. She was even lovelier than he remembered, her hair of captured sunlight toppling to the dark moons of her nipples hidden by her gown, and he wanted to embrace her again at long last. But she was right to hold him off for an explanation. "Lucinda, I would never force you to anything. If you come with me, you will not lose your freedom. I mean only to add to it."

The caring in his voice lured her closer.

"Won't you come with me, Lucinda?" Jaki pleaded, daring to place his hand on hers. His heart soared when she did not recoil from his chilled touch. "I have diamonds, enough for us to live well all our days. Come away with me."

Blurs of hope and need crossed through Lucinda, and she wanted to abandon the anger that had boiled in her since they had parted in the lion garden. But instead she said, "Love is broken by pain. If I stay here, I will find my way back to Europe and a comfortable if premature dotage as a gentleman's wife. And if I go with you now into the night — will you let me walk away again the next time you must make a choice?"

Jaki bent over and pressed his face against her hand. She smelled of mint grass, and the memory of that scent filled him with desperation. "I want you," he said, lifting his face to look into her questioning gaze. "I've wanted you before I knew you. But my past took me from you. And now my past is dead." He took the amber ring from his thumb and held it up. "If you will come back to me, I will give my life to you. No one will come between us again."

She took the ring from him and traced it with her fingers. "Where will we go? My father will pursue us."

"We'll change our names and live in Switzerland."

"No. Switzerland is not far enough for a man like my father."

"Does it matter?" Jaki asked. "You have forgiven me."

"Yes, I forgive you. How could I not? You've come back for me, the one man I have ever loved."

A surge of joy filled Jaki's head. He bent to kiss her but held back when he saw the look on Maud's face as she watched them.

"My lady, your father will kill him if you go," Maud interjected, her heart skipping with her daring.

"He must find us first. We will go to the New World. Even William Quarles cannot reach us there."

Maud threw herself to her knees before her mistress. "Luci, please, say you are not serious. You cannot go with this man. He is a pirate. What kind of life will you have with him?"

"Maud, you have caused me enough grief," Lucinda said. "Would we be here now if you had kept your silence with my father?"

"How could I have been silent when he was beating you?" The maid's hands clutched at Lucinda's gown. "If you go, he will kill me."

Lucinda regarded her levelly. "You will come with us, then."

Maud's jaw trembled. "Go with you — and this pirate? No, I would rather die."

"Leave her here, Lucinda," Jaki said. "We don't want her troubling us on our journey."

Lucinda shook her head and looked at Maud with cold appraisal. "My father may very well kill her if we leave her. He is that arrogant and cold-hearted. Besides, I am a lady. I need a maid. And she is a good one. Her family served ours for many generations before we lost our estate." That thought softened her gaze, and she put a hand on Maud's shivering shoulder. "Come with us in good faith, Maud. I need you."

"Lady, I beg you, don't ask this of me."

"I promise you, Maud, we will live at least as well as we have aboard ship. Believe me." Her gentle countenance darkened. "You have left me no choice. If I leave you here, you will alert the guard, and they will hunt us down."

Maud shook her head vigorously. "I will say nothing."

"I believe you would mean to say nothing," Lucinda said kindly. "But our guard has ways of making you talk. You must come with us. You have no choice, gentle sister. Prepare your things."

"I will scream," Maud threatened.

A knife jumped to Jaki's hand as if from nowhere. One moment he had been sitting still, and the next he was pointing the blade at her throat. Wawa whimpered.

"Jaki!" Lucinda put a firm hand on his arm. A wave of alarm iced through her. "Maud, get your things."

The maid crawled backward from the knife and stood up. When she turned away, Jaki put the blade back in its sheath under his shirt. He winked at Lucinda, but his movement had been so swift and precise that she believed the wink was meant to calm her and not disavow his intent. "When will your boat meet us?" she asked.

Jaki went to the window. The cat star blinked on the horizon. "Soon," he replied, and vainly searched the dark sea for the prau.

While Jaki stood at the window knotting bedsheets, Lucinda gathered her favorite gowns and bound them together. She packed her jewels in a camphorwood box: a ruby salamander brooch, pearl hairpins, a necklace of ice-bright emeralds, earrings of topaz, white jade, and starry sapphires, bracelets of fine-chain Italian gold, and radiant gem rings. When Lucinda caught Maud furtively glancing at the door and the bedstand blocking it, she laid a hand on her maid's arm. "Forget that foolishness, Maud. He will kill you to save me. And if he does not, my father will in his rage. Come with us peacefully." A smile warmed her face. "Sister, we have endured much together since we were children. You know my love for you is true. When we have reached our first port, if you are still unhappy, I will send you back to England with riches of your own."

Maud gripped her arm. "Luci, my sense forebodes ill."

"If I stay here, Maud," Lucinda said, "I know what will become of me. I will be expediently married to some pompous old man with minor influence in the court, and I will live out my days as mistress of a chilly manor, mothering other little ladies and gentlemen so they may grow up to do the same. Have we come to that, after all the wonders and glories we have seen in this wide world? If I were a man, I daresay it would be different for me. But I am a woman, and so I must obey. Well, I will not obey. I defy fate. I will have my own life in my own hands — and I will make my own great house."

Maud cast a glance at Jaki. "He hardly seems the pillar of a great house, my lady."

"That is why I need you, Maud. He is rough material, suitable for the tough times ahead. Refinement will be our task. A hard task, but our lives will be in our own hands. And we will be free to make something of life rather than be made by it."

"The ship approaches," Jaki called. The prau bobbed on the swells, and by its slow advance Jaki could see that it would soon fall back. "We must leave at once."

Lucinda looked out at the night sea, trying to make out the smudged shadow that was the prau. She put her hand on his where he was securing the rope of bedsheets to the frame of the window. "Before I go with you, true child, you must promise me a thing." She nodded to the sea drifts under the swirl of stars. "I am at your mercy out there, Jaki. You must swear never to abandon me. When we leave, we go as husband and wife."

Jaki held the ring in his hand. "As husband and wife," he promised, and his eyes met hers, clouded with emotion. He was feeling the bond in their blood and wanted to tell her then how he was at her mercy, too. His whole life he had been journeying to this moment. At the worst, he had doubted the Life would ever reveal this to him. But now the spirit that had climbed with him to the clouds and had led him through the jungle and over the sea had carried him to the tip of being. He wanted to tell her all this. But she knew. Her eyes were shining like rain. He put the ring on her finger, but she pressed it back into his palm. "When we are truly wed, I will wear this," she said, and kissed him, the incense straw of his scent enclosing her.

Jaki tested the knotted bedsheets, then lifted the mattress he had tied to the far end. He secured the bundle of gowns, the box of gems, and the maid's satchel to the twisted sheets crisscrossing the mattress and dropped it out the window. The rope went taut as the mattress flopped into the sea, where it wobbled in the wake of the carrack.

"Maud, you're going down first," Jaki said, taking her hand. She resisted, but the shadows of his broad-boned face frightened her, and she relented.

"Use your feet," Jaki advised. "Slide from knot to knot. And don't be afraid. If you fall you'll not be hurt. Go now, quickly. Your mistress will be right above you."

Maud slid clumsily down the cloth rope and flopped in a muffled splash onto the mattress.

"Now you, love," Jaki said, and helped Lucinda through the window. She descended more ably, sliding onto the soaked bedding opposite Maud so their balanced weights would keep it afloat — but it had already begun to sink.

Jaki grabbed a leather bottle filled with drinking water and then sent Wawa out the window ahead of him. He placed the handle of the bottle between his teeth, leaving his hands free to grip the rope. He swirled down after Wawa and cut the tie as he descended into the water.

Freed of the ship, the mattress spun away. "Kick your legs!" Jaki urged, and the women thrashed with him as the wake of the carrack settled back to the placid glass of the sea.

"Sorcerer!" Kota's voice tripped out of the dark.

Maud shrieked.

"Sorcerer," Kota called again, and the prau lifted over the next swell and drifted toward them.

Wawa leaped into the boat. Mang and Kota helped the women aboard, and Jaki passed over the water bottle, the camphorwood box, and the maid's satchel. Then he grabbed the gunwale and heaved himself aboard.

"My gowns!" Lucinda gasped, and grabbed an oar to reach for the floundering mattress.

Jaki took the oar from her. "Let them go. The seawater has ruined them anyway. We will have new gowns made for you."

The men rotated the rowing until dawn, when the tide came in and carried them into the marsh isles. Kota sat at the stern using an oar to steer; Mang lay curled up at the prow, stupefied with exhaustion, and Maud, her auburn hair strung in coils across her face, sat hunched over her knees. Rain rising with the light whorled in purple drafts among the knobby islets, and the red shadow of day flowed through the mangrove trees and cane grass.

"This is the most beautiful morning of my life," Lucinda said, breathing the loamy land breeze.

Jaki cradled her in his arms, feeling the gratitude of a man returned from the dead. He smiled. The Life was big enough not only to hold them but a whole world that was new. From this morning, he belonged to this woman and that new world, and the past belonged wholly to its ghosts.

*

By noon, they had found their way to a marsh village, where Jaki traded trinkets from Lucinda's camphorwood box for a larger skiff with a crude sail. Jaki gave Kota and Mang a diamond each, as he had promised, and told them they were free to leave. But they wanted to be nowhere else. Jaki's shrewd sense of survival and these diamonds were incentive enough to stay with him. Together they spent the rest of that day making the skiff seaworthy and trading with the villagers for food and water.

They sailed the next day with the green dawn at their backs.

"Where are you taking us now?" Maud wanted to know.

"We will sail up the Malacca Strait," Jaki said. "We will stay in sight of the coast. In a month — or less, depending on the weather — we will reach Dagon, where we can trade diamonds for a larger boat and a crew. Dagon's a big port."

"I know that," Maud said with a taint of indignation. "We have been to Dagon. There's an English factor there. But I think you will not get even that far. By now our guard knows we are kidnaped, and he will prevail upon the Dutch to turn back and inform Captain Quarles. *The Fateful Sisters* will run you down for the pirate you are."

Jaki lowered his face and leaned against the rail. "*The Fateful Sisters* is no more."

Maud turned about sharply, and Lucinda's face darkened.

"It was destroyed in Serangoon Harbor two days ago," Jaki murmured.

"I do not believe you," Maud spat.

Lucinda searched Jaki's face for the truth. He nodded, and she brought her hands to her mouth, afraid to hear the rest. "Father?"

"He is alive," Jaki said. "Far as I know, no one was killed."

"How?"

He described the collision of the big ships in the harbor. "Your father had time to abandon ship," he assured her. "It is unlikely he was harmed."

"Then the Bantam must be furious," she said, relieved that the man she loved was not her father's murderer. She wanted to flee her past but she did not have the heart to kill it.

"The Bantam cannot blame your father for what happened. News will have reached Dagon by the time we arrive. We will know about your father then."

"You are a monster," Maud said. "You cannot say you love her when you strike so fiercely at her family."

"No, Maud," Lucinda responded. "Father was knighted before we left England. He came here as a warrior to extend the influence of the crown. The Bantam employed him to stalk pirates. Jaki faced him on his own terms. Whose loss was worse — my father losing his ship or my husband losing his captain?"

Maud glared at Lucinda. "You belittle your father who partakes of a king's strength — and you call this pirate your husband. Lady, you have lost sense. You are untuned."

Her maid's hot disparagement of Jaki inflamed Lucinda. Her hand flashed and she slapped Maud. "Watch your tongue. Remember who you are."

"I know who I am," Maud blurted through her tears. "You have forgotten yourself. I was the maid of a lady. And I am yet a maid."

Lucinda watched Maud curl into a corner in the stern of the skiff and sob into her hair. Her sudden fury drained away, leaving her chilled. "Hold me, Jaki. I am afraid."

Jaki pressed himself against her. "Don't be frightened. Nothing has changed between us. Maud is upset because she is alone."

"She does not like you," Lucinda muttered into his shoulder. "She thinks I am foolish for loving you — and she will not call you my husband."

"I am your husband. No matter what she or anyone else thinks. We must believe in each other and be strong to make our own way in this world."

"I believe in you," she promised, her fingers bracing against his solidity. "No matter what has happened to my father, I do not blame you. He is a cruel man, who lives by the sword. In my heart, I have put him aside for you."

Jaki squeezed her tighter. "We are truly one, then."

"As you believe in me, Jaki, there is one thing we must do." She stroked the wind-tossed hair from his face. "When we reach Dagon, we must have a wedding. I want to be wed before everyone — before Maud, before the English factor. I want my father to know. If he knows, the world will know that we belong to each other."

Jaki agreed and rocked Lucinda in his embrace, feeling the anxiety in her tight grip on him. From the corner of his eye he saw Maud still bent over, quaking with fear. When was the last time he had been afraid?

He thought back through the bitter trance that had helped him to destroy his enemy's ships in Serangoon, through Pym's execution, through the daredeviltry that had almost killed him when he had tried to save Pym, and he realized he had felt no fear then, though there had been plenty of cause for fear. He thought back through his misadventures with Shirazi and the death-brink they had pranced together, and he found no fear.

The last time he had been afraid was in Njurat with Pym, when they were under the strong eye. He had been terrified by the dragon. The mother of life, Jabalwan had called her. He had known the purest of terror under her gaze — but what he had seen then had cured him of fear. What was it? He fetched back and recalled the horrifying vividness of her presence. That was what had purged him of fear, and remembering that dreadful vision he heard again the voice of Jabalwan's ghost: *Look at the mother. Her beauty is terrible. She is the Life's beauty — the terrible beauty of all departure.*

He hugged Lucinda tighter, understanding at last. He had seen then the void that sustained everything. The woman he held in his arms was already vanishing. The breath in their nostrils, the warmth in their flesh, was already wisping away with the clouds. Each instant created itself anew and was gone in the next moment. All of life was departure. And that realization held him freely yet firmly, like the deep blue reaches of the sky.

Sadness undercut this wisdom, because he knew he could never convey it to Lucinda, to anyone. This perception could come only from the mother, from the beauty of mystery. But what sane, sober person would seek such terrible beauty? Fear jealously guarded this knowing.

The rarity of Jabalwan's legacy became poignantly obvious to him then. Only a sorcerer would purposefully seek out the pain and the fear that led to the mother; and only the mother, the child's first departure, the Life's ceaseless birthing, could impart the fearless beauty he was feeling. Clarity is what it was, a pellucid objectivity that liberated the heart from its fear.

Now Jaki knew what he owed his wife. She was afraid and would be until they could find their way home, wherever that was. Her fear belonged to him now. He had married it, and he would need all his sorcerer's wiles and fearlessness to hold on to her as long as he could in the spell of departure that entranced everything alive. The wedding would be the first healing ritual, his first chance to take some of her fear onto himself.

"In Dagon we will have a wedding all of Asia will hear of," he promised her. And to himself he vowed to remember she was afraid, that Maud was afraid, and Mang and Kota, and the whole world around him was afraid. And though fear was done with him, he had only begun to work with it.

With rain in its teeth, the wind scampered across Serangoon Harbor, driving Chinese merchants into their lorchas and Malaysian fisherfolk under the frond-leaf awnings of their praus. William Quarles stood defiantly erect at the prow of a sampan heaped high with trash. Rotted pig and dog carcasses found bloated in the harbor after the destruction of the big ships were mounded on the sampan among fecal rags and bloody bandages from the wounded.

The garbage skow tacked slowly into the wet wind, crowded with the

English crew who had been ordered by the enraged Bantam to ride with the refuse twelve miles out of the harbor to where a British vessel would be allowed to pick them up. Quarles surveyed the scorched harbor, bile biting the back of his throat as he looked for a last time at the mammoth ribs of his ship turned up like a dead claw among the rubble of the shattered sea wall. The stench of the refuse matched the fetor of hate that had been rising in him since the boy-pirate had crashed *Black Light* into his ship. Only death could repay this crime. *Only death*, he swore.

"Jaki Gefjon," he said to the mazed trees, bitterly recalling the name his daughter's maid had told him. At least he had had the foresight to send Lucinda ahead to Jakarta, sparing her the agony of his debacle. She was safely on her way and would know nothing of this until the Admiralty were appraised of his tragedy and he had the time to formulate a strategy that would snare the wily pirate. "I will find you, Jaki Gefjon — and I will hang you as I hanged your captain." The words spoken aloud helped keep his humiliation at bay, and he repeated them, the stench of garbage rising about him.

Under the orchard of stars, the skiff with Jaki and his companions sailed north up the Strait of Malacca and into the Andaman Sea. Jaki steered by the constellations as Pym had taught him, a night-sorcerer with skills that Jabalwan would have admired. By day, the skiff put into jungle coves out of sight of the sea and men-of-war, and the travelers bathed, slept, ate, and sometimes bartered with the natives.

Several times at dusk, setting in or out of their hiding places, their little vessel was crossed by pirates, fierce, Byzantine-eyed men with brandy-burned stares and necklaces of human ears and noses. But each time, the sight of Wyvern, the reckless bat shape dripping feathers and snakecoils, had sagged the pirates as though their bones had gone damp, and no one harmed them.

Most days were empty of any encounters, and during the long uneventful night journeys, Jaki and Lucinda discussed what they would do when they reached Dagon. They decided to sell some of Jaki's diamonds to buy clothes and to book passage to the New World, Guiana or Curacao — any of the warm Dutch colonies. Of all the powers, the Dutch were the most tolerant, and Lucinda was convinced that among them, she and Jaki could establish an estate, live well, and rear their children free of the European prejudices that had stultified her childhood.

Maud kept to herself, angry at Lucinda for forcing her to endure this harsh voyage and fearful that Mang and Kota would molest her. When she contracted jungle fever, she abjured all help and tried to cure herself by fasting and bathing in eucalyptus water. Only after she was too weak to stand did she accept help. Mang and Kota took turns waving fronds to cool her, Lucinda swabbed the stinging sweat from her flesh, and Jaki prepared plasters with seaweed and forest herbs that soothed the blisters scalding her body. Through a river-reed, she sipped a root broth Jaki prepared that tasted like midnight and that quelled her scorching fever within hours. Her resentment and fear yielded, and, with her health renewed, she felt ashamed of the selfish anger that had isolated her. She returned docilely to her duties as Lucinda's maid, laundering her mistress's clothes and helping the others with the campfire and the foraging.

When her strength was fully returned, Maud sought forgiveness from Lucinda. "I had forgotten who I was," she said when she and Lucinda were bathing alone in a jungle pool. "I had hopes when your father sent us off in the carrack that we were returning to England — and I would see my Aunt Timotha again. And when I was stolen away with you, I forgot my place. Will you forgive me, my lady?"

"Mousie, you are easily forgiven," Lucinda said. "You are my only true friend. I could not bear to lose you — to fever or to spite."

Maud touched toes with Lucinda under the water. "I was afraid. But this voyage, for all its hardships, is not as terrible as I had feared."

"The worst is over," Lucinda reassured her, and blue-winged butterflies traipsed between them as if in confirmation. "Jaki will provide for us until we reach Dagon. And then, if you want, you may return to England, as I promised."

Maud shook her head. "I was wrong to want to be apart from you, Lucinda. I had truly forgotten my lot. In the fever, I remembered. And now, I will go where your fate leads us. It would be a blessing if it could always be like this." She spread her arms under the jungle wall of torn sunlight and brazen flowers.

"We've Mister Gefjon to thank for that. Though I know you think him a pirate, he has been most civil and accommodating."

"He is not the man I always imagined you would marry," Maud admitted. "But he is daring and generous. He cared well for me in my fever. And he is handsome, Lucinda. I am sorry I questioned your virtue in choosing him."

"And I am sorry, too, for having struck you." That apology stilled the last ill feeling in Lucinda's heart, and she settled deeper into the pool, her hair fanning in the water like a platinum lotus.

On his forty-seventh birthday, a week after *The Fateful Sisters* was destroyed in Serangoon Harbor, William Quarles arrived in Jakarta. The English cargo ship that had retrieved him and his crew from the garbage skow was a cramped, stinking vessel, not designed to convey so many men; his sailors had been obliged to sleep on the planks and accept half rations. No one complained, but Quarles could see in their tight faces that they thought ill of him. Rather than anchor safely in the mouth of the strait, he had ordered *The Fateful Sisters* to moor at the sea wall so that he might have the satisfaction of hanging Pym in full view of the entire settlement. A scaffold on the wharves would have served just as well. His arrogance had lost them their ship and their pride, and they awaited his sentencing before the British factor in Jakarta with ironic anticipation.

The morning they put into port, he was on the first longboat that rowed into the harbor, so that he would arrive before his crew could disembark and have the satisfaction of seeing him announce his failure.

Though the heat was smothering, Quarles dressed with full decorum in puffed satin breeches, a blue captain's baldric draped across his red velvet doublet, and a broad officer's hat plumed with a white feather. But at the dock, no delegation waited for him, though the ship's signal banners had announced important intelligence. Had some swifter vessel carried the news of his ignominy ahead of him? He knew that sultans used messenger pigeons among themselves. Did all of Asia already know of his loss? A pang sharpened in his stomach at the thought that he had fallen so far from favor that he was beyond ceremony. He mounted the dock ladder with the solemnity of a condemned man.

The wharves were busy. Lading ships glided languidly over the brown water of the harbor toward the newly arrived vessel, and Javanese stevedores, in headwraps and waistcloths, squatted in the meager shade of the bollards on the loading platform. Farther down the cluttered harbor, three Dutch ships stood regal as cathedrals at their moorings, and the dockhands bustled in the shade of wide canopies and awnings. Quarles recognized the carrack that had carried his daughter from Serangoon, and he realized that she had probably already heard of his defeat. Would she gloat too? He had struck her, and he had deceived her with her maid to capture her lover. But he had failed to capture the scoundrel *and* he had lost his magnificent ship. Certainly, like the crew he had dominated since leaving England, she would abandon him to his misery.

At the gabled trademaster's station, British naval officers lounged on padded cane sofas, cooling themselves beneath a punkah, a large frond fan rigged to wave as an elderly Malay man gently worked the pulley. Their banter dulled when Quarles entered, and a whisper circled the chamber. He had never had many friends among the other captains. He had neither college affiliations nor family members at court, and he had never made an effort to ingratiate himself with those who had. Now, he ignored them.

At the desk of the trademaster's secretary, Quarles made arrangements for lodgings and compensation for his shipless crew. As he was standing there, he overheard his daughter's name among the officers' whisperings. He laid a heavy stare on the man who had uttered Lucinda's name. "Sir, do you speak of my daughter?"

The whole room hushed, and everyone's attention fixed on Quarles. The man who had been addressed remained seated and cocked one surprised eyebrow. "Captain — are you unaware of your daughter's fate?"

Quarles moved his square body one ponderous step toward the seated man. "How do you mean?"

"Pirates have taken her, man. Have you not heard?"

Quarles's heart staggered. He seized the seated man and hauled him upright. "Speak the truth, devil, or by God —"

Shouts rang through the room, and Quarles was grabbed from behind and pulled away.

The secretary rose from his desk and approached Quarles. In a confidential whisper he said, "Your daughter and her maid were not aboard the Dutch carrack when it docked. The guard who accompanied them denies any knowledge of their disappearance. The factor interrogated the man himself. You would do well to speak with him."

With a shrug, Quarles broke free of the men holding him, bowed curtly to the secretary, and barged out of the station. He half believed that some mistake had been made. Even so, he set off at a run toward the cobbled boulevard that led to the embassy houses.

At the English factor's residence, he barged through the front door without knocking, shoved past the doorman, and shouldered open the double doors of the factor's chambers.

The factor, a wispy man with vaporous chin whiskers and hooded, drowsy eyes, was bent over his desk, quill in hand. He looked up without alarm. "Quarles," he said in a flat voice, and laid his quill down. He motioned to a cushioned chair beside his desk. "Please — sit."

Quarles ignored the chair and stood close to the desk. "What has become of my daughter?"

"Sit down, William." The factor, despite his size, commanded a resonant voice. When Quarles was seated, the factor said, "No one notified me that *The Fateful Sisters* was in harbor. I would have met you at dockside with full pomp."

Quarles closed his eyes and lowered his head. "*The Fateful Sisters* is not in harbor." He removed a sweat-rumpled parchment from his doublet and laid it on the desk. "My ship was gutted by pirates in Serangoon Harbor. The full account is here."

The factor sat back and seemed to wrinkle smaller. "*The Fateful Sisters* lost?" He pinched the bridge of his nose and was silent for a full minute. "Oh, piteous fortune — the Admiralty will be gravely disappointed to take this loss. The king is already skeptical of the expense of our naval ventures in the East. This may very well decide him against further support for company trade."

Quarles sat impassively, though his insides were molten. "Lucinda is my only family," he said, quietly.

The factor sighed and nodded. "Yes — of course. This is a black time for us all." He placed his bony hands on the desk, one atop the other. "I have placed the guard you sent with your daughter and her maid in the harbor jail so that you might interrogate him yourself. The man claims he had heard suspicious noises in your daughter's cabin but was reassured by her and the maid. But an hour later, when he checked in on them again, they were gone, the stern casement open and trailing a rope of bedsheets. This was off Pulau-Pulau Riouw. We can surmise that your daughter dropped into a small ship. The greater mystery is where the small ship came from to steal her away — and who would be so bold."

"I know who stole her away," Quarles said with chilled certainty. "She has a lover. A pirate. The very one who gutted my ship."

The factor's eyebrows rose. "How can that be? You sent your daughter away before the disaster occurred, did you not?"

"Yes, of course," Quarles replied, agitated and helpless-looking. "The pirate could have rowed through the shoals and intercepted her."

"That's hardly possible, William. No small ship could negotiate that distance so quickly. I have interviewed the Dutch captain and his officers, and they assure me that they were not complicit in this. There is no evidence to disbelieve them. If they had not found a rope attached to the chainwale, obviously thrown from the outside, they would have deemed it impossible for a man to mount their ship unseen."

"This . . . is not an ordinary man." Pain winced in Quarles's voice, and the factor looked at him with curiosity and concern.

"So extraordinary as to steal your daughter from a Dutch ship under full sail? But where can they go? I will send notice to the company agents throughout Asia. Two Englishwomen cannot appear in a port without being noticed."

"Should they appear in a port." Quarles's nostrils flared as if smelling something vile. "This pirate is jungle bred. He may take my daughter with him into the wilds."

The factor shook his head, and a fatherly smile deepened the creases in his gaunt cheeks. "My dear William, if I may be so bold to say, I have met Lucinda, and for all her virtues, she is not one to embrace a life in the jungle. If this heathen is her lover, he will bend to her way. Believe me. If they are alive at all, I suspect they are this very hour in Serangoon. There you are disgraced, and they believe that you cannot pursue them."

"Aye." Quarles slumped dejectedly into his chair. "As my report will detail, the Bantam's love for the English would seem to be exhausted. Only foreign powers openly exultant over my loss have access to that port now."

The factor sat back and stroked his sparse whiskers. "You forget that all ports are yet open to the Thieves' Church."

Quarles's quizzical look hardened to a stare. "You —"

"I do believe that your family once shared my faith."

"Sir," Quarles responded stiffly, "I am loyal only to the Church of England."

"Of course, of course." The factor smiled almost glumly. "But the Church of the Two Thieves owes a great debt to your noble Uncle Samuel for his services in our cause. That debt devolves to you, dear William. I will see that our contacts in Siam and Singapore keep an eye open for your daughter. In the interim, we have this messy business of *The Fateful Sisters* to conclude. The Admiralty will call for your immediate censure and return to England. I will forward your report as slowly as I can, but news of this magnitude has its own wings. We must put you to sea again before you can be recalled. Naval business is out of the question, but I believe the company can find some work for a captain of your skills and stature."

Quarles sat silent for some moments, pondering the implications of his complicity with the Thieves' Church. Affiliation with the papists who had inspired his Uncle Samuel's downfall galled him — yet he could bring to mind no other way of retrieving his daughter — if she was alive at all. At last, in a slow, strangulated voice, he said, "Sir, I would be most grateful."

"Yes." A smile floated like an illusion on the factor's skeletal face and was gone. "The Thieves' Church guards her own."

Dagon was celestial. Mosques, temples, and pagodas rose among flame trees, delta lakes, scarlet-lacquered wood bridges, and boulevards. Canals lined by stout, flat-topped trees mazed the city. Sunlight smashed off the great golden pile of the Shwedagon, a pagoda of pure gold that rose high above the city. Beneath its radiance, a karst-cliff of hanging gardens and looming teak trees brooded like a tapestry. The gold stupa was the center of the city. Its first neighbors were the pantile-roofed cantonments where the wealthy merchants and foreign traders lived. A labyrinth of cluttered clay houses with thatch roofs jumbled to the Irrawaddy River, fronted by rice mills and ironwood wharves.

After weeks of sailing up the wild coast, the travelers eagerly climbed ashore and set off down the wharf lane, leaving Kota and Mang behind with orders to sell the skiff for whatever they could get. Lucinda hailed a palanquin, and they followed the wide, cobbled river road to the gold stupa that lorded over the city.

At the Shwedagon, Jaki displayed a large diamond to the wizened patriarch, who disappeared and returned shortly in the company of a bejeweled prince with silver whiskers that stood like bristles from his mahogany face. He took the diamond and gave the bedraggled travelers the use of one of his residences, a palatial, colonnaded house not far from the gold stupa.

Servants, brightly garbed in billowy pyjamas and puggaree headscarfs, ushered them up a wide, scalloped stairway into the vast house. Pink marble panels adorned the bracketed pillars, painted calico hangings covered the walls with mythical scenes, and the floors were black polished flagstones. Each room was a unique arrangement of richly dyed rugs, rosewood furniture, and Chinese porcelain. Jaki marveled at every turn and immediately sent a servant to fetch Kota and Mang from the wharves.

Lucinda and Maud were greeted by women servants and were taken to a bath of colored marble with piscine faucets breathing steam.

After Jaki had bathed in a similar chamber, a manservant led him to a feast laid out on a table inlaid with jade. Before him were mounds of fragrant rice, aubergines, yams, dishes of dhal, prawns, curried meats, fruit chutneys, yogurt, curds mixed with sugar and ground almonds, and a glazed pot of black tea. The steward grinned solicitously beside a Dutch chair of carved ebony.

Jaki sat, tossed a fruit to Wawa, and was reaching to help himself when a man in bucket-top boots, slashed doublet, and feathered cap strode into the room, his spurs and sword jangling. The steward approached him and was brusquely shoved aside. "Where is Mistress Quarles?" he asked in English.

Jaki rose. "Who asks?"

"I am Robert Fletcher, British factor to Burma," he announced. "I am informed that the daughter of Captain William Quarles has newly arrived here. I came at once. And by the authority of the British Crown, I demand to see her."

Jaki regarded the man silently a moment, reading the indignation in the thin lips behind his trim mustache and forked beard. "We are in Asia, Mister Fletcher. Your Crown means nothing here."

Fletcher's eyebrows pinched tightly. "Who are you?"

"He is my husband," Lucinda said, entering the room. She was wearing a blue sari, with her hair gathered to one side and hanging over her shoulder. Maud, her eyes wide with concern, followed behind.

Fletcher turned and bowed. "My lady." He removed his hat, and his long, dark hair fell over his shoulders. "I am Robert Fletcher. Your father is gravely concerned for your well-being. Every British factor in Asia has been alerted to your peril."

"Mister Fletcher, I am in no peril," Lucinda said, going to Jaki's side. "My maid and I are now members of the household of Jaki Gefjon."

Jaki gave a humorously curt bow.

Fletcher stared at them, befuddled. "Mistress Quarles, do you know who this man is?"

"I've told you," she replied. "He is my husband."

"Your husband?" Fletcher said, aghast. "My God, woman, he is a pirate. This man is responsible for the destruction of *The Fateful Sisters*." His face was hard. "We know of him from the pirate ship's surgeon, who confessed before his execution. I do not know what he has told you to lure you away, but I assure you he is not worthy of you. He is not only a pirate but a Dutch merchant's bastard, birthed on a blackamoor heathen." He spat the last sentence with vehemence and paused several beats, expecting a fight. When the demeanor of those before him did not change, he stepped back. "Your father will be poisoned to learn of this."

"My father is well, then?" Lucinda asked in a chill voice.

"Well? Hardly so. He has lost his ship, the pride of our Asian fleet. He has been disgraced in Singapore, and he and his crew have been ejected by the Bantam. Years of diplomacy that have won us a toehold in Malaysia have been squandered. Now his whole obsession is to recover you. So long as his only daughter, his only kin, is in the sway of this fiend, he will not rest. He has defied the king's order to return to England."

Lucinda stepped to Fletcher, who mistook her concern as anxiety for her father. "Mister Fletcher, you must inform my father at once that I am not a prisoner. I have chosen to live my own life rather than be married off at his whim."

The factor flinched with surprise. "Lady, he is your *father*. You are bound by honor and love to obey him."

"Then call me dishonorable and unloving, but I am not here unwillingly." She removed her hand. "Tell him I hold no malice against him. He *is* my father, and I have loved him as a daughter. But his heart is too hard. My life beckons me elsewhere, and I have given myself to Jaki Gefjon with a loving heart and a free will."

"I think it best, my lady, if you tell him yourself," Fletcher said, and drew his sword. He snatched Lucinda by the arm and yanked her to his side. He slashed the sword angrily to stop Maud from rushing forward.

Before Jaki could lunge for him, Fletcher went stiff and dropped his weapon.

Kota stepped from behind him, the tip of his parang poking the back of the Englishman's head. He prodded with the blade until Fletcher released Lucinda. Mang, a cocked flintlock in his hand, entered and picked up the fallen sword. "Chop?" Kota asked Jaki.

Jaki shook his head. "No, don't kill him. He has a message to deliver."

Lucinda faced Fletcher with glittering fury. "You have quickly lost my trust, Mister Fletcher. Yet I invite you to attend my formal wedding. A week from now. On the grounds behind this house. I trust you will be there so that I can be assured my father will receive a full account of my betrothal."

"Leave your weapons and soldiers behind," Jaki warned. "I do not want to have to kill at my wedding."

Fletcher snatched his sword from Mang, plucked up his fallen hat, and departed. The steward bowed apologetically, snapping admonitions to the servants clogged in the doorway to return to work.

Jaki drew a long breath to slow his pounding heart. "So our wedding is to be in a week?" he said, pulling a seat for Lucinda.

"Was I wrong not to consult you first?" Lucinda asked, recovering her composure and waving for the others to join them at the table.

Jaki shook his head with a grin. "I promised you a wedding. I had hoped to do it sooner." He spooned curry on a thin disc of bread. "Why wait a week? We should be getting a boat and out to sea. You heard Fletcher. Your father is looking for us."

"Yes, but a week is hardly time for him to receive Fletcher's news and respond," she replied. "And we will need that time to ready ourselves for the next leg of our journey to the New World. After we've dined, we shall pay a visit to an acquaintance of my father's, who I believe will be more amenable to our plans."

A rickshaw took Jaki and Lucinda along a terrace road beside the gold pagoda, and they viewed the clusters of stockaded settlement houses grouped around mosques, shrines, and monasteries, all jammed against the elbow of the river. Not far away they came to a house where intricate moldings dressed the eaves and the Dutch tricolor was displayed. Lucinda stopped the driver and asked him to wait.

She spoke in English to the elderly Burmese servant who opened the door. "Tell the factor's secretary that Lucinda Quarles, the daughter of the English captain William Quarles, is here on urgent business. Tell him, please, this is a matter of trade."

The door closed and opened again almost immediately and they were greeted by the factor himself, a portly, red-haired man with an arrowhead nose pinched by scissored spectacles. Lucinda had met him the year before at the English factory where the Dutch had ratified their truce in Burma with the British, and he remembered her well. He took her hand, kissed it, and said, "Your defiance of your father has usurped all other gossip in this sleepy town. I did not think you would appear here. How ever did you manage to elude the pirates along the coast?"

Lucinda looked to Jaki. "My husband provided me safe passage."

The factor bowed to Jaki and introduced himself. "I am Jakob Boeck, in the service of the Dutch East India Company." With a squint of curiosity, he said to Jaki, "Your name is Dutch, is it not?"

"My father was a captain with your company — " he began.

Boeck cut him off with a cold laugh and said in Dutch, "A man with a love for the natives, I read from your face." When he saw Jaki's incomprehension and Lucinda's annoyance, he asked in English, "Is he still alive?"

"No. He was killed by pirates before I was born."

The factor shook his head and waved them into his office, a capacious chamber with a beamed ceiling and wall hangings of cut velvet and watered silk. They sat down in cushioned chairs, and he fixed his stare again on Jaki. "Now you are yourself a pirate."

Jaki met the factor's somber gaze evenly. "Any European ship with weapons in Asia is a pirate."

Boeck leaned forward to hear such outlandish cynicism. "Sir, you speak thoughtlessly. Though perhaps in your years as a pirate you never learned the distinction between ships of trade armed to protect themselves and ships of predation."

"The European powers prey on each other," Jaki answered, ignoring the restraining hand Lucinda had placed on his thigh. "Dutch, English, Portuguese, Spanish — they not only murder and steal among themselves, their greed ravages the native peoples far worse than the coastal pirates who were here countless centuries before you arrived. It is your armed European vessels in Asia that are the true pirates, it seems to me."

Boeck tugged at his chin whiskers and turned to the woman. Lucinda was a woman of delicate beauty, with attentiveness in her every gesture. She was also — he reminded himself — the daughter of a powerful English captain with whom he had signed a treaty of mutual compliance two years before. If he could return her to Quarles, the gratitude of the English would be an advantage in the next trade dispute. For that reason, he constrained his revulsion at the primitive she had chosen to squander her virtue upon. "Mister Gefjon, you are failing to consider the role of government. The sultans and lords that we found in place when we arrived here are the very sovereigns with whom we trade. They are not reluctant to receive our goods in exchange for theirs. As for the disputes among the nations of Europe, that is an ancient rivalry."

"The fang and claw of the forest," Jaki said calmly, seeing the anger ticking at the Dutchman's temples. "Peoples have preyed upon each other from the beginning of time. The Bible shows us that truth. Only might distinguishes sovereigns from pirates."

"What an archaic attitude," Boeck said with vexation. "Mistress Quarles, my servant tells me you wish to discuss a matter of trade."

"Yes." She removed her hand from Jaki's leg, where her nails had bitten his flesh trying to inhibit him. Only now did she realize just how much her husband was wanting in diplomatic finesse, and she wished she had come on this errand alone. "As you know," she began, nodding to Boeck with deference, "I am no longer a part of my father's household, having decided to wed the man I love."

"An untraditional and grievous choice, if the gossips are to be believed."

"Fortunately, I am here to counter the gossips," she replied with a charming smile. "My husband and I are indeed untraditional, and to avoid a grievous fate we are seeking a legitimate means to establish ourselves in the world."

"A worthy endeavor surely, Mistress Quarles," Boeck conceded. "But how can you possibly manage that by defying your father and convention?"

"That is precisely why we are here, Mynheer Boeck. We are looking for your sanction."

"Mine?" His hand covered the ruff at his throat and his eyes widened. "You don't mean to appeal to me for sanctuary?"

"Oh, no," Lucinda said quickly. "Certainly my father would bring pressures to bear on you if we were to stay here. I understand that. Wherever we go in Asia or Europe, he will pursue. That is why we need your help. We look to the New World."

Boeck's brow crinkled with surprise. "That is a bold move, my lady."

"This is a bold age."

"But how may I help you?"

"You can issue us shares in one of the Dutch settlements in the New World," Lucinda said in one hopeful breath. "In trade, of course, for goods of value that we can offer you now. A typical transaction for a factor."

"Yes, but not typically initiated by a woman fleeing her father." He twisted the point of his beard and regarded her from the corner of his eye. "What goods of value have you?"

Jaki reached into his medicine bag and came out with a handful of large diamonds. He placed the smoke-colored rocks on the ebony tabletop.

Boeck picked up one of the gems and assessed it closely, as though skeptical. In fact, he had often seen diamonds in his family's jewelry guild back in Amstel, and he knew the one chunk he was holding could alone buy the entire guild from his mother's greedy brothers, who dominated the family business and had obliged him to accept foreign service. Even so... He put the stone down. "I cannot accept these in trade for shares," he said with genuine glumness.

"But why not?" Lucinda blurted. "These are extraordinary stones. The best you've seen, I daresay."

"Indeed, they are remarkable gems," Boeck conceded. "But if I accept them, they will only be taken from me by your father. Or at least he will try. Our treaty forbids us to trade for pirated goods."

"These are not stolen," Jaki said. "They are the legacy of my tribal people. They are mine by birthright."

"Sir," Boeck said, allowing some of his anger to burr his words, "you are a pirate. Whatever you may wish to think of your heritage or of the European powers, you remain a pirate. Your actions in Serangoon demonstrated before all of Asia that you are a dangerous man. No government will trade with you — for if it did it would be ostracized by all the other sovereignties you call pirates."

Lucinda put a firm hand on Jaki's arm, and he abandoned his reply with an exasperated huff. Then she turned to the factor. "Mynheer Boeck, who is to know these diamonds are from us? We certainly will be in no position to be identified with them once we are in the New World. With your connections, these gems can readily find their way to where they belong, in the Netherlands, among the finest jewel cutters in Europe."

"My lady, you are not a naive woman. Why are you acting the part? Everyone knows you are here in Dagon with — your husband. Soon your father shall know. He, too, has his connections. How can I hide such a transaction from him? No, these gems will renew hostilities between the Dutch and the English, and that cost will far exceed their worth."

Lucinda sank back in her seat, her face drawn. Jaki took her hand and made to rise, determined to find his own way to the New World. Diamonds were diamonds. Someone would buy them, and he and Lucinda would get the funds they needed. The same thought entered Lucinda at his touch, and she rose abruptly. "I thought you were a shrewder businessman, Mynheer Boeck," she said brightly. "We will not be daunted in our effort to reach the New World. With or without your help we will succeed. You merely deny yourself." Jaki offered his arm and they walked to the door.

"Please," Boeck said, standing. "I cannot accept a pirate's booty. But I am willing to help you, if I can."

"How?" Jaki asked.

Boeck paid him no heed and spoke to Lucinda. "I will issue you shares in our colony in Brazil, enough shares to own your own homestead in the New World, from which you can make a handsome start — if you will offer me goods of value other than pirate's booty."

"If these diamonds are not good enough —" Jake shot back, but Lucinda stayed him.

"What goods of value do you have in mind?" she asked.

"None that you own — yet," Boeck replied, signing for them to be seated. "I am responsible for a caravan that will be leaving Dagon shortly, traveling north along the Irrawaddy. After conducting trade in Burma, the caravan will continue west into India, bound for the great Moghul capitals of Benares, Agra, and Lahore. The journey is long and arduous — but potentially lucrative as well. Usually, a company agent travels with the caravan, but this season I am shorthanded and none of my staff wish to make such a difficult trek to barter kettles and jerkins for indigo and ginger. I believe you, the daughter of a trading captain, are not unfamiliar with both European and Asian exchange rates for such goods — hm?"

"A short hundredweight of indigo plants commanded five pounds sterling when we left London three years ago," Lucinda said, proudly. "The current rate in Jakarta is less than one-tenth that, about eight shillings. Fresh ginger sealed in earthen pots is more valuable than gold in Europe and can be had in most Asian ports for about three pennies an ounce, four shillings a pound."

Boeck smiled and nodded, impressed. "Your presence would assure my venture of an intelligent and capable negotiator, which I am thus far sorely lacking. In return for your services, I am prepared to issue you company shares in our Brazil holdings as well as safe passage from Surat, on India's west coast, to the New World. In that way I will have helped you to achieve your goal without breaking the terms of agreement I have with your father. And your father will be no threat to you in the interior of Asia."

When Jaki saw that Lucinda was actually contemplating the offer, he spoke irately. "Only fools ignorant of the wilderness would accept your bid. We have suffered enough in the wilds getting here. I will not subject my wife to such dangers again."

"Sir, I think the lady is neither a fool nor willing to dismiss my proposal." He turned a favorable countenance on Lucinda. "With your diamonds, you can assure that your accommodations in the caravan will be most comfortable. The foreman and the animal handlers are capable, and your only task will be to supervise the trading in the capital cities. When you finally arrive in Surat, you will have earned your own place in the world — a rare accomplishment for a man, let alone a woman — yet not above the reach of William Quarles's daughter. Will you at least consider it?"

Lucinda ventured a smile. "I will — but only on the condition that we are regarded and treated as owners by the foreman, crew, and sojourners."

"Owner — yes, of course. I will have your name inscribed as chief representative of the company."

Lucinda rose and offered her hand. "Your proposal is dangerous,

Mynheer Boeck, but I knew there would be danger when I chose to flaunt convention for the adventure of love. And what is adventure, after all, but the dignity of danger."

"A poetic truth," Boeck said, kissing her hand and knocking on the table for his servant. "I hope you will finally accept my offer, despite its dangers, for I believe there will be less danger for you in the caravan than you will surely find at sea, where your father's allies are everywhere."

After Lucinda and Jaki left, Jakob Boeck sat down at his desk and took out the manifest for the caravan he hoped to lure Lucinda into. With a pensive stare he reviewed the list of men who would be conveying the company's cargo of broadcloth and kettles into the interior of Burma. Somewhere among them must be a man with the attributes he needed to seize this heavensent opportunity. The man would have to be treacherously skilled enough to dispatch the half-breed and take his diamonds and yet intelligent and loyal enough to return the diamonds and the silly Englishwoman to Dagon. Many men could kill but few could see the wisdom in cooperating with a man of power like himself. They would rape the woman, murder her, and flee with the diamonds, only to be apprehended by one of the many sultans loyal to the company for the weapons the Dutch provided in their incessant feudal wars. One name did stand out, a man who had worked for the company and the sultans and who knew how to obey as well as kill. Boeck called out to his servant. "Send me Ganger Sint."

Jaki was peeved. "Lucinda, the wilderness is brutal. Our diamonds will count for nothing more than rock in the jungle."

Lucinda consoled him by taking his hand and stroking his fingers. They were sitting on a balcony in the great house overlooking Dagon, a kelpy breeze from the river lifting around them. The evening sky shimmered like a pond, and the gold pagoda glowed supernally above the terraced hills. "Just yesterday we were still at sea," Lucinda said. "At any time my father's men could have swept over the horizon and assailed us. This caravan will be no more dangerous than that and somewhat less if we use our wealth wisely to make ourselves comfortable."

Jaki looked into her tranquil face, her eyes looking back at him with hopeful daring. "I had thought to protect you from further hardship," he said, dropping his gaze to her hands and almost shocked to see her delicate wrists mottled with sunburn and sloughed skin. "Life aboard ship is something you are familiar with. How much less strenuous it would be for us to go from here aboard a big ship."

"But where would we get such a ship? You saw the few big ships there are in the harbor. Dutch and English, all of them. We could never buy passage without walking right into my father's grasp."

"We don't need to buy passage," Jaki said, and looked beyond her, a plan beginning to form in his mind.

"What are you talking about?" she asked with a tinge of alarm.

"My men and I will seize a ship. We will sail it across the Bay of Bengal to the Maldives. Pym told me about their pirate coves. Under the banner of Wyvern, we can get the provisions and the crew we need to round Africa and cross the Atlantic to the New World."

Lucinda's face narrowed with incredulity. "You are but three men in all. You cannot possibly seize an ocean-crossing vessel with two men, let alone manage it on the high seas."

"Give me two days on the wharves and I will gather us a crew," he promised excitedly.

"Pirates." Lucinda shook her head. "I did not come with you to live as a pirate."

Jaki sat back into the large pillows strewn about the balcony. "The Spanish are pirates to the English. The English are pirates to the Dutch. The Dutch are pirates to the Portuguese. What does it matter? I say we take a Dutch vessel, sail it across the Bay of Bengal, and turn it over to the Portuguese in Goa as a war prize. Then we'll be praised as heroes, not pirates, and we'll use our diamonds there to book passage to the New World."

"No, Jaki." Lucinda locked her arms across her body in adamant refusal, inflexible as an idol. "I left my father's world to be with you, because I thought you were a caring man. Not a man who cares for power, but for me and the children we would have together. I will work hard with you to earn that family and the home we want far from the conflicts of empire — but I will not pirate for it." She uncrossed her arms and reached for him. "True child, have you forgotten the days and nights we spent together, talking about what is important to us?"

Her touch was firm and gentle, soothing the bruises of Jaki's long wandering. Her voice was so sure, her face the very shape of his desires, and in the fading light, with a halo of darkness about her luminant hair, she was the worshipful center of the world to him. Could their two bodies equal their dream? Everything he had learned about life from Mala, Jabalwan, and Pym bespoke violence. *The Life is secret,* he remembered, *but what is known is violent.* Or was that his fear muttering? He had thought he had left fear behind in Njurat. He looked again to his wife, her face a shadow now in the failing light. *The shadow of departure.* The thought chirped from the back of his skull, and he realized that he had not lost his fear. Not at all. His fear had stepped out of him and taken up residence in this woman. Fear gawked back at him from the loveliness of her small, lean body, her fragile hands and feet, her eyes like delicate mirrors. He was afraid for her.

"Lucinda, listen to me. I am not a pirate, but I know of their ways. Once we are safe, I promise you . . ."

She stopped him by kneeling forward and placing two fingers on his lips. "Hush. No more suasion, Jaki. Remember you told me that in your tribe, when a man marries a woman among your people, he goes with her to her family and lives under her roof." She brushed her lips against his cheek, and her voice softened to a whisper. "You are married to me now. Live with me under my roof."

Jaki took her in his arms then and lifted his face to the liquid fire of evening. She knew the slow scales of his soul. She knew him. When she rocked in his arms, her birdbright weight against his chest, he exhaled the unspent words of his will and smiled with sad comprehension into the gathering thickness of the night.

Now that her mistress was alone in the world, with neither English-speaking domestics nor a patriarch to contour the day's duties, Maud eagerly busied herself with the myriad chores of arranging the wedding Lucinda dreamed aloud for her during the sweltering afternoons when they lay together in their jasmine-petaled baths.

Over the next four days, the landscaped grounds behind the mansion were arrayed with canopies, tree-awnings, and pavilions. With the steward as escort and interpreter, Maud arranged for the head monk at Shwedagon to officiate, and then visited the monasteries and mosques in Dagon to hire drum players, chanters, and dervish dancers to perform at the ceremony.

The day before the wedding, Jaki chanced to meet a blind monger on the wharves who bought and sold goods that pirates had seized from merchant ships and could sell nowhere else. Jaki found in his bag of wares an English translation of the Bible bound in brown calfskin, which he bought and presented to Lucinda as a wedding gift. That night, he opened the Book to Isaiah and read to her: "As the bridegroom rejoices over the bride, so shall God rejoice over us."

On the day of the wedding, it rained. Opalescent sheets of mist swirled across the sward, and heat fog crawled up from the river and smothered the grounds. Maud fretted and wanted to postpone the ceremony, but Lucinda and Jaki were undaunted. The monks assured them that the downpour was a favorable omen and, as if to prove it, marched into the torrent with upturned, beatific faces, raindrops sparking off their shaved heads, drums pulsing, and cymbals clanging. The curious guests watched from the verandah. As Lucinda had anticipated, the entire European population of the settlement had turned out, including Robert Fletcher, who had come, like the other factors, with his

Burmese wife, children, and servants. Wawa pranced among them, tugging at skirts and plucking tidbits from the burdened banquet tables that had been moved inside.

Lucinda wore a sheer yellow veil under a crown of wisteria and a pearl-studded gown of Chinese silk embroidered with silver-threaded designs of clouds and wind-vapors to honor her husband's vision. Within moments, the rain turned it opal, and it clung to her shiningly. Jaki stood resolute but drenched at the altar, water dripping from the fawn hat Lucinda had insisted he wear.

The steward presented the bride, and Jaki stood with his arm about her in the rain while the Buddhist priest intoned sutras and Maud wept with ambivalence. Jaki placed the amber asphodel ring on Lucinda's finger and lifted her veil. As their eyes met, Jaki suddenly saw his destiny with such sharp clarity that he might have been on a mountaintop at dawn, high above the dark world, afire with the first glimpse of the sun. He had survived the wilds of the night, and now his way would be clear the whole long day of his life.

Lucinda recognized the joy in her husband's gaze from every restless dream of love she had wandered since she was a girl. The dream was over now, and where it had been, there was a place to live where all the tasks of the future seemed possible.

They kissed, a clangor erupted from the monks' orchestra, and Kota and Mang fired their flintlocks into the air.. Dervish dancers spilled onto the sward, whirling with the torrent, and Jaki and Lucinda retreated to the house among them.

On the verandah, Robert Fletcher was the first to greet them, his face wrinkled in a forced smile. "Today will be a great disappointment to your father," he said, taking her hand, "but he will be proud of your bravura. I hope you will not regret this. On his behalf, I offer you the traditional English blessing: Bread for life and pudding forever."

Lucinda smiled coolly. "The only blessing I ask of you, Mister Fletcher, is that you convey to my father the happiness you see here."

For a wedding gift, Jakob Boeck presented Lucinda with the manifest for her caravan and the overseer's papers that guaranteed her diplomatic passage through Burma and India. By accepting them, she signaled her readiness for the trek, and the Dutchman's round face radiated satisfaction as he kissed her hand and slapped Jaki's shoulder. "As we say in Burma, keep your gaze straight ahead and the demons will not catch you."

Lucinda was pleased to have her future in her hands, and Jaki was happy to see the woman he loved satisfied with all he had promised. They mingled merrily with their guests, and the festivities in the great house rambled long into the night under the applause of rain.

*

The manifest papers that Lucinda reviewed were dated *May A.D. 1627*, and the hot, damp wind from the south announced that the monsoon season was about to begin. Jaki and Lucinda stood with Jakob Boeck on the wharf where the caravan had gathered, and Wawa pranced on one of the bollards, squawking at the crates of pigs being rafted into midstream to be taken up by the caravan vessels.

The newlyweds were well dressed for their journey. Lucinda did not wish to wear boots, but Jaki had insisted, horrifying her with tales of jungle leeches and scorpions. She also wore a straw hat faced with green-gold satin set over a turned-back lace cap which could be lowered to ward off mosquitoes. In a wine-colored skirt and a black jacket, she was elegant and yet ready for the wilderness. Standing there next to her husband, who had his bonebeaded medicine bag slung over his shoulder and was leaning on his eight-foot-long blowgun, she seemed ready to meet a caliph or trade with an aborigine.

Four barges, with eyes painted on their hulls and smiles of thick rope connecting them stem to stern, waited in the cinnamon waters of the river. The broad decks were laden with bales, crates, animals, pilgrims, and a crew of Burmese porters busy securing guide ropes to the water buffalo on the shore, who would pull the barges upstream for the first leg of the journey.

"As agreed," Boeck was saying, his spectacles pinching the tip of his pointy nose, "you are listed as the company's chief representative on this caravan, Mistress Gefjon. And you alone will be responsible for trade negotiations at each market, so that at the caravan's final destination of Surat you will principally have determined the profit or loss of this venture. Barring natural disasters, this should be a most profitable enterprise. I am confident that with your diplomatic experience the trading will go exceedingly well." Peglike teeth glistened in a narrow smile. "As for the daily chores of the journey, the native crew and the foreman will attend to the particulars of moving the cargo. You need not concern yourself with that. The foreman is a company man who has made this journey before, and he will decide the order of march and the stopping places."

"Subject, of course, to my best judgment," Lucinda said, "if I am to be truly responsible for this venture."

Jaki smiled to see the factor's pout fall back into his beard when Lucinda refused to relent. "Of course," he conceded. "But you would be wise to do as he says. He knows the route and the dangers. Trust him."

Boeck waved to a knot of men loading the lorcha that would house the Gefjons on the river journey, and a large man with a hooked jaw and a chest as deeply keeled as a bull's strode toward them. He wore a short-waisted doublet, brown sailor's trousers that fell to his knees, shoes laced tight to his ankles, an earring in his left ear, and a flat hat, with greasy blond hair wisping from underneath. His shaven face was dented with pockmarks, and his ash-colored eyes were long and devilish like a mule's with its ears laid back. "This is Ganger Sint," said Boeck.

The burly man looked at them as if from a distance, his face impassive, his eyes drowsy. He neither bowed nor offered his hand, and Lucinda's gaze slipped off him and back to Boeck. But Jaki, leaning casually on his long blowgun, kept his stare on the man and observed the relics of much jungle travel on his body: bleached patches on his shins above his boots where leeches and swamp fungus had scarred him, a scar on his forearm with the distinctive twin nailhole pits where a large snake had struck, and the piss-bright yellow in the whites of his eyes attesting to fevers.

"I will do all I can to make this journey comfortable for you," Sint said in raspily accented English. "Are you ready to go aboard? We should be on our way."

Boeck watched from the wharf as the lorcha shoved off and Ganger Sint bellowed for the caravan to begin. The drivers ashore snapped their whips, and the buffalo strained against their ties, nudging the line of barges against the stream.

The river journey had been timed to carry them upriver before the monsoons flooded the banks, clogging the shoals with forest debris and making barge travel impossible. For these first ten days of the journey, until the barges reached the unbreachable mud flats of Prome, there was little for Lucinda or Jaki to do but sit in the bow of the lorcha and watch the shanks of the river slip by. The air was filled with damp, algal smells, the wauk of monkeys from the trees, and the bleating of the animals on the barges behind them. Occasionally the wind shifted, and they would smell the stink of the penned animals and the sweet taint of opium that the crew and some of the pilgrims smoked.

Jaki opened the Bible that he had given Lucinda and tested his reading skills, glowing with nostalgia as he waded through the Book's familiar stories.

Lucinda reviewed the maps Boeck had given her with the manifest papers and consulted with Ganger Sint about the pace of the caravan. Already the buffalo were being pushed hard, and she wondered if they could relax the pace for the sake of the beasts.

"Not possible, ma'am," Sint answered. "We must reach Prome before the heavy rains or we'll be flooded and lose most of our cargo."

"But after that," she said, running her finger along the sketchy route on the map, "perhaps we could take this leg slower. Mynheer Boeck must have etched this passage too hastily. Thirty miles a day seems far too arduous."

Ganger Sint placed a blunt finger on the map where she had been pointing and said, "This is Mon territory, ma'am. If we linger there we run the risk of facing off with the natives. That can be dangerous, at the best expensive, for their tolls are steep. The rains will be coming on strong by then. That may keep most of the Mon bands dry at home while we move through their territory."

"But can the crew and the animals keep such a pace?"

"Leave that to me, ma'am. You concern yourself with a trade strategy for Prome. We'll be needing to convert our barges there to pack animals. And the merchants can be tough as rhino hide since they know we must leave the barges."

When Sint had left them alone, Jaki said, "Why don't you take a tender back to the barges and review the crew? See what they think about the Mon and thirty-mile days."

Lucinda wrinkled her nose. "My father taught me otherwise. Command is jeopardized when officers mingle with the crew."

Jaki considered this, then said, "Well, I'm not an officer for the company. I'll go and let you know how the crew and passengers feel about the pace."

"I wish you wouldn't," Lucinda said. "That's Mister Sint's job."

"Do you trust him then?"

"Why ever not?"

"Well, he's a company man. He's here to do Boeck's bidding, not tend to the crew."

Lucinda's face clouded. "Only pirates rule by majority, Jaki. We are not going to do things Pym's way on this caravan. Authority commands here. Let Ganger Sint do his job, and we shall do ours."

"You mean, you will do yours. I'm not in command here. Boeck believes me a pirate still. My name is not written on those papers of yours. And he calls you yet by your father's name. I travel on this caravan only because you do. Let me mingle with the others."

"Jaki —"

"I'll wear my hat," he said, consoling her, taking the fawn hat from the belaying pin where it hung. At first he had protested Lucinda's insistence that he not walk about bareheaded like a beggar. Even peasants wore hats of some sort, she had argued, to which Jaki countered with Pym's rebuttal that hats were authoritarian emblems symbolic of the dominion of men over men and that doffing them displayed an enlightened liberation from imperial rule. "Anarchy," she had moaned. But Jaki knew she had never seen the barracoons in the swamps of Bandjermasin, where the tribesfolk were penned at night like animals after slaving in the fields for the Dutch. Her father had not shown her the Portuguese chain gangs that continuously dredged the harbor in Macao, nor had she ever been a prisoner aboard a Lanun galley, reduced to a thing for the lusts of men with hats. So when Jaki had replied that he infinitely preferred anarchy to the subjugation of other men, she had looked at him with total incomprehension, mortified to have such a shamelessly bareheaded husband.

Jaki took Wawa with him in the tender, and they floated downstream from the lorcha to the first barge, where Kota and Mang had a canopy for shade and were lounging with their new Burmese wives. Jaki had expected them to go their own way in Dagon, crazed with the bags of gold that had been traded for the diamonds he had given them. But at the wedding, shrewd-eyed Mang, dressed as richly as a merchant from Venice, had approached a group of importers and, with a few whispers, exchanged his gold for their spices, textiles, and hardware. Kota followed suit shortly thereafter, having intended all along to follow Jaki wherever he went. Now the two of them sat like pashas, hauling their goods north to be traded at a steep gain in the isolated and gold-rich northern cities.

"From lawless pirates to respectable merchants, eh?" Jaki teased them after tying off the tender and climbing a rope ladder aboard. In their pink satin vests and feathered hats, the grim-faced men looked no less dangerous. Lifelong hardship had impressed their features with a wildness that their newly coifed beards could not hide.

They chatted while Wawa plucked dates from the bunches that hung on the canopy poles, delighting the women. None of the Burmese and few of the pilgrims had ever seen a silver-furred gibbon, and soon a small crowd had gathered around the canopy. Wawa did tricks, affording Jaki the opportunity to mingle with the travelers and gauge their temper. They were a motley group, monks and nuns, tinkers, soldiers whose Portuguese muskets were all that was left of their tribes and their causes, grain traders, sojourning prostitutes, thieves in the guise of jugglers, animal herders taking their fattened beasts along as provisions for the caravan and to be traded upcountry for coin.

The spicy stink of their gathered bodies drove Jaki to the stern, where the caravan crew — mostly slaves, indentured criminals, and war prizes — poled the river mud, dislodging the flotsam that tangled between the barges. Jaki took up an unused shaft and helped them for a spell, until they became curious and began talking to him. In a Malay patois, he began to explain who he was, but they already knew. His destruction of the big ships in Serangoon had made him famous among the tribal seamen, and they wanted to know why he was not with his European wife in the luxury lorcha.

"We not like you," a blister-mouthed tribesman said, indicating Jaki's fine clothes.

"No, we are different in some ways," Jaki said, and reached into his medicine bag. He took out a small tortoiseshell packed with a mash of tubers and leaves that he had concocted at stops along their skiff journey up the Malaysian coast, and he smeared it on the tribesman's blistered leg. "Yet — we are the same. We are both from tribes. Only with others who know tribal ways am I at ease."

Days would pass before this man would trust him, but each day, he allowed Jaki to treat his sores. In time, word circulated that the pirate of Serangoon was a healer and, what was more, once a tribesman. Jaki visited each of the barges and befriended the crewmen he met by sitting with them and sharing their meals of fish and rice chaff. Occasionally, he brought them vegetables from the lorcha. At twilight, when the barges were lashed to trees on the shore, he joined in the storytelling. And the crew liked him all the better that he was not afraid of Ganger Sint. It was widely known that the big Dutchman had killed defiant crewmen on other caravans and that he was quick to use his switch. His size and reputation intimidated the tribespeople, and when he passed, a breathless silence muted the crew.

"It's not right you be mingling like this," Ganger Sint told Jaki when he was helping pole a barge around a bend of stunted rain trees. The air was lashed with rainbows from the turbulent river, and the tropic sun was shattered into fire among the crowns of higher, solitary trees.

"They are my friends," Jaki answered, concentrating on his shaft pronging the mud, not looking at the large man.

"It's not right that your wife be alone so often," Sint added, stepping closer.

Jaki lifted his shaft, laid it on the gunwale, and turned to face Ganger Sint's cold stare. "My wife's maid attends her. And I'm with her at night. Why should it concern you?"

"I don't like other men doing my work."

Jaki lifted the shaft and prodded it toward the foreman. "You pole, then."

Sint slapped the shaft aside. "I manage the men. You stay out of my way. And keep your bag of tricks to yourself. If these heathen see the diamonds you have in there, they'll cut your throat for sure."

The wind shifted that evening, and the air went sweet and hot. A squall crashed over the forest and kicked the river into a choppy froth. Wawa cowered between Jaki's legs when he rowed the tender from the barges to the lorcha at sunfall. As he was tying off to the lorcha's stern, a mournful groan jumped across the slashing wind, and Wawa screamed. Out of the swirling rain, the lorcha's aft mast came crashing down toward Jaki. He hurled himself overboard, and the tender burst apart as the mast bashed into it. Spinning chunks of timber whirred around him, and he dunked himself. When he came up, Wawa was splashing toward him, clinging to his fawn hat, and he grabbed the animal and clutched at the lorcha's hull.

Overhead, Ganger Sint's harsh face appeared. He was looking at the shattered tender, which was wallowing in the chop. From where he bent over the taffrail, he could not see Jaki and Wawa bobbing beside the hull. With a hooked pole, he reached overboard and snagged Jaki's medicine bag.

Jaki shoved out from the hull and grabbed the pole, almost ripping it from Sint's hand. For a moment they faced off, and Jaki felt the other man brace his grip as if to ram him with the staff. Instead, he hauled back, pulling Jaki closer to the lorcha. A moment later he threw down a coil of rope. Wawa scampered up it first, and Jaki followed.

"Stiff wind," Ganger Sint said, his black hat slung over his shoulder by its strap and his wispy hair flaring in the blow. "You're in God's shadow to be alive now."

Jaki grabbed the medicine bag away from Sint and shoved past him. At the post of the fallen mast he stooped and examined the deck. The iron pegs that held the mast brace were uprooted.

Lucinda and Maud had rushed out at the sound of the crash, and now Jaki assured them he was all right as he drew Lucinda back into the cabin. Maud took the gibbon below deck to towel him dry, and Jaki stripped off his wet clothes.

"Sint tried to kill me," he told Lucinda. "The mast pegs were taken out."

"And how do you know it was Sint who did that?" she said, rubbing him down with a towel. "The wind's been jarring this mast all day and no one's examined it since we came aboard that I know of."

Jaki shook his head. "The wind wouldn't have tugged those pegs out."

Lucinda said nothing, but Jaki could read the uncertainty in her silence.

"Why was Sint aboard?" he asked. "He's supposed to be on the barges, minding the crew."

She glared at him. "You were there on the barges — and no one was here when the wind picked up. He came to secure the lorcha."

"He came to take those pegs out and club me when I came aside."

"Mast pegs rock out of their cradles when they're not tended," Lucinda said with annoyance. "You're blaming Sint because you haven't been watching after our lorcha and that almost cost you your life."

"Do you really think that?" Jaki's nostrils flared. "If Sint had come aboard to secure the lorcha, why didn't he see the pegs then?"

"He has been busy wrapping canvas and battening portholes. It was not his responsibility anyway — it is yours."

Jaki swallowed his anger. "Earlier today he told me to be careful about showing the diamonds in my medicine bag. I never told him I had diamonds in there. How does he know?"

"Boeck must have told him."

"Yes." Jaki nodded with satisfaction and finished drying himself. "That's what I figure. No one else knows. And if I had died tonight, those diamonds would be on their way back to Dagon in Sint's pouch — and he'd have taken you with them."

"Why are you speaking such nonsense?" Lucinda's cheeks were smudged red with anger. "I am an owner on this caravan. I have Boeck's papers to prove it. He would not renege."

Disbelief sharpened Jaki's features. "Do you think that once I'm out of the way Boeck would hesitate to seize you and make a favorable deal for himself with your father?"

Lucinda's jaw was set. "You're wrong, Jaki Gefjon. You think all men are pirates because that's all you've known. Boeck is a factor and a gentleman. I have his word in writing."

"You're a woman, Lucinda. His word to you means nothing to him."

"You are speaking like a heathen."

"That's what I am, then. But I am not going to be easy prey for Ganger Sint. Not anymore."

"What are you going to do?"

Jaki dumped the contents of his medicine bag onto the floor and separated out the diamonds. There were eleven of them. "Tomorrow everyone is going to know I have these diamonds. And they're going to know they are mine and what they mean to me."

"Why? Why make a spectacle of yourself before these primitives?"

"Because they are not just primitives. They are people, like you and me and Sint. Once they know about these, they cannot be stolen without everyone knowing they are stolen."

Lucinda stared at her husband, flushed with withheld anger. Jaki's eyes were bright. He seemed so intent on being right. "In many ways, Jaki Gefjon, you are a child."

Jaki stiffened. He gathered his diamonds, snakeskins, twigs, roots, berries, and leaves, and dumped them back in his bag. Without looking at Lucinda, he put on his trousers, slung his bag and shirt over his shoulder, and picked up a black vest and his wet hat. He walked to the door where his blowgun had been leaning since they had first boarded the lorcha.

"Where are you going?" she asked.

"Let me be," he said without looking back. He took his blowgun and closed the door after him.

He strode angily through the warm rain to the stern hatch, checked to see that the anchor was secure, and glanced about for Ganger Sint. No one was on deck. Again he looked at the mast-mounting, bent down and picked up the dislodged iron pegs. The wind could have knocked the mast out of its support, but he did not think so. He lifted the stern hatch and went below deck.

All the port and larboard hatches were open, and the air was flecked with raindrops. Still, a mustiness hung in the lanternglow, a stink of cooking fires, sweat, and rotting timber. The smell of people. It had been the same in the longhouses, and it made him yearn for the marl scent of the jungle, the gloat of rain in the canopy, the opal mists leaking from the trees and glowing like starlight. How far away that life seemed now.

The Burmese crew sat and sprawled about an iron stove where a black pot was bubbling with monkey stew. Ganger Sint lay in a hammock, his hands behind his head, his boots flopped on the ground beneath him. The crew and the foreman watched Jaki as he stood under the deck brace where the mast had lifted out. If the wind had shook the mast free, the brace would be loose, too. He prodded the brace with his blowgun. The wooden strut creaked as it shook.

Jaki looked at Ganger Sint, who was watching him with sleepy eyes. *Am I wrong about this monkeyface?* he asked himself, and the hostile shadow in the Dutchman's eyes answered him — or was that, too, an illusion? Jaki walked past Sint and through a tight companionway to the forward cabin where the provisions were kept.

Maud was there with Wawa. She had dried the gibbon off with a corner of spare canvas, and she was feeding the animal coconut milk and yellow plums. "Are you all right?" she asked. "Wawa is still scared."

"Wawa is happiest in the jungle." Jaki laid down his blowgun and medicine bag and put on his shirt. "Have you seen the stitching kit?" he asked.

Maud removed a leather bag from beside a stack of canvas bolts and handed it to him. Jaki sat on a coil of rope, placed his hat and black vest before him, and removed a needle and a spool of black thread from the stitching kit. Slowly, with great care, he took out his mountains' tears and, by the wan light of the oil lamp hung from a rafter, began to stitch them over the buttons on his vest.

Maud left him there with Wawa and returned to the forecastle cabin. She found Lucinda weeping into her pillow and coaxed her to sit up. "Why does he go his own way?" Lucinda sobbed. "Why did he marry me if he isn't going to stay by me?"

"He is a man of the wilderness," Maud said, wiping the tears from her face.

"But he was so reasonable before. Why does he insist now on loitering with the foul-smelling crew?"

"Let us sleep now," Maud counseled her. "Jaki will come around. He is a man of the wilds, very much like my Aunt Timotha's kin, with their straw poppets for inducing the grain to grow. They have their own wisdom, which seems foolishness to us. He is your husband now. And he does love you. But in his way. You must trust him."

Maud blew out the lamp. In the rain-drumming dark, the future seemed suddenly strange and uncaring. "We will make it to the New World, Maud," Lucinda said, her voice stronger for her uncertainty. "And by the time we get there, Jaki will be a man of grace and authority and not wildness anymore."

"Yes," Maud said, afraid that it would be so. "His English is very good already. And he goes everywhere with a hat now."

Jaki appeared on deck the following dawn in a black vest with four big diamond buttons and a fawn hat with seven diamonds circling the brim. The crew were agog at the sight of uncut gems of such size, and Ganger Sint put his hands on his hips and ground his teeth to see Jaki displaying the diamonds the foreman already considered his own. Boeck had told him about the jewels and said that a list and description of each of them was deposited in a company vault. But Sint believed that was a lie, for the factor had refused to tell him how many diamonds there were. Sint had decided to take all but three for himself, and he had worked out an elaborate plan to return to Europe with them and sell them to the highest bidder outside the company. Now that the whole crew knew about them, though, an accident befalling Jaki would not be enough. He would have to murder him away from all the others during the jungle crossing after Prome, where he could claim the diamonds were lost. That would be a more troublesome effort, yet it pleased Sint, for then he would have the pleasure of killing the arrogant pirate with his own hands.

Prome was two days away, and the crew decided not to repair the stern mast of the lorcha but tug the vessel behind the last barge instead. Jaki visited each of the barges, telling the story of his mountains' tears to anyone who would listen. Mang and Kota, impressed with his bravura, accompanied him during his storytelling, burnishing their renown as the Pirates of Serangoon.

Lucinda was disenchanted with Jaki. No mood fit perfectly — not anger or even regret. She loved him for his daring, and yet feared his bravado. She desired his strong embrace, and still doubted his constancy. She wanted him but could not quell her ideals to take him as he was.

The night before they were to arrive in Prome, he returned to her cabin. Without her, he felt like a child without parents. He had slept alone two nights in the provision hold and had used the darkness and solitude to ponder how he had found his way to her and what she really meant to him. Was it simply her beauty that had attracted him? Was that all she was to him? But that was so much. Her beauty was like the high plateaus of Borneo, vistas wider than a lifetime, distances holy with woodlands, magisterial crags, weather fronts, and the sea barbed with the sun's gold. But to enter into that beauty, to walk down into the vista and become a part of it, was laborious. He resolved to return more sincerely to his journey with her and entered her cabin like a thief returning with what he had stolen.

Lucinda was reviewing the manifest by lamplight, shaping a trading strategy for the next day's bargaining in the marketplace of Prome. Maud was sitting beside her, sewing, and when she saw Jaki she rose and excused herself.

"I have come to apologize," Jaki began.

Lucinda straightened. "Apologize for what?"

Jaki closed the door behind him and took off his hat. In the lamp-glow, the diamonds on his hat and vest burned like stars. "For these," he said, indicating the diamonds.

"They're your gems. If you want to wear them provocatively, you should."

"I defied you," he said. "I followed my instincts instead."

"Perhaps that was not a bad thing," she replied, and stood up.

He forced himself to speak distinctly. "Whatever separates us is wrong."

She recognized the strength he had exerted to find those words, and a profound sympathy for him swept through her. She reached out, and he pulled her against him, clutching her hair. "Stay with me," she muttered into his chest. "There is no peace without you. Stay with me, true child."

Always, he wanted to promise, and held her tighter. *Always,* he wanted to say, but the fear in that word made his heart feel like a fruit splitting to seed.

When rain lowered over the sea like a harp into the hands of the wind, Quarles believed his daughter was dead. And on days when from the gunwale of his ship he could see staves of sunlight glowing in the depths of the jungle islands, he was certain that the heathen pirate had stolen her away into the wilderness, where she lived as a forest princess. She was his only family. She was all that his suffering could ever redeem, and she was dead, or worse, lost.

He did not grieve her absence any more than he had mourned when her mother had died of plague in his arms. He had spent all his lamentations as a child in Chatham bemoaning his life as a dockhand, and he had no grief left in him, only defiance. But how did one defy the plague that hides in smoke or the pirates that the jungle births? He had decided that ignorance was the god that had snatched from him his wife and his daughter. Already in the capitals of Europe plague was being routed by a better understanding of humors and flux. But though he had killed the pirate king Trevor Pym, and other civilized captains were using the latest developments in marine warfare to flush out pirate nests throughout Asia, the jungle remained wild. Someday, not in his lifetime but in a future he cherished, the jungle would be tamed by empire and pirates would be extinct. To that goal, he devoted his life.

For the first months after the loss of his daughter, his devotion to empire had him captaining slave barges. The company had found work for him transporting savages from the entrepôt at Surabaja to the Dutch and English agrarian colonies in the Spice Islands. Many of the local natives in the Moluccas had been decimated by European diseases or were too truculent to apply themselves to field work, so manual labor had to be imported from Africa, where slavery had long been a practice among the tribes. Quarles's spirit of stern command was well suited for this work, and he applied himself vigorously to satisfying the company's commission.

But on drear days and when he was in sight of the jungle, his memories of Lucinda troubled him. Then he would sit alone in his cabin and remove from his sea chest the Bible cover of Jaki Gefjon's that he had taken from Pym. It was the only trace he had of the enemy who had stolen his daughter. He wondered where its pages had gone, why it had a nailhole through its spine, and what the enigmatic phrases meant in the space where Jaki's name belonged. That the pirate had desecrated the Book seemed obvious to him, and though Quarles had abandoned all faith early in life and privately scoffed at religion, he swore to the God of the abused Book that he would avenge the Lord if only the villain and the women he had kidnaped were delivered into his hands. It was the most ardent prayer of his life.

After his third voyage, on his return to Surabaja, a letter packet awaited him at the trademaster's station sealed with the stamp of the English factor at Jakarta. Inside were two papers. The first informed him that his daughter, her maid, and the pirate Jaki Gefjon had been seen by Robert Fletcher in Dagon. The second was an Admiralty order commanding him to return to England to personally account for the loss of *The Fateful Sisters.*

Prome was a cluttered river village of frond-roofed huts bunched beneath the enormous wall of a rain forest. From a distance, the air around it looked greasy with the smoke of cooking fires and the miasmic mists of the jungle. On either side of the river were mountain ranges clothed in shambling vegetation, steep, verdant crags towering into the sky like a dream's minarets. To the west, the cliffwall, threaded with waterfalls, was a pillar of wonder, while the fang-shaped palisade of the east seemed a pillar of horror and the trash-heap village squatting beneath it an unclean offering.

Jaki stared at the abrupt chasms above him, and a chill snaked through him. Here was a gateway to the netherworld. The forest path guarded by these towers was the threshold of his life, the deceptive borderland between past and future. *The light of the jungle is deadlier than darkness.* Jabalwan spoke with the slim voice of memory, and Jaki gripped his blowgun more strongly.

Lucinda saw the apprehension in Jaki's tense jaw, and she felt a moment of uneasiness about insisting that he journey on this caravan. The sorcerers' prophecy had said his future was outside the jungle. She knew he would have been happier at sea, in the world of his spirit father and of everything new and European. He was still becoming European — that was her promise for his fulfillment, the best that she could offer him. But fate decreed they return to the jungle first. Lucinda promised herself she would be more tolerant of his primitive ways until the forest was behind them. The cultivated kingdom of India would be a better place to continue the refinement of her husband. For now she would strive simply to keep him close and as untroubled as possible in the shadow of his jungle past.

A reveler's scream lifted Lucinda from her brooding. Villagers in bright sarongs and headcloths crowded the black mudbanks of the Irrawaddy, waving ti leaves as the caravan buffalo slogged among them and the barges came aground on the sandbars. The crowd, alerted to the approach of the caravan days earlier by drum songs, swarmed about the barges and the lorcha, and planks of teak were laid over the shallows so the travelers could come ashore.

Ganger Sint was the first one into the village, leading the crew to the feast hut erected among the ruins of an ancient temple. Lucinda, leading Jaki, Maud, and Wawa from the lorcha, was greeted at the end of the teak walkway by a narrow, turbaned man with skin dark as the river mud, a bristly black beard, and black eyes wet with alertness. At the sight of Jaki's diamonds, he cried with wonder. He bowed to Jaki and greeted him in Dutch. Jaki shook his head, stepped back, and tilted his long staff toward Lucinda. She explained in garbled Dutch that she was the owner and presented him with the letter of passage Boeck had given her. The man studied the letter intently for several moments, then bowed extravagantly to Lucinda, making her understand that he was the local merchant responsible for outfitting the caravans that continued north from here by land. The merchant put both of his hands on his chest, bowed again, and introduced himself. "Prah."

He lifted his whiskered chin toward the eager villagers who had gathered on the mudbank, and at his signal they swept through the water, clambered aboard the laden barges, and began unloading the bales of textiles and the crates of hardware.

Prah led them into the village, a half circle of stilt-raised huts and mud streets lively with pigs, dogs, and children. Jaki reeled with memories of the many jungle villages he had visited in the forest. But the people here had not gathered reverentially to greet him; they were intent only on the cargo, which they carried to shore with all the respect due holy vessels.

European goods appeared everywhere. The nearby trees and shrubs were hung with colorful strips of linen, all of the huts had battered pots and chipped mirrors hanging in their windows, and the married women wore woolen shawls in the sullen heat. The young women were in the feast hut among the ruins, favoring the caravan crew. The old ones and the very young, who had not run down to the barges, gawked at the cargo with cheerful vacuousness. The grinning emptiness of their grimy faces shot an uncontrollable shiver through Jaki. This was the future of all villages — a merchant headman, their women given freely to strangers, and reverence only for things. Jaki's ribs ached with that thought, and he was glad when Lucinda took his hand.

They came to Prah's dwelling, a large bark-roofed hut, the doorway curtained with beads, the windows screened with blue-dyed muslin. The interior was carpeted in antelope hide, and they removed their footwear before entering. Incense twined from dragonhead censers set on cast-iron Chinese trivets, a Swiss pendule clock chittered softly atop a Dutch chest of drawers, and an agate vase of Persian design graced a corner shelf behind a lacquered chess table with pieces of green and white jade. Prah invited them to sit on a pallet of indigo cushions. He clapped his hands, and a dour Burmese woman entered with a tray of porcelain cups from Delft and a steaming blue kettle of Japanese ceramic.

While they sipped green tea, they discussed the conversion of the caravan from river to land, using a clay tablet to draw images of what they were trading. The bartering went slowly, less for the lack of a common language than for Prah's dogged persistence on maximizing his profit. Lucinda was determined to take her caravan through Burma's jungles to the Manipur pass and into India with as little loss as possible, and she did not want to begin her land trek by squandering her goods on an avaricious village merchant. She scanned the European and Moghul artifacts in the hut, and when her eyes alighted on the ranks of chess pieces an idea flourished in her. She pointed to the chess table and motioned an opening move. Prah's eyes winced smaller, and he pursed his lips. He looked directly at Jaki's diamonds and back to Lucinda. She shook her head and removed a chamois satchel strung about her waist. She spilled her gems onto the pallet, and Prah fingered the brooches, rings, and hairpins and turned up his palm, wanting more. Lucinda shrugged, emptyhanded, and Prah looked over to where Maud was feeding crackers to Wawa. Lucinda frowned, thought for a moment, then nodded. Prah stood up and went to the chess table.

"What are you doing?" Jaki asked as she moved to rise.

"I am going to play a game of chess for the elephants we need," she answered and looked to Maud. "Wish me luck. I have naught to play with but my trinkets — and you, Maud."

Maud's face jumped. "Lucinda, you wouldn't!"

"It seems you are all I have that he's interested in, Maud," she said. She tried putting the curl of a laugh in her voice to ease the fear she saw in her maid, but she sounded callous and quickly added: "There is no risk at all. You know I won't lose. I've been playing with Father since I was nine. There's no risk."

"Here — take one of the diamonds," Jaki said, urgently. "That's what he really wants."

"Certainly not," Lucinda said, firmly. "I'll not have you buying what I need. I can succeed with what is already mine."

Maud took Lucinda's hands as she stood up. "Please, my lady, I beseech you, do not gamble with me."

"Maud." Lucinda squeezed her hands. "I am not gambling. I would never gamble with you, Mousie. But you must help me now. I need a lure — and he finds you attractive. Nothing will come of it. You are bait."

"Oh, my lady, I could not bear to be with *him*." Maud fisted her hands over her stomach to suppress a chill of nausea. "Must it be this way?"

"I need to do this on my own," Lucinda said. "This is my caravan. I'll not use Jaki's diamonds when he himself did not want this trek. You are all I have. Won't you help me?"

"I am afraid."

"Trust me."

Lucinda sat down at the chess table opposite Prah and chose the right hand of the two fists he held before her. It held the green piece and gave Prah the first move. The game went swiftly. Prah, a skilled player, opened with a horse attack that took the center, while Lucinda countered with a phalanx of pawns on the queen's side, hoping to pin the knights. But Prah's knights were merely a diversion for his real attack, a sliding bishop coordinated with a rook that trapped Lucinda's king.

Lucinda sat back, her heart buzzing in her chest to have been duped so easily.

Maud wept, and Jaki tore off a diamond from his vest and clacked it onto the chess table. "Play again."

Prah shook his head, his keen eyes gauging the intensity of Maud's discomfort and Jaki's responsiveness to it. Jaki tore off a second diamond and a third and dropped them onto the table. Prah smiled.

Maud and Jaki hunched beside Lucinda, as she drew green again.

Out came Prah's slashing horse attack, but this time Lucinda made no attempt to block him. Instead she retreated, moving her pieces to the side, and with each setback, Maud stifled a cry. She could not bear any longer to watch Prah's grin glisten brighter with each advance, and she shut her eyes. The movement of the pieces clicked in her mind like divinatory bones casting her fate. When she dared to peek again, the merchant was not smiling. His chessmen cluttered the center and were getting in each other's way. They had become targets for Lucinda's surrounding army.

Jaki could tell from the pile of captured pieces before Lucinda that she was winning, and he observed her interested calm, her willingness to sacrifice pieces now that she had her enemy trapped. She had treated Maud with as much serenity, trading her like a chess piece for the elephants she needed to find her way to India. Anger mixed with his love for her, and he felt a chill enter his passion. The numb touch at the center of his chest was reminiscent of the bitter love he had felt for Jabalwan, forever his teacher, his doorway to life in the wilderness, forever the murderer of his mother.

"Mate!" Lucinda called. She picked up the diamonds and handed them to Jaki. Maud hugged her and sobbed, and she stroked her maid's hair.

Prah was still staring at the board, his lips moving behind his beard. At last he looked up. "You have won," he said in Dutch, slowly enough for her to understand, "as I won the last game. Let us play a decisive third."

Lucinda shook her head. "No more games," she said in a mix of English and Dutch. "I took the risk with my maid and my husband's diamonds, and I have won."

Prah stood up abruptly. "You must play me another game!"

"We will have our elephants now, if you please," Lucinda said, rising.

Prah shouted something none of them understood, and two men with their faces hidden by the ravelings of their white turbans entered from the back door with drawn blades. Maud screamed, and Jaki jumped forward and whirled his blowgun.

The intruders dropped their weapons, and Prah's wrathful face slackened. In the front doorway, Kota and Mang stood with cocked flintlocks in their hands.

Noon heat stifled the village, and the work of loading the elephants went slowly. Ganger Sint staggered drunkenly from the feast hut to the grassy field where the villagers were loading the elephants and buffalo with the caravan's goods. He had to trouble his besotted brain to count the beasts; there seemed too many of them. Prah stood on the verandah of his hut, and Sint swaggered over to him and sprawled on the steps while he questioned the merchant. "You dolt!" Sint roared when he heard what had happened. "You should have skinned her — not played games! She's a woman! How many good Dutchmen have come through here with me and you've skinned them all, for every guilder you could get. You — " He reeled to his feet. "You could have skinned them and ended this whole farce right here."

With one hand, Prah shoved Sint backward, and the foreman tumbled down the stairs and landed on his back in the mud. Prah signaled his two men, and they dragged Sint out into the field among the milling workers. Jaki approached and bent over him. He was unconscious. "Strap him to a buffalo," he told Kota. "We can't wait for him."

Mang spat. "Leave him here. His shadow we do not need over us."

"He will come after us," Jaki said. "I'd rather see him than be looking for him."

Jaki walked back toward the elephants. Lucinda was talking to the mahout, who was showing her how he used his hook to bring an elephant to its knees so it could be mounted. Jaki had seen these huge creatures in Bandjermasin, where the Dutch used them as stevedores. They were sad giants, the color of the thunderclouds above.

Jaki lifted his attention to the sky to read the future in the luminously dark clouds and was startled to see the tribes. *Of course,* he chided himself, *where would they have gone?* Blowing backward from the future was a horde of people slouching nearer, their possessions strewn behind them, their visages haggard with famine.

He dropped his gaze back to earth. The pilgrims loitering at the cavernous mouth of the rain forest and the merchants gathered by their beasts waiting for the order of march were contemplating the shadowy gateway, each appealing to his own god for aid — and no one doubted they would need supernatural help on the journey ahead. The calls of wild animals wounded the deep silence of the forest, and the tenebrous light squeaking through the dense trees defied the sense of sight so invaluable on river and sea. The jungle offered only shadows. Jungle travel relied on the lowest senses, scent, taste, and touch. Jaki had to steel himself to return to the blindness of the jungle, and a smile hovered up in him as he recalled his clumsy first moons following Jabalwan, when the sorcerer blindfolded him and Wawa's voice became his eyes. He whistled for the gibbon.

The rains began as the caravan entered the jungle. The incantatory rhythms of raindrops sifting through the canopy became the chant of the journey, a melancholy cadence that matched the wistful spirit of the elephants. Lucinda and Maud rode in a canopied litter atop the lead elephant with the mahout and his wife. The children and some pilgrims were carried in a buffalo-driven cart behind the lead elephant, and the merchants with their cargo-laden beasts marched after them. Kota and Mang alternated as rear guard. Jaki took the lead, sending Wawa ahead yet continually urging him to stay close. This forest was unlike any jungle they had known in Borneo. Here unfamiliar plants mingled with the eerie calls of strange creatures, and the mood of the wilderness was tense.

Toward nightfall, as camp was being made, the whistle came from Mang that Ganger Sint was awake. Unstrapped from the back of a buffalo, he staggered around, astonished to find himself in the gloom.

Sint squinted through the ache between his eyes, looking for Lucinda, and when he found her sitting by the fire with her maid and the mahout's wife, he saw her as if for the first time. She was a lovely woman, all right, with her fair hair and a face as downy gold as any in Holland. He had thought her a tawdry runaway until now. But in the dozen times he had passed through Prome, no one had gotten so much as a bowl of beetle-leg soup from Prah without paying handsomely. And she had gotten elephants and paid nothing! He wanted to speak with her, to express his respect. But, already, he knew the outcome of that. She was an English captain's daughter, a willful lass who had taken a fierce and pretty-faced half-breed for a husband. Like all the good things of this world, she was beyond him.

He knew then that killing her insolent pirate husband would not be enough. She would have to suffer by his own hand to redeem the sense of loss she called up in him. He squatted at the fire of the Burmese crew and surreptitiously observed Lucinda as she ate the pan-fried bread, leeks, and snakemeat prepared by the mahout. Jaki entered the firelight with his two pirate friends, and they sat among the women. In Jaki's hand the three gems he had torn from his vest glinted. Sint watched astounded as the young pirate handed a diamond to each of his men and one to the maid.

Maud took the diamond with astonishment. "Mister Gefjon, why are you giving me this?"

"Enough of this mistering," Jaki protested. "Call me Jaki as my friends do."

"Jaki," Maud said, peeking at him with shy eyes. "I cannot take riches from you."

"I am giving this to you for your help today." Jaki nodded to his two men, acknowledging their grateful grins. "Now, like Kota and Mang, you are free. You have something of your own. Stay with us as long as you will. Go when you please."

Maud looked to Lucinda, who reluctantly nodded her head. "I lost you today, Maud," she said, and the humility in her voice surprised the maid. "Without Jaki, I'd have lost you forever. Take the diamond.

And yes, when we reach Surat, if you wish to return to England, you may go with my blessing."

"Not until you teach me chess," Maud said around a smile, "and I can best you."

Lucinda passed a sore look at her husband, and he grinned and handed her his hat with its band of seven diamonds. "I'll keep the one on my vest," he told her. "The rest are yours. Take them now if you wish."

She tossed the hat back to him, and Sint could read the pique in her set jaw. Jaki had seen the dimple that appeared in her chin before, on the Irrawaddy, when she had called him a child for displaying his diamonds, and he was not surprised when she said tightly, "Sometimes you make me feel so cold inside, as if you'd never shown me your heart, as if I were sleeping with Satan and love counted for nothing. I did not marry you for your diamonds, silly. Go ahead and give them all away. Make our servants as wealthy as we. I will still love you." She said that with a defiant blush that made Jaki reach out and trace the hurt dent of her chin. His gentle touch broke the spell of scorn she felt for his childlike magnanimity, and she looked deep into his eyes, admiring the animal quiet and freedom of him. "You love me best when you try to understand my heart," she said. "And now I feel I must try to understand yours."

Ganger Sint did not understand the friendship he spied. Nor did he comprehend the love that would take a desirable woman like Lucinda from a comfortable life of influence and place her here in the mud and mosquitoes. Death he knew far better than love, and his memory was long. He remembered the Spanish burning his village in Holland, his father thrown headfirst into the well, his mother screaming as the armored men in dark beards dragged her into the barn. Sint was nine, big for his age, big enough to be brained and gutted by the invaders if he was caught, yet small enough to have stayed hidden under the burning house until the last moment. In the black smoke stampeding the town, the enemy never saw him, and by the time he had shouted into the well and heard nothing but his own screams coming back, and by the time he had crawled weeping to the barn, the flames were high and the Spanish were gone. He had found his mother, naked, her blue bowels in her lap.

He had toured hell that winter and saw enough of war and famine and plague to forget he was a boy. In the spring he joined a Dutch brigade for food, not vengeance. The army fed him, clothed him, trained him to kill — and he knew a grim satisfaction that was as close to happiness as he would ever get. When the company needed soldiers to project and protect their interests in Asia, he volunteered, wanting to get as far away as possible from winter and the well and the barn.

Sint withheld his loathing from Jaki and his company, and over the following days he kept his distance, marching to the rear, yet just close enough to see all he wanted of his prey. Watching Jaki striding with ease through the green shadows, laughingly reassuring his wife and her maid at the raucous cries of birds and monkeys, Sint experienced a wrath he had felt before only in battle. Jaki was too alive, too delighted with his life. He was Sint's shadow, a mockery of all Sint was not. And he waited, like a spider he waited.

Jaki was aware of Ganger Sint's attentiveness. The man's belligerence was silent but palpable, and several times Jaki had even considered stabbing his jugular with a poison thorn while he slept. Only the fear of losing his wife's respect restrained him. Lucinda had agreed to do her best to bring the caravan into India safely, and the loss of the head foreman would be a loss of face for her. So Jaki decided to avoid killing him as long as he could. By day, he had Kota and Mang watch Sint and alert Jaki to the foreman's movements with whistle signals.

Jaki could tell by Lucinda's subtle remoteness that she was still annoyed about the diamonds he had given away in Prome. Maud sensed this and tried several times to return the gem. Jaki would not take it back, and Lucinda insisted Maud keep it. At night when Jaki and Lucinda were alone in their tent of broad leaves, the rain chattering around them, they were happy, and she told him she did not care what he did with his diamonds. Inside that yes, however, he heard a no, restrained and far away. He knew she was withholding her disapproval, restraining her education of him, until they had found their way clear of the jungle. He was grateful for that and did not press her.

The jungle waged constant battle against the caravan. Fever harrowed Lucinda as well as many of the merchants and pilgrims, and Jaki was glad for Maud's knowledge of plant remedies, learned from her Aunt Timotha. Without her help he could not have administered to all the ill. The incessant rains slurred the trail, and the ferny vegetation and vine-grip seemed to flourish before their eyes so that the crew had to hack a path with their broad blades. Once, a girl gathering blossoms was bitten by a cobra. She collapsed in a convulsion of terror, her flesh discoloring in black bands, and Jaki was forced to stab a hole in her throat and insert a reed tube to breathe for her until the toxin relented.

Giant pug marks began to appear. Jaki had never seen cat prints so massive. By clawspan and stride he knew the panther was over ten feet long. "Tiger," the mahout announced when Jaki called him over to view the spoor. "Tell no one. Panic. Very bad."

Jaki kept the secret two days, but on the third a crewman disappeared at the watering pool. Ganger Sint found the prints beside the pool, and he felt as though his wrath had gone beyond him and taken bestial form in the hollows of the jungle.

The caravan grouped more tightly, and side journeys from the trail to fetch water were escorted by men with flintlocks. Yet the next night another crewman vanished from the tail of the caravan.

Three days passed before the tiger approached again. Each night, Jaki had set up a lean-to of atap leaves at the back of the caravan and propped his blowgun between his legs, waiting for the beast. When its eyes appeared in the darkness like two drips of fire, Jaki was dizzy with drowsiness and only Wawa's screech alerted him.

Jaki lifted his blowgun, sighted the flickering sparks of eyelight, and huffed with a breath from the core of his belly. A roar bawled from the darkness so loud the elephants trumpeted in fear, Wawa leaped into Jaki's arms, and the slumbering travelers woke with shouts. The eyeglints were gone, and the roaring came again from farther away.

Sint, half naked, with a flintlock in his hand, and the mahout, gripping a kris in one hand, a hatchet in the other, jumped to Jaki's side, toppling his lean-to. "What have you done?" the mahout cried.

"He hit the tiger with a dart." Sint spat in disgust. "You're not hunting pigs now, half-breed. That is a Bengal tiger out there. If you hit it three times with your puny darts you wouldn't kill it. You fool heathen." He stood up and scanned the jungle night. "Now we'll have to go after it."

"No, no," the mahout warned, waving his kris. "The jungle is the mouth of the tiger."

Lucinda and Maud stepped through the gathering crowd of nervous travelers, Kota and Mang behind them. "Have we lost anyone?" Lucinda asked anxiously.

"Strengthen the fires," Sint ordered. He turned abruptly and announced to the caravan, "The aborigine wounded the tiger with a dart. As the poison inflames the creature, it will strike more boldly — not to eat, but to kill. Get close to the fire — and arm yourselves."

A roar jumped from the jungle, sonorous and crazed. The elephants bellowed, and the people rushed for the smoldering fires and fed the flames with branches.

"We have no choice now," Sint went on, squinting warily. "At first light, we will have to track it or no one will be safe."

"No," Lucinda said. "No one is going after it." She spoke directly to Sint, with iron authority. "We will stay together and go forward. We will use the elephants as a moving barrier and mount bowmen and musketeers to guard our perimeter fastidiously. No one will be lost."

Sint stared at her in the slithery light. "Lady, you are not playing chess now. Every piece you sacrifice will be a human life."

"I am the owner," Lucinda said, and another roar flashed from the darkness, vile with hurt. Lucinda ignored it and said, "I will not permit a hunt. If we lose you, we lose our weapons, and we will truly be helpless."

A merchant called out from beside a fire gushing with new kindling. "The foreman is our protection. The company sent him for that. Let him decide."

Murmurs of agreement billowed from the crowd.

"The foreman is under my command," Lucinda insisted, with a cadence of authority she had learned from her father. "*I* decide what is best for the caravan. We will stay together and guard our flanks. No one will leave the camp." She stared hard at Ganger Sint and met his small, deadly eyes unflinchingly. "Are we agreed, Mister Sint?"

The foreman stifled his surprise with a sullen nod and barked orders at the men with flintlocks, positioning them on the perimeter before hunkering down beside a fire, his flintlock across his knees.

Lucinda had torches propped at the edge of the camp and arranged the people in a circle facing out from the fire, their jittery stares searching the darkness for movement.

Jaki sat with Maud and Wawa, and nearby Kota and Mang herded their young wives between them. No one spoke. When Lucinda joined them, Jaki was too ashamed to meet her gaze, and he accepted her consoling hand on his knee by tightening his grip on the blowgun beside him. He wanted to be alone with his shame, but there was nowhere to go.

"You did what you could," Lucinda whispered to him. "That is more than anyone else."

"It's my fault," he muttered. His face glinted as if frosted, and his eyes were dark and twitchy.

"You did not create the tiger," she assured him.

"But I wounded it. I made it more terrible."

The demonic cry burned again in the darkness. The elephants stamped and snorted fearfully, and Wawa clung tightly to Jaki's leg.

Kota handed Jaki one of his flintlocks, and he passed it to Lucinda and gentled Wawa by scratching his ears. "I had my shot at the beast tonight," he said.

She accepted the gun with a sad frown. "This should be your weapon now, Jaki. Your blowgun cannot help you anymore."

He did not look at her. Instead, he kept his gaze on the thriving darkness of the jungle, one hand on Wawa, the other on his blowgun. She was right, he knew. He could not carry his past with him anymore. But he hated that truth. The blowgun had been Jabalwan's, and to surrender it was to relinquish his last physical bond with his beloved teacher. The Life had led him far from all he had learned as a sorcerer, yet still he clung to the old weapon, the old way. But where, where truly, was his place in this kingdom of guns, big ships, and money? The answer had her hand on him — but he could not face her yet. He was ashamed that he was still owned by his past.

He would have to begin his life again — but not until he had righted what he had made wrong. He decided then that he would meet the tiger as he had met the savagery of the monkeyfaces on the high seas, and, before that, the Spider. He would go alone at first light into the jungle.

In the apricot light of dawn, while Lucinda circled through the camp readying the caravan for that day's journey, Jaki put on his hat, picked up his spear and a flintlock, and sent Wawa into the jungle ahead. The gibbon came hurtling back through the treetops shouting its cry that it had seen a man.

Jaki sent Wawa ahead again and followed with Mang and Kota. Around the next bend, a bald, squat man popped up from behind a toppled altar stone where he had been relieving himself. Hurriedly lowering his orange robe, he hobbled from behind the rock, tripped over a braid of knotweed, bounced over the rocky ground, and sprang back to his feet, a hapless smile pressed into his rotund face as he bowed before the armed men.

When a startled Jaki returned the bow, the clumsy monk proceeded to jabber away in a singsong dialect. Jaki, not getting a word of it, tried English, the smattering of Dutch he knew, and finally, in exasperation, Spanish.

"Ah, so you speak the Jesuits' tongue," the monk replied in crisp Spanish. "Might I have a drink from your flagon?" Jaki signed for Kota to give his water to the monk. When he had drunk, the bald man said, "I came here to pray two weeks ago, when the tiger began to harry my fellow travelers — and the tiger trapped me in these ruins. The caravan I was journeying with dispersed into the jungle, and no one returned for me. I heard your elephants last night, and the tiger troubling you. I added you to my prayers."

"Who are you?" Jaki asked.

"I am Dhup," the monk replied through his relentless smile, "a monk wandering the palm lines of the Buddha. I am traveling to Sarnath, the Deer Park in India where the Buddha first revealed his wisdom."

Gunshots and screams erupted from the camp, and Jaki and his men rushed back down the trail, Wawa scampering after them.

The camp was in an uproar. Buffalo kicked their hoofs high, and most of the elephants had snapped their restraints and were pressing together despite the loud protests and blows of the mahout. People scattered to get out of the way of the alarmed elephants. Children wailed, men shouted. Jaki searched wildly for Lucinda and, not finding her in the turmoil, howled her name.

He headed through the melee of animals and people to a knot of men with flintlocks and spears. Ganger Sint was at their center, his big, chipped face strained with yelling. Lucinda was before him, shaking her head, her arms outstretched, trying to hold the group together. As Jaki hurried closer, he spotted the latest casualty: the mangled body of a young girl — the young girl he had saved from snakebite.

"You!" Sint bellowed when Jaki shoved to Lucinda's side. "You've brought this on us! We're going after that tiger now." The foreman trained a brittle stare on Jaki. "And you are coming with us."

"No one is going," Lucinda insisted. "We will kill it the next time it attacks."

"Three of us are dead," Sint challenged, veins clicking at his temples. "How many more will die while we cower behind these elephants?" He returned his vengeful gaze to Jaki. "You're a hunter. You can stalk this creature."

"I will," Jaki said.

Lucinda pulled at his vest until he turned about. "You are my husband. I forbid you to go."

With a stricken expression, Jaki shook his head. "I would be useless to you if I stayed."

"You cannot protect me out there," she said quietly to him. "I need you here to stand with me against Sint. Affirm my authority, Jaki, or we will have a mutiny."

He put a hand at the back of her neck and bowed his face close to hers. "I serve you best by meeting the evil I have created."

"Jaki — you are leaving me again as you did in Singapore for your pirate captain. Do not do this to me. If you truly love me, stay with me."

His hand tightened at the back of her neck. "I do love you, Lucinda. That is why we are here and not at sea now." He dropped his hand. "I must do what it is within me to do."

"Jaki —"

"No more will die because of me," he said loudly, looking around him. The monk had edged into the crowd, little noticed, and watched impassively as Jaki declared, "I will go after it alone."

"That's stupid," Sint scoffed. "You can track it, but you'll need men with flintlocks and bows to bring it down."

"Kota," he called, and the small, stout man stepped forward, his tall companion sagging with relief. "You stay with my wife and protect her with your life. Mang, you will wear tiger fangs today."

Mang jerked as if struck. "Or they will wear me," he grumbled and shuffled forward.

"Everyone else stays here," Jaki ordered, "or I will not go. I will not have the whole caravan crashing through the jungle with me."

Ganger Sint allowed himself a grin that dimmed slightly when Jaki removed his hat and handed it to Lucinda. "The tiger will overlook my informality," he told his wife.

She took his hand with the hat. "Do not go, Jaki," she begged, tears sparkling. "Stay with me."

He wanted to console her, but words balked. He twisted his hand free, took the flintlock from Kota's grip, and gave it to Lucinda. "I will be back."

The tiger's spoor was easy to follow, even in the smudgy light of early morning, the prints were so huge. Wawa chirruped from ahead, Mang and Sint staggering noisily behind him. Jaki signed for them to hold back and separate. He knew that exposing his back to Sint was dangerous, but blundering through the jungle like this was certain death. He signed for Sint to move to his left and hoped that Mang would spy any treachery early enough to save him.

The hunt demanded full alertness. Jaki had a flintlock, one shot, and his spear, which he trusted more. *Hope has no tribe,* he heard Jabalwan whisper far back in his head. Always before when he had abandoned hope and charged heedless of his life into battle, he had lived. If he had cherished any hope during any of those fights, he might never have known the beauty of Lucinda or the dream of their future. He paused to think this through and heard Mang and Sint bumbling behind him. He had to give up hope. He had to find his place at the desperate center of the world where passion was single-minded. That was where the tiger lived.

Wawa chirruped from ahead, and Jaki slinked forward so silently that the men behind him did not realize he was gone. Wawa cried again, more urgently this time, and Jaki froze. He whistled for the gibbon to come to him. Wawa called back his signal for danger.

Jaki whistled again, more loudly, this time commanding Wawa to wait.

Wawa screamed then as he never had before. Jaki abandoned caution and charged through the jungle. He smelled it then — the musky fetor of the giant cat. A roar banged over him, and he swung around. But he was alone. The beast's cry had come from above him. Jaki looked up. Wawa was dangling from a branch, his bowels hanging in a scarlet tangle.

Jaki howled, and the roar crashed again from above. The tiger was in the canopy, an ember of yellow light melting among the leaves. Jaki fired his flintlock. Twigs flapped, and he dropped his gun. With his spear, he lowered Wawa's body to the ground.

Jaki bowed over the animal, shaking with grief. The gibbon's little hand twitched and grabbed a lock of Jaki's hair. Wiping his tears, the youth peered into Wawa's staring black eyes. "Rest," he whispered, beginning the intonation for the dying. "The wind knows your name now. You are part of the song it sings to the stars. Rest." Wawa's hand relaxed, and its eyes widened darkly. Jaki choked and pressed his face to the warm muzzle of his animal.

The tiger snarled from somewhere behind. Jaki rose from Wawa's carcass with rageful intensity, not bothering to pick up the flintlock. He barged through the vine-tangle, his spear thrust forward, a war cry spiking from his lungs.

In the clearing, he found Mang sprawled forward, the right side of his neck torn away, his head twisted at a brutal angle. The wind in the treetops dropped the hot stink of the predator. Another squall of tiger rage battered the glade, and Jaki shouted back with all his might.

The canopy rustled behind him, and he spun about. The tiger flashed into sight in midleap, claws outstretched, fangs bared. Jaki swung his spear up and rooted himself to his death, the agony of all his losses bursting from him in one mad cry.

The beast collided with him, heaving him to the ground. Claws furied, rending his doublet, slashing his flesh. Raving jaws chewed the spear beside his head. And then they were gone. Jaki lay in the leaf litter, his heart a gusher of pain. His blowgun was split open, and he gazed at the white woodmeat as into sunglare, just comprehending that he was still alive.

He struggled to sit up and saw Ganger Sint emerge, grinning, from the nearby brush.

The foreman raised his flintlock and aimed it at Jaki's head. As he fired, another roar crashed through the trees behind him, and his shot went wild. He whirled about just as the tiger charged like a lightning stroke through the vine wall.

Ganger Sint's mouth worked a silent scream, and he ran three pathetic steps before the giant pounced on him. A livid howl of agony escaped him before his life was smothered under the monster shape.

Jaki squirmed to his feet as the big cat finished mauling Ganger Sint and turned with gorged rage at him.

Slowly, Jaki slid into the curtain of vines dangling from the high trees. The animal loped toward him, and he flew over the root humps and leaf drifts, growls spilling like a drum song behind him. The wind veered, carrying the underworld smell of the cat.

Ahead, the caravan burst into view, and in an explosion of clarity he saw that he was going to be torn apart in front of everyone. Squirting cold sweat, he threw himself into the clearing.

The elephants swung aside and people scattered, shrieking. All but one, who stood fast. Terror had blinded him until the flintlock blasted his hearing; now he glimpsed Lucinda, still aiming her flintlock, the smoke and gunfire rushing from it. Her blond face was an arrow of concentration suddenly obscured by smoke. A great weight struck Jaki from behind, and he collapsed.

Lucinda was at his side in an instant, pulling him away from the claws that had dug into the back of his boots. Jaki sat up and looked at the giant tiger sprawled behind him, the socket of one eye caved in where Lucinda had shot it. The stub of his own poison dart was still embedded in the tufted brow between the green flame-cored eyes of the brute.

The last shiver of fear wavered from him with the touch of his wife's hand on his shoulder, and he realized that he was gawking at the dead beast with an open mouth and wide eyes. After Njurat, he thought he had defeated fear. How terribly wrong he had been. *Life is afraid— and not to feel fear is to move closer to death.* His face relaxed, and he felt a void inside of him, the scooped-out space of his soul where he had touched the world. With the fear gone, all other emotions were paralyzed, all feeling was numb.

Jaki wobbled to his feet and clutched Lucinda to him, his bones still buzzing with the deep screams of the tiger. Blood soaked his shirt and torn doublet, and the deep gouges in his flesh yelled with pain now that his terror had quelled. "It is over," Lucinda said, the sound of her voice calming him. Locked in the grimace of its sudden death, the ten-foot tiger looked like a bestial thunderbolt, jagged with black strokes on silver and gold fur.

"Old tiger, lah." Kota prodded the dead cat with his parang, lifting its long silvery jowl whiskers.

The numbness in Jaki's chest was immense as he signed for Lucinda to wait, then led Kota and several of the crewmen to the dead bodies in the jungle. While Mang and Sint were carried to the camp, Jaki returned to where Wawa lay. He crouched over the gutted gibbon, waving off the flies. A great sob escaped him and was met by a small cry from behind. He looked over his shoulder and saw Lucinda, her hand to her mouth.

"Wawa," she breathed as if she might call him back. She knelt beside her husband then, and wept with him.

The Burmese crew fashioned several vests and a jerkin from the tiger skin, and with the claws and fangs they crafted an impressive necklace, which they stitched to the tiger's beard and presented to Lucinda. She wanted to give it to Jaki, but he insisted that she wear it. "If not for you, I would be with Wawa now," he told her as he fastened the necklace about her throat. "You were right about waiting. I will listen to you more carefully now."

Jaki meant it. With the death of Wawa, whatever remained of his tribal soul had left him. Jabalwan's shattered blowgun was the final sign that he had broken with his life as Matubrembrem. He left the two halves of the blowgun stuck in the ground where Wawa had been killed. Looking back, he realized that the break with the dying tribes had been inbred in him and was in fact the legacy of his Dutch father. His life as a tribesman, which had begun to die when he lost Jabalwan, was truly finished now, and he resolved to go forward as Jaki Gefjon, his father's son.

But his resolve was thin as water. The emptiness that had filled him after he had fallen under the claws of the tiger persisted. He would be dead, except that his wife had saved him — but he felt now as if only his body remained. The blast of the flintlock that had smashed the tiger's brain seemed to have carried off his soul. And though he knew that his life as a tribesman was long gone, he could not find himself. His chest was empty. Not even sadness flinched when he thought of Wawa or their years of wandering. He was hollowed out.

For days, Jaki meandered listlessly with the caravan, oblivious to Lucinda's caresses and the teas Maud offered. The others ignored him, believing his power had gone over to his wife when she slayed the beast who had fixed him in its wrath. *What would Jabalwan do?* he asked himself over and over. He prayed to the ancestors. He sacrificed betel nut to Wawa's spirit. He grieved alone in the dark avenues of the jungle. But he was dead inside. Nothing was effective and nothing was resolved. Ashamed of his dejection, he kept to himself, wandering far ahead of the caravan or, when the jungle closed in, keeping the company of the lead buffalo, where Dhup, the clumsy monk, stationed himself. With the monk, he felt at ease. Dhup, stumbling over every root, laughing at himself as he dodged dangling vines only to crash through thornbrush, was preoccupied just watching after himself and paid no heed to the sorcerer.

At a bend in the river, Jaki found the death that had been stalking him since Lucinda had killed the tiger in his shadow. He had gone ahead of the caravan and had stopped to gather berries.

The emptiness in Jaki decanted into the distant blueness above the tangled trees and vines, and alertness filled him: someone was stumbling through the forest on the bluff above the river. Before he could shout a warning, ferns above him rustled, an orange robe flapped like licks of flame, and Dhup careened into view. He had followed Jaki but had apparently lost his trail on the high ground. The next instant, his arms shot up for balance; he seized a creeper, which snapped in his grip, and then he plummeted over the brink, falling with a splash into the running water. He surfaced closer to Jaki, his face gaping with panic, one arm clutching at nothing. He disappeared.

Jaki dropped his hat filled with berries, and dove into the hurrying river. The water was cold and enraptured with its own will. It hoisted Jaki free of his muscles and swept him away like a broken tree. By chance alone he collided with Dhup, who was twisting and kicking to keep his head above the rushing water. Dhup seized Jaki by his arms, and the two men sank.

Jaki struggled to break Dhup's frantic grip, freed one arm, and was immediately clutched about the neck. The two rolled and tumbled, legs interlocking, faces mashed together. Most of Jaki's air gushed from him, and he was crushed by pain. Light wheeled beside them, split into blue fire and a lopsided glance at the jungle wall, spidery clouds, stars exploding from the pain in his lungs. He gasped, and Dhup pulled him down again. As they sank, Jaki wrenched his whole body, but Dhup was locked onto him. He relaxed, hoping they would rise again. But the blue shadow of the surface was darkening as the current pulled them deeper.

How stupid to die like this, Jaki thought, weighted down by someone else's fear. Better the tiger had taken him and spared his wife this unknowing. The light was purpling, and a new silence was filling his body. She would never know what had become of him.

All thoughts shrank to pain then. The last breath bubbled from him violently, hurt and jagged.

Baffled noises erupted, and air scalded his lungs. His body bucked above the water like a breeching whale, throwing off the monk's death-hold, and with horrified strength thrashed for shore. But his legs beat heavily, and his arms were shackled. He convulsed and perceived that he was already ashore. The current had swept them downstream to a mudbank, and they were both sprawled belly-down.

Jaki lurched to his side, his chest aching with his pounding breaths. Dhup was beside him, vomiting water. Slurred sensations sharpened: he saw sunlight flitting like music in the shore trees, clouds drifting overhead, egrets plucking at the shallows. A laugh lanced him, and he flopped to his back and opened his arms to the world.

When Jaki limped up the bank, arm in arm with Dhup, the depression he had endured after Wawa's death was gone. They staggered back to the caravan laughing at the conspiring shadows that kept tripping the monk, singing in Spanish about the beautiful river and how they were too ugly for it to keep.

Jaki was determined to fulfill the promise of his reprieved life, and he immediately doffed all nostalgia for his earlier existence as a tribesman and embraced the spirit of his father with a passion. Ready now to devote himself to his wife as wholly as he had once served Jabalwan, he removed the diamonds from his hat and returned them to his medicine bag. Instead of scouting and foraging, he stayed by Lucinda's side and applied himself to dressing and behaving as a European. He spoke only in English, even to himself, forsaking the tribal voice he used to speak with the clouds. The clouds had nothing new to say anyway: the tribes of the sky still wandered like cattle, reckless to the walls rising around them, heedless to the hawk-faced Europeans herding them in. Sitting atop their elephant mount, he queried his wife about England and the countries she had visited with her father. He was determined to cover his memories with a future, to replace the past with the new.

The terrain seemed to match Jaki's resolve. The forest relented and became a dry, flat pan the color of a scab. For several weeks they traveled the hard-packed trail among bronze tufts of sand grass and large, calm sheets of red rock, journeying across the desert lying between the riverbends. Where the river met the desert, fruit groves and quince arbors effloresced in terraces above the rocks, irrigated by the villagers who lived along the banks. The orchards had been cultivated centuries earlier as resting places for the caravans that crisscrossed on the plain from China, India, and Indonesia. At each village the natives welcomed the nomads with skins of rice wine, fruit brandies, and chilled fresh water.

Traveling was easier without the rains, the jungle terrors, and the menace of Ganger Sint. Lucinda began a journal, and at night the travelers learned chess by firelight and listened to stories under the cool moon.

Maud told a tale she had heard from her Aunt Timotha about the Barley King who ruled a village for a year and was denied nothing until the following spring, when his throat was ritually cut and his blood used to enrich the fields. Kota related frightful tales from his years as a pirate, and Jaki recounted the arrogant reign of Batuh and the final battle with the Rain Wanderers, when Jabalwan returned from the dead. But only when Lucinda spoke about her visits with her father to the ports of India did the fire-circle talk become truly animated.

Jaki listened attentively, wanting to know what kingdom lay before them, and what he heard amazed him. The Moghul Empire was immense, stretching across all of India to the Persian mountains and the ocean that led to Africa. And the empire was extravagant. Lucinda described marble palaces unrivaled anywhere in the world, and other travelers spoke of fountains of wine and groves hung with fruit carved from opium. The kingdom was Muslim, yet its emperor was an alcoholic despot and a drug addict, who delighted to see his enemies pulled apart by elephants.

Dhup, too, had a story, and it stayed with Jaki, though he heard it very late one night. Dhup had carried a curse. As a child he was the only one to survive a plague that destroyed his mountain village. He wandered after that, and each village he visited was harrowed by the plague, which never touched him. He became notorious among the hill tribes and would have been killed on sight had not a Buddhist monastery granted him sanctuary. There, too, the plague struck, but the monks did not drive him out. Instead they made him minister to the stricken monks and taught him how to heal with teas and compotes made of moldy fruit. A few died, most survived, and Dhup applied the cure to himself. After that, no one became sick around him again.

"Evil climbs down from heaven," Dhup told him, "just as blessings do. Only the arrogant think they are evil — or good."

"You speak like a teacher of mine," Jaki said.

"Perhaps I have had the same teacher."

Jaki felt excitement kindle in him. Though the clumsiness of this man had almost drowned him, it had also returned him more fully to life, and Jaki felt a kinship with the monk. Perhaps he too was a sorcerer. "Why does heaven send evil?" he asked.

"Who knows the truth? We simply name evil."

Jake nodded. "So I believe." He sensed that this short, awkward man understood the same truths as he — and maybe more, for his quiet smile implied a wisdom that belonged to this world. "The Life is secret," Jaki went on. "But our small lives are in our hands and we must choose. How does one choose when one is evil? My people call me the son of the devil, and they must be right. I have seen, again and again, a terrible destruction coming to all the tribes. That evil must be in me or I would not see it. I have tried to choose good — yet I do not understand good or evil, and in the eyes of others I am a pirate and a devil's son, someone to be killed." He looked up at the stars and let his thoughts flow. "My mother tried to teach me of God. But he is a terrible God who kills his own children. My mother accepted this, and she was killed because I, the devil's child, was her son. That is irony — God's justice. Now all I can tell myself is that the Life is secret and cannot be known, only lived. That does not seem enough. How do I live with the evil that is in me?"

"You already know." Dhup grinned. "Like the diamonds you once wore on your hat, you live around your flaws. Evil consumes itself, while good perseveres. Continue to choose the good and let evil exhaust itself."

"How does one know good from evil?"

Dhup's grin widened to a smile full of crooked teeth. He reached out and, with a blunt finger that felt like steel, touched the down between Jaki's eyes. "That is all one really knows." His smile dropped away, and he withdrew his hand. "But one knows it only for oneself." He bowed and lay down in the dirt beside the spent fire to sleep.

*

"Monday 12 October 1627." Lucinda began a new leaf of rice paper in her leather-bound log. The brown ink set like dried blood.

"We traveled nineteen miles today and camped at a caravansary on the crest of the Imphal pass. To the north, majestic ice mountains watch us, and the nights are cold. We are glad now for the yak-fur blankets got so cheaply in the sweltering lowlands.

"From this promontory, we have enjoyed our first glimpse of India far below us. Gossip of war among the Moghuls disturbs the merchants, but there is no turning back for us. Boeck would only too gladly despoil us of our profits while declaring our contract moot for not attaining our agreed objective of Surat.

"I, too, am disturbed, though not by the Moghuls' strife. I have visited India before, with Father, and the sight of that vast and splenetic country reminds me of him and my fright of his rage. The very virtues I admired in him when I was a child — his will, his imposing physical presence and command of men, his great stamina — are my bane now, even now almost six months since fleeing him.

"This half year has been the happiest of my life, for I have never before known freedom and love — yet my joy is tainted by woeful memory of what Father called love — his dismal strictures imposed by violent threat. I have no doubt that he is pursuing me and if he finds me will exert all his mad strength to bend me to his command. I fear that not even brave Jaki with all his primordial powers could withstand the fury of this vehement man whose ship he destroyed and daughter he stole. How righteous Father's wrath must seem to him. Lord forfend I ever face that bitter man again.

"Jaki, ever diligent to make of himself a gentleman in the European manner, reads a page or more of the Bible every day. Or when he reads not, he sets the book in the sunlight, sits before it, and watches it as if it were an animal. I have learned not to inquire too searchingly of his motives, as he is wont to much metaphysical discourse. That, I know, is his legacy as a sorcerer of his tribe, yet I find his talks about the sad stories in the passage of the clouds tiring. Again today, he told me how books are a wall that turn us from the open God-given world to the confines of the man-made. My reply that God has given us dominion and that the wall of books is our rampart against chaos befuddled him. How strange for me to discover, Jaki has no notion of chaos. As if the world, with all its miseries, were not to be perfected! Sometimes I do believe he would be happier with his tribe if only he had not been burdened with Dutch paternity. Yet he is earnest to be his own father, to parent himself as a European, and he continues to obey me most excellently, as though I were his docent. I pray daily that I not misguide this innocent, sincere man.

"Maud was with great mirth today to see the last of Burma, which she liked not. She well remembers India and the lavish opulence of the princes who feted us when we visited with Father. I share her hope that the journey henceforth will be more comfortable."

Lucinda laid down her stylus and looked about her. Nearby, bareheaded Jaki sat on a flat ledge among thrusts of rusty rock, scowling at the open Book. Maud was busy with several of the merchants' dusky wives, boiling lentils and barley in a kettle for that evening's meal, giggling at some bawdy story they were sharing. The caravan's pavilions fluttered in the breeze, and a flute ditty traipsed from the camp on a whiff of opium. On a lower slope where a grove of silver pine and mountain sedges provided fodder, the elephants cluttered like boulders. Snow pigeons plummeted in white bursts from the sun and flocked in wide circles over the steep hillsides and farm terraces. Silver peaks burned across the northern brim of the world, and beneath them the cluttered valleys and long plains of India shimmered with forest haze, river glints, and the purple smoke of horizons. Lucinda breathed the resin smells rising from the lustrous land and smiled with the peace of a faithful pilgrim.

"The jungle will defeat you," Jakob Boeck warned. He was standing with William Quarles and Robert Fletcher on a stone levee along the swollen Irrawaddy. The raft that the Englishmen had outfitted to take them upriver to Prome was moored below them. The three men were dressed in ruffed collars, slit-seamed sleeves, satin breeches, garter bows, polished boots, and feathered hats. The coach that had carried them to the river's edge waited on the wharf road, a brown silhouette against Dagon's diadem of torchlight. "Last night I received word from Prome that the foreman I had sent with your daughter's caravan was killed by a tiger. The merchants who found his grave turned back."

"We will not turn back," Quarles asserted, staring down the portly, sharp-nosed ambassador. "And if anyone should have been dissuaded from this perilous journey *that* should have been my daughter. I will not forget that it was you, Mister Boeck, who sent her forth into the wilderness."

"Captain Quarles, please." Boeck placed his hand on Quarles's arm and was startled to feel the iron of it. "Your daughter was determined to escape you. If I had not helped her, she would have gone to the Portuguese. The pirate has diamonds. He would have bought passage out of Asia. She was talking of going to the New World. They would have eluded you entirely. Now, at least, you know they are on the spice trails in Burma. Let me send a message ahead to my contact in India. Why risk your lives in the jungle when you can await their arrival in Surat?"

Fletcher nodded his agreement. He viewed this entire escapade with foreboding, yet duty and the hope of promotion obliged him to accompany Quarles. "Sir," he ventured hopefully, "the factor's counsel is sage. I have been to Prome. It is a primitive place. And beyond it, the so-called spice trails vanish in dense jungle before attaining the high country to the north. With that heathen pirate born to the jungle guiding the caravan, we are unlikely to overtake them."

Quarles turned his back on the two men and stared hard at the silks of sunrise unraveling over the river. Boeck's words had stung him with a truth that had long burned him but had yet to pierce his heart: Lucinda was escaping him. He had driven her away with — what? Wanting her to marry a gentleman? Wanting fortune for her? Outrage at her betrayal boiled in him, and he groped for understanding. He had struck her, as any good father would when his child strays toward danger. Yet he had protected her and sustained her all her life. More. He had educated her. He had made her worthy of nobility. In his mind, his love was beyond reproach, and that fired his determination. He would not let her go. She was *his* daughter, flushed from his own body. No pirate would take her from him.

On the slave barge in the Moluccas, when he had believed she was dead or a jungle princess, he had attempted simply to surrender his life to a greater cause. For him, it had been empire, the expansion of civilization against the chaos of jungles, plagues, and pirates. But now, what cause was greater than his own flesh and blood? Empire did not need him. Destiny would carry empire forward. His daughter, stubborn child-woman, ensorceled by a pirate and her own misguided willfulness, was suffering now in some remote jungle hellscape. She needed him. Who would save her from herself if he did not?

Quarles turned about decisively. "Mister Fletcher, get into the raft and see that the crew understand their duties. Mister Boeck, I will return with my daughter."

Jaki was devoted to his wife, determined to live his destiny through her because he believed she was a portal to the world of his fathers. So eager was he to leave behind his history of grief and attain the status of a European that he obeyed her even when she contradicted his experience. Though Pym had taught him the advantages of democratic rule, he submitted without reservation to his wife's insistence on managing the caravan autocratically. At smaller caravansaries where the mules brayed angrily because they disliked the smell of camels, Jaki turned out into the night camels and merchants who had journeyed with them from Dagon, even though the mule owners had only recently joined the caravan. The mule migrants had offered Lucinda better trade rates, and she was an aggressive and opportunistic negotiator.

By the time the caravan had wended among the spice villages and silk hamlets of Manipur and had entered India through the craggy Imphal pass, two elephants and three camels were required to carry their profits alone.

Temples and shrines proliferated under the blue shadows of the great mountains to the north. Vedic missionaries, haggard men with rasorial faces, joined the caravan and preached their creed of sky gods, wind deities, and the powers of light, demonstrating their comprehension of cosmic continuity by bloodlessly piercing their flesh with needles, walking on fire, contorting their bodies in knots as if their limbs were so much rope. Jaki engaged in long conversation with these sorcerers called *fakirs;* Dhup simply blessed them with his grin. When the caravan rested, he ambled off to sit on the steps of dark temples and watch golden dragonflies flitting among dung heaps, while Lucinda traded with the long-eared abbots of the carved stone chapels that peeked from behind lush groves of banyan and pipal.

Maud busied herself gathering hibiscus, frangipani, bougainvillea, mango blossoms, and every useful plant she could find. Jaki was intrigued by her European versions of remedies Jabalwan had taught him. Together they sought out local healers and learned the use of unfamiliar roots and herbs. They shared cures and taught each other by campfire and riverbank. Jaki even began carrying his medicine bag again, making room among his personal relics — Pym's, the Wyvern banner, and his flintlock — for the new plants.

Lucinda was indifferent to their passion for plants and spent most of her time at the village marketplaces competing with the other merchants. Her blond hair was an advantage since few villagers had ever seen anyone like her, and the opportunity to trade with her was irresistible. By now she had become adept at gauging the needs and desires of the local people, and she huckstered so well that by the time they reached the temple city of Sarnath, they were burdened with possessions.

Sarnath was two dark, ancient towers on a river plain crowded with ruins, the tents of pilgrims, the stalls of merchants streaming with bright banners, and the mats of spiritual teachers who were gathering students by demonstrating *siddhis,* supernatural powers. One loinclothed teacher threw a rope into the air and it fell back as a snake. Another threw a rope up, and it went stiff as bamboo. He climbed it and sat perkily on top, pulling blossoms out of the empty air and casting them to the boisterous crowd. Diseased and destitute natives mingled among the shouting curious, desperate for miracles.

The two great towers, empty for centuries, were shrouded in vines and vetch; a tree sprouted near the crown of one of them. Closer to the ground, pilgrims had cleared away swatches of the overgrowth, revealing stone panels carved with lotus scrolls, human figures, and animals, all stained black with time, mutilated and broken.

Dhup wandered into the gusts of incense smoke from offerings the numerous pilgrims burned on exhumed bricks. After stumbling over the basket of a snake charmer and startling the crowd almost to a stampede, he found a perch on the steps of a pillar supporting a stone elephant, and from there he looked out over the Deer Park with its noisy merchants, listless mendicants, shrunken sick, and gaunt dogs challenging carrion pigs for the human excrement that lay everywhere among the ruins. His invincible smile blazed. Here, two thousand years earlier, the Wheel of the Law had first been expounded — and still the Wheel ground on, whirling with the cries of babies, the loud importunities of traders, and the moans of the dying. Above the vivid smells of the bazaar's spicy foods, incense, and offal, the sweet char of human flesh lufted on the breeze from the south, from the Ganga, the river, where the burning ghats cremated corpses on the holy water and liberated souls from the welter of the world.

Jaki and Maud strolled through the crowd, inspecting the fakirs and wonder-workers and purchasing elixirs and powders. In the shriek and stink of the crowded ruins, all of human life seemed to be jammed: an old woman squatted with her sari pulled up to her hips while she emptied her bowels beside a sculptured lion; a beggar boy with warped legs played a passionate dance ditty on a reed flute; mothers and babies with faces caved in from starvation gazed benignly from where they sat in the shadows of huge white cows.

Jaki read the distress in Maud's face and tried to reassure her. "All of India is not this gruesome. Sarnath is the threshold to India's grave. Five miles south, Dhup says, is a holy river where the natives believe that if they are cremated they will not be reborn. The dying come here from every hamlet in the land."

When they returned to the caravan, the cargo from the lead elephants was being carted off by skeletal porters. Lucinda stood smiling beside a Chinese merchant in a green, long-sleeved silk gown. The merchant bowed to Jaki.

"Why is he taking our profits?" Jaki asked his wife.

"I have traded them," she answered with a proud smile. "The load was too much for the elephants — and now we have room to pick up and carry more."

"Traded our profits for what? The elephants are going to have to carry whatever he's given us — unless it's gems."

"Better," Lucinda said, reaching into the velvet pouch where she kept her jewels. She removed a handful of rice paper roweled with Chinese characters. "Flying money. That is what the Chinese call it. Trade bills."

"That's paper," Jaki objected, seizing one of the bills and examining both sides. "It's worthless."

Lucinda took back the bill and returned it with the others to her pouch. "When we get to western India, any of the Chinese factors there will exchange these bills for gold, silver, or goods."

"He told you that?" Jaki asked, cocking an eyebrow at the fragile, parchment-skinned merchant.

"It is an ingenious idea," Lucinda said. "The Dutch have been doing the same thing in Europe for the last thirty years. That is why their empire is expanding so swiftly."

Jaki pursed his lips skeptically. He was about to say, "You are the owner," but a swirl of activity distracted them.

The mahout was shouting at a clot of men, women, and children in rags who were trying to approach the gold-haired people. Jaki walked over to see who they were, and the Chinese merchant hurried his porters away.

"Gypsies," the mahout said. "Drive them away. They evil."

They looked evil, dwarfish, with bow legs and trollishly large hands. The men had long heads, ape-sloped brows, eyes like inky glass, and mangy beards curled over eel-gray skin. The three women were veiled and held their children tightly to their dark skirts. One of the two men broke free of the mahout's restraining grasp and shuffled swiftly past Jaki to Lucinda and Maud. He threw himself in the dust at their feet, and Lucinda bent and urged him to rise. She plucked a gold coin from her pouch and pressed it into his thick hand.

The gypsy's loose, purple lips grinned a broken-toothed smile. "Thank you, lady," he said in droning Spanish. "You are generous to wanderers in need." He nodded, but the light in his eyes was nasty.

Maud tugged at Lucinda's sleeve. "Come away, Lucinda."

"Lucinda!" the gypsy brayed. "The name of light. You are a daybreak child. Let me award you with a glimpse of the supernal light of what is yet to be."

Jaki stepped to Lucinda's side and watched the bedraggled beggar tug a green cloth from under his shirt. The cloth unknotted to reveal a sheaf of green-backed cards, each card colorfully illustrated, depicting regal figures and fabulous beasts.

"Who are you?" Jaki asked in Spanish.

"A beggar this lady has pitied," the man replied. "I will spread the cards for her, if she will allow."

"Come away, lady," Maud urged again. "This man is evil. Truly. I smell it."

Jaki agreed. The air around him had a sharp taint of ammonia that cut through the fetid smells of the bazaar and the musk of the caravan animals. "You've paid him. Let him be."

But Lucinda did not move. The mysteriously beautiful images of the cards held her rapt, and she was curious to see what he would do with them. "Let me accept his offering," she said. "He will feel less a beggar that way." She gestured to a stool in front of her yellow canvas tent, walked over to it, and sat down. "Spread your cards for me."

Maud and Jaki exchanged dark glances, and Jaki knelt at Lucinda's side. "Is this English?" He took her hand in his dry, hard grasp. "This smells of the sorcery I've left behind to be with you. We must not look back. Remember Lot's wife."

"You are being superstitious, Jaki," Lucinda said quietly. "I will not eschew this man's magicking tricks, because I do not fear them. I am English. My fate is in God's hands. No sorcery can change that."

Jaki stood up and stepped back. Maud took his arm, and together they watched over Lucinda's shoulder.

The gypsy knelt in the dust and offered her the cards. "You must shuffle them."

The greasy cards exuded an earthy, acrid fragrance, like coal dust, and her hands stopped abruptly, before she had expected. She handed the cards back.

The gypsy fanned five cards on the ground: The Tower, A Pack of Hounds, Three Swords, Five Cups, and The Sun. He pressed a charred thumb to the first card, showing a stone minaret shattered by a jag of lightning and a white horse bolting from it. "The broken wall," he muttered. "You are free from the laborious steps of the stark tower, the high lonely tower where you were a queen on the ancestral stair — and a prisoner. But you are free now — free —"

Lucinda stole a glance at Jaki and saw him scowling with alertness. Maud beside him was biting her knuckle.

The gypsy's thumb-stump pressed the second card — hunting dogs in full run, ears and tails streaming, eyes sparks of intent, sleek bodies honed to the wind. "You love what you love — and you run with your heart's desire. But there is no way you can own that loveliness." His thumb hopped to the next card, three swords stabbing a heart to a splintery post. "For you are the sacrifice, thrall to the tree of life, beauty's cruelty, the heart torn out and doomed — " The black thumb struck the fourth card, three cups spilled on a riverbank, two standing on eroded soil, a tar-bubbled toad between them, and across the river a willow of bellropes. "Doomed, another soul lost to God's fever. On the journey to your desire's home, you will die . . ."

Jaki swooped forward and grabbed the gypsy by his shirt so fiercely the garment tore and the man fell backward in the dust. His face twisted with fear, the gypsy went for his knife. But Lucinda stood and restrained her husband, wrapping her arms about him. "Jaki! This is just a beggar's ploy for more money. Be calm, my love."

Jaki let Lucinda pull him back, but he kept his angry gaze firmly on the gypsy. The man lifted the last card and turned it for them to see. "The Sun," he said. "Two hearts that beat as one bleed when they are torn apart but — look! — the Sun!" His hand shook, yet the image was clear: a naked child prancing on a flowery knoll under a languorous, lion-colored sun and the sky around it slick with sparks. "You will die, generous lady. You have tasted your freedom and you will die. But your seed will live. Where the sea eats the dunes, your seed is chained to the stars. What more can any of us damned expect?"

Jaki shook off Lucinda's hold and kicked the cards into a dusty cloud. "Get away from us, devil!" The gypsy frantically gathered his cards, and Jaki seized him by the hair and dragged him several paces before heaving him away. The gypsy was lifted to his feet by his family and stared back at Jaki with rueful fervor, wagging his burnt thumb, before they hustled him away.

Maud, who had watched aghast, dashed for her tent. Then she turned and, seeing Lucinda berating Jaki for his uncouth behavior, ran behind the elephants. She lifted her skirt and hurried after the gypsies.

"Wait," she said in English, then summoning her halting Spanish, "I have something for you."

The gypsies, angry and afraid, kept their hands close to their weapons, but the beggar who had read Lucinda's fortune stepped forward. The ammonia stench widened as he removed his hands from inside his shirt and held them out. He expected another gold coin to lift the doomful weight of her mistress's future, and when she placed a rock in his hand, he almost dropped it. "What is this?" he asked in disgust.

"It is a diamond," she answered, her face pale. She ransacked her brain for the Spanish she needed. "It is an uncut gem. Very valuable. Take it. But spare my lady your curse. Spare her."

The gypsy moved the gray rock among his fingers, his bottom lip jutting. "You must love her truly."

"She is my whole life. I am her maid, her follower."

The gypsy rubbed the rock against his sooty beard and then pocketed it. "It is done. She will find her own fate now."

Maud sobbed a sigh. "Thank you."

The gypsy family surrounded the fortuneteller as Maud turned away and walked slowly back toward her tent. This moment felt right to her. Lucinda had not wanted her to have the gem anyway, and now it had been spent to spare her. She swept her gaze across the caravan, saw elephants powdering their backs with the bright dust and scratching themselves on the banyan's strut branches, saw the lackeys gathering kindling for that night's cooking fires. Relief heightened everything, the montage of colorful tents, the spice wind from the bazaar, the yapping of monkeys from the blue haze of hill trees.

Her open stare narrowed to one face among the workers — the broad, furtive visage of Kota. He had been watching her all along from the open flap of his tent, and he scampered across the camp to Jaki, his chemise open to the navel and his pants unbuckled and held by one hand. A pang of anxiety shot through her, and she lifted her skirt again and ran. But by the time she reached Lucinda, Kota had already whispered in his master's ear.

Jaki's face cramped with anger. "You gave the gypsy your diamond?"

Lucinda rose from her seat in disbelief. "Maud — "

"It is true, my lady," Maud said to Lucinda's red boots. "The gypsy has lifted his curse. You will be safe now."

"You fool!" Lucinda snapped. "You squandered your fortune."

"I did it for you." Maud's eyes flashed with tears. "I wanted him to spare you."

Lucinda was outraged. "My fate is not touched by that grub's insignificant power." She took Maud's quivering face in her hand and lifted it so her brimming eyes met Lucinda's vehement gaze. "You will go to that gypsy and retrieve your diamond."

Maud shook her head, and her eyebrows lifted pleadfully. "No, my lady!"

"Do not defy me, Maud!"

"Please, Luci, do not make me do this. I do not want the diamond."

"You will get it," Lucinda demanded, "or you will stay here in Sarnath and beg your way to England."

Maud cringed at that thought and turned away, weeping.

"Get your flintlocks," Jaki told Kota before he ducked into his tent. He shouldered his medicine bag and unsheathed the sword he had purchased in Dagon. Lucinda's stare as he stalked past her reproached him for witlessly giving a servant girl a diamond. He did not stop to dispute her, but in his heart the admiration he had been feeling for Maud since they had begun to study together flared brighter. When he caught up with her, he took her by the arm. "Forgive me for showing you anger," he said. "You did right." She wiped away the tears from her cheeks. "But what you did, I should have done. Go back to your tent. I will attend to the gypsy."

"No." She put her hand on his swordarm, amazed at the courage this man fired in her. "I will go with you. I must."

Kota ran to their side, a flintlock in each hand. "Gypsies, lah!" He pointed a gun toward a rash of beggars scurrying among the toppled stones of a dark shrine. They disappeared in a vault shaggy with creepers.

"Tuck your guns in your waistband," Jaki said. "I want no one killed over this — unless our lives depend on it." He motioned Maud behind him and handed her a flintlock. "Stay here. Use this if you must." He winked to allay the trepidation wrinkling her brow and sauntered across the sunny field. The shrine's broken archway was littered with bones, and human skulls leered from the worn façade of the temple walls. *A death temple!* Jaki balked, feeling the revulsion of the tribesman within him. The gypsies were living in a grave. No other tribe would molest them here, he knew, stepping willfully into the cold heat of the shrine. *I am a European,* he told himself. *Father, be with me now.*

Eyeglints flared like fireflies in the shadows. A monkey shrieked, and the gypsies rushed from the dark and clustered around the intruders, palms up.

Jaki raised his sword, and the beggars scattered. Across the dark vault and its silver rods of sunlight, he recognized the gypsy family who had confronted them at the caravan, and he burst toward them. The veiled women screamed, and the gypsies snatched their children and scattered into the black mouth of the inner temple. Jaki charged the fortuneteller, who confronted him with his cutlass drawn. The edge barbed a wire of sunlight. But Jaki did not hesitate. He slammed the gypsy's cutlass from his grip, whirled deftly, parried with his forearm the smashing blow of the gypsy's fist, and slammed him against the pillar's twisted stone.

"The diamond," Jaki demanded in Spanish, fitting his swordtip under the gypsy's jaw.

The stunned man coughed breathlessly and began weeping. "It was given freely," he sobbed, his head lifted on the bladepoint. "Do not steal the first hope God has given the damned. Our children suffer."

The sword twisted, and the gypsy jerked straighter. Tears squirted from his wincing eyes, and he yanked the gem from his sash. "Take the diamond and be cursed to a living death," the gypsy choked. "Take my life and my curse will corrupt your children."

Jaki plucked the gem from his fingers and lowered his sword. "I want only the lady's diamond."

Emboldened by the removal of the sword, the gypsy whined grievously: "The diamond is rightfully mine. I did not steal it. The lady gave it to me."

"Wanting you to change a fate you have no power to curse." Jaki backed away and signed for Kota to move out, too.

The pirate shuffled crabwise through the arch, keeping an eye on the gypsy, but as he stepped over the threshold, swords swung through the darkness. Kota blocked the blows with his guns, discharging both of them aimlessly. He bounded back through the door, shoving his gun muzzles into his sash and drawing his parang. Jaki stood in the middle of the vault, sword raised.

The fortuneteller's wrung face lifted into a grinning snarl as he stooped and retrieved his sword, while gypsies with scimitars and axes advanced with slow intent from the dim alcoves.

"Return the diamond," the fortuneteller commanded, "or we will cut your hearts from you and take it anyway."

Jaki and Kota edged toward the exit, back to back, blades poised. "Run for the door," Jaki whispered in Malay. "Save Maud."

"No," Kota replied with hot determination. "Our blood will mingle here."

The fortuneteller let out a howl, and the gypsies charged. Jaki and Kota were engulfed, and only by whirling their weapons in wide strokes did they hold the enemy off. But there were too many shrieking demons, and when the intruders' swords clanged against the scimitars, gypsies sidled closer and swiped viciously at Jaki's and Kota's legs. In moments they would be hacked meat.

An explosion shook the dark chamber to startled silence and sent bats shooting into the searing day. From the doorway, sunlight flapped about Maud's silhouette as she lowered the flintlock she had fired.

Jaki and Kota leaped through the opening that the gunshot had sheared and bounded up the stairs that led out.

The fortuneteller hissed at the pirates on the stairs and the maid who stood fast in the sunhaze behind them. He circled his burnt thumb in the air. "My curse is on that diamond. The shadow of death goes with it from here!"

Jaki grinned, reached into his medicine bag, and tugged out the pirate banner Pym had bequeathed him. Even in the dense shadows of the shrine, the oppressive image of the dragonhawk was distinct enough to elicit moans from the gypsies. "My curse for yours!" Jaki shouted, and his echoes tripped over the answering cries of the despairing beggars as they fled into the depths of the temple, tumbling over each other like frantic rats.

Jaki sheathed his sword and bowed to Maud. "We owe you our lives," he said with open relief.

Maud blew a happy sigh and helped Kota and Jaki fold Wyvern. Her breath sharpened. "This is the flag that spared us from the pirates at sea. What is this beast?"

"Life's talons," Jaki answered and added, with a glint of mischief in his eye. "Our mother."

"She looks so terrible."

"She is. She loves us to death." Jaki handed her the diamond. "And this *is* yours, Maud. Keep it or trade it for fair value."

Maud clasped her hands. "I will not take it, Jaki. Lucinda does not want me to have it."

"I want you to have it."

They wobbled arm in arm back toward the camp, Kota walking

backward behind them to see they were not attacked. "Why, Mister Gefjon, do you want me to have this diamond?" Maud asked.

"We have many diamonds. You are part of our family, why should you not have one?"

"You honor me so, but I am only a servant, not family."

"Not in my eyes." Jaki stopped and faced her. "I have married Lucinda but not all her ways — though she thinks she is changing me. And I suppose she is. But one thing will never change, and that is what belongs together. In my tribe, a family shares all it has. To me, you shall always be Lucinda's sister, not her servant. Take the diamond. Lucinda sent you back for it. It is yours."

A shiver narrowed through her bones. "It is cursed. Lucinda will die."

"All life is cursed. The mother of life is terrible. She eats her young. Shall we then deny ourselves?"

"Jaki, I cannot take it." She tugged at her mass of brown curls. "I am only a maid. It is my station, and so I will always be a maid. No amount of diamonds will change that. But —" She lowered her gaze, searching for the courage to speak. "Your concern, that wishes on me this wealth, that I do accept. It is a gift I cannot possibly misplace and no one can steal. As I am in your eyes Lucinda's sister then you are in my eyes a brother. I will cherish that." She looked up then, and she saw a smile lurking on Jaki's lips and understanding in his eyes.

Lucinda was waiting for them. She had paced there while they were gone, counting her failures. Why was he so resistant to her wisdom? Why did he still insist on mixing high and low? The obvious answer depressed her: Jaki himself was low, a primitive, a child of unalloyed nature whom she could never redeem. Yet now, with the necessity she felt growing from within her, Jaki's civilizing was more vital than ever.

"The diamond," Jaki said, presenting her with the chunk of cloudy rock. "Maud will not take it back. She believes it is cursed. Will you have it?"

Lucinda took the gem. "I will. And I will wear it as you once wore yours."

Maud groaned. "Luci, the gypsy cursed it."

"Maud, go and prepare supper." Lucinda shooed her away and dismissed Kota with a wave.

"You have no fear of the curse or the gypsy's frightful prophecy?" Jaki asked, escorting her back toward their tent.

She chuckled. "As a child I used to hide in my father's study when he met with members of a secret society who had tried to recruit him." Her laugh dazzled. "The Church of the Two Thieves, they called themselves. They wore robes and tall hats, burned incense and read ancient tomes about angels, prophecy, and the hidden hand of God. But still they were just men. No ghosts appeared. No auguries came true. And when they were done, they took their robes and hats off, drank wine, and stumbled home like the besotted men they were. That cured me early of any faith in the supernatural. I fear no curses. And neither do I fear death. What is there to fear? When I die, I will be as I was before I was born, in God's grace."

Just outside their tent, she took Jaki's face in her hands. "Love, I must tell you a thing."

There was some turbulence in her eyes, and his stomach fisted.

"I am not afraid of death," she said. "But I am afraid of life. It is so cruel. We must strive hard to find our way to the New World and there make a home — a real home."

"We will, my antelope. Do not be afraid."

"I am not afraid for me. But I am afraid for another — the one I carry within me."

Jaki's tongue thickened. "You are with child?"

"Yes," she nodded. "I have not bled since we crossed into India."

"That is only two moons."

"That is enough. I feel the changes." The heat of her pride burned like a rash at the sides of her neck. Jaki pulled her closer and she could feel the passionate hope of his embrace.

The raft that carried William Quarles and Robert Fletcher up the Irrawaddy returned to Dagon six weeks later with both Englishmen swaddled in rags and shivering with malaria. They had reached Prome though the river was bloated with the monsoon run-off, but the journey had taken much longer than Quarles had estimated. The swollen river was clogged with uprooted trees and dead animals, and the long portages exhausted their supplies. Prah, the merchant who had lost his best elephants playing chess with Lucinda, took his revenge on the white woman's father by extracting from him his sword and all his gold for an old, cantankerous elephant and a lame guide that no one else would employ.

When they faced the wall of the jungle, wholly grown over since the passage of Lucinda's caravan two months earlier, Fletcher did his best to dissuade Quarles from going any farther. The air had thickened and gone still, and the monsoon rains had thinned to a perpetual mist that hung in tatters among the root burls of the dripping, sparkling forest. Quarles insisted on barging relentlessly through the jungle with the dim hope of catching Lucinda while she tarried in the highlands meeting her trading obligations.

Fletcher briefly entertained the notion of returning by himself when he saw that Quarles was determined beyond reason to find his daughter. But he had aspirations beyond foreign service and hoped for a commendation from the captain, who, despite his defeat at Serangoon, was renowned throughout Asia as a man of power. Only after they had entered the eternal twilight of the jungle — when Quarles began to rave about pirates as parasites, and a cold vacancy in his chest that only his daughter's touch could heal — did Fletcher understand that the captain was not simply ambitious beyond reason, he was mad.

The following night, the irascible elephant that had sulked for days bolted while they slept, taking with it their sacks of rice, their skins of fresh water, and their compass. Even then, Quarles wanted to go on by foot, but the lame guide could not, and the Englishmen would be lost without him. With great reluctance, Quarles agreed to return to Prome. Yet even that proved nearly impossible, for the chill in his chest expanded throughout his body and he had to be dragged in a makeshift litter.

Two days later, Fletcher also caught the chills, and the two of them were reduced to hobbling feebly after their guide. Without him, they would certainly have died, for they were too weak to forage for food or even to build a fire. When they staggered into Prome, reeling like drunks, staring with yellow, crazed eyes from under hair that had shriveled to mats of ash, the villagers did not recognize them, and they were almost butchered for evil forest spirits. Prah took pity and sent them downriver in the raft they had come up in, provisioning them with rice and fruit.

In Dagon, Jakob Boeck was alarmed to hear of the arrival of the Englishmen. Afraid that they would die and that his involvement with them might constitute a fractious political incident, he immediately notified the English factor newly arrived from Jakarta.

"You were a fool to chase into the jungle after your impetuous daughter," the English factor told Quarles when the captain had gained enough strength to sit up in bed and listen. Quarles clutched the Bible cover that he carried with him as an emblem of the pirate he stalked. The inscription within it had come clear to him at the height of his fever. Then he saw that death was his only reason to live — that the mine of signature was the treasure of one's name, one's honor. That insight, written by the hand of the pirate's own father, had pushed him to go on until the shadow of death had stopped him. The Bible cover had become his assurance that only the death of Jaki Gefjon could guard his honor now that the pirate had destroyed *The Fateful Sisters* and taken Lucinda as plunder.

"You ignored the Admiralty's order that I sent you in Surabaja." The factor's voice came from a cottony distance. "That was most foolish of all."

Quarles gazed up at the ceiling as if at a holy fresco. "I cannot go back," he croaked. "I have nothing. Only my daughter."

"Nonsense, William." The factor's wrinkled face and vivid blue eyes loomed closer. "You have a name. And you have the ancestral estate in Devon that you won back with your life's effort. You must defend those — or you will lose them."

Quarles's gaze roamed across the room's carved lime-wood garlands and swags, poor rhymes of the jungle vegetation that he could still see behind his closed lids, just as he could still smell the acid stink of the forest compost, the decay of all things, the signature of death.

"William, are you listening to me?" The factor's eyes were cold as nailheads. "Shall we speak later?"

Quarles rested his gaze on the airy flowers carved at the edge of the ceiling, and he willed himself out of the hot tunnels of the forest and into this hornet-colored room. "I cannot return to England without my daughter," he said in a vicious voice. "My name — my estate — they mean nothing to me without her."

The factor averted his eyes with understanding. "I have anticipated that, and I have already sent a letter of explanation to the Admiralty informing them that you are engaged in a vital diplomatic mission. I have purchased you some time."

Quarles passed him a weary, querying look.

"The Thieves' Church is your ally, William."

"I am sworn to the Church of —"

"England — yes, I know. You have repeatedly refused our call." The factor nodded impatiently. "But will the Church of England save you now? Have they a plan for recovering both your reputation and your wayward daughter?" He smiled paternally to see the captain's emaciated face relax with wondering, and he bent closer. "You do not understand the Church of the Two Thieves. You think her some papist device. I assure you, she is far older than the Church of Rome. Far older than Rome. Ah, you squint with incredulity." He sighed a silent laugh. "When the Romans invaded Britain, they toppled our shrines, defaced our worship-stones, and forced their religion upon us. But our Celtic faith did not die with the Romans. Our gods took their names. And when Rome became Christian, so did the names of our craft. We are the children of the forest. Like the two thieves that hung beside Christ, we are both of this world and the afterworld. No crown claims our fealty. We serve life herself — the struggle of light and life, prosperity and fertility, against poverty and defeat. For those who believe in life against death — both in this world and the next — we are their guardians. That was the faith your Uncle Samuel embraced, William."

"What is your plan?" Quarles asked in a flat and hopeless voice.

The factor clamped his jaw and sat back. Quarles would be no man's minion, he realized, but he wanted something desperately and that was as good. "Boeck informs us that Lucinda's caravan has trade papers that will admit them into the Moghul kingdom, then across India to Surat. As you must know, the Moghuls are in turmoil now, with Jahangir dying or already dead and no heir apparent. The Moghuls despise foreigners and will not allow us free access to their domains. But the Thieves' Church has made contact with a Moghul faction that has a strong chance of assuming leadership when Jahangir passes. Their chance will be much enhanced if they can acquire flintlocks to arm their supporters. We have twenty-three cases of Dutch flintlocks — one hundred and fifteen guns — seized from a Portuguese prize that in turn had taken the guns during their raid on Amboina last year. I will send a message to the Moghuls that we will exchange these weapons for your daughter and subsequent trading rights when they assume power." The factor cocked his head to mark the simplicity of the plan.

Quarles narrowed his eyes suspiciously. "You do not need me for this plan."

"Oh, but we do, William. As I said, the Moghuls are in turmoil. The outcome is uncertain. England can make no formal partisan declaration at this risky time. We must hedge now, mustn't we? Your mission will be a personal one, without the sanction of the crown. If you succeed, you will have your daughter back, and England may have an ally on the Peacock Throne. If you fail — you may forfeit your life. But that must hardly seem a risk to a man who intrepidly defied an Admiralty order and plunged headlong into the jungles of Burma." His eyes sank deeper into his skull. "Shall I make arrangements for your mission to Surat?"

Quarles closed his eyes, and the brackish stench of the jungle swelled through him. With a breathless gasp, he hissed, "Yes."

Lucinda had a jeweler in Varanasi clasp the retrieved diamond to a gold filigree necklace fine as two strands of braided hair, and she wore it with her tiger's beard necklace. The bold display of these emblems of power impressed the humble villagers, and soon fabulous stories of the Tiger Lady traveled on a road of tongues ahead of the caravan. Crowds gathered in the hamlets to see the woman with hair like the sun's harp, the woman who had purged Manipur of tigers.

Lucinda knew a great deal about the empire they were crossing because two years previous, while touring the English factories at Ajmere and Ahmadabad with her father, she had read the journals of the first English ambassador to India, Thomas Roe. Ten years ago, Roe had won trading rights at Surat after much intrigue in the court of the century-old Moghul Empire. Many nights beside the fire, Lucinda enthralled Maud and Jaki with tales of a strange emperor named Jahangir who surrounded himself with paintings of Saint Bernardino of Siena, Saint Anthony, and John the Baptist. Jahangir was a friend of Portuguese Jesuits and a Muslim — yet he drank wine and smoked opium all day in his opulent palace while watching elephants fight. At night he retired to a seraglio of a hundred women who could not be seen in public and were guarded by eunuchs. Jahangir's favorite wife, Nur Jahan, ruled him and inspired his fiendish cruelty toward his enemies, even against his eldest son, who had attempted rebellion and was punished by having his eyelids sewn shut.

Weeks earlier, while they were still in view of the ice peaks to the north, the village markets had been abuzz with the death of Jahangir. The Moghul Empire was in turmoil, and now they were marching into a battlefield where the sons of Jahangir were fighting for power. On the mountain range overlooking the purple, hazy crofts and valleys of India, Jaki had wanted to turn back. "We have profits enough for Boeck," he had said to Lucinda. "Let us return to Dagon and buy passage to the New World."

Lucinda would not be persuaded. With her tiger's beard across her chest, her veiled hat strung over her shoulders like a cowl, and her cloudpale hair diaphanous in the breeze, she seemed worthy as a priestess. "War is different in India," she explained. "Unlike Europe, where the Spanish devastate whole countrysides, putting harvests to the torch to make winter a weapon, the battles here are strictly between warriors. A whole class of men are reared simply to fight, and they do all the fighting. Farmers remain farmers, even in war. Our caravan will travel unmolested. In fact, we will be welcome, as even in war men are hungry for the new. Perhaps more so, seeing with their swords the fleetness of life." She had swept her arm across the empurpled sheen of rain, heat, and the forests' slow exhalations. "We will earn a great profit in this land."

The caravan was met far outside the newly built Moghul city of Mirzapur by eager traders, and the train of elephants, camels, mules, and oxen crossed the river to the unfinished marketplace like a rowdy festival, surrounded by a jabbering crowd of hawkers and mongers. Lucinda rode atop the lead elephant with Maud in a canopied howdah, delighted with all the attention. In the two days since they had left Sarnath, Lucinda had burdened the elephant behind her with new merchandise — bolts of Chinese silk and nankeens, bales of indigo plants, cinnabar, kaolin, teas both green and black, orpiment and xanthin, slabs of rare lumber: sandalwood, camphor, bosmellia, balsam gum. And here in this city shaping itself to life on the riverbank, she would double her profits.

As the caravan sloshed ashore, gunshots cracked the still heat of the river plain. Elephants trumpeted with alarm, and the jubilant roar of the crowd faded as people peeled aside to allow two black stallions with mounted swordsmen through. The swordsmen, their faces masked by black turbans, had their scimitars unsheathed, raised to their shoulders, and they pranced through the wet crowd directly toward Lucinda's elephant.

Jaki and Kota moved their hands reflexively to their flintlocks — but did not dare draw them: the river bluffs were suddenly cluttered with men in black pyjamas and turbans who overlooked the riverbank with long-barreled muskets. Their commander rode through the corridor that his horsemen had opened in the crowd and brought his mount alongside Lucinda's elephant. "I am Subahdar Hadi," he said in English aromatic with open vowels. Standing in his silver-trimmed saddle to face her, he scrutinized her diamond, her tigerskin bodice with its necklace of claws and fangs, and her features muted by the shade of her hat-net. His eyebrows lifted and his tiny eyes widened just perceptibly. "You are the famous Lucinda Quarles. Yes, I know your name. Ambassador Boeck of the Dutch Company alerted me months ago that you were journeying here. But I hardly believed it until the rumors began arriving of a Tiger Lady with white-gold hair. I am honored to welcome you to the kingdom of Uttar Pradesh, where I am the servant of the great Moghul emperor Shahryar."

"Thank you, Subahdar Hadi," Lucinda replied to the war chief with a courteous bow of her head and a glance to her husband to be certain that he and Kota had not drawn their weapons. "We are not worthy of such a glorious reception as this. Ambassador Boeck must have told you we are merely traders on our way to the Dutch factory in Surat. We hardly expected to be greeted by a potentate and certainly not by one who speaks English so fluently."

A smile flashed in the Subahdar's beard. "I am not a potentate, Mistress Quarles. I serve the Moghul as *Farrash Khanah,* simply a tender of the tents — a camp-maker. It is my master's current pleasure that I oversee the construction of this new port on the Ganges." His face was decorated with eyepaint and lipstain, and a ruby glinted from his right ear. "Some fifteen years ago it was the emperor Jahangir's desire that I accompany and set camp for your countryman Sir William Hawkins, when he toured our empire. He stayed with us for three years, and thus I have acquired some facility with your language. Will you accept my hospitality in Mirzapur?"

"You are too generous, my lord," Lucinda deferred with lowered gaze. "We are a common caravan, not worthy of your attention. I myself am no longer Mistress Quarles. Did the ambassador tell you that? I have married Jaki Gefjon." She smiled down at her husband, and he stepped forward, swept off his hat, and executed the low bow that Pym had taught him was appropriate for dignitaries.

"Ah, the pirate," the Subahdar said with a soft ripple of laughter as Jaki rose stiffly from his bow. "Of course Mynheer Boeck told me of you, but even if he had not, I would have known you. In the last few months, your notoriety has spiced the gossip in tents throughout the empire. The Bantam of Malaya, whose harbor at Serangoon you are said to have destroyed single-handedly, warns that you are an unpredictable savage. Is it true you were reared by headhunters in the jungles of Borneo?"

Jaki looked up at the Subahdar and smiled. "Are any of us responsible for the accidents of our birth?"

The Subahdar laughed, a staccato of grunts that broke the hush of the caravan crowd into titters of polite relief. "Well put, sir." He hissed a command, and the two armed horsemen flanking the lead elephant sheathed their swords and spun away. "Please join me in our camp, out of this oppressive heat. Your merchants may trade in our new marketplace while I have the honor of entertaining you."

Lucinda prodded her elephant, and it knelt on its front right leg and raised its left so she and Maud could step down. Jaki and Kota, infected by the Moghul pageantry, walked to the head of the elephant and helped them to the ground.

The Subahdar sighed loudly and thrust his open palm first at Maud and then at Kota. "Alas." He shook his head. "I cannot extend my invitation to your companions. I have just this day been recalled to Mandu, and my servants are burdened with the necessities of our coming march. You must forgive me, but I can personally entertain only the two of you. Your companions will have to accompany the caravan into Mirzapur."

Jaki faced the Subahdar with a frown of suspicion. But before he could speak, Lucinda said, "I am sure we will have no need of servants in your household." To Maud, she said, "When you go to the market, try to keep your mind off spices and teas and see if you can exchange that glassware for some textiles."

Jaki handed his musket to his companion. Years of battle had creased menace into the Subahdar's brow, and Kota was relieved not to have to go with him. He tucked the second musket into his sash and slipped into the crowd.

The Subahdar pointed toward two black saddled horses, and his smile flashed again as he watched Jaki cumbersomely mount. Lucinda rode with her skirt pulled up, to the shock of the attendants who had never seen a woman ride or, for that matter, anyone with sunpale hair and eyes that seemed to reflect the sky.

"I have heard that in Burma you wore an unusual hatband, Sir Gefjon," the Subahdar noted casually as they began their ride up the river-wall trail. "Few men but kings or fools would wear diamonds on their hat. Why do you challenge the avarice of men?"

"I no longer display them," Jaki said.

"But the whole world knows you carry diamonds," Hadi insisted with a bemused grin.

"Those are sacred stones," Jaki replied, riding bent forward, clutching the pommel. "My people call them mountains' tears and believe that they are the sorrow of life's suffering. They are all I have left of my legacy. If another man's avarice took them from me, he would take their sorrow as well — and perhaps that would be best for me."

The Subahdar shook his head and squinted sadly at Jaki. "Young pirate, you are thinking like a primitive. I am surprised you have kept your sacred stones and their sorrow this long." He looked over at Lucinda and the diamond about her neck. "You are both so very young. Are you yet twenty? I am thrice your age, and I have seen fools and kings suffer because they have misjudged evil. I am glad Allah sent you to me before you were found by one of the many despotic governors who rule these impoverished fiefdoms. Their men are bandits and you are wearing their favorite god for an ornament."

"But is this not your kingdom?" Lucinda asked. "Are not all the governors Muslim and thus moral? The Koran forbids stealing even from infidels."

"Your knowledge of the Holy Book is a sign of your civility," the Subahdar said, guiding his horse closer to her, gazing with admiration into her wide face. "But the Koran also says no one shall be forced to the faith. Though we rule these lands by law, we have not forced civility on anyone — and so, I thank Allah you are with me, for I will see that you are treated justly."

Blue, green, and yellow tents, big as houses, loomed into view on the bluffs overlooking a deep bend in the river. "Your trading, Mistress Gefjon, will take place aboard our floating shops," Subahdar Hadi said, pointing to the shadowy southern bank, where barges in the shapes of predatory birds were anchored. "There you will have an opportunity to exchange your crude eastern goods for the finest merchandise of our empire."

They dismounted and were led across colorful carpets to the camp's bazaar. Taking their cue from the Subahdar, Jaki and Lucinda removed their boots and followed him into a tent raised on a dozen green-lacquered pillars, eighteen feet tall, supporting a wooden platform that served as a second story. Brocade and velvet swathed the pillars, and tapestries hung from beneath lattices that spilled sunlight onto peach-bright carpets. Cloth screens stitched with hunting and battle scenes divided the vast tent into twelve chambers. "The signs of the zodiac," the Subahdar informed them, ascending an anchored rope ladder. "And up there, where we shall dine, the empyrean heaven which covers the lower sky. But before you join me, please, refresh yourselves."

He clapped, and a female servant in a blue sari emerged from one of the chambers and greeted Lucinda; a manservant in an open tan robe stepped from an opposite compartment and bowed to Jaki. In their separate screened cubicles were wooden tubs inlaid with mother-of-pearl and filled with steaming water. They shed their dusty clothes and were stretched out on deerskin-padded tables. Their muscles were kneaded, their skin rubbed with astringent fruits, their teeth and gums massaged with almond paste, and Jaki's stubbly beard shaved; then they were bathed in the clove-tinted water. Emerging ruddy and glistening, they were dried with rough cotton cloths, anointed with aloe and more perfumed oil, and dressed in local garments: an apricot-tinted sari for Lucinda and a patterned shirt of Dacca muslin and blue trousers for Jaki. They stepped out simultaneously and laughed to see each other dressed as Moghuls, their skin glowing and their eyes brighter for the dark collyrium the servants had stroked on their eyelids.

The upper story was plush with bright cushions, pillows, and bolsters, and a feast was being laid out on a varnished reed mat. At the top of the rope stairway a servant with a pearl-handled dagger sheathed at his hip in damask and gold admitted Lucinda but stopped Jaki. He put a hand on the sorcerer's medicine bag, and Jaki yanked it free.

The Subahdar stepped from behind a latticework screen and exchanged blunt phrases with the guard. "I am sorry," he finally said to Jaki, "but my captain is too suspicious a man to allow you to bring your sack into the dining hall unopened. Will you appease him by showing us what you are carrying?"

"That's only his charm pouch." Lucinda giggled, giddy with the luxuriant glow of the hot oil rubdown.

Jaki lifted the bulky bag off his shoulder and laid it on the carpet. Before opening it, he delivered the speech about the elemental forces that he had first heard from Jabalwan. "It is made of snake leather, and the design stitched on it with serpent teeth, shell, and boneheads are the powers of the world." He opened the bag. His hat was on top, and inside it were the seven diamonds. "The mountains' tears I've told you about." Below were the Bible and Pym's spyglass, both of which the captain scrutinized for hidden blades. Beneath the Book and the spyglass were the medicine satchels: leafrolls, bark sheafs, slivered root bundles, bamboo canisters filled with herbs, and also the phials of extracts and powders he had purchased in the bazaars. Under the clutter of medicines was the carved ivory canister that held Pym's maps of the New World. That intrigued Hadi, and he unrolled each of the maps but did not study them, for beneath them, at the bottom of the bag, was a triangle of folded canvas that could have held a weapon. The guard insisted on opening it, and when the Subahdar saw that it was the pirates' banner, he shouted a laugh.

"Will you allow me to display it while we eat? It is our custom to hang the tapestries of our guests." Hadi was genuinely impressed with the craftsmanship of the embroidery and guessed the handiwork was Chinese even before Jaki told him. The image was frightfully detailed, the eagle-stare of the beast a vertigo of white flame, its tangled serpent legs dragon-circles of jet and jade, wings spread like the inexorable geometry of night, talons slashing. Hadi regarded the young pirate with a fresh scrutiny while they chatted about trade and dined on black partridge, fatted kid, quail, fawn, camel's milk, yogurt, coconut and pistachio mash, mounds of vegetables, chilled wine, and betel nut wrapped in mint.

Dressed in clothes familiar to Hadi, Jaki's youth was more apparent to the Subahdar — as were his primitive strengths. This striking crossbreed of northern barbarian and southern aborigine was almost a child, not even old enough for a full beard. And without his boots, his feet revealed that he was of humankind's lowest caste, a forest dweller with broad calloused soles and big toes splayed like thumbs. His hands, too, were bossed with callus, and powerfully sinewed as an ape's. The muslin shirt exposed the phosphorous glints of scars on his shoulder. And the youth's face was as avian as the monster on his banner. Here was a man who was as much animal — a man meant for respect but not honor.

The Subahdar shifted his gaze to the woman and was pleased to see no signs of the beast on her. She seemed to ignore her mate's primitive appearance, his feline slouch-walk, and his childlike beliefs. What was it then she found appealing in him? The message that the Subahdar had received weeks before from Boeck had informed him that an English rajah's daughter had run away with a pirate she loved, and Hadi had expected to meet a man of authority, with a beard, regal bearing, and the courtly manner of the English ambassadors he had entertained in the court of the Moghul. What was before him was farcical, and he laughed at himself for the anxiety he had indulged when he first decided to retrieve the lady for the powerful English rajah.

"You must stay in Mirzapur while I am gone," he said to Lucinda. "The roads are too dangerous to go on from here without a military escort. Rest until I return, and I will arrange for a guard to accompany you to Surat."

"Oh, we cannot stay here, Subahdar," Lucinda said with a glance at Jaki. "I am to have a child in the spring. Soon after, my husband and I will be in the New World."

"A child? Ah!" Hadi stroked his beard. "But isn't the New World a dangerous place for a child? I have been told that it is a land of wilderness, religious fanatics, pirates, and savages."

"That is why she is going there with me," Jaki interjected, dunking a rolled leaf of bread and sliced quail in orange sauce, "since I am all of that." He spoke with a smile, but he was tense with doubt. He did not like the Subahdar's calculating gaze, which did not hide his contempt.

Lucinda chuckled and squeezed Jaki's knee. "The New World is also colonies, Subahdar, outposts of empire, and we have arranged with the Dutch to settle in Brazil."

"Then you cannot linger here if you are to travel to the other side of the world in half a year!" Hadi lifted his goblet of lemon water and toasted them as he had learned from the English emissaries. "You must come with me tomorrow. Leave the caravan behind. I will write you notes of trade for your goods and you can travel by horse with me to Mandu. Prince Dawar Bakhsh is pleased to meet foreigners. You will conduct excellent business with him, and he will provide a small army to escort you to the coast. And they will not only protect you from brigands but also introduce you to the wealthiest rajahs along the way."

Lucinda accepted happily after ascertaining that their servants could accompany them, but Jaki, unable to contain his mounting dread of the Persian war chief, stood up and walked to the trellis window, where a telescope pointed toward the river. He peered through the eyepiece and saw the river trees amuck with sunlight, the Ganges' brown thigh, punting boatmen with sweat in the cracks of their faces. As the Subahdar prattled about the telescope and its advantage in battle, Jaki spotted Maud haggling with a trader over a basket of goat tufts, the world's softest fur, imported from Kashmir. High above, on a dusty ridge, the gunmen who had surrounded them earlier drilled, gracefully kneeling and rising through enfilade maneuvers.

Hadi nudged Jaki aside and peeked through the eyepiece. "These Rawalpindi marksmen are the pride of the Moghul's army. Their maneuvers are a crown secret."

"You need not fear us breeching your trust, Subahdar," Lucinda ventured. "We are bound far from empire."

"For kings, no corner of the earth is too far." The Subahdar smiled and cupped some lentils with a chard leaf. "Even the New World is touched by the Old."

"In the marketplace," Jaki said, "they say the former Moghul had two sons, and they are fighting for the throne. Is this war why you are called away from here?"

Hadi's eyes narrowed. "You spy on my soldiers, young pirate, and you ask about war —" He thought momentarily of simply having this distasteful heathen taken away and hanged, but knew that the English rajah's daughter would be far easier to transport with her lover than without — and he smiled numbly. "You are lucky to be married to so civilized a wife. She will enrich you." He clapped and servants brought bowls of jasmine water to rinse their hands.

"Tonight you will stay in my camp," the Subahdar announced at the end of the meal. "Your servants will be summoned and outfitted for our journey. Tomorrow at dawn, we begin for Saugor."

Later that evening, after Lucinda had traded her raw materials for tapestries, ivory sculptures, silk garments, and jewelry, she and Jaki were quartered in the zodiac tent with a decanter of wine and a black lump of opium big as a toe. Jaki glowered at his wife. "I do not like this Subahdar."

"How can you not after the gifts and hospitality he has bestowed on us?"

"Because he *has* bestowed such gifts on us," Jaki grumbled. "He wants us with him to protect not us but his gifts. And besides —" His frown was dark as Cain's brand. "He looks on you with too much favor."

Lucinda chuckled and grabbed Jaki by the ear. "Are you jealous?"

"Is the prey jealous of the hunter?"

She kissed him. "You are too suspicious. Our host is gracious. He has entertained English before. Let us enjoy his gifts." She poured a goblet of wine, sipped it, and passed it to him.

Jaki took Lucinda's hand with the goblet. "Lucinda, we are in danger here. I feel it. We must find a way to get free of Hadi."

Lucinda squeezed Jaki's wrist. "You are a silly boy sometimes. We have found wealth here. Is that not why we have journeyed this far? This is our fortune, Jaki. This is the wealth of our children. I will not give this up because you are afraid."

"I am not often afraid."

"In the jungle you were fearless and that almost widowed me. Now you are afraid and we may lose all we have suffered for." She brushed the long hair from his eyes. "I have grown up among ambassadors and dignitaries. Hadi is a diplomat. Though he is a foreigner, I know his ways. Trust me, true child, and behave like the honored guest you are."

"We are not guests, Lucinda. We are prisoners."

Lucinda shook her head wistfully. "You have much to learn. I'm glad I am your teacher."

Jaki took a deep draft, hoping to calm his apprehensions, and picked up the lump of opium. It smelled like animal sorrow, like earth where something had died the season before. Pym had not allowed the smoking of opium on board *Silenos,* but Jaki had glimpsed the dark dens of smokers in Macao and Chan-chiang when he had gone with Blackheart to round up the crew after shore leave. He stabbed a morsel with a stylet from the velvet smoking kit and held the black crumb to the lantern flame on the trivet between them. When the opium bubbled into smoke, he inserted it in the long-stemmed pipe and drew deeply.

The celestial smell pervaded his lungs with a cool exultation. He held out the pipe to Lucinda.

"No," she said. "Riding elephants and horses is all I ask of the child in me. Opium is more than our baby needs."

Jaki drew another lungful. Colors steepened, and he gazed up through the trellis at the ribbons of sunset. The last heat of day soughed languidly through the tent, not even wiggling the loose tooth of flame in the lantern.

A chill blurred through Jaki, and he stood up. "I'm going to walk about," he said, and his voice sounded shadowy. "Shall we accept our host's offer to stroll his garden?"

Lucinda declined by unhooking her bodice and lying back on the mounded pillows. "The fragrance of the smoke has calmed me so. I will rest here. Do not stay long. The Subahdar says we mount at dawn, and he seems a punctual fellow."

Jaki smiled, the opium's peace softening his features and making him look younger, like a long-eyed child. Barefoot, he crossed the court and followed a path that wended among knobby trees to a garden maze of flowery shrubs.

The garden was a spiral, with rows of lemon trees enclosing a whorl of trimmed yew hedges. Evenly tapered cypresses rose like jets of black flame from among boulders shaggy with lichen. Maroon clouds bulked above the sprays of hibiscus hedges where the blossoms had wrinkled closed for the night. Far ahead in the dusk, the Ganges gleamed like a glass snake.

Jaki sat on a stone bench at the center of the garden and watched the first hour of night eddying in the clouds. The reverie of the opium disembodied him, and he seemed to hover in the nightbreak. A cry came from the grove cypresses behind him, and he startled: the call was Wawa's alert for approaching men.

Jaki dipped to his knees and peeked over the bench into the silver darkness. The serenity of fear held him breathless for a long spell while he listened with his bones for another cry. *Wawa is dead,* he heard Lucinda say crisply in his mind. Vanilla moonlight swirled among the trees, and moths floated like flakes of ash. Men were approaching. He saw their shadows gathering on the lane, smoky shapes in the moonmist, no more real than Wawa's cry.

"Yes," Jaki hissed in English as he comprehended that the opium was opening the light between worlds to the Longhouse of the Souls. The slender cypresses became the struts lifting the Longhouse above the jungle floor; the stars became lamps glimpsed through bamboo slats; the cauldron moon shone from the doorway in a ring of rainbow: it was the cooking fire at the center of the Longhouse, the glowing cooking pot with the melted child inside it. He could see the fetal shadow of the child in the translucence of the pot, the markings of the moon.

The mating of vision and actuality troubled him, and he stood up and called upon all his reason to see clearly. The moon was the moon, the trees, trees. No one was approaching. He was alone in the dark. He sat down.

But he heard Wawa's plaintive warning again. Jaki sat still. The dead were filing from the Longhouse behind him into the luminous sky.

The opium had opened his strong eye, and this time he did not resist. To his left he watched the lanky silhouette of Mang slump past, his hands to his tiger-clawed throat. The shade's face was placid, intent on the gateway to the other world shining sullenly in the west.

A growly laugh to his right made him turn his whole body. Pym, the beads in his rattail hair sparking with last light, stared at Jaki over his snap-necked shoulder, gazing directly backward like a broken puppet as he ambled into the twilight's kelp. "I am worm-dirt, I am. As you too shall be soon enough. Life breeds death. Mindless. Blind."

Anguish clotted Jaki's cry. "Wait!"

Pym laughed again. "It takes weight to wait, lad. Hah! It's too late for that." The darkness absorbed him.

"Your heart leaps as if it will live forever," a familiar voice called from behind. Jaki turned slowly, shaken from his vision of broken-necked Pym and confronted a melancholy young man with a strong nose and coiling black locks.

"Shirazi," Jaki exhaled. "You find me a prisoner again."

The youth paused in his walk and shook his head wistfully. "Is this what you dream?" he asked. "To become as your father? I knew you to be a pirate out of the jungle. Are you doing what you dream here in the heart of the empire? Indeed you are a prisoner, but not of the Subahdar, Jaki. You are a prisoner of your own heart."

Jaki moved to speak again, but Shirazi turned away and disappeared among the lace of shrubs.

Jaki turned to see who was passing next from the Longhouse of Souls. The square profile of Batuh flitted by, his eyes daggerpoints of hostility, flashing for an instant as he spotted Jaki on his dash through the garden. Jaki glimpsed other slinky shadows and knew they were men he had killed. Except for Batuh, none saw him, so determined were they on fleeing the Longhouse.

"Legion, is that not what the Book calls them that are unclean?" Jabalwan asked.

Jaki walked on the balls of his feet toward the voice. Jabalwan and Mala were standing hand in hand before the notched-log stairway of the Longhouse; they looked burnished in the moonlight, sweatslick.

"Are you of the many, Matubrembrem?" Jabalwan asked. "Is that why we find the last of the sorcerers here among the unclean, the makers of war, the worshipers of power?"

"Teacher!" Jaki cried. "Mother!" The magic of their encounter stole his breath, and he had to draw deep to pull his thoughts together. "I am alone. I have no tribe. No people know me for their own. I must make my life from whatever I can find. I have chosen with my heart, Mother. Am I wrong?"

"The Book says in Ecclesiastes, 'The hearts of men are full of evil,' " Mala said, " 'and madness is in their hearts while they live — and after that, they go to the dead.' "

"Mother, do not speak against me," Jaki pleaded, his sight smearing with tears. "My heart is true. I love Lucinda. I love the child she carries that is mine." He looked to Jabalwan. "Teacher, the Mother of Life blessed me Herself in the last hour of Njurat. She told me to go into the world and make my life full. A sorcerer is only half of what I am. I have a father as well as a mother. It is his spirit I must live now to be all that I can." He peered sadly at the ghosts. "Am I wrong?"

Jabalwan led Mala aside, and they began to pare into mist. Jabalwan gestured toward the Longhouse before they vanished. "Go then to your father, and see why you are named child of the devil."

Wiping away tears, Jaki gazed up at the Longhouse of the Dead. His father was visible in the doorway, kneeling over the lunar cooking pot. A bareheaded, golden-haired ghost with skin pale as starlight, he was dressed as a Dutchman of his age and station, with flare-topped boots, knee breeches of shimmery satin, longcoat with brocaded buttonholes and tucked-back tail so his sword could hang free. His hands were in the cooking pot.

"Father!" Jaki called, but the ghost did not respond. "Pieter Gefjon — it is I, your son, Jaki."

The ghost looked over his shoulder, annoyed. His face was bold, eyebrows tufted, beard streaked back from years of facing into the wind. At the sight of Jaki, the stern features softened to the point of love.

"Father, I need your help. I —" Jaki stepped closer. "I want your blessing. How else can I find my way through your world?"

Pieter Gefjon rose to one knee and lifted his hands from the cooking pot. He was holding the melted child. It was dead, its gluey features fixed in a stare of outraged horror. Captain Gefjon twisted off one of its sticky arms and ate the glutinous flesh.

Jaki squeezed his eyes shut and sank to the ground. When he looked up again, he made himself see cypress trees and the moon. He closed his strong eye and sat, cold inside, watching clouds snaring the stars.

*

The road from the port city of Surat wound clumsily among river gorges where the autumn rains lunged from the mountains toward the sea. William Quarles, still thin and trembly from the malaria that had wasted him four months earlier, rode a sable mare whose mane was braided with red ribbons. Moghul guides — black-robed men with scimitars and turbans wrapped about spiked helmets — picked their way carefully over the shale ledges on jittery steeds. Behind, a wagon narrow as a coffin was lugged by a one-eyed mule. Stacked with the horns and heads of slaughtered goats, the wagon was painted in garish designs signifying the demoness Durga, the black Kali, empress of all mortal horrors. None of the Rajput bandits who haunted these steep trails would raid an offering to the black Kali, so the one hundred and fifteen flintlocks in the wagon were safe — so long as the one-eyed mule did not misstep and plunge into the roaring canyon.

One of the guides shouted and pointed up to a blue-white rag tumbling through the bramble of overhanging clifftrees. Closer, Quarles saw that it was a pigeon. It alighted among the goats' heads, pecked at a skull, and hopped to the driver's shoulder so he could remove the coil of parchment wrapped about its leg. The Moghul nearest Quarles dismounted and dashed to the wagon. He retrieved the ribbon of parchment, glanced at it, and passed it to Quarles. The captain was astonished to see that the message was written in English and signed by the official that the Thieves' Church had contacted among the Moghuls. All prior communications had been by word of mouth through emissaries in Surat, because the official was a subahdar, high-ranking enough to represent princes and therefore too politic to commit anything to writing. This missive indicated that Quarles had reached the Subahdar's demesne and would learn something of the truth of their agreement. He read, "Esteemed Captain — your daughter is safe and in my protection. I write to warn you that she is most obviously enamored of her pirate consort and bears the pirate's child. I trust that this does not thwart our prior arrangement. Please inform me of your intent that I may adjust my own strategy. Shall I dispatch the pirate? By the glory of Allah — Hadi Fath Izar."

The Moghul who had passed him the note waited attentively, an inkstone, quill, and small writing board in his hands, ready to return the pigeon to the sky with the Englishman's message. Quarles peered down through a tumult of pines into the water rush and felt his soul rise into his throat. The thought of Lucinda with child — with the heathen-pirate's child — almost toppled him from his mount, and he clutched the pommel with all his might. All that kept him upright was the knowledge that his daughter was at last in his grasp again.

A sob rose in his chest, but he would not utter it. He had endured every suffering voicelessly: poverty, the death of his wife, the destruction of his ship, his daughter's disappearance, the jungle's brutality. He would not weep now.

On the back of the parchment strip, he wrote, "Noble Subahdar, our strategy remains the same. Kali herself conveys the instruments of your prince's victory. Spare the pirate that I may face my tormentor and claim his life with my own hand. Your servant, William Quarles."

Jaki's hands were restless. In the four months since he had lost Wawa and left the pieces of Jabalwan's broken blowgun stuck in the jungle floor, he had taught himself to play chess, to work the reins of a horse, to appraise grades of goat fur, even to write a few words of English. For four months, his hands had been busy, but now they ached to hold again the familiar weapon and to stroke his faithful jungle friend.

It was after Jaki's opium visit to the Longhouse of the Dead that he began again to use his hands as he had in the wilds of his childhood. At first, his fingers were content to work plant fiber into lacy knots and to carve soft reed wood into tiny mouth whistles. But as the journey through the Moghul Empire carried him farther from Mirzapur without diminishing the fright of his opium vision, he realized that his hands were not merely nostalgic — they were making a weapon. The hollow and bore-grooved reed, tiny enough to fit behind his teeth, was not the musical toy he had supposed but a miniature blowgun, no bigger than what was left of his animal soul.

Surreptitiously, Jaki set to work preparing a dart for his minuscule weapon. He quietly gathered poisonous berries and leaves and stewed them under the campfire rocks to a black gum. Night after night, the gum thickened blackly, and yet he continued to cook it, until the resin was as viscously concentrated as the opium that had led him to the Longhouse of the Dead.

"Sunday 31 January 1628," Lucinda wrote in her rice paper journal. She sat under the canopy of her tent, facing the tiny valley of Saugor and beyond, on the next rise, the grim fortress wall behind which the whole town had gathered to greet the Subahdar's party. Raucous cries, pipe music, and the occasional trumpet of an elephant drifted through the pine and sal trees.

Subahdar Hadi trotted into the camp's grove accompanied by two officers. Maud stood up from the racks of plants she was placing out to dry, and Kota appeared in the doorway of his tent, bare chested and sleepy eyed. The Subahdar ignored them as he dismounted. He bowed to Lucinda, and she closed her journal and rose to greet him. "Please, do not stand for me. Surely we are old acquaintances by now. Our shared journey has made us brethren. Sit, sit."

"Why are you not in the fortress to receive the welcome of this city's people?" she asked, settling back on her cushioned mat. "My husband left for there with his monk friend an hour ago."

"I am on my way there," he replied, sitting cross-legged before her. "But first I had to meet with my scouts. And though you are a woman, I will speak with you as openly as I would a man, if that pleases you. We are far from Agra, dear Lucinda, and this territory is overseen by Rajputs, Hindus. My scouts have ascertained that they are hospitable to their Muslim lords, but I needed to be sure. You see, I must go ahead to Mandu this very day. You and your husband will follow. I have received assurances that the Rajputs will not interfere in your passage. Nevertheless, you will be accompanied by my guards."

"What is your urgency in reaching Mandu, Subahdar?"

Hadi clasped his hands and lowered his head. "As I have told you, I am the tender of the tents for the unlucky Shahryar, who has been replaced as Moghul this very month by his brother, Shah Jahan. Prince Dawar Bakhsh, who will be your host in Mandu, is, like myself, an ally of Shahryar. We are to meet within the week with emissaries from our new lord, the Moghul Shah Jahan. I cannot expect you in your condition to travel that swiftly to Mandu, so I will go on ahead of you."

"Are you in disfavor, Subahdar?" she asked with a frown of ingenuous concern.

Hadi dismissed her apprehension with a smile. "Lady, this is not England, where misplaced loyalty can cost one's head. The great weakness of our empire is that the right of succession is not clearly defined in our laws. England is ruled by primogeniture, I believe. Our warrior tradition leaves the sons and even the nephews of the dead Moghul to contest among themselves for rule. I served the old Moghul well. And I am a Muslim in a Hindu country. My life and service are too valuable to be sacrificed for political reasons alone. The prince and I are to meet with our new lord's emissaries that we might swear our allegiance to Shah Jahan. By the time you arrive in Mandu, the transition to the new order will be complete."

Lucinda nodded her understanding. "Forgive me for pressing my curiosity on you."

Hadi smiled warmly. "Your curiosity is natural. It affords me the chance to be curious in return. May I ask you about your husband?"

Lucinda blinked with surprise. "What of him, Subahdar?"

"He is not nearly as couth as you, Mistress Gefjon. Rather, there is something of the animal in him. I do not understand why one as cultured as you would give your life to such a man."

"What you call animal, Subahdar, I consider human nature untrammeled by the arbitrary conventions of society." She felt the heat of her opinion rising in her, and she cut herself short.

"Is that why you are fleeing to the New World to have your child?"

he inquired, holding her defiant stare with his lazy gaze. "To escape convention?"

"For a woman, convention restrains as a prison does. I would have no freedom in my father's world, so I am forced to seek a world of my own. Jaki is the only man I have met who understands freedom."

"Perhaps because he has no tradition by which conventions are born."

"What tradition he had was destroyed by traders who have no respect but for their own profits."

Hadi tugged at the pearl in his right ear and monitored Lucinda's expression, reading her anger and seeing within it a willfulness he marveled at. "Are all the women of England as forthright and strong-minded as you?"

"You mean as arrogant?" She grinned and shook her head. "I must give credit to my father for my possessing any mind at all. He reared me as though I were a son, taking me with him wherever he went instead of entrusting me to a convent or a governess's care. I am a peculiarity among my people, and it is a better fate for me that I never return to England."

"But what kind of life will you have in the wilderness?"

"Whatever we can make of it," she answered, pausing slyly, "rather than what is made of us."

"Then I wish you well," the Subahdar said quietly. Though his face betrayed no emotion, he imagined her haughty face when he turned her over to her father in Mandu. The Koran was clear about the place of women, and such a one as this was an abomination, a heresy.

Lucinda watched the Subahdar and his men gallop away toward the fortress, then turned back to her journal. She wrote: "The Subahdar himself goes ahead of us to Mandu to make peace with the new Moghul. Truly we are blessed to have him as our protector in this calamitous land."

The journey southwest to Mandu was serenely beautiful. The Vindhya Mountains, blunt cliffs and pinnacles of green amber, separated the great plains of sal forest and the Ganges basin on the north from the Deccan, the vast and primeval territory to the south. The bunched mountains were the barriers of empire, beyond which the Moghul domination did not extend. "Even in ancient times," Dhup informed Jaki, "the Vindhya stopped the Aryan invaders from the north who brought with them Sanskrit and the mysteries of the wind."

Jaki wanted only to flee with Lucinda to those green-gold mountains and beyond, eluding the grasp of the Subahdar. With Kota thrashing a decoy trail, he could get Lucinda and Maud deep into the forest with little or nothing for the soldiers to follow. Somehow, he was convinced, they would make their way successfully to the coast and commandeer a vessel. But Lucinda would give no thought to escape. "What are we fleeing?" she asked with sincere bafflement. "The Subahdar has given us a fortune in trade bills. When we cashier these in Surat, we will buy two ships and still have wealth left from the rajahs we've yet to trade with."

"Wealth," Jaki sighed. They were sitting together on a flat boulder, their bare feet dangling in a roadside stream. Every five miles, almost on each hour, the carriage carrying Lucinda and the Muslim officers' wives would make a rest stop on orders from the Subahdar's surgeon, who was solicitous of Lucinda's pregnancy. The dozen guards the Subahdar had commanded to escort them were instructed to tend to all her needs, and *sharbat,* a green lemon drink, was brought to them with fried mango, saffron rice, jellied fruits, and assorted cooked meats from the villages ahead. "Has Hadi bought us, then?"

"Of course," Lucinda answered. "We are conducting business under papers from the Netherlands. Their East India Company has already made a small fortune by dint of our effort. Why should we not profit ourselves and our children? I am quite pleased by the Subahdar's generosity. He has not once done us an unkindness. If we flee from him, as you wish, then we also flee from our fortune. As well as forsaking all the treasures earned these last eight months, we may very well be ambushed and killed without the protection of these soldiers."

She was right, Jaki knew, and he conceded with a nod and another sigh. They were the Subahdar's prisoners, manacled with gold, caged by wilderness. Unless Lucinda and he were willing to abandon their fortune, what choice did they have but to go forward?

Jaki was sullen despite Lucinda's confidence. He was a prisoner of his heart, the opium had shown him that with hallucinatory clarity. He lacked Lucinda's faith in civilization, convinced that they would be better off alone in the mountains and penniless than wealthy and watched by armed men. But that was the animal in him talking — and that animal had squandered his life in the jungles of Burma. He would be tiger's scat now if Lucinda had not saved him. She knew this world of walls, of cities and empire, of money and barter. She knew to wait for the tiger. And he knew well enough now to trust her. So he tried to stop thinking of running away from the walls, remembering a vision he had shared once with Jabalwan that soon the whole world would become a wall. In his loneliness, he confided in Dhup.

The monk had been given a horse and, in fact, he rode better than he walked. He and Jaki followed Lucinda's carriage together, talking about the world's wall and how the obstacles and limits imposed by the world were the very shape of one's identity.

"What did you mean by *wind* when you warned me that wind follows the tiger?" the sorcerer asked.

Dhup stared at Jaki with a look of wonder. "You remember that?"

"At the time, I thought you meant I could sense the tiger by its scent. But you meant something more, didn't you?"

"Why do you think that?"

"Kota told me once of a Chinese seaman who could break spars with his bare hand. He said he held the wind in his belly. Also, I have watched your clumsiness. You are no ordinary man."

"We are all ordinary," the monk replied. "What is extraordinary is that so many of us ignore what few strengths lie within us."

The memory of the fakirs performing their *siddhis* came to Jaki's mind. But he knew that the monk was not referring to miracles. Jaki said, "My teacher, toward the end of his life, once took me to the mountains to show me a strength within that he called spirit fist. He dangled from cliffsides like a hummingbird and once punched me senseless without touching me. He said the power was ordinary, and that it was an energy that moved in our bones, that heals our wounds and grows our hair. He called it a spirit wind. Do you know of it?"

"For a man with a wife and a child coming" — Dhup smiled wearily and shook his square head — "you should be thinking of the strength within as the perseverance of peace with the mystery. You are, after all, enacting the rites. You are a husband. Soon you will be a father. Now is not the time to be thinking of yourself and the power growing your hair. Leave that for those who live alone, who have married the force growing their hair. You are married to the world. Make your place in the mystery, Jaki, and think hard on those around you. What holds people together is a pain that has no wound. All your love grows from this pain. Those who understand this are wiser than good or evil. Do secret good."

After that, Dhup deflected all conversation about spirit wind by quoting the sutras on the wounds of wanting. Jaki preferred to ride in silence, certain only that his wife was leading them to ruin, uncertain about everything else. If the heart, with its hungers, was madness, what was love? Was Dhup right? Was love the child of pain? Was that the meaning in the opium image of his father eating the melted child? Could all of human life be coming to that? Was there nothing ahead of them but a world of walls and an apocalypse of fiery clouds, a long murder called life?

These black thoughts churned within Jaki, but he strove to hide them. Dhup spoke truth: now was not the time to be thinking of himself. Ahead lay Mandu and peril to all he loved. Once he was certain that Lucinda could not be dissuaded from following the Subahdar, he spent his time with her at the frequent roadside stops extending his chess game, while keeping his darkest strategies to himself.

Mandu rose from the southwest sky, its mosque domes and palace turrets lit by golden daybreak. Perched along the crest of the Vindhya

Mountains, the Muslim city gleamed like a bed of pebbles under the sky's vast river. The battlemented wall ribboned across the horizon, appearing and disappearing among the folds and rills of the mountains.

"Mandu is eight English miles long," the Subahdar declared to the travelers. "The circuit of the wall is almost twenty-three miles," he said, sweeping his gem-knuckled hand across the long vista. He had charged into their camp the night before with twenty horsemen and relieved the soldiers who had escorted them from Saugor. When he waved parchment sheets at Lucinda, trading papers for the rajahs on the road to Surat, she was luminous with joy. Jaki was glad to see her happy, but he had not been impressed by the papers. They were just paper. The view of Mandu this morning, however, awed him. The city was glorious and huge. For an hour they traveled through a valley of ancient pines, where night still hung like a beard among the boughs. Near a pine bog, the Subahdar called the procession to a stop so that the women could rest. He dismounted, and his men followed, knotting their reins together and dispersing along dim paths into the scraggly underbrush to relieve themselves.

Jaki tied his horse to Lucinda's carriage and with his medicine bag slung over his shoulder wandered over the rock outwash of a cliffwall into the darkness of willow flats. He hunkered under a tree as if to empty his bowels and removed a leaf bundle from his medicine bag. Inside was the hollow reed he had shaped into a blowpipe as tiny as his fingernail and, embedded in treewax, a needle-thin thorntip he had soaked in poison. He peeled away the wax, inserted the dart in the blowpipe, and capped the pipe at both ends with the wax. When he was certain no one was watching, he thumbed the bee weapon into the vault of his mouth and used the wax to affix it to his palate. The risk was that the casing would break and the poison would take him. But he accepted that as the price of his suspicion. This, he knew, was to be their last stop before reaching Mandu, and he had to be certain that in the capital of his enemy he at least had the power to sting.

Jaki tucked his diamonds into the pocket of the folded Wyvern standard and buried the cloth under gravel and willow leaves. He marked the spot with three stones that he leaned into a pyramid. Then he returned to the group with his medicine bag weighted down with rocks.

They rode for another hour before the trail lifted through a glen of sunslants, swirling butterflies, and stately trees. A herald's trumpet blared from ahead, and its echoes bounced among the canyons. With the next bend, the cliffwalls fell away, and the sky opened to a cloudless blue panoply above massive ramparts the color of dried blood.

On a high turret above the arched entryway, a herald blared on his trumpet again, and the sentries posted in the open gateway raised their pikes in formal salute to the Subahdar. The trail had widened enough for four horsemen to ride abreast, and Jaki and Dhup, flanked by soldiers, entered the mountain city behind the women's carriage and Kota's painted wagon. As they trotted under the stone archway into the city, he observed archers in the battlements and musketmen patrolling the tree-lined boulevard inside the wall. Beyond the trees, nailed to warped planks crossed in X's and leaning against the parapet, were a dozen naked bodies aswarm with carrion birds, their ripped flesh dangling like rags, their eyesockets gouged empty.

"Whoever has found the world has found a corpse," Dhup quoted in English from the sutras, and urged his horse closer to the Subahdar's. "Who are these unfortunates?"

"Rebels," Hadi answered, not averting his gaze from the saluting troopers who flanked the boulevard. "Fanatical supporters of Shahryar — men who shared the same devotion as myself and Prince Dawar Bakhsh but who were not politic enough to accept the new Moghul Shah Jahan. I would be nailed there myself but that I am wise enough to abandon preference and to serve whoever sits on the Peacock Throne."

Dhup dismounted as soon as they had passed the site of the execution. "I will stop here to pray before these corpses," he told the Subahdar and Jaki. "And then I will visit the shrines of Mandu. I am just a monk. I am not suited for the company of princes. Will you excuse me that I may serve the dead with my chants as I do the living?"

"The dead best serve themselves," the Subahdar said. "But do as you must." Hadi waved to his troopers to let the monk pass. Dhup pressed his palms together, bowed, and wandered into the morning glare toward the corpses.

Lucinda and Maud had not seen the bodies from their carriage, so entranced were they by the marble buildings and the garden-lined avenues. Kota, at the reins of his wagon, had turned his head from the crucified men and he was smiling broadly with forced bravura, trying to blot the ill omen by imagining the bounty they would cull from this opulent city. Limp garlands and the shattered rags of fireworks festooned the gutters, and Hadi explained that these were the remnants of the three-day celebration honoring the new Moghul's coronation.

The Subahdar guided them to a palace of blue marble that shone like ice. "Here you will leave all your weapons," he commanded, "and I will accompany you into the presence of Prince Dawar Bakhsh."

Jaki stood up in his saddle and nudged back his fawnskin hat. "Why must we leave our weapons?" he asked. "We have dined together before with our weapons at our sides."

"Yes," Hadi acknowledged with a judicious nod, "but never before with a prince. My men will collect your weapons here, and you will come with me into the reception garden."

When Hadi pulled away to give this order to his men, Jaki dismounted and frowned at Lucinda. "This is not good."

"We need no weapons here, Jaki," Lucinda told him. "We are in the protection of the Subahdar and his prince."

Jaki hummed skeptically and removed his buckler. "Even so, I want you to stay close to me. I need your strength, Lucinda."

The Subahdar motioned for them to follow him up the white stairs, but Jaki restrained Lucinda with a hand on her arm. "Maud and Kota will join us, of course," he said to Hadi.

The Subahdar frowned. "You are meeting a prince. Have some consideration for his sensibility. He will not want to share his presence with your servants."

"They are not our servants," Lucinda insisted, and Jaki regarded her with surprise. "We have traveled together from Dagon, thousands of miles, through jungle and over desert and mountains. If they are not deemed worthy of the prince, then neither are we. Convey our apologies to Prince Dawar and show us where we will be staying while we are your guests here."

The Subahdar lifted his hands in exasperation. "My apologies," he said with contempt. "Bring your companions. We will not detain the prince any longer."

Jaki waved Kota to his side. "Be sharp now," he whispered to the swarthy man. "We are in the dragon's lair. Stay close to the women."

They climbed the glassy stairs and entered the palace beneath a speartipped marble dome. Plasterwork galleries arched overhead, illumined by oil lamps in nets of iron lace. Jaki pretended to admire their filigree while he noted the six archers who took up positions behind them at the only exit.

They waited a long time before a massive bronze door while the Subahdar spoke softly with the archers at the end of the portico. Sparrows flitted among the galleries. Sunlight climbed two more stairs, and at last the immense metal door swung outward on giant hinges. Blue-robed men in white turbans bowed to the Subahdar and stood aside to admit him. They ignored the sword at his side but meticulously searched each of his four guests. They took Jaki's medicine bag and, at the Subahdar's signal, left it beside the door. From Kota they removed a dagger hidden in his boot cuff. Lucinda frowned at him. "You are no longer a pirate, Kota," she berated him. "Has your wealth done nothing to soften your bellicosity?" He shrugged and winked at Jaki, who placed a consoling hand on his shoulder.

Hadi strode over the onyx threshold, and the others followed into an expansive courtyard open to the sky. At the center was a curtained gazebo with a brilliant blue awning tasseled with pearls, beneath which sat the prince, backed by two men with scimitars. He was a splinter of a man, whose exquisite silk robes hung bulkily on his frame. He motioned them closer. Hadi strode four paces and dropped to his knees, face lowered, palms face up. Lucinda and Maud curtsied, and Jaki and Kota removed their hats and lowered their heads, both of them searching the courtyard from the corners of their eyes, placing the guards.

Prince Dawar stroked his whiskers with long fingers and spoke softly in Persian to Hadi. Behind him, the curtain of the gazebo parted, and William Quarles stepped out. Jungle fever had harrowed his face to a waxy mask behind a singed beard, and the cold stars of his gray eyes fastened on his daughter, full of sparkling concentration. He held his square hand out for her.

"Father!" Lucinda exhaled, almost soundlessly. The shock of seeing him whirred through her veins, and she sagged against Jaki.

The Subahdar jumped to his feet and stood before them with a sharp smile. "Deception brought you here more safely than force, Mistress Quarles," he said as the guards closed in from the edges of the chamber. "Go quietly now to your father." He looked to Jaki. "Let her go and spare her the sight of your spilled blood."

Anger burst through Lucinda's surprise, and she glared past the Subahdar at her father. "You cannot have me back!" she yelled. "I am married now. I won't go back!"

Quarles's outstretched arm beckoned her, and he shook his haggard head. "Come, Lucinda," he said in his bass rumble. "You are still my child. Come to me."

"Never!" she shouted past the guards who had stopped before her. "I belong with my husband. I am carrying his child. I will not leave him."

Jaki searched for an opening among the closely ranked guards and saw none. Kota, who had also been looking, caught his eye and shook his head. At a signal from the Subahdar, the guards grabbed Lucinda, and she shrieked as they pulled her away.

With his tongue, Jaki dislodged the reed waxed to the roof of his mouth, bit off the gum caps, and clenched the tiny blowpipe firmly. The metallic flavor of the poison wrinkled his mouth and stung his tongue. The guards closed in on him swiftly, and he stepped forward as if to meet them, but actually angling for a clear shot at the Subahdar. He held his head high, peering over the guards' shoulders as they seized him. They converged on him with such force he was hoisted off his feet. Lucinda was dragged toward her father, her stricken face craning to see him. Maud and Kota did not struggle and were led docilely away.

Jaki looked around him. The poison was leaking into his mouth and had already numbed his tongue. He had to act quickly or he would die himself. But he would not kill a hapless guard; he wanted the Subahdar.

A slap resounded in the courtyard, and Lucinda's cries stopped. He turned and saw his wife slumped over between two Moghuls, Quarles clutching her long hair and lifting her face to meet his furious stare. He tore the tiger's beard from her throat and threw it to the floor. Jaki's sight dizzied, and he realized that he had waited too long. The poison was paralyzing his brain. He sagged, and the flanking guards bolstered him.

The Subahdar's regal figure appeared suddenly before him holding the medicine bag he had retrieved from the door. Jaki pulled back as if to avoid the man, and, as he had hoped, the guards lugged him firmly forward. He reversed himself abruptly, sprang ahead, his whole body outstretched, and spat through the reed blowpipe.

The dart spun wild and dropped harmlessly to the floor beside the Subahdar's boots. Jaki gagged and let the tainted reed drop from his numb mouth. Swords hissed and flashed, and the Subahdar's shout stopped them as metal bit the flesh under Jaki's ribs. Hadi opened the bag and yelped when he saw the stones. He gripped Jaki's face in a gruff hand and stared into his sickened eyes. He barked something in Turki, then said loudly in English, "The fool has poisoned himself trying to kill me." His own sword came up and nicked Jaki's throat.

"Stop!" Quarles called. He looked to the prince, who had watched the seizure from his throne with slumberous opium-eyes. The prince lifted a frail finger, and the Subahdar lowered his sword. Quarles nodded for the guards to take his daughter away, and he approached the pirate. He looked even younger than Quarles had remembered him from the night of the duel in Macao. He searched the heathen's face for the pugnacity that he had expected to confront and saw only a boy dopey with defeat. "Do not kill him yet," he told the Subahdar. "I must speak with my daughter first before I will know how he must die."

The Subahdar waved the guards away, and they dragged Jaki across the courtyard in the opposite direction from where Lucinda had been hauled. The poison invaded his brain, and with the mosaics of the floor shuttling under his gaze, he slid into darkness.

Lucinda sat sobbing on a marble bench in an enclosed garden while Maud hovered nearby, fretfully scanning the enclosure for the inevitable approach of William Quarles. When he did arrive, she gasped at the sight of him. He was hatless, a state she had rarely seen him in, and he looked gaunt and severe.

Lucinda lifted a contemptuous stare to her father and did not rise. "You have no right to take me from my husband," she said with a tight jaw.

Quarles stood before her with his hands fisted at his sides. Anger gilded his stomach and his lungs with acid. "Are you truly carrying his child?"

She thrust her face toward him. "Yes." Her lip flinched, expecting a blow.

But Quarles did not move. The months of anguish that he had endured, tracking her through malarial jungles and across mountains, had all concentrated to this moment. Yet now, looking into her scornful face, he did not recognize her. Her escape had changed her. Her sun-streaked hair and burnished features were not those of the girl he had reared. And the vacuum in his chest that he had expected her to fill only swelled tighter against his ribs.

"You are mad," he said then, and his hands unclenched as a flush of pity tempered his rage. "The lustings of flesh have shaken you, Lucinda. You are not the daughter I knew."

"I am not mad," she replied hotly. "You are mad to pull asunder husband and wife."

"Hope now is my only delight, daughter." He extended an open hand to touch her cheek, but she pulled away. "I can only hope that time will heal your madness. For surely you have lost your wits to throw yourself away on a pirate and a pirate's life of hardship. You are not meant by heaven or precedent to live in the wilderness. What you think love is the ambition of lust, an inward fury that has blasted your reason."

"And the child that I carry?" she demanded. "Will you pretend that my child is madness?"

"Wisdom must bear what our flesh cannot banish. You will have the child in England."

"No!" she said, furiously. "I will have this child with my husband, the man I married before God. You have no right to separate us."

"Daughter," he said in a gasp of sorrow. "You will bless me for saving you when you are right again." He turned away from the stiff face that condemned him. "We leave on the morrow."

"I will not!" she shouted after him. "I will kill myself first!"

He did not look back, but her threat held her face before him, and he imagined her hanged by the neck, curled about poison in a puddle of vomit, dashed among rocks . . . he put a hand to his damp brow. She would have to be watched closely until she recovered from her madness. And she would recover. He needed that faith. Or she would be better dead — and he could not bear that. At least Providence had delivered her into his hands, and fate had granted him the term of her pregnancy to heal her of her imbalance. He knew her well enough to believe she would not kill her child, and he prayed that, despite her threat, despite his great fear that she might never recover, she would grant him an heir to bless his pitiless life.

Jaki and Kota were strapped to wagon wheels in the plaza before the palace and tilted on posts to face the sun. Kota called words of encouragement to the sorcerer, but Jaki was only half conscious and did not respond. Soon the heat silenced Kota, and the thought of death shut him in behind his glared eyes.

When Jaki came to, the sun had climbed down the sky, and he was shivering. Kota called for him, and he turned his head but could not find his companion. Nausea pulled his eyes shut, and he was almost torn apart by a fit of vomiting.

The seizure spun him into a trance, and he thought he saw Pieter Gefjon's broad body gliding toward him among blue shafts of fire. He came straight for him, hatless but dressed in ruff and knee breeches. Vibrations of strength ushered about him like heat waves.

Jaki fought the great weariness of the poison to reach for him, and the tongs binding his wrists gnashed his flesh. "Father!" he called, and the effort broke the vision and he saw William Quarles standing before him in the gloaming.

"Father?" Quarles echoed, derisively. "You think I am your father because my daughter has taken you for her demon lover?" He spat and stepped closer to gaze more keenly into the face of the creature that had ruined his life. His hands lusted to attack his throat and squeeze the life from him, but he restrained himself. He wanted to see this face alive, to remember it clearly so he would know it when he saw it again in the face of his grandchild. He put his hands to the sides of the pirate's face and peered into the blackly dilated eyes. "You are going to die. But you will be blessed when I am done with you, for you will be dead — while I must live in the corruption you have made of my life. And so I will kill you slowly, that you may taste some of the suffering you have inflicted on me."

From under his doublet, he removed the Bible cover that he had carried since Selangor and held it before the pirate's eyes. "You remember this. Your father's tree is here." Quarles smiled coldly to see the recognition in the monster's eyes. "Yes, you do remember. Then you recall what is inscribed in here. You must then know that *I* am the lion of your final moment, Jaki Gefjon. *I* guard my name, my honor, as hotly as any good man. Only death, and death alone, can guard the treasure of the Quarleses' reputation. And that is why I have chased you across the earth, plunderer."

Jaki's mouth worked to speak, but his voice would not comply. He wanted to explain that he loved Lucinda and their child, that his whole life had been a coming to love. His breath jumped from him in a grunt, and Quarles pushed the Bible cover against Jaki's face with such force that the boy's skull hit on the spoke behind him, and he passed out.

Quarles spat again and tucked the Bible's cover under his doublet.

Hanging beside Jaki, Kota watched, and his blood moldered to see the hate in Quarles's face. He shut his eyes softly and from far back in his mind began a death chant.

*

Deep in Mandu, within the maze of cobbled streets and gaunt stone houses of the city's most populous quarter, Dhup meandered. Earlier, after chanting sutras before the executed men under the south wall of the palace district, he had ambled off, with the thought that Mandu was a good place for him to take his leave of Jaki and his party. To continue any farther with them would take him south into the Deccan, away from the great plains of the north, the palm of the Buddha. But as he moved through the streets, he observed that he was being followed. A black-robed figure with a veiled face trailed him on the terraced avenues that led away from the palace. In the merchants' quarter, among the frantic mongers, Dhup tripped over a vendor's stool, slammed into a rickety stand piled too high with winter melons, and ducked under a wagon to escape the avalanche of fruit. He scurried on his belly under the packed carts in the jammed market square, startling monkeys and doves, and tumbled into the street among the bustling crowd far from the man trailing him.

Dhup was certain that the Subahdar had ordered him followed, and he began to make inquiries in the marketplace. Immediately he learned that the crucified men were not rebels against the Moghul Shah Jahan, as the Subahdar had claimed, but rather rebels against the pretenders Prince Dawar Bakhsh and Shahryar. Dhup assumed Hadi had lied to deceive the foreign travelers, and the monk decided he must return to the palace.

But that night, as Dhup made his way to the palace, he was jumped. Supporters of the new Moghul, determined to oust the rebellious prince, had watched him inquire about their dead comrades. When they learned that he had arrived with the Subahdar, a renowned advocate of the prince, they had concluded he was a spy for their enemies. They leaped at him as if he were a sturdy palace soldier, and he collapsed before them like windblown paper. The rebels and the monk crashed into a weaver who was bent over his loom, toppling the cane stand supporting the weaver's oil lamp. The spilled oil flashed into flame over a pile of raffia, and fire sheeted into the overhanging tapestries with the jubilant sigh of a loosed genie.

The screaming merchant struck at the rebels with his cording comb, and Dhup kicked over the burning baskets, hoping to smother the flames but instead scattering them in a fuming arc. Within minutes the brisk mountain winds had quickened the fire into a holocaust.

Across Mandu, the partisans who had been waiting for Shah Jahan's army to sweep into the city and depose the unfaithful prince mistook the firestorm for the beginning of that assault. Green fireworks splashed in the sky, the signal to the Moghul's supporters to rise up and bring down the evil prince. The soldiers on the battlements were stoned, roped, shot with arrows. Armories in every quarter were attacked and matchlocks distributed to the partisans who knew how to shoot. Brandishing the weapons, the partisans rallied the mob to storm the palace. At the court, Shah Jahan's agents exploded the prince's arsenal, and the blast collapsed the battlements along the north wall and rocked the granite pedestals of the building.

The spasm of earthquake shook Lucinda loose from her grief. She rose and hurried through a drizzle of crushed sandstone leaking from the seams in the ceiling to the veiled doorway of her chamber. Screams resounded from farther down the corridor, and gongs and shouts of alarm folded through each other from across the palace. She stuck her head out, expecting to face the guard posted at her door, but the corridor was empty.

Lucinda stepped across the marble hall to Maud's chamber as more explosions boomed from inside the palace. Bellowed orders and the clangor of steel could be heard amidst the dull rumbling of caving walls.

"Come away," Lucinda called. "We must escape."

"Escape?" Maud pulled on her leather slippers and scampered to the door. She looked down the empty corridor. "Which way shall we go?"

Lucinda took Maud's arm and they headed away from the commotion into the garden. Beyond the first lotus doorway, they found their guard lying on his back, his blouse black with blood from his slashed throat. Maud stifled a scream as Lucinda crouched over the dead man and unsheathed his curved dagger.

"That is where we came in," she whispered, pointing the blade at a dark portal beyond the persimmon tree. They paused in the doorway, listening to the screams and the cracking of musketfire. Lucinda edged into the blackness, feeling along the wall until she saw the gray shine of night in the shape of an oval window. Through it she could see black-robed figures flitting across the plaza, sprinting to the stairs that mounted to the palace. The battle was in the front chamber just below where they stood.

"Lucinda," Maud whimpered, and pointed to the far end of the plaza were Jaki and Kota were bound.

Lucinda turned back into the darkness, toward the sound of the clashing swords behind them. A curved stairway dropped deeper into the gloom at their feet, and they hurried down into the reception garden where they had been taken prisoner. Warriors whirled like shadows among the potted trees, their scimitars flashing in the dark. Three guards lay dead on the steps of the gazebo. Gunfire flared from the balcony rooms, and in the glare they spotted the open bronze doors that led to the portico above the plaza.

Lucinda squeezed Maud's hand reassuringly, and whispered, "Stay with me." Then she bolted. At the open doors, they slowed to step over fallen bodies. A panel shattered beside their heads, and the explosion sent them flying down the broad steps toward the torchlit plaza. As they ran, they could see flames lapping from palace rooms and red shadows scuttering across the plaza. Saddled, riderless horses galloped in a panic across the courtyard, and musketfire flashed from the garrets. Everywhere men were being swatted to the ground and trampled, their cries stabbing from the clamor.

When the women finally reached the captives, Kota was alert, and he grunted with surprise at the sight of Maud clawing at the knot beside his wrist. Jaki stirred, awake but stupefied. A screaming man careened past like a wraith and was gone. Bitter smoke tumbled around them in a windshift as Lucinda bent over her dagger and began sawing at the leather binding Jaki's ankle.

Maud cried out and grabbed Lucinda by her shoulder. She glanced up at the riot of beasts and men. From the midst of the melee strode William Quarles, his cutlass in hand.

From his window, Quarles had seen the first swarm of rioters ascend the stairs to the tree-flanked boulevard of the palace. Immediately, he had recognized that the attack was coordinated and that internal subversion was certain. He had snatched his saber and charged from the room to get his daughter. By the time he had reached Lucinda's chamber, his daughter had crossed the plaza.

Now she lunged upright at the sight of him. He advanced on her, shouting. "Lucinda! Put the knife aside!"

She stood hard, breathing fast through her mouth. Her knife jerked before the thundering command of her father, but she did not relent. She braced herself, her face bent with wrath, and raised her dagger.

This was what Dhup saw as he ascended the last of the terrace steps and staggered onto the boulevard. He had been carried east with the rioters to the palace steps, and he acted at once to avert murder. Dhup weaved among the wandering animals and came up behind Quarles, a sash from his robe looped in his hand. Shrieking, he pounced on the Englishman's back, snagged his knife hand with the sash, and jerked it behind him.

Quarles clawed at his back with his free hand, and Dhup hooked that, too, in the sash, pulling it tight about Quarles's wrists and dropping him to his knees. The monk unclasped a cloth belt from under his robe and swiftly lashed together Quarles's ankles.

Lucinda stepped back in amazement before her father's bellows. While Dhup grabbed for the reins of riderless horses ambling aimlessly on the boulevard, Lucinda cut loose Kota, and he helped her unbind Jaki. Together they secured him belly down on a horse's saddle and mounted the other horses Dhup had steadied. Dhup trotted to the lead, holding the reins of Jaki's horse. Lucinda turned in her saddle and looked back at her father, her face triumphant but not gloating. Quarles's enraged screams pursued them to the south gates at the end of the boulevard. But Quarles suddenly fell silent along with the rest of the rioters when the gates lurched open and they saw, with alarm, that Shah Jahan's army was nowhere in sight.

The horses budged through the confused crowd and into the night. They followed the road by which they had come the day before, descending with the trail into deeper darkness. When Mandu was a slim glow in the sky behind them, they paused and unstrapped Jaki. He was stunned, yet cogent enough to recognize where they were. He pulled Kota close and instructed him to retrieve Wyvern and the diamonds at the pyramid marker in the willow flats.

"We have lost everything because I did not heed you." Lucinda wept, stroking the hair from Jaki's eyes and leaning her forehead against his temple. "Do not die, true child."

"He will not die," Dhup promised. "Fate frees a man to serve life."

"Lah." Kota stepped from the darkness and handed the folded Wyvern to Jaki.

With bruised hands, he opened it to expose the diamond chunks. "Mountains' tears," he muttered in a smoky voice, and offered them to Lucinda.

She accepted the diamonds with wet eyes. "Yes, these belong to us now." She clutched Wyvern and the diamonds to her heart. "They were wept for us."

Rain met them in the pass through the mountains, but by the next morning they had found their way to a sunny meadow where the horses could graze and Maud and Dhup could gather vegetables and stream water for soup. Dhup found a hive; Kota smoked it, and they ate honeycombs and dandelion soup. They bathed in the stream and dried themselves in the warm grass.

The food revived Jaki, and Lucinda sat with him, fretting like a mother. She cradled his head in her arms, trying to let go of the fright of their escape.

"You were right all along," she said, needing to atone for her misplaced trust in the Subahdar. "You predicted our grief, but I would not listen. Only when I lost you, true child — only then did I see the horror of my greed."

"You are not to blame." Jaki soothed her. "All would be well if your father would let us be."

"I was too like him in my willfulness. He thinks me mad! I believe he would kill me before he would let us be free together."

"He will never have that chance again," Jaki vowed.

"From hence, we will strive together, always." She pressed her face to his chest. "I will heed your subtle senses."

"And I your reason." He smiled at her and touched her frown. "Our first wedding was in water. Now we have been married in fire. And though that fire consumed all we earned on the caravan, the price was small."

"You still have your diamonds," she said, "and I have these." From her dress pocket, she produced a wad of paper bills. "The flying money. Father never knew I had it."

"Diamonds and money." Jaki laughed, opening his arms to the wild peaks. "And a whole world to spend them in!"

They resumed their flight from Mandu refreshed, exhilarated to be alive. Spurred by the fear that patrols had been sent to hunt for them, they traveled quickly and did not stop again until they made camp late that afternoon on a high pasture overlooking a broad, slow river.

"The Narbada," Dhup said. He was sitting on a sedgy hillock a thousand feet above the dense forest of the riverbank. Behind him, the horses were browsing, Lucinda and Maud were gathering edible grasses, and Kota was building a fire. The scene flushed Jaki with a warmth he had not felt since his days aboard *Silenos.* "Tomorrow we will part there." Dhup cracked two wild walnuts together in his palm and threw the shells over the edge. "You will follow the river to your destiny. It is a holy river, second only to the sacred Ganges. You will see many shrines and pilgrims, and they will help if you need them. The Narbada flows west and empties into the sea two hundred and more miles from here. You are capable. Your way will become clear from there."

"And you?" Jaki asked, accepting two wings of walnut meat.

Dhup circled his hand in the air. "I must return to Mandu. I participated in setting the city afire. I must see what I can do to set things aright."

Jaki nodded, though he did not understand. "Who are you — really?"

Dhup's smile drew tight over his crooked teeth. "I am what you see: a monk who minds the noble truths."

Jaki scrutinized the bronze-skinned man beside him. Nothing extraordinary offered itself. The man was clumsy, thin limbed, almost weak. "In Mandu you saved our lives. How did you know —"

Dhup interrupted with a little wave. "You were in my care. You have been in my care since Burma."

"Then you were not drowning in the jungle river when I dove in to save you."

"No."

Jaki's eyebrows flinched with bafflement. "But why?"

"How else could I have saved you? You were drowning in your losses."

Jaki's perplexed squint relented, and he took the monk's hand. "How can we repay you?"

Dhup's smile showed his jammed teeth. "Do secret good."

On the switchbacking trail down into the river gorge, a woman's corpse lay in the middle of the road. As the horses approached, crows swirled from the dead woman and sailed into the shadows of a cinnamon grove. The woman stared with empty sockets at the riders, her stiff arms stretched out beseechingly in the dirt, her shriveled flesh clinging to her bones like seaweed. Dhup immediately dismounted and left his reins to trail while he knelt beside the corpse and began chanting.

Jaki led the others around the monk and the shrunken body in its nest of black rags, and helped them to dismount around the next bend and start a fire for the noon meal. Then he returned to help Dhup bury the woman. They gouged a grave with flat rocks, and Dhup chanted as they covered the body with soil and the bough of a camphor tree.

Kota believed the corpse was a grim portent. He would not eat the tuber Jaki had found while digging the grave, and then, irritable from hunger, he sulked when no one would heed his pleas to return to the meadows and find another path down to the river. Dhup wagged a finger at him. "The world is a corpse. There is no getting around it."

Late in the afternoon, when the sun was a fiery crown in the trees, they reached the river. Powder-blue cranes stalked among the water lettuce on spidery legs, and farther out the brown current glinted with white plovers. Reed and mud shanties littered a rocky spit a half mile away, their cooking fires smudging the wind. Kota, his stomach brambly with hunger, spurred his steed to a gallop, and the others followed with laughing shouts.

The villagers marveled at their blond visitors, and the travelers slept that night on reed pallets in the best hut. In the hour before the sun rose, they sat with the village leaders and bargained their way onto the river. In exchange for the five horses, the fishing village gave their largest raft — a square, thatch-roofed float of vine-lashed timber and bamboo — and agreed to stock it with a basketful of green mangoes, three sacks of rice, and twine and hooks for fishing.

At first light, Jaki and Lucinda sat with Dhup while he chanted his morning sutras. Afterward, he embraced each of his comrades and then untied the raft's tether from the tongue tree, pressed his palms together, and bowed. They floated away under a sunrise brown as wine, and Jaki gazed at the monk watching them until a bend in the river parted them forever. An ominous misery tainted him, and he feared that Kota's warning about the corpse on the road had perhaps been valid somehow, that its evil was not yet exhausted.

His foreboding was confirmed when Maud emerged from the bamboo cabin an hour later, her face drawn, and announced to him that Lucinda was bleeding.

Though the day was hot, she was shivering. The blood had first appeared two days before, just after their hard ride from Mandu, but it had been only a spotting, and Lucinda had prayed that it would abate. On the river, cramps began and the flow thickened. Now, lying with her legs propped on rice sacks, she cursed Hadi, Fletcher, and her father, and prayed for the life of her child.

They tied off at the bank, and Kota boiled water while Jaki and Maud foraged for viburnum leaves, barberry roots, and clumps of sphagnum moss to make styptic sponges. But the bleeding was too profuse. Lucinda believed the baby was lost with her fortune. The fists of pain pummeling her from inside were the rage at her betrayal by her father. In Mandu she had lost her chance to be her own provider, to refute her father's mastery of her by making her own way in the world. Without her fortune, she was as all women were, as she had always been — an unnecessary embellishment. She hung from her father's will and now she would hang from her husband's — and, as much as she loved him, that galled her. When the glisteny clot that was her baby slid from her threaded with veins and maroon as a liver, she felt all the melancholy she could ever feel for herself or the world.

Jaki wrapped the fetus in a palm leaf, built a pyre of silver deadwood on the mudbank, and watched the flames shake the unborn child to blue smoke. The smoke curved in the wind and rustled to the shape of a child, bringing Jaki to his knees in the mud with awe. He watched the childshape rise through the noonlight and begin to fill the emptiness as it flowed into the other world. The specter of his descendant smiled at him, it seemed, its arms clutching at the emptiness, reaching for him. He smiled back, sadly, his arms rising toward the ghostly child, and his fingertips went cold, touched by the presence in the grasp of departure. Did he imagine or actually hear a young voice say, "I belong to you. I have never left"?

Maud heated the pebble of opium Jaki had kept with his diamonds since Mirzapur, mixed it with mashed figs, and fed it to Lucinda to allay the pain of her convulsed womb. By the time Jaki returned from the pyre, his wife was glassy-eyed, muttering about her father killing her child.

Tears came then. He pulled Lucinda into his arms, and they held each other. "I saw the child-spirit, Lucinda. It told me it belongs to us. It said it is still with us." Jaki stroked her hair. "We will have another child."

He believed that, Lucinda saw in the glow of his face. And in that moment, her blood drubbed with opium, she saw deep into him, saw his heartsore need for her, for her love, for all that she could give to fill the void of *his* loss. They were both orphaned, she understood then, and she wept again, pressing her fingers to his face and feeling the irreversible sorrows of their lives. They were vanishing together; even as they hugged, they were vanishing, as everything under the astral stare they called a sky was vanishing. He was right. He had been right in Mirzapur about the treachery of the Subahdar — he had even been right in Burma to walk into the jungle and face the tiger, face the emptiness dissolving the future.

"No," Jaki said in a hushed voice, and she realized she had been ranting aloud. "You were right to wait then. I was wrong, and I learned to trust you. Until that day I followed you out of duty. Since then, I have followed with respect."

"But I was wrong about Hadi. Without Dhup, we would have been killed."

He quieted her with a hand to her brow. *Yes,* he thought, *Mandu has shown us the limits of trust.* But he did not say that. She looked haggard. In the many months of their travels, her hands had toughened, leaving her nails broken-mooned, and her face, without its powders and paints, was innocent as a boy's, freckled from the sun and hollower of cheek. He loved her all the more, and his heart was spelled with the pain she had endured to be with him. He had to overcome the nightmare of their homelessness before it was too late, and make a place for them in the world where they could live their vanishing together and leave behind children.

Weeks later, deep in the night, the wanderers reached the sea. Kota and Jaki moored in a covert of tule grass opposite a splash of lights that gleamed in the dark river's mouth like a casket of spilled jewels. Lucinda and Maud wanted to sleep, but Jaki was eager to investigate the city shining on the far shore. Leaving Kota to guard the raft, he wandered into the dark.

As the stars dimmed, he returned rowing a canoe of treebark. Behind him, silver clouds crisscrossed the gray sky above the sea. He drank some tea with Kota, and the women heard his excited voice and emerged from the cabin, rubbing sleep from their eyes. "We will have an ocean-worthy vessel in two days," he said in greeting. "And a crew to man her."

Kota poured more tea, and they sat on the raft's bulwark, lifting their faces from the steam to smell the heat of the river quarreling with the cool sea. "I spent most of our fishhooks to rent a canoe from a man I found torch fishing, and I rowed into the city he called Bharoch.

In the harbor I met drunken Portuguese sailors who called the city Broach. It's an open port — Spaniards, Portuguese, Dutch, and English all have houses and slips. And no one fights. The old Moghul had them agree to a truce while in port. Now they are waiting for the new Moghul to award trading rights to the companies of his choice."

"I see no big ships, lah." Kota pointed across the river.

"Tomorrow a Dutch carrack will arrive," Jaki said with a confident smile. "I overheard sailors in a barge tavern say that the Portuguese were alerted by smoke signal from their scouts on the north coast of Gujarat. *Amaranth* appeared off Porbandar yesterday and will make port here tomorrow night. She's three hundred tons, with light armament, five or six twelve-pounders, and the usual Dutch flummery and low draft."

"Slow, lah. What cargo?"

"She's out of Aden. An African slave ship. Her cargo is meant for the Portuguese, which is why they know so much about her. They need laborers to work their estates in Goa to the south, and they are trading diamonds from their mines to the north. The arrangement is perfect."

"What do you mean?" Lucinda asked, looking across the river to the immense tidewall and the long wooden warehouses above the revetment. Company banners in bold colors and broad canvas were stretched on bamboo stanchions and posted before each docking berth.

"Are we not Dutch agents?" Jaki said. "Today you will introduce yourself to the Dutch factor."

"Dressed in rags?" Lucinda asked.

"You and Maud will get new clothes. We will trade the raft."

Lucinda's eyes danced as she opened her waist pouch and removed a roll of paper twined with vine. "The flying money," she grinned. "From the Chinese merchant in Sarnath. If we can find a Chinese merchant here, we can have clothes, food, even gold."

Jaki's face brightened, and he kissed his wife. "Just what we need. You see, it is said the Europeans in Broach are all sick and sweating blood."

"The red flux," Maud gasped.

"Yes, so it must be. The malignant spirits are in the water, and they drink it without the ritual fire that sets the evil free. Many have died. The rest are weak. I figure the crew on the *Amaranth* will be famished as well. They have not eaten good food in weeks. And that will be our weapon. A feast!"

Lucinda's face was dark. "You mean to lure the Dutch crew from their ship with food —"

"And while they dine, we take *Amaranth* for our own," Jaki completed, triumphantly.

"What of the slaves?" Maud asked.

"They will be our crew."

"It is a mad idea." Lucinda sighed. "Mad enough that it may in truth succeed."

After these weeks on the river, the four travelers shared understanding deeper than words. Lucinda and Maud decried any use of violence, but they had learned from Mandu to let Jaki and Kota do what they could not do for themselves. The men, for their part, had not forgotten the tiger in Burma, and they remembered from Lucinda's chess game that, more often than not, luring the enemy was far better than attacking. With the resolve of the inevitable, all four of them embraced Jaki's plan and set about completing it.

They poled their raft across the river, left the canoe with a fisherman on a reedy crannog near the wharves, and traded the raft for gold. They found a Chinese merchant in a riverside warehouse fronted with stone lions. He scowled when he saw the flying money, yet he honored his countryman's calligraphy and exchanged each bill in gold coin.

That afternoon, properly attired in new European clothes, the travelers rented palanquins and toured the European cantonment, seeking an adequate hall for their scheme. The inn they chose was situated on the hill overlooking the harbor and featured a large windowless gallery. Once the kitchen services had been secured from the happily startled owner, Kota set out with the cook for the market to purchase food. Meanwhile, Jaki began preparing the gallery and Lucinda and Maud took a palanquin to the house of the Dutch factor.

The Dutch Company house was shuttered against the red flux, and Maud had to knock a long while before the door was opened. The flux had killed the factor a week earlier, and his secretary had assumed his functions. The weary man was overjoyed to meet hale Europeans, young women at that, and he bade them to tell their story.

"We did not all of us escape the flux," Lucinda said, placing a carved cedar box she had brought as a gift on the table. She opened the box, revealing the sheaf of trade bills from the caravan. The secretary was delighted to learn of the profits she had earned for the company and which, she told him, the Moghul Shah Jahan was holding for them. "All of those silks and rare woods mean nothing to me now that my husband is dead," she told him, relating how Jaki had died of fever during their river journey. "We, too, have suffered from the flux. But now that we have survived to reach this port, we will give thanks to God with a feast. We have hired a large hall not far from here, and we will have every kind of delicacy we can procure from the harbor merchants. Will you join us tomorrow night?" Once she had the factor's exuberant acceptance, she added, "The whole town is talking about the carrack due tomorrow. As I mentioned, my father is a sea captain, and I know too well the travails of the sea. Please extend our invitation to the captain and officers of the *Amaranth.* While the crew has the pleasures of shore leave, their superiors are too often without comfort. I would like to honor them." The factor gave his hearty promise, and Lucinda and Maud left him cheerfully leafing through the trade bills.

Back at the inn, the women found Jaki examining the doors to the gallery. "Lisbon oak." Jaki knocked on a panel, and the door resounded thickly. "They are strong. And once we wedge them, they will hold our drunken guests for a spell."

Kota returned with a wagonload of vegetables and animals and joined Jaki in the gallery. They fit wedges Jaki had fashioned under each of the two doors. Kota shook the doors and felt their strength. "Not enough."

Jaki smiled. "This is only the first door. Come." He led Kota outside and showed him crates of bamboo segments. "The Indians call them *charkhi,* used to control their elephants in battle. The Chinese ward off demons with them. The merchant who took the flying money says these will raise dragons."

Kota pulled the cap from one bamboo cylinder and poured out thick-grained gunpowder. The heavy lines of his face hoisted a smile. "Fire-works. Lah."

They slept that night in the gallery and spent most of the following day arranging the banquet hall and supervising the innkeeper's preparation of the meal. Outside in the yard, under the bougainvillea shrubs and over the tufted swards, Jaki and Kota strung the *charkhi.*

When the harbor bell rang the arrival of the slave ship, Jaki had already spotted it from the roof. With a spyglass he had purchased from the Chinese, he watched it come into port. *Amaranth* rode easily at anchor a quarter mile from shore behind the black tidewall that jutted farthest into the estuary and held back the silt. The path along the tidewall out to the ship was as crowded with people as the waters around the ship were with small boats. Through his spyglass, Jaki saw merchants waving their goods, the Dutch secretary surrounded by musketmen in the tan uniforms of the Dutch Company, and the scurvy-blotched crew disembarking.

"The Dutch will be here soon," Jaki called as he climbed down from his perch. "One last check to make certain all is ready — and then Kota and I will be off to the dock. You know what to do."

"Unless the Butterboxes qualm at feasting in a shut room," Maud said. "How can we hold thirty men in here?"

"The Dutch are as afraid of the flux as any European," Jaki said, leading them to the gallery. "Just be sure to remind them that a windowless chamber is the safest place in India to dine."

Kota sniffed the aromas of the braised capon and stewing mutton, and he showed his purple teeth. "Good food, lah. Hungry stomach louder than fearful heart. Not worry."

They stood at the doorway and appraised their two days' work: in the radiant lanternlight, the tapestries' keen colors were a festive backdrop for the long banquet table laden with chappati, steaming biryani rice, bowls of fruit, tankards of arrack, and an empty centerplace where the lamb and capon would be served.

Jaki turned to go, and Lucinda grabbed his arm. He countered the fear he saw in her face with a quick smile. "We cannot fail," he said with certainty. "We are working together."

"If anything happens to you —"

"If we are not back here before the last course," he repeated, more for his peace than for hers, "politely excuse yourselves and go immediately to the fisherman at the harbor bazaar who bought our raft. Pay him with the gold you have left, and he will take you both to Surat. It's less than twenty miles south of here. You have the diamonds." He placed his hand against her bodice pocket and felt the rocks there. Before she could speak again, he looked to Kota and Maud. "You won't have to use them. Our plan will carry us." Lucinda hugged him, and Maud watched dolefully. "And be of cheerful countenance. Our guests must feel wanted." He nodded for Kota to leave, kissed his wife, and backed out the door.

The tang of the sea wind cleared Jaki's head as he walked around to the kitchen to pick up the twenty-pound sack of rice he had set aside earlier. In the yard beside the inn, they checked the array of fireworks, carefully noting where the fuses were under the shrubs. Jaki tucked a flintstriker in his doublet under the Indian caftan he had put on. Then they clicked the blades of their hand knives together. "We cannot fail," Jaki said in Malay.

With a gray turban covering his ash-blond hair, no one took particular notice of Jaki in the falling darkness, and he and Kota merged with the crowd of Indians who were shoved aside as the Dutch secretary's carriage with the ship's officers inside rolled past, followed by the troops of laughing crewmen.

The canoe that Jaki had left with a fisherman was waiting for them. They paid him with the bag of rice and rowed out toward the big ship. Many small ships bobbed about *Amaranth,* their crews astonished by her size and inspecting her swollen hull grain and huge anchor chain. No one singled out the canoe with its two scarfed men. Kota spotted an open gunport facing the breakwater, and Jaki guided the canoe between the giant hull and the black stone tidewall.

Neither bothered to secure the canoe when they grabbed on to the splintery hull and began to scale it. They both knew that either this ship would be theirs within the hour or they would need no vessel of any kind. The tidewall hid them from view up to the gunports, and there they crawled through the open port they had spotted from the canoe.

The stink was hot and sharp, and Jaki had to gnash his teeth to keep from gagging. Kota checked the low-ceilinged gun room and found no one. In the gangway, the groans of the slaves rose from below with a fetor of feces and corpses. Jaki jerked his thumb topside, and they took separate gangways to the upper deck.

Jaki emerged under the quarterdeck. From there he could see the watch on the forecastle and on the main deck facing the tidewall. Kota's squat shadow appeared on the main deck beside the bell. He signed to Jaki that there was a guard behind him on the quarterdeck, and Jaki signaled him about the forecastle guard. From his doublet, Jaki removed a velvet wallet stuck with poison thorns, each thorn meticulously threaded to a spool of cotton fiber. He fit a thorn into the reed pipe he carried in his turban. The feel of the ship breathing beneath him revived memories of his years on the boards, reeving rope high on the main mast, sliding along the decks on a rolling sea, dangling like a star from the crosstrees. He rose with the sway of his bones, his muscles twisting to the tilt of the deck, and he sidled backward up the steps to the quarterdeck.

The guard leaning on the taffrail, watching the milling crowd below, jerked upright with the needling pain at the side of his neck. Jaki had yanked the thorn free with the thread attached to it, and when the guard slapped his flesh, nothing was there. A biting insect, he thought. Jaki waited hunched behind the binnacle until the poison began its work. Finally the watch leaned heavily against the rail and slumped.

Kota, relying only on his dagger, had already killed the watch on the forecastle and, like Jaki, propped the body at its station. They converged on the last deck watch, who guarded the gangway onto the tidewall. Jaki struck the guard in the throat with the dart. When the man staggered as if hit on the head, Kota rushed to him and tripped him onto his dagger. They sat the dead man against the chainwale so he was visible from the tidewall and hurried for the hold.

The malodor of rotted flesh was a glaze in the chutes of the companionways, slick as the air of hell, and the two men descended with clenched jaws. Moans and feeble voices shifted in the dark. Kota found an oil lantern hanging from a rafter, and Jaki lit it with the flintstriker. In the papery glow, they gasped to see men dark as soil chained to the floors and shackled to the walls for as far as the lanternlight reached. The sparks of eyes winced at them, and Jaki shuffled forward among them.

Another light flapped from across the deck as a fourth guard stepped up through the gangway to the orlop deck. The bullish man in sailor's trousers and leather vest bellowed in Dutch, hung his lantern from a rafter, and unwound the whip hooked to his belt. He surged forward, and the first snap of the whip cut Kota across his jaw and flung him backward against the stairs.

Jaki slammed the lantern onto a step, dousing himself in darkness, and ducked aside as the whip snapped again where he had been standing. He tripped over the body of a slave, collapsed to his face, and the whip lashed across his back, slashing like a razor and rending his caftan. Jaki bounced to his feet with the pain and dove for the guard. The Dutchman drew a parang. Jaki pulled short and had to cover his face with his arms as the whip swiped at him again. The pain tore his sleeves away, and he felt blood run to his elbows.

The slaves were shouting now, and Jaki prayed there were no other guards aboard. The whip lashed again, caught Jaki's knife hand, and ripped the dagger from his grip. He dashed for it, and the whip bit his thigh and dropped him flat. His fingers curled on the dagger, and he writhed to avoid the downsweeping parang, which shattered the plank behind his head. Jaki struck with his knife, catching the guard's swordarm. The Dutchman yowled and dropped his weapon.

Kota, back on his feet, saw the parang stuck in the deck and bounded for it. The whip garroted him — and Jaki seized the leather lash, pulled himself along it, and drove his dagger into the guard's chest.

Jaki searched the charred faces of the slaves for a leader. He found three men who were not cheering, simply watching. He knelt before them and shook their chains. They pointed to the post of the mainmast, and Jaki retrieved the keys from there. He freed a dozen men who seemed to have the clarity and strength he would need to get the ship out of the harbor. The black men, naked but for loincloths and grimed in their own feces, stood up and staggered like crones. They signed that the others should be freed, but Jaki shook his head and with his hands made them understand the boat had to return to sea first. Reluctantly, the enfeebled black men agreed and quieted the frenzied slaves.

Jaki guided them up the companionway to the top deck and showed them the dead guards. With Kota's help he communicated that the officers and crew were ashore. "Stay with them," Jaki told Kota. "And try to make the Africans understand what we have to do to raise anchor. See if there are any fit enough to climb the masts. I'm going for the women."

Jaki removed his torn caftan, revealing the doublet and breeches of a gentleman, smoothed back his hair, and walked down the gangway from the ship to the tidewall. The crowd stood aside as if he were a Dutchman, and he hurried through them and jogged up the cobbled wharf street toward the inn on the hill.

The feast was going well when Jaki arrived. The factor's secretary was at one end of the banquet table, the captain at the other, and the officers crowded around it raising their tankards in toast while the crew ranged through the gallery, gorging themselves on the food that Maud and the unsuspecting innkeeper were serving from trays. Jaki caught

Maud's eye from the doorway, and she signaled Lucinda, who was sitting beside the secretary. With a courteous smile, she excused herself, chatted briefly with an officer, nodded to the crewmen she passed, and exited the room with Maud.

Lucinda and Maud took one door and Jaki the other, and they swiftly closed the room. The laughing and happy yelling went on even as they fit the wedges into place, and only as they fled down the stairs did they hear the first shout of alarm when someone tried the door and it would not budge. The doors rattled, the plank held firm, and the festive noise in the gallery became angry cries. As Jaki located the fuses to the *charkhi,* they heard the crashing of trays as the banquet table was cleared and lifted to be used as a battering ram. The first blows of the table against the doors were muffled by the sudden explosions of the *charkhi.*

Following Jaki, Lucinda and Maud sprinted down the hill toward the wharf. Behind them, the night erupted into flowers of fire, white and red explosions, and the sirens of rocket flares. People from the surrounding houses emerged, and the crowd at the wharves turned and began to climb the hill toward the splashing flames.

At the gangway to the ship, Jaki looked back and saw the inn lit eerily by garlands of silver fire, the mob so dense the Dutchmen would have trouble leaving the building.

The freed slaves slipped the moorings as Jaki and the women ran aboard. Kota had sent three men up into the masts already and had deployed eight at the anchor wynch. As they had planned, Lucinda took the helm, Maud at her side to help her handle the whipstaff, while Jaki and Kota climbed up the shrouds and began to unfurl canvas.

The wind was low and steady from over the grasslands, and the sails filled quickly and tugged the big ship into the river's current. The tide was ebbing, the small boats peeled aside, and the open sea climbed before them.

From the spars, Jaki looked back and watched the smoke from the *charkhi* dissolving in the moonlight. The Dutchmen were just breaking through the crowd and scrambling to the wharf's edge to see their ship sailing away. Jaki crossed among the spars, shifting canvas, until the ship glided through the moonslick estuary and gained the seaway.

Lucinda was weeping at the whipstaff. When Jaki stepped onto the quarterdeck, she relinquished the helm to Maud and clutched at him. "We're free, and I am truly a brigand now," she sobbed, and he held her to him.

"And so are the three hundred men with us," Jaki said into her hair, his heart thudding with energy. "All of us brigands and free! We'll tack north from here. In Karachi or Gwadar we'll sell the diamonds to buy more boats so these Africans can sail like men." He reached out and put an arm around Maud, too. "We are free because we strove together."

"Good-by, India," Maud called to the retreating lights of Bharoch. "Good-by, land. *Amaranth* is our home now."

"Not *Amaranth,*" Lucinda said. "We should christen her with a new name."

"I have just the name for our first ship," Jaki said, his eyes flashing. "In Burma you once said a thing that hurt me, that I have carried in my heart since. But as my heart has changed and I have learned to love you more, the hurt has become respect. Let us call this ship *Sleeping with Satan.*"

Maud huffed with alarm, but Lucinda laughed. "Yes, I said that. That was how it was with you when you wore your diamonds brazenly and shared your sorcery with peasants. Anger burned hotly between us then." The darkness circled them, and she said quietly, "Our pain has become our bond, true child. Let this ship be called *Sleeping with Satan.*"

The Moon Is a Horn We Blow with Our Last Breath

Later, when Adam wondered how light
had been created, God gave him two stones
— of Darkness and of the Shadow of Death —
which he struck together. Fire issued
from them. "Thus it was done," said God.

— MIDRASH TEHILLIM

WIND SIZZLED across the grasslands under the tangled stars, and William Quarles lay on his back in his tent, his mind retracing the miles he had traveled. His hands were crossed atop his chest, his fingers locked in the tiger's beard he wore over his shoulders. Where was Lucinda? He had traveled the road to Surat emptying his coffers among the Rajput chieftains, expecting them to use their forces to help snare Lucinda and Jaki. But the anarchy he had left behind in Mandu rode ahead of him: marauding gangs loyal to the new Moghul swarmed the districts, challenging every rajah's authority and provoking uprisings. All of the search parties that he had meticulously organized dissolved quickly, and he reached Surat without having caught even a rumor of his daughter.

Quarles ignored the cold spanglings of malaria that occupied his body and lay staring through the open flap of his tent, pondering where to turn next. He had hired porters and skilled hunters to accompany him into the cattle savannah along the Tapti River east of Surat. He had read Lucinda's journal, and he knew that she was determined to complete her business agreement with the Dutch. The goods she had earned on her caravan were still in Mandu, and her only hope of claiming them was to appeal to the new Moghul through the Dutch factor in Surat. The Tapti was the most direct route to the port city.

What robbed Quarles of sleep was the knowledge that the pirate still had diamonds. Boeck had seen them and said they were big as radishes.

The Subahdar had seen them, too — as well as the monstrous Wyvern colors — but the banner and the diamonds had been missing from the pirate's sack. The mystery of their disappearance troubled Quarles with visions of his daughter suckling her baby in the shadow of the dragon flag while her pirate lover commanded a frigate bought from the Portuguese with his diamonds.

Hoofbeats mumbled under the wind, and Quarles sat up and crawled out of his tent, cursing the inner cold that jarred his muscles. He put on his hat and boots, seized the saber, and trudged through the tall grass to the trail that led from Surat. Most of the camp followed him.

The lead horsemen pulled aside at the sight of Quarles, and the gharry they were leading rolled to a stop. The door opened, and a pallid, sunken face under a broad hat swam into the fluttery torchlight. Quarles recognized the English factor from whom he had learned of Lucinda's disappearance a year earlier in Bantam and who had met him in Dagon after his horrific journey up the Irrawaddy. The factor frowned. "William, what are you doing out here on the moors? I had to learn from the Dutch where you were. Have you entirely abandoned England along with your good sense?"

"Sir," Quarles almost shouted with surprise, and removed his hat. He passed his saber to a porter and helped the elderly man from the carriage. "I am searching for my daughter. She eluded me in Mandu. I —"

"I know all about Mandu." With gingerly disdain the factor touched the tiger's beard hanging from Quarles's neck. "And this? Do you sleep with this native gear every night? You look like a frightful woolly-head." He gestured impatiently toward the camp, and the horsemen dismounted. Quarles saw that they were Rajput soldiers in billowy trousers and brocaded vests, with knives at their hips and flintlocks strapped to their backs. The soldiers led the way up to the camp, and the factor took Quarles's arm to steady himself in the dark. In an annoyed voice, he said, "I have received a full report from the porters who returned with you from Mandu. I would have preferred to learn of your failure from you directly."

"The weapons were delivered," Quarles replied with a flash of indignation. "I fulfilled my diplomatic mission."

"Have you not heard?" The factor stared piteously at Quarles. "Mandu has fallen to the new Moghul. The Subahdar and his prince have been put to death, and their heads were paraded on the road to Surat days after your return. Your mission was an utter failure. If you had reported to the British trademaster instead of hurrying off on your own you would have found this out."

"I did not think that you would be in Surat," Quarles said as they entered the camp. "I was intent on finding my daughter."

"Equally intent, I dare say, on avoiding the Admiralty's wrath." The factor motioned, and the Rajput soldiers set their torches in the earth, forming a circle in the cleared space where the camp's fire had collapsed to a ring of ash. The soldiers unfolded two canvas seats and placed them facing each other. The factor signed for Quarles to sit and lowered himself into the other chair. "William, your pursuit of your daughter is finished." From under his doublet the factor removed a flattened roll of parchment. "This is the Admiralty's order for your arrest."

Quarles stood, swept a harsh stare at the surrounding soldiers, and glowered at the old man. "You will take a corpse from this place."

"Sit down, William."

"I will not go freely."

"Sit down, I say."

Quarles sat, a malarial shiver defeating the fiery swell of his anger. "Is that why you are in Surat — and why you have hurried out here in the midst of the night — to take me defenseless?"

"I am in Surat for you," the factor acknowledged, and waved the arrest order. "This is but a copy, one of many that have been distributed to factors across Asia. I came to Surat from Dagon as soon as I received it. But not to arrest you, William." He tossed the parchment to Quarles. "I should not like to see you dragged in irons before the Admiralty court. After a session on the rack, you may be inclined to reveal things better kept secret. No, my friend. The Thieves' Church is responsible for your being here, and we will see that you elude capture until this unfortunate matter is resolved in your favor."

"But how can that ever be?" Quarles held the open parchment to the light. "I am here charged with *treason* for ignoring the Admiralty's direct command. Treason!" He hurled his hat to the ground and propped his head against his fist while he read on. "This also declares that I have been found guilty in absentia for the negligent destruction of *The Fateful Sisters*!" He looked to the factor. "These offenses will put my head to the block."

The factor agreed with a solemn nod. "Unless the charges are refuted, you will be deemed a traitor. Yet this very day there are lawyers in England laboring to clear your name. When the time is right, you will have to make an appearance before the Admiralty. To that end, you must return to England at once. Only there can the Thieves' Church properly defend you. This will be more difficult without the sop of a diplomatic tie to the Peacock Throne, but with your outstanding prior accomplishments, I am certain that eventually you will be exonerated."

"And my daughter? What is to become of her whilst I cower in England waiting for your lawyers to save my head?"

The factor lowered his face and stared at Quarles from under his spidery eyebrows. "William, do you not yet see? Your daughter has no love for you. She is a woman now, and she has fled you. You must relinquish her and act to save your own head."

"I will never relinquish her!" He swung his fists before him, his square knuckles white with resolve. "She is my life, my only heir. All I suffer, I endure for her."

"Just so. But she thinks otherwise, William, or she would not have fled from you so decisively in Mandu."

"She is awry. Her wits are muddled. I will not abandon her to her madness."

"*You* are mad if you continue to defy the Admiralty. The British factor in Surat has his own copy of this warrant for your arrest, and he will certainly pursue you. That is why I have come at this dark hour. You must flee before our fellow countrymen discover that you are here."

"Then I will bribe the Rajputs for papers of passage and journey up the Tapti. Lucinda must still be in the interior."

The factor plucked at his wispy chin hairs, making a decision. "Your daughter is no longer in India," he said. "She and her pirate cohort commandeered a Dutch slaver in Broach a fortnight past. They are now far at sea, bound for parts unknown."

"Broach?" Quarles rose, a trembly hand to his brow. "Then she came down the Narbada. Brassy. The Portuguese control that river."

"You regard our competitors too highly — and your daughter too lightly. Since the old Moghul died, all treaties are in question. To protect their interests, the Portuguese have moved south to Swally and Goa, and the Dutch want to replace them. Perhaps they will reconsider now that they have lost a fully loaded slave ship." The factor frowned to see Quarles pacing, the fingers of one hand tangled in his beard, the other clutching the tiger's pelt. "You should be proud of your daughter. She has taken a vessel from the finest navy in the world. Be proud of her and release her. You cannot pursue her any farther, for who knows where she will voyage now."

Quarles scowled at the factor. "I should be proud that my daughter is a pirate? Never. The pirate who stole her from me, he is responsible for seizing the Dutch ship. Of that, I am certain. Pym was right indeed to deem the boy worthy of fear. I should have feared him more when he was in my grasp and killed him then."

The factor rebuked him with a stern stare. "Sit, William. You speak with an arrant tongue."

"I will not sit," Quarles said with surprising enthusiasm. "I am already on my way. And this time I will not fail."

"On your way? Where? The world is far bigger than your arrogance."

"I will find them," Quarles insisted, not looking at the factor, his mind already at sea, remembering from his daughter's journal her ambition to reach the New World.

"How? You will be arrested in Surat."

"The Portuguese have ships in Swally. I have enough gold squared away for a frigate and a crew."

"Such talk will be your undoing. Your entire fortune will be spent for some worm-riven Portuguese timber and a crew no better than pirates. William —" The factor beseeched him with wide eyes. "You will become the very knave you despise in your daughter's heathen. You will be a fugitive, flying from port to port in pursuit of — what? A daughter who loves you not."

Quarles knelt before the factor. "You must not try to stop me," he said, and cast a glance at the soldiers.

"The Church of the Two Thieves owns no cure for madness. If you insist on throwing your life away, I can do nothing."

Quarles relaxed and stroked his grizzled beard. "There is a thing you may do for me." He bit his lip, steeling himself. "When you return to England, you can arrange for my estate in Devon to be sold. I will need the funds when I have recovered my daughter."

The factor blinked. "If you flee now, you can never return to England."

Quarles nodded. "I will use the funds to make a life for my family elsewhere. Will you do this for me?"

The factor hooded his eyes against Quarles's fanatic gaze. "I will need your authorization."

"Then let us prepare a draft now. I must be away by first light. My fate is already at sea."

Sunlight gleamed from the sea's facets, gulls bobbled on strings of wind, and *Sleeping with Satan* soared. At the crown of his kingdom, Jaki stood in the crosstrees, his arms open to heaven, and stared at clouds upon clouds rafting overhead.

The bright celestial fathoms enraptured Jaki, and he hung like a bug in the gaze of the spider, frail, strumming with hopeless passion. He would be free. Though the world itself was a cage of walls, he would be free. The sheets below him boasted of April's northeast monsoon, and the whistling strain of the spars was freedom crying in the chains of the wind.

That was the cry he had first heard aboard *Silenos* up in the luminous light of the shrouds where his fathers had hunted whales and empires. Pym had shown him the same radiant height in his own head: the falcon-view of time called history, where ideas were prey stalked among the centuries.

Jaki wondered at the future's sorcery. As a boy and a sorcerer he had had no future; there was only *now,* endlessly repeating — until he had learned he was the last sorcerer. After Jabalwan, time would never be the same, and each generation would bewilder the next, just as he had bewildered the sorcerers at Njurat. *Life is mystery.* As a pirate, he had endured his ignorance with dignity. But now, with a wife, a sister, and a vessel jammed with broken tribes, he burned to know where they were going.

Mala, Jabalwan, Pym, Mang, *Silenos,* his father — all were ghosts now and could not help him. But the visions they had shared with him would be his wings and would carry him above the fangs and poisons of empire to freedom in the unconquered west.

That was Jaki's conviction in April 1628, as he watched the clouds split above him and the prow of the ship slicing the dark water below to silver wings.

Jaki had decided against sailing to Surat, for he could not find in himself any trust for his father's people. Instead, he took *Sleeping with Satan* north along the Gujarat coast and came to shore in a ferny cove behind a giant bluff from which vantage sentries could peer over the horizon and warn of approaching ships. The Africans, some of whom had not been off ship in five harrowing weeks, ambled like dreamers among the scalloped dunes and windbent trees. Many buried themselves in the sand; others fashioned amulets from the crystals of shells and rocks broken by the tide. No one would go back on board to help with refitting the ship because they believed ghosts haunted the decks. Chains clanked in the bulwarks, they said, though all the chains, shackles, and body racks had been thrown overboard in the first hour that the Africans were free. Cries snapped from the top mast when no one was there. Blood dewed on the planks where people had died, and voices seeped through the hull from the bilges.

None of this had been witnessed by Jaki, but he believed there must be ghosts because everyone but Lucinda believed. "You are a sorcerer," she told him after their second day alone on the anchored ship, where they had confronted nothing more ominous than scuttling rats. "Do whatever you must to clear the decks of ghosts before some warship finds us here." So the next morning, Jaki stripped to a loincloth, smutched his body head to toe with soot and scarlet berry paste till he gleamed like a salamander. Then he took the canvas from the new medicine pouch he had fashioned from a crocodile skin, and carried it up the main mast. He rigged the rolled canvas to the yardarm with a pulley release, and when the first sea breeze rustled across the dull day, he snapped the sheet in the wind. Wyvern rippled into the morning like a mirage in the maritime gust, a hot-eyed viper pinioned to wings raggedly uplifted in a crest of black fire. The Africans moaned from the shore.

Jaki paced the decks, stopping every few steps to kneel and burn bark peelings laced with gunpowder. He did the work slowly and purposefully, reliving the jungle rituals he had performed with Jabalwan.

The exorcism took all day, and it was as much for his own sanity as for the others. The sorcerer in him had been troubled since his opium night in the gardens of Mirzapur and even more so after Lucinda's miscarriage. What did the future hold for them? Hard as he stared, he saw nothing. The world smothered spirit in earthliness, as Pym had claimed till his end. *All is emptiness. Life breeds life and nourishes death. No wisdom but power, lad. No power but dominion.*

Step by step, throughout the slave ship with its fulsome stench, Jaki confronted his apprehensions and made peace with his future. By nightfall, when he was running up and down the companionways with a torch in each hand, chanting Rain Wanderer hunt songs at the top of his lungs, whatever spirits there were had abandoned ship in the upsurge of his enthusiasm. At midnight, he climbed to the crosstrees with both torches in one hand and danced a circle-hop with the flames, frenzied in his victory over the dead.

The tribesfolk onshore marched to the tenders and were carried out to the ship in jubilant choruses. That night the bilges were drained by bucket crews, and the next day the squalid decks were purified with holystones and caustic water leeched from wood ash.

Finding a crew among the two hundred and forty-eight bewildered Africans was a more formidable task than exorcising ghosts. Tribal loyalties and disputes had endured the Africans' months of slavery, and *Sleeping with Satan* was immediately partitioned among friends and enemies. Only unanimous respect for the people who had liberated them, as well as the certainty that other slavers stalked the horizon, prevented outright battling. Jaki, who well remembered the ferocious competition for heads among the tribes of his childhood, defied his ignorance of the black people's languages and aggressively intervened in their quarrels, gesticulating passionately to communicate the grave danger of their ship alone at sea, prey to storms as well as slavers. Begrudgingly at first, and later with the fervor of a people allied against extinction, the squabbling tribes relinquished their animosity in favor of Jaki's leadership.

In those tumultuous first days, the sky was blessedly free of squalls, and Jaki and Kota were all business, training the most able tribesmen to catch the wind by working the sheets of canvas in synchrony. The Africans took easily to the shrouds and handled the spars with the graceful attentiveness of men familiar with the wiles of physical things. While the men learned to sail and to fire the cannon, Lucinda and Maud worked with the women, organizing them into foraging parties, cooks, clothes-makers, and caretakers of those who were broken from the thirty-six days of confinement. By the time the carrack left the cove, the crowded ship was boisterous with the shared hope of going home.

Jaki was hoping for an opportunity to seize a sturdy galleon, or a slow but capacious sailing barge, but two days north of the Portuguese fortress at Diu, *Sleeping with Satan* encountered a sleek, forty-gun Portuguese caravel manned with bellicose Persians. They tried to flee from the warship, but the fleet caravel cut off *Satan*'s sea approach and pinned her against the silt banks. The carrack would have been blown to splinters then if they had been flying Wyvern, but at the sight of the warship Jaki had ordered the banner draped from the bowsprit, signaling surrender. He kept the gunports closed, ordered the armed crew below decks, and stood some of the Africans along the rail so the Persians could see that their prize was a valuable slaver.

Jaki leaned on the taffrail, bareheaded to display his Dutch hair. Grapnel hooks crashed to the decks, and the first wave of red-turbaned seamen leaped aboard, blades between their teeth, short-barrel muskets crossed in their sashes. Jaki drew his saber as if to surrender it, waited until the planks were laid between the ships' rails, then shouted the order for the Africans to attack.

The deck hatches burst aside, and in moments the decks were teeming with two hundred armed warriors. The Persians collapsed beneath the hacking African swords, and their mates on their own ship tried to cut free and pull away to use their cannon. But Jaki leaned hard on the whipstaff, tilting the bulky carrack into the outbound tide, and slammed the caravel. Kota, with a musket in each hand and a scimitar strapped to his back, led the Africans onto the Persian ship.

The Persians fought savagely, cutting down many warriors, and soon the decks and companionways were slippery with blood and clogged with corpses. Without room to maneuver, the last Persians were quickly isolated and killed. With huge voices, the Africans declared their victory and stripped the Persian banners from the masts.

Jaki and Kota, on deck with the dancing warriors, had no idea what the Africans were shouting in their a cappella chant. Later, when they had learned something of the tribal tongues, the cry would become familiar to them all, the Africans' song of triumph that defied death: "We dance in the jaws of the serpent!"

The Africans decided among themselves who would sail in the new vessel, but they deferred to Jaki for the selection of their captain. Several of the leaders among the Africans appeared worthy of the captaincy, but one reminded Jaki of Jabalwan — a man younger than most, but one who had consistently looked after the weakest and who could not be bullied by the strongest and wiliest. The man had a weather of his own, appearing bored as a shaman, yet always involved, whether fighting the Persians or quietly mediating tribal squabbles. He was a striking man, tall as a spear, black as the eternal sky between the stars, and with a face as bony and smooth as a fish skull's. His name was Axo

Ndjobo, which meant Bitten by the Stars. Once Jaki nominated him for the captaincy of the caravel, the great majority of the Africans voted exuberantly for him.

Kota wore a face dark as a bat's after that. He had worked hard training the Africans to handle the whipstaff and the rigging, and he had expected to be named captain of the new ship. He had even troubled to dress for the role, in a large plumed hat cocked on one side, a red satin waistcoat, and a closed ruff about his throat pilfered from the caravel's wardrobe.

"You cannot captain the Africans," Jaki told him. "The tribespeople need their own leader."

"I know them," Kota insisted. "I show them how to steal wind, how to steer, and they obey. Lah. I am wise sailor."

"Yes," Jaki agreed, clapping an arm about the small man's thick shoulders and guiding him up the steps to the quarterdeck of *Sleeping with Satan.* "That's why I want you to captain this ship. The crew here is African as well, and they need a captain who is experienced."

Kota blinked like a turtle. "You are captain, lah?"

"No." Jaki jerked his thumb over the rail to where Lucinda and Maud could be seen fitting curtains to the open windows of the stern stateroom. "My wife and I had enough of that on the caravan. You will be the captain now. I will navigate. Lucinda will be quartermaster. And if we do our jobs right, the Africans in their own ship will learn enough by example not to be lost in the first high seas."

Kota swelled like a frog. For the first two days and nights of their thousand-mile journey across the Arabian Sea, he rode aboard the caravel, supervising the Africans. They were eager learners, having been tempered in the forge of despair, and by the third blue day with the northeaster bucketing their sails and the sea parting from their bows, they were exultant enough to name their ship. To a twelve-gun salute from *Sleeping with Satan* and a clamorous choral chant from the Africans, the caravel was dubbed *Children of the Serpent* and the name was branded on the bow in English.

"That name's as ghastly as ours," Lucinda said from the quarterdeck as the smoke from the cannon salute rushed by like specters. "Why ever do they want to call it that?"

"Fa," Kota answered. "Their magic, lah. From it they learn everything. They know this world sit on a serpent. The serpent live in the sea and hold up all land, all mountain, all jungle. When serpent hungry, it eat iron, shit gold. When restless, it move and earth shake. These people — lah." He held a satin-sleeved arm toward the caravel. "They far from home, far from gods. Only serpent under sea to carry them, carry them back. Yes, they children of the serpent."

"Fa," Maud said aloud, waving to the impassioned Africans on the caravel and on the decks below. "We must learn their magic, Jaki."

Lucinda smiled wryly. "On the contrary, it is *our* magic the Africans had best learn — if they are to find their way home and not be enslaved again."

Maud nodded mutely and looked to Jaki, recalling the night over a year ago when Jaki and his silver gibbon had surreptitiously boarded their vessel to claim Lucinda for his bride. Maud smiled wanly to think of her fright then and with what grave reluctance she had followed Lucinda into the night sea. The wanderer's life she had dreaded had been grander than she could have guessed, despite the moments of desperation, and the pirate she had loathed a year before had won her heart. Jaki was the first man to treat her like a lady. At first that had been a happy novelty, but their friendship had deepened during their months together, studying herbs and roots, exploring markets, tending the ills of the caravan while Lucinda bartered with local merchants. With great reluctance, Maud admitted to herself that she had grown to love Jaki. His furzy scent left her breathless when he leaned close to show her the seeds in the clenched fist of a bud, or took her hands in his to guide her fingers as she learned the secrets of knots.

She never showed him her feelings. Not even Lucinda knew. Maud's busy days and easy laughter hid her ardor, and she watched Jaki with a hopefulness he did not see.

Jaki was too rapt with the responsibilities of life at sea to notice Maud's growing affection for him. He spent hours alone in the crosstrees observing his ships and the dazzling solemnity of the clouds. Sweetly drunk on the sparkling days and star-whorled nights, he greeted everyone on the crowded ship with smiles.

Lucinda saw a side of her husband she had never met before. He was euphoric just sitting on the planks in a circle of Africans, studying their language and customs and teaching them in return. He happily moved among chores all day, washing clothes by towing them astern, fishing with a trailing line, mending sails, marking the sun with Lucinda's help, and frequently disappearing up the mainmast to the top basket on the crosstrees. At night, he slept deeply in his hammock beside Lucinda's in the crammed stateroom, and she watched him in the slanted moonlight, his hair like a rhyme of her own, his mother's bones pressing against the animal tenderness of his face with her enduring love.

Time alone with him was not possible on the decks, even in sleep, since every habitable niche was filled with Africans. On a sparkling morning four days out into the Arabian Sea, Lucinda watched as Jaki clambered up the shrouds to relieve the watch in the crosstrees, and her blood shimmered. Her father had always forbidden her to climb the rigging, though she had never once had any desire to mount a rope ladder on a rolling ship, until now. The crosstrees was the only place on board where she could be alone with Jaki, and she was determined to be with him.

Elated with her own ardor and resolve, she returned to the stateroom and put on a pair of Jaki's tar-speckled canvas pants. She pulled a blue puff-sleeved blouse over her head, and with a strand of jute tied her sun-bleached hair in a topknot. At the port chainwale she removed her sandals, stepped to the rail where the standing rigging was lashed, and gazed up at the mainmast tottering against the towering clouds.

Fear thrilled through her as she followed the ascent with her eyes. She took hold of the prickly shroud and stepped to the ratline. Churning clouds swelled across the sky, and she had to seize the stiff rope with the very iron in her blood to stave off vertigo.

The shrouds leaned in toward the mast, and the climbing went easier than she had guessed. She mounted the first flight from the deck to the yard of the lower topsail quickly, not looking down or up, keeping her stare fixed on the rungs of twisted hemp. Her hands, toughened from a year of managing elephants, camels, and mules, were uncomplaining, but her feet winced on the coarse ratlines, and her shoulder bones strained in their sockets with a searing ache.

On the yard top, where the first flight of shrouds converged to a slatted platform and the next flight of rigging began, she thought of going back down. Then she spotted the Africans gawking at her from the tops of the fore- and mizzenmasts. And there was Kota on the quarterdeck. He had not seen her yet and was directing the pilot in the binnacle. He would call her down if he saw her, and she took hold of the shrouds and started up the second flight.

Her feet stinging, she paused on the platform above the upper topsail and watched the clouds boiling gently. Booming shouts hurtled from below. Kota had spotted her. Mustering her strength, she pulled herself up the last flight, twenty-five ratlines to the round wicker-rope basket on the traverse beams of the crosstrees.

Jaki, who had been lying on his back staring into heaven, sat up when the shroud ties squeaked someone's approach. He peered over the brim, and Lucinda laughed to see him leap to his feet with alarm. "What are you doing?" he cried, looping his arm under her shoulders and helping her into the basket.

"I want to be with you," she answered, her voice vibrating with the rush of the ship. She looked out to see *Children of the Serpent* rocking to starboard and the following sea laced with scud, the chop lifting the flat sterns high and quickly dropping them again, surging the ships forward. The power of the wind and the hurrying current exhilarated her, and she hugged Jaki. "It's beautiful." She waved to Kota, who was standing arms akimbo at the binnacle, a red petal among the brown leaves of Africans.

Jaki shook his head, smiling with delight and admiration. "I would never have hoped to be here with you. I've never seen you on the shrouds."

She chuckled hopelessly. "This is my first time. Father forbade it. I don't see why. It's not so very difficult."

Jaki held her at arm's length and regarded her in her oversized garments with vibrant attentiveness and a crooked smile. "You look splendid, wife."

She pulled him to her, and they swayed for a moment overlooking a world of crestspray and raffish sunlight. The gravity of their embrace drew them to their knees, and the whole world lifted above them to a crown of ransacked clouds.

Their passion for each other had been stymied for weeks since Lucinda's miscarriage on the Narbada, and they gazed at each other now with interminable desire. Slowly, in expectant anxiety, they took off each other's clothes so that they were kneeling naked on their shucked garments under the bright smoke of the sky.

Jaki's breath sharpened to see again the pale, curved grandeur of his wife's nakedness, and he lowered his face to her breasts and breathed her soft warmth. Her fingertips trailed the carved lines of his chest and the cobbled curve of his belly. He rolled atop her and let her hands fit him to her slick heat. The roll of the ship joined them in a slippery, glittering pang, and their bodies arched, his head thrown back, her legs lifted to the snug poise of their embrace.

They sagged together in a vast chill grace. For a long spell, they lay listening to the wind ruffling the sails and sloughing over the crosstrees heathery with silence.

Lucinda rolled to her back and looked up into the clouds. "What do you see up there?" she asked.

"Wind and storm," he mumbled.

"I want to see what you see."

"Your father must have shown you the weather."

"You see more than the weather or you wouldn't stare so long."

"Dhup would say we see the sky, and it is clear until our seeing makes it cloudy."

"And what do you say?"

She felt him tighten, and he said, "I do not understand what I see."

She kissed his fingers and measured him with a passionate stare. "What do you *think* you see?"

Jaki was silent so long she almost asked again, but when he felt her breath coiling to speak, he said, "The story of the world." He sat up and brushed his hair back with both hands. The carefree childlight was gone from his face. "We are living a great change. It is the end of the ancient ways that go back to the beginning of time. The end for them —" He lifted his chin to point through the wicker basket to where *Children of the Serpent* was pacing them. "As it is the end for my people."

Lucinda sat up into a frown. Jaki's touch on her cheek was so gentle, when he stopped it ached. "What is ahead for us, sorcerer — in the story of the world?"

"A home," he answered at once. "Pym used to say that the hearth was the only true altar. Among his beloved Greeks, the hearth was the one god without a form, for she is the home, our place on the earth. The cooking pot and its fire. Every tribe worships there."

The shadow did not depart her face, but her loveliness was not diminished by it, and when she reached for him, he pulled her so close their bones knocked. "Hold me, Jaki. I am afraid. We have defied so many powers to be together. What will become of us? Like these ships — or those clouds — we go where the fateful winds take us."

He faced her squarely, with a truthfulness in his blue stare beyond all doubt or revelation. "Then take comfort in knowing that wherever we are going, heaven or hell, or any of the kingdoms between, we go together."

They embraced, and the static of their lovemaking rustled louder in their blood, easing their apprehensions, and warming the promises in their hearts, as though they would live forever.

The wind led *Sleeping with Satan* and *Children of the Serpent* over the horizon's dark depths, through briny days and starslick nights, to the Horn of Africa.

"Too many of our people have died in this place for us to pass here in peace," Axo Ndjobo told Jaki on the night that they lay off the littoral trading towns in the Gulf of Aden. During the two-week crossing, Ndjobo had consolidated his command of the Africans. Though only a handful of the men were from his western tribe and most of the Africans were from disparate tribes in the eastern kingdoms of Makonde and Nyamwezi, Ndjobo's majestic mien and wisdom in settling disputes won the fealty of all.

"With the light of day, we will see Ras Khanzira, the port where we were loaded aboard this very ship like cargo. We will see what ships are in the harbor, and we will use our cannon to take or destroy any who fly the flags of our enemies."

Ndjobo and a bevy of Africans were seated on the floor of the stateroom with the pirates who had liberated them. Three weeks of working the wind and the sea with the Africans had mitigated the white people's ignorance of Bantu and its dialects, but communication was still clumsy and slow. The captain's message was repeated several times in varying idioms and with clarifying gestures by the Africans who had worked most closely with the whites.

Jaki looked to Lucinda as their meaning became clear. She took his hand. "Jaki, he wants vengeance."

"Axo," Jaki began slowly, "war is more dangerous at sea than on land. Our crews can sail with the wind, but they've never been tried in a storm or even a real head wind, let alone in battle. Whoever we fight will have more experienced crews."

"More experienced," Ndjobo agreed when he understood, "but not more fierce. We — all of us — are ready to fight. It is our duty to the dead. You know how to fight at sea. Together, we will destroy our enemies."

"Jaki —" Lucinda protested.

Jaki deferred to her with a nod. "Tell *him*."

Lucinda stared flatly at the captain. "Axo — we cannot fight because we cannot afford to lose. If either of our ships is hit squarely with even one shot, the vessel could sink and your people will drown. And if we are not sunk but merely damaged, then we will be captured and everyone will be enslaved again."

Axo stirred under Lucinda's stare while he listened to his advisers hectically trying to translate. He understood and silenced them with a finger. "It is our duty," he said. "We will not leave this place without breaking the enemy who are killing and enslaving my people."

"Then you will fight with your ship alone," Lucinda said bluntly.

Jaki leaned toward her. "My love, there are four of us and more than two hundred of them. Where's the diplomacy you displayed so ably in India?"

Lucinda would not give in. "Have we come this far to be killed in a vendetta?"

"That would be sad but heroic," Jaki said softly to her. "If Axo maroons us here among the slavers and the pirates, that will just be sad."

Lucinda ignored him. "Axo, we saved you from slavery to return you and the others to your lands, not to murder and plunder."

Ndjobo's bony face was placid as stone. "We will fulfill our duty to the dead," he said at last. "You have been our friends, and we would have no ship at all without you. But if we do not fight here, we will have trouble with all who have gone before us across the black river of time." He fixed Jaki with a penetrating stare. "You fought with your hands to free us. Does your woman speak for you?"

Jaki raised his palms and lowered his gaze. "Axo, she is my life."

Axo shifted his solemn gaze to Kota. "And you, captain?"

Kota had been listening nervously, fingering the wrinkled leather of his seaboots. Under Axo's heavy regard, he quailed and looked to Jaki. "What to say, sorcerer?"

"You are captain, Kota," Jaki replied. "Is this the crew you want with you in a sea battle?"

The idea of plunder appealed strongly to Kota, and he mentally assessed the strengths of the crew and the ships. "*Serpent Children* is warship, lah," he said to Jaki. "Forty gun. And the blacks can handle the big guns now."

Jaki turned to Axo. "The captain of our ship will go with you. He has fought many sea battles. Obey him and you will not fail."

"And this ship?" Axo asked. "You will not help us?"

Lucinda shook her head. "We will not fight. Take from us your people who must avenge their dead, and leave with us your women and those who have no place in a battle. We will return them to their lands if you do not return."

The black captain nodded stiffly as though she had cursed him.

Kota turned to Jaki with an appeal. "Cover from sea — lah?"

Before Lucinda could deny him, Jaki spoke. "We will stand off the gulf and guard your back. But you will be alone on your raid. Choose your targets wisely, Kota — and if you are outgunned, stay here and send them in alone."

No one slept that night, waiting for dawn to reveal the coast ports on the headland. In the crosstrees, the African watch scanned the mist-hung shore with a spyglass. He counted six ships, three cargo barges, and three warships, all flying Dutch Company banners.

"Three — many warships," Kota moaned. But when Ndjobo called his warriors on *Sleeping with Satan* to join him, the pirate captain stood beside him. At the tender, Kota clutched Jaki to him. "I go with Pym, lah."

Jaki smiled without mirth. "Yes, Pym would not hesitate to pin three warships at anchor. He's with you, all right. And be sure to listen to him and stay upwind. He fought with cunning, not arrogance. Remember."

The tender carried Ndjobo, Kota, and his warriors to *Children of the Serpent.* Several trips were required to convey all the Africans who wanted to partake in the raid, and even then there were more who pressed against the rails to go — but there was no time. The Dutch in the harbor had seen the two ships off their coast flying pirate flags, and their warships were stirring.

Jaki, Lucinda, and Maud watched from the quarterdeck as *Children of the Serpent* weighed anchor and unfurled canvas. Rain blew in sheets from the sea, smoking over the decks. In the stiff torrent, *Children of the Serpent* swooped toward Ras Khanzira, and all aboard *Sleeping with Satan* were silent as the Dutch ships came out to meet her. Sparks glinted as the Dutch forecastle guns fired. The shots splashed short. "Turn now," Jaki urged aloud, seeing the Dutch begin their tack. "Catch them with their sides open." But *Children of the Serpent* barreled straight toward them, flying within range of the Dutch cannon.

"Kota is gambling on the stormwind to dampen the Dutch guns' trajectories," Lucinda said, almost breathless. "It's a mistake. The Dutch have the most powerful cannon in the world."

As the Dutch ships tacked and presented their sides, their cannon winced flames. The topgallant on the Africans' foremast snapped away and rigging lashed into the air. *Children of the Serpent* turned athwart the wind, and her twenty larboard guns flared. At that close range and with the stormwind behind them, each shot found its mark, shredding the sails of the lead Dutch ship, smashing her binnacle, stalling her tack, and bashing in most of her cannon. But the other two defenders completed their tack and moved apart to pincer their foe.

Jaki was half overboard, leaning on the rail with apprehension, and he threw himself back when he saw the enclosing Dutch fire their forecastle guns simultaneously. The crossfire smashed the foremast of *Children of the Serpent* and kicked timber and crewmen into the rain-spinning morning.

"They're crippled," Lucinda groaned.

Flames spurted from the prow of the African warship, whipped by the wind, and the royal sheets on the mainmast collapsed. "Fire!" Jaki cried. "They'll have to fight the fire and leave their cannon unmanned." But the wind feeding the flames also swept *Children of the Serpent* hard by the Dutch ship, closing on her port. The African port guns boomed—the men in the gundeck had not abandoned their posts even though flames were licking around them, threatening to ignite their powder hold. Astounded by the Africans' suicidal fervor, Jaki and Lucinda shouted warnings as the shots from the broadside caved in the gunwale of the Dutch ship. With a sundering roar, the powder hold ignited, and the Dutch vessel erupted into a convulsion of fire and black smoke.

The Africans on *Sleeping with Satan* bellowed a cheer, then in the next instant fell silent as the other Dutch defender fired her cannon and the Africans' bowsprit was sheared away. *Children of the Serpent* veered off, her prow braiding smoke. Her gunners now had left their cannon to keep the onboard fire from gutting them as it had the Dutch. The crew in the masts were scurrying to replace shredded canvas and catch enough wind to avoid the oncoming Dutch ship.

"They cannot pull off fast enough," Lucinda said. "Jaki, we have got to go in after them."

Jaki cast her a startled look, saw the concern honing her stare, and barked orders to weigh anchor. The Africans flew to their posts with a hurrah. But hard as they worked, they could not catch wind before the Dutch closed in on *Children of the Serpent.* Cannonfire thundered across the bay, and the masts of the African ship were blasted to stumps. With gut-wrenching slowness, *Sleeping with Satan* turned into the wind while *Children of the Serpent* lay helpless before her enemy's barrage. The Dutch fired two more rounds, collapsing the Africans' main deck, before swerving off to confront *Sleeping with Satan.*

"Hard ahead!" Jaki shouted. "Full canvas!"

Lucinda took his arm. "The wind is too stiff," she warned. "We'll throw ourselves past the Dutch, and they will rip us apart when we come around downwind."

Jaki smiled coldly. "And that's what the Dutch are thinking." He waved Maud to him. "Go below, both of you."

Lucinda protested, but Maud, heeding his grim insistence, took Lucinda in a firm embrace and guided her off the quarterdeck.

The rain and the Africans were Jaki's strategy. But timing would be crucial, and he stood atop the binnacle to gauge speed and distance, realizing that he had just enough time to call the Africans down from the masts. They came reluctantly, not comprehending why he would command them to abandon their posts at that crucial moment. He ordered the pilot on the whipstaff to hold a hard course, and he ran to the voice tube and shouted for swords to be brought up. When the gun crew scrambled to the main deck, their arms full of swords, he gave one to each of the men on the masts and sent them up again with the order to cut the free rigging at his command. Then he sent the gun crew back to their cannon, ran to the quarterdeck, and leaped atop the binnacle again.

Timing was all now. Too soon and their shots would fall short. Too late and they would be helpless, for he was going to cut their ship's wings. It was a gamble, but it was their only chance to crush the Dutch without a long battle.

Face raised to the stormclouds, he prayed aloud. "Powers of the world, strike with me. Lend me your strength as always."

The moment to act loomed as the Dutch held their fire and did not tack, fully expecting *Sleeping with Satan* to glide past them. "Cut the free rigging!" Jaki yelled.

The Africans hacked at the ropes bracing the canvas, and all the sails suddenly dropped away, muffling the speed of the carrack as she narrowed closer to the Dutch warship.

"Hard alee!" he shouted to the pilot below him, and the big ship tilted suddenly, almost careening. Jaki leaped from the binnacle and threw himself at the voice tube. "Gundeck, fire! All larboard guns fire!"

Sleeping with Satan cut before the Dutch vessel so suddenly and so closely that Jaki could see the shock on the faces of the crew — men with blond hair like himself, like his father. For a moment, guilt overcame him. Then his ship's guns blasted, and the Dutch vessel was lost in the smoke. Her cannon replied before the smoke cleared, but the guns were misaimed and the rainy wind cut the shots' spin. *Sleeping with Satan*'s guns roared again, the wind tattered the gunsmoke, and the Dutch vessel appeared in a whirlwind of flames. Her crew were rushing madly to leap overboard, but few made it before the powder hold caught fire. Stunning blasts rent through the warship in a rising crescendo of destruction. *Sleeping with Satan* accepted her surrender.

Jaki's ship towed the Dutch vessel and *Children of the Serpent* into the harbor of Ras Khanzira. There the Dutch factor was waiting at the wharves to relinquish the port for the lives of the men saved from the futile defense. Men in beards and ruffs stood in a nervous cluster at the levee under a red leather canopy drooling rain.

Trailed by his African clansmen still bloody from the battle, Captain Kota, and the three whites, Axo Ndjobo stepped ashore. The astonished Dutch commanders were solicitous of the safety of their people and readily accepted Ndjobo's conditions: the yielding of arms and the release of all slaves in the town. Jaki acted as translator, assuring the factor of the security and well-being of the small Dutch population in exchange for the cargo then in port and for use of the harbor in repairing his ships.

The African wounded were treated and conveyed by horse-drawn wagon in a caravan bound for the interior from where they had come. Most of the slaves and the crew from the pirate ships went with them. The ones who remained were those, like Axo, whose people were on the other side of the continent; they would sail around the Cape to the rocky coast of Whydah. Under Kota's direction, they dry-docked *Sleeping with Satan, Children of the Serpent,* and the captured Dutch warship and rebuilt them.

For Jaki and Lucinda, the three weeks ashore were a giddy respite from the crowded life of the crossing. They stayed in an elegant Muslim-style house with tiered rooms, flame-shaped windows and doors, all enclosed by an oasis garden overlooking the sea. It was just a year earlier that they had been married in Dagon, and they celebrated their first anniversary with a party. Axo Ndjobo got drunk, wept for the broken tribes of the world, and, in a tranceful swell of prophecy, declared that Lucinda was with child and would birth a girl destined to begin a dynasty.

Lucinda was pleased with Ndjobo's prediction, for she very much wanted a child to go with her into her new life. The morning that they departed Ras Khanzira in three well-provisioned and seaworthy ships, leaving the slave harbor in flames behind them, she declared that she wanted her child born in the New World, and she began plotting an itinerary that would hurry them around Africa and across the Atlantic to the Antilles within nine months.

Sobered, Ndjobo was embarrassed that Lucinda had taken his exuberant babbling so seriously. But she was indeed with child, and to pacify his own conscience, he promised the unborn child his scepter, a manta ray stinger with which to rule her kingdom in the New World.

Ras Khanzira was a city of ghosts when William Quarles arrived. The Dutch had emerged from their compound to find that nothing of the harbor remained to be salvaged. Fire had gutted the anchorage, and the powder kegs that the pirates had exploded in the breakwater had clogged the channel with boulders. The company decided to abandon the port, and the Arab merchants gathered their goods and moved west to Djibouti. Quarles arrived to find monkey hordes occupying the empty buildings and goats foraging in the sorghum fields.

Quarles's ship was a massive galleon he had dubbed *Revenge*. The vessel had cost him all the gold he had saved from his years of naval service, and to pay his dangerous crew — Hindu and Persian felons, Portuguese drunks, miscreants retrieved from the colony jail — he had promised them booty. But in the fortnight since departing Swally, no prey had offered itself, and the crew grieved for plunder. At Ras Khanzira, Quarles turned them loose. They ravaged the deserted port, and before they returned to the ship they set the city ablaze in their frustration at finding nothing worth pillaging.

Quarles cruised the Horn, capturing dhows and interrogating their occupants about the fate of the ghost harbor. Upon learning that Wyvern was responsible for driving off the Dutch and sacking the port, he ordered full canvas slapped on. The satisfaction of closing again on his mad daughter and her pirate lover was cold in his veins, and he determined with silent ferocity that this time they would not elude him. He stood on the quarterdeck, spyglass to his eye, and resolutely searched for ships on the horizon.

One morning mirrorflash messages spiked the air with urgent warnings of a galleon flying British colors that had harried the vessels trailing *Sleeping with Satan* during the night and had taken one of the caravels. "It's Father," Lucinda said at once. Jaki was dubious, and he and Axo Ndjobo organized a defensive ploy to trap the galleon. A cargo galley lingered behind the fleet as a lure, and Axo's two warships waited on the horizon for signals of an attack. The signal came at dusk, and the warships swooped in to smash the galleon. But the British ship was not there. Instead, the pirates found the caravel that had been lost the night before, now outfitted with a new crew and harassing the cargo galley.

Only after the warships had closed in did the British galleon loom out of the gathering night, cannons ablaze. The pirate ships were pinned against the shallow coast, and after a brief exchange of cannonfire, the tide began to sweep them landward. One warship squeaked out of the inbound current by taking a battering from the galleon and limped northward to rejoin *Sleeping with Satan* and Axo's flagship.

Aboard the galleon, William Quarles watched the burning pirate ship until he was certain she was retreating. Then he gave the command to stand off the floundering galley and warship. By midnight the pirates had run aground, abandoned their vessels, and scattered into the African jungle. Quarles's crew were ecstatic. After weeks of relentless pursuit and no booty but the livestock they rustled from seacoast villages, they had taken three ships in two days.

In the green light of dawn, the captain lumbered to his stateroom and laid out the few remnants of Lucinda's life that he possessed: the tiger's beard necklace, Lucinda's tawed leather journal of her caravan trek, her calfskin-bound English Bible, and the Bible cover with the nailhole in its spine and Gefjon's family tree inscribed within. Wounded with malaria and desperation, he let his hands flutter over these meager tokens.

"Is it Father who is pursuing us?" Lucinda asked, but Jaki did not know for sure. After the loss of three ships to the mysterious British galleon, *Sleeping with Satan* and Axo's two vessels flurried north more swiftly. Off the turbulent coast of Whydah on the Bight of Benin, Axo Ndjobo was returned to his people, and *Sleeping with Satan* picked up a crew of Africans eager to cross the sea to the New World. The pirate flotilla dispersed, many of the captured ships adopting the colors of coastal kingdoms and becoming vessels of trade. Two warships elected to accompany *Sleeping with Satan* to the Americas.

Before parting, Axo Ndjobo presented Jaki — who had saved his life and returned him to his people — with a parchment sheet and a roll of black velvet. The velvet unwound, and Jaki held up a polished gold dagger that tapered seamlessly from a serpent-coil haft with cross-folded wings.

The parchment, a page from a ship's log written in a floriate Spanish hand, listed booty from a ship Ndjobo's crew had fleeced as she cruised out of the Atlantic on her way home from the New World. At the head of the page was written: *Aztec treasure recovered from the wreck of the galleon* Dona Luisa, *discovered among the shoals of Cozumel in* A.D. *1627*. One entry was underlined, and Jaki read it aloud: "From the Isle of Sacrifices, a gold dagger, described in the log of the *Dona Luisa,* 20 September 1522, taken during an Indian religious ceremony where it had been used to cut the living hearts from the breasts of human sacrifices . . ." Jaki's voice trailed off, and he lowered the parchment.

Lucinda and Maud were aghast, but Jaki felt the power of this gift. He thanked Ndjobo and held the dagger against his thudding heart; it seemed to him the claw of Wyvern, the portion of the world's evil that he had been born to carry. He saw the protests in the faces of Lucinda and Maud, and he knew they would beg him to cast the evil instrument overboard. Yet he also knew he would not discard this frightful idol of death. It was a tooth from the Mother of Life, a morbid token of all the violence in the blood of every living thing. To discard it would put it back into the unknown, into the very hands of the jealous dead. Only by holding it, by cherishing it and using it, could he touch the hand that rose from the bottom of all things.

"Throw it overboard," Maud pleaded with Jaki the morning that they left Africa behind them.

He disregarded her, staring ahead into a stormgray sky, reading the surge of lowering clouds. "There's no way out of it but through," he muttered.

"Jaki, are you listening to me?" Maud put a hand on his shoulder. "That dagger you wear at your hip has the blood of human sacrifice on it. If you keep it, there will be more sacrifice."

Jaki nodded contemplatively. "You are right, young sister. But our destiny is sacrifice. A cruel word. Devotion means the same. We are devoted, all of us, to our journey. We have sacrificed much to be together. And our devotion will have to be strong for us to reach the New World and then to survive there by our own strength. If I throw this emblem of our sacrifice into the sea, the emblem becomes the sea. And that is too vast. At least this dagger fits my hand."

Maud bit her upper lip. "You are too cunning for me, Jaki. I am but a peasant girl who knows only what she has seen. Have you forgotten that the baneful prophecy of the gypsy in Sarnath has come to pass? Lucinda conceived and lost a child, as the gypsy augured. And still you carry the cursed diamond." She peered hard at him, not understanding how he could know so much of the hidden powers and yet act so heedlessly. "I fear all emblems of sacrifice. Jaki, throw the evil thing overboard before we share the fate of the *Dona Luisa* and the galleon that found her and dared to carry this cruel instrument. Let us trust in God instead."

"God —" Jaki huffed. "Maker of mosquitoes, sharks, and serpents. I do indeed trust in God, Maud. That is why I wear the gold blade. Pure chance, God's most deft tool, has recovered it from a century of sleep in the carcass of a Spanish galleon so that Axo Ndjobo might take it as a prize on the high seas and present it to me at our parting. Shall I spite God then and throw it away?"

A puzzled expression weighted Maud's features. "You are truly a sorcerer, Jaki Gefjon. I'll not argue with you anymore. I do believe you think the devil could be a friend."

She turned and padded away, leaving Jaki chilled with her apprehensions. In an angry flash, he drew the gold knife from the leather scabbard at his hip. Its edge caught the graying light and held it; the flexed coils of the hilt and the folded wings breathed stillness. As he had known from the very first moment he had touched it, the knife was more than itself: the spooled energies within it were untwining into the curved paths of his life, widening into the storm ahead and all the storms beyond. Maud's fear riled him — because she echoed his own most secret fear.

Since Njurat, when even skeptical Pym had glimpsed the secret order of the Life and been awed, Jaki had tried to live above his fear. That had almost killed him in Burma, when the tiger trapped him in his fearlessness. Even now, a year later, he was still dreaming of Wawa, his truest friend, who would still be with him if he had not forgotten his fear.

"Damn fear!" he barked at the smoky sky and the wind-bellied Wyvern. "I am not fear's puppet." He strode to the prow, swung his legs over the bulwark of the forecastle, and crawled out on the bowsprit as far as he dared go in the bucking sea. Clutching the spar with his knees, he pulled the silk cord from the grommets of his shirt and lashed the gold dagger to the bowsprit, point forward, stabbing the future. "Powers of the world," he called as he knotted the cord. "All life is your sacrifice. The whole world is your altar. Stab this ship into the New World. Stab us across the sea and into the wild earth."

Lightning jagged ahead, and by the time Jaki crept backward to the forecastle, thunder rumbled over the ship. The storm was less than an hour away, and he walked the length of the ship shouting orders to prepare for the approaching blow. At the stern, he gazed back from where they had come, at the sea flashing in gempoints of sunlight. The Old World was three days behind, and the New World was over thirty days ahead. His three ships were spanking dauntlessly across the Atlantic — and he was determined not to let omens and portents obstruct them.

Lucinda agreed with her husband. She was as indifferent to the sacrificial gold dagger as she had been to the gypsy's frightful prophecy. In a blithe mood, she named the knife Chrysaor, after the gold sword of Greek legend that Cronos wielded to shave time into months, days, and hours, and she referred to it as the ship's figurehead.

While the first storm of their Atlantic voyage raged about them, Maud and Lucinda reminisced below deck about their childhood travels together in the Mediterranean, while Jaki and Kota mulled over maps of the Atlantic and the Caribbean taken from Spanish prizes, wishing they had not lost Pym's maps in Mandu. The chanting of the Africans swelled louder as the storm mounted, but by nightfall even their stalwart spirits were silenced by the monster winds. The tempest ripped away hatches and standing rigging, prying loose planks, and spinning the ship like a toy. At the worst of it, Jaki folded up the maps and crouched in prayer with Kota on the floor of the stateroom while Maud moaned about God's disfavor and Lucinda battled seasickness. Fearing another miscarriage, Jaki and Kota lashed her bed to the walls to keep it from shaking too violently.

For two days they were thrashed, and when the sky cleared, they were one boat less. The companion ship that remained had lost two masts and her holds had been flooded, spoiling her provisions. She turned about to return to Africa, and *Sleeping with Satan,* battered but whole, went on alone, drifting slowly for another three days in desultory breezes. During that time, the crew repaired the hatches and the rigging and renewed their spirits with a drum-dance ceremony before Wyvern, thanking the god of storms for delivering them sound from its fierce winds. The lull broke that night. Ripple breezes tugged at the flaccid canvas and by dawn freshened into a northeast trade that cracked the sails to full-bellied windnets and lurched the ship forward.

The black crew, some of them veterans from the African cruise, were expert now at snatching every available gust, and *Sleeping with Satan* flew swiftly, the gold-daggered bowsprit resolutely piercing the way. The tribesmen were pleased at first that Jaki had placed their leader's gift at the very prow of the ship, and, with their companions lost and fallen back, they were determined to see Chrysaor shoot across the sea and gouge the soil that their people had been enslaved to till.

But Kota agreed with Maud. From the day that the sorcerer affixed the ritual blade to the bowsprit, bad luck had dogged the ship. After the storm sheared away her companions, *Sleeping with Satan*'s pummeled timbers began weeping seawater. Caulking leaks became a full-time job for three crewmen. On the rigging, a block split suddenly, disjointing a halyard and plunging a man to his death on the main deck. The blood that grimed the oak where his head shattered could not be cleansed though men scrubbed it with lye. Spiders appeared on all the decks and in all the cabins overnight, small, muscular red mites that dropped from the rafters and left blistery trails of scalp bites. Weevils materialized in the grain barrels. And fever flared through the crew.

Maud brewed febrifuge teas for the sick to drink while she swabbed their bodies with brandy. Kota was convinced the fever was the cold fist of Death that held Chrysaor, the knife of sacrifices. "Why do the dying feel cold, lah?" he asked Jaki. They were in the ship's galley supervising the crewmen Jaki had ordered to bucket the scuttlebutt's water from a barrel to a cauldron. The ports and hatches gaped wide, but the air was torrid with steam from two other boiling kettles. "Their flesh burns to touch. What-is-evil sucks the heat from them."

"Yes, what-is-evil will kill us too if we drink this water."

"But this water boiled ashore, lah? Same as always. Same as Africa. Same as India. Same as Pym."

"That's why we are here now, captain. To be certain it is done right this time."

"Maybe not water. Maybe what-is-evil is what Maid Maud says. Lah. Chrysaor took lives for the gods. Made to take lives for spirits."

Jaki shook his head. "The gold dagger belongs to Wyvern now, not the Aztec gods. What-is-evil is polluted water."

Kota hummed pensively, stared at the flames kicking in the iron stove, and said, "What-is-evil is bad water. Lah. But captain must think of ship with heart and head. The heart of captain unhappy with sacrifice knife at bow."

Jaki peered down at Kota, eyebrows lifted. "Are you ordering me to remove the dagger?"

Kota shuffled uneasily. "No, sorcerer, not that. I am captain. I must think with heart and head. Captain must think of this."

"If boiling this water does not break the sickness onboard," Jaki declared, "I will cut loose that tragic knife and throw it in the sea."

Kota was not satisfied. He had listened to all the answers that Jaki and Lucinda had offered for the ill turns of fate: storm damage opened the leaks; their weeks at sea had been time enough for spiderlings to hatch; the bloodstained oak was a knot-whorl that the lye had scored. Still, he believed Maud was right. Chrysaor was unholy. Kota determined to remove the knife himself.

After the candles had been snuffed that night in the cabin of the sorcerer and his wife, and most of the crew were asleep, Kota removed his broad hat, put a knife between his teeth, climbed over the forecastle's bulwark, and crept out to where Chrysaor was lashed. But before he could cut it free, the ship jarred over a swell in an abrupt windshift, and he lost his grip. The watch in the crosstrees did not see him, and only the half-dozen sailors who bunked in the orlop cabins heard, in their sleep, his body slam against the hull before it was dragged into the blind depths. The next day, Jaki found Kota's hat in the forecastle and felt his blood go heavy as he understood what had happened.

For three days and nights, Jaki sat in the crosstrees with only a flagon of water, his gaze lost in the wool of the sea. He wore Kota's hat and tried to feel his friend's revulsion for the gold dagger so he would have the strength to complete what his companion had died to do and throw the knife of sacrifices into the sea. But all he felt was fear seeking flesh, dread wanting a hand of its own. The ghostly feeling was so very much Jaki's memory of Kota that at night he expected to see his ghost glaring at him from the shrouds. Instead, the stars glinted like cardamon seeds, moonshadows fluttered on the swells, and the fear seemed to descend on him from the fog of the Milky Way. At dawn on the fourth day, he came down from the top, filled his flagon with wine, fit it into the plumed hat, and threw it overboard.

Revenge and her three prizes sailed north far from shore to avoid the pirate flotilla. Now that Quarles had secured a small fortune in booty, he was eager to find a friendly port where he could outfit his ship for the Atlantic crossing. The week before Christmas, he put into the Cape Verde Islands, his Union Jack squared away and nonallied trade colors flying from the masts of his ship and his prizes. The Portuguese warmly received him and gladly exchanged his plunder of ivory, hides, and spices for bigger cannon and provisions. Among the adventurers in the blue-tile-roofed seaport of Ribeira Grande, an expert crew was readily assembled with the promise of pirate-stalking in the New World, and *Revenge* was caulked, heavily armed, and provendered for a Christmas Day departure.

The night before he set out, Quarles was visited aboard ship by a richly dressed merchant with black flowing hair and a permanent frown knitting his thick eyebrows. "My name is unimportant," he said in heavily spiced English, "as we will never meet again." Quarles had granted the man permission to board because he claimed to have news from the English factor in Asia who had championed him. Once they were alone in Quarles's stateroom, the merchant removed his hat and told Quarles, "The English factor you served is dead, lost in his sleep on his way back to England. A happy death at his advanced age. The news ran ahead of you through the Red Sea."

Quarles regarded the foreigner through a narrow stare. "And you? You know of this because you share his faith?"

"Yes. The Church of the Two Thieves has charged me to convey this to you." He removed a thin envelope from his doublet and lay it on the captain's desk. Quarles picked it up and examined the insignia of the Dutch West India Company pressed into the sealing wax. The merchant continued, "The Thieves' Church has sold your English estate, as you requested, and converted its worth to land in the Dutch colony of New Holland. As we did not know where you would next appear, this is but a claim. Numerous copies have been distributed to our members in outposts where you were likely to seek haven. When you present this to the governor at Fort Amsterdam, you will be granted title to your new lands."

Quarles queried the merchant thoroughly, but the man had no further information about Quarles's status in England or the property he had acquired in the New World. When he was alone again, he examined the claim delicately as though it were a poison-ink letter. The paper represented the end of his ancestral ties to Britain. Father beyond father had fulfilled their fates in England — and before the Normans, in France, back into the smoke of time. The old way ended here. No— the ruthless truth asserted itself in him with angry vigor — his legacy had ended cruelly in Serangoon Harbor when *The Fateful Sisters* was destroyed.

The malarial twitch in his fingers jangled louder, and he tucked the claim into Lucinda's Bible. A life awaited him in the New World. And mad as she was, Lucinda was his only prayer for a future there.

As if Kota's death had somehow appeased the dark forces, the misfortunes aboard *Sleeping with Satan* relented. The timbers stopped leaking, trays of fuming olibanum smoked out all the spider nests, the fevers vanished, and the weevils were sifted from the grains and cooked in a gruel with quince pulp that the Africans found sumptuous.

Lucinda's pregnancy bloomed prodigiously into its eighth month, and Jaki joked about a stowaway. Maud cared for the expectant mother attentively, insisting that she rest and dosing her with balm of Gilead and Java plum tea at every meal. The baby was active, rolling in Lucinda's belly like the sea that was carrying them, and Lucinda was happier than she had ever been before. By day, Jaki propped her before the open stern windows, Maud bundled her in quilts, and she pleasured herself watching the opals of the sea change colors. At night, when the stirrings of the baby roused her, she listened to the soughing of nearby porpoises and occasionally the sigh of a whale as it blew.

Running log lines behind the ship, Jaki estimated that they were crossing a hundred and twenty-five miles a day. Their latitude, if the shots of the midday sun from the crest of swells were accurate, put them directly on a line with the Antilles, nameless islands on the captured maps arcing south from Porto Rico to the Spanish Main, Tierra Firme, and El Dorado. Three weeks after new year and two days before the maps promised the chain islands, mewing sea birds whirled about the masts and the loamy scent of land haunted the ship. Antlers of driftwood scraped the hull, and the first tarpon were caught on the fishing lines, silver-plated and big as armored men.

Lucinda would not stay in the stateroom, and Jaki assembled a cot for her on the quarterdeck so they could sight the New World together. The western clouds were skulking close to the horizon, streaming off the island peaks beyond the earth's curve, lighting up at sunset in green rays and violet ribbons. A winter storm was mounting, and the winds shifted to the west and blew against them, forcing them to tack. During the night, the stars vanished, and the sea buckled into steep swells.

The next day, with the ship kicking like a stallion on the storm crests, the watch in the foremast top cried "Island!" and claimed the pouch of gold Lucinda had tied to the ship's bell for the first to sight land. She made an entry in the log: "Saturday 22 January 1629, forty-two days after leaving the Whydah coast, Hevioso has sighted an island at" — "Time?" she asked Jaki, and he snapped open an oval pocket watch from where it hung on the side of the binnacle.

"Twenty minutes past the ninth hour."

She filled in the time and their approximate position from the previous day's speed calculations and the last sunshot before the sky clouded over: "9:20 A.M., N11°15′ W62°23′. We have crossed three thousand four hundred and eighty-six miles of ocean to enter the New World with the new year."

Lucinda wrote with bravura to counter her fear of the stiff wind blowing them aslant their sighting. A wave crashed into the hull with a roar, knocking the logbook from her hand and spilling the ink phial. Through the spyglass Jaki could see the island's treeline bowing before the westerly blow. He slammed the glass shut against his palm. "Get below decks, Luci. Maud, help Lucinda."

Lucinda's face looked green in the shadow of her floppy hat. "What are you going to do?"

"We'll reverse," Jaki replied. "We have to run before the storm or it will shatter us." He looked up at Wyvern, its million-year fury blazing in the stormlight. "Full about on this tack," he told the pilot. "Let the wind carry us."

Jaki helped Lucinda to her feet, and she clung to him, her face a furrow of despair. "Jaki, we're so close."

The hurt in her voice engulfed him, an icy fire of fear and rage—fear for the fragile being in his arms, the drum of her pregnancy vibrant against him. Gently, he said, "Go below," and he looked to Maud, who took Lucinda by the shoulders. Jaki turned away and shouted for the sheets to be reefed, Wyvern to be taken down and tied to the stern, and the pilot to turn and hold steady.

Sleeping with Satan tacked into the wind and cut hard away from the island, bearing north into the vast sea as Jaki stood entranced at the rail. *What would Pym do?* he asked himself, and the groaning timbers and whining spars answered. *Silenos* was a weapon; *Sleeping with Satan* a leaky slave ship tired from its forty days at sea.

No! he defied himself. *What would Pym do?* Of course *Silenos* was a weapon: Pym had built her — murderous captain, pitiless Pym. Wyvern's devil would know how to break free of the storm's grip, and Jaki closed his eyes and looked for that ghost in him. Nothing. The light behind his eyes was the color of old shoes. The spars coughed. He opened his eyes and squinted against the daggers of glare from a rent in the stormclouds.

In the next six hours, Jaki and his crew plied every swerve of the wind. But they could not stay ahead of the storm, and finally the gale winds swept over them. "All we can do is batten down and ride out the great winds," Lucinda said when Jaki cursed their ill fortune. He had come to sit with her by the lashed window in the stateroom and was surprised to find Lucinda seraphically calm and clear-headed. "We are far safer at sea than we would be on land. We are fortunate the storm caught us before we made landfall. *Sleeping with Satan* has carried us through one tempest. I dare say, she'll hold us through another. Let us trust in our fate," Lucinda said, crossing her hands over the child within her.

Jaki stared numbly at her. The powers of the world had led him to this precarious crest, and now all his dizzied thoughts and molten feelings were crammed into this one inexhaustible moment. *Life is blind,* Pym echoed from far away. *Alone in a world of accidents, luck is a monster.* Jaki kissed his wife and returned to his place on the rocking quarterdeck.

Lightning jagged overhead, thunder punctured the black afternoon, and *Sleeping with Satan* jumped with the impact of the shattered sky. The crew, who had worked fervidly to outpace the storm, were exhausted and scared, and when Jaki called, "All hands below! Mash wine for all who can stomach it! Today we dance in the jaws of the serpent!" a shout went up.

A mountainous swell hammered the hull, cracking timber and setting the whole ship gonging. Jaki sent the pilot below and tied off the tiller. Whirlwind rain blinded him, and he bowed before it and prayed. But his prayer was lost in the howling wind.

"Fire!" A scream flashed from below, and Jaki saw black smoke snarling from the prow. He cursed and had to lean into the wind to shoulder his way to the hold. Below deck, the crew jammed the companionways, frantic to staunch the leaks that gushed from the weakened hull and to reach the fire before it raged to the gundeck. Stinging smoke blurred the air, and Jaki covered his nose and mouth with the crook of his elbow and shoved forward.

A shriek that burst hearing threw everyone to the planks, and the ship pitched to her side. With a thundercrack, the vessel righted herself, and a gargantuan shout of ripped wood from the depths of the ship announced that the mainmast had sheared away. The next instant, the main deck caved in under the debris of the fallen masts. Rafters collapsed from above, crushing four seamen.

Jaki pushed to his feet, amazed that he was still alive. His breathing ached with the acid fumes of the hull's burning tar as he clambered over bodies and debris toward the aft and Lucinda. The captain's companionway was undamaged, and he flew to the stateroom and crashed through the door to find Lucinda and Maud huddled in the bed, clutching each other. He joined them, shouting comfort they could not hear, and the three of them clung desperately together inside the maelstrom.

By dawn, the great winds had blown over, and the sun rose small and glassy. *Sleeping with Satan* hovered in the water, stern high, prow sunk to where her mainmast had been. Lucinda was wrung from the night-long ordeal, too weak to leave her bed, and Jaki left her there with Maud while he went to survey the damage.

Crewmen were scurrying over the shattered deck, lifting the wounded from the smoking holds. The fire that had been creeping toward the powder hold had been quelled by the corpses the crew had stacked against the blazing timbers. The seawater was stifling the flames in the mash of timbers below them. Jaki watched the water spit through the buckled hull, and his heart jammed against his ribs. In hours, the ship would keel and sink.

"We have to lighten the ship," he said in a foggy voice. He gestured to make his meaning clear, and the weary men set to work sifting through the ruins for what they could lift overboard. Jaki left them chanting a dolorous song for the dead and pressed back through the cluttered gangway toward the stateroom.

Along the way, a dazed crewman stopped him and held up the gold dagger that had been lashed to the bowsprit. In the vapor-wrinkled shadows, the knife seemed lit from its inside. The cord that had held it was still tied about the haft. The sailor mumbled something in African, a few words in English, and Jaki understood that he had retrieved Chrysaor when the bowsprit had been kicked onto the foredeck. Jaki took the blade, nodded his thanks, and budged past the crewman. The cursed knife felt intensely heavy. He slipped it between his belt strap and his hip and hurried on.

The stern of the ship was intact, as if protected by Wyvern, whose ensign still hung from the taffrail. Jaki was estimating how much time the ship could remain afloat and how far they would have to drift to reach land when he met Maud outside the stateroom door. She laid a shivering hand on his arm. "Lucinda's begun labor. The baby has dropped. It won't wait for landfall."

He found Lucinda sitting up, clutching her distended belly, her face flushed and sparking sweat. When she saw him, her hands shot out for him.

Maud hastily set to boiling water on the trivet stove they had carried into the stateroom days before. Jaki held Lucinda to him, and she bit the collar of his shirt, tearing the fabric. He stroked her head, then lay a strong hand on her belly. He felt the head of the baby low and silently prayed his thanks. "Luci, everything will be all right," he assured her. "I have seen babies birthed before. And ours is a healthy one. It has already turned to enter the world." He eased her back until she was lying down and brushed the hair from her glazed eyes. "We will work together now."

The birthing was slow. Hours passed in spasms as the ship shuddered and jolted in the becalmed sea, and Jaki left his wife only briefly to assure himself that the lightened wreck was not capsizing. Night fell, and still Lucinda's birthhold was not fully dilated, though her water had broken. Pain came to her in wracking waves, hour after hour, until her limbs felt made of glass. The walls lurched violently, and she yanked Jaki closer. "The ship," she rasped.

"The flooding has stopped," he lied. "By dawn, we will sight land. Ease your mind."

The ship bucked as the rising water in the bilges shifted the debris about, and Jaki stole time from Lucinda to go out on deck and order a tender prepared for her. Only two tenders had survived the attack, and there was no drinking water left and no edible food. But the flooding had slowed as the rubbish in the holds swelled against the buckled timbers.

At midnight, the baby's head appeared. Jaki was grateful for the hours he had spent listening to the tales the tribal mothers told of childbirth, for men were never allowed in the birthing hut. He remembered enough to keep the crowning head from rushing forward, and he coaxed Lucinda to breathe the head out. The wounded ship rocked viciously, and the shuddering headhold sucked the child into its grip in a drooze of blood. The skin of the taint had turned white with strain and was about to rip. Jaki took the gold blade and lifted it to cut the blanched skin.

Maud, who was helping hold Lucinda's legs, hissed and shook her head. "Not that knife," she mouthed.

"It will give life this time," he said, and waited for the ship to steady. With his finger placed to protect the crowning head, he nicked the stretched skin at the height of a rush. The head emerged face down, and Lucinda shrieked. Jaki lifted the birthcord over the baby's top shoulder as its head turned to face its mother's blood-grimed thigh; then, with a gentle pull, he freed the lower shoulder. The ship shook again, and the child, purple in the shawl of its birthsac, skidded into his hands.

Jaki cleared away the shiny membrane and held the child up for Lucinda to see — a girl, her face a slit-eyed scowl cheesy with afterbirth. She squirmed a long moment and sucked air, turning bluer, and abruptly shook out a scream. Maud offered a blanket, and Jaki laid her in it. With Chrysaor, he cut the umbilical cord.

While Maud presented the baby to Lucinda, Jaki attended the stunned flesh of her birth channel. A gush of dark red blood accompanied the placenta that had slid out with the child, and he gingerly felt the contracted uteral wall and nudged it back in. The bleeding did not stop.

Dawn lit the horizon before Jaki had cleared away the clots of blood and staunched the bleeding from his small incision. Still, blood was draining from higher, pulsing in bright spurts. Maud prepared a poultice of dried moss soaked in the broth of astringent herbs, and Jaki washed his hands and sat with his wife and daughter.

The tiny creature was rose-pink, clear-eyed, and glad for its mother's milk. Lucinda, shivering with aftertremors, smiled through her pain. The room had brightened with more than dawnlight. An astral radiance seemed to suffuse the air, the glow of her life touching the world. The pain had changed color as soon as the baby was born, and the glimmers of hurt in her body felt like wind-humming energy blowing outward from inside her.

Jaki gave her a pain-stifling root to chew, and she worked it wearily with her teeth until its quieting power steadied her trembling. The hungry baby at her breast was all her longing — pure hunger for life — and the little human gave her the strength she needed to close her eyes and sleep.

Dripping pain into the tarry darkness, she rose. Rainbow light uncurled about her, lifting her, and she began to drift beyond sleep. Toilings of fire wavered, unfocused, and — trembling like rain — she sped toward that mute enormity of radiance.

I'm dying, she realized without fear or loneliness. *Death is just as true child has said: a river that bears us away.*

As that thought unfolded, the blurry vista before her snapped to a lucid overview of the brightening sea, and she stared at swells like sapphires and strings of sunlight pulled taut through iron cloudbanks. With a jolt of astonishment, she saw below her the wreck of *Sleeping with Satan.* The ship was floundering among the waves, miles of debris sprawled behind her. She looked like a storm-torn tree adrift.

Under the sooty veils of dawn, a purple armada of islands rose from the horizon, the dreamy upsurge of the New World. *Sleeping with Satan* was only hours from landfall. She yearned to return and shout their triumph to Jaki and Maud, but the current carrying her was too strong, and she rose higher into the fire-rinsed empyrean. The glim of the dawning sky was a blue warmth that smelled of spring and everything hopeful. True peace saturated her.

The astounded silence trembled with diaphanous voices — Maud and Jaki whispering over her. Their words were too remote to understand — but she heard them, and they were enough to anchor her. She stopped rising. The urgency to help the ones she loved gave her the power to pull herself down into the razoring cold. Her being trembled tighter about her, freezing as she pushed against the gravity of freedom. And as she descended, she felt again the loneliness of life, the fear, and the welter of suffering in the grease of flesh — and she wished for her baby and her husband the imperishable gift of the peace she had found beyond life.

As soon as Lucinda's breathing drowsed, Maud dried her tears and pulled away. She bolstered the cot so the baby would not topple with the lurching of the damaged ship, and she gently examined the poultice she had fixed between Lucinda's legs. The moss was dripping blood. She looked to Jaki and saw the black recognition in his clenched face. "She is dying," she whispered.

Jaki pressed his fists to his eyes. He stood stiff with anguish, reaching hard within for the powers of healing and strength that could save her. But inside was only empty torment. He shuffled out of the stateroom and up the tilted stairs to the quarterdeck. The tortured crew had worked all night to clear the debris and lighten the sinking ship; now they sat in a huddle on the intact portion of the main deck, nursing the wounded. Moans and dirgeful singing lilted in the glassy air.

Jaki mounted the frayed shrouds and relieved the watch in the mizzenmast top. From there, he searched the sky and his own heart for some sign, some clue of the spirit powers.

"She is my wife," he begged the invisibles. "No. More. She is my life. Without her I would be a useless sorcerer in the jungle, mending bullet wounds and herding the people deeper into the wilderness. You spared me that. You gave me her. Please, don't take her away now. She is a mother now. Her baby needs her. Take me in her stead." He spread his arms wide. "Slay me now and give her life back!"

The careless wind puffed his shirt and scattered his hair. A sea bird mewled from the topgallant spar. He sagged, and a sob of hopelessness wracked him. Only the fear that Lucinda might wake and find him gone withheld the gathering madness of grief. He lifted himself out of the top and crept down the shrouds.

When he returned to the stateroom, his breath shattered in his lungs. Lucinda was awake and sitting up. She smiled at him, pale as grass, and he stumbled to her like a drunk. Her fingers were icy and he squeezed them in his rough palms. With her free hand, she nudged her blanket lower so he could see their baby asleep at her breast. The infant looked almost a specter of the sunlight itself, golden and frail. He bent to touch her fists and smelled her glisteny scent. "She's beautiful," Jaki said, and brushed her whorl of blond hair. "What shall we name her?"

"I leave that to you," Lucinda said, tucking the blanket closer to the child. The cold had emptied her of almost all feeling but cold, and she strained not to shiver.

Maud approached with a cup of steaming brew. "Drink," she pressed. "This will warm you."

Lucinda took a tremulous sip and handed the bitter tea back. "Thank you, Mousie, but I have no need of this anymore." Dizziness tugged at her blood.

"You must try to drink," Maud insisted. "This will quell you."

She refused with a slow shake of her head. "Not necessary. I am dying."

With all his tenderness, Jaki stroked her disheveled hair, as if tenderness enough could magically heal her. "You are not going to die. We will take care of you."

"Jaki," she said with hurt incredulity. "You most of all should know. I am not afraid. You are here for our child. And Maud. You will go on. I have seen that. But the mystery is over for me."

Maud shared a frightened glance with Jaki and placed the teacup down.

"Lucinda, please —" Jaki's voice swelled louder. "You must try to live."

"True child, don't." She closed her eyes against a wave of numbness as the chill of the world soaked her bones. "Speak honestly with me now as you always have before." When she opened her eyes, she saw him smiling, his stare brimming with hot tears. "Why are you crying? Oh, listen to me." She pulled him closer with her wispy strength. "I think I have already died. I have felt the sky-river that carries us to heaven — just as you've said. True child, it is real. More real than this. You mustn't despair for me. I am happy."

He pressed his burning face against her cheek. "I love you, Lucinda," he breathed. "I cannot live without you."

"Silly sorcerer," she laughed in his ear, and her voice thinned like smoke. "You must live, or what will become of our child? Do not frighten me."

"Lucinda —" He gagged, and she patted him and tangled her fingers in his hair.

"Listen, true child." She spoke in a deepening whisper. "From heaven I saw the New World. It is as beautiful and wild as we have always dreamed." She had to draw deeply to speak, her eyes wincing with the effort, and her words were vaporous, barely audible: "You are not far from there now. Do not give up. Do not ever give up. I have seen . . ." Her breath faltered, and her hand fell from his hair.

He looked up to face her, and her last sigh kissed him.

"Lucinda!" he called in a panic and seized her face between his palms. She was cold, and her sleepy eyes were empty. Maud lifted the baby away. Jaki pressed his wet cheek to Lucinda's. His eyes squeezed shut and his mouth opened soundlessly, a cry too huge for his voice rising through him.

The weary Africans watched as Jaki slammed ripped planks into a dirgeraft with a mallet. Maud watched, too, with the infant in her arms, swaddled in a wool blanket though the blunt heat of the day was wrinkling the air on the horizon. *He's mad,* she thought, appalled by the ferocity of his banging. Twice already she had approached him for help with the hours-old child, but he had ignored her.

The crewmen had found a she-goat with its head above water among the bobbing pens in the shattered animal hold, and Maud squeaked milk from its shrunken dugs and fed it to the baby; meanwhile, the sailors built a fire from broken timber on the sagging deck and roasted the drowned chickens, drinking the blood for want of fresh water. Jaki did not even glance up from his wild pounding when they offered him food. Hands bloodied from splinters, he struggled to lift the raft over the side, angrily shoving away the men who gathered to help. Then, his strength spent, he curled up like a dried leaf. Quietly, some of the crew lashed the raft to the railing with a length of cut rigging, and it knocked dolorously against the hull.

Finally, Jaki stood up and disappeared into the stateroom, emerging with Lucinda's body in his arms. Her limbs were already stiffening, and he held her against him like a brace of sticks. Two men took her shoulders and ankles while Jaki lowered himself into the raft. The body was handed down to him, and he laid her on the warped planks and arranged her hair, sucking air through his teeth not to smell her corruption. He lifted her hand to remove the amber asphodel ring, but the scorching sun had already swelled the flesh about it. With the gold dagger from his hip, he cut a lock of her hair long enough to knot about his wrist. She was lovely even in death, sugar-blond, proud-boned — and young, so much younger than she had seemed in life. Her childlike face was serene as a sleeper's.

"I was not worthy of you, Lucinda," he told her. "The powers of the world took you from me. And the rains will never bring you back." He lifted his tear-washed face to the gulls fluting above them, and his heart clenched so tightly his ears ached. He looked down at her a last time, the beautiful woman of his father's people, the beautiful woman who had died for loving him. "Forgive me, Lucinda. I never knew what I was doing. I never —" His tongue choked him. His knees unlocked, and he had to clutch at the mooring to keep from falling beside her. He hauled himself back aboard the drowning ship and cast off the line.

A spiritless breeze dragged *Sleeping with Satan* west, away from the deathraft, and Jaki chanted loudly in his tribal tongue: "I was your child, Lucinda — but I was not true. I was not your true child, after all. I led you to death. You shared your life with me — and I killed you. Now I will live your death." He ripped his shirt from his body and threw it into the sea. "Oh, Mother — take my wife into your house. Father! Father — take my wife into your big house. And make a place for me. I will be with her again — soon, I swear it."

Revenge weathered the western gale with no serious losses and damage only to her standing rigging. William Quarles stood in the forecastle lee, tasting the wind and watching the dark towers of cloud circle the horizon. The air smelled green with land, yet the gray horizon was empty and haunted with flashes of lightning. Another strong blow was mounting, and he cursed Jaki Gefjon for daring to sail into the jaws of winter.

From the logs of Jaki's ships that Quarles had taken off Africa, he knew the name of his prey was *Sleeping with Satan*. Had the pirate made landfall before these storms crashed out of hell? Quarles opened his telescope and scanned the horizon under the storm crests. Through the lens he spotted driftwood on the bruised swells and called a pikeman to retrieve it. For two days now, vegetation kicked out to sea by the winter storms had been sighted, and by the condition of the woodmeat the captain could gauge how long it had been drifting and how far they were from land.

"Captain!" the pikeman shouted with surprise as he hauled in the debris. "Flotsam!"

Quarles examined a plank that the pikeman had hauled in. The tar-stained grain and the numerous teredo wormholes told him that the timber had come from below a ship's water line. His years of dockyard work helped him to identify the plank as a garboard strake, which meant the vessel it had come from had almost certainly sunk.

While he was studying the plank, a cry from the top alerted him to a small craft on the horizon. Through his telescope he saw a crude raft rocking in the stormswell. *Revenge* steered for it, and when she pulled near, grapnel lines were thrown and the raft pulled alongside. Quarles peered down, and a powerless cry jerked from his entrails — a blind roar filled his ears — and he stared and stared at his dead daughter.

"Foul!" he howled to see Lucinda's face mottled as the moon. "Oh, foul murderer!" He heaved himself over the rail and skirled down the grapnel line. With her stiff body in his arms and the terrible stench invading his sinuses, he shook on his bones and almost blacked out.

The crew of *Revenge* gazed helplessly at each other. The religious crossed themselves, and many looked away.

Quarles lowered the corpse and stood aghast over it, sobs clawing from inside his chest. Eighteen years earlier, his wife had lain dead in his arms, cold as a mirror, and he had not wept, he had not shed a tear — he had not yet learned how. Lucinda had taught him how to weep in Mandu, when he believed he had stolen her back from the pirate. Now the tears flowed freely, for he could never steal her away from this pirate.

Quarles removed his hat and laid it over her ghastly face. Then he bellowed for chain and the colors. He weighted her rigid legs with the shackles and draped her in the Union Jack. Then he went to his state-room and returned with Lucinda's Bible, journal, and tiger's beard. He wrapped the journal in the tiger pelt and dropped it at the foot of her draped body. He opened the Bible to the Psalms, and in a voice like grinding stones, he read: "The cords of death encompassed me, the torrents of perdition assailed me. In my distress I called upon the Lord — and my cry reached his ears."

He decided to keep his daughter's Bible, but from his pocket he removed the timeworn Bible cover inscribed with Pieter Gefjon's family tree and cast it, too, into the raft. "You shall sleep with your lover," he whispered as a promise. "You shall sleep with him under the windings of the sea."

Without taking his eyes from the deathraft, he nodded to the men holding the ropes. The grapnel lines were pulled, the raft tilted, and Lucinda's body plunged into the deep.

Clouds quilted the sky, ruffled by a high wind, but the sea was still as a mirror. On the wreck of *Sleeping with Satan,* two becalmed days after Lucinda's death, most of the wounded were dead, too, and had been jettisoned. The sunstroked survivors quivered like rodents in the florid heat.

The prow of the ship was submerged, the castle of grand bay windows and the neck of the rudder lifted high with the air trapped in the holds. But as the air leaked away, the ship eased stem-first into the depths. What was left of the oak deck stern of the mainmast rode inches from the sea, a jagged float of lumber glinting with salt crystals, too hot to touch. The tattered canvas from the mizzenmast had been cut down and stretched on stalks of split wood to cast shade. Seventeen crewmen lay stupefied in the flimsy shadows.

The stateroom, even with all the windows open, was an oven of trapped air — and that was where Jaki lay, on the cot where Lucinda had died. In the smothering heat, awash in sweat, craven with heartache, he thought of his wife and the times they had made love in this cot, straddling each other as if they could have ridden their bodies through this violent and random world. And the heat baked those thoughts until they were calcined and crumbly, then there was nothing. The dust of his body baked in the stiff bed.

Maud knew that Jaki wanted to die and that he was indifferent to the child whose birth had killed his wife, but she did not leave him alone. She needed his help with the infant. She had tethered the goat to the taffrail, under a rag of propped canvas, and had been feeding it moldy barley grit salvaged from the galley before it had flooded. Without water, the animal's milk had dried up, and the crew wanted to butcher it while it was still alive and its blood uncongealed. They closed in to take the goat, and she rasped a scream for Jaki.

He appeared at the steps of the tilted quarterdeck naked but for a scrap loincloth, his enraged face gaunt and wolf-eyed. He said nothing. And the crewmen crawled back to their shreds of shade.

Jaki turned his stare on the baby in Maud's arms, disappointed she was still alive to suffer, her wrinkled eyes goggling at the world. Maud pleaded with her eyes for him to approach, and he hobbled up the stairs. "She has not cried in a day," Jaki said, kneeling beside them.

"She is too weak." Maud handed her fan to Jaki and let her arm flop to her side. "It is time you named her."

Jaki feebly fanned his daughter, and she closed her eyes into the breeze. "She is dying, like all of us. Why burden her with a name? By nightfall she will be with her mother."

Maud grasped his arm with a harsh strength that startled Jaki. He looked into her scorched face and met a disdainful anger. "Where is your proud talk of the Life now, sorcerer?" Her lips quivered. "Name your child."

He looked away across the still sea, and his face when he turned back was blurred, drugged with desolation. "She shall be called Lucinda."

"No." Maud's voice cracked. "You'll not name her after the dead."

"Her name is Lucinda," Jaki said with finality. He touched the softness between Lucinda's eyes. "She is named by her father." He climbed to his feet and shuffled back down the stairs to the deathbed.

That very hour, a breeze stirred, flurrying the sea, and wuthering within minutes to a rain-swirling wind. The crewmen pranced along the broken deck catching rain with their mouths and turning lopsided kegs upright to hold the fresh water. Men who had been too weary to stand danced, faces open to heaven. One of them jumped to stillness, both arms pointing to the horizon. "Sails!"

Jaki staggered to the quarterdeck at the cry, spyglass in hand. The flash of rain had dimmed, and sunlight glimmered on the water. The sails climbing the horizon were triple-masted to a heavily gunned bark flying the red-and-white cross. "Warship," he declared. "English."

"Will they see us?" Maud asked from behind him. "We must light a fire."

Jaki slammed the glass closed against the rail and cast the tube into the sea. "They've already seen us. We are in their line. They will reach us in the hour."

"Then, we are saved," Maud cried.

"You are — and Lucinda," Jaki said and looked over the seventeen Africans lapping water from their palms. "They will find no freedom aboard that ship. And I will share Pym's fate — if they take me." He regarded the sullen clouds in the southeast. "Another bank of rain is closing. A storm. If we ride that we may lose them in the longboat." He went to the taffrail and began unlashing the ensign banner that bore Wyvern.

"What are you doing?" Maud asked hotly.

"We will need a sail," he answered. "This will do."

"A sail?" She frowned with bewilderment and looked across the smashed carcass of the ship at the inundated debris and the longboat floating there. "You think to flee a three-master in that?"

"It is ugly," he admitted, freeing the salt-chymed banner. "But it is handsomer than the scaffold. Stand back."

The crewmen at his side helped him to draw in Wyvern, and he ordered the others to lug the tender over the side and to gather all the matchlocks.

"Jaki," Maud shrilled. "You will be captured. You cannot escape."

Jaki jerked a thumb at the sky. "The storm will cover us. And with this wind, we may yet reach the islands. I believe we are only leagues away. By dawn, we may well be in the New World."

Maud bit her lip to keep from answering him. He was mad, greedy for death. She knew she could not dissuade him. The rain had refreshed the infant enough for her to whimper with hunger, and Maud sat down with her beside the binnacle and bared her breast. "There's nothing here for you, young creature," she said, gentling the anxious face. "But you will be safe soon." The child mouthed her halfheartedly and began to cry. "Good girl. You've fight left in you yet." *Like your parents,* she thought.

Jaki and the Africans secured a makeshift mast to the longboat's thwarts with fish netting for rope. It took them all of an hour to fasten it properly and to pulley-rig their banner. By then, the English warship was cutting across the wind toward them.

Sleeping with Satan was so low in the water that the tender glided easily through the blasted gap of the prow. Jaki marshaled the six men who wanted to flee. The others were too weak to face a sea journey in a storm-driven longboat, or they loved life more than they feared slavery. While those who were going gathered what remained of the rain spill, Jaki climbed to the quarterdeck and knelt beside Maud and the wailing Lucinda. "I will cherish you in my memory, young sister."

"And your daughter?" she asked, her eyes playing angrily over his face.

Jaki put his thumb to the baby's crying mouth. Animated, she displayed the wide facebones of his forest ancestors. "You have earned her life. She is your daughter now."

"Stay," Maud begged, clutching him with one hand at the back of his neck.

"And be hanged?" He leaned into her grasp and kissed her cheek. "No, it is better that Lucinda's father run and hide. I will seek you out when I am free."

"How? The world is vast."

He smiled plaintively and stood up. "I am a Rain Wanderer. I will find you." And then he was gone, limping down the steps and curling his long body over the rail and into the masted longboat. As he stood in the stern and waved to her, she recognized the cold glow on his face and the pale aura of death that had passed to him from his wife — and she did not wave back.

Wyvern caught the gusty rain and carried Jaki and his comrades away. Across Jaki's naked chest, a snakeskin strap hung the medicine bag he had made in Africa, and in his right fist Chrysaor caught the sunlight. Maud stood up to follow the longboat's glide into the distance. For a while, she believed the English galleon would ignore the fleeing boat — the bark was furling her sheets and turning to come alongside the wreck. Maud waved to the mariners on the ship's poop deck, one of them studying her with a telescope, and she held the baby up for them to see.

Quarles recognized Maud and ordered *Revenge* to drop anchor beside *Sleeping with Satan.* His heart thrashed at the sight of the infant. Since finding his daughter's corpse the day before, he had been tortured with memories of her as a child — a princess of life, clever and frisky — and he was the first to board the sinking pirate vessel, hurrying down the grappling net, saber in hand.

At the sight of him, Maud almost dropped to her knees. "God in Heaven," she whimpered. "Captain Quarles!"

Quarles bolstered her with one arm, attentive to the terror and the weakness in her face. "Bear up, Maid Rufoote," he urged, and his voice startled her alert. "I'm not going to harm you." He stared down at the ruddy infant and a luminous strength swelled in him. "Is this Lucinda's child?"

"Yes," Maud whispered. "But she — she . . ."

"I know she's dead," said he. "We buried her yesterday at sea. Where is the heathen who murdered her?" His gaze was ferocious, and she quailed. "Water," he yelled, and knelt with her into her faint, supporting the baby with his swordarm. "Bring water!"

The infant spluttered a cry, alarmed by Quarles's shouts, and he dropped his saber and lifted her frail weight. The pink buds of her fists shook, and her eyes squeezed tight with the vigor of her cry. "There, child," he muttered, and put a thumb to her chin. "You're with your grandfather now. Your suffering is at its end. No harm will come to you so long as I live."

A flagon was passed to him, and he unstoppered it and tried unsuccessfully to tip water to the baby's lips. Then he splashed water over Maud's face, and she blinked and roused. "Drink, Maid Rufoote. Not too deeply. Good. Now help me with this child. I fear she's fevered."

Maud sat up groggily and took the flagon. With her finger over the spout she dribbled water to the infant's lips while Quarles held her. In a moment the child quieted and looked up at the bearded face above her. "She's weak. She needs milk."

"We've goats aboard," Quarles said. "There will be milk for her." He gazed down, and a trembling of love surprised him, trespassing the solitude of his grief and anger. "How old is she now?"

"This is her third day in the world."

"And is she named?"

Maud met Quarles's keen stare. "She's named after her mother."

Quarles swallowed and half nodded. "So be it. Take her aboard." He signed for the sailors who had been watching, handed Maud the infant, and the seamen escorted her up the grappling net. Quarles looked after them until they were free of the wreck.

The ominous sky rattled with lightning, and the rain stiffened. Quarles had his men hurry the Africans aboard *Revenge.* He stood on the sinking deck, rain veiling from the brim of his hat, and swept his far gaze over the frothing sea. Among the feathery crests, he picked out the distant sail of the longboat he had seen jettison as *Revenge* approached. *Sleeping with Satan* groaned mightily and wobbled. He banged his boot against her gunwale, cursed the very wood, and abandoned the wreck.

The Africans were dropped into the animal hold where food and water was lowered to them. Maud and the baby were ushered below deck to the surgeon's cabin. And Quarles hollered commands to set *Revenge* in pursuit of the longboat.

Jaki grimly observed the warship sliding after them. Where was the rain that was supposed to blanket them? To the east, mauve clouds released rain in opalescent auroras, sheeting the galleon. "Fight or surrender?" he asked aloud, facing the six men in the longboat.

They scowled back at him with unanimous defiance and raised their matchlocks. "Death before slavery!" they shouted. "We dance in the jaws of the serpent."

"Hold your fire, then," Jaki commanded, "until each shot will take a slaver with us to the afterworld. Prime your guns, men. Today is the end of our suffering."

The galleon sliced toward them with the stormclouds behind it. The rising wind on the port beams carried pinpoints of warm rain and veils of cold spray. A plover appeared overhead, and the Africans whooped with joy for the omen. The sea bird tilted into the wind and flew ahead of the longboat as if showing the way.

"Land!" the crewman in the prow yelled, and all hands looked away from the pursuing galleon to the western horizon, where purple smoke edged the horizon.

The British ship was gaining swiftly, and the men in the longboat could see sailors with muskets at the gunwale aiming at them. Jaki stepped to the stern and pointed Chrysaor at the galleon. If anyone was to be shot, he would be first. Lucinda was a heartbeat away.

"Jaki Gefjon!" a gruff voice rode the high wind. "Drop your sail! Come about!"

Jaki straitened to hear his name, and the cold thought pierced him that the British man-of-war was William Quarles's. He cupped a hand to shield his eyes from the scudding spray. At the forecastle rail was a man in a white-plumed hat, a spyglass to his eye.

"Ready on Wyvern," Jaki called. He watched the warship bear down on them and Lucinda's father come clearly into view, the strength of his hatred apparent even at this distance. "They're going to ram us if we hold." Jaki swelled before the swoop of death, eager for it, feeling it in the motion of waves and wind, shoreless, infinite.

"Broach to! Drop your sail! Or we will run you down!" Quarles shouted.

The wind steepened, and the warship's bow foamed closer, its name visible, laid in scarlet on the bow: *Revenge.* "Tack alee!" Jaki cried. The sailors reefed Wyvern, pulled the hoist line to leeward, and dropped the banner into the wind in time to cut out of the galleon's direct path.

Musketmen rushed to the rail of *Revenge* as the longboat slid past. The smoke of their gunfire leaped forward with the wet wind, and the tillerman sitting below Jaki fell from the longboat before he could fire his matchlock. Jaki dropped into his place as the Africans fired. Two of the matchlocks clicked uselessly in the rain; three flared loudly. Two musketmen on the galleon snapped away before their comrades' second round crackled. Musketballs punched through Wyvern and crashed into the trammeled spar that served as a mast. One struck a sailor in his thigh, and he fell with a scream.

Jaki hooked his leg over the tiller, hoisted the fallen matchlock, and squeezed the trigger. One of the musketmen dropped. Jaki flung the matchlock aside and steered across the wind behind the big ship. A squeal of ripping wood leaped from the damaged mast. The pole snapped, dropping Wyvern onto the prow.

From the porthole in the surgeon's cabin, Maud saw musketballs crash into the longboat and spun aside with a cry. Staggering with the ship's roll, she clutched the frightened baby to her and barged for the door.

On deck, sailors bustled through the rain to bring *Revenge* about. Quarles, striding along the main deck and exhorting his men, was frantic to destroy the longboat. When he saw Maud and the child, he hollered, "Get below!"

"No!" she screamed. "You are killing this baby's father."

"He is a murderer!" Quarles shouted back. "He slayed my daughter, my only child."

"No! Lucinda loved him. She died loving him. You must not kill him."

Quarles's face warped with rage. He waved at a seaman. "Take her below and lock her in the surgeon's cabin. Be quick."

The five pirates had used this brief respite to pull farther into the shallow water, and Quarles realized as he turned upon them again that pursuit would risk grounding the deep-drafted galleon. The storm sky clouded the water, disguising sandbars and coral shoals, and he ran to the pilot and ordered the big ship to pull away. "Port cannon!" he bellowed to his officers. "Blast that longboat to hell!"

Revenge sheered off abruptly, and her gunports clacked open. Jaki knew the fight was over. He abandoned the tiller, cut the rigging from the canvas with his gold dagger, and muscled the cracked mast overboard. The Africans were huddling now, oars up, staring dolefully across the swells at the warship's cannon.

Jaki lifted Wyvern and wrapped the sheet about him so that the viper-hawk's visage gloated from his chest. Over it he hung his medicine bag by its strap. With a tight smile, he turned to the cowering men and raised his knife. "We dance in the jaws of the serpent."

The men mumbled the chant hollowly, and Jaki faced the line of gunmen, the wet fingers of the dead on him.

The cannon kicked fire and blusterous smoke, and the siren cries of metal hurtling through the rain's iridescence lifted the Africans to their feet. The impact heaved the sea into the sky and scribbled the stormy air with burst timber, orts of flesh, and a spray of blood.

When the cannonsmoke cleared, only shards of the longboat remained, tossed by the swells. William Quarles exulted.

Revenge rode the gale winds through the Antilles and arrived in the Dutch colony on Santa Cruz two days later. The crew, who had signed aboard in Ribeira Grande for passage to the New World and plunder, were disgruntled that their captain had no further intention of stalking prizes and planned instead to winter in the Caribbean and sail north in the spring to the distant Dutch colony of New Holland. They demanded payment, and Quarles, having no other sizable assets, was obliged to relinquish command of *Revenge* to the crew, who elected their own captain and sailed at once to despoil the Spanish silver *flota* off Cuba.

The Dutch colony on Santa Cruz was a small European village of gabled chalets with rubble walls in pastel colors and yards crowded with Ixora shrubs and zinnia hedges. The populace earned their livelihood managing sugar cane fields, and there was little work for an exiled British captain. Quarles banged a hut together from weathered ship's lumber and used his meager funds to provide for himself, his granddaughter, and his somnolent maid.

Maud rarely spoke with Quarles. She had witnessed the destruction of the longboat from the surgeon's porthole — torn bodies tossed into the air, the broken vessel and its passengers scattered like rubbish into the storm — and she tried hard to forget. She busied herself tending the infant and fishing on the sparkling cape. She longed to return to

England and her Aunt Timotha, but Quarles could not manage the child without her. Finally, in an attempt to appease her, he sent for the old woman through the Dutch governor of Santa Cruz. In the spring, with the remainder of his gold, he bought passage for himself, Maud, and the child on a Dutch frigate bound for New Holland. When they arrived in Fort Amsterdam in May, Aunt Timotha was on the wharf waiting for them.

Craggy as a pine cone, ruddy and alert, Timotha Firth was the first true joy Maud knew since leaving Africa. She bounced in the old woman's embrace, and Timotha lay hands the color of musty wheat on the baby's head and sang a blessing in the old tongue. Her gap-toothed smile warmed even Quarles. Without title or fortune, their lot would be difficult, and that grieved him for the sake of the little girl. Yet when he saw the crone from his childhood, an inexplicable hope opened in him.

That confidence did not last the day. Fort Amsterdam was a stockaded hamlet with rutted dirt roads still muddy from the spring rains. The ditches outside the barricades festered with mounded refuse, offal from the butchers, gurry from the wharves, and ordure from the chamber pots of the town. Flies swarmed. The Dutch stared suspiciously at the rattily dressed English and their three goats, and the governor had them wait among the stinging flies an hour before he reviewed Quarles's claim. A provisional deed was drafted requiring Quarles to develop his property within a year or forfeit it, and the English were dispatched downriver in a dinghy. The ferryman carried them past lush meadowland and walnut groves and deposited them with their goats and their two crates of worldly possessions on the banks of a marshland.

"I have been duped!" Quarles shouted. "My Devon estate, fifty acres of cultivated land, three miles square of woodland and chase, taken from me in barter for this — this swamp! I am duped! The Thieves' Church has swindled me!"

"Aye, so they have," Timotha cackled, gawking about at the shaggy kingdom of swamp grass and reckless trees. "And what hope had you, a man of honor, in a church of thieves?"

Quarles glowered, but Timotha was not looking at him. She and Maud stood in awe before the primeval beauty of the land. Streams shimmered unbound by banks over sandbars tufted with copses of willow and swales of reeds. On higher ground, trees loomed in melancholy grandeur like the ancient forests of Britain. No ax had ever been wielded in these jammed groves, and huge, fantastically contorted limbs meshed with the verdure of young boughs. Wanton grapevines coiled to the top of the tallest trees and swung in the breeze like the ragged shrouds of a ship. Everywhere giant wildwoods were lifting from their roots in the marshy soil and toppled trees lay in ruins under gilled mushrooms and a profusion of brilliant flowers that glowed hotly in the gloom. Spotted deer crouched among the thickets and waterfowl burst into flight at their approach.

In a glade on a high knoll overlooking the marsh and the river, Quarles and Maud set up camp, erecting a tent from waxed sail canvas. While Timotha built a fire and Maud milked the goats, Quarles took his musket and, muttering imprecations at the Thieves' Church, stalked off to hunt them a meal. Old meanings had lost their hold. Everything he had learned as a mariner and a sea captain was useless to him now. All his life he had struggled to survive — but never like this, gun in hand, not knowing where to begin in the trackless forest.

He paused and gazed down on the marsh and the slow swerve of the river. When the sour riverscent reached him, he began to see in his mind a harbor, right there in the tidewater at the edge of his land. He had had enough experience as a dockhand to know that the site was ideal — close enough to the fort for a ferry, yet far enough from the clutter of the narrows to anchor many more big ships than the fort could, without clogging the causeway. The fantasy flexed in his brain with such lucidity he forgot his despair and allowed himself to dream. He knew that if he did not build this harbor himself, some opportune Dutchman would.

He envisioned the work that lay ahead. If he could do it, perhaps he would return to where he had begun as a youth — an earthly price to pay for a man who had taken supreme vengeance into his own hands. He slapped the mosquitoes stinging his cheeks and thought of Jaki Gefjon, who had lived wild all his life. The pirate's ghost would get full satisfaction from the humbling years that Quarles would have to endure to earn a life for the young Lucinda from this wilderness, and that thought eased him. He grimly saluted the riverbend, where the future was gathering its tasks, and turned back into the forest.

Night. Darkness sleek and black as a beetle. Far away the blood beat — quiet as the pulse of a flame.

Jaki sat up and found himself propped by a staghorn of driftwood. Before him, phosphorescent waves sizzled across a pebbly beach. Beside him sprawled one of the Africans who had stood with him in the longboat when the cannon fired. He was still hugging the plank that had carried him on the tide to this beach.

Jaki looked down at himself and ran his hands over the tattered flag of Wyvern, which barely covered his nakedness. He remembered the cannonshot striking the prow of the longboat and hurling him out of the stern and into the water as the hull burst over him. Fléchettes of the exploded longboat had gashed him, but he was whole — yet again, the powers of the world had spared him. He lay back into the bramble of driftwood and stared up into the shreds of stormcloud dissolving in the trade wind. Far out at sea, out over the Old World, the sun was rising.

The African, too, was intact, scathed by splinters but whole. When he woke, he wept for those who would not wake and bowed in gratitude to the climbing sun. Together, Jaki and the African explored the islet. Great, muscular trees and clacking palms overlooked them from the limestone scarp above the beach, obedient to the stream hidden beneath them. Cactus and palmetto thronged on the coral marl of the moon-colored bluffs. And the emerald sounds of the long reef bobbed with white birds.

Snagged among the driftwood was his medicine bag. The ripped pouch was emptied of its herbs and only the mountains' tears remained, weighted with the heavy-heartedness of the first people. One was missing, claimed by the sea. Seven were left. Under the torn bag, snagged among knotted snakeskin, was the gold ritual dagger, Chrysaor.

Jaki jerked the cursed knife free. As he raised it to hurl it into the green water, a sunburst smote him from the blade's mirror, reminding him of the defiance of death. Here was all the world's grief in one loathsome object. He lowered the knife and gazed into its gold surface.

The sober face that stared back was someone new. He recognized his mother in the spacious bonecurve between the vivid blue eyes, and he felt the oddity she had felt when she stared into his father's foreign face. He saw not his spirit father but the father of his flesh, the one who had been seized by an irrepressible desire for her beyond all the disciplines of strangeness.

His hand opened, and he examined the pinioned serpent that formed the knife's hilt. The dragonhawk was Wyvern, the monstered fusion of life and death. The serpent tail was everything close to the earth—the mineral madness of roots sprouting jungles, animals, and tribes, while the eagle head and winged claws were all that lofted into the invisible. And he saw that he was himself Wyvern. He had sensed it from the first, but now that certainty winced like a bubble in his heart. Mothered by the jungle, fathered by the wind, he was half serpent sorcerer and half raptor pirate — a child of lust and deception — the earth aching with the effort of heaven.

Jaki's fist closed on the hilt. It was just a knife, he reminded himself, and he tucked the blade into his waistcloth. He was just a man. And all these thoughts that leaped up in him were only the noises of his cry.

The islet was barren but for a few mighty trees, blue turtles, and some crocodiles who sulked among lionheaded willows. On the north shore, Jaki and the African discovered the ruins of a tribal settlement — charred huts, shattered drying racks, wind-rubbed skeletons with bashed skulls, and a dented conquistador's helmet.

The African retreated to the forest to gather breadfruit, and Jaki sat among the skeletons and raised his face to the high cumulus. The garbage dumps of the future were there in the sky, the tribes foraging among them, their big-bellied children aimlessly wandering through the slosh of smoldering trash where rain forests had once stood. In the distance were the shining glass towers of the new cities, the sky-tall houses where the grandchildren of the conquerors lived. And beyond the spires loomed the horrible firecloud of death, a vastly evil tree of purple lightning and orange billowings. The melted child emerged, glossy with burns, its broken mouth bubbling with blisters. And Jaki did not look away. He watched the child curl into a mollusk of cinders, one hand reaching out for him — and in its crisp fingers, blackening in the heat, was Chrysaor.

Jaki understood then the horrible vision that his terror had always deafened before. The conquered world, many children away, was immolating itself. The future was a vast sacrifice — a ritual of destruction that would tear the world apart between the opposing gods of sky and earth. And he knew then why these visions had come to him and what they had been riddling: the future needed Wyvern, the god that was both sky and earth. The heavenly god of the Book, whom Mala had loved, was not enough, for that high god trampled the snake underfoot and subjugated the earth and her tribes. As a child, Jaki had sensed that the angry god of the Book, who ritually murdered his own son, was not his god. Now he knew that was true. The future of humanity, if it was to survive at all, needed Wyvern, and it needed him and half-breeds like him, who had learned from both the cunning mansnake who loved the earth and from the rapacious hawkman who loved high places.

But Jaki felt that the truth of these visions had come clear too late for him. Under the weight of his mourning, he had no hope for the future. What difference could one soul make to the enormous suffering he had glimpsed? His own pain seemed more than he could bear, and he spent three days doubled up under the palms, eating nothing, drinking only the rain that fell over him in the green sunsets.

The African was angry that Jaki scorned the gift of life that the gods had freely given; *he* did not want to die on this lonely atoll. When Jaki began to wither, he force-fed him and harassed him until the sorcerer at last found living easier than dying. He began to eat again to appease his tormentor, and as his strength returned he realized that the animal inside his body would not let him die. He would have to live with his grief, and he silenced the African by busying himself making stone axes and hacking at the powerful trees. He spent all of himself in his work, hoping to weary his sorrow. He grew stronger, and within a fortnight the two of them had built a crude vessel to bear them over the moon-drawn paths of the sea.

The catamaran that Jaki and the African lashed together from tamarind logs carried them south through the Antilles to Misteriosa Cays, a stammer of islands where they found a cove of blacks who had escaped from slavery in the Spanish Main. The African chose to stay among them with the Arawak Indians, who regarded the blacks as beloved of the night goddess and therefore sacred.

Jaki lingered there three moons, the vision of the world's sacrificial death withering before the brutal grief of losing Lucinda. What could the future really come to for him without her? Mourning lay heavy as sludge in his lungs, and he could breathe clearly only in the jungle. The biting insects and the persistent malarial tremors that he refused to treat were the companions of his sorrow. His years at sea with Pym and Lucinda had softened him, and the ache of his bare feet among the root burls, thorns, and scorpions was welcome.

Finally, though, his grief was no more faithful than life. And one morning, he saw a sight that flung him out of the jungle. In the stumbling water of a brook, Arawak maidens were bathing themselves for some dawn ritual. The girls stroked each other's breasts, their laughter flashing through the trees like startled birds. Their playful eroticism surprised him, and his body ached with desire as if for the first time.

Jaki was annoyed at the urgency of the life force in him, irate that he could feel any desire after the death of the woman he loved. He scolded himself for his infidelity, accusing himself of being no better a man than the salacious fop who had spawned him. In his dreams, he was visited by the Arawak maidens and the paddy girls of his adolescence, and when he woke he hungered more for the softness of a woman's embrace than for food. He had to admit then that if he was to prove himself better than his father, he could no longer hide from his fate in the jungle. Life would have its way with him — as always before.

Something strong carried the sun, the moon, and the stars through the sky — whatever Pym had said about the world spinning like a ball, whatever Jabalwan had said about the firebird dancing its victory around the body of the nighthawk — and something powerful was carrying him through his sorrow. But he would not forget Lucinda. No matter how strong the desire for life grew in him, he would not forget his wife. And the only way he could think to remember her now that the grief was molting to life was to find their daughter and to be for her the father he had always yearned to find for himself.

*

Jaki bathed in the brook where he had seen the maidens frolicking, cut the burrs from his hair with Chrysaor, and returned to the Arawak village where he and the African had first arrived. The tribesfolk were happy to outfit the catamaran with a sail and to see the sad spiritman leave their island.

Jaki steered south, remembering from his maps that his father's people, the Dutch, had colonies on the northeast coast of South America. Five moons after *Revenge* had exploded the longboat from under him, Jaki surfed into the mouth of a river, following a Dutch brigantine that led him upstream to a log-walled fortress. Naked but for a loincloth, he arrived at Fort Kyk on the Essequibo River in Guiana on a luminous morning in July 1629.

Jaki was the color of brass as he stepped from the catamaran onto wharves of lashed logs, where slaves were unloading wagons and heaping barges with bales of indigo and cotton. Jaki's blue eyes and sunbleached hair admitted him to the fort, and he went directly to the largest building, a three-tiered mansion with Dutch gables and the tan and green company flag hanging limply before it. His Dutch was meager but sufficient to request an audience with the governor. The sunburned secretary laughed at the naked youth, until Jaki showed him the smallest of the diamonds, a cloudy chunk the size of a walnut.

The governor wore his wide ruff low around his neck in deference to the ponderous heat. He had scaly eyepouches like a lizard, and he spoke English and Spanish. With the precise eye for value and opportunity that had created the Dutch empire from the avarice of merchants, he greeted Jaki with avuncular affection and a sincere interest in his story.

In his two years of watching Lucinda bargain, Jaki had learned how to gauge the trustworthiness of men, and when he was convinced that the governor was a man of traditional European honor whose greed could not be overestimated, he placed three of the seven mountains' tears on the polished rosewood table. The governor's face opened like a blossom.

"These are the woes of all the sorcerers who came before me," Jaki explained. "I have named them after my own sorrows."

He pushed the three across the table one at a time, and with each one he spoke a name, "*Malawangkuchingang — Jabalwan — Wawa.* With these I would buy a ship. I believe they are sufficient for a large, seaworthy vessel."

"Indeed," the governor agreed, holding the smoky gems to the light, reading the worth of several fully outfitted carracks in them. "These are gems of the first water. You will have your ship, Mister Gefjon."

Jaki reached into his pouch and held up a rough, round diamond. "*Pym's Lost Eye,*" he called it, and smiled wanly. "With this I want the funds for a crew."

"Done," the governor said, plucking the gem from Jaki's fingers. Its weight startled him, and he decided that the crew would be paid for from his own coffers and the incomparably more valuable gem would accompany him on his triumphant return to Amsterdam.

"I have other diamonds," Jaki announced. "And they will be yours, once I have a ship and crew and the necessary papers to assert my rights as the ship's owner and master."

The governor smiled at Jaki's caution. "You have learned well from your English wife, Jaki Gefjon." After instructing the secretary to draft the papers, the governor escorted Jaki to the wharves.

The vessel that Jaki had purchased was the smallest but most modern merchant ship in the harbor, taken as a prize from the British six months earlier, a twenty-four-gun frigate. Jaki immediately dubbed her *Lucinda.* He arranged to have the whipstaff replaced with a wheel and to paint the hull dolphin blue, the color of the horizon. While that work was being done, the governor sent a dispatch at Jaki's request to all the Dutch ports in the Caribbean, inquiring about *Revenge.* A month later, when *Lucinda* was ready to sail, Jaki knew that his daughter was alive and that William Quarles had claimed the infant and taken her with him, north to the new colonies in the primeval forests of America.

With the authorized ownership documents for *Lucinda* in his hands, Jaki met the governor in his office and produced two more diamonds. They were the largest, one square as a boottip, the other long as a goblet's stem, and when he clicked them together sparks flashed in the governor's eyes. *Pieter Gefjon's Faith,* he named the square one, and the long one he called *Jan van Noot's Penis.* "With Gefjon's, full provisions for my crew and sufficient cargo to earn our welcome in ports of trade. That is what my spirit father would have wanted." At the governor's nod, he handed over Pieter Gefjon's gem. "For the second, I want gold."

The September day *Lucinda* sailed from Fort Kyk, her holds were filled with indigo, tobacco, and cocoa from the jungle plantations of Guiana and furniture and Delft tile from Europe. Captain Jaki Gefjon held bills of trade for a dozen ports on his cruise through the islands and up the Atlantic coast to the Dutch settlement of Fort Amsterdam. Twenty-two years after he had lost his head, Pieter Gefjon's ambition for the wealth of diamonds and precious cargo was attained by his namesake, half a world from where his blood had spilled.

But another ghost was more apparently present on that late summer voyage. At Fort Kyk, Jaki had commissioned a tailor, a bootmaker, and a barber, and he stood on the bridge of his frigate in pythonskin boots cupped low on the calf, white mariner's trousers, and black jacket trimmed in scarlet with the secret designs of the Rain Wanderers. He avoided ruff but wore lace and falling bands at his stiff collar. On his head, he fitted a black brimmed hat cocked and plumed with blue parrot feathers. At the front of the hat, he attached the last of the mountains' tears, the diamond that had belonged to Lucinda and that Maud believed bewitched, the one he had named *The Gypsy's Curse*. With his coifed hair and the frosty beard he had grown since his wife's death and trimmed to the clean edge of his jaw, he was the apparition of Jan van Noot.

The Dutch named the river the Mauritius, but Quarles insisted that it should be named after its English discoverer, and he called it the Hudson. In the five months since Quarles and the two women had been left on this shore, they had lived off the abundant land. Maud and Timotha fed the baby with goat milk, tuber mush, and berry pulp. Quarles was an excellent shot, and the women dressed the skins of the animals he hunted. Once a month he carried to Fort Amsterdam the buckskins and hare pelts they did not need and traded them for more shot and powder.

They had done little to improve the land because survival alone required their full efforts. Nonetheless, Quarles and Maud together had managed to clear the knoll overlooking the river, fell trees, roll logs, and construct a crude cabin with a roof of waxed canvas and rush reeds and a hearth of river slate and rocks. The effort had almost broken them, and they ached continually in every joint.

Each day Quarles made some effort toward creating the pier he had envisioned on the riverbend. Without draft animals, his efforts to clear the embankment and drive posts were pathetic, and the approach of winter only drove him harder. But with the first deep chill of October, Lucinda became ill, and Quarles's vision of a river estate withered like a mirage.

From the first, the child had been hardy, eager to toddle, attentive to every seed tuft or leaf that the wind gifted her. But fever dulled her watchful stare. She wailed in spasms and whimpered day and night. Timotha bathed her in evergreen teas to cool the fever and Maud dribbled nettle extract into her broth to fortify the infant, but nothing helped.

"I am sore afraid," Maud whispered to her aunt, and Quarles's heart throttled to hear Timotha reply, " 'Tis the black fever, Maud, and there be nought we can do but pray — pray God take her swiftly from her suffering."

Quarles stumbled into the forest and collapsed on the sodden ground, shivering with anguish. Timotha's words came back on him: *There be nought we can do but pray*. He prayed. Always before he had mocked the faith of those who had prayed, but now he prayed. Though he knew nothing of his own soul, he prayed that the life of this infant be spared. Though his prayer felt like wind blowing through a hole in a plank, he begged to the unseen high one. Though he could find no more words than *Spare this girl-child, Lord of Life,* he worshiped until his breath thickened in his throat and he gagged on his faithlessness.

That night, the fever broke. *Chance fortune,* Quarles told himself, but he could not believe that anymore. His joy was too strong, and he danced with the baby in his arms. The next morning, he shaved his beard to signify his humility before the Lord and the prodigious change within him, and he began to read his dead daughter's Bible. Maud and Timotha were astonished — suddenly William Quarles was eager to speak with them of God's providence, the corruption of life since the Fall, and their supreme fortune in having each other to share the work of redemption.

From the Bible, Quarles learned the necessity of forgiveness, and he found a chapel for himself in the forest where he could purge his soul of its hatred and clear the way for God's intervention in his life. Kneeling under the rays of sunlight, the leaves bright as stained glass in the trees, he forgave the Church of the Two Thieves for cheating him — and he thanked the Lord for his home in the mild haze of the marsh and for the wild things that had given their lives to become food and clothing. At last he had the strength to forgive the pirate Trevor Pym for slaying Uncle Samuel and depriving him of the privileged life that would have been his birthright. And he forgave Uncle Samuel for his dissipation of the family fortune and his desperate betrayal of Drake's fleet. And he forgave himself for his iron will that love could not bend, that had driven his daughter from him. The calm ferocity of his forbearance opened another chamber in his lungs, and he breathed deeply and struggled to forgive Jaki Gefjon for his destruction of *The Fateful Sisters.*

He squeezed his eyes shut tight, and the stars' white fire glistened inside him. Aloud, he said, "I forgive you, Jaki Gefjon — I forgive you for taking my daughter from me." A sob wrenched through him, and he doubled over.

When the pain unclenched in his chest, he looked up. The air was dizzy with leaves unlatched by the wind. And he felt more lonely and more alive than anyone on earth.

Quarles was on his hands and knees in the mud, wrestling a flat boulder into its place in his rude tidewall, when the blue-hulled frigate cruised up the Narrows. The beauty of the vessel lifted him to his feet, and he stood in the summery breeze that had surprised November and admired the fleet rake of the masts.

He mounted the slick rocks of the jetty to better view the ship as she glided past, and he noted her Dutch Company colors, though the wide cut of the courses and the slim strake seemed the latest British innovations. She was a prize, he realized, and a flinch of patriotic hurt troubled him despite his exile. He squinted to read her name and almost toppled from his perch when he saw etched in gold on the prow *Lucinda.*

He hailed, "Lucinda!" But the frigate was too far and he was yelling into the wind. A deckhand waved at him, and he knew what a pitiful sight he must look, grimed in mud atop his rockpile. He watched until the ship vanished around the bend that would take her to Fort Amsterdam. Was it sheer chance that the Dutch had given a British prize his dead daughter's name? Or was God putting him to the ultimate test and resurrecting his direst enemy? Could that be? He had blown up Jaki Gefjon at sea — but he had not seen the man's body. The seastorm had swept the debris into the shoals.

A saline bitterness climbed in his throat, a taste like blood, as he picked his way carefully down the rocks. He needed the scripture's nakedness, the truth stripped of his anguish and fragility, and he hurried toward the cabin over the scraggy bogland, waist-deep in rushes and marsh weeds.

Maud was lugging home a bucket of stream water when Quarles scuttled out of the cabin, the Bible clasped to his breast, and disappeared into the forest. She looked to Timotha, who was amusing the baby by the woodpile, and the old woman shrugged. In the last month, since Lucinda's recovery, the captain had been a different man entirely, reshaped by his new-found faith. He whistled jaunty tunes when he returned from the hunt, crawled laughing on the ground for hours with his grandchild, and read long passages from the Bible to the women while they quilted or shucked walnuts. He had found a poor peace in himself — that was how Timotha explained it to Maud. "A poor peace he's found counting his denials." And Maud felt pity for him each morning that he slogged out to the riverbank to lash rocks, drag them through the mud, and lever them into the breakwater.

"How can he build an anchorage with his bare hands?" she asked her aunt one drizzly morning when the slosh of the river was plucking the rocks away from the jetty as fast as he was stacking them. "What is to become of his dream?"

"What becomes of all our dreams," Timotha replied. "We reach for the moon if we have any dreams at all. But the moon is a horn we blow with our last breath, and 'tis not till then we know the worth of our striving. Leave him to his dreams, and they will carry him."

Quarles knelt among the trees and read, "Thou shalt not avenge, nor bear any grudge . . ." And the words wavered on the page like a vibration in the powdery sunlight. "My name is Legion, for we are many." But images of Lucinda disfigured by death jammed his heart — her eyelids charred black, her skullshrunk lips, the stink of her putrid flesh — and he sat entranced in the tremulous light, no consolation rising from the open Book on the ground.

*

Lucinda arrived at Fort Amsterdam among the svelte breezes of a warm November morning. Jaki stood at the starboard rail, awed by the beauty of the New World that his wife had not lived to see. Gray cliffs paled the western bank above a rubble of red sandstone and bosks of blue willow. To the east were the hills of Manhattan, blotched crimson and gold, delirious hues. Hunched below the soft hills was a rookery of docks, moored trade ships, and shabby warehouses over which brooded Fort Amsterdam, a ponderous citadel of piked oak with tall garrets for keeping a seawatch over the sound. *Lucinda* was met by a bevy of dinghies and guided to a slip where burly men in wool caps and wooden shoes waited to unload her cargo.

Meticulously dressed in black and red and wearing his diamond-fronted hat, Jaki stepped down from the gangway to the larboard pier and shivered though the air was warm and redolent with autumn. He had arrived in the afterworld of Lucinda's dreams, and he looked about with wonder.

Wooden shoes clopped loudly on the pier as the stevedores approached, and Jaki was hailed by a stout man in elaborate ruff, slit jerkin, and knee-high boots. The man swept off his hat, and his silver hair flared as he bowed his head. "I am Peter Minnewit," he announced smoothly in Spanish. "I am the fort's governor. Your ship's devices inform me the captain speaks Spanish. I had expected a swarthier man."

"Spanish was my mother's tongue," replied Jaki, and he doffed his hat. "I am honored to be greeted by the governor."

"You are kind to say so," Minnewit said, noting the chunk of rough diamond on Jaki's hatband. "But this is a very humble colony, and we are rarely visited by a vessel as richly laded as yours. You carry tobacco?"

"Three long hundredweights."

The governor smiled lavishly. "Then your stay will assuredly be a lucrative one. There's been a dearth of the divine weed in our colony this season." He gestured toward the wharf road, where a coach awaited them. "Accompany me to my house that I may hear how you came to wear a Dutch name and visage and yet speak this foul language of our oppressors."

In the coach, jouncing over the rutted road that climbed toward the fort, Jaki gripped the velvet squabs of his seat as much to bear the burden of his story as to steady himself. He began with the arrival in Borneo of Pieter Gefjon and Jan van Noot, as he had first heard the tale from Jabalwan. When he concluded his account in the governor's office beneath large windows of diamond-shaped leaded lights, the Dutchman said, "Your wife would be proud of what has become of your mountains' tears — and you." He pinched his dented chin, wanting to act for this world-wanderer's benefit, this bastard son of the

Lowlands. "Your daughter is with her grandfather in the marshland south of here. I will dispatch a guard with you to retrieve her."

"Thank you," Jaki said. "I must go alone."

The governor shook his head. "You think that is wise? The English are a bellicose lot. And Captain Quarles struck me as particularly pugnacious. He will most certainly try to kill you."

"I must give him that chance."

"Why?" Minnewit boomed, his head rocking back with incomprehension. "Leave the dead to bury the dead. Claim your daughter and grace her with the benefit of your mountains' tears. That is what both your fathers — what any sensible Dutchman — would do."

"But I am also my mother's son, governor. I am a sorcerer. I fear life and its imperishable mystery more than I fear death."

"Bah. Your grief has addled you. All men fear death. You have wealth now. Do not squander your life for the satisfaction of some brutal Englishman. Listen to me, Jaki Gefjon, and live. Do not deny your daughter her father."

"With your help, she will not be denied her fortune." Jaki withdrew a folded sheet of paper. "Here is a copy of a testament I drafted aboard ship. Will you execute it if I do not return?"

Minnewit accepted the paper with a scowl. "You war on yourself, young man," he scolded. "You can only win this fight by losing. I do not understand how any man with health and wealth, sorcerer or not, can choose death over life. Yet I respect your long suffering, and I will protect your survivor."

Jaki left the governor's house determined to meet his fate that day, while the winds were warm and the clouds so deeply pearl. Outside, he paused and stared up at the large stone and timber house with its hipped roof and eave cornices, and he saw in that cumbrous structure how impossible it was for the governor to understand him. The governor's house was built to last, like the ambitions of Jaki's fathers, which had reached greedily into faraway territories, wanting to claim the whole world for their homeland. But within him persisted something homeless that he had inherited from his mother, something the Rain Wanderers had sought on their unmarked roads in the jungle.

How strange it must have seemed to his fathers to see longhouses built to be used for a season and then returned to the jungle. How strange for them to discover kingdoms without borders, land without owners. His life was like that, a longhouse built to house his love. He was owned by his love for his wife. That had been Jabalwan's despair of him, and that was why he could never be a true sorcerer. He could not marry the sky and her clouds, for he belonged, from the first, to a woman. And now that she was gone, his life belonged to the wilds. It was never meant to last. How could he have explained to the governor his vision in Njurat, when he saw that life's enemy was not death but indifference? Since losing Lucinda, he had become indifferent. Only Quarles could cure him of that.

A ferry carried Jaki south across the Narrows to the marshland. Strange birds cawed from the fire-colored woods. Jaki lifted his face into the sun and scanned the cliffs on the far shore, the sheer palisades that towered over the river like the broken wall of the planet, the end of all maps. He knew then that he had reached the end of his journey. The dreams of his fathers had found their way to earth in him, and now all that remained was the last mystery.

Death's perfected landscape lay all about him, weirder than any of the strong eye's visions. Twilight bloomed in the trees, though the sun still climbed toward noon. Clouds of fuchsia and orange leaves clumped like cumulus for as far as he could see, wisping even from the rock wall of the bold cliffs. Through the spectral landscape, he was calm, alert to the unfamiliar beauty around him, deep enough in his life to be free of the creature of his mind while he rode the river. The future browsed nearby, waiting for him like a change of horse.

Jaki was certain that Quarles would kill him on sight, but he did not want to die until he had seen baby Lucinda and given Maud the ship's papers and the stamped trade bills from his journey north. When he spotted smoke blurring into the riverwind, he had the ferryman pole to shore, and he disembarked and sent the ferry back. He followed the river edge until he reached the crude tidewall and heard remote voices, then walked up the bank and into the forest's whiskery light.

From the woods, he looked over the humble camp perched on the river bluff, and was saddened by the paltry cabin, the gaps between the unhewed logs stuffed with dried mud and grass, the sagging roof of reeds, the rubble chimney oozing smoke. Maud appeared from the far side of the cabin, dressed in a clever patchwork of rags and fawnskin, her hair mussy. She was carrying Lucinda in a pouch on her back. At the sight of his child, Jaki dizzied with longing and could not comprehend how he had ever been separated from her. He wanted to burst out of the covert and claim her, but he stayed his tense muscles and dared himself to watch, like a sorcerer.

Maud was strolling with an old woman who wore a brown sack dress, and they were carrying a bucket between them, on their way to the stream that Jaki heard curkling in the distance. As they passed, he stepped from his hiding place and walked up behind them soundlessly, keeping his eyes on his watchful daughter, who had turned in her seat and was laughing at him as if with sudden recall.

Her perfect face was shining from somewhere inside, radiant with innocence. She was the uncrowned queen of life, sovereign of freedom, not yet enslaved by dreams. In her smile he glimpsed the shameless future that did not need him. He had returned to award her the legacy of his long journey — but that was his own willful dream. She did not need that; she was free of grief, free of any attachments but the animal simplicities that would sustain her even after the longing came on, the invisible pain of loss that had no home in the body.

Maud glanced over her shoulder at the laughing baby and found herself staring, instead, at a man. She did not recognize him. He smiled when he saw the unknowing in her face, and Maud's inquisitive expression melted in a hot blush. "Jaki —"

Jaki nodded, arms open. Maud collapsed into his strength, and he held her, then stepped back, still clutching her strong hands, and admired the courage in her calluses, the miles in her summer-colored face. "You have lived, strong and brave," he told her, and kissed her begrimed fingers.

Timotha looked on coolly. She had imagined from Maud's stories that Jaki was a larger, craggier man. Under the black wing of his hat, his twenty-year-old face was boyishly lucid.

"The child is well?" he inquired, and when she nodded, he asked, "You?"

"Yes," she answered, still overcome with surprise. "I saw you blown up. The whole longboat blown up before the storm."

"God spared me."

"Aye, God," Timotha said, and compressed a laugh to a grunt. "God carries our fortunes and our dead."

"My aunt," Maud introduced her, unstrapping the infant from her back. "Timotha Firth."

Jaki held his cooing daughter in his arms, and he kissed the child and quieted her with a blue feather from his hat. He faced the old woman and saw her weary flesh folded like honey, her swollen eyelids, and her upper lip glinting like the hairs on a horse chestnut. In his arms was a life's beginning and before him its furthest reach. Baby and crone, clinging like leaves to the tree of generation, completing themselves in each other. He could see that truth in the crone's sunken face when she caught the baby's eye and something thriving and eternal passed between them. That perception swelled his heart with caring for everything alive, and he stepped closer, laying a hand on the old woman's arm. "Thank you for helping my child."

She nodded, unexpectedly moved by the timbre of his voice.

"I thank you," the old woman replied, and put a raspy hand on his. "Your daughter is a beautiful creature, Mister Jaki Gefjon — the world's promise — aye, and a love that heals the passing of a used-up woman like me."

Maud took his arm. "Captain Quarles —" She spoke her fear. "Does Captain Quarles know you are alive?"

"No," Jaki answered impassively.

"Then we must flee at once, before he sees you." Maud pulled on his arm to guide him toward the trees, but he would not move.

"I owe a debt to William Quarles," Jaki said dryly. "And I am going to find him after you and I have talked."

"It will be murder," Timotha quacked.

"If that is in him."

"It is, Jaki," Maud warned, her face opening with fear. "He keeps a primed musket in his sea chest and he is a fine shot. These months of hunting have only sharpened his eye."

"The Quarles family have always been excellent shots," Timotha agreed, rubbing her jowls. "But they ill choose their targets. Unhappy targets."

Jaki shaded Maud's frown by leaning the brim of his hat on her head and peering playfully into her eyes. "I have come here to face Lucinda's father." He smiled at the double meaning and lifted the baby between them. "Before I do, I need to see Lucinda and know she is loved. And I see that." He nestled the child in one arm and with his free hand removed a packet of papers from inside his jacket. "These are for her. Her legacy. I have named you to the Dutch Company as her financial guardian."

Maud would not touch the papers, and Timotha took them from his hand. "You speak as though you were dead," Maud whispered bitterly.

Timotha handed the papers to Maud, wagging her empty hands in the air as though the papers' mortal dust had smut her fingers. "A rare traveler is he what knows where his journey has taken him."

"Hush, Auntie," Maud scolded. Her blood was jumpy, itching at the tips of her body, and she spoke as though she had held her breath too long. "Captain Quarles is old and embittered. Of late he has found succor in God. He is best left believing you are dead."

Jaki shook his head and looked away, across the field to the red and yellow trees champing in the wind. He felt like a fish, all touch and staring, rubbing through the ocean dark, shiny and alert. Death was too big a thought for his head. "No more talk of death." He held Lucinda high, and she reached for his hat and tugged at its brim, trying to grasp the cloudy rock tied to the hatband. "I am here to see Lucinda and remember our friendship, Maud. Come, let us walk." He took Maud's arm, glad for the strength he felt in her.

They headed into the forest, Maud quiet, searching for hope, and Jaki and Timotha chatting about babies and the north woods and the watchful lives hidden in them.

William Quarles was weary. Since sighting the British prize with his daughter's name on its prow, he had tried to stave off his fear that Jaki

Gefjon was alive by hauling more rocks to his jetty. But his apprehensions persisted even after his strength was spent. Now, as he drowsed on the straw tick in the cabin, a premonition stiffened in him. He sat up and stared through the window for the women and the child.

They were walking far across the field toward the forest, with a stranger who looked to be, at that distance, a wealthy Dutchman. Quarles frowned and withdrew his spyglass from the battered sea chest beside his tick.

The clipped beard and the elegant clothing did not baffle Quarles for an instant — he recognized that face. The glass dropped from his stunned fingers. He reached for his musket, nauseated with the disbelief and shock that his daughter's murderer was truly alive and holding her child in his arms. Twice he tried to drop the gun and even shouted at his hand: "Evil begets evil!" But the hand would not let go. The hard-edged memories of his grief steadied him, and he checked that the gun was primed. His mind groped to explain this sudden horror as he lumbered from the cabin. He was going to kill a ghost.

Jaki saw Quarles striding through the buffed grass, musket in hand, and all his calm vanished. Quarles was not as he remembered him. He had the stride of a man used to the weight of a sword, but he was dressed as the commonest sailor. Even his mustache and beard had been shaved away to reveal stubbled jowls and a mouth tight as a scar.

Fear fluttered in Jaki. He handed Lucinda to Maud and looked into her brown-gold eyes. The child caught the fright in his suddenness and began to cry.

"Take Lucinda into the trees," he pleaded, and when he saw Maud's insistence to be near him stiffening through her, he looked to Timotha.

She laid her hands on her niece's shoulders. "Come away now, Maud," she said firmly. "We must protect the child." And to Jaki she said in parting, her arms crossed around Maud, "Life and death are not enemies but one friend."

Jaki faced away and stepped to meet William Quarles, breaking into feathers of sweat.

Quarles raised his musket. He waited for Jaki to bolt so he could catch him in a flare of dismay and greedy fear. But the pirate just stood there. That stymied Quarles's blood lust, and he raged hotter at this show of contempt even as a cold whisper of sanity urged him to drop the musket.

Quarles drew back the musket's hammer and sighted Jaki's crown, settling his aim into the brim-shadow of his hat where the pirate's stare glistened. Maud screamed for him to stop, and the baby's cry kicked loudly. Jaki met the sky's stare and yearned for the madness that had lifted him in defiance before *Revenge*'s cannon. The stroke of his heart almost wrenched him off his feet until he recalled Lucinda's death. His fear calmed; this was the stillness his whole life had led him to.

The baby's cry wobbled closer, and Jaki's peaceful death soured as he realized that Maud was hurtling toward him, hurrying Quarles's shot. He imagined Maud colliding with him as the shot meant for him burst her life, or the child's, and a cold energy brushed through him from his feet to his scalp.

The alarm on Jaki's face was the signal Quarles had been waiting for — and the trigger surrendered to his caress. But at that moment, Maud ran into the line of fire, and Quarles jerked back as the charge exploded.

Jaki grabbed her, and she clutched the baby tighter to her chest under the jolting blast. The musketball whistled over their heads and into the forest. Maud crimped a scream. They stared into the gunsmoke. Quarles was stunned, a shadow nesting in his grievous face.

"Shame!" Timotha shouted at him, berating him as she crossed the field, her cries competing with the baby's.

"Wait with her," Jaki said quietly, and stepped toward Quarles.

The sight of the pirate's face alight with relief rekindled Quarles's rage, and when the boy stepped close enough, he struck out with the musket.

Jaki snagged his gun wrist with a deft hand and twisted the gun loose. "You had your chance to kill me, *Father,*" he whispered with effort. He bent Quarles's wrist until the older man sagged, and they knelt together in the grass. "Why did you spare me?"

Tears sprung in Quarles's eyes. Jaki released his arm, but the old man continued to weep, his face warped and wet, his shoulders shrugging, shaking loose the months of infuriated bewilderment that had followed Lucinda's death. He had lost himself then. He had thrown away honor, career, and fortune to retrieve Lucinda, and her death had snuffed the lamp in his chest. Now he was reduced to a murderer—and he *was* a murderer, he was convinced: his intent had been to kill with vengeance an unarmed man. He covered his face with both hands, ashamed of the weakness of his body, the poverty of his soul. Always, he had served only himself; now, madness glittered across his brain with the insight that he had misspent his whole life.

"I aimed to kill," Quarles sobbed.

Jaki's hands, firm as iron, gripped Quarles's arms. "Get up. We must talk."

Maud and Timotha were hunched around the baby, peering coldly at Quarles. The child was watching him with her bright, attentive eyes. He turned away, hollowed by shame, and with Jaki's arm across his shoulders slouched toward the forest.

They sat down on a fallen tree out of sight of the clearing. Quarles clutched his hands between his knees and looked dully at the man he would have murdered. "What do you want of me, devil?"

"I am no devil," Jaki said, straddling the log to face Quarles. "I am just a man." He pushed back the cuff of his left sleeve and showed the braid of Lucinda's hair on his wrist. "I am the husband of your daughter."

Quarles violently shook his head. "You stole her."

"You know better." Jaki pressed all his love for his wife into words. "Lucinda was too strong for anyone to steal. You know that."

Quarles sat like stone. Of course Lucinda was too strong to be stolen; her willfulness was his own bequest to her. And with that admission, he turned to look, as though for the first time, upon the man she had chosen.

"Then you *are* my father," Jaki said, and searched for that recognition in Quarles's hooded eyes. When he did not see it, he went on. "I never had a father — because I kept looking for him in one man. And that man was dead. And he was not even my real father, who was also dead. Is death my father? I wondered about that, until now. You are my father, if anyone, because you are alive and we share a deep loss."

Quarles studied him with slow tortoise eyes, perceiving the grief turning in the boy like a soft river. He flinched inside, outraged that this stranger dared to claim his suffering. He spoke monotonously. "I tried to kill you."

"But you didn't."

"The woman interfered," Quarles groaned. "I aimed to kill."

Jaki reached into his jacket to where Chrysaor was sheathed at his hip, and in one fluid stroke removed the gold dagger and lay it on the log between them.

"Kill me, then," Jaki said. "I know from the root of my breath that I loved your daughter. Lucinda and I made a child between us, and that killed her. If I must die for that, then do it now."

Quarles's little eyes tightened dangerously. "You think I wouldn't." He seized the knife with his right hand, Jaki's hair with his left, and with a black strength threw him to the ground and stabbed. A fury as wild as it was hopeless thrust the blade into the lace at Jaki's throat and held the point to the ruby of blood shining there. Quarles pressed his face close to Jaki's. "You would let me kill you?" he panted, and jabbed deeper, flushed to see Jaki's eyes wince shut and his mouth despair.

Jaki's suffering staggered Quarles's rage; he let the knife drop and hunkered in the auburn duff, horrified by what he had done.

Jaki sat up, hand to his neck. The knife had lanced his flesh but not punctured his throat. He picked up the dagger and sheathed it, then looked to Quarles, squatting in the leaf drift like a bewildered animal. They sat silently listening to crows caw while leaves fell around them nicked with sunlight.

"I was wrong," Quarles said at last, wiping the numbness from his worn face. "Not about you." He passed him a harsh frown and looked away. "About myself. I thought I was better than this. But no one is spared, no one lifted above life's cruelties." He looked to Jaki, saw the wily understanding in his boyish features, and glimpsed the pain he must have endured. "This world is a shuckheap." He spit. "A shuckheap of all we've pared away to create our noble dreams. The dreams go on. Love. Sacrifice. God. They go on, all right, life after life. We —" He struck his chest fiercely. "We are what is left behind, left to plunder what remains when our dreams leave us." He rocked mournfully as a bear and stood up. "We are all pirates," he said with exasperation, and offered a thick hand to Jaki.

Jaki looked at the hand — the fingers bruised from work, the palm open with hope — and he took it and pulled himself to his feet. A light shot up in the bores of his eyes, and a smile flickered in his beard. He squeezed Quarles's hand and agreed: "Pirates."

After the first snowfall, Jaki stood at the edge of the field where Quarles's shot had been thwarted. Lucinda rode on her father's shoulders, bundled in goose-down pants and bodice, her alert face petaled by a red wool scarf pulled up as a hood. Neither of them had seen snow before, and they stared with wonder at the drifts saddling the open spaces, castellating the forest and tinkling like moondust in the tail of the wind.

The morning was still dark when Lucinda had awakened, crying to be held. Rather than waking the others, Jaki had bundled the child and taken her out under the starry sky. The horizon of sleeping trees shone silver in the dawn. Jaki felt giddy before the unearthly beauty of the snow, with the giddy weight of his daughter on his shoulders. He danced across the smooth expanse, reeling toward groves of walnut and mammoth chestnut. Billows of snowflakes fumed brightly around him in the dim light. Lucinda clung to his hair with her fisted mittens, squealing when Jaki's twirling dance kicked snow. Today, she was one year old.

Behind them, in the split-log cabin crowned in snow and icicles, windowlight sharpened like stars as lamps were lit in the kitchen. The cabin was all that Jaki's crew had time to build before the snows began. Though hastily constructed, the log cottage was comfortable for their first winter in the New World: Maud and Timotha had dressed the five rooms with tapestries, lace curtains, and shining Dutch furniture. Quarles had carved Lucinda's cradle from the log where he had learned pity. And masons from the fort had built a hearth big enough to burn stumps. The seething blaze opened bright treasures of warmth and vision before which Jaki sat at night, feeling the tree deep inside his body putting forth new leaves.

The survey lines for a much grander house were staked out on the glade where Jaki danced. The foundation marks were hidden in the snow, rooting his dream in the cold earth. In spring, a home would rise here. Blown by time's winds, Jaki Gefjon and his family would sail the swells of winter and summer through the years, through the generations, into the glare of the future.

But Jaki was not thinking of that now. His heart and mind were in his dance as it led him and Lucinda across the emptiness that held their future. Their laughter circled with the opal wind into the wilds, vanishing into clearings where not long ago tribesfolk in eagle masks and snakeband leggings had danced their stories.

Jaki twirled to a stop at the edge of the glade among ricks of frozen ironweed. The cleared ground was on a broad knoll above a tract of marshy sedge and forest that the Dutch called Breuckelen — Brookland, which his English father pronounced Brooklyn. From the hillock, Jaki looked down on the firth where Quarles had designed a pier. The ice on the river gleamed in the gathering light, and the sea wall that Jaki and his men had built to extend the wharf was banked with snow dunes.

Above the estuary, violet light limned the western cliffs, as the night sunk into the creek beds under the forests. The sinking darkness drew Jaki after it. Watching it go, hearing the great trees around him creaking, smelling the sea and the earth in the wind, Jaki thinned out of his body and into the cold, restless wind.

Lucinda sat patiently on her father's shoulders. In the three months since he had returned for her, they had become close, and usually she tolerated his sudden still watchfulness, at least briefly. She was a watchful being herself, quietly attentive to the world's details, becoming her mother's image around her father's soul. But now she was cold, and she did not see the hope he saw in the gray horizon. She pulled at his long hair and fussed for him to move.

Whatever omens were unfolding in the sky, Jaki ignored them. He swung his daughter down from his shoulders and cradled her in his arms. The look of her pollen-bright face inspired magic in him, so that blood jumped to the roots of his hair when he held her. He wanted to teach her the crafty lore he had won as Matubrembrem, and he was hungry to learn all she already knew of love. She was the Life, the eternal story the clouds were dreaming, and he told her that in his first language, the tongue of her tribal grandmother. "How Bright Air Between the Palms would have treasured you," he said, wading back toward the cabin, smiling to see the serenity that seized her when he spoke the language of the shadow people.

Lucinda felt the love brighten in her father whenever he spoke to her in that rounder voice, and she lay quietly in his embrace listening. Since he had appeared, she had sensed a new security, and the fear that she had sometimes heard pummeling her mother's heart she heard no more.

Yellow windowlight lay tall on the blue snow, and Jaki lowered Lucinda to the stamped trail so she could toddle alongside him to the cabin. The fragrance of breakfast unfolded in the downdraft from the chimney, and Lucinda tugged harder at Jaki's finger, wobbling to where Maud had appeared in the doorway. Maud swooped the child into her arms, smiled at Jaki, and began to brush the snow from Lucinda's hair. In the spring, Jaki would ask Maud to marry him. Lucinda's ghost had been counseling that since the cabin was finished and he had first glimpsed her among the torn veils of the hearthfire. *In time,* he had promised the ghost. *In time, mystery closes all questions.*

When Maud had disappeared inside, Jaki turned and looked back toward the white field. For the first time in weeks, he felt expansive. Working with Quarles to build a dockyard in the wilderness had taxed all his resources and left little strength for trances. His entire fortune was invested in the harbor; he had spent all the gold converted from his diamonds to buy materiel and to pay laborers. He, Quarles, and the crewmen who had returned to Brooklyn after sheltering *Lucinda* at Fort Amsterdam for the winter had worked restlessly. They had dredged the marsh, poldered the estuary, and erected jetties to shape an anchorage on the Upper Bay. By spring, the harbor would be worthy of *Lucinda* and the big ships that would arrive from Europe and the Caribbean. Each day, he had given all of himself to a home in the New World.

But today was his daughter's birthday — the anniversary of his wife's death — and the glory of the snowbound world loosened Jaki's daily concerns enough for him to think like a sorcerer again. The renewing wisdom came back on him strongest when he thought about Lucinda and Maud, despite the suffering that had joined them, and he told himself in the language Mala would have understood: *We cannot bear life without a mother. Does not all happiness remember the first, the ultimate intimacy of the mother when life was whole with her, inside her, and not even breathing was necessary? Pym was right, after all: the greatest tragedy is to be born, to be pushed out of the mother and to be cut from her. That is the first defeat. And that is how we live, by being defeated, by never again succeeding to the whole and accomplished life inside the mother. Yet we remember — and by that memory we endure. Our defeats are building a greater victory. Her love is all we need to go on.*

His thoughts sounded loud in the steep silence of the snowy world, and he quieted himself. He walked back into the open space where next winter his house would stand, and he bent down and picked up a handful of snow. His bare fingers burned as he held the white powder to his mouth and tasted its numb energy. Close up, he saw the tiny palaces of ice, the halls of mirrors. Among the frozen lavings, he glimpsed faces thistly with colors — Mala, Jabalwan, Wawa, Pym, Lucinda — *The dead return as prophecy with the rains,* the sorcerers believed. He held the handful of frozen rain as though each flake were an instant of his life, and he scattered the powder over the field where he had been willing to die to find this life. The spontaneous rite inspired him to believe that the dead were listening. He stared at the snowdust that clung to his hand, each mote a star stretched over nothing, vanishing in the dawn-pink of his palm. The dead had placed life firmly in his hands now.

Jaki blew a triumphant sigh, and the cloud of his breath vanished in the cold. Another day's work loomed ahead, and the winter morning's reveries scattered among practical thoughts of surveying the sea wall for ice damage, cataloguing the new supplies purchased at Fort Amsterdam, and arranging a birthday celebration for Lucinda. He turned toward the cabin. But before leaving the field, he stooped and wiped the snow from the sign he had posted on a stump before the glade. It was a ship's plank that he had scorched with the name of the house he would build here, the plume of the serpent's flight, the signature of mystery, the sign of his dream:

WYVERN 1630